QUÉ

THE MAMMOTH BOOK OF
EXTREME FANTASY

THE MAMMOTH BOOK OF
EXTREME FANTASY
TO THE ULTIMATE LIMIT

EDITED BY
MIKE ASHLEY

RUNNING PRESS
PHILADELPHIA · LONDON

Constable & Robinson Ltd
3 The Lanchesters
162 Fulham Palace Road
London W6 9ER
www.constablerobinson.com

First published in the UK by Robinson,
an imprint of Constable & Robinson, 2008

A copy of the British Library Cataloguing in Publication
Data is available from the British Library

UK ISBN 978-1-84529-806-7

1 3 5 7 9 10 8 6 4 2

First published in the United States in 2008 by Running Press Book Publishers

US Library of Congress number: 2008926372
US ISBN 978-0-7624-3383-4

Running Press Book Publishers
2300 Chestnut Street
Philadelphia, PA 19103-4371

Visit us on the web!

www.runningpress.com

Printed and bound in the EU

CONTENTS

BEYOND THE IMPOSSIBLE
Mike Ashley

I N MY PREVIOUS ANTHOLOGY, *The Mammoth Book of Extreme Science Fiction*, I defined "extreme" as those stories that took a basic idea, whether simple or complicated, and developed it to some extreme, beyond what the reader might normally expect. I've used that same basis here.

However, whereas the content of a science fiction story is limited by the rules of science (no matter how much the author may try and bend them), in fantasy there are no limits other than those which the writer himself may impose. So while science fiction is the literature of the possible, no matter how extreme, fantasy is the literature of the impossible, which means it's pretty extreme to start with.

And that's the fun of this anthology. In all of the stories, the authors have taken a fantastic idea – and I mean fantastic in both its senses – and then seen how far they can push it. My one criterion is that they must still be readable stories. I did not want anything that was incomprehensible.

All the stories here are straight narratives. It's the ideas and how they are developed that are extreme, and though the authors have applied a certain logic as a hand-brake on their imagination, that doesn't stop them taking things beyond the impossible.

The kind of ideas you will encounter include:
- a cartoon character who becomes aware of his readers;
- a world of darkness where any concept of light means death;
- a man who decides to live all ages at once;
- an occult experiment to recreate the Crucifixion that goes wrong;

And those are the relatively straightforward ones.

In recent years, ever since the phenomenal success of *Lord of the Rings*, fantasy has become associated in many people's minds as relating solely to wizards and elves and dwarves in worlds where magic works. This overlooks that vast wealth of fantasy fiction that has been appearing for centuries, much of which has nothing to do with elves or fairies.

Fantasy is the most liberated form of fiction. It allows the writer to free their own and the readers' imaginations and go for broke. In fantasy anything can happen, anything at all. In fantasy reality gives way to the unreal.

The challenge to the writer is to make it into a meaningful story which the reader can still understand and which could even seem real, no matter how extreme. There are stories here, even the most extreme ones, which manage to suspend the reader's disbelief enough that, for a moment, you believe it could happen. And that's one of the pleasures of fantasy. For that moment as the story engulfs you, you can live in the world of the impossible. Masters of fantasy in the past have included H G Wells, John Collier, Algernon Blackwood, H P Lovecraft and Stephen Vincent Benet – none of whom wrote about elves and fairies. However, for this volume I wanted to include stories primarily by the modern masters. Over half the stories have been written in the past ten years. The oldest story is by William Hope Hodgson who was so forward thinking that the story reads as almost contemporary. Contributors include those masters of the unusual and bizarre Orson Scott Card, Peter Crowther, Paul Di Filippo, Rhys Hughes, R A Lafferty, Michael Moorcock, Christopher Priest, Michael Swanwick and Howard Waldrop.

As with the previous volume I have presented the stories in sequence from the least to the most extreme, so your imagination can expand as you work through the book. Dip in at a later story at your peril!

However, in order to bring you back safely into this world the final story serves as a form of *digestif*, allowing a mental calming down. But otherwise, the brakes are off. Prepare yourself for a wild and exuberant ride.

Mike Ashley
November 2007

SENATOR BILBO
Andy Duncan

We begin our journey in what ought to be the relative safety of the Shire. But we are generations on from the days of Bilbo and Frodo and the Shire finds itself infected by politics and politicians. Andy Duncan wondered what it might be like if Theodore Bilbo, the segregationist and member of the Ku Klux Klan, who was a US senator from 1935 to 1947, had been related to Bilbo Baggins.

Andy Duncan (b. 1964) is a native of South Carolina. He is a former journalist and currently a college teacher who has been winning a swathe of awards since his first fiction appeared in 1996, including the World Fantasy Award for his collection Belthahatchie and Other Stories *(2000). His website is at www.angelfire.com/al/andyduncan/*

"It regrettably has become necessary for us now, my friends, to consider seriously and to discuss openly the most pressing question facing our homeland since the War. By that I mean, of course, the race question."

In the hour before dawn, the galleries were empty, and the floor of the Shire-moot was nearly so. Scattered about the chamber, a dozen or so of the Senator's allies – a few more than needed to maintain the quorum, just to be safe – lounged at their writing-desks, feet up, fingers laced, pipes stuffed with the best Bywater leaf, picnic baskets within reach: veterans, all. Only young Appledore from Bridge Inn was snoring and slowly folding in on himself; the chestnut curls atop his head nearly met those atop his feet. The Senator jotted down Appledore's name without pause. He could get a lot of work done while making speeches – even a filibuster nine hours long (and counting).

"There are forces at work today, my friends, without and within our homeland, that are attempting to destroy all boundaries between our proud, noble race and all the mule-gnawing, cave-squatting, light-shunning, pit-spawned scum of the East."

The Senator's voice cracked on "East," so he turned aside for a quaff from his (purely medicinal) pocket flask. His allies did not miss their cue. "Hear, hear," they rumbled, thumping the desktops with their calloused heels. "Hear, hear."

"This latest proposal," the Senator continued, "this so-called immigration bill – which, as I have said, would force even our innocent daughters to suffer the reeking lusts of all the ditch-bred legions of darkness – why, this baldfooted attempt originated where, my friends?"

"Buckland!" came the dutiful cry.

"Why, with the delegation from *Buckland*…long known to us all as a hotbed of book-mongers, one-Earthers, elvish sympathizers, and other off-brands of the halfling race."

This last was for the benefit of the newly arrived Fredegar Bracegirdle, the unusually portly junior member of the Buckland delegation. He huffed his way down the aisle, having drawn the short straw in the hourly backroom ritual.

"Will the distinguished Senator," Bracegirdle managed to squeak out, before succumbing to a coughing fit. He waved his bladder-like hands in a futile attempt to disperse the thick purplish clouds that hung in the chamber like the vapors of the Eastmarsh. Since a Buckland-sponsored bill to ban tobacco from the floor had been defeated by the Senator three Shire-moots previous, his allies' pipe-smoking had been indefatigable. Finally Bracegirdle sputtered: "Will the distinguished Senator from the Hill kindly yield the floor?"

In response, the Senator lowered his spectacles and looked across the chamber to the Thain of the Shire, who recited around his tomato sandwich: "Does the distinguished Senator from the Hill so yield?"

"I do not," the Senator replied, cordially.

"The request is denied, and the distinguished Senator from the Hill retains the floor," recited the Thain of the Shire, who then took another hearty bite of his sandwich. The Senator's party had re-written the rules of order, making this recitation the storied Thain's only remaining duty.

"Oh, hell and hogsheads," Bracegirdle muttered, already trundling back up the aisle. As he passed Gorhendad Bolger from the Brockenborings, that Senator's man like his father before him kindly offered Bracegirdle a pickle, which Bracegirdle accepted with ill grace.

"Now that the distinguished gentleman from the Misty Mountains has been heard from," the Senator said, waiting for the laugh, "let me turn now to the evidence – the overwhelming evidence, my friends – that many of the orkish persuasion currently living among us have been, in fact, active agents of the Dark Lord…"

As the Senator plowed on, seldom referring to his notes, inventing statistics and other facts as needed, secure that this immigration bill, like so many bills before it, would wither and die once the Bucklanders' patience was exhausted, his self-confidence faltered only once, unnoticed by anyone else in the chamber. A half-hour into his denunciation of the orkish threat, the Senator noticed a movement – no, more a shift of light, a *glimmer* – in the corner of his eye. He instinctively turned his head towards the source, and saw, or *thought* he saw, sitting in the farthest, darkest corner of the otherwise empty gallery, a man-sized figure in a cloak and pointed hat, who held what must have been (*could* have been) a staff; but in the next blink, that corner held only shadows, and the Senator dismissed the whatever-it-was as a fancy born of exhilaration and weariness. Yet he was left with a lingering chill, as if (so his old mother, a Took, used to say) a dragon had hovered over his grave.

At noon, the Bucklanders abandoned their shameful effort to open the High Hay, the Brandywine Bridge, and the other entry gates along the Bounds to every misbegotten so-called "refugee," be he halfling, man, elf, orc, warg, Barrow-wight, or worse. Why, it would mean the end of Shire culture, and the mongrelization of the halfling race! No, sir! Not today – not while the Senator was on the job.

Triumphant but weary, the champion of Shire heritage worked his way, amid a throng of supplicants, aides, well-wishers, reporters, and yes-men, through the maze of tunnels that led to his Hill-side suite of offices. These were the largest and nicest of any senator's, with the most pantries and the most windows facing the Bywater, but they also were the farthest from the Shire-moot floor. The Senator's famous ancestor and namesake had been hale and hearty even in his eleventy-first year; the Senator, pushing ninety, was determined to beat that record. But every time he left the chamber, the office seemed farther away.

"Gogluk carry?" one bodyguard asked.

"Gogluk *not* carry," the Senator retorted. The day he'd let a troll haul him through the corridors like luggage would be the day he'd sailed oversea for good.

All the Senator's usual tunnels had been enlarged to accommodate the bulk of his two bodyguards, who nevertheless had to stoop, their scaly shoulders scraping the ceiling. Loyal, dim-witted, and huge – more than five feet in height – the Senator's trolls were nearly as well known in the Shire as the Senator himself, thanks partially to the Senator's perennial answer to a perennial question from the press at election time: "Racist? Me? Why, I love Gogluk and Grishzog, here, as if they were my own flesh and blood, and they love me just the same, don't you, boys? See? Here, boys, have another biscuit."

Later, once the trolls had retired for the evening, the Senator would elaborate. Trolls, now, you could train them, they were teachable; they had their uses, same as those swishy elves, who were so good with numbers. Even considered as a race, the trolls weren't much of a threat – no one had seen a baby troll in ages. But those orcs? They did nothing but breed.

Carry the Senator they certainly did not, but by the time the trolls reached the door of the Senator's outermost office (no mannish rectangular door, but a traditional Shire-door, round and green with a shiny brass knob in the middle), they were virtually holding the weary old halfling upright and propelling him forward, like a child pushed to kiss an ugly aunt.

Only the Senator's mouth was tireless. He continued to greet constituents, compliment babies, rap orders to flunkies, and rhapsodise about the glorious inheritance of the Shire as the procession squeezed its way through the increasingly small rooms of the Senator's warren-like suite, shedding followers like snakeskin. The only ones who made it from the innermost outer office to the outermost inner office were the Senator, the trolls, and four reporters, all of whom considered themselves savvy under-Hill insiders for being allowed so far into the great man's sanctum.

The Senator further graced these reporters by reciting the usual answers to the usual questions as he looked through his mail, pocketing the fat envelopes and putting the thin ones in a pile for his intern, Miss Boffin. The Senator got almost as much work done during press conferences as during speeches.

"Senator, some members of the Buckland delegation have insinuated, off the record, that you are being investigated for alleged bribe-taking. Do you have a comment?"

"You can tell old Gerontius Brownlock that he needn't hide behind a façade of anonymity, and further that I said he was begotten in an orkish graveyard at midnight, suckled by a warg-bitch and educated by a fool. That's off the record, of course."

"Senator, what do you think of your chances for re-election next fall?"

"The only time I have ever been defeated in a campaign, my dear, was my first one. Back when your grandmother was a whelp, I lost a clerkship to a veteran of the Battle of Bywater. A one-armed veteran. I started to vote for him myself. But unless a one-armed veteran comes forward pretty soon, little lady, I'm in no hurry to pack."

The press loved the Senator. He was quotable, which was all the press required of a public official.

"Now, gentle folk, ladies, the business of the Shire awaits. Time for just one more question."

An unfamiliar voice aged and sharp as Mirkwood cheese rang out: *"They say your ancestor took a fairy wife."*

The Senator looked up, his face even rounder and redder than usual. The reporters backed away. "It's a lie!" the Senator cried. "Who said such a thing? Come, come. Who said that?"

"Said what, Senator?" asked the most senior reporter (Bracklebore, of the *Bywater Battle Cry*), his voice piping as if through a reed. "I was just asking about the quarterly sawmill-production report. If I may continue…"

"Goodbye," said the Senator. On cue, the trolls snatched up the reporters, tossed them into the innermost outer office, and slammed and locked the door. Bracklebore, ousted too quickly to notice, finished his question in the next room, voice muffled by the intervening wood. The trolls dusted their hands.

"Goodbye," said Gogluk – or was that Grishzog?

"Goodbye," said Grishzog – or was that Gogluk?

Which meant, of course, "Mission accomplished, Senator," in the pidgin Common Speech customary among trolls.

"No visitors," snapped the Senator, still nettled by that disembodied voice, as he pulled a large brass key from his waistcoat-pocket and unlocked the door to his personal apartments. Behind him, the trolls assumed position, folded their arms, and turned to stone.

"Imagination," the Senator muttered as he entered his private tunnel.

"Hearing things," he added as he locked the door behind.

"Must be tired," he said as he plodded into the sitting-room, yawning and rubbing his hip.

He desired nothing more in all the earth but a draught of ale, a pipe, and a long snooze in his armchair, and so he was all the more taken aback to find that armchair already occupied by a white-bearded Big Person in a tall pointed blue hat, an ankle-length gray cloak, and immense black boots, a thick oaken staff laid across his knees.

"'Struth!" the Senator cried.

The wizard — for wizard he surely was — slowly stood, eyes like lanterns, bristling gray brows knotted in a thunderous scowl, a meteor shower flashing through the weave of his cloak, one gnarled index finger pointed at the Senator — who was, once the element of surprise passed, unimpressed. The meteor effect lasted only a few seconds, and thereafter the intruder was an ordinary old man, though with fingernails longer and more yellow than most.

"Do you remember me?" the wizard asked. His voice crackled like burning husks. The Senator recognized that voice.

"Should I?" he retorted. "What's the meaning of piping insults into my head? And spying on me in the Shire-moot? Don't deny it; I saw you flitting about the galleries like a bad dream. Come on, show me you have a tongue — else I'll have the trolls rummage for it." The Senator was enjoying himself; he hadn't had to eject an intruder since those singing elves occupied the outer office three sessions ago.

"You appointed me, some years back," the wizard said, "to the University, in return for some localized weather effects on Election Day."

So that was all. Another disgruntled officeholder. "I may have done," the Senator snapped. "What of it?" The old-timer showed no inclination to reseat himself, so the Senator plumped down in the armchair. Its cushions now stank of men. The Senator kicked the wizard's staff from underfoot and jerked his leg back; he fancied something had nipped his toe.

The staff rolled to the feet of the wizard. As he picked it up, the wider end flared with an internal blue glow. He commenced shuffling about the room, picking up knickknacks and setting them down again as he spoke.

"These are hard times for wizards," the wizard rasped. "New powers are abroad in the world, and as the powers of wind and rock, water and tree are ebbing, we ebb with them. Still, we taught our handfuls of students respect for the old ways. Alas, no longer!"

The Senator, half-listening, whistled through his eyeteeth and chased a flea across the top of his foot.

"The entire thaumaturgical department – laid off! With the most insulting of pensions! A flock of old men feebler than I, unable even to transport themselves to your chambers, as I have wearily done – to ask you, to demand of you, why?"

The Senator yawned. His administrative purging of the Shire's only university, in Michel Delving, had been a complex business with a complex rationale. In recent years, the faculty had got queer Eastern notions into their heads and their classrooms – muddleheaded claims that all races were close kin, that orcs and trolls had not been separately bred by the Dark Power, that the Dark Power's very existence was mythical. Then the faculty quit paying the campaign contributions required of all public employees, thus threatening the Senator's famed "Deduct Box." Worst of all, the faculty demanded "open admissions for qualified non-halflings," and the battle was joined. After years of bruising politics, the Senator's appointees now controlled the university board, and a long-overdue housecleaning was underway. Not that the Senator needed to recapitulate all this to an unemployed spell-mumbler. All the Senator said was:

"It's the board that's cut the budget, not me." With a cry of triumph, he purpled a fingernail with the flea. "Besides," he added, "they kept all the *popular* departments. Maybe you could pick up a few sections of Heritage 101."

This was a new, mandatory class that drilled students on the unique and superior nature of halfling culture and on the perils of immigration, economic development, and travel. The wizard's response was: "Pah!"

The Senator shrugged. "Suit yourself. I'm told the Anduin gambling-houses are hiring. Know any card tricks?"

The wizard stared at him with rheumy eyes, then shook his head. "Very well," he said. "I see my time is done. Only the Grey Havens are left to me and my kind. We should have gone there long since. But your time, too, is passing. No fence, no border patrol – not even you, Senator – can keep all change from coming to the Shire."

"Oh, we can't, can we?" the Senator retorted. As he got worked up, his Bywater accent got thicker. "We sure did keep those Bucklanders from putting over that so-called Fair Distribution System, taking people's hard-earned crops away and handing 'em over to lazy trash to eat. We sure did keep those ugly up-and-down man houses from being built all over the Hill as shelter for immigrant rabble what ain't fully halfling or fully human or fully anything. Better to be some evil race than no race at all."

"There are no evil races," said the wizard.

The Senator snorted. "I don't know how *you* were raised, but I was raised on the Red Book of Westmarch, chapter and verse, and it says so right there in the Red Book, orcs are mockeries of men, filthy cannibals spawned by the Enemy, bent on overrunning the world…"

He went on in this vein, having lapsed, as he often did in conversation, into his tried-and-true stump speech, galvanized by the memories of a thousand cheering halfling crowds. "Oh, there's enemies everywhere to our good solid Shire-life," he finally cried, punching the air, "enemies outside and inside, but we'll keep on beating 'em back and fighting the good fight our ancestors fought at the Battle of Bywater. Remember their cry:

"Awake! Awake! Fear, Fire, Foes! Awake!
"Fire, Foes! Awake!"

The cheers receded, leaving only the echo of his own voice in the Senator's ears. His fists above his head were bloated and mottled – a corpse's fists. Flushed and dazed, the Senator looked around the room, blinking, slightly embarrassed – and, suddenly, exhausted. At some point he had stood up; now his legs gave way and he fell back into the armchair, raising a puff of tobacco. On the rug, just out of reach, was the pipe he must have dropped, lying at one end of a spray of cooling ashes. He did not reach for it; he did not have the energy. With his handkerchief he mopped at his spittle-laced chin.

The wizard regarded him, wrinkled fingers interlaced atop his staff.

"I don't even know why I'm talking to you," the Senator mumbled. He leaned forward, eyes closed, feeling queasy. "You make my head hurt."

"Inhibiting spell," the wizard said. "It prevented your throwing me out. Temporary, of course. One bumps against it, as against a low ceiling."

"Leave me alone," the Senator moaned.

"Such talents," the wizard murmured. "Such energy, and for what?"

"At least I'm a halfling," the Senator said.

"Largely, yes," the wizard said. "Is genealogy one of your interests, Senator? We wizards have a knack for it. We can see bloodlines, just by looking. Do you really want to know how…*interesting*…your bloodline is?"

The Senator mustered all his energy to shout, "Get out!" – but heard nothing. Wizardry kept the words in his mouth, unspoken.

"There are no evil races," the wizard repeated, "however convenient the notion to patriots, and priests, and storytellers. You may summon your trolls now." His gesture was half shrug, half convulsion.

Suddenly the Senator had his voice back. "Boys!" he squawked. "Boys! Come quick! Help!" As he hollered, the wizard seemed to roll up like a windowshade, then become a tubular swarm of fireflies. By the time the trolls knocked the door into flinders, most of the fireflies were gone. The last dying sparks winked out on their scaly shoulders as the trolls halted, uncertain what to pulverize. The Senator could hear their lids scrape their eyeballs as they blinked once, twice. The troll on the left asked:

"Gogluk help?"

"Gogluk too *late* to help, thank you very much!" the Senator snarled. The trolls tried to assist as he struggled out of the armchair, but he slapped them away, hissing, in a fine rage now. "Stone ears or no, did you not hear me shouting? Who did you think I was talking to?"

The trolls exchanged glances. Then Grishzog said, quietly: "Senator talk when alone a lot."

"A lot," Gogluk elaborated.

The Senator might have clouted them both had he not been distracted by the wizard's staff. Dropped amid the fireworks, it had rolled beneath a table. Not knowing why, the Senator reached for it, eyes shining. The smooth oak was warm to the touch: heat-filled, like a living thing. Then, with a yelp, the Senator yanked back his hand. The damn thing *definitely* had bitten him this time; blood trickled down his right palm. As three pairs of eyes stared, the staff sank into the carpet like a melting icicle, and was gone.

"Magic," said the trolls as one, impressed.

"Magic?" the senator cried. "Magic?" He swung his fists and punched the trolls, kicked them, wounding only their dignity; their looming hulks managed to cower, like dogs. "If it's magic you want, I'll give you magic!" He swung one last time, lost his balance, and fell into the trolls' arms in a dead faint.

The Bunce Inn, now in the hands of its founder's great-granddaughter, had been the favored public house of the Shire-moot crowd for generations. The Senator had not been inside the place in months. He pleaded matters of state, the truth being he needed a lot more sleep nowadays. But when he woke from his faint to find the trolls fussing over him, he demanded to be taken to the Bunce Inn for a quick one before retiring. The Senator's right hand smarted a bit beneath its bandage, but otherwise the unpleasant interlude with the wizard seemed a bad dream, was already melting away like the staff. The Senator's little troll-cart jounced through the warm honeysuckle-scented night, along the cobbled streets of the capital, in and out of the warm glows cast by round windows behind which fine happy halfling families settled down to halfling dinners and halfling games and halfling dreams.

The inn itself was as crowded as ever, but the trolls' baleful stares quickly prompted a group of dawdlers to drink up and vacate their table. The trolls retreated to a nearby corner, out of the way but ever-present, as bodyguards should be. The Senator sat back with a sigh and a tankard and a plate of chips and surveyed the frenzy all around, pleased to be a part of none of it. The weight of the brimming pewter tankard in his unaccustomed left hand surprised him, so that he spilled a few drops of Bunce's best en route to his mouth. *Aah.* Just as he remembered. Smacking foam from his lips, he took another deep draught – and promptly choked. Not six feet away, busy cleaning a vacant table, was an orc.

And not just any orc. This one clearly had some man in its bloodline somewhere. The Senator had seen to it that the Shire's laws against miscegenation had stayed on the books, their penalties stiffened, but elsewhere in the world, alas, traditional moral values had declined to the point that such blasphemous commingling had become all too frequent. This creature was no doubt an orc – the hulking torso and bowlegs, the flat nose and flared nostrils, the broad face, the slanting eyes, the coarse hair, the monstrous hooked teeth at the corners of the mouth – but the way the orc's arms moved as it stacked dirty plates was uncomfortably man-like. It had genuine hands as well, with long delicate fingers, and as its head turned, the Senator saw that its pupils were not the catlike slits of a true orc, but rounded, like the pupils of dwarves, and men, and halflings. It was like seeing some poor trapped halfling peering out from a monstrous bestial shell, as in those children's stories where the hero gets swallowed whole by the ogre and cries for help from within. The orc, as it worked, began to whistle.

The Senator shuddered, felt his gorge rise. His injured hand throbbed with each heartbeat. A filthy half-breed orc, working at the Bunce Inn! Old Bunce would turn in his grave. Catching sight of young Miss Bunce bustling through the crowd, the Senator tried to wave her over, to give her a piece of his mind. But she seemed to have eyes only for the orc. She placed her hand on its shoulder and said, in a sparkling gay voice: "Please, sir, don't be tasking yourself, you're too kind. I'll clean the table; you just settle yourself, please, and tell me what you'll have. The lamb stew is very nice today, and no mistake."

"Always pleased to help out, ma'am," said the orc, plopping its foul rump onto the creaking bench. "I can see how busy you are. Seems to me you're busier every time I come through the Shire."

"There's some as say I needs a man about," Miss Bunce said, her arms now laden with plates, "but cor! Then I'd be busier still, wouldn't I?" The orc laughed a horrid burbling mucus-filled laugh as Miss Bunce sashayed away, buttocks swinging, glancing back to twinkle at her grotesque customer, and wink.

At this inauspicious moment, someone gave the Senator a hearty clap on the back. It was Fredegar Bracegirdle, a foaming mug in his hand and a foolish grin on his fat red face. Drink put Bracegirdle in a regrettable bipartisan mood. "Hello, Senator," Bracegirdle chirped, as he clapped the Senator's back again and again. "Opponents in the legislature, drinking buddies after hours, eh, Senator, eh, friend, eh, pal?"

"Stop pounding me," the Senator said. "I am not choking. Listen, Bracegirdle. What is that, that...*creature*...doing here?"

Bracegirdle's bleary gaze slowly followed the Senator's pointing finger, as a dying flame follows a damp fuse. "Why, he's a-looking at the bill of fare, and having himself a pint, same as us."

"You know what I mean! Look at those hands. He talks as if someone, somewhere, has given him schooling. Where'd he come from?"

As he answered, Bracegirdle helped himself to the Senator's chips. "Don't recall his name, but he hails from Dunland, from one of those new, what-do-you-call-'em, investment companies, their hands in a little of everything. Run by orcs and dwarves, mostly, but they're hiring all sorts. My oldest, Bungo, he's put his application in, and I said, you go to it, son, there's no work in the Shire for a smart lad like yourself, and your dear gaffer won't be eating any less in his old age. Young Bunce, she's a wizard at these chips, she is. Could you pass the vinegar?"

The Senator already had risen and stalked over to the orc's table, where the fanged monster, having ordered, was working one of the little pegboard games Miss Bunce left on the tables for patrons' amusement. The orc raised its massive head as it registered the Senator's presence.

"A good evening to you, sir," it said. "You can be my witness. Look at that, will you? Only one peg left, and it in the center. I've never managed *that* before!"

The Senator cleared his throat and spat in the orc's face. A brown gob rolled down its flattened nose. The orc gathered its napkin, wiped its face, and stood, the scrape of the bench audible in the otherwise silent room. The orc was easily twice as wide as the Senator, and twice as tall, yet it did not have to stoop. Since the Senator's last visit, Miss Bunce had had the ceiling raised. Looking up at the unreadable, brutish face, the Senator stood his ground, his own face hot with rage, secure in the knowledge that the trolls were right behind him. Someone across the room coughed. The orc glanced in that direction, blinked, shook its head once, twice, like a horse bedeviled by flies. Then it expelled a breath, its fat upper lip flapping like a child's noisemaker, and sat down. It slid the pegboard closer and re-inserted the pegs, one after the other after the other, then, as the Senator watched, resumed its game.

The Senator, cheated of his fight, was unsure what to do. He could not remember when last he had been so utterly ignored. He opened his mouth to tell the orc a thing or two, but felt a tug at his sleeve so violent that it hushed him. It was Miss Bunce, lips thin, face pale, twin red spots livid on her cheeks. "It's late, Senator," she said, very quietly. "I think you'd best be going home."

Behind her were a hundred staring faces. Most of them were strangers. Not all of them were halfings. The Senator looked for support in the faces in the crowd, and for the first time in his life, did not find it. He found only hostility, curiosity, indifference. He felt his face grow even hotter, but not with rage.

He nearly told the Bunce slut what he thought of her and her orc-loving clientele – but best to leave it for the Shire-moot. Best to turn his back on this pesthole. Glaring at everyone before him, he gestured for the trolls to clear a path, and muttered: "Let's go, boys."

Nothing happened.

The Senator slowly turned his head. The trolls weren't there. The trolls were nowhere to be seen. Only more hostile strangers' faces. The Senator felt a single trickle of sweat slide past his shoulder blades. The orc jumped pegs, removed pegs: *snick, snick.*

So. The Senator forced himself to smile, to hold his head high. He nodded, patted Miss Bunce's shoulder (she seemed not to relish the contact), and walked towards the door. The crowd, still silent, parted for him. He smiled at those he knew. Few smiled back. As he moved through the crowd, a murmur of conversation arose. By the time he reached the exit, the normal hubbub had returned to the Bunce Inn, the Senator's once-favorite tavern, where he had been recruited long ago to run for clerk on the Shire First ticket. He would never set foot in the place again. He stood on the threshold, listening to the noise behind, then cut it off by closing the door.

The night air was hot and rank and stifling. Amid the waiting wagons and carriages and mules and two-wheeled pedal devices that the smart set rode nowadays, the Senator's little troll-cart looked foolish in the lamplight. As did his two truant bodyguards, who were leaning against a sagging, creaking carriage, locked in a passionate embrace. The Senator decided he hadn't seen that; he had seen enough today. He cleared his throat, and the trolls leaped apart with much coughing and harrumphing.

"Home," the Senator snapped. Eyeing the uneven pavement, he stepped with care to the cart, sat down in it, and waited. Nothing happened. The trolls just looked at one another, shifted from foot to foot. The Senator sighed and, against his better judgment, asked: "What is it?"

The trolls exchanged another glance. Then the one on the right threw back his shoulders – a startling gesture, given the size of the shoulders involved – and said: "Gogluk quit." He immediately turned to the other troll and said: "There, I said it."

"And you know that goes double for me," said the other troll. "Let's go, hon. Maybe some fine purebred halfling will take this old reprobate home."

Numb but for his dangling right hand, which felt as swollen as a pumpkin, the Senator watched the trolls walk away arm in arm. One told the other: "*Spitting* on people, yet! I thought I would just *die*." As they strolled out of the lamplight, the Senator rubbed his face with his left hand, massaged his wrinkled brow. He had been taught in school, long ago, that the skulls of trolls ossified in childhood, making sophisticated language skills impossible. If it wasn't true, it ought to be. There ought to be a law. He would write one as soon as he got home.

But how was he to *get* home? He'd never make it on foot, and he certainly couldn't creep back into the tavern to ask the egregious Bracegirdle for a ride. Besides, he couldn't see to walk at the moment; his eyes were watering. He wiped them on his sleeve. It wasn't that he would *miss* the trolls, certainly not, no more than he would miss, say, the andirons, were they to rise up, snarl insults, wound him to the heart, the wretches, and abandon him. One could always buy a new set. But at the thought of the andirons, the cozy hearth, the armchair, the Senator's eyes brimmed anew. He was so tired, and so confused; he just wanted to go home. And his hand hurt. He kept his head down as he mopped his eyes, in case of passers-by. There were no passers-by. The streetlamp flared as a buzzing insect flew into it. He wished he had fired those worthless trolls. He certainly would, if he ever saw them again.

"Ungratefulness," the Senator said aloud, "is the curse of this age." A mule whickered in reply.

Across the street, in the black expanse of the Party Field, a lone mallorn-tree was silhouetted against the starlit sky. Enchanted elven dust had caused the mallorn and all the other trees planted after the War to grow full and tall in a single season, so that within the year the Shire was once again green and beautiful − or so went the fable, which the Senator's party had eliminated from the schoolbooks years ago. The Senator blew his nose with vigor. The Shire needed nothing from elves.

When the tavern door banged open, the Senator felt a surge of hope that died quickly as the hulking orc-shape shambled forth. The bastard creature had looked repellent enough inside; now, alone in the lamplit street, it was the stuff of a thousand halfling nightmares, its bristling shoulders as broad as hogsheads, its knuckles nearly scraping the cobbles, a single red eye guttering in the center of its face. No, wait. That was its cigar. The orc reared back on its absurd bowlegs and blew smoke rings at the streetlamp − rings worthy of any halfling, but what of it? Even a dog can be trained, after a fashion, to dance. The orc extended its horrid manlike hand and tapped ashes into the lamp. Then, arm still raised, it swiveled its great jowly head and looked directly at the Senator. Even a half-orc could see in the dark.

The Senator gasped. He was old and alone, no bodyguards. Now the orc was walking towards him! The Senator looked for help, found none. Had the wizard's visit been an omen? Had the confusticated old charm tosser left a curse behind with his sharp-toothed staff? As the Senator cowered, heard the inexorable click of the orc's claws on the stones, his scream died in his throat − not because of any damned and be-bothered wizard's trickery, but because of fear, plain and simple fear. He somehow always had known the orcs would get him in the end. He gasped, shrank back. The orc loomed over him, its pointed head blocking the lamplight. The orc laid one awful hand, oh so gently, on the Senator's right shoulder, the only points of contact the fingertips – rounded, mannish, hellish fingertips. The Senator shuddered as if the orc's arm were a lightning rod. The Senator spasmed and stared and fancied the orc-hand and his own injured halfling hand were flickering blue in tandem, like the ends of a wizard's staff. The great mouth cracked the orc's leathered face, blue-lit from below, and a voice rumbled forth like a subterranean river: "Senator? Is that you? Are you all right?"

Sprawled there in the cart, pinned by the creature's gentle hand as by a spear, the Senator began to cry, in great sucking sobs of rage and pain and humiliation, as he realized this damned orc was not going to splinter his limbs and crush his skull and slurp his brains. How far have I fallen, the Senator thought. This morning the four corners of the Shire were my own ten toes, to wiggle as I pleased. Tonight I'm pitied by an orc.

SANDMAGIC
Orson Scott Card

Orson Scott Card (b. 1951) has been a major writer of fantasy and science fiction since his first story sale, "Ender's Game" in 1977. The following year he received the John W Campbell Award as Best New Writer and has since won over a score of awards for his work.

Card subsequently developed that first story into the novel Ender's Game *(1985). Other novels include* Songmaster *(1980),* Wyrms *(1987),* The Lost Boys *(1992) and the alternate-world series about Alvin Maker that began with* Seventh Son *(1987). His fantasies include* Hart's Hope *(1983),* Magic Street *(2005) and the upcoming* The Lost Gate *(2008). The last is part of Card's Mithermages series which has been long in the planning.*

The series began nearly thirty years ago with this story, "Sandmagic". On the surface it may seem just another otherworldly fantasy but, as one comes to expect from Card, he takes it just that little bit further. Card's website is at www.hatrack.com/osc/bibliography/index.shtml

The great domes of the city of Gyree dazzled blue and red when the sun shone through a break in the clouds, and for a moment Cer Cemreet thought he saw some of the glory his uncles talked about in the late night tales of the old days of Greet. But the capital did not look dazzling up close, Cer remembered bitterly. Now dogs ran in the streets and rats lived in the wreckage of the palace, and the King of Greet lived in New Gyree in the hills far to the north, where the armies of the enemy could not go. Yet.

The sun went back behind a cloud and the city looked dark again. A Nefyr patrol was riding briskly on the Hetterwee Road far to the north. Cer turned his gaze to the lush grass on the hill where he sat. The clouds meant rain, but probably not here, he thought. He always thought of something else when he saw a Nefyr patrol. Yes, it was too early in Hrickan for rains to fall here.

This rain would fall to the north, perhaps in the land of the King of the High Mountains, or on the vast plain of Westwold where they said horses ran free but were tame for any man to ride at need. But no rain would fall in Greet until Doonse, three weeks from now. By then the wheat would all be stored and the hay would be piled in vast ricks as tall as the hill Cer sat on.

In the old days, they said, all during Doonse the great wagons from Westwold would come and carry off the hay to last them through the snow season. But not now, Cer remembered. This year and last year and the year before the wagons had come from the south and east, two-wheeled wagons with drivers who spoke, not High Westil, but the barbarian Fyrd language. Fyrd or firt, thought Cer, and laughed, for firt was a word he could not say in front of his parents. They spoke firt.

Cer looked out over the plain again. The Nefyr patrol had turned from the highway and were on the road to the hills.

The road to the hills. Cer leaped to his feet and raced down the track leading home. A patrol heading for the hills could only mean trouble.

He stopped to rest only once, when the pain in his side was too bad to bear. But the patrol had horses, and he arrived home only to see the horses of the Nefyrre gathered at his father's gate.

Where are the uncles? Cer thought. The uncles must come.

But the uncles were not there, and Cer heard a terrible scream from inside the garden walls. He had never heard his mother scream before, but somehow he knew it was his mother, and he ran to the gate. A Nefyr soldier seized him and called out, "Here's the boy!" in a thick accent of High Westil, so that Cer's parents could understand. Cer's mother screamed again, and now Cer saw why.

His father had been stripped naked, his arms and legs held by two tall Nefyrre. The Nefyr captain held his viciously curved short-sword, point up, pressing against Cer's father's hard-muscled stomach. As Cer and his mother watched, the sword drew blood, and the captain pushed it in to the hilt, then pulled it up to the ribs. Blood gushed. The captain had been careful not to touch the heart, and now they thrust a spear into the huge wound, and lifted it high, Cer's father dangling from the end. They lashed the spear to the gatepost, and the blood and bowels stained the gates and the walls.

For five minutes more Cer's father lived, his chest heaving in the agony of breath. He may have died of pain, but Cer did not think so, for his father was not the kind to give in to pain. He may have died of suffocation, for one lung was gone and every breath was excruciating, but Cer did not think so, for his father kept breathing to the end. It was loss of blood, Cer decided, weeks later. It was when his body was dry, when the veins collapsed, that Cer's father died.

He never uttered a sound. Cer's father would never let the Nefyrre hear him so much as sigh in pain.

Cer's mother screamed and screamed until blood came from her mouth and she fainted.

Cer stood in silence until his father died. Then when the captain, a smirk on his face, walked near Cer and looked in his face, Cer kicked him in the groin.

They cut off Cer's great toes, but like his father, Cer made no sound.

Then the Nefyrre left and the uncles came.

Uncle Forwin vomited. Uncle Erwin wept. Uncle Crune put his arm around Cer's shoulder as the servants bound his maimed feet and said, "Your father was a great, a brave man. He killed many Nefyrre, and burned many wagons. But the Nefyrre are strong."

Uncle Crune squeezed Cer's shoulder. "Your father was stronger. But he was one, and they were many."

Cer looked away.

"Will you not look at your uncle?" Uncle Crune asked.

"My father," Cer said, "did not think that he was alone."

Uncle Crune got up and walked away. Cer never saw the uncles again.

He and his mother had to leave the house and the fields, for a Nefyr farmer had been given the land to farm for the King of Nefyryd. With no money, they had to move south, across the River Greebeck into the drylands near the desert, where no rivers flowed and so only the hardiest plants lived. They lived the winter on the charity of the desperately poor. In the summer, when the heat came, so did the Poor Plague, which swept the drylands. The cure was fresh fruits, but fresh fruits came from Yffyrd and Suffyrd and only the rich could buy them, and the poor died by the thousands. Cer's mother was one of them.

They took her out on the sand to burn her body and free her spirit. As they painted her with tar (tar, at least, cost nothing, if a man had a bucket), five horsemen came to the brow of a dune to watch. At first Cer thought they were Nefyrre, but no. The poor people looked up and saluted the strangers, which Greetmen never do to the enemy. These, then, were desert men, the Abadapnur nomads, who raided the rich farms of Greet during dry years, but who never harmed the poor.

We hated them, Cer thought, when we were rich. But now we are poor, and they are our friends.

His mother burned as the sun set.

Cer watched until the flames went out. The moon was high for the second time that night. Cer said a prayer to the moonlady over his mother's bones and ashes and then he turned and left.

He stopped at their hut and gathered the little food they had, and put on his father's tin ring, which the Nefyrre had thought was valueless, but which Cer knew was the sign of the Cemreet family's authority since forever ago.

Then Cer walked north.

He lived by killing rats in barns and cooking them. He lived by begging at poor farmer's doors, for the rich farmers had servants to turn away beggars. That, at least, Cer remembered, his father had never done. Beggars always had a meal at his father's house.

Cer also lived by stealing when he could hunt or beg no food. He stole handfuls of raw wheat. He stole carrots from gardens. He stole water from wells, for which he could have lost his life in the rainless season. He stole, one time, a fruit from a rich man's food wagon.

It burned his mouth, it was so cold and the acid so strong. It dribbled down his chin. As a poor man and a thief, Cer thought, I now eat a thing so dear that even my father, who was called wealthy, could never buy it.

And at last he saw the mountains in the north. He walked on, and in a week the mountains were great cliffs and steep slopes of shale. The Mitherkame, where the king of the High Mountains reigned, and Cer began to climb.

He climbed all day and slept in a cleft of a rock. He moved slowly, for climbing in sandals was clumsy, and without his great toes Cer could not climb barefoot. The next morning he climbed more. Though he nearly fell one time when falling would have meant crashing a mile down into the distant plain, at last he reached the knifelike top of the Mitherkame, and heaven.

For of a sudden the stone gave way to soil. Not the pale sandy soil of the drylands, nor the red soil of the Greet, but the dark black soil of the old songs from the north, the soil that could not be left alone for a day or it would sprout plants that in a week would be a forest.

And there *was* a forest, and the ground was thick with grass. Cer had seen only a few trees in his life, and they had been olive trees, short and gnarled, and fig sycamores, that were three times the height of a man. These were twenty times the height of a man and ten steps around, and the young trees shot up straight and tall so that not a sapling was as small as Cer, who for twelve years old was not considered small.

To Cer, who had known only wheat and hay and olive orchards, the forest was more magnificent than the mountain or the city or the river or the moon.

He slept under a huge tree. He was very cold that night. And in the morning he realized that in a forest he would find no farms, and where there were no farms there was no food for him. He got up and walked deeper into the forest. There were people in the High Mountains, else there would be no king, and Cer would find them. If he didn't, he would die. But at least he would not die in the realms of the Nefyrre.

He passed many bushes with edible berries, but he did not know they could be eaten so he did not eat. He passed many streams with slow stupid fish that he could have caught, but in Greet fish were never eaten, because it always carried disease, and so Cer caught no fish.

And on the third day, when he began to feel so weak from hunger that he could walk no longer, he met the treemage.

He met him because it was the coldest night yet, and at last Cer tore branches from a tree to make a fire. But the wood did not light, and when Cer looked up he saw that the trees had moved. They were coming closer, surrounding him tightly. He watched them, and they did not move as he watched, but when he turned around the ones he had not been watching were closer yet.

He tried to run, but the low branches made a tight fence he could not get through. He couldn't climb, either, because the branches all stabbed downward. Bleeding from the twigs he had scraped, Cer went back to his camping place and watched as the trees at last made a solid wall around him.

And he waited. What else could he do in his wooden prison?

In the morning he heard a man singing, and he called for help.

"Oh ho," he heard a voice say in a strange accent. "Oh ho, a tree cutter and a firemaker, a branch killer and a forest hater."

"I'm none of those," Cer said. "It was cold, and I tried to build a fire only to keep warm."

"A fire, a fire," the voice said. "In this small part of the world there are no fires of wood. But that's a young voice I hear, and I doubt there's a beard beneath the words."

"I have no beard," Cer answered. "I have no weapon, except a knife too small to harm you."

"A knife? A knife that tears sap from living limbs, Redwood says. A knife that cuts twigs like soft manfingers, says Elm. A knife that stabs bark till it bleeds, says Sweet Aspen. Break your knife," said the voice outside the trees, "and I will open your prison."

"But it's my only knife," Cer protested, "and I need it."

"You need it here like you need fog on a dark night. Break it or you'll die before these trees move again."

Cer broke his knife.

Behind him a heard a sound, and he turned to see a fat old man standing in a clear space between the trees. A moment before there had been no clear space.

"A child," said the man.

"A fat old man," said Cer, angry at being considered as young as his years.

"An illbred child at that," said the man. "But perhaps he knows no better, for from the accent of his speech I would say he comes from Greetland, and from his clothing I would say he was poor, and it's well known in Mitherwee that there are no manners in Greet."

Cer snatched up the blade of his knife and ran at the man. Somehow there were many sharp-pointed branches in the way, and his hand ran into a hard limb, knocking the blade to the ground.

"Oh, my child," said the man kindly. "There is death in your heart."

The branches were gone, and the man reached out his hands and touched Cer's face. Cer jerked away.

"And the touch of a man brings pain to you." The man sighed. "How inside out your world must be."

Cer looked at the man coldly. He could endure taunting. But was that kindness in the old man's eyes?

"You look hungry," said the old man.

Cer said nothing.

"If you care to follow me, you may. I have food for you, if you like."

Cer followed him.

They went through the forest, and Cer noticed that the old man stopped to touch many of the trees. And a few he pointedly snubbed, turning his back or taking a wider route around them. Once he stopped and spoke to a tree that had lost a large limb – recently, too, Cer thought, because the tar on the stump was still soft. "Soon there'll be no pain at all," the old man said to the tree. Then the old man sighed again. "Ah, yes, I know. And many a walnut in the falling season."

Then they reached a house. If it could be called a house, Cer thought. Stones were the walls, which was common enough in Greet, but the roof was living wood – thick branches from nine tall trees, interwoven and heavily leaved, so that Cer was sure no drop of rain could ever come inside.

"You admire my roof?" the old man asked. "So tight that even in the winter, when the leaves are gone, the snow cannot come in. But *we* can," he said, and led the way through a door into a single room.

The old man kept up a constant chatter as he fixed breakfast: berries and cream, stewed acorns, and thick slices of cornbread. The old man named all the foods for Cer, because except for the cream it was all strange to him. But it was good, and it filled him.

"Acorn from the Oaks," said the old man. "Walnuts from the trees of that name. And berries from the bushes, and neartrees. Corn, of course, comes from an untree, a weak plant with no wood, which dies every year."

"The trees don't die every year, then, even though it snows?" Cer asked, for he had heard of snow.

"Their leaves turn bright colors, and then they fall, and perhaps that's a kind of death," said the man. "But in Eanan the snow melts and by Blowan there are leaves again on all the trees."

Cer did not believe him, but he didn't disbelieve him either. Trees were strange things.

"I never knew that trees in the High Mountains could move."

"Oh ho," laughed the old man. "And neither can they, except here, and other woods that a treemage tends."

"A treemage? Is there magic then?"

"Magic. Oh ho," the man laughed again. "Ah yes, magic, many magics, and mine is the magic of trees."

Cer squinted. The man did not look like a man of power, and yet the trees had penned an intruder in. "You rule the trees here?"

"Rule?" the old man asked, startled. "What a thought. Indeed no. I serve them. I protect them. I give them the power in me, and they give me the power in them, and it makes us all a good deal more powerful. But rule? That just doesn't enter into magic. What a thought."

Then the old man chattered about the doings of the silly squirrels this year, and when Cer was through eating the old man gave him a bucket and they spent the morning gathering berries. "Leave a berry on the bush for every one you pick," the old man said. "They're for the birds in the fall and for the soil in the Kamesun, when new bushes grow."

And so Cer, quite accidentally, began his life with the treemage, and it was as happy a time as Cer ever had in his life, except when he was a child and his mother sang to him and except for the time his father took him hunting deer in the hills of Wetfell.

And after the autumn when Cer marvelled at the colours of the leaves, and after the winter when Cer tramped through the snow with the treemage to tend to ice-splintered branches, and after the spring when Cer thinned the new plants so the forest did not become overgrown, the treemage began to think that the dark places in Cer's heart were filled with light, or at least put away where they could not be found.

He was wrong. For as he gathered leaves for the winter's fires Cer dreamed he was gathering the bones of his enemies. And as he tramped the snow he dreamed he was marching into battle to wreak death on the Nefyrre. And as he thinned the treestarts Cer dreamed of slaying each of the uncles as his father had been slain, because none of them had stood by him in his danger.

Cer dreamed of vengeance, and his heart grew darker even as the wood was filled with the bright light of the summer sun.

One day he said to the treemage, "I want to learn magic."

The treemage smiled with hope. "You're learning it," he said, "and I'll gladly teach you more."

"I want to learn things of power."

"Ah," said the treemage, disappointed. "Ah, then, you can have no magic."

"You have power," said Cer. "I want it also."

"Oh, indeed," said the treemage. "I have the power of two legs and two arms, the power to heat tar over a peat fire to stop the sap flow from broken limbs, the power to cut off diseased branches to save the tree, the power to teach the trees how and when to protect themselves. All the rest is the power of the trees, and none of it is mine."

"But they do your bidding," said Cer.

"Because I do theirs!" the treemage said, suddenly angry. "Do you think that there is slavery in this wood? Do you think I am a king? Only men allow men to rule them. Here in this wood there is only love, and on that love and by that love the trees and I have the magic of the wood."

Cer looked down, disappointed. The treemage misunderstood, and thought that Cer was contrite.

"Ah, my boy," said the treemage. "You haven't learned it, I see. The root of magic is love, the trunk is service. The treemages love the trees and serve them and then they share treemagic with the trees. Lightmages love the sun and make fires at night, and the fire serves them as they serve the fire. Horsemages love and serve horses, and they ride freely whither they will because of the magic in the herd. There is field magic and plain magic, and the magic of rocks and metals, songs and dances, the magic of winds and weathers. All built on love, all growing through service."

"I must have magic," said Cer.

"Must you?" asked the treemage. "Must you have magic? There are kinds of magic, then, that you might have. But I can't teach them to you."

"What are they?"

"No," said the treemage, and he wouldn't speak again.

Cer thought and thought. What magic could be demanded against anyone's will?

And at last, when he had badgered and nagged the treemage for weeks, the treemage angrily gave in. "Will you know then?" the treemage snapped. "I will tell you. There is seamagic, where the wicked sailors serve the monsters of the deep by feeding them living flesh. Would you do that?" But Cer only waited for more.

"So that appeals to you," said the treemage. "Then you will be delighted at desert magic."

And now Cer saw a magic he might use. "How is that performed?"

"*I* know not," said the treemage icily. "It is the blackest of the magics to men of *my* kind, though your dark heart might leap to it. There's only one magic darker."

"And what is that?" asked Cer.

"What a fool I was to take you in," said the treemage. "The wounds in your heart, you don't want them to heal; you love to pick at them and let them fester."

"What is the darkest magic?" demanded Cer.

"The darkest magic," said the treemage, "is one, thank the moon, that you can never practice. For to do it you have to love men and love the love of men more than your own life. And love is as far from you as the sea is from the mountains, as the earth is from the sky."

"The sky touches the earth," said Cer.

"Touches, but never do they meet," said the treemage.

Then the treemage handed Cer a basket, which he had just filled with bread and berries and a flagon of streamwater. "Now go."

"Go?" asked Cer.

"I hoped to cure you, but you won't have a cure. You clutch at your suffering too much to be healed."

Cer reached out his foot towards the treemage, the crusty scars still a deep red where his great toe had been.

"As well you might try to restore my foot."

"Restore?" asked the treemage. "I restore nothing. But I staunch, and heal, and I help the trees forget their lost limbs. For if they insist on rushing sap to the limb as if it were still there, they lose all their sap; they dry, they wither, they die."

Cer took the basket.

"Thank you for your kindness," said Cer. "I'm sorry that you don't understand. But just as the tree can never forgive the axe or the flame, there are those that must die before I can truly live again."

"Get out of my wood," said the treemage. "Such darkness has no place here."

And Cer left, and in three days came to the edge of the Mitherkame, and in two days reached the bottom of the cliffs, and in a few weeks reached the desert. For he would learn desertmagic. He would serve the sand, and the sand would serve him.

On the way the soldiers of Nefyryd stopped him and searched him. Now all the farms were farmed by Nefyrre, men of the south who had never owned land before. They drove him away, afraid that he might steal. So he snuck back in the night and from his father's storehouse stole meat and from his father's barn stole a chicken.

He crossed the Greebeck to the drylands and gave the meat and the chicken to the poor people there. He lived with them for a few days. And then he went out into the desert.

He wandered in the desert for a week before he ran out of food and water. He tried everything to find the desertmage. He spoke to the hot sand and the burning rocks as the treemage had spoken to the trees. But the sand was never injured and did not need a healing touch, and the rocks could not be harmed and so they needed no protection. There was no answer when Cer talked, except the wind which cast sand in his eyes. And at last Cer lay dying on the sand, his skin caked and chafed and burnt, his clothing long since tattered away into nothing, his flagon burning hot and filled with sand, his eyes blind from the whiteness of the desert.

He could neither love nor serve the desert, for the desert needed nothing from him and there was neither beauty nor kindness to love.

But he refused to die without having vengeance. Refused to die so long that he was still alive when the Abadapnu tribesmen found him. They gave him water and nursed him back to health. It took weeks, and they had to carry him on a sledge from waterhole to waterhole.

And as they travelled with their herds and their horses, the Abadapnur carried Cer farther, and farther away from the Nefyrre and the land of Greet.

Cer regained his senses slowly, and learned the Abadapnu language even more slowly. But at last, as the clouds began to gather for the winter rains, Cer was one of the tribe, considered a man because he had a beard, considered wise because of the dark look on his face that remained even on those rare times when he laughed.

He never spoke of his past, though the Abadapnur knew well enough what the tin ring on his finger meant and why he had only eight toes. And they, with the perfect courtesy of the incurious, asked him nothing.

He learned their ways. He learned that starving on the desert was foolish, that dying of thirst was unnecessary. He learned how to trick the desert into yielding up life. "For," said the tribemaster, "the desert is never willing that anything should live."

Cer remembered that. The desert wanted nothing to live. And he wondered if that was a key to desertmagic. Or was it merely a locked door that he could never open? How can you serve and be served by the sand that wants only your death? How could he get vengeance if he was dead? "Though I would gladly die if my dying could kill my father's killers," he said to his horse one day. The horse hung her head, and would only walk for the rest of the day, though Cer kicked her to try to make her run.

Finally one day, impatient that he was doing nothing to achieve his revenge, Cer went to the tribemaster and asked him how one learned the magic of sand.

"Sandmagic? You're mad," said the tribemaster. For days the tribemaster refused to look at him, let alone answer his questions, and Cer realized that here on the desert the sandmagic was hated as badly as the treemage hated it. Why? Wouldn't such power make the Abadapnur great?

Or did the tribemaster refuse to speak because the Abadapnur did not know the sandmagic?

But they knew it.

And one day the tribemaster came to Cer and told him to mount and follow.

They rode in the early morning before the sun was high, then slept in a cave in a rocky hill during the heat of the day. In the dusk they rode again, and at night they came to the city.

"Ettuie," whispered the tribemaster, and then they rode their horses to the edge of the ruins.

The sand had buried the buildings up to half their height, inside and out, and even now the breezes of evening stirred the sand and built little dunes against the walls. The buildings were made of stone, rising not to domes like the great cities of the Greetmen but to spires, tall towers that seemed to pierce the sky.

"Ikikietar," whispered the tribemaster, "Ikikiaiai re dapii. O ikikiai etetur o abadapnur, ikikiai re dapii."

"What are the 'knives'?" asked Cer. "And how could the sand kill them?"

"The knives are these towers, but they are also the stars of power."

"What power?" asked Cer eagerly.

"No power for you. Only power for Etetur, for they were wise. They had the manmagic."

Manmagic. Was that the darkest magic spoken of by the treemage?

"Is there a magic more powerful than manmagic?" Cer asked.

"In the mountains, no," said the tribemaster. "On the well-watered plain, in the forest, on the sea, no."

"But in the desert?"

"A huu par eiti ununura," muttered the tribemaster, making the sign against death. "Only the desert power. Only the magic of the sand."

"I want to know," said Cer.

"Once," the tribemaster said, "once there was a mighty empire here. Once a great river flowed here, and rain fell, and the soil was rich and red like the soil of Greet, and a million people lived under the rule of the King of Ettue Dappa. But not all, for far to the west there lived a few who hated Ettue and the manmagic of the kings, and they forget the tools that undid this city.

"They made the wind blow from the desert. They made the rains run off the earth. By their power the river sank into the desert sand, and the fields bore no fruit, and at last the King of Ettue surrendered, and half his kingdom was given to the sandmages. To the dapinur. That western kingdom became Dapnu Dap."

"A kingdom?" said Cer, surprised. "But now the great desert bears that name."

"And once the great desert was no desert, but a land of grasses and grains like your homeland to the north. The sandmages weren't content with half a kingdom, and they used their sandmagic to make a desert of Ettue, and they covered the lands of rebels with sand, until at last the victory of the desert was complete, and Ettue fell to the armies of Greet and Nefyryd – they were allies then – and we of Dapnu Dap became nomads, living off that tiny bit of life that even the harshest desert cannot help but yield."

"And what of the sandmages?" asked Cer.

"We killed them."

"All?"

"All," said the tribemaster. "And if any man will practice sandmagic, today, we will kill him. For what happened to us we will let happen to no other people."

Cer saw the knife in the tribemaster's hand.

"I will have your vow," said the tribemaster. "Swear before these stars and this sand and the ghosts of all who lived in this city that you will seek no sandmagic."

"I swear," said Cer, and the tribemaster put his knife away.

The next day Cer took his horse and a bow and arrows and all the food he could steal and in the heat of the day when everyone slept he went out into the desert. They followed him, but he slew two with arrows and the survivors lost his trail.

Word spread through the tribes of the Abadapnur that a would-be sandmage was loose in the desert, and all were ready to kill him if he came. But he did not come.

For he knew now how to serve the desert, and how to make the desert serve him. For the desert loved death, and hated grasses and trees and water and the things of life.

So in service of the sand Cer went to the edge of the land of the Nefyrre, east of the desert. There he fouled wells with the bodies of diseased animals. He burned fields when the wind was blowing off the desert, a dry wind that pushed the flames into the cities. He cut down trees. He killed sheep and cattle. And when the Nefyrre patrols chased him he fled onto the desert where they could not follow.

His destruction was annoying, and impoverished many a farmer, but alone it would have done little to hurt the Nefyrre. Except that Cer felt his power over the desert growing. For he was feeding the desert the only things it hungered for; death and dryness.

He began to speak to the sand again, not kindly, but of land to the east that the sand could cover. And the wind followed his words, whipping the sand, moving the dunes. Where he stood the wind did not touch him, but all around him the dunes moved like waves of the sea.

Moving eastward.

Moving into the lands of the Nefyrre.

And now the hungry desert could do in a night a hundred times more than Cer could do alone with a torch or a knife. It ate olive groves in an hour. The sand borne on the wind filled houses in a night, buried cities in a week, and in only three months had driven the Nefyrre across the Greebeck and the Nefyr River, where they thought the terrible sandstorms could not follow.

But the storms followed. Cer taught the desert almost to fill the river, so that the water spread out a foot deep and miles wide, flooding some lands that had been dry, but also leaving more water surface for the sun to drink from; and before the river reached the sea it was dry, and the desert swept across into the heart of Nefyryd.

The Nefyrre had always fought with the force of arms, and cruelty was their companion in war. But against the desert they were helpless. They could not fight the sand. If Cer could have known it, he would have gloried in the fact that, untaught, he was the most powerful sandmage who had ever lived. For hate was a greater teacher than any of the books of dark lore, and Cer lived on hate.

And on hate alone, for now he ate and drank nothing, sustaining his body through the power of the wind and the heat of the sun. He was utterly dry, and the blood no longer coursed through his veins. He lived on the energy of the storms he unleashed. And the desert eagerly fed him, because he was feeding the desert.

He followed his storms, and walked through the deserted towns of the Nefyrre. He saw the refugees rushing north and east to the high ground. He saw the corpses of those caught in the storm. And he sang at night the old songs of Greet, the war songs. He wrote his father's name with chalk on the wall of every city he destroyed. He wrote his mother's name in the sand, and where he had written her name the wind did not blow and the sand did not shift, but preserved the writing as if it had been incised on rock.

Then one day, in a lull between his storms, Cer saw a man coming towards him from the east. Abadapnu, he wondered, or Nefyrre? Either way he drew his knife, and fit the nock of an arrow on his bowstring.

But the man came with his hands extended, and he called out, "Cer Cemreet."

It had never occurred to Cer that anyone knew his name.

"Sandmage Cer Cemreet," said the man when he was close. "We have found who you are."

Cer said nothing, but only watched the man's eyes.

"I have come to tell you that your vengeance is full. Nefyryd is at its knees. We have signed a treaty with Greet and we no longer raid into Hetterwee. Driplin has seized our westernmost lands."

Cer smiled. "I care nothing for your empire."

"Then for our people. The deaths of your father and mother have been avenged a hundred thousand times, for over two hundred thousand people have died at your hands."

Cer chuckled. "I care nothing for your people."

"Then for the soldiers who did the deed. Though they acted under orders, they have been arrested and killed, as have the men who gave them those orders, even our first general, all at the command of the King so that your vengeance will be complete. I have brought you their ears as proof of it," said the man, and he took a pouch from his waist.

"I care nothing for the soldiers, nor for proof of vengeance," said Cer.

"Then what do you care for?" asked the man quietly.

"Death," said Cer.

"Then I bring you that, too," said the man, and a knife was in his hand, and he plunged the knife into Cer's breast where his heart should have been. But when the man pulled the knife out no blood followed, and Cer only smiled.

"Indeed you brought it to me," said Cer, and he stabbed the man where his father had been stabbed, and drew the knife up as it had been drawn through his father's body, except that he touched the man's heart, and he died.

As Cer watched the blood soaking into the sand, he heard in his ears his mother's screams, which he had silenced for these years. He heard her screams and now, remembering his father and his mother and himself as a child he began to cry, and he held the body of the man he had killed and rocked back and forth on the sand as the blood clotted on his clothing and his skin. His tears mixed with the blood and poured into the sand and Cer realized that this was the first time since his father's death that he had shed any tears at all.

I am not dry, thought Cer. There is water under me still for the desert to drink.

He looked at his dry hands, covered with the man's blood, and tried to scrub off the clotted blood with sand. But the blood stayed, and the sand could not clean him.

He wept again. And then he stood and faced the desert to the west, and he said, "Come."

A breeze began.

"Come," he said to the desert, "come and dry my eyes."

And the wind came up, and the sand came, and Cer Cemreet was buried in the sand, and his eyes became dry, and the last life passed from his body, and the last sandmage passed from the world.

Then came the winter rains, and the refugees of Nefyryd returned to their land. The soldiers were called home, for the wars were over, and now their weapons were the shovel and the plow. They redug the trench of the Nefyr and the Greebeck, and the river soon flowed deep again to the sea. They scattered grass seed and cleaned their houses of sand. They carried water into the ruined fields with ditches and aqueducts.

Slowly life returned to Nefyryd.

And the desert, having lost its mage, retreated quietly to its old borders, never again to seek death where there was life. Plenty of death already where nothing lived, plenty of dryness to drink where there was no water.

In a wood a little way from the crest of the Mitherkame, a treemage heard the news from a wandering tinker.

The treemage went out into the forest and spoke softly to the Elm, to the Oak, to the Redwood, to the Sweet Aspen. And when all had heard the news, the forest wept for Cer Cemreet, and each tree gave a twig to be burned in his memory, and shed sap to sink into the ground in his name.

DREAM A LITTLE DREAM FOR ME...
Peter Crowther

---

*Although a Yorkshireman through and through, Peter Crowther (b.
1949) seems as much at home in the United States, where many of
his stories are set. His fascination for the machinery that runs the
world makes me think of him as the British Ray Bradbury. He has
worked in IT, journalism and PR, but has been writing his
idiosyncratic stories since the 1980s. His books include* Escardy Gap
(1996), written with James Lovegrove, Lonesome Roads *(1999)
and* The Spaces Between the Lines *(2007). Not content with
writing he has also edited a number of anthologies and has turned
publisher with the award-winning PS Publishing which, in
addition to its many excellent books, also publishes the quarterly
magazine* Postscripts. *Several stories from that are included
elsewhere in this volume.*

*This is not the first extreme fantasy of Peter's that I have
published. There was "The Eternal Altercation" in* The Mammoth
Book of Sorcerer's Tales. *This story might seem a little closer to home
but don't be misled. Not only will you go to Hell and back, but you'll
see the end of all...well, you'll see.*

His website is at http://store.pspublishing.co.uk/

We are such stuff
As dreams are made on; and our little life
Is rounded with a sleep.
– William Shakespeare, *The Tempest*

Behold, this dreamer cometh.
– *The Book of Genesis,* 37:19

Everybody has a dream; everybody dreams. The man who told me that – the same man who spent his time showing an old dog-eared piece of card around in Vinzenz Richter's Wine Tavern, in the long shadow of Meissen's Albrecht Castle – was a long way from home…always assuming, of course, that the dead have someplace to hang their hat at the end of a busy working day. And something to do when they get there.

When I was in full time employment, for a big financial organization, all I ever wanted to do when *I* got home from work was write.

Every evening I would finish dinner as fast as I could reasonably chew it, and then high-tail it into my small book-lined office and boot up the trusty computer. Seems I had more energy for writing then, though that seems ridiculous when all I have to do now is write.

Back then, when I was in and out of meetings filled with corporate types who felt they needed permission to break wind, I made silent (and sometimes not so silent) promises to whatever deities ruled the world that if I could ever get out of the mindless slog of listening to minutes being read out day in, day out, and into a silent world of my own thoughts and words I would never ever complain again. And, when it happened, I didn't. I was true to my word. For a while. Well, why not: after all, I had nurtured a dream – as the woman by the statue of the pissing boy in Hamburg had known…among many things, as it turned out – and my dream had become a reality.

But it was the dead man with the old card that was to enable me to recognize that my dream was not the only one. Nor was it the most important.

But first things first.

My first novel, a minor espionage epic set in Britain, Holland and the United States and over which I had pondered and sweated and agonized for almost three years, sold to the third publisher who read it. And it sold well, made a second printing in hardcover and a couple of nice book club sales and then went into a paperback edition which hovered around the lower edges of the bestsellers listing for almost two months. The all-important second book was eagerly awaited. Mostly by my publisher.

"So how's the book coming along?" James Farraday asked me a couple of weeks before events were set in motion to change my life forever. He posed the question as nonchalantly as the mouthful of tossed salad would allow.

We were in a small restaurant off Columbus Circle, sitting in the smoking section – and there's not many of those around these days – and I was pulling on a Salem Light and pushing olives around on my plate like toy soldiers on a military campaign map. He waited a few seconds, washing most of the salad from his teeth with a mouthful of Shiraz, before grunting, "Well?"

The truth was, the book hadn't been coming along too well at all. In fact, the book wasn't actually started as such. After four months, since the day I had proudly announced in Farraday's office that I would be starting that very afternoon, typing in those mystical and terrifying words "Chapter One", I still had nothing. Worse still, since the advent of computers and word processors, I couldn't even take him back to my apartment and show off a full wastepaper basket brimming with scrunched-up starts. With the exception of a loose-leaf notebook containing a few pages of scribbled notes, I had zilch. Nada.

"Well," I started, pacing the lie so that it tumbled out easy and sounded more like the Artist's reluctance to say too much about his next project until the final period was typed in and pored over a while, "it's coming along. It's coming along a little slower than I'd like but, you know, it's coming along."

James nodded and splashed more wine into our glasses. "Yeah?"

"Yeah."

We were as close as most authors and their editor could reasonably hope to be, and closer than many. We had shared other bottles of wine and other meal-table chats, some even when there was no real need for him to be there. But I think he saw something in me that struck a chord. Just as I think there were few people he could call real friends. His real friends, I believe, were the books he worked on.

"But it is coming along," he said, returning to the promised novel.

I nodded. "But like I say, slow."

"Mmm." He forked a piece of pasta into a mound of lettuce and transferred it to his waiting mouth. "Is it started?"

His expression told me that he knew the answer already but I decided to persevere. "Let's just say it's not going as well as I'd hoped."

For a long minute, he said nothing. Then, "You know," he said, chewing, "maybe you need to take a break. You thought about doing that? Taking a break?"

I stubbed out my cigarette and thought about lighting another, but it was difficult enough making him out through the haze I had already created. I pushed the ashtray away from me and thanked whatever god looked after diners that most good restaurants train their staff to empty ashtrays after each butt. Sure enough, a young man with a smile that looked like it had come from a catalog appeared as if by magic and replaced the offending item with a clean version. Before I could say anything, James leaned forward and, with a sly wink, said, "You could put it down as research." He straightened up again and forked the last of the salad onto the final few strands of linguini. "Think about it. Somewhere you've always wanted to go. Shoe-horn it into the book someplace and write it off." He laid his fork on the cleared plate and snapped his fingers. "Just like that. Say four weeks. Six maybe. Then we can see how things are coming along when you get back." He lifted his glass, swirling the wine around as he studied me. "Can you think of anywhere?"

I could.

The air in Europe smells of confectionery, my father had told me. *Even in the bars where it mixes in with the smell of alcohol, cologne, perfume and the pungent aroma of French and German tobacco, you can smell candy. Makes you feel like a kid all over again.*

He had been right, as I was to find out. But my first week had failed to ignite the same enthusiasm in me as it had in him and already I was showing signs of being homesick.

At night, in the sumptuous hotel rooms, you could look out of the open window and have to strain to hear anything. No planes flying overhead, no stilted rap music from passing cars and not even the distant wail of police sirens prowling the concrete corridors of Manhattan looking for transgressors. Or the perfect cup of coffee.

The fact was, the coffee tasted too bitter and there probably weren't any transgressors here. And believe me, when a New Yorker starts to get misty-eyed about the prospect of not being mugged then you know something's wrong. I'd known it pretty well since the second day. But it hadn't really hit home until a chance meeting with a middle-aged but very attractive woman with a hauntingly soothing purple hair-colouring.

It was my eighth day in Europe.

We happened to be standing next to each other in Neugartenstrasse, an otherwise empty street, staring at a cherubic statue of a naked young boy. In fact, I had been so engrossed in the statue that I had not even seen the woman approaching: one minute I had considered myself alone and the next she was there.

The boy had his hands held aloft behind his head and his pelvis thrust forward, an abundant and constant stream of water fountaining from his little delicately sculptured penis and rattling noisily into the small lake around his feet. Presumably the water was circulated by means of a system of tubes and pumps, though no evidence was visible. I didn't know and was beginning to care even less. This lack of interest had undoubtedly been heightened – if not caused entirely – by the fact that, somewhat foolishly, I had bought a German – French phrasebook and so was having a hard time making sense of anything. But the pictures were vaguely interesting.

The woman glanced up the street and produced from her coat pocket a small tin cup which she then held beneath the stream until it filled. Turning to me, the cup already lifted to her lips, she said, "On ne sait jamais, paraît qu'en buvant de cette eau, on trouve un bon mari." Then, with a throaty laugh, she drained the cup and turned to me, smiling proudly. "Ah," she said, dabbing at her lips with a gloved hand, "c'est magnifique, non?"

I frowned, smiled and shook my head. "I'm sorry, I don't understand." The words came out as a rattling stammer and I made a mental note to spend some time studying foreign languages before I next ventured behind Europe's lace underskirts.

"You are not French, monsieur?" She looked shocked.

I shook my head. "American. New York," I added, as though the first admission were not a sufficiently heinous crime.

She frowned and pointed to the guide book in my hand. "Then why do you have a French translation book?"

I waved the book and gave a small laugh, feeling my ears turning bright red. "Ah, yes," I began. "A. Mistake. I. Bought. It. In. Error," I explained, separating the words as though teaching rudimentary English to a visiting Martian…one of those saucer-eyed, spindly-legged figures that habitually stop cars on Nevada highways in order to engage in a little anal exploration with passing hayseeds driving pick-ups, called

Duane or Clyde – the hayseeds, not the pick-ups. "What was it that you were saying?"

"I said, legend has it that by drinking this water one will find a good husband."

"Ah." Her English was perfect which meant that any further utterances from me could be effected in a fraction of the time I might otherwise have taken. But no further utterances seemed to be forthcoming.

"You are here on holiday, yes?"

"Vacation, yes." I waved a hand at the urinating statue. "Seeing the sights."

She frowned again and smiled a little slyly as she returned the tin cup to her ample coat pocket. "But you are looking for something, yes? You are not simply on holiday."

I shrugged and shook my head. "No... I mean, yes. I'm just taking a break."

She took hold of my arm at the elbow and leaned close. I could smell peppermint and perfume, a heady and intoxicating mixture, and, just for a second, I felt my pulse quicken. "I know," she confided, confirming this revelation with a series of sharp nods. "You are looking for something. You are chasing a dream.

"We are all chasing dreams, Mons – I am sorry, Sir. But it is only when one learns not to look that one can truly find. When you have mastered that, perhaps you will have success. You must go to Meissen."

"Meissen?" It sounded like something Dick Dastardly's dog, Muttley might have said, his teeth clamped on some unfortunate's pants-seat.

She lifted her shoulders and made a sad shape with her mouth. "Perhaps, perhaps not," she said, answering some unspoken question as she looked me up and down. "But most everyone finds what they are looking for in Meissen. There is a magic there that...oh, I don't know." She laughed. Then I laughed.

We could have been sitting in a bar off Fifth Avenue, drinking

margaritas and discussing a new Neil Simon play. But we weren't, and
suddenly that fact hit me: I was a long way from home.

Her face became serious. "You must find the dream," she said. "But
take care for there are those who would take it from you." The light in
her eyes gave them a momentarily fearful glint, and then it was gone.

I smiled respectfully and considered several responses, none of which
seemed appropriate. Instead, I decided to stone-wall it out and wait for
her to say something else.

She removed her hand from my elbow and patted the bulge in her
pocket. "Ah well, perhaps you will wish me luck in finding my own
dream, eh? And I wish you luck with yours, whatever and wherever you
eventually find it to be." Then she was on her way, her high-heeled shoes
clacking on the paving slabs, sashaying up the street like a would-be
movie star. But in truth, she was already fading and still looking for her
leading man.

I left the phrase book beside the statue. Maybe it would turn out to
be somebody else's dream.

That night I tried to figure out just what my own dream was.

By three o'clock in the morning, an empty bottle of hoc and a full
ashtray on the table beside me, I had decided, in that wonderfully lightheaded and euphoric way that only comes after too much alcohol, that
the woman had probably been right. I had to go to Meissen. Why not?

I'd done the galleries and sidewalk cafes of Paris and Brussels, and
now Hamburg, until I was cultured out, and I'd seen and marveled at
enough gargoyle-festooned architecture to make even Frank Lloyd
Wright yawn and ask what was on at the movies. My mind was made up
and it felt good. A decision had been made. I pulled off my trousers and
stretched out on the bed.

Sleep came immediately. Beneath its sheet of oblivion my father
came into my hotel room and sat beside me. It was a very clear

dream...so clear that I saw the light shining briefly into the room from the corridor outside. Then the darkness returned and I saw only my father's shape until he reached the bed. Then, in the glow of the moon through the windows, I saw him in his entirety.

He was wearing an army uniform and though he was much younger than when I had last seen him – lying in a hospital bed surrounded by drips and blinking machines that were busy stealing him from me – I recognized him right away.

When you see this, he whispered to me, *you must look at it.*

I could see something in his hand but couldn't make out what it was. But whatever it was, it wasn't very big. *What is it?* I asked.

A dream, he said. *It's only a dream. But it is not yours alone. It belongs to everyone. And you must show it to them.*

If he said anything more, I don't remember it.

Feeling groggy, even after breakfast and several cups of black coffee plus a half-pack of Salem, I caught a train later than I had planned, packing my suitcase in a haphazard fashion that I was sure I would regret when it came time to remove the clothes so casually thrown inside. Then, with the memory of my late father's nocturnal visit still as fresh in my mind as though it had really happened, I arrived in Dresden where I boarded the *Theodor Fontaine*, one of only two cruisers built to negotiate Germany's second-longest river, and set off along the Elbe to Meissen.

It was like sailing into a children's story book.

My guidebook – this time an English language edition – told me that the city of Meissen had escaped the Second World War with barely a cup and saucer being rattled. It showed.

On either side of the river, wild flowers grew in such abundance that it was hard to imagine humans living there at all. Ubiquitous herons and buzzards and kites seemed to support such a conclusion and the occasional Hansel-and-Gretel riverside houses, and the barely glimpsed spired churches and turreted castles nestled as though forgotten deep in the lush woodland heightened the feeling of being deliciously trapped inside a fairy tale. I sat transfixed watching it all float by, daring myself time after time to jump ship. Like the man in the old *Twilight Zone* episode, I felt I had found my very own Willoughby – a magical domain that waited for anyone brave enough to relinquish all that had gone before and take a chance on finding true happiness.

We stepped off the boat and into this fairyland grotto speaking in the hushed and reverent tones of acolytes seeking an audience with their God. And well might it have been so.

If God had decided to spend his time making pottery instead of people, he would first have had to create somewhere like Meissen. The city is home to the oldest china factory in Europe, where some 600 artists are employed to hand-paint each item. But with price tags that range from $100 for a thimble to around $8,000 for a six-piece floral coffee set, it's a hobby that's affordable to only a few. Gods included.

Following a brief check-in at my guest-house and the welcome putting down of my bags, I washed and hit the streets. There was a stillness and calm about the place, drifting up the narrow house-lined streets and down cobbled alleyways in which the very air itself seemed to have lain undisturbed since the dawn of time. Fragmented footsteps echoed desultorily, hunched rooftop gargoyles stared with wide and unmoving eyes, beveled store-front windows reflected our passing images like funhouse mirrors, making the resulting elongations and distortions somehow more in keeping. And so it was, road-weary but mentally alive and even strangely rested with the onset of twilight, I came across the welcome glow and muted hum that characterizes a bar in any country in the world.

Vinzenz Richter established his notorious wine tavern on Am der Frauenkirche in 1873, notorious because of the array of weapons and instruments of torture housed in its cellar…the function of every item explained in gory detail (though thankfully not demonstrated) nightly by the current owner, one Gottfried Herrlich.

It was here, drinking my third stein of Muller Thurgau, that I saw Dennis Dannerman.

The last time I had seen Dennis was maybe five years earlier, in Salsa Posada, a small Mexican eatery on Thompson Street, right across from El Rincon de Espana – what a delight: the best Mexican or Spanish food in town and right across from each other.

Dennis tended bar at Salsa's, seeing to folks while they waited for a table, feeding them Gold and Silver Label tequila, copious amounts of Dos Equus or Tecate beers, and mixing cocktails for the folks who like to go to Mexican restaurants to drink them (and who, presumably, like to go to cocktail bars to listen to Los Lobos on the PA system). And all the time, he could carry on a conversation – a real conversation, not one of those cheesy streams of polite but vacuous niceties you get from some bartenders – and he'd laugh and take drink orders for the tables already eating and not miss a single beat or get a single order wrong. And best of all, he didn't throw the bottles around, though I always believed he could have done if he'd wanted to because I believed he was a special person, one of those people you come across maybe only two or three times in a lifetime.

But there were two more things that made Dennis special, at least as far as I was concerned: the first was that, like me, he loved jazz music, particularly anything by Horace Silver or Chet Baker; and the second was that we both shared the same birthdate – the Fourth of July. I didn't find the second one out until, when I had been going into Salsa Posada for several years, Nick Hassam and I had called in there just for a few slammers to celebrate my birthday – the fortieth – before continuing around a few well-chosen dives in the Village to get completely blitzed. When I asked where Dennis was, the girl behind the bar explained that he'd taken the night off to celebrate his own special event, the Big Three O. I couldn't wait to call in again when he was on duty, just to compare notes…in that strangely metaphysical way that many Cancerians seem to do. But I never did get the chance.

It was maybe a month later, six weeks at the most, that I finally got back to Salsa Posada, again with Nick. Still no Dennis. This time, when I asked about him, the girl behind the counter gave me a strange smile and sidled off to the woman by the payments desk. A brief hushed conversation resulted in the woman coming up to me and telling me, in a tone of muted respect, that Dennis was dead. He'd piled his Corvette into a road sign on the Brooklyn-Queens Expressway on his birthday.

And now here he was shuffling around a tavern in Meissen, Germany.

At first, I figured it must be Dennis's double.

But, as I watched him going up to different people – not everyone, just one or two, seemingly picked out after careful consideration – and showing them something, talking to them quietly, holding onto their coat sleeves, I decided that, no matter what we're taught about dead people being considerably immobile – not to mention silent – this one was the exception.

There was no question that it was Dennis so, obviously, the announcement of his death was somewhat exaggerated. Clearly, a mistake must have been made. Maybe he'd lent his car to someone and they'd totaled it, destroying any evidence to the contrary in the resulting conflagration. Maybe it suited him to be "dead" – after all, here he was several thousand miles away from New York apparently immersed in another life. Lots of maybes. But I decided to bite the bullet and speak to him.

When he finished talking to an elderly couple over by the bar, the man nodded and placed his drink on the counter. Then the man took his wife's drink – I assumed the woman was his wife – and, even though neither glass was empty, the two of them just turned around and walked out. I recorded all this at the time but it didn't seem particularly significant. At least, not then.

I picked up my own glass and wandered across to Dennis, approaching him from his right side as he surveyed the other people. He was just standing there, not doing anything, no drink, nothing. Just as I was reaching out, I saw that he was holding a piece of old card in his right hand. Then I made contact.

He didn't turn to me but simply glanced in my direction and then his eyes faced front again.

"*Er fragt, wo man am besten isst,*" he said without looking around. He laughed and shook his head. "*Und was kann ich fur Sie tun?*"

"Dennis?"

Still he didn't turn but when he spoke his voice was almost a whisper. "Is it *really* you?"

I moved around so that I was facing him. "That's what I thought about *you*. How are you?"

He stepped back a little so that he could get a good look at me, which also enabled me to get a good look at *him*. "I'm fine. How about you? How's New York?"

"Same as ever. It's just New York"

"New York is never only 'just' *any*thing."

"No, I guess you're right there."

He nodded, gave a small smile and started to look some more at the people around us.

"They told me you were dead," I said. His expression didn't alter and he continued to scan the room. "The woman in Salsa Posada."

"Cheryl."

"Cheryl," I echoed. "She said you'd crashed the car."

Still nothing. I followed his gaze and scanned the faces. They were just people having a good time, drinking the beer, talking, making out.

Pretty much like any bar I'd ever been to. Without turning, I said, "You waiting for someone?"

"Kind of," he said.

I turned back to face him. "Do you live here now?"

His eyes shifted back to look at me. "Look," he said, "I'm really busy right now. Can we do this some other time?"

I shook my head in a mixture of annoyance and amazement. "I don't get it. They tell me you're dead and then I find you in a bar in…"

"Meissen," he offered.

"In Meissen, and you won't even pass the time of day." I pulled out my pack of Salem and lit one. "I had something to tell you that I thought you mi…"

"We both have the same birthdate. Fourth of July."

"How did you know that?"

"I know everything." He waited a minute or so and then went on. "I knew you were here, for example…here in Germany."

"How?"

He sighed. "Siglinde Erhard told me." Then he said, "And I knew she had told you to come to Meissen."

Siglinde Erhard had wanted a man to care for and to care for her more than anything else in the world. This was what Dennis Dannerman told me as we walked along the bank of the River Elbe, the moonlight playing amidst the ripples in the water.

Although she had been forsaken – Dennis's word – by many men in her life, she had never lost the hope that she might find someone worthy of her affections. But eventually every abstinence, whether forced or voluntary, must have a respite, and without that respite things just go from bad to worse.

So it was, on an evening when she was feeling particularly desperate, Siglinde Erhard hanged herself in her apartment with a pair of her own nylon stockings. She thought it would be a release. But she was wrong.

The bitterness and resentment and desperation that had so fueled her life continued to run thick and strong even when she was dead. And so she still walked the streets of her beloved Hamburg, looking for someone in whom she recognized a basic goodness. One of her favorite visiting spots when she was alive was the statue of the pissing boy in Neugartenstrasse. The statue still held an attraction for her in death, perhaps even more so.

"Jesus Christ," I said, "isn't there *any*one here who's alive?"

"The percentages are the same wherever you are, whatever country you're in," Dennis said. "It's just..." He seemed to search for the appropriate words. "It's just that we usually don't get sent back to the place we left. Too many people might recognize us."

Over on the opposite bank, a heron flapped its wings wildly.

If Dennis Dannerman thought this was supposed to explain things to me, he was wrong. But he would not give any further explanations. "Don't ask me to say any more," he said.

We walked in silence for a while and then Dennis said, "Siglinde is not like me. She's just a ghost."

"And what are you? Can you tell me that, at least?"

He shrugged. "How about an angel?"

"An *angel*?"

"It's as good a description as anything. I know I don't have any wings but they went out with the Ark. I'm just..." He paused, again searching for some meaningful word or phrase. "I'm just doing a job. That's what Heaven should be all about, doing jobs. A big company, run like any other big company." There was something in the way he spoke that made me feel a little uneasy. Or maybe it was just that *I* had worked for a big company, and I didn't like it. Office politics, backstabbing, lying and cheating...surely the Elysian Fields were above all that.

"And what job are you doing?"

"What angels have always done: teaching people how to live for others and not be selfish." He seemed to consider this for a few seconds and then added, "But it's not always a popular occupation."

As we carried on walking I tried to reconcile such altruism with the grubby self-serving reality of Big Business. I failed miserably. The two concepts seemed mutually contradictory.

Perhaps sensing my confusion, Dennis stopped and turned to me. Producing from his jacket pocket the piece of card I had seen him showing in the tavern, he held it out to me. "Take a look, tell me what you see." I frowned and took an involuntary step backwards. "Go ahead," he said, thrusting the card towards me. "But you may not keep it."

I took the card and turned it over.

It was either some kind of out-of-focus photograph or a painting, dog-eared and stained with use, the image creased and faded. "What is it?"

"What it is isn't important. It's what you can see...that's the important thing."

I shifted around so that the moon's glow was directly behind me. "It looks like...it looks like some kind of blur." That was the best way I could describe it. The card was a haze of swirling shapes and shades and tones...maybe in colour, although I had no way of knowing that in the moonlight.

In fact, maybe it was the moonlight that made the thing seem to move on the card, like billowing dry ice smoke or graveyard mist...and was it my own shadow cast on the card or was there something behind the mist? Something big and...old, though I wondered what it was that made me think that; something which seemed as eager to see me as I was to see it. "I don't know," I said, handing the card back. "I have no idea what I can see."

Dennis took the card and slipped it back into his pocket. "It'll come to you, but when it does you must look with your heart, not with your eyes."

"And how do I do that?"

He smiled. "Like I say, it'll come to you."

I started walking, suddenly aware that the night had turned cold. Pulling my coat tightly around me and speaking over my shoulder, I asked Dennis what he had meant when he said that what it was wasn't important.

But it was my father's voice that answered. *A dream*, it whispered. *It's only a dream.*

When I turned around the path was empty. Dennis Dannerman had gone.

I walked around for a half-hour or so looking for him, smoking cigarettes and wondering, each time I passed someone, whether they were truly alive or simply shadows of themselves.

I considered returning to the tavern but decided I had had enough of crowds for one day, and so I went back to my guest house.

In truth, it was more than a guest house: cozy, pleasant and warm, a spice-smelling reassuring bolt-hole of sheets, frilly table-covers and flocked wallpaper, and, in Frau Maier, a bustling somewhat burly woman who smelled of mothballs and had a habit of making tiny humming sounds when she was listening to me. Her English was every bit as perfect as anyone else's and this further emphasized my need to learn at least the basic fundamentals before making such a trip again.

She welcomed me in personally, as though I were a long-lost relative returning from some fabled war fought on horseback and with oversized cutlery. Her hands clasped at her stomach, her back ramrod-straight and her smile tight but genuine, she asked if I would like any refreshment before retiring to bed – so much more eloquent and image-conjuring than simply "hitting the sack". But I declined. Already the beer I had consumed was making me feel a little woozy...but maybe the conversation I had had with Dennis Dannerman on the banks of the river had contributed to that. I bade her goodnight and went up to my room. Within minutes, I was tucked up in bed. Sleep seemed to come almost immediately.

Colours were everywhere, swirling around me, so deep and dense they were taking my breath away. The shapes billowed and withdrew, wafting suddenly one way and then the other, and all the time there were other shapes – real shapes, shapes of people – just behind the haze, standing there watching me.

When I opened my eyes again the room was dark. But not so dark that I couldn't make out the shape sitting in the chair by the window. I knew right away who it was.

I wanted to ask how he had got into my room but such questions seemed a little redundant when asked of an angel. And anyway, maybe I was still asleep. I reached for the pack of Salem. "Forget something, Dennis?"

He sighed. "We've stopped dreaming for others," he said. "All I wanted to do was put things right…or, at least, make them a little better."

"Dennis," I said, blowing smoke and hiking myself up in bed, "you're going to have to bear with me a little here. What do you mean about our stopping dreaming for others?"

He got to his feet and walked across to the window. "It's a cyclical thing, Charles," he said. "Most of the time, people care for each other pretty well but things tend to get run down." I could see his head turn around to look at me but I couldn't see his face. "And it starts when they're asleep.

"People don't know it's happening most of the time," he said, "they're just reacting to the way things are around them. Times get tough, and the people get tougher. It's a fact of life. They dream for themselves…they dream of success and wealth…about winning the lottery or being promoted; they dream of nice clothes and great vacations; about making out with people they've always wanted to make out with. They stop dreaming about the other poor shmuck who's maybe got even less than they have because they want it for themselves...and they want it all. Then, when the dreaming gets selfish enough, they stop even *thinking* about other folks." He looked back out of the window. "And that's where things are right about now. The collective dreaming for others stopped a long, long time ago. Collective thinking will follow soon."

I didn't say anything for a moment. "If you think that explains things then you've been away too long," I said at last.

"I'm not through," he said.

He walked back to the chair and I switched on the lamp by the side of the bed. The dim light gave the room a slightly surreal tone, as though everything that could be trusted was here within the parameter of its glow...and everything beyond it was hard and cold and dangerous. I shivered involuntarily, even though I was still fully clothed, and hoisted the sheet up to my chin.

He settled deeper into the chair. "Got a cigarette?"

"But you're an angel?"

"So?"

I tossed the pack across and followed it with the matchbook.

Dennis lit up and blew out smoke, sighing dreamily. "Good," he said. "Okay, let's say I've been a little economical with the truth. I'll take it from the top. Two things: first, the Dream."

He waved a hand. "Oh, I'm going back hundreds – thousands – of years. Back to the beginning, almost. In the beginning, there wasn't The Word...or even *a* word. There was only a dream, a dream for mankind. It was God's dream. He felt that men should bond amongst themselves, look after and out for each other. But what works in theory doesn't always work in practice. Where individuality exists – and individuality is the essence of existence – there will always be strife, struggle, and envy.

"Of course," he went on, "there was no way he could give a collective intelligence to men – that stuff only works in science fiction...and not always even then – because there were too many distractions. But only too many distractions while they were fully aware of them."

"I don't follow."

"He figured that if he could stop those distractions, just for a while, he could get them to bond...become almost a sentient multi-multi-headed creature. And so he hit on an idea – two ideas, actually. The first was to remove the diversions and the distractions, and the second was to place something – one thing – in their stead.

"And so," Dennis Dannerman said as he stubbed out his cigarette, "God invented sleep, and he created something to fill that void of existence...a dream of togetherness to bond people together."

"Jesus Christ, Dennis, what are you telling me here? I feel like Spencer Tracy in *Inherit The Wind*. What happened to Darwin in all this?"

"Oh, evolution happened just the way that Darwin said it did. But God gave us sleep, and the ability to dream. What we've lost over the millennia, is *The* dream...the one that God gave us to bond us all together."

Dennis explained that God had over-stretched the dream idea. What had worked when the entire world population was but a few hundred thousand didn't work so well when it numbered into the millions. There were now too many people for the collective dream to be effective.

"So God decided that the original concept of the dream had to be recorded somewhere as a physical entity, and that it must then be shown to people, unlocking the seed and the ability he had planted in the first of mankind at the beginning, and which had been passed down – 'genetically', if you will...albeit in an increasingly diluted fashion – as a kind of race memory. After a lot of work, he finally did it. In other words, he managed to give substance to the insubstantial."

Dennis produced the piece of card from out of his pocket and held it up. "And here it is."

I stared at the card and made my single biggest mistake of the evening: I said...

"You said there were two things. What's the second?"

He looked at me, smiled tiredly and said, "The second thing I wanted to tell you about is the Devil wants the Dream."

I was probably expected to say something there but I couldn't bring myself to do it.

Dennis Dannerman stood up and walked across to the window, leaning on the sill like a man who had run a marathon. "When Lucifer was expelled from...from the other side, he took something with him. Just one thing."

"Why do I think I know what that was?"

"Right. He took the dream. And he's kept it all these thousands of years. Kept it 'down below' to use the theatrical term for Hell." Dennis turned around.

I was frowning. "But you've...So how did you get hold of the Dream?"

"It's like nothing you could imagine, Charles," he said. "Down there. Nothing in your wildest nightmare can prepare you for that place. Just...just a void, an empty space filled with crags and rocks and tunnels, hot...hotter than – and I know I'm repeating myself – hotter than you could think hot could be. No sky, no ground, just rock everywhere, dark tunnels which glow with some kind of half-light, and all we do is crawl through them, minute after minute, hour after hour, day after day, looking for a way out."

"*You* crawled through them? But I thought..."

"That's where I went. When I died. I wanted to keep it from you but there's no way to do that."

"Why did you want to keep it from me?"

He looked down at his tightly-clenched hands. "Because I was ashamed."

"Is that why you gave me all that other stuff...the 'angel' stuff? Because you were ashamed?"

He nodded. "Partly."

"And what was the other part?"

"I want you to do something for me and I didn't think you'd want to do it if you thought I was bad."

"Do what?"

He waved a hand. "When I died, all the things I'd done caught up with me. I won't bore you with the details but suffice to say the scales were weighted against me. I accepted my lot with some reluctance, but I did accept it. When you hear the list of charges, it's difficult not to be contrite." He shook his head and let out a small laugh, though it was entirely without humor. "Some of those things I didn't even remember. But there was no arguing against them. And anyway, most of them I did remember. So…

"The rumor of a way out of Hell has been circulating down there for as long as Hell has existed. As has the rumor of the Great First Dream, the blueprint for humanity's goodness, lost to the Gods since the time Lucifer was sent packing. It was held, the stories went, in some inner sanctum looked over by the Devil itself." He waited for that to sink in for a few minutes and then added, "And I found it.

"There were three of us, a mercenary from 8th century Antigua called Paul Theolomides and a heroin dealer from 1960s Madrid – Salvatore something-or-other.

"We came across the small cave separately, dropping into it from three different holes in the wall pretty much at the same time. There's no sleep down there – although you're tired all the time…I mean dog-tired, falling down dead tired. And there are no meals, no coffee breaks, even though you're always thirsty and always hungry – thirsty like a man crawling the desert for days, hungry like someone who hasn't eaten for weeks. But not sleeping and not drinking or eating doesn't harm you in any way. You just go on…tired and thirsty and hungry.

"Anyway, we dropped into the cavern and there it was, sitting on an outcrop of rock."

"The dream? That piece of card you carry?"

He nodded. It was glowing like fairy lights, casting shimmering shadows around the walls, throwing hues of colour across the ground like light ripples on a still lake. And the whole cave was hissing, a permanent state of anger and mistrust, and maybe even fear.

"Paul recognized it pretty much straight away. Sal didn't know shit about anything, even though he'd been there years longer than me."

"And where was..." I hesitated: what the hell was I talking about? "Where was the Devil?"

Dennis shrugged. "Taking a dump? Checking the furnaces? Who knows? All I know is that when each of us took this thing in our hands we could feel it, you know? We could feel the power of it, feel the light and the warmth, feel...feel the goodness.

"They – Paul and Sal – wanted to use it as a bargaining chip...strike up a deal with 'the authorities'. But I wanted to take it away from that hateful cave, wanted to take it away from Hell forever, maybe restore it to its rightful owners. There was a scuffle – we all have bodies there, bodies which cannot be inflicted with pain from each other, but which are in pain every minute of every day...bullet-wound pain, back pain, chest pain, headache, gut ache, nausea, pancreatic cancer, gout, hangnails and Tequila hangovers...all rolled into one. All the time. God, you wouldn't believe.

"Anyway, there was this scuffle and I got the Dream. I scurried back up one of the tunnels and, though they followed me in, I soon lost them, turning first this way and then that, then another, keeping going all the time, the card jammed into my mouth. Pretty soon I was alone, or as alone as you ever get down there...occasionally coming up on some other guy's bare backside swaying to and fro in front until you take a different path.

"Then, without any warning – I have no idea how long I was crawling that way, crawling with the card – there was a light up ahead, and the crawlspace was getting wider." He raised his arms in the air. "And I was out, bare-ass naked, but out. In a cave in Rheinisches Schiefergebirge – the Rhenish Slate Mountains: I didn't know that at the time, of course, only later.

"I made my way down the highlands into Hunsruck, through Taunus, Eifel and Westerwald, down through the wine-growing region, until at last I came upon houses. Under cover of darkness I stole clothes – still don't need food, still don't need sleep…but the pains have stopped, and the tiredness and the hunger and thirst – and eventually I made my way to Hamburg and, eventually, here to Meissen. By the time I found out what day and year it was, I'd been out for four days, sleeping out in the fields and the woods. It was the fourteenth of July 1995 – 10 days after my death. Which meant I had been in Hell for five or six days." He gave an involuntary shudder. "And I thought I had been there for years…years and years.

"My mother found me in Hamburg, only she wasn't my mother. 'She' was the Devil itself, come to retrieve the dream…and me.

"He was wearing a disguise?"

"Not 'he', 'it'. When Lucifer went down he was simply pissed off. The ensuing time spent forging a domain out of hard rock and reflecting on how badly he felt he had been treated turned the pissed off into pure madness. The Devil probably doesn't even recall its life as a God. Doesn't recognize the name Lucifer."

"So how did you manage to…"

"It was your father that saved me."

"My father? How?"

"The word had gotten out. The Dream had been rescued from Hell and the Gods knew all about it. After he had introduced himself, in a silvery spidery voice that whispered in my head, your father told me that the woman was not who she pretended to be. And that I must not give the card to her. I must not give the card to anyone. Instead, I must use it…must carry the message forward to all that would listen."

"But why didn't she – I mean, 'it' – why didn't the Devil just take it? And how did you get away?"

"The Devil may only take what is offered to him voluntarily. When I told this *thing* that I had been informed that she was not my mother, there were some tears – how could I say that of her? and all that – but eventually, she showed her true form." He shuddered again and I had no wish for further explanation.

"I left late at night, running down the streets of Hamburg carrying only what I wore on my back...plus the card containing the Dream. And that is where I met Siglinde Erhard. She told me that she had been waiting for a man in whom she could trust and that voices had told her that I was that man. I must leave Hamburg that night, she explained, and forever do good work. She said that it was only through good work that I may be redeemed. And she told me to go to Meissen."

He paused for breath and sat down in the chair once more. "Since then, I have passed the card around to all that would listen...letting them touch it, feel the power, but each time telling them that they may not keep it. You see, I could trust no-one...and yet the very nature of my task was such that I had to trust everyone. Your father told me that the end to my work was near. Someone was coming, he said. Someone who could take my burden from me."

I didn't say anything, just raised my eyebrows questioningly.

He pointed a finger. "That someone is you."

"*Me*? Jesus Christ, what's going on *here*?" I jumped up off the bed and walked to the bureau where my spare cigarette packs were stacked up like reassuring bricks of normality. "Why doesn't someone from Heaven come down and just take the damned card back?"

"Because nothing that has ever been in Hell may enter Heaven. It's tainted...but it can still be used here on Earth."

"But you said... I mean, your redemption? Doesn't that mean *you're* going to go there? And *you've* been in Hell." I waited for a few seconds, watching Dennis Dannerman's vacant expression, and then something began to gnaw at me. "And if I take the card – which I have no intention of doing, let me add – what happens to you?"

"I can't answer any of those questions. What is it they say about 'faith'? I only know this: you are to take the card – of your own free will – and…you are to release me."

I lit a cigarette. "And what will happen to you?"

He held the card out to me. "No idea."

Then the door opened and my father came into the room.

"Take it, son," my father said. "Let him go. He has earned his rest."

In the years since my father's death I had forgotten what he looked like. Forgotten the sound of his voice.

I had photographs, of course, and, occasionally, when I was feeling in the mood or when I stumbled across an old photo album while looking for something else, I would flick through the images of him – photographs taken sometimes with me, sometimes with my mother and sometimes just by himself.

But those static reminders can serve against memory and not for it. You forget the movement of the mouth, the adjustment of hair, the turning of the head. A million tiny movements and affectations that make the person who he or she really is. No amount of photographs can reproduce that.

In the small room in the Meissen guest-house the memories of my life with this man came flooding back to me. How I wished, in that instant, for my mother to be magically whisked from the rest home in Wells on the Maine coastline, and carried halfway across the world to my room. But then, in that same instant, I wondered how she would feel…her a frail but still beautiful woman in her eighties and him a relatively young man not quite 60 years old. Just the way he had been when he had been taken from her – from *us* – all that time ago.

"Oh…" I began, not quite knowing what to say, placing my cigarette on the ashtray and preparing myself to lunge across at him and take him in my arms.

He shook his head as though sensing my thoughts. "Accept the dream, Charles," he said, pointing to the card. "Accept your destiny."

Without further hesitation, I stepped across to where Dennis sat, still holding the dog-eared piece of card that contained God's first dream for mankind, and I took it between my fingers, feeling, with a momentary puzzlement, some reluctance on Dennis Dannerman's part to let it go. Perhaps, I thought, when the chips were down, his faith had deserted him...just for a second. Perhaps he was wondering where he would be transported to, wondering whether he would open his eyes onto pastoral fields or would suddenly find himself crouching once more in the labyrinthine stone tunnels of eternal damnation.

As I pulled, I saw his lips begin a word, a "Ch..." word...and then he was gone. The chair was empty.

I looked down at the card and watched the shapes swirl and eddy, felt the shifting of sound and the movement of light, heard the unmistakable serenity of silence and smelled the depth of hope. It made me want to cry...but to cry with joy.

"Let me see it," my father said. "Let me look upon it, son."

And, may God have mercy on me, I handed the First Dream to my father.

But it wasn't him at all.

Most of the rest of it is a blur now. But, sometimes in an unguarded moment, particularly in the warmth of my bed where I lay, another deadline missed, waiting for sleep but praying that no dreams will come to haunt me, I replay those final seconds. I still hear, in my memory, the sharp intake of breath of the man who accepted the card I had voluntarily passed to him, a sound not like any sound I had ever heard from any human being...let alone from my father. And whatever tricks the memory might play, that is something of which I am certain.

And the deep voice that said, in a sarcastic tone, "Thank you," and then added, with a hint of gleeful humor, "I look forward to meeting you again", was no voice I had ever heard around my childhood home, not even when my father was telling me scary stories of shambling monsters made from piles of rain-soaked fall leaves and a chance bolt of lightning, while I lay beside him tucked in my bed, eyes as wide as saucers.

I suppose the immediate vanishment of my "father" – and the card – should have been accompanied by a maniacal laugh, a puff of reddish smoke and the unmistakable odour of brimstone, but there were none of these Vaudevillian staples and Hollywood CGI effects.

There was only a stark emptiness. And the imagined silent tears of the Gods raining on a beautiful and endless plain somewhere far, far away... Somewhere I may never see.

LOST WAX
Leah Bobet

Leah Bobet is Toronto born and bred. When not working in Canada's oldest science-fiction bookshop, or on her degree in linguistics, she tells me her time is divided between "studying belly-dance, learning to knit, a windowsill herb garden that's spilling off both windowsills and onto the kitchen table, an old blue acoustic guitar, gourmet cooking, and an obsession with urban (local) history and urban exploration." I'm surprised she gets any writing done at all, but she has been selling stories and poems to a variety of magazines since 2001. The following story shows how you may get your just desserts, but not necessarily in the way you might expect.

Her website is at www.leahbobet.com

In the Factory at Calendar Point, the carvers and the wizards and the casters make magic. Simon sweeps up.

The wax is carted in from beekeepers scattered across the country, each licensed and watched and reporting to the provost every season on the movement of their flocks. Simon washes the floors after the carters have come and gone. He helps carry the crates to the carvers, sometimes, and the book-dusty theoreticians, one sketching the sigils from diagrams on brittle parchment and the others taking knife to wax, molding them in three dimensions. He gathers the curls of spare wax from the floor and burns them in the fire that feeds the casting crucible.

In the afternoons, Simon brings water to the potters, who paint clay carefully on the carved wax molds; in the evenings he scrubs their wheels and tools, soaking them in water until his fingers wrinkle. He does not clean the casting crucible; that is Jan's work, stoop-shouldered and sure-fingered, and old as his grandfather was on the day the farm passed to his father and his own indenture began in truth.

At the precise trembling moment between day and dusk, the sigils and guardians are cast. Wax puddles out of the molds, spreads across the catchbasin, and molten metal is poured in its place. Simon never sees the finished product. He empties the catchbasins, one by one, pouring thick and lazy drops of wax into the reservoir. The magic is in the wax, he's heard them say. He is careful. He does not spill a drop.

Come morning, the orders are delivered to students, wizards, kings and rich men by couriers in dashing clothes of all colours, none ever the same: it would not do to identify a Factory courier to footpads and thieves. Some days Simon thinks he might become a courier in lord's livery, and when he thinks this he sweeps harder and harder until the Factory shines like the moon. Jan watches him with even looks when this bright mood is upon him, and sends him away: check the carvers' floor one more time, perhaps empty the chamberpots, dust the lintels so the specks do not get in the molds. Jan is old and his hands are covered in soot. Simon does not get angry when he invents these tasks.

It is a great honour to work at the Factory. It is a great honour to carry its broom in your hands, for even brooms can be full of magic.

Simon comes home at dusk, smelling of smoke and sweat and honest labour. He lets a room in a boardinghouse off Progress Square that was still Bear's Heart Square when he arrived, but people call it Progress already and the old name is near-forgotten. He eats in the kitchen there, simple clean country food a day or two paler from the long trip to bring it to Calendar Point, or from a street vendor when it is middle-month or end-month and his pockets hold a neat packet of coins. There is smoke in the streets, and music. He practices his letters reading pamphlets pasted on walls or drifting through the streets, and dreams of attending lectures, of fairs bursting with wild animals and sleight-of-hand shows. He pays his rent, and sends money home to his family to pay for his labour lost, and hoards the rest in a box beneath his bed against a lack of imagination for luxury.

Every night Simon shuts his doors, pulls the curtain over his rounded quartered-compass window, and draws the curls of used wax from the stitching of his pocket.

He comes home with pockets heavy with wax: they are torn and mended and torn again once his clumsy stitching wears away or breaks – he is too timid to ask the house laundress to mend them true. The boardinghouse-mistress and the herb lady do not watch him as he slips into his penny-garret; they privately wonder over tea if he is smuggling opium or casting-metals, and just as quickly dismiss those thoughts: were Simon Lake a smuggler, he would not pay his rent in such small, well-fingered coins. The mistress's daughter fancies that he carries books, that he is a man of words and deep river-thoughts, but she is of the right age to fill a silent young man's figure with ideas that were never there.

Over gaslight he melts the fragments into his wooden wash-bowl until they are soft and ready, and molds them close into the cloudy block that started off a finger's width, then a palm's width, then an imperfect factory standard size. The mistress's dishwasher does not report him: he knows all the ways to remove wax from wood, from stone, from cloth.

It has taken him time to learn to carve wax: it is softer than wood, and cannot be whittled. It is harder than dirt, and cannot be molded. His rejects he burns in the crucible fires, eased back into the Factory in bits and crumbled pieces. This time, he thinks, every time the block grows strong and whole. This time will be the one, and he wishes.

The knife flicks, and he whispers the words into the cracks made by his tiny fingernail blade: *Give me a better life. Bring me a better life. Bring me something, a sign, a hope.*

The greyish wax breathes, and sighs, but there is no smell of magic,

just a faint hint of rotten rosemary from the street where the herb lady
has dumped her unsold and unsellable wares. Simon taps it with a finger,
and it does not reach out, or speak, or scowl. Leftover magic, defective
and drained. The wax used before casting is buttery and soft-golden and
smells like the best breakfast you never had.

The bed creaks, and his hand trembles, and the house shifts on its
foundations in its sleep. Simon puts his half-formed sigil in the drawer
beneath his holiday clothes, and sleeps, and dreams of candlelight.

Simon sweeps the factory floor as the long afternoon moves on, shifting
shadows so he is never sure which planks he has caressed with the straw
broom and which left untouched. He stares at the curling shards
longingly, treasure and firelight around his feet. The guards will collect
his dustpan at the end of the morning; he has never dared palm even a
sliver of virgin wax.

The penalty – in the bindings they would place on his hands and the
shame he would place on himself for having to beg again for a position
– is too great. But the wizards who watch the factory and grounds do not
clap him in irons for seditious thought; his mind is filled with lake
stillness.

Jan sees through it, sees past it, and takes the broom from him. He
sends Simon to wash the potter's tables again, six hours ahead of normal,
and threatens the whip if there remains a speck of grey upon the
polished, varnished, scarred wood tables. Simon inhales clay dust that
coats his tongue and throat, smoke from the kilns, smoke from the
crucibles in the sheltered room next door. The air in the Factory tastes
like something tangible, not alive but perhaps conscious. The sound of
the whistle that calls end to day's work knows that it has a name.

Today, they call his name, only to his ears. Today, they murmur to
him, and nobody else hears, but the wizards on duty frown and tap
instruments, smell the air, consult their heavy necklaces and pocket-

watch-chains of charms, their good clean bowler hats just slightly askew. *Simon Lake, Simon Lake* meanders through his consciousness. The shards in the dustpan spell it out. The dust on the tables vibrates with it, and when he pours the day's wax from the catchbasin into the reservoir, it hits with a note that reminds him of his own voice raised in laughter, or anger, or debate.

Magic is everywhere you look for it in the Factory. It is the motion of the air. At shift's end, Simon follows the air and the whistle and the dust-kin out the door, and into the streets of the city.

Steam-trains run into the stockyards, and he smells the low moaning of cattle imported to the slaughterhouses for meat and leather. Farmer's carts rattle along the roads, bringing in the produce to be sold at market the next morning; the sound stirs memory in him, and the urge to flee to ground. Sweaty and dirt-smeared men laugh and joke along the streets, leaving jobs at other factories, ones that make more mundane things. He sees them, and sees what he might be in ten years, or twenty, and shudders.

Why did you come to the city? a keening, whispering voice asks. Simon looks around, but there is nobody there to speak so clean and fairly: nothing but the wind. His heart quickens: perhaps it is a wizard-voice. Perhaps he has been chosen for a great task.

Perhaps it is his sign.

"I came, sir," he tells it, clearing his throat as if addressing the foreman, "to gain a better life."

And have you found it? ask the cobblestones, and the spaces between them, ground with manure and dust and grass-seeds.

He clutches his hands in front of his body, tight in one another. He has a room and hot potatoes with cheese on pay day. He is paying off his indenture to the soil. The house-mistress's daughter seems to like him. His parents, if not proud, are not disappointed.

He shakes his head. "I've taken wax," he confesses, not knowing to who, but knowing he should, he must be honest now. "If I had magic…"

There is magic in a bear's heart, so the name has been erased. There is magic in a falcon's claw, clutched at the moment of dying. There is magic in things and not just symbols, it whispers, and he listens. *Factory magic is not your kind of magic.*

"Then what shall I do?" he whispers, his carving hand growing stiff from tension.

We have been looking some time, it says, pondering and sweet, *for a vessel, a mold, a thing well-designed and willing. Are you willing?* it asks, and he draws in a breath.

"Yes," he says, elated and terrified and strung tight with delicious vindication – his sign is here at last. "Oh yes."

Look to where things are still, the murmur says, tasting of sweet peas at first picking and old blood and sunshine. *You will find your advancement there.*

A pair of beat cops come around the corner, one twirling his baton idly, chattering away to the other. Simon closes his mouth, shoves his hands in his pockets, and makes his long way home to Progress Square, vowing in his head to call it Bear's Heart Square forever more.

There are a lot of stillnesses in his head: it is why he is permitted to work in the Factory. He spreads out on his mattress that night and dives into them, dives deep.

There is no magic there. His dreams are of floorboards, and rafters, and shaped, squared things. He dreams in symbols and metal and wax, and when he wakes, he weeps.

He touches his knife to the wax that night, and whispers new words into the scores and cuts and careful curves. *Give me magic. Let me touch magic.*

That is not the way, the hissing voice of wild magic whispers, but it is the only way he knows. The knife slips, draws blood, and he bandages the finger and keeps going. The night falls silent. He carves until dawn.

———————————————

Simon goes to the factory sleepy-eyed and haggard. There is wax beneath his fingernails, and he does not notice or care. Jan takes him aside immediately and sends him to scrub, and chastises him loudly for not doing so the night before. Simon knows he is trying to help. Simon knows he is trying to save his job and his prospects. He scrubs with a knot of resentment building in his belly, and comes out to report sullen and with his eyes downcast.

Jan takes him into the potters' room, where the workers have not yet come in for the day. "What," he asks, "has happened to make you so prickly and careless?"

"There is no magic in me," Simon whispers, realizing that Jan has known all along about his small thefts of wax, about his yearning and sleepless evenings, and clenches his fists tighter.

"There is no magic in anyone," Jan says, severe, drawn-faced. "They just borrow it for a while."

Simon looks down at the older man's hands, curled around the broom like a falcon's claw at the moment of dying. "We could make it," he says. "We could make our own and get out of here. It spoke to me…" he says, and Jan holds up a hand.

"Magic isn't to be wanted. Magic is to be feared," he says, soft, between the murmuring creaks of machinery and the shouts of vendors in the city outside the Factory gates. "Anything that must be chained to serve will destroy you, and anything worth chaining to serve can do the job right and full."

Simon looks at his feet, at the unravelling leather shoes that they gave him on his first day at the Factory. He did not know Jan felt himself a philosopher. "Wizards," he says, "wear fine suits, and cast spells to their own design. They pay in gold. I've seen their houses…" and he has, everyone who lives or dwells a while in Calendar Point has seen those graceful, towering spires "…and their children. They never frown, except when they're thinking of something terrible and great."

Jan is silent for a long time. "Sometimes I forget how young you are," he says roughly, and puts his curled and ruined hand on Simon's shoulder.

He pulls away. He leaves the Factory, his broom still in the cubby. He goes into the stockyards, into the sewers, into the streets, looking for somewhere that is truly still, and by nightfall he is truly lost. Darkened buildings rise above him like forest trees; there are no gaslights on these streets, and there are no signs, and no smells to light his way to somewhere cleaner and bigger and less secret.

"Magic?" he calls out, not knowing it by any older or other name.

Simon Lake, it murmurs, heady and hesitant. *What is it you truly want?*

"Magic," he says again, closing his eyes. "I don't want to be a farmhand anymore. I don't want to be a cleaner. I want to be like them – the people who are always smiling."

You want to be special. You want to inspire: fear, or hope, or doubt.

"I want to be an honour," he says, and the words come formal to his lips, and for the first time, he is very afraid indeed. But the wanting is stronger, the wanting was always stronger: to be more than one is, to be great, to be the cause of something. The wild magic smells that, and despairs, and rejoices.

Very well, the magic says, grim and sad and ready. *Very well.*

Simon lifts his head up to the sky, opens his mouth and his arms, closes his eyes. *Come in*, he cries out to it, voiceless, all the lake stillness gone forever from his mind. *Come into me.*

The world rushes into flame and light.

The mages find him at sunrise, legs deer-quick, ears wolf-sharp, only his eyes still his own. They bring him before the wizard-magistrate, who looks upon him and calls him Simon Lake, who works in the Factory (an honour, that), who rents off Progress Square. They find his hoard of pennies, and they find his hoard of wax, half-carved into trees, into civic fountains, into the houses of the great and the small animals that haunt the lake country, stealing corn and nuts and fruit. The boardinghouse-mistress watches the wizards with eyes round as a rabbit's, and her daughter cries. The herb lady nods as if some great mystery is resolved, and flirts with the inspector, and is turned away back to her tea and wares.

There is no trial. There never is, with magic involved.

They hang him at high noon, and the wild magic whispers in his ear, *hush hush*, as the trap opens and the knot tightens and his legs kick in the air. The papers say hangings are a quick death, the knot striking one just so and the suffering brief. Simon strangles slowly as the goodwives and children watch. His hands clench like those of a dying falcon, and his bear's heart bursts, and the blood bubbles at his mouth before they cut him down and pronounce him.

"This," call out the street preachers, the dervishes, the mad, "is why it is foolish to toy with stolen magic. This is how you lose your soul!"

The crowd wails and shudders in terrified glee. A few young ones turn away, lips twisted. A few more of them follow the wind than might have otherwise: cobbler's boys, and shop clerks, and a heavy young woman who bastes fine gowns together for the third best seamstress in the city. They dream of bees that night, and wake up hungry, and do not go to hangings anymore. They meet, and marry, and open up public houses and greenhouses and places where things are still, and they allow no man-made magic in their homes, and they never speak of this day.

They mark their doors with a sprig of rosemary, for remembrance, until they forget what it means or who hung their cutting first. Nobody who writes in decades to come about the Rosemary Revolution speaks of this day, or this hanging; it is forgotten by its own historians. It sleeps in peace, and it is still.

His parents come for his body, his mother weeping, his father's face hard as cobblestone streets. They bury him on the farm, and plant an apple tree atop the grave. The roots twist down and empty his coffin of those things that fall away in earth, leaving good hard applewood and bone in the shape of a man, a young man, one barely past his fifteenth birthday. The substance drains out of him, dirtied and spent into the catchbasin of the soil, and something else fills the gap that is left behind.

The apple tree bears bewitching fruit. Those who bite into it go a little mad, for a while: they smell things that are not there; they see things that have never graced the lake country, machines and dirty streets and the way a night sky looks through haze and smoke. They mostly go to the city: they stay in certain public houses, they eat fruit from certain greenhouses. They make friends, and they do not visit home. They never quite fit into the lake country again, after that taste.

There is a storm on the night ten years after Simon's death. The apple tree cracks and falls, splitting into two at the touch of lightning. The children from the farms and the village crowd around it, all afraid to touch: the children are afraid of that spot. Already they do not remember why.

The stump is uprooted and they find the roots broken, the space between them cradling the shape of a man, the bones of a man poured out on the ground between them like lost wax after the casting.

They split the mold, but there is nothing inside at all.

It remembers brooms. It remembers that things should always be clean and clear and true. Falcon's-Claw-Bear's-Heart, smelling of apples and rain and moving like wind and purpose, takes its first steps towards the taste of the city.

SAVE A PLACE IN THE LIFEBOAT FOR ME

Howard Waldrop

---

*When I began planning this anthology one of the very first authors
I considered for inclusion was Howard Waldrop. I was, though,
spoiled for choice. Waldrop (b. 1946) is one of those writers who is
incapable of writing anything normal, thank goodness. All of his
stories are wild and unpredictable but, because of that, there were
few magazine markets for his kind of madness. Much of his material
appeared in small-press magazines like the beautiful* Shayol *or*
Nickelodeon *— the latter published by Tom Reamy who appears
elsewhere in this anthology. Waldrop's work did appear occasionally
in original anthologies and his "The Ugly Chickens" in Terry Carr's*
Universe 10 *in 1980 went on to win the Nebula and World Fantasy
awards for that year. He has published a couple of novels,* Them
Bones *(1984) and* The Texas-Israeli War *(1999) and maybe some
day we'll see* I, John Mandeville, *which he's been working on
since forever. Thankfully many of his short stories have been
collected in various volumes, including* Howard Who? *(1986),* All
About Strange Monsters of the Recent Past *(1987), and* Night of
the Cooters *(1990), all essential reading for devotees of the bizarre
and unusual. The following story, which depicts several of our
favourite silver-screen comedians in search of their destiny, is just a
taster.*

The hill was high and cold when they appeared there, and the first thing they did was to look around.

It had snowed the night before, and the ground was covered about a foot deep.

Arthur looked at Leonard and Leonard looked at Arthur.

"Whatsa matter you? You wearin' funny clothes again!" said Leonard.

Arthur listened, his mouth open. He reached down to the bulbhorn tucked in his belt.

Honk Honk went Arthur.

"Whatsa matter us?" asked Leonard. "Look ata us! We back inna vaudeville?"

Leonard was dressed in pants two sizes too small, and a jacket which didn't match. He wore a tiny pointed felt hat which stood on his head like a roof on a silo.

Arthur was dressed in a huge coat which dragged the ground, balloon pants, big shoes, and above his moppy red hair was a silk tophat, its crown broken out.

"It's a fine-a mess he's gots us in disa time!"

Arthur nodded agreement.

"Quackenbush, he's-a gonna hear about this!" said Leonard.

Honk Honk went Arthur.

The truck backed into the parking lot and ran into the car parked just inside the entrance. The glass panels which were being carried on the truck fell and shattered into thousands of slivers in the snowy street. Cars slushing down the early morning road swerved to avoid the pieces.

"Ohh, Bud, Bud!" said the short baby-faced man behind the wheel. He was trying to back the truck over the glass and get it out of the way of the dodging cars.

A tall thin man with a rat's mustache ran from the glass company office and yelled at the driver.

"Look what you've done. Now you'll make me lose this job, too! Mr. Crabapple will…" He paused, looked at the little fat man, swallowed a few times.

"Uh…hello, Lou," he said, a tear running into his eye and brimming down his face. He turned away, pulled a handkerchief from his coveralls and wiped his eyes.

"Hello, Bud," said the little man, brightly. "I don'…don'… understand it either, Bud. But the man said we got something to do, and I came here to get you." He looked around him at the littered glass. "Bud, I been a *baaad* boy!"

"It doesn't matter, Lou," said Bud, climbing around to the passenger side of the truck. "Let's get going before somebody gets us arrested."

"Oh, Bud?" asked Lou, as they drove through the town. "Did you ever get out of your contract?"

"Yeah, Lou. Watch where you're going! Do I have to drive myself?"

They pulled out of Peoria at eight in the morning.

———————————————

The two men beside the road were dressed in black suits and derby hats. They stood; one fat, the other thin. The rotund one put on a most pleasant face and smiled at the passing traffic. He lifted his thumb politely, as would a gentleman, and held it as each vehicle roared past.

When a car whizzed by, he politely tipped his hat.

The thin man looked distraught. He tried at first to strike the same pose as the larger man, but soon became flustered. He couldn't hold his thumb right, or let his arm droop too far.

"No, no, no, Stanley," said the larger, mustached man, as if he were talking to a child. "Let me show you the way a man of gentle breeding asks for a ride. Politely. Gently. Thus."

He struck the same pose he had before.

A car bore down on them doing eighty miles an hour. There was no chance in the world it would stop.

Stanley tried to strike the same pose. He checked himself against the larger man's attitude. He found himself lacking. He rubbed his ears and looked as if he would cry.

The car roared past, whipping their hats off.

They bent to pick them up and bumped heads. They straightened, each signaling that the other should go ahead. They simultaneously bent and bumped heads again.

The large man stood stock still and did a slow burn. Stanley looked flustered. Their eyes were off each other. Then they both leaped for the hats and bumped heads once more.

They grabbed up the hats and jumped to their feet.

They had the wrong hats on. Stanley's derby made the larger man look like a tulip bulb. The large derby covered Stanley down to his chin. He looked like a thumbtack.

The large man grabbed the hat away and threw Stanley's derby to the ground.

"MMMMMM-MMMMMM-MMMMM!" said the large man.

Stanley retrieved his hat. "But Ollie..." he said, then began whimpering. His hat was broken.

Suddenly Stanley pulled Ollie's hat off and stomped it. Ollie did another slow burn, then turned and ripped off Stanley's tie.

Stanley kicked Ollie in the shin. The large man jumped around and punched Stanley in the kneecap.

A car stopped, and the driver jumped out to see what the trouble was.

Ollie kicked *him* in the shin. *He* ripped off Stanley's coat.

A woman pulled over and slammed into the man's parked car. He ran over and kicked out her headlight. Stanley threw a rock through *his* windshield.

Twenty minutes later, Stanley and Ollie were looking down from a hill. A thousand people were milling around on the turnpike below, tearing each other's cars to pieces. Parts of trucks and motorcycles littered the roadway. The two watched a policeman pull up. He jumped out and yelled through a bullhorn to the people, too far away for the two men to hear what he said.

As one, the crowd jumped him, and pieces of police car began to bounce off the blacktop.

Ollie dusted off his clothing as meticulously as possible. His and Stanley's clothes consisted of torn underwear and crushed derby hats.

"That's another fine mess you've gotten us in, Stanley," he said. He looked north.

"And it looks like it shall soon snow. Mmmm-mmmm-mmmm!"

They went over the hill as the wail of sirens began to fill the air.

Hello, a-Central, givva me Heaven. ETcumspiri 220."

The switchboard hummed and crackled. Sparks leaped off the receiver of the public phone booth in the roadside park. Arthur did a back flip and jumped behind a trash can.

The sun was out, though snow was still on the ground. It was a cold February day, and they were the only people in the park.

The noise died down at the other end and Leonard said:

"Hallo, Boss! Hey, Boss! We doin'-a like you tell us, but you no send us to the right place. You no send us to Iowa. You send us to Idaho, where they grow the patooties."

Arthur came up beside his brother and listened. He honked his horn.

On the other end of the line, Rufus T. Quackenbush spoke:

"Is that a goose with you, or do you have a cold?"

"Oh, no, Boss. You funnin'-a me. That's-a Bagatelle."

"Then who are you?" asked Quackenbush.

"Oh, you know who this is. I gives you three guesses."

"Three guesses, huh? Hmmmm, let's see…you're not Babe Ruth, are you?"

"Hah, Boss. Babe Ruth, that's-a chocolate bar."

"Hmmm. You're not Demosthenes, are you?"

"Nah, Boss. Demosthenes can do is bend in the middle of your leg."

"I should have known," said Quackenbush. "This is Rampolini, isn't it?"

"You got it, Boss."

Arthur whistled and clapped his hands in the background.

"Is that a hamster with you, Rampolini?"

"Do-a hamsters whistle, Boss?"

"Only when brought to a boil," said Quackenbush.

"Ahh, you too good-a for me, Boss!"

"I know. And if I weren't too good for you, I wouldn't be good enough for anybody. Which is more than I can say for you."

"Did-a we wake you up, Boss?"

"No, to be perfectly honest, I had to get up to answer the phone anyway. What do you want?"

"Like I said, Boss Man, you put us inna wrong place. We no inna Iowa. We inna Idaho."

"That's out of the Bronx, isn't it? What should I do about it?"

"Well-a, we don't know. Even if-a we did, we know we can't-a do it anyway, because we ain't there. An if-a we was, we couldn't get it done no ways."

"How do you know that?"

"Did-a you ever see one of our pictures, Boss?"

There was a pause. "I see what you mean," said Quackenbush.

"Why for you send-a us, anyway? We was-a sleep, an then we inna Idaho!"

"I looked at my calendar this morning. One of the dates was circled. And it didn't have pits, either. Anyway, I just remembered that something very important shouldn't take place today."

"What's-a that got to do with us two?"

"Well…I know it's a little late, but I really would appreciate it if you two could manage to stop it."

"What's-a gonna happen if we don't?"

"Uh, ha ha. Oh, small thing, really. The Universe'll come to an end several million years too soon. A nice boy like you wouldn't want that, would you? Of course not!"

"What for I care the Universe'll come to an end? We-a work for Paramount."

"No, no. Not the studio. The big one!"

"M-a GM?"

"No. The Universe. All that stuff out there. Look around you."

"You mean-a Idaho?"

"No, no, Rampolini. Everything will end soon, too soon. You may not be concerned. A couple of million years is nothing to somebody like you. But what about me? I'm leasing this office, you know?"

"Why-a us?"

"I should have sent someone earlier, but I've…I've been so terrible busy. I was having a pedicure, you see, and the time just *flew* by."

"What-a do the two of us do to-a stop this?"

"Oh, I just know you'll think of something. And you'll both be happy to know I'm sending you lots of help."

"Is this help any good, Boss?"

"I don't know if they're any good," said Quackenbush. "But they're cheap."

"What-a we do inna meantime?"

"Be mean, like everybody else."

"Nah, nah. (That's-a really good one, Boss.) I mean, about-a the thing?"

"Well, I'd suggest you get to Iowa. Then give me another call."

"But what iffa you no there?"

"Well, my secretary will take the message."

"Ah, Boss, if-a you no there, your secretary's-a no gonna be there neither."

"Hmmm. I guess you're right. Well, why don't you give me the message now, and I'll give it to my secretary. Then I'll give her the answer, and she can call you when you get to Iowa!"

"Hey, that's-a good idea, Boss!"

"I thought you'd think so."

Outside the phone booth, Arthur was lolling his tongue out and banging his head with the side of his hand, trying to keep up with the conversation.

There were two lumps of snow beside the highway. The snow shook itself, and Stan and Ollie stepped out of it.

"Brr," said Ollie. "Stanley, we must get to some shelter soon."

"But I don't know where any is, Ollie!"

"This is all your fault, Stanley. It's up to you to find us some clothing and a cheery fireside."

"But, Ollie, I didn't have any idea we'd end up like this."

Ollie shivered. "I suppose you're right, Stanley. It's not your fault we're here."

"I don't even remember what we were doing before we were on that road this morning, Ollie. Where have you been lately?"

"Oh...don't you remember, Stanley?"

"Not very well, Ollie."

"Oh," said Ollie. He looked very tired, very suddenly. "It's very strange, but neither do I, Stanley."

The cold was forgotten then, and they were fully clothed in their black suits and derbys. They thought nothing of it, because they were thinking of something else.

"I suppose now we shall really have to hurry and find a ride, Stanley."

"I know," said the thin man. "We have to go to Iowa."

"Yes," said Ollie, "and our wives will be none the wiser."

The Iowa they headed for was pulling itself from under a snowstorm which had dumped eleven inches in the last two days. It was bitterly cold there. Crew-cut boys shoveled snow off walks and new '59 cars so their fathers could get to work. It was almost impossible. Snowplows had been out all night, and many of them were stalled. The National Guard had been called out in some sections and was feeding livestock and rescuing stranded motorists. It was not a day for travel.

At noon, the small town of Cedar Oaks was barely functioning. The gleaming sun brought no heat. But the town stirred inside, underneath the snows which sagged the roofs.

The *All-Star Caravan* was in town that day. The teenagers had prayed and hoped that the weather would break during the two days of ice. The *Caravan* was a rock 'n' roll show that travelled around the country, doing one-night stands.

The show had been advertised for a month: All the businesses around the two high schools and junior highs were covered with the blazing orange posters. They had been since New Year's Day.

So the kids waited, and built up hopes for it, and almost had them dashed as the weather had closed in.

But Mary Ann Pickett's mother, who worked the night desk at the Holiday Inn, had called her daughter at eleven the night before: The *All-Star Caravan* had landed at the airport in the clearing night, and all the singers had checked in.

Mary Ann asked her mother, "What does Donny Bottoms look like?"

Her mother didn't know. They were all different-looking, and she wasn't familiar with the singer anyway.

Five minutes after Mary Ann rang off, the word was spreading over Cedar Oaks. The *All-Star Caravan* was there. Now it could snow forever. Maybe if it did, they would have to stay there, rather than start their USO tour of Alaska.

Bud and Lou slid and slipped their way over the snows in the truck.

"Watch where you're going!" said Bud. "Do you have anything to eat?"

"I got some cheese crackers and some Life Savers, Bud. But we'll have to divide them, because…" His voice took on a little-boy petulance "…because I haven't had anything to eat in a long time, Bud."

"Okay, okay. We'll share. Give me half the cheese crackers. You take these."

Lou was trying to drive. There was a munching sound.

"Some friend you are," said Bud. "You have two cheese crackers and I don't have any."

Lou coughed. "But, Bud! I just *gave* you two cheese crackers!"

"Do I look like I have any cheese crackers?" asked Bud, wiping crumbs from his chin.

"Okay," said Lou. "Have this cheese cracker, Bud. Because you're my friend, and I want to share."

Again, the sound of eating filled the cab.

"Look, Lou. I don't mind you having all the Life Savers, but can't you give me half your cheese cracker?"

Lou puffed out his cheeks while watching the road. "But, Bud! I just gave you *three* cheese crackers!"

"Some friend," said Bud, looking at the snowbound landscape. "He has a cheese cracker and won't share it with his only friend."

"Okay! Okay!" said Lou. "Take half this cheese cracker! Take it!"

He drove on.

"Boy…" said Bud.

Lou took the whole roll of Life Savers and stuffed them in his mouth, paper and all. He began to choke.

Bud began beating him on the back. The truck swerved across the road, then back on. They continued towards Cedar Oaks, Iowa.

There were giants in the *All-Star Caravan*. Donny Bottoms, from

Amarillo, Texas; his backup group, the Mosquitos, most from Amarillo Cooper High School, his old classmates. Then there was Val Ritchie, who'd had one fantastic hit song, which had a beat and created a world all the teenagers wanted to escape to.

The third act, biggest among many more, was a middle-aged man calling himself The Large Charge. His act was strange, even among that set. He performed with a guitar and a telephone. He pretended to be talking to a girl on the other end of the line. It was billed as a comedy act. Everybody knew what was really involved – The Large Charge was rock 'n' roll's first dirty old man. His real name was Elmo Simpson and he came from Bridge City, Texas.

Others on the bill included the Pipettes, three guys and two girls from Stuttgart, Arkansas who up until three months ago had sung only at church socials; Jimmy Wailon, who was having a hard time deciding whether to sing "Blue Suede Shoes" for the hundredth time, or strike out into country music where the real money was. Plus the Champagnes, who'd had a hit song three years before, and Rip Dover, the show's MC.

The *Caravan* was the biggest thing that had happened to Cedar Oaks since Bill Haley and the Comets came through a year and a half ago, and one of Haley's road men had been arrested for DWI.

"What's-a matter us?" asked Leonard for the fiftieth time that morning. "We really no talka like dis! We was-a grown up mens, with jobs and-a everything."

Whonka whonka went Arthur sadly, as they walked through the town of Friedersville, Idaho.

Arthur stopped dead, then put his hands in his pockets and began whistling. There was a police car at the corner. It turned onto the road where they walked. And slowed.

Leonard nonchalantly tipped his pointy felt hat forward and put his hands in his pockets.

The cop car stopped.

The two ran into the nearest store. *Hadley's Music Shop*. Arthur ran around behind a set of drums and hid. Leonard sat down at a piano and began to play with one finger, "You've Taught Me a New Kind of Love."

The store manager came from the back room and leaned against the doorjamb, listening.

Arthur saw a harp in the corner, ran to it and began to play. He joined in the song with Leonard.

The two cops came in and watched them play. Leonard was playing with his foot and nose. Arthur was plucking the harp strings with his teeth.

The police shrugged and left.

"Boy, I'm-a tellin' you," said Leonard, as he waited for the cops to turn the corner. "Quackenbush, he's-a messed up dis-a time! Why we gots to do this?" With one hand he was wiping his face, and with the other he was playing as he never had before.

————————————————

Donny Bottoms was a scrawny-looking kid from West Texas. He didn't stand out in a crowd, unless you knew where to look. He had a long neck and an Adam's apple that stuck out of his collar. He was twenty-four years old and still had acne. But he was one of the hottest new singers around, and the *All-Star Caravan* was going to be his last road tour for a while.

He'd just married his high school sweetheart, a girl named Dottie, and he had not really wanted to come on the tour without her. But she was finishing nurse's training and could not leave. At two in the afternoon, he and the other members of the *Caravan* were trying the sound in the Municipal Auditorium.

He and the Mosquitos ran through a couple of their numbers. Bottoms' style was unique, even in a field as wild and novelty-eating as rock 'n' roll. It had a good boogie beat, but Bottoms worked hard with the music, and the Mosquitoes were really good. They turned out a good synthesis of primitive and sophisticated styles.

The main thing they had for them was Donny's voice. It was high and nasal when he talked, but, singing, that all went away. He had good range, and he did strange things with his throat.

A critic once said that he dry-humped every syllable till it begged for mercy.

Val Ritchie had one thing he did well, exactly one: that was a song called "Los Niños." He'd taken an old Mexican folk song, got a drummer to beat hell out of a conga, and yelled the words over his own screaming guitar.

It was all he did well. He did some other people's standards, and some Everly Brothers' stuff by himself, but he always finished his set with "Los Niños" and it always brought the house down and had them dancing in the aisles.

He was the next-to-last act before Bottoms and the Mosquitos.

He was a tough act to follow.

But he was always on right before The Large Charge, and *he* was the toughest act in rock 'n' roll.

They had turned the auditorium upside down and had finally found a church key to open a beer for The Large Charge.

Elmo Simpson was dressed, at the sound rehearsal, in a pair of baggy pants, a checked cowboy shirt, and a string tie with a Texas-shaped tieclasp. Tonight, on stage, he would be wearing the same thing.

Elmo's sound rehearsal consisted of chinging away a few chords, doing the first two bars of "Jailhouse Rock" and then going into his dirty-old-man voice.

His song was called "Hello, Baby!" and he used a prop telephone. He ran through the first two verses, which were him talking in a cultured, decadent nasty voice, and he had the sound man rolling in his control chair before he finished.

Elmo sweated like a hog. He'd been doing this act for two years, he'd even had to lip-synch it on Dick Clark's "American Bandstand" a couple of times. He was still nervous, though he could do the routine in his sleep. He was always nervous. He was in his late thirties. Fame had come late to him, and he couldn't believe it. So he was still nervous.

Bud and Lou were hurrying west in the panel truck, through snowslides, slush and stalled cars.

Stan and Ollie had hitched a ride on a Mayflower moving van, against all that company's policies, and were speeding towards Cedar Oaks from the south-southeast.

Leonard and Arthur, alias Rampolini and Bagatelle, were leaving an Idaho airport in a converted crop duster which hadn't been flown since the end of the Korean War. It happened like this:

"We gots to find us a pilot-a to fly us where the Boss wants us," said Leonard, as they ran onto a small municipal field.

Whonk? asked Arthur.

"We's gots to find us a pilot, pilot."

Arthur pulled a saber from the fold of his coat, and putting a black poker chip over his eye, began swordfighting his shadow.

"Notta pirate. Pilot! A man whatsa flies in the aeroplanes," said Leonard.

A man in coveralls, wearing a WWII surplus aviator's cloth helmet, walked from the operations room.

"There's-a one now!" said Leonard. "What's about we gets him?"

Without a honk, Arthur ran and tackled the flyer.

"What the hell's the matter with him?" asked the man as Arthur grinned and smiled and pointed.

"You gots to-a excuse him," said Leonard, pulling his tophatted brother off him. "He's-a taken too many vitsamins."

"Well, keep him away from me!" said the flyer.

"We's a gots you a prepositions," said Leonard, conspiratorially.

"What?"

"A prepositions. You fly-a us to Iowa, anda we no break-a you arms."

"What's going on? Is this some kind of gag?"

"No, it's-a my brother. He's a very dangerous man. Show him how dangerous you are, Bagatelle."

Arthur popped his eyes out, squinted his face up into a million rolls of flesh, flared his nostrils and snorted at each breath.

"Keep him away from me!" said the man. "You oughtn't to let him out on the streets."

"He's-a no listen to me, Bagatelle. Get tough with him."

Arthur hunched his shoulders, intensified his breathing, stepped up into the pilot's face.

"No, that's-a no tough enough. Get really tough with him."

Arthur squnched over, stood on tiptoe, flared his nostrils until they filled all his face except for the eyes, panted, and passed out for lack of breath.

The pilot ran across the field and into a hangar.

"Hey, wake-a up!" said Leonard. "He's-a getting the plane ready. Let's-a go."

When they got there, the pilot was warming the crop duster up for a preflight check.

Arthur climbed in the aft cockpit, grabbed the stick, started jumping up and down.

"Hey! Get outta there!" yelled the pilot. "I'm gonna call the cops!"

"Hey, Bagatelle. Get-a tough with him again!"

Leonard was climbing into the forward cockpit. Arthur started to get up. His knees hit the controls. The plane lurched.

Leonard fell into the cockpit head first, his feet sticking out.

Arthur sat back down and laughed. He pulled the throttle.

The pilot just had time to open the hangar door before the plane roared out, plowed through a snowbank, ricocheted back onto the field and took off.

It was heading east towards Iowa.

At three in the afternoon, the rehearsals over, most of the entertainers were back in their rooms at the Holiday Inn. Already the hotel detective had had to chase out several dozen girls and boys who had been roaming up and down the halls looking for members of the *All-Star Caravan*.

Some of them found Jimmy Wailon in the corridor and were getting his autograph. He had been on the way down the hall, going to meet one of the lady reservation clerks.

"Two of yours is worth one Large Charge," said one of the girls as he signed her scrapbook.

"What's that?" he asked, his eyes twinkling. He pushed his cowlick out of his eyes.

"Two of your autographs are worth one of Donny's," she said.

"Oh," he said. "That's nice." He scribbled his usual "With Best Wishes to My Friend…" then asked, "What's the name, honey?"

"Sarah Sue," she said. "And please put the date."

"Sure will, baby. How old are you?"

"I'm eighteen!" she said. All her friends giggled.

"Sure," he said. "There go!"

He hurried off to the room the lady reservation clerk had gotten for them.

"Did you hear that?" the girl asked behind him as he disappeared around the corner. "He called me 'honey.'"

Jimmy Wailon was smiling long before he got to Room 112.

Elmo was sitting in Donny's room with three of the Mosquitoes. Donny had gone to a phone booth to call his wife collect rather than put up with the noise in the room.

"Have another beer, Elmo?" asked Skeeter, the head Mosquito.

"Naw, thanks, Skeeter," he said. "I won't be worth a diddly-shit if I do." Already, Elmo was sweating profusely at the thought of another performance.

"I'll sure be glad when we get on that tour," he continued, after a pause. "Though it'll be colder than a monkey's ass."

"Yeh," said Skeeter. They were watching television, "The Millionaire," the daytime reruns, and John Beresford Tipton was telling Mike what to do with the money with his usual corncob-up-the-butt humor. Skeeter was highly interested in the show. He'd had arguments with people many times about whether the show was real or not, or based on some real person. He was sure somewhere there was a John Beresford Tipton, and a Silverstone, and that one of those checks had his name on it.

"Look at that, will you?" asked Skeeter a few minutes later. "He's giving it to a guy whose kid is dying."

But Elmo Simpson, The Large Charge, from Bridge City, Texas, was lying on his back, fast asleep. Snores began to form inside his mouth, and every few minutes, one would escape.

Donny talked to his wife over the phone out in the motel lobby. They told each other how much they missed each other, and Donny asked about the new record of his coming out this week, and Dottie said she wished he'd come home soon rather than going on the tour, and they told each other they loved each other, and he hung up.

Val Ritchie was sitting in a drugstore just down the street, eating a chocolate sundae and wishing he were home. Instead of going to do a show tonight, then fly with one or another load of musicians off to Alaska for two weeks for the USO.

He was wearing some of his old clothes and looked out of place in the booth. He thought most northern people overdressed anyway, even kids going to school. *I mean, like they were all ready for church or Uncle Fred's funeral.*

He hadn't been recognized yet, and wouldn't be. He always looked like a twenty-year-old garage mechanic on a coffee break.

Bud and Lou swerved to avoid a snowdrift. They had turned onto the giant highway a few miles back and had it almost to themselves. Ice glistened everywhere in the late afternoon sun, blindingly. Soon the sun would fall and it would become pitch black outside.

"How much further is it, Bud?" asked Lou. His stomach was growling.

"I don't know. It's around here somewhere. I'm just following what's-his-name's orders."

"Why doesn't he give better orders, Bud?"

"Because he never worked for Universal."

Stan and Ollie did not know what was happening when the doors of the moving van opened and carpets started dropping off the top of the racks. Then the van slammed into another vehicle. They felt it through the sides of the truck.

The driver was already out. He was walking towards a small truck with two men in it.

Stan and Ollie climbed out of the back of the Mayflower truck and saw who the other two were.

The four regarded each other, and the truck driver surveyed the damage to the carpets, which was minor.

They helped him load the truck back up, then Stan and Ollie climbed in the small van with Bud and Lou.

"I wonder what Quackenbush is up to now?" asked Bud, as he scrunched himself up with the others. With Lou and Ollie taking up so much room, he and Stan had to share a space hardly big enough for a lap dog. Somehow, they managed.

"I really don't know," said Ollie. "He seems quite intent on keeping this thing from happening."

"But, why us, Bud?" asked Lou. "We been *goood* boys since…well, we been good boys. He could have sent so many others."

"That's quite all right with me," said Stanley. "He didn't seem to want just *anybody* for this."

"I don't know about you two, but Lou and I were sent from Peoria. That's a long way. What's this guy got against us?"

"Well, there's actually no telling," said Stanley. "Ollie and I have been travelling all day, haven't we, Ollie?"

"Quite right, Stanley."

"But what I don't get," said Bud, working at his pencil-thin mustache, "is that I remember when all this happened the first time."

"So do I," said Stanley.

"But not us two," said Lou, indicating Ollie and himself, and trying to keep the truck on the road.

"Well, that's because you two had…had…left before them. But that doesn't matter. What matters is that he sent us back here to… Come to think of it, I don't understand, either."

"Or me," said Lou.

"Quackenbush moves in mysterious ways," said Bud.

"Right you are," said Stan.

"Mmmm Mmmmm Mmmmm," said Ollie.

By the time they saw they were in the air they also realized the pilot wasn't aboard.

Leonard was still stuck upside down in the forward cockpit. Arthur managed to fly the plane straight while his brother crawled out and sat upright.

Looping and swirling, they flew on through the late afternoon towards Cedar Oaks.

The line started forming in front of the doors of the civic auditorium at five, though it was still bitterly cold.

The manager looked outside at 5.15 pm. It was just dark, and there must be a hundred and fifty kids out there already, tickets in hand. He hadn't been at the sound rehearsal and hadn't seen the performers. All he knew was what he heard about them: they were the hottest rock and roll musicians since Elvis Presley and Chuck Berry.

The show went on at 7.00 pm as advertised, and it was a complete sellout. The crowd was ready, and when Rip Dover introduced the Champagnes, the people yelled and screamed even at their tired *doo-wah* act.

Then came Wailon, and they were polite for him, except that they kept yelling "Rock 'n' roll! Rock 'n' roll!" and he kept singing "Young Love" and the like.

Then other acts, then Val Ritchie, who jogged his way through several standards and launched into "Los Niños." He tore the place apart. They wouldn't let him go, they were dancing in the aisles. He did "Los Niños" until he was hoarse. They dropped the spots on him, finally, and the kids quit screaming. It got quiet. Then there was the sound of a mike being turned on and a voice, greasy in the magnificence, filled the hall:

"Helloooooooooooo, baby!"

It was long past dark, and the truck swerved down the road, the forms of Stan, Ollie, Bud and Lou illuminated by the dome light. Bud had a map unfolded in front of the windshield and Ollie's arms were in Lou's way.

"It's here somewhere," said Bud. "I know it's here somewhere!"

Overhead was the whining, droning sound of an old aeroplane, sometimes close to the ground, sometimes far above. Every once in a while was a yell of "Watch-a youself! Watcha where you go!" and a *whonk whonk*.

The truck below passed a sign which said:

WELCOME TO CEDAR OAKS
Speed Limit 30 mph

After The Large Charge hung up the telephone receiver, and they let him offstage to thunderous ovation, the back curtain parted and there were Donny Bottoms and the Mosquitoes.

And the first song they sang was "Dottie," the song Bottoms had written for his wife while they were still high school sweethearts. Then "Roller Coaster Days" and "Miss America" and all his classics. And the crowd went crazy and…

––––––––––––––––––

The truck roared into the snowy, jampacked parking lot of the auditorium, skidded sideways, wiped out a '57 cherry-red Merc and punched out the moon window of a T-Bird. The cops on parking lot duty ran towards the wreck.

Halfway there, they jumped under other cars to get away from the noise.

The noise was that of an airplane going to crash very soon, very close.

At the last second, the sound stopped.

The cops looked up.

An old biplane was sitting still in a parking space in the lot, its propeller still spinning. Two guys in funny clothes were climbing down from it, one whistling and *honking* to the other, who was trying to get a pointy hat off his ears.

The doors of the truck which had crashed opened, and four guys tumbled out all over each other.

They ran towards the auditorium, and the two from the plane saw them and whistled and ran towards them. They joined halfway across the lot, the six of them, and ran towards the civic hall.

The police were running for them like a berserk football team and then...

The auditorium doors were thrown open by the ushers, lances of light gleamed out on the snow and parked cars, and the mob spilled out onto the concrete and snow, laughing, yelling, pushing, shoving in an effort to get home.

The six running figures melted into the oncoming throng, the police right behind them.

Above the cop whistles and the mob noise was an occasional "Ollie, oh, Ollie!" or "Hey, Bud! Hey, Bud!" or *whonk whonk* and...

The six made it into the auditorium as the maintenance men were turning out the lights, and they ran up to the manager's office and inside.

The thin manager was watching TV. He looked up to the six, and thought it must be some sort of a publicity stunt.

On TV came the theme music of "You Bet Your Duck."

"It's-a Quackenbush!" said Leonard.

The TV show host looked up from his rostrum. "Hi, folks. And tonight what's the secret woids?" Here a large merganser puppet flopped down and the audience applauded. The show host turned the word card around and lifted his eyebrows, looked at the screen and said:

"That's right. Tonight, the woids are Inexorable Fate. I knew I should've hired someone else. You guys are too late."

Then he turned to the announcer and asked, "George, who's our first guest?" as the duck was pulled back overhead on its strings.

The six men tore from the office and out to the parking lot, through the last of the mob. Stan, Ollie, Bud and Lou jumped in the truck which a wrecker attendant was just connecting to a winch, right under the nose of the astonished police chief.

Arthur and Leonard, whistling and yelling, jumped in the plane, backed it out, and took off after circling the crowded parking lot. They rose into the air to many a loud scream.

The truck and plane headed for the airport.

The crowd was milling about the airport fence. Inside the barrier, musicians waited to get aboard a DC-3, their instrument cases scattered about the concourse.

The truck with four men in it crashed through the fence, strewing wire and posts to the sides.

It twisted around on its wheels, skidded sideways, almost hitting the musicians, and came to a halt. The four looked like the Keystone Firemen as they climbed out.

There was a roar in the air, and the biplane came out of the runway lights, landed and taxied to a stop less than an inch from the nose of the passenger plane.

"We not-a too late! We not-a too late!" yelled Leonard, as he climbed down. "Arthur, get tough with-a that plane. Don't let it take off!"

Arthur climbed to the front of the crop duster and repeated the facial expressions he'd gone through earlier with the pilot. This time at the frightened pilot of the DC-3, through the windshield.

Leonard, Bud, Lou, Stan and Ollie ran to the musicians and found Wailon.

"Where's Bottoms?" asked Bud.

"Huh?" asked Jimmy Wailon, still a little distraught by the skidding truck and aeroplane. "Bottoms? Bottoms left on the first plane."

"The first plane?" asked Ollie. "The first aeroplane?"

"Uh, yeah. Simpson and Ritchie were already on. Donny wanted to wait for this one, but I gave him my seat. I'm waiting for someone." He looked at them; they had not moved. "I gave him my seat on the first plane," he said. Then he looked them over in the dim lights. "You friends of his?"

"No," said Stanley, "but I'm sure we'll be seeing him again very soon."

Overhead, the plane which had taken off a few minutes before circled and headed northwest for Alaska.

They listened to it fade in the distance.

Whonk went Arthur.

They drove back through the dark February night, all six of them jammed into the seat and the small back compartment. After they heard the news for the first time, they turned the radio down and talked about the old days.

"This fellow Quackenbush," asked Ollie. "Is he in the habit of doing things such as this?"

"Ah, the Boss? There's-a no tellin' what the boss man willa do!"

"He must not be a *nice* man," said Lou.

"Oh, he's probably all right," said Bud. "He just has a mind like a producer."

"A contradiction in terms," said Stanley.

"You're *so* right," said Ollie.

"Pardon me," said the hitchhiker for whom they stopped. "Could you fellows find it in your hearts to give me a ride? I feel a bit weary after the affairs of the day, and should like to nestle in the arms of Morpheus for a short while."

"Sure," said Lou. "Hop in."

"Ah yes," said the rotund hitchhiker in the beaver hat. "Been chasing about the interior of this state all day. Some fool errand, yes indeed. Reminds me of the time on safari in Afghanistan…" He looked at the six men, leaned forward, tapping a deck of cards with his gloved hands. "Would any of you gentlemen be interested in a little game of chance?"

"No thanks," said Bud. "You wouldn't like the way I play."

They drove through the night. They didn't need to stop for the next hitchhiker, because they knew him. They saw him in the headlights, on the railroad tracks beside the road. He was kicking a broken-down locomotive. He came down the embankment, stood beside the road as they bore down on him.

He was dressed in a straw hat, a vest and a pair of tight pants. He wore the same countenance all the time, a great stone face.

The truck came roaring down on him, and was even with him, and was almost by, when he reached out with one hand and grabbed the back door handle and with the other clamped his straw hat to his head.

His feet flew up off the pavement and for a second he was parallel to the ground, then he pulled himself into the spare tire holder and curled up asleep.

He had never changed expression.

Over the hill went the eight men, some of them talking, some dozing, towards the dawn. Just before the truck went out of sight there was a sound, so high, so thin it did not carry well.

It went *honk honk.*

I AM BONARO
John Niendorff

This story has haunted me for over forty years. It first appeared in Fantastic *in December 1964. It intrigued me then, and it has continued to intrigue me ever since. Although I looked for other work by the author I found none, and even suspected he might have used an alias. Not until the advent of the internet did I discover that Niendorff (b. 1939) had written several episodes for the TV western series* The High Chaparral *and* Death Valley Days *in the later 1960s and subsequently became editor of* Science of Mind *magazine, which deals with practical spirituality. Some of his writings for that magazine were collected as* Listen to the Light *(1980). But I knew none of that until recently when I stumbled upon the author's website at www.john-niendorff.com. This story may be short, but then, so are splinters.*

Only the ticket agent saw the old man as he was thrown from the motionless boxcar and tumbled crazily to the gravel-covered earth. The train hissed and wheezed for a moment as it gathered energy for movement then began crawling away from the station.

Slamming the lid of his cashbox closed, the agent ran from the tiny office to track-side where the old man lay. He paused for a long breath then called, "You okay, Mister?"

The old man stirred noiselessly. Dressed in faded coveralls, he had long white hair that fell in tangled disarray to his rounded shoulders; his matted, filth-encrusted beard was the same white as his hair.

"You need any help, old man?"

Painfully slowly, the old man rose to his knees, pushed his arms hard against the ground, and shoved his body erect. The agent took a startled step backward when he saw the face: the most pitiful, wretched face he had ever seen. Brittle skin, like old parchment, was shrunk against the bone and eroded with deep wrinkles; and eyes that were hollow, empty and desperately sad.

Across the front of his shirt, a crudely-lettered cardboard sign, pinned carelessly onto the wrinkled cloth, proclaimed simply, "I AM BONARO."

"Bonaro? That your name?"

The old man gave no sign of recognition, for he was incapable of even that elementary act. He only began to dig deep into his trouser pocket, bringing out a soiled yellow mass that he gripped tightly in one withered hand. It was a sponge.

He held it out.

The agent tentatively reached out his own hand. "For me?"

Bonaro said nothing, but held out the sponge until he was certain that the agent did not understand then he drew it back and let the hand fall limply.

"Bonaro? I guess that's your name. If you'd like some coffee, I've got a pot inside. Otherwise, you'd better beat it."

Bonaro's face remained immobile. Not even his empty eyes altered their fixed stare.

"Look, friend, if you don't need help, at least stay away from the tracks. They're dangerous. You understand that? Dangerous. You'll get hurt if you fool around here without knowing what you're doing."

Bonaro swayed uncertainly as though he were going to fall then he held out the sponge once more, hesitated a moment, and began to pad silently away from the tracks, holding the dirty sponge in front of him as if it were a guidepost by which he steered.

Old Bonaro was not aware of having been thrown from the train; he was not aware of having met the ticket agent. He only knew that he was Somewhere…and that which he sought might be anywhere.

He had been five years old when he first wished himself different. The place he had lived was high above the asphalt streets, a slim wooden shambles squeezed between rotting tenements. He had distant memories of a thing called Father: a loud, dirty man who never shaved and snored raucously. And Mother: a screaming, anxious assortment of abrupt nervous reactions like spank and slap and swear.

Bonaro recalled being locked in a closet because he had cursed at his father; a closet that was small and dark, where spiders crawled and tickled his skin and the groans of the tired walls were magnified until they filled his head with droning, foreign speech.

He sat there for longer than he knew, without moving, until he saw a tiny sliver of dusty light along the bottom of the closet door, and crouching down with his ear close to the splintery floor, he could almost see outside.

Young Bonaro knew that he could never escape through that crack beneath the door. A piece of paper could. A coat hanger would slide through there. A slippery gob of mud could do it. So Bonaro wished himself a slippery gob of mud, spreading himself out thinly on the floor. It was difficult at first, forcing each particle of himself through that slim slit, but finally he oozed the last drop out of the closet and wished himself Bonaro.

His father had beaten him for getting out; after carefully examining the lock on the closet door, he had beaten Young Bonaro with a long board until the boy was strangling on his own blood.

The Old Man thought of that time as he walked away from the train station and into a wide main street.

When did he next wish...? When he had been about twelve. Bad-father had taught him to steal, while Bad-mother laughed. Stealing was easy for Bonaro when he learned how to run away and hide, and he was never caught until that time when he was twelve and stole the Man's wallet.

He had run for many blocks until his body refused to carry him further, and he collapsed into a soft pile of rags and trash. Seeing the walls high around him meant nothing until he saw the men coming after him, then jerking his body upright, he flung his eyes violently in every direction where escape might lie.

A high brick wall...a building...a wooden fence twice his own height...there was no way out and the men were after him. So Bonaro did the only thing he could: he wished himself part of that pile of trash and they never found him.

The train station was far behind.

"'Scuse me, fella. You okay?"

To Bonaro, the policeman was only another form to which he held out the sponge.

"You can't talk, is that it?" The policeman pulled a note pad and pencil from the pocket of his uniform. "Maybe you need help. Can you write?"

The hand in which Bonaro held the sponge began to quiver.

"Now, look here, old man. I guess I don't understand, but you darned near caused about five accidents by walking across that street without watching the traffic. You be careful from now on."

Then, as the policeman went away, Bonaro's thoughts went back.

On his twentieth birthday he had first seen the words "socially incorrigible" on his progress chart in the juvenile home. He learned that his father had died, his mother was arrested for a reason he didn't understand. But Bonaro never cared, because he could always wish.

Hang-Pants, the hoodlum, had thought Bonaro an easy mark – one fist to put him senseless on the sidewalk – when Bonaro had wished himself a big rock. Hang-Pants left with a broken hand. That was funny.

Bonaro had killed the priest in front of a hundred worshippers and laughed as he wished himself a gleaming golden cross.

"I AM BONARO."

The sign flapped on his chest as he stepped into the diner and sat down on a tiny stool. The young waitress looked suspiciously at his bedraggled appearance.

"Help you, sir?"

She suddenly jerked her body back as he thrust out the mouldy sponge.

Bonaro's memories were vague in his head as he thought of the many, many fears of being alive. A dark night and a dog's bark – *fear* – wish to be a lion. Steep stairs, slippery – *fear* – wish to be a rubber ball. Many…so many each day…uncounted when life was steal and kill and wish-different to escape.

"Help you, sir?" the waitress asked again.

They had come after him that final night with torches. Because they knew it was Bonaro who had killed their little girl. Bonaro stood tall, boldly on the wide concrete highway as they came for him. He saw the mob crunching closer, their kerosene torches flaming and flashing in the darkness. They marched across the field onto the road where he stood.

What could he become? To hide on this barren hardness?

One torch wiggled and sailed like an exploding star above the mob, arcing high towards Bonaro. He saw it streak down and felt it hitting his chest, the pungent odour of the kerosene filling his head as flame attacked his shirt. His body was heat and fire, as he pounded open palms against the growing horror of burning flesh as his clothes ignited.

Water! Water, said his mind as he dissolved himself into a puddle, seeping away from the scorching clothes, gathering in a pool on the road. He felt cool as a tender breeze caressed his dampness and he waited until he felt the warmth that meant sun. Sun meant time had passed. The mob would be gone and he wished himself Bonaro again.

Water, a puddle in the road, is drawn into the wind...evaporates. Bonaro almost screamed knowing why he had felt the coolness. What part had gone away with the wind? Eyes? Arms? No...his body was whole, but something still was gone.

Gone in water which goes on the wind, then to clouds, to rain. Rain comes back. Water is never gone...just lost.

He would find it, searching many, many more years until his body died. He would recognize that water because it was part of him. He would *know*.

The waitress set up a glass.

"Help you, sir?"

Bonaro held out the sponge hopefully.

THE OLD HOUSE UNDER THE SNOW

Rhys Hughes

Rhys Hughes (b. 1966) is a master of the surreal and has written scores of short stories noted for their magical word play. His blogsite is at rhysaurus.blogspot.com. He has set himself the target of writing exactly 1,000 short stories, and he's already nearly halfway there. A sampling will be found in his collections Worming the Harpy *(1995),* The Smell of Telescopes *(2000) and* At the Molehills of Madness *(2006). Many of his stories are surreal or absurdist in nature, as exampled by "The Deaths of Robin Hood" included in the fourth volume of my* Mammoth Book of Comic Fantasy. *The following is one of his longer escapades and is somewhat reminiscent of* Alice in Wonderland – *at its most nightmarish!*

"Get your spade."

I won't say Curtis was a mean man, but that's how he wanted to be remembered. His face was gentle and round and inspired only good humour in the people he wanted to annoy or dominate. Not that he was soft, but his basic nature was too pleasant and relaxed to give him the reputation he craved, which was that of a tough adventurer, an outdoors type, rugged and unforgiving.

He worked hard to keep himself in shape and his expression always betrayed his inner dismay at a life of enforced marches over hills and early morning baths in icy ponds. His stamina and frugality were contrived. As for myself, I had less than half his love of trekking, camping and the wilderness in general, but this was enough to ensure I joined one of his expeditions every month.

"Where are we going?" I asked.

"Not far this time. Just up to the crater. The place where it's always winter and the snow is extra fine."

"What's there? Nothing, if I recall."

He tried to fix me with an intimidating stare, failed and rubbed his eyes. Then he pulled out a folded sheet of paper from his pocket and handed it to me. I opened it and found myself blinking at a map. It was old and the ink had faded but I recognised the local mountains. There was something else.

"Where did you get this?" I wondered.

Curtis licked his lips and nodded with childish glee. "Bought a cabinet in an antique store from a senile fool last week. It didn't look quite right in any of my rooms, I can't say why, so I kept moving it about and I guess all that vibration activated some hidden springs. A secret compartment popped out and this was inside. It reminded me of the legend and made me think that maybe there's truth in it after all."

I examined the map more closely. "This certainly looks like a house."

"I'm sure it's the Baron's place. He must have sold the cabinet without realizing the map was in it. More than a century ago!"

I sighed. In the rather thin folklore of our region the tale of the missing mansion was the most prominent fable. I couldn't account for its popularity, for it lacked plot and moral and was utterly inconclusive. The Baron was an immigrant from somewhere in Central or Eastern Europe, only he wasn't a real aristocrat but a rich merchant with aspirations to a title. He built a large house in the mountains and the labourers who worked on it were recruited from a lunatic asylum, so that its location would become a sort of secret, for they were bound to disagree on where it was. And so it was finished and nobody had seen it since.

Curtis enjoyed relating the different endings of this myth.

"The madmen built it inside out and it collapsed. Or the Baron was hiding from the devil, who disguised himself as a labourer and remained behind, to greet the new owner when he opened the door, though this doesn't explain why it vanished. Or some sort of experiment went wrong and shrank it to the size of an eyeball. They said the Baron was a magician or scientist."

I tapped the map with a finger. "But here is a more mundane explanation."

"Yes and it suits our purpose. The crater isn't above the snowline but the surrounding peaks mean it is always in shade. It must have been empty when the Baron built his house there. Then an avalanche filled the crater and buried it under tons of snow for a hundred years."

I laughed. "That's so simple!"

"The snow won't melt but will just keep getting deeper until the crater is full. We have about thirty feet to dig through. My guess is that the building is in perfect condition down there. And all the stuff in the rooms untouched."

"Do you mean treasure?" I mumbled.

He offered me a wry smile. "The Baron was a wealthy man and I doubt he deposited his money in a bank. It wasn't the way they did things back then. Maybe there's nothing of any value but it can't hurt to take a look."

"Worth it for the adventure," I said.

He slapped me on the back. "That's the spirit! Let's gather some equipment. Ropes to climb into the crater and flashlights for our work."

I checked my watch. "It's getting late."

"All the more reason to hurry. Come on, Warren!"

I needed no further encouragement. Within an hour my backpack was full and my hiking boots were laced tightly to my feet. We tramped through the town to the outskirts and found the path which led into the foothills. Nobody we passed gave us a second glance. They were used to seeing us embark on expeditions, but it was an odd hour to be setting off, with the sun already low in the west, and we had no tents. I welcomed the lighter load and I know Curtis did too, though he would never admit it.

The path was strewn with small stones and as we slowly ascended my ankles began to ache from the constant stumbling, but I didn't complain. Soon we turned off and followed the equally rocky bed of a narrow stream. This was a quicker route to the crater. The chill penetrated my boots but I had got into the rhythm of walking and felt at peace with nature, enjoying the weak warmth on the back of my neck and the smell of the air, which was clean and exhilarating.

I was shocked out of my complacency by a sudden crash from ahead. The note of violence boomed around the mountains in a prolonged echo. I paused and was nearly overwhelmed with fatigue and doubts.

Curtis kept going. "Just an avalanche. Nothing special."

I nodded and caught him up, the spade on my backpack swinging and slapping my flank as if I was a mule that needed to be goaded.

THE SUN WENT DOWN...

But we went up, higher and higher, until we were truly in the mountains and could permit ourselves a rest without feeling guilt. We sat and shared a flask of coffee and marvelled at the rosy clouds and the darkening sky.

Our progress would become more difficult, but we were fairly close to our destination. One more hour and we would be standing on the rim of the crater. We had both made this journey many times before, but rarely at night and always on the way somewhere else. Although an impressive geographical feature, the crater had previously held scant interest for us, being little more than a deep hole stuffed with snow.

Now we had a different opinion of it. Greed had blessed it.

We resumed our trek, picking our way between boulders and over the trunks of fallen trees. It was exciting but there was a hollowness in my stomach. I expected to be disappointed, to learn the map was a hoax or that the house had been crushed flat and its supposed treasures ruined. I knew Curtis was dreaming of gold bars but I thought paper money more likely.

The moon appeared through a rent in the clouds. Nearly full it was a great assistance to our uncertain feet and the path became less perilous. When we reached the crater and peered over, the snow below glimmered brightly. Our flashlights were surplus to requirements, but we were confronted with our first major problem. The avalanche we had heard earlier had taken place right here.

"More than thirty feet now!" I blurted.

Curtis grunted and pointed at the dark shapes that littered the fresh snow like giant limbs and heads. They were large rocks and parts of trees. Silently we secured our ropes to an overhanging crag and climbed down. Then we wandered among the debris to the exact centre of the crater and unslung our backpacks. According to the map the mansion was directly below us, but neither of us felt like digging.

The eyes of my companion glinted and his round face broke into a smile. He had picked up his own spade but now his grip relaxed and it dangled idly from his fingers. He indicated a boulder which had tumbled from a neighbouring peak. It was black and smooth and rested on the snow with an absurd elegance but on one side there was a wide indentation where a fragment had broken off in the fall.

"I have an idea. Look at the shape of this rock."

"Like an overthrown altar," I commented.

"Not quite, but it might resemble one more closely in a few minutes. Help me turn it so that the depression is facing upward."

"I don't understand," I replied.

He ignored me and began digging under one corner of the boulder and his heavy breathing was so sincere I felt sorry for him and joined in.

I used my spade as a lever and together we managed to shift the position of the enormous stone. Tiny crystals on its surface sparkled magically as Curtis roamed the surrounding area to collect wood. We piled branches into the depression and I finally understood his plan. It took several failed attempts with matches before a few of the smaller and drier twigs caught.

But the fire rapidly took hold.

I backed away but Curtis said, "Use the blade of your spade to reflect the heat back onto the boulder. It would be better to start a fire underneath it, but we can't do that."

"Some rocks explode when heated," I pointed out.

He shrugged. "That's the risk."

I watched as he added more branches to the blaze. The crater glowed with the pulsing light as if it was breathing and blushing. Within the orange of the flames appeared other colours, purple and green, but there was no smoke. I grew tired of holding my spade at an awkward angle and lowered it briefly. It grazed the surface of the snow and I was startled by an angry hiss. Meanwhile the snow around the base of the boulder began to crackle and give off wisps of steam.

Then the rock started to sink.

It dropped through the snow smoothly and Curtis threw on a final log before it sank out of view. The moon was still bright but now the crater seemed gloomy and unfriendly. We moved closer and gazed into the shaft. The boulder was already far below us, spitting sparks, and I briefly imagined I was observing a rocket barging into the sky. This optical illusion confused me and I staggered before regaining my senses. Hot air rose up the shaft and brushed my face and studded my brow with jewels of sweat.

"It's certainly warm enough now."

Curtis turned and strode off. "We'll use one of our ropes to climb after it and keep the other in place to get us out of the crater."

By the time he returned and tied one of the ropes to the trunk of what had been a mighty tree, the boulder had vanished from sight. We scratched our heads. Instead of flames or at least embers, the base of the shaft was occupied by something dark and shaped differently from the rock. But when we listened, the hiss of melting now was still faintly audible.

"I'll go first," declared Curtis.

I declined to argue and he took hold of the rope and lowered himself into the shaft. I followed close behind. We must have gone down more than sixty feet when he suddenly announced he had reached the bottom. He described it as a hard surface slanted at a steep angle. Then he added that there was another tunnel in the snow which ran parallel to this incline. All this mystery resolved itself in my mind when he next spoke.

"I'm standing on the roof!"

"The roof of the mansion?" I gasped.

"Of course. The boulder didn't stop here but slid sideways to the edge. It probably tipped over the side and has melted another shaft down to the base of the crater. If we follow the path it has made we can be sure of standing next to the house. Then it's just a question of finding a way inside!"

I panted my agreement and he crawled along the tunnel, still supporting himself with the rope. I touched down on the roof myself and followed his example. A beam of light told me he had switched on his flashlight. This beam shook and wobbled as he reached the next vertical shaft. I sensed the tons of snow above me and controlled my trembling, which had less to do with cold than fear. Then I also reached the edge of the roof.

To my astonishment, Curtis was standing a few feet below me. I wondered aloud if the mansion was really a cottage and if legend alone had expanded its size, but from the expression on his face, which was ghostly in the electric light, I realised this wasn't the case. He confirmed it with his next words.

"I'm not standing on the ground."

"What happened?" I asked.

"The boulder has come to rest on an upper balcony. I'm balancing on it right now. Falling snow has extinguished the embers but it's still hot. I can't stay here much longer. If I can't get into the house I'll have to come back up."

"Is there a window?"

I heard him fumbling among the shadows. "Yes and it has a handle. Let's hope it opens inwards. I'll give it a try now."

He did and the resultant creak was like a laugh. Then he vanished and the flashlight went with him. I found myself staring down at the top of the boulder and the ash which filled its indentation. He had entered safely. I hastened to join him.

THE HOUSE WAS EMPTY

The Baron was absent and nobody else was at home. I closed the window behind me and crossed the room to where Curtis stood. The cold was intense and the floor and walls were coated with frost. This was obviously the highest floor of the mansion and the room was relatively small and bare. It contained a bed, desk, chair and a few other small items of modest furniture.

But Curtis was excited. "Look at this, Warren!"

He played the beam of his flashlight over a cabinet in the corner. I saw nothing remarkable in its contours and simple decoration.

"I don't understand," I replied.

"It's almost identical to the one I purchased in that antique store. I guess the Baron must have sold some of his possessions before he disappeared. I hope this doesn't mean he was short of money. I'd hate to think this adventure was pointless!"

"Never that," I answered. "Shall we go down?"

He nodded and we passed through the open door onto a wide landing. We instinctively knew the house was too large to explore all at once. We desired to find the main rooms and become familiar with those first and we assumed they were located on the ground floor. We passed a table on which stood a candelabrum holding two candles. Curtis reached into his pocket for matches and lit the wicks. The glow was weak but welcome.

"One hundred years old," he muttered.

We reached the stairway and began our descent. There were brackets set into the wall also holding candles, some mere stubs, and we lit these too on our way. We decided to light every candle we encountered to chase away the perennial night. Because of the frost it was impossible to say whether there were carpets beneath our feet. I was inclined to the belief the stairs were bare. The lower we went, the colder it became.

When we reached the next floor down we took a detour through some of the rooms before returning to the stairway. We followed this procedure for every floor. In the wavering glow of the candles above us I felt I was swimming through an undersea grotto. Certainly I hadn't been this cold since the caving trip I undertook with Curtis a few years previously, a trip which involved diving into pools that had never seen the sun. Stamping my feet did little to warm them. I was numb all over.

After a while, an odd thought occurred to me.

"The layout of this house is regular. The shapes of the rooms and their relative positions are conventional. I was expecting unnatural angles and corridors that go nowhere. After all, it was built by lunatics."

"Yes but it wasn't designed by them. The Baron designed it and he was mad too. Doubtless his design was mad and they constructed it in a mad way. The two madnesses cancelled each other out. Thus the result is unintentionally normal."

I snorted. "How grotesque!"

We finally reached the ground floor and wandered together into an enormous room. This was what we had dreamed about, a chamber filled with the trappings of wealth. One wall was dominated by a monumental hearth. A marble mantelpiece held ornaments that demanded closer inspection. A grandfather clock, utterly silent now, stood in the middle of the opposite wall. Between them a couple of elegant chairs were arranged at pleasing angles. A chandelier hung from the ceiling and burst into a cluster of tiny suns as the flashlight caught it.

Smirking at each other we pointed at a table which held two silver goblets and a bottle of wine. Before sampling this vintage we rested on the chairs. But something wasn't right and we remained tense.

"I'm too weary to search for treasure now."

Curtis didn't argue. "Yes and it's too cold to relax properly. That wine won't really warm us. How about if we start a fire and get this room warmed up? Then we can sleep for an hour or two and be refreshed for the plundering later. There are some books over there. We'll use the paper to get the blaze going."

I sat rigid, trying not to let my teeth chatter, my hands gripping the frosty arms of my chair. "But the chimney isn't open to the sky."

"Do you think the smoke will come back down? If it does, we'll vacate this room and shut the door tight. I still think it's worth a try. Fetch the books and I'll break up some furniture. Here are the matches. I wonder why the snow didn't fall down the flue and fill the house? I guess there must be a grille at the top of the chimney."

I rose stiffly and approached the bookcase. I had expected volumes of science or magic in a foreign language but these tomes were ordinary enough, encyclopedias and works on local history and geography. I tore out the pages and cast them into the fireplace. Curtis searched a cabinet and after convincing himself it held no money or anything else of value he flung it to the floor, repeating this action until it shattered.

We crouched before the hearth, warming our hands and faces.

Soon we were able to add the remnants of another cabinet and a table. There was almost no smoke in the fire and I was grateful for this, but the flames contained unexpected colours. Now we were warm enough to try the wine. I had a corkscrew on my pocket knife and managed to work the frozen cork out.

"Wait! Did you hear that? A gurgling sound!"

"It's the wine in the bottle!" laughed Curtis.

I shook my head. "It's coming from the wall above the hearth."

Moving closer I placed my hands on the wall and quickly drew them away. Then I moved to the side and tried again. I bit my lower lip nervously.

Curtis had already poured and tasted. "Not bad. Well?"

"Blisters. It's red hot."

"What do you expect? You touched the wall directly above the hearth."

"No, it's spreading. I don't think this is an ordinary fireplace. There seems to be liquid behind it. Probably oil of some kind in a tank. There must be a network of pipes embedded in the brick."

I followed the moving heat into the shadows. I realised it was spreading along the floor and ceiling too. Curtis unbuttoned his jacket.

"What do you think it means?"

"The entire room is a giant radiator. Maybe the whole house."

"So what? The Baron was eccentric."

I stepped to the window and pressed my face against the glass. A sudden crash made me spin around. Curtis was adding more fuel to the fire. I strode over to stop him but then questioned my caution. There seemed no harm in the idea of turning our domestic climate from polar to tropical. I assisted him and we removed our outer clothes item by item, pausing only to finish the bottle. I offered to search for more wine. One wall was now so hot it glowed dully. I discovered that the warmth really had spread beyond the limits of this room. Out in the hall I found another bottle, this time of brandy, idle on a table.

Curtis had taken my place by the window. He beckoned to me.

"A gap of several inches has opened between the house and the snow outside. If this continues we'll be able to melt our way out of the crater!"

"And expose the secret to everyone," I pointed out.

"We'll claim the treasure first anyway. And you have to admit this is an easier way of getting back out."

I did. While I was doing so there was a powerful lurch.

"What was that?" I cried.

Curtis answered, "I think the house is sinking."

"There must be more snow beneath it. How can this be? Let's extinguish the fire and stop it going any deeper. We'd better hurry!"

"There's nothing to put it out with. And even if we douse the flames the house will remain hot for a long time yet."

I grabbed his arm. "Upstairs quick! We can get out through a window at the top and still be at our original level. It's our best chance."

But I knew this was a forlorn hope and so did he. The house was sinking faster and more smoothly now, though it groaned and creaked as it gathered speed. In fact we just stared at each other and didn't move a muscle, apart from those necessary to keep us alive and form a pair of very frightened smiles. Then we regained something of our normal composure and sighed softly at our predicament and remarked on how ironic it was.

"I wonder how deep the snow is?" I muttered.

He returned to the window and there was a snapping noise which I assumed was his foot treading on a piece of broken furniture that had somehow escaped becoming fuel. But it wasn't. He stood for a long time at the glass, rubbing his hands which were behind his back. I didn't care for this mannerism and told him so but he ignored me and mumbled something about the amount of oxygen contained in all the cubic space in the house and how long it would last two men and the fire they had to feed.

Finally he looked over his shoulder and answered me.

"It's not snow now. It's ice. The Baron must have constructed his mansion on the surface of a frozen pool. Not a normal frozen pool but one solid all the way through. We're melting our way into it and the ice is doubtlessly sealing itself again above us. If we extinguish the fire we'll eventually cool and slow down and stop and be entombed forever. We have no choice but to keep burning the furniture. It's a one way ride."

I was incredulous. "To where? The bottom of the lake? What good will that do us? It's death either way."

The mansion shuddered and I nearly lost my balance.

"The pressure outside is enormous," he said. "It can only get worse. I'm truly sorry for dragging you on this trip. You were my friend."

"I still am!" I spluttered.

His tone became thoughtful, even slightly mystical. "Very well. We both know that the story of the Baron and his missing mansion is the most popular of our local legends. But there are others. I am currently thinking about one in particular. I've always wondered about this crater and what made it. The result of volcanic activity or the wound inflicted by an ancient meteorite? I never imagined it might be the special lake."

I took his meaning and went very pale.

He added, "The one rumoured to be bottomless."

THE DAYS PASSED

We dropped like a hot boulder in the shape of an altar. But the only indentations were in our hearts. Ice opened below us and clenched above like a sequence of blue-white fists. And we wandered our domain, our prison, collecting fuel and searching for food. We smashed wardrobes and clocks and existed on sherry and spirits. But in a corner of the kitchen where the heat had not yet spread I found a ham and a tin of biscuits preserved in the frost. We ate without pleasure and listened to our own teeth in despair.

At least we had stopped accelerating. The pressure of the ice squeezed the house but the hot oil in its veins expanded it and this balance was expressed as a shallow breathing of our total environment, the breathing of a man ready for his coffin, though in fact it was we who were buried. We discussed the legend of the bottomless pool. There was nothing to it really and perhaps that is why it was so terrible. I'm not sure if either of us hoped for anything. We kept ourselves busy.

The air grew stale in time but we discovered that fresh oxygen could be obtained by going into a spare room, one we had not yet entered, and there were plenty of those, but we rationed these gulps of purity carefully. I think I was most afraid of breaking through the ice into ordinary water and drowning in one of the rooms, but this seemed increasingly unlikely. The legend insisted the lake was completely solid, an infinite icecube in nothingness, and that is what I gradually came to believe.

We still looked for treasure, without success.

I was reading one of the Baron's books, tearing out each page as I finished it and casting it to the flames, when Curtis suddenly shouted.

He was standing at the window, a duty we took in turns, and I glanced at him with a mixture of gloom and wild optimism.

"There's something out there. It has gone now."

"What was it?" I asked.

"It might have been a submarine. An early design. We've passed it so I suppose we'll never know for certain."

Then he burst into tears. It was the first time I had seen him weep and I was grateful he had surrendered to the impulse before me, but I couldn't think of a way to comfort him. Words were useless. I decided to rely on the brandy bottle or whatever alcohol came to hand. There was nothing available in this room so I rose and departed and passed into the hall. Most of the original candles had burned out but we had found spares and some were monsters, whole legs of wax which could last months. Yet we were conscious of the need to preserve air and we had blown many out, abandoning the majority of the house to shadows.

I returned with a bottle of rum and some interesting news.

"I've discovered a study beyond the kitchens. It contains a telephone! One of the first practical models. The Baron was clearly a man of the moment. I don't mean to sound ridiculous but what if it still works?"

Curtis had dried his eyes and was manly again, but his cheeks were damp and his efforts to appear in control were mostly wasted.

"I saw no cables leading into the crater," he declared.

"True. But I'm going to try. Nothing else to do today. Come with me. Won't it be a relief just to dial a number?"

He meekly nodded and followed me to the study. The telephone was a contraption fitted inside a cabinet bolted to the wall. It was a primitive device but recognisable enough, with a mouthpiece and dial. I opened the cabinet doors and stood there awkwardly, trying to operate the mechanism and rehearsing what to say.

"Who are you ringing? The police?"

"My wife in Kamloops. I want her to know first."

Curtis scowled and paced in agitation as I pressed the earpiece to the side of my head and dialled the number. It was answered almost immediately. There was no need for me to talk. I listened with a frown and then replaced the receiver.

"What happened? What did she say?"

"It was a wrong number. I got a man. He said, 'Who? What? Eh! He's not at home. Haha!' Then he hung up."

"Let me try," demanded Curtis.

I shrugged and he took my place and his fingers were busy with the dial. Though he held the earpiece I distinctly heard the voice at the other end of the line.

"Who? What? Eh! He's not at home. Haha!"

I was bewildered but Curtis was terrified. The colour drained from his skin. He staggered back and clutched me to steady himself.

"There's something about that voice," he stammered.

"Yes it does sound peculiar, almost artificial."

Voicing this thought gave me an idea. I groped behind the cabinet for the cable at the back of the telephone. Then I followed it along the wall and through a side door into a short corridor. I turned a sharp bend and entered another room, little more than a recess, bare apart from a table on which sat an antique gramophone. The disc was spinning and the arm that held the needle was raised above it. The cable stopped here. I called back to Curtis to ring a number, any number, and he replied that he would. Hidden relays in the gramophone clicked and the needle lowered onto the disc. The thin voice came again and then the arm raised itself. It was a trick.

I wandered back to Curtis. "The Baron must have made that recording and invented an automatic device to set it in motion whenever anyone used the telephone. But why? It's an obscure joke. I'm not laughing."

"Nor me. I recognise that voice."

"Impossible. The Baron vanished a century ago."

Curtis had calmed down. He moved away slowly, out of the study and through the kitchens. The gleam of a bottle on a high shelf caught his attention and he reached for it. He bore his prize back to the chamber that contained the fire. On the way he paused at every window to look out. This had become a habit for both of us. The dark ice slid past. Back in the furnace room, for such had we termed it, we sat in the two remaining chairs and vainly attempted to drink our troubles away. Then he chuckled sourly.

"It was the voice of the man in the antique store."

I blinked. "The senile old fool?"

"None other. I never imagined the Baron might still be alive. We made a big mistake. He never dwelled in this mansion. He built it as a trap, not a habitation. He became a shopkeeper and existed in humble isolation."

"Well he certainly never attracted any attention."

Curtis nodded. "That was the idea."

"Who was the trap intended for?" I pressed.

"Remember that other ending to the legend? The devil came for him and that's why he disappeared. But in fact the Baron outwitted the devil. He didn't construct his house in a secret location to escape his fate but to entice it. Once his enemy found it and entered and activated the trigger by lighting the fire the whole edifice would sink into the eternal ice."

"I can't believe the Baron is more than a century old."

"Come on, Warren! Is that any stranger than what has happened to us?"

I began to lose my temper. I didn't want superstition to endanger our hopes of survival more than necessary. "It doesn't matter. The devil didn't come."

"Are you sure about that?"

"The house was still on the surface of the lake when we found it."

Curtis cried in perverse triumph, "Precisely! We entered and sprung the trap. And now we are entombed. What does this mean?"

"That one of us is the devil?" I whispered.

He jumped up. "Not you! Coming here was my idea! It's my fault. I always felt there was something wrong with me, even when I was a child, a discomfort with my own being. I had an urge to be mean to people. I was too shy to do it properly but now I know the reason for the faults in my character. I'm the devil."

I didn't disappoint him by objecting to this.

Instead I stood and strode to the window. It was a way of avoiding further conversation. I expected to see just the tedium and horror of endless ice, but I was confronted with something startling. I made no comment but waited to observe what might happen. I shut my eyes tight and took a dozen deep breaths. Then I opened them again. What I had seen was no illusion. At last I felt ready to share the revelation.

"There's a shape down there. It's getting bigger."

"The bottom?" suggested Curtis.

I shook my head and held tightly to one of the curtains. My shallow breathing was loud in my ears but it didn't mist the glass. By its very nature a bottomless lake was infinitely deep. I wondered if we might be entering a region of opaque ice, impure and toxic. Not that this made much difference to our situation. I watched as the shape slowly filled my field of vision with blackness. I bit my lip.

The collision was milder than I feared. Every ornament on every surface jumped once and then there was silence. Even the logs on the fire seemed to stop crackling. I turned and exchanged a long glance with Curtis. He smiled weakly and I relinquished my hold on the curtain. I began to walk over to him, but before I was halfway to his chair the house gave another lurch. The sound was terrible. I imagined the cellar under our feet had become filled with pigs, but I knew that our stones were sliding over slates.

"What's going on?" whimpered Curtis.

"There's another house below us. We've touched down on its roof. That's the only explanation."

"Be sensible. It would have to be gigantic."

"I'm sure it is. And it has a sloping roof. We're sliding to the edge."

"And after that? Down again!"

I nodded and counted away the minutes. After so much plunging, this lateral movement came as a shock. I think we both felt nauseous. Then the sliding stopped and we resumed our purely vertical motion. But within less than an hour we stopped again. I knew this was the final destination of this particular house. Beneath us now was stone, not ice, and however hot we made the fire our mansion was stuck here. I ran through the room and the hall beyond to a window in the far wall. Curtis protested weakly behind me.

"Let's get some fresh air!" I called back to him.

"What are you doing, Warren?"

I opened our window and reached for the handle of the window beyond. Fortunately both swung inward. I heard the sudden intake of breath of my companion. He had followed me reluctantly and now attempted to restrain me by clutching my arm. I shrugged him off and climbed through the two windows into an enormous room. In design and furnishings it was similar to one of our own bedrooms but it was much bigger. I drank the clean air with delight and howled in celebration.

A VAST PALACE

Our own house had come to rest on one of its upper balconies. The structure was so large it confounded the senses but most of the objects it contained had normal dimensions. They were simply more numerous. A few, such as the candles, were scaled up. We lit a pair as thick as big men that stood in a corner. The light they provided was generous and enabled us to understand we didn't wish to remain here. We wanted to explore. We ventured onto the landing and reached an immense staircase.

We repeated the procedure of lighting candles on the way down. The individual steps were large but not unmanageable. This palace had not been created for giants. It had a more complex layout than the Baron's home and we found ourselves crossing open galleries suspended above the distant ground floor or passing through sequences of unusually shaped cells, some circular or polygonal, a few trapezoid and disturbing. I can't describe the place as deliberately confusing but it possessed some of the playful malevolence of a labyrinth.

It was unbearably cold. We had become used to working near the mouth of a furnace and the frost that coated every surface was like an unwelcome memory. The voyage to the ground floor was heroic or pathetic, I am unsure which, but we eventually reached the base of the staircase. A thought had occurred to us and we searched for the kitchens. Here was the obligatory ham and biscuits, but also cheese and bowls of dried fruit. They were more perfectly preserved than their counterparts in the Baron's mansion had been.

Out of habit we bore as much as we could carry to the chamber that contained the fireplace. We gasped on the threshold of this room. It resembled a gutted cathedral. There were chairs and silent clocks and dozens of cabinets but only one fireplace. It was a monster. A man might erect a tent inside it and set up camp. It was so tall the ornaments on its mantelpiece were beyond my reach, but from previous experience I surmised they were porcelain vases and jade animals and framed photographs blurred by age and chemical decay to sepia blooms of pure abstraction. I sat and waited for our food to thaw, knowing it never would.

"I'm much happier here," I remarked.

"The air is fresh. But it's so cold! This isn't our fate."

"I know what you mean," I conceded.

"Eventually this oxygen will go stale too and the food and drink run out. We've only bought a little time coming in here. A few weeks."

I cast an eye at the anticipated bookcase. Curtis interpreted this gesture as permission to fetch a few volumes and pass them to me. I opened one. It was an encyclopedia but written in a form of English that was almost incomprehensible. I felt too emotional to attempt reading further. With a mixture of resignation and delight I ripped out a handful of pages and ignited them with a match. Then I stood and approached the hearth and cast them in. At this signal, Curtis went to work.

He added the other books and splintered a chair. This was followed by a table and several cabinets. His enthusiasm was contagious and I joined in, but the gurgling above the hearth was slow to begin. A building this size would require a fiercer blaze to heat up sufficiently. We worked harder, hurling in entire pieces without breaking them up. We even added one of the clocks. It burned away to a skeleton of cogs and springs and loomed upright through the flames like a phantom of the lost cycles of day and night, now dead to us. We no longer bothered to search anything for treasure first.

The palace shuddered and we felt it begin to melt the ice that encased it. We continued to pile on the fuel. Then the descent commenced. With an eerie crackling, we accelerated into the frozen abyss. It was peculiar and horrible but also something of a relief. We quickly attained a velocity greater than the maximum of the Baron's mansion. Whether this was connected to our greater mass, the outer shape of the palace or a change in the nature of the ice, I couldn't say. Curtis became cheerful in the presence of the furnace, standing closer to it than I would dare.

"It's my proper environment now."

"It's not yet proven you're the devil," I responded.

He sighed. "How far do you think we'll go? Surely we can't go beyond the centre of the planet? That's the point of greatest gravitational attraction. Whether this lake is bottomless or not, we'll have to come to a stop there. Will it be like hitting an invisible barrier?"

"No. Our momentum will carry us beyond it."

"How far beyond? All the way to the other side? If so, will we be inverted when we come out? How much momentum will we need?"

"There's no other side to infinity," I replied.

This kept him quiet. We returned to work, adding fuel to the inferno. When we were confident we could leave it unattended for a short time, we vacated the room and located the kitchens. We passed through them to the room beyond. We wanted to see if there was a telephone here as well, but the layout was different. It wasn't a study but a storeroom. No telephone but a large selection of tools. Some of these were a great help in breaking up the furniture. We helped ourselves to a pair of axes, a big hammer and a wheelbarrow. Now we were equipped to rip up floorboards and demolish bannisters if necessary.

Our habit so far had been to stay close together, even sleeping in the same room. But with a larger fire to tend it became more convenient to sleep in shifts and more peaceful for one of us to bed down in the hall or a side room while the other worked. Slowly we grew more independent of each other but without any resentment or bad feelings. What he did when I wasn't around, apart from work and sleep and eat, was unknown to me. I never asked. Nor did he show much curiosity about my own methods of passing time. I began a systematic exploration of the lower levels of the palace. I planned to make a map.

I was reluctant to stray too far from the furnace room for obvious reasons. The fire required a lot of physical toil to keep the building at a sufficient temperature to melt the ice. In the end my project proved impossible. There was simply too much space to chart. But I did make a complete circuit of the cellars. Flinging back a trapdoor I climbed down into a network of stone cells. I took my flashlight with me, for there were no candles here. Hundreds of bottles of wine in racks mocked our previous lengthy searches in corners of ordinary rooms. Beneath the floor I heard the grinding and hissing of the ice.

It was in this honeycomb of untrodden dust and unlabelled vintages that I first thought I heard a voice ahead of me. I passed into the next cell, expecting to discover that Curtis had preceded me, but it was empty. Now the voice was still ahead, one cell further on. It was faint and unintelligible. I stepped forward again and once more found only emptiness. I decided it was an echo, an acoustical trick which meant its source might be miles distant. I also concluded it was not a human voice but a wall flexing under the enormous outside pressure and acting like a membrane, pumping weird but random sounds into the basement hive.

I returned from this minor exploit with as many bottles as I could carry, one slipping from under my armpit and smashing on the flagstones. I delivered them to Curtis. He had gone back to the storeroom for a pitchfork and was standing next to a mound of chairs, pieces of tables and all manner of flammable objects. With a fluid motion he forked them into the blaze, pausing only occasionally to wipe the sweat from his brow with a grimy hand. I didn't mention the illusory voice. It was my turn to take over but he insisted on working a double shift. My protests were ineffectual.

I wandered off again. It occurred to me that if I could find a laboratory among the innumerable rooms I might be able to make air from ice. I knew there were methods of releasing oxygen from water. The possibility of suffocation was still one of my major concerns despite the vastness of the palace. I entered at least fifty new rooms. My energies were wasted, for suddenly a powerful jolt hurled me to the floor. Then the building started sliding sideways. I knew what was coming. I rose and seated myself in a chair to await the second vertical drop to the next balcony. This amplification of my previous experience was both satisfying and grotesque.

A LOST CITY

This is how it seemed to us as we passed through the windows into the distorted bedroom and from here down the stairway to the ground floor. A metropolis under the ice, enclosed by walls and covered with a roof. The building was so large it couldn't be described as a palace. At the very least it was a collection of palaces fused together, but in truth a capital city was a closer analogy. Enough rooms to house several million people.

The eccentricities in the design were more pronounced than in the edifice we had just left. The angles and the layout were utterly strange. A multitude of lesser staircases intersected with the main one, curving away like spare horizons, and the candles resembled pillars, the columns of an ancient temple. More agile than me, Curtis swarmed up them to light the wicks.

I remember reading a story about a man trapped in a deserted city. He also felt horror at its design, the product of whim rather than function. He described the routes between its cupolas as the paths of an "exiguous and nitid" labyrinth. At the time I imagined a garden maze with woollen hedges. I had taken the book that contained this story on a hiking trip and had no dictionary to reveal the meanings of unknown words, but now I was in a similar situation for real and although this new sequence of rooms and corridors could never be defined as exiguous it certainly became nitid, for the wicks in the candles were as thick as ropes and flared brightly.

Tiring of the descent, Curtis grasped the bannister and swung one leg over. He whooped as he let himself go and slid out of sight. For some reason this action unnerved me. I toppled a giant candle and soaked one of my handkerchiefs in the pool of wax under the wick. Then I squeezed the cloth into a ball, ignited it and dropped it over the side of the stairwell. It hissed as it streaked down into the pit like an economy comet. I watched as it briefly illuminated each level it passed. Finally I glimpsed the form of Curtis far below. The flames bathed his laughing cheeks a sooty orange. He was travelling at a perilous velocity.

I heard his shrieks as he thundered around each corner, unable to brake. If he wasn't killed by this foolish impulse he would reach the bottom long before me. I debated whether to follow his example. In truth I was scared. I continued to walk down as normal, but I was less proficient at climbing the candle-pillars than Curtis and soon I was groping in thick dusk, the light of the higher levels fading more slowly than the shrieks below but with graver consequences for my progress. At last it was a choice between tripping or sliding. I gripped the bannister between my thighs and attempted to control my speed by tensing my muscles, but I was too tired and abandoned the struggle.

I rushed into the cold depths. The friction was welcome, warming me to a comfortable temperature. Curtis had already melted much of the frost from the bannister with his own descent but the polished wood beneath was almost as slippery. After a long while I saw twinkling stars below.

He had reached the bottom and ignited dozens of candles. But I felt no blast of heat. He had not yet started the fire in the grate. For a moment I feared that perhaps this house was different from the others and lacked a fireplace. We were taking the similarities between the buildings for granted. But in fact the hearth was there. Curtis had found another reason for not creating an immediate blaze.

He was engaged in constructing a ramp from tables and cabinets. With the tools he had carried with him he was nailing lengths of wood together. Part of this ramp consisted of rollers made from the circular legs of certain chairs. The ramp led from the base of the gargantuan hearth and out of what we now always called the furnace room. He worked like a demon, cutting and hammering. I helped him and eventually the end of the ramp terminated some ten feet above the ground, directly under the stairwell. Then we returned to the furnace room and I selected a shelf of books. I examined a few. They were written in a very peculiar English which included a handful of extra letters. We ignited them in the hearth and hastened back to the other end of the ramp.

"This building is so immense I don't think we can warm it up the usual way. We simply can't work that hard."

I nodded. "So the ramp will help us?"

Curtis looked down. He had trodden in the ash of my extinguished handkerchief. "Absolutely. We can climb to higher levels and push items of furniture over the edge. They will land on the ramp and slide into the fire. Whether they smash or not with the impact doesn't matter. This fire will be very hungry."

We set to work and his system proved remarkably effective. First we knocked out the struts of the bannister and cast them on, then we roamed the rooms of the floor one level above the ground. It was no longer necessary to break up wardrobes and beds and carry the pieces back. We simply shoved them out of their corners onto the landing and over the side. Finally the familiar lurching motion came again and we knew we had done enough to earn ourselves a rest. The continuous impacts had damaged the ramp and Curtis decided to repair it. I took this chance to wander off alone.

I was troubled by voices again. Louder than they had been in the cellars of the previous house, they seemed both mocking and profound. I almost caught the meanings of some of the words. Then I realised they were talking in the language of the books, an evolved or decayed version of my own natural tongue.

I called after them, "Anyone at home?"

But they remained always ahead, out of reach. I felt increasingly reluctant to rejoin Curtis. I preferred the companionship of the voices, malicious as they sometimes seemed. I stopped by one window and watched the ice sliding past. The inertia of such an enormous building was incalculable to one so little schooled in physics as myself but I guessed it would be more than sufficient to carry us beyond the centre of the planet. I fell into a reverie. I wondered if I had caught a fever. I decided to return to the ramp and enter the furnace room. If I was ill I would welcome the attentions of Curtis despite my growing distaste for his presence. It was a question of priorities.

I was nearly there when the collision happened. I had been wandering in a delirium for a week. I called out to Curtis and he answered from afar. We were sliding sideways across an unseen roof. Hours later we began the shorter drop to the next balcony. I felt my companion lift me under the arms. I shouted that I didn't want to be hurled onto the ramp. He laughed and I saw he had removed all his clothes. He was dressed only in oily sweat and grime. A mad stoker.

"Fresh air is what you need. Lean on me and I'll take you across to the next house."

A SUNKEN NATION

I recovered quickly. Curtis had made elaborate preparations for entering a building as large as a small country. Once through the windows he lit the candles in the bedroom with a device he had constructed himself, a taper fixed to the end of a telescopic pole. Out on the plaza of the landing we didn't bother starting down the steps. Curtis attached ropes to the bannister and dropped them into the stairwell.

During my fevered absence chasing voices he had discovered

storerooms containing not only climbing and mining equipment but explosives and inflammable liquids. We lowered a selection of choice items into the darkness. We followed like spiders on threads. This house was so vast and the stairwell so deep there was a substantial difference in air pressure between the level of the balcony and the ground.

Despite the frost Curtis still refused to wear clothes. He was playing his new role properly. When we reached the bottom he scurried and leapt like a wild goat. I wondered how long it would be before he trimmed his beard into a point or fork. With his previous experience he constructed a new ramp in astonishingly fast time. The fireplace we had to tend was a cavern as wide and high as the crater we had originally entered that fateful night. The amount of fuel needed to warm this house was staggering.

I flicked through some of the books on the multitude of shelves that stretched for miles to the end of the furnace room. They were written in an alphabet which contained at least sixty letters. Very few words were pronounceable, let alone meaningful. I was called away by Curtis.

He had already started a fire in the hearth. He had plans to dynamite part of the stairs and next highest floor, bringing tons of wood down on the rollers of the ramp. I took cover in the kitchens, searching for food and voices.

I consumed most of a bottle of brandy, calling for the unseen people to stop hiding. But they always eluded me. Far away, like a storm in an adjacent valley, the rumble of an explosion vibrated the floorboards. In a series of trapezoid studies I discovered collections of musical instruments. There were no telephones here but I found the inlets and outlets of speaking tubes. They connected different sections of the intolerably large house. From one I heard Curtis singing as he worked. I kept silent and didn't reply to him. I tried to estimate the dimensions of the house but the answers were always ridiculous.

I knew I had to find Curtis before we reached the next balcony. I was lost in a tangle of corridors and galleries. The laughter of my companion was no clue as to which direction to choose, for frequently it emerged from the trumpet of a speaking tube. I took long detours for little or no profit. I came across rooms decorated with wallpaper so freakish it infected my dreams. The yellow of stained cups and mummified eyes, the orange of dying suns and the blushes of executioners. I strummed a lute as I went, attempting to teach myself tunes at the back of my memory.

There were too many unanswerable questions. If the frozen lake was bottomless how could it be contained within the sphere of our world? How many houses existed in the lake? Who had built them and would they continue to get bigger indefinitely? I wondered if I would ever lose count of them, forgetting the exact number of balconies, bedrooms, stairs and hearths. Already there were more clocks in the furnace room than rooms in the original mansion. Such pointless repetition deeply oppressed my sanity.

At last the anticipated lurch came and the house began to slip into the ice. I sat on the floor as it accelerated to a horrible speed. It had taken Curtis a long time to make a hot enough blaze to set this building on its way. Even with my assistance I thought it unlikely we could get the next house moving. This possibility had evidently occurred to him. I finally found him squatting on the apex of a pyramid of broken furniture. His lips were curved in a smile but his eyes were humourless.

"I used too much dynamite. Brought down more than I expected."

"We're dropping at a fearsome rate."

He maintained his false smile. "There's an inferno in the hearth."

"Do you believe that explosives and accelerants will be enough for the fifth house? It might be the size of a continent!"

"Fifth did you say? Don't you mean the thirteenth?"

"I don't follow you," I replied.

He peered at me more closely and rubbed his eyes with blistered knuckles. "You've lost count somewhere. This is the twelfth mansion.

We're heading towards number thirteen now. If you weren't so young I'd say you had gone a little senile! Maybe it was that fever you caught a while back? I don't get things like that anymore. I'm the devil. My immune system is too strong."

I shrugged. I was convinced the error was his but I didn't care to argue with a madman. I was mildly amused to note he had trimmed his beard. Curtis always did the most with what he had, but nothing would ever cause him to grow horns and a tail. His face was less round now. He was learning real hardness, the bake of the furnace and constant physical exertion. He fell silent and probed a tooth with his tongue. I saw that two or three of his incisors were chipped. Then I noticed the gash on his neck, probably an effect of the blast. Even the devil should be careful with explosives.

"It doesn't really matter," I said.

He leaned his head to one side. "What doesn't?"

I frowned. I had forgotten the subject of our conversation. Flinching from his earlier remark about senility I countered, "Don't you remember?"

He sighed. "Listen Warren, I'm really looking forward to reaching the next house, whatever its number. I want to keep going for as long as we can. Do you know why? Because one day we'll reach a mansion so vast it will be as big as the world! If we can't get back to the surface, that will be the next best thing, a perfect substitute. A house with as much surface area as the world but more compact because all that space will be arranged on many levels. Like tectonic plates stacked above each other."

"But we'll never be able to make fires big enough to reach it."

"Not on our own, true."

I answered slowly, "I don't think we are alone here. I believe there are other beings, possibly people, in some of the rooms. There may even be a great many of them. A tribe. A civilisation, hiding or waiting. I don't know if we could enlist their help but it might be worth a try. We don't have a choice really. If we don't find them our next stop will be our last. Our final destination."

"I don't want that. I want to keep going until we reach a house as big as an entire world. It will be my equivalent of going home."

I nodded but I suspected his real motives were different from his stated ones. I imagined he wanted to rule a private empire, a personal pandemonium, a replica of hell in the ice. In our position our ambitions were understandably warped. But at least Curtis had a definite wish. My own desires were vague, as if they sought without success to crystallize in a brain of sluggish lava. I turned away but I didn't embark on another minor expedition yet. I went down into the nearest cellar and crouched with my fingertips on the flagstones, foolishly hoping to feel the presence of the next house as we hurtled towards it.

A BRAND NEW WORLD

And Curtis led the way again through the windows into the bedroom. We despaired of reaching the ground floor even by ropes and distracted ourselves from thinking about starting the voyage by searching the wardrobes arranged along the wall. They stood like hollow megaliths in the shadows all the way to the remote door which led to the landing, each sixty foot tall and yet only a fraction as high as the ceiling. As we walked past, the vibrations of our feet set the wire coathangers inside tinkling, a soft sound like the stilts of insane acrobats wading through lagoons of mercury.

We opened doors indiscriminately. Most were empty or contained a few jackets and trousers, undecayed but useless, for they all had at least three arms and legs. But in the interior of one I discovered another wardrobe and inside this another. We passed through a nest of concealed boxes.

Inside the final one I noticed a lever and a key set into the floor. I remarked that this wardrobe resembled a primitive elevator and Curtis nodded thoughtfully. Then he stooped next to me, grasped the key and twisted it.

"A clockwork device," he grunted.

"Wind it tight and then I'll pull the lever. Maybe this is what all those clocks are kept for? Spare cogs and springs."

When he had finished I released the brake. We dropped down a hidden shaft, the wardrobe rattling and screeching. I wanted to clasp Curtis for reassurance but his nudity repulsed me. After a long time we began to slow and finally came to a halt. We stumbled out into the murk at the base of the stairwell, our ears ringing. The portal to the furnace room was less than one hour's walk from here. I don't know which of us was most confused. I had started to believe this was the thirteenth house but Curtis now insisted it was only the fifth. We had swapped delusions.

"You have a reasonable excuse for your forgetfulness," I said. "Memory is something that evolved for its survival value. Learning from experience is a useful tool. But the devil didn't evolve from anything. He was always the way he is now. I can't defend my own senility in the same way. I'm just a weak mortal."

We entered the furnace room and gasped. At the very limit of the beams of our flashlights the immense cliff of the hearth reared up. The frost on the mantelpiece glittered like perpetual snows on the peaks of a high mountain range. In vain I looked for tigers and smugglers loaded with chests of tea. I mopped my face with my sleeve. I was perspiring despite the low temperature. My fever had not entirely dissipated. Curtis took a few steps forward, paused and looked back over his shoulder.

"This fireplace will defeat us. However hard we work we'll never fill it. There's no point even trying on our own. I'm not a giant."

"Nor I. There's only one thing we can do."

There was an uneasy silence, then we clasped hands.

"We'll split up. We must promise not to return here until we find some other beings to help us. It might take weeks, months, years."

"Goodbye Curtis. Best of luck."

"Thanks Warren. Take care of yourself. Sorry for getting you into this fix in the first place. I took your world away from you. I'll do my best to replace it. You'll be my deputy in pandemonium. I'll make you my successor."

I released his hand. Before I left the furnace room I decided to satisfy my curiosity in one other regard. I set off on the trek towards the region of bookcases. When I reached it my suspicions were confirmed. Every letter in each word in the volumes I inspected was completely different from all the others. They had descended into pure gibberish. I couldn't imagine what creatures might speak such a language, but I didn't need to, for neither Curtis nor myself stood a chance of actually encountering them. Until that moment I would do my best not to speculate. There was no point wasting thoughts.

I passed out of the furnace room through an obscure side door. I found myself in a corridor that constantly altered its width from very narrow to very wide and which ran straight for no more than fifty paces at a time before sloping or veering off at an acute angle. My flashlight died. I ran in darkness, bruising my knees and elbows against the walls. There must have been speaking tubes here also or else the passage itself possessed its own weird acoustical properties, for as the days passed I infrequently heard the voice of Curtis as if the man or devil himself stood behind one of my shoulders.

He was calling out, "Anyone at home?"

At last the corridor spluttered me out into light. I stood on the landing of an upper level. Candles as high as power pylons blazed far above me, the wicks hissing like coal suns. Curtis must have already passed this way. I ascended a short staircase and roamed through a warren of ovoid rooms.

The final one contained an observatory. A powerful reflecting telescope rested on a tripod with legs as thick as girders. I climbed a ladder to the eyepiece and adjusted the focus. The chamber was studded with windows but none faced out onto the endless ice. The observatory was located near the centre of the building. I studied burning candelabra in unimaginably remote rooms with the interest an astronomer might reserve for nebulae. I swung the telescope and explored other vistas, the distant reaches of carpeted corridors and spiral stairways.

Once I thought I detected a cluster of moving shapes. They vanished before I could be sure of their nature. Equally hopelessly I looked for Curtis.

Abandoning the telescope I vacated the room and continued my journey. Within a week I heard the voices again. It was still impossible to catch up with them.

On a whim I decided to violate the pact I had made with Curtis and return to the furnace room alone. The passages blended into one and all I could rely on to estimate the distance I walked was the complex unearthly melody I created from the squeaky floorboards I occasionally trod upon, each one a slightly different note, sometimes less than one thousandth of a tone apart. Or so I guessed. And then I discovered a bicycle leaning against a hatstand. My average speed increased dramatically.

The unseen voices returned and grew louder. This time they didn't seem to be hiding from me. I rang my bell but they were still a journey of several days ahead. I was pedalling a course I had already examined with the telescope, a channel of inner space. The air slowly became warmer around me. I felt sick. My smugness melted with the ice that pressed upon the house. Curtis had done something truly diabolical. I forced myself to dismount and rest, sheltering under a table in a recess of the panelled wall. Beneath the hissing pylons I slept fitfully.

I woke and resumed my race into the cacophony and heat. The sounds of industry were ferocious, an unbearable clatter of hammering and sawing. I bounced down a staircase and crossed an immense carpeted plain. Shadows danced across the threshold of a portal. I braked and came to a halt on the edge of this room. It pulsed with fire. It was the furnace room and it was full. Nightmare figures capered everywhere, cutting up furniture and casting it into the fire. Sometimes they threw in one of their own kind by mistake. And the house was sliding down, building up speed. I knew for sure our inertia was sufficient to carry us beyond the gravitational centre of the planet. And I suddenly understood something Curtis hadn't even suspected.

I felt an arm on my shoulder.

"Speak of the devil," I joked feebly.

"I was wondering when you'd come back. Look at what I've created, Warren! Just like hell now, isn't it? We're on our way to the next house. I've discussed it with my demons and they all disagree on which number this one is. I've decided to take the average of five and thirteen and call it the ninth."

"You've become a wise ruler," I said.

"Why not? There's no reason for the devil to be obtuse. Come in and I'll introduce you. The next house down will be as big as our world."

"I'll pass on that offer. It's too crowded in here for comfort."

He made no effort to detain me. "Very well. Tell you what, I'll appoint you my envoy to the farthest reaches of my realm. That way you can go off exploring without feeling you have let me down. What do you say?"

I turned and wheeled my bicycle away. As I mounted it the barely concealed rage in my former companion's voice seemed to push me along. I accelerated from the mouth of a domestic tartarus.

Still he boomed after me, "You are a useful servant of the crown of hell. I salute you, my trusted envoy. Who knows what regions and tribes you might come across? May your mission succeed!"

I laughed to myself as I escaped him forever.

I had plans of my own, less grandiose than his but no less surprising. The development of a puncture halfway across a room so large it contained clouds and entire weather patterns did nothing to deter me. I continued on foot. I sheltered from the rain under a glass coffee table as wide as a lake. One by one the candles were extinguished. Lightning relit them and moved behind a range of sofas. My beard grew ragged as I pressed on. I was looking good for my age, but my skin felt thirsty for the sun. The simple pleasures of life on the surface haunted me. Autumn leaves, the moon.

There were no more houses below us. I was confident of this fact. This was the last one. I had worked it out carefully.

Each time we touched down on the roof of a building we slid sideways. Part of our motion had been horizontal as well as vertical. This horizontal displacement had added up to many miles. It was something we had mostly overlooked. And yet the consequences were remarkable and exciting.

If a man moves horizontally across the face of the globe he will eventually find himself at the antipodes, on the far side of the world, but he won't fall off because the direction called "down" is determined by the centre of the planet, the point of greatest gravitational attraction. The deeper into the earth he goes the less horizontal movement he will need to circle this point. This also holds true for houses.

We were falling back up.

We had reached a position opposite the crater in which had stood the Baron's mansion. We had reached a point directly below the far side of the world. The antipodes were above us. Now our inertia would carry us beyond the centre of the earth and back through the ice the way we had come. But we wouldn't collide with any houses as we went because this house had already collected them. The way was clear. We would break through into the crater and the real world. Upside down.

At any rate this was my theory.

There were problems with it but I chose not to dwell on those. For instance Curtis had seriously underestimated the dimensions of this building. From my experience in the observatory I calculated it as already several sizes larger than the planet that contained it. One of life's awkward paradoxes, I guess. Thus it was impossible to imagine what might happen when the house surfaced.

But whatever the result I felt deep pity for the owner of the antique store who had sold Curtis his cabinet. The devil was bound to want revenge on the man who tricked him. The fool would be completely defenceless. And yet if the Baron was really still alive he surely would have employed his magical or scientific powers to disguise himself with the appearance of youth. There was no better way to divert suspicion, even if his desiccated brain did make the occasional mistake.

I had always been very clever and senility would take some getting used to. Fortunately I had been clever enough to foresee my own senility and take it into account. I had forgotten my own identity and abode, even my original language and desires, but I was still being controlled by a plan I had invented in my youth. I was my own puppet. At least this was the best option remaining to me. I might as well embrace it. The role of devil had already been taken.

I chuckled to myself. Everything had come together very well. I would resolve the inconsistencies at my leisure. Only one difficult task remained to make my satisfaction complete. I would return to the original mansion. Stored at the end of a sequence of diminishing balconies, forgotten by the devil and unsuspected by his minions, beyond innumerable stairways and corridors and rooms, it waited modestly for me to take up my rightful residence at last.

I was going home.

BANQUET OF THE
LORDS OF NIGHT
Liz Williams

Liz Williams delights in proclaiming that her father was a stage magician and her mother a gothic novelist. Inevitably the result was a mistress of dark fantasy. She has been producing short fiction since 1997, several of which have been nominated for awards. Her books include The Ghost Sister *(2001) and* The Poison Master *(2003), the last of which is related to the following story. It takes us to a world of perpetual night and how one individual seeks to restore light despite the cost. Liz's other books include a wonderful series about Inspector Chen, a detective whose cases take him between this world and the next, and whose adventures are chronicled in* Snake Agent *(2005),* The Demon and the City *(2006) and others. Liz Williams's website is at* www.arkady.btinternet.co.uk

Severin de Rais hurries through thistledown light, with the dangerous parcel clutched close to his heart, hoping that he won't turn a corner and come face to face with an Unpriest. He's already late, and the Isle de Saint Luce is forbidden territory. Yet even in the midst of his terror, de Rais still thinks it's a pity that he can't pause and marvel, for the Isle is, by old decree of the Lords of Night, the only place in all Paris where light is permitted at this hour. But de Rais cannot stop to admire the lamps; he's running out of time, and if an Unpriest should find what he is carrying…de Rais does not even dare think about it. A death sentence, surely. He glances with swift unease up at the shattered stump of Notre Dame, imagining it as it might have looked five hundred years before, filled with candles and prayers and light, before the Lords came and brought the darkness with them, conjuring the great shell which covers the world. The shell lies above the churning stormclouds, too high even to be seen, and de Rais drags his quivering attention back to the present. The metal cover of the precious, precarious parcel is sharp against his chest; the unspells which protect it burn his skin. He wonders in a delirious moment if it will rust if the rain touches it; rust and crumble into nothing more than red ash, like old blood.

The growing rain blurs the lamps of the Isle de Saint Luce so that they look like dandelion clocks, their down blown away on the wind. The light makes de Rais squint and peer, but the parcel warms his breast, in spite of the rain. Heat seeps through him like the taste of honey. The world spins briefly to summer, leaving raindrops scattered in the void. De Rais blinks at this first taste of a season he has never seen, and clasps the parcel even more tightly to his chest. Crossing the bridge which bisects the Seine and leads into the Rue Moins Pitie, de Rais pauses reeling for a moment to catch his unsteady breath. The Seine runs fast with rainswell: a mass of branches tumbles in the current, turning the water to bramble and briar. The risk that he is about to take makes de Rais wonder for a moment if it would be wiser simply to drop the parcel in the river and let the torrent carry it back to the sea, but then he turns away. Above de Rais' head, the curfew bell begins to chime out through the darkness, telling seven o'clock through the gloom. De Rais hurries on towards the Palais.

Behind him, the lights of the Isle are soon lost as he crosses onto the familiar territory of the right bank. De Rais makes his way through dark streets, following his path with meticulously counted steps: along the Quai, down the Tuileries, into the heart of the Lords' Quarter. Should he deviate from that path, he runs the risk of becoming lost in the maze of the city. Occasionally, he detects the faintest gleam of light upon the wet surface of a wall; neon in a blacked-out basement, a candle flickering in a secret room. And then his fears come true. Hastening around the corner into the Rue de Louvre, de Rais runs right into a group of Unpriests. Their long leather coats rustle against the pavement; their heads swivel from side to side. They are clicking like insects in a termite mound, and de Rais shrinks back against the wall, his heart hammering. But their gaze, concealed behind their black lenses, does not turn his way and in a moment they are gone. Why should they challenge him, after all? He's only a lowly pastry chef, and he's not on forbidden ground any more. He's entitled to be in this quarter, the honour signified by the ribbons on his coat. Breathing a long and tremulous sigh, de Rais continues on his way.

He reaches the kitchens of the Palais shortly afterwards, and his lateness is rewarded by a bellow of rage from the head chef. Mumbling insults and excuses beneath his breath, de Rais sidles through the outskirts of the kitchens to collect his work clothes from the store. He fastens the midnight jacket around himself and adjusts the tall smoke-coloured hat in the dim reflection of the mirror. His pinched, pale face seems a picture of guilt, but the parcel remains for now in the pocket of his overcoat. De Rais plans to remove it surreptitiously when things quieten down, and hide it at the bottom of the little bread oven in his own small domain. Stepping around the corner of the table, he picks up the chopping board and begins work.

De Rais is a methodical pastry chef, who believes in preparation and planning. The ingredients for today's desserts and pastries have been assembled the night before; the last chores performed by de Rais before he made his weary way homewards. On an ordinary day, tonight and tomorrow would follow the same pattern: home to the attic room in the old Latin Quarter; a few hours snatched sleep, broken by the sounds from the dingy cafe downstairs, then back to the Palais early in the morning, with perhaps a stolen hour towards twilight when de Rais can go to the library or snatch a pastis in one of the dreary licensed cafes. But today, things changed. Today, de Rais went to meet the girl: the terrorist, the rebel, the one who gave him the parcel, and perhaps because of that tomorrow will be different too, de Rais thinks with a sudden uplift of his spirits that must surely be noticeable clear across the kitchen. He starts guiltily, and thinks careful, neutral thoughts, but it's not easy to see the expressions on the faces of those who inhabit the kitchens. The head chef jealously guards the ration of candles; everyone else must work in the cold glow of the ovens or simply by touch. It isn't as though they haven't had practice, after all.

Opening the refrigerator, de Rais takes out a container and places it on the table. He opens it carefully, not wanting the essence to escape. The container is full of ice: glassy dark ice from the seas near the southern pole, a place that de Rais knows only from legend. It seems to hold its own glow: it's almost green, like the stories the old folk tell about dawn. With a sharp scalpel, de Rais touches the edge of the sheet of ice, so that it splits and cracks into a nest of slivers. De Rais arranges the shards of ice in the centre of each of the twenty seven sorbet dishes, then reaches back inside the refrigerator for the ingredients of the sauce. He plans a complex, subtle accompaniment to the simple ice: a touch of fragrant Indonesian darkness, gathered close to midnight, redolent of cinnamon and incense and spiced smoke. Placing the darkness in a bowl, he adds a pinch of flavours: twilight from Japan, warm and clouded, with a hint of star anise. Then a touch of evening from the Sinang Delta, water-clear and cool. De Rais stirs all of these elements nine times with an ebony spoon, then pours the swirl of darkness into a silver pan and lights the chilly flame beneath it. He waits, frowning, as a drift of smoke begins to rise from the sauce and then he casts it in a spiral around the little columns of ice and claps his hands imperiously for the serving staff to take it into the dining hall, where the Lords of Night are waiting. The head chef looks up, once, as the procession passes by, and gives a single grudging nod of approval.

Having dispensed with the appetisers, the responsibility for the meal passes on to the head chef for a time, while de Rais busies himself with the desserts. He hopes to get the chance to take the parcel from his overcoat pocket and slip it into the oven, but the head chef has got the apprentices out of his fevered way by sending them over to work in de Rais' corner, a not-uncommon occurrence. Frustrated, de Rais gets on with his own tasks.

He prepares fondants of gloom, sorbets of shadows, and sherbets of dusk; each one gathered from the far and unseen corners of the Earth. Then de Rais wipes his weary hands on his apron and steps back to admire his handiwork. Behind him, the booming voice of the head chef says, "Not bad. Perhaps there's some promise in you after all."

De Rais jumps like a tortured hare. Turning, he snaps, "Don't do that! You startled me."

"Why?" The head chef thrusts his cadaverous face close to that of de Rais. "Nervous? Been doing something you shouldn't? Been gobbing in the fondants again?"

De Rais bridles; he'd never dream of doing such a thing and the head chef knows it.

"Get over there, boy, when you've finished. I want some help to scrub the floors."

The head chef's head jerks in the direction of the apprentices and they scramble after him as he ambles back towards the cold crimson glow of his own territory. Heart pounding, de Rais sidles into the store, retrieves the parcel at last and slides it underneath the iron floor of the little oven. The package is still warm. It seems to radiate its own heat, and de Rais is relieved when at last it's safely out of sight. Then, he goes to where the head chef is waiting and begins to rinse the stone floor clean of blood. He keeps thinking about the package lying in the oven. Once more he rehearses the plan that has been steeping in his mind ever since the girl gave him the parcel.

Once the kitchens are quiet, and everyone has left for the night, de Rais will take the package out of the oven. And then, he will begin to cook. He'll prepare a special dish for the next banquet of the Lords of Night, which will take place tomorrow, on a day that was once called Midsummer. De Rais thinks of the eternal, plunging rain, which he fancies he can hear beating on the pavements above the dungeons of the kitchen, and he shivers as he swabs the bloodstained floor. Mechanically, he goes over the plan once more in his mind, but in the next few minutes, he realizes it might be too late to even think about executing it. The Unpriests have arrived.

They slither down the kitchen stairs, boot-heels clicking on the expensive tiles. De Rais risks a glance, and the nape of his neck grows cold. The people in this group are no ordinary Unpriests. Their long coats bear the Lords' own insignia, and there is a woman with them, dressed in black velvet riding breeches and a leather cuirass. A single dark pearl dangles from one ear, like a bead of jet. Her eyes are hidden behind thick dark lenses. Her head swivels from side to side.

This is the closest that de Rais has ever been to one of the creatures of the Lords of Night, and she makes him feel hollow and numb. He stares grimly down at the high, polished heels of her boots. The language that she speaks is archaic, formal, and barely intelligible; she enunciates slowly, evidently for the benefit of the head chef who, as a mere servant, might not be expected to understand her.

"The Unchurch has had word that an attempt is to be made on the lives of the Lords of Night, by non-persons, by dream-sellers, by ghosts. The servants must submit to be searched."

"An attempt on – ?" The head chef's thin face quivers in shock. "By whom?"

"I told you. Non-persons. Those who deny darkness, who seek That which is Not."

"By what means?"

"Unknown," the Unpriest says, stiffly, then concedes "By myself, at least. The Lords, of course, know all, but in their black wisdom they have not divulged the answer to one as lowly as myself and were I to know that answer, I would be no more likely to divulge it to you. Now. Prepare to be searched."

From beneath the folds of her coat, she takes a device that de Rais has never seen before. It consists of an extending tube, at the end of which is a round, glistening lens. The woman raises it to the level of the head chef's face, and passes it down his body, from the crown of his head to his toes. Fascinated, de Rais nonetheless stares straight ahead, afraid of attracting undue attention, but he glimpses from the corner of his eye the chef's cadaverous form, surrounded for a moment by black energy; an aura of unlight. One by one, the woman passes the device along the rows of apprentices: darkness crackles and snaps. At last she reaches de Rais. She stares at him for a moment, and, swallowing, he raises his gaze to hers but sees nothing. Her eyes are entirely concealed behind the thick obsidian lenses.

She says, caressingly, "You look alarmed, boy. Are you afraid?"

De Rais says what is no more than the truth. "Yes. I am afraid. I have been afraid ever since I can remember."

A thin charcoal brow arches above the lenses. The woman says, "Indeed? Of what?"

Boldly, de Rais answers, "Of not matching the expectations of the Lords of Night. Of not meeting the standards that I myself set to serve them."

"You talk like an artist," the woman says, brows still raised.

"I am an artist, madam," de Rais says, with the bravery of absolute fear. "I am an artist of culinary colour and its absence, a master of texture and shade, of monochrome uniformity. I drain the delicacies that I prepare of the touch of light and fire and brightness that is bestowed upon them by the flames on which they are conjured into being, so that the palates of the Lords of Night may not be seared for one moment by the tiniest spark of light."

To de Rais' infinite surprise, the head chef turns his head and says, "It's true, my lady. The food that this man prepares is a paradigm of unlight. His concoctions are as dark and smooth and rich as the galaxy's core itself." His glance catches that of de Rais: *I don't like you. But you're still one of us.*

The woman bows her head in mocking acknowledgement. "Well, then, I am honoured. But you must still be scrutinised."

She raises the device once more and the lens rotates along its appointed track. The woman puts her head on one side, studies him.

"You absorb light, you say? You purify the foods of darkness?"

"I do."

Something long and thin whips from the tube which holds the lens and lashes de Rais across the face. The impact spins him around and he sprawls backwards, stunned. The Unpriest says, "It shows. There are cracks and flickers along the edges of your soul. It is dangerous work that you do, M'sieu…?"

"My name is de Rais," he says, through bleeding teeth.

"M'sieu de Rais. I had not thought that the life of a pastry chef would be so fraught with hazard. Take care that you visit the Unpriests more regularly, to purge your soul of traces of light as effectively as you purify the foods that you prepare." She turns away.

The rest of the kitchen is searched methodically, and de Rais' heart skips and hops as an investigation is made of his work area, including the little stove. The Unpriest lingers as she examines the pastries and sorbets, and de Rais hides a bruised smile as he sees her stealthy fingers creep out and flick a piece of brittle icing to her mouth. But the metal binding of the package remains secure, hidden beneath the iron floor of the little oven and guarded with unspells. The woman heads for the stairs with an angry flounce and de Rais inclines his head until the beetle-click of her boot-heels betrays her absence. No-one says a word after that, except the head chef, who turns to de Rais and says brusquely, "You. Have you finished?"

"The floor is clean. I have my preparations to complete for tomorrow."

"Go and do It, then."

One by one, the apprentices leave the kitchen. De Rais hovers over his tasks, lingering on slicing and moulding and freezing, until the head chef snaps a curt goodnight, along with instructions to lock up. De Rais listens as the chef's heavy footsteps pound up the stairs and the door slams behind him, then he runs to the stove and takes out the package. It's so hot that it burns even de Rais' callused hands. Cursing beneath his breath, he drops the package on the table and flicks open the complex locks until the inside of the package is revealed. He stares for a moment. The girl who gave the package to de Rais has told him: you will see nothing. Do not expect to be witness to a miracle. It is latent, nothing more. But you will be able to touch it. Cautiously, de Rais reaches inside the hot metal binding and feels something smooth and soft and warm. He lifts it from the binding, and to his surprise it comes away easily. He feels it glide across the table and has to put out a hand to stop it from falling onto the floor.

Then, working quickly in case it dissipates, de Rais takes his sharp knife and begins to chop, his hand moving faster and faster with a chef's practised speed until the contents of the package are in tiny pieces. And then de Rais begins his final great work; the last work that, if all goes well, he will ever perform in the palace of the Lords of Night. He begins to sculpt the substance into sugars and candies, into creams and shadows. At last he passes his hand over the surface of the chopping block and finds only a minute sliver, like a splinter of glass. De Rais is sorely tempted to pop it in his mouth, but he resists the temptation and drifts it onto the curling pinnacle of a sugar tower instead. And then he slips everything into the darkest, coldest recesses of the refrigerator, to wait there till morning. As he turns to leave, he fancies that when he next opens the door of the refrigerator, it will have begun to glow.

Early next morning, before the waking bells toll out across the city, de Rais rises from a troubled night, bundles himself into his clothes and hurries back to the Palais. The rain has stopped, but a thin wind rips down the Tuileries, snatching at de Rais' untidy hair. He does not think he slept, and yet his head is filled with dreams that defy the darkening day; dreams of something that flickers golden down the rainy air. When de Rais reaches the Palais, the head chef greets him with a grunt and a tilt of the head; their yesterday truce still fragile as spider silk.

Quietly, unobtrusively, de Rais slides into his chef's jacket. He takes a deep, shaky breath and opens the refrigerator. It is still and dim within, and undisturbed. De Rais relaxes a little, and his breath mists cold metal. He rests his hands on the top of the refrigerator for a moment, to steady them. Then, he goes about the remaining preparations for this evening's banquet; the less critical, less dangerous things, a frenzy of slicing and moulding for the hundred guests of the Lords of Night.

When evening comes, everything is ready. De Rais stands back and exchanges triumphant glances with the head chef, whose face is blue with cold. De Rais dispatches perfumed bowls of dusk to the dining hall, and joins the apprentices for a surreptitious glimpse of the guests as they arrive. His hands are trembling again. He watches as something glides through the great double doors at the end of the vast hall. It stands seven feet high and its armoured head drifts from side to side. Its mandibles exude a faint and musty fragrance. Huge smooth claws rustle beneath its midnight robes. It moves with ponderous, swinging slowness down the hall, and in its wake the air seems suddenly thin and darker, as though it breathes in health and light, and gives out nothing. Another follows through the double doors: female, this time. De Rais catches sight of the long out-thrust jaw and the slotted vertebrae of her throat beneath her hood. She places a delicately jointed foot on the thick carpet and teeters forward. De Rais melts back into the shadows. Three hours to go, before the clock strikes midnight.

Downstairs again, and silent in his corner of the kitchen, de Rais watches as the dishes of the main course are carried upstairs. The head chef has excelled himself. The foods he has prepared are rarefied to their finest extreme: all blood and essence. De Rais does not like to think where such food has come from, but he doubts that it has been produced by the meatracks at the edges of the city. Wild things, he thinks, reared in the deep growth of the forests which surround Paris, hunted down. The clock ticks on. The seemingly endless parade of dishes is borne from view. At last it is time for dessert.

De Rais hovers anxiously as the sorbets, each one with its cool, deceptive pool of night around the incarnadined ice, are taken upstairs by the serving staff. Then, still in his dark jacket, he waits for a frozen moment until he is certain that the attention of the head chef is elsewhere, and slips after the serving staff. Apart from a pair of servitors at the far end of the hallway, their glacial gaze fixed on the great bronze doors, the hallway is empty.

De Rais hastens to the dining hall, his footsteps muffled by the carpet. He puts his eye to the crack of the dining room door. He knows the risk, he thinks, but he still has to see. Inside, it is almost dark. A faint phosphorescence illuminates the high, echoing vaults of the hall. Beneath, the shadowy presences of the Lords of Night dine on the last of the meat essences. There is a susurrus of anticipation as the desserts are passed around the hall by the silent serving staff, who then troop from the hall. De Rais, his hearing fine-tuned by anticipation, hears the tiny crack as the first silver spoon touches the first sorbet, and the minute crunch of mandibles upon ice. De Rais takes a single breath. Followed by the rest of its companions, the Lord swallows a single spoonful of captured evening. And explodes.

Latent light, ingested by perfect darkness, electrifies every filament of the Lord's body before it flares up into a great column of brilliance. De Rais, thrown back against the wall, can see nothing but the shattered form of the Lord branded upon his retinas, but he can taste the light which streams out from the dining hall: the hard, clear sunlight of mountain peaks; the roseate depths of sundown over ocean; the golden, glittering brightness of the sun at midsummer noon. It has worked. The Lords are gone in a moment of fire, consumed in the forbidden, latent light so carefully concealed in darkness and ice by the skilful hands of Severin de Rais. And in the eye of his mind de Rais sees that light pouring up from the heart of the banqueting hall, gilding every wall in Paris and running liquid into the river, distributing itself in immaculate proportion until the shell of shadow that covers the world is broken and the hidden sun revealed. Darkness and light, night and day, in balance once again, for everyone.

Except de Rais. For he knows, as soon as that first blaze of magnificence has passed, that the light has been too much for his shadow-born eyes. Once the flashing echoes have faded from the ruin of his sight, there is only night once more: familiar, relentless, and cold. But as de Rais turns to grope his way along the hallway, he is smiling, for in his imagination and his heart and his soul there is nothing but the sun.

CHARLIE THE PURPLE GIRAFFE
WAS ACTING STRANGELY
David D Levine

Like the previous author, David Levine has been selling short fiction since 2001. Several of his stories have been nominated for awards and he won the Hugo Award for best short story with "Tk'tk'tk", published in 2005. He lives in Portland, Oregon and, with his wife, produces the fanzine Bento.

Also like the previous story, this tale first appeared in Realms of Fantasy, *one of the best magazines for a wide range of original fantasy fiction. The story questions the very nature of reality.*

His website is www.spiritone.com/~dlevine/sfindex.html

Jerry the orange squirrel was walking down the sidewalk one day when he saw some word balloons floating above the hedge beside him. It was the voice of his friend Charlie the purple giraffe. "A man has to have a proper garden, doesn't he?" Charlie was saying. "And what makes a proper garden? Proper plants! And what do you need for proper plants?"

After each question, Charlie seemed to be waiting for an answer. But no response was visible.

"You need proper dirt!" Charlie continued. "And what do you have to have for proper dirt?"

Intrigued, Jerry scampered to the top of the hedge and stared down. What he saw made little lines of surprise come out of his head.

"You have to have proper worms!" Bent double, Charlie was busily tying a Windsor knot around the neck of a common garden worm.

Beside him, a large tin can – its ragged-edged lid tilted at a rakish angle – squirmed with hundreds of worms in tiny top hats, spats, and bustles.

It wasn't the worms that surprised Jerry, though – Charlie did that sort of thing all the time. It was the fact that Charlie was speaking into thin air.

"Who ya talkin' to, Charlie?" said Jerry.

Charlie was so startled that his eyes momentarily jumped out of his head. But he quickly regained his composure. "The worms?"

"Worms don't have ears."

"Uh… I was talkin' to *you*, Jerry."

"You didn't even know I was here."

"Sure I did! I was just pretendin' I didn't."

"Uh huh." Jerry's words dripped frost. One linen-clad worm raised a parasol against the drips.

"As a matter of fact, I was just about to invite you in for tea. Care to join me?"

"Yeah. We can have a nice chat."

They walked from the yard into Charlie's cozy one-room bungalow. It was pink today, with cheerful curves to its walls and roof, and was surrounded by smiling purple flowers. The entire interior was wallpapered in blue and yellow stripes, which clashed with the green and black stripes of Charlie's suit.

Charlie poured tea for the two of them, holding the tiny teapot delicately between white-gloved finger and thumb. A musical note came from the pot as he set it down. He seated himself and raised his cup, pinky raised – though he did not drink, for his arms were too short to reach his head. "What brings you out on this fine morning?" he asked. His words were sprinkled with rainbows and candy canes.

Jerry sipped his tea for a moment. "Charlie…you have to admit you've been acting a little strange lately."

"Strange?" Charlie's eyes darted to one side, then returned to Jerry. Jerry set down his cup. "You've been talking to yourself."

"Me? Talk to myself?" He slapped his knee and laughed, not very convincingly. "Why should I talk to myself, when you're so much more interesting than I am?"

"I've seen you do it. Like just now."

"I told you, I was talking to you."

"What about last week, when you were working on your car? I saw you from three blocks away. Every once in a while you'd wave your wrench and pontificate. It was like you were trying to convince someone of something, but there was nobody there."

"I was…rehearsing. I'm giving a speech to the Rotary Club next week."

Jerry hopped up on the table. "Charlie, there is no Rotary Club in this town."

"It's in…another town."

"What other town?"

Charlie passed his cup from hand to hand. He stared fixedly at a point on the wall. It was as though he were staring out a window, but there wasn't even a painting there – just the wallpaper, which was now patterned in pink and white polka-dots. His expression was grim, almost angry. Finally he brought his head down to Jerry's level, cupped his glove to his mouth, and whispered "I wasn't talking to myself."

"Oh?"

Charlie peered theatrically from side to side, then leaned in even closer. "I was talking to the readers."

Jerry crossed his arms on his chest. "There's nobody here by that name."

"It's not a name. It's…what they do. Readers. People who read."

"Who read what?"

A change came over Charlie then, like a cloud passing in front of the sun. He placed his hands flat in his lap, straightened his neck, and took a deep breath. "Us," he said at last. "They read us."

"I don't understand."

Charlie stood up and began to pace, his hands tightly clenched behind his back. His strides were long, and the house was tiny; he could only take two or three steps in each direction before having to turn around. "Jerry," he began, then paused. "Look…do you ever ask yourself, why am I here? What is the meaning of life?"

"Sure. Sometimes. Doesn't everyone?"

Charlie stopped pacing, turned suddenly and leaned down to Jerry again. "We make them laugh." His tone was deadly serious.

"Them."

"The readers. We were created to entertain them."

Jerry waved his tiny paws in a broad gesture of negation. "Whoa there, big guy. Jerry the squirrel is nobody's creation and nobody's patsy. I'm here for *me*."

"Sorry, Jerry, but it's the honest truth. We're just characters in a comic book."

Jerry fixed Charlie with a hard, beady stare. "Prove it."

Charlie's eyes closed and his shoulders slumped. He turned away from Jerry. "I can't."

"Then how do you know it's true?"

"I've always known, I think, in the back of my head somewhere. But then one day…" He turned back to Jerry, and his eyes were two black pits of fear and despair. "I had just said good-bye to Hermione the hedgehog, I turned back to go into my house, and then…suddenly everything was black. I couldn't move. I couldn't see. I was squashed flat. But somehow I knew that all around me, piled above and below me like a huge stack of pancakes, was everyone and everything I have ever cared about. They were all squashed flat too, but I was the only one who knew it. That went on for a moment that seemed like forever. And then I was right back in my house, as though nothing had happened."

A thought balloon appeared above Jerry's head: "He's bonkers!"

"I know it sounds crazy. But it was as real as anything. And ever since then… I know we're being read, and we're being laughed at."

"I get it," Jerry said with false cheer. "When you talk to yourself you are telling them jokes!"

"No!" Charlie's hands bunched into fists, and he pounded the air ineffectually. "I'm trying to *explain* myself!"

Jerry scratched his head, and a few question marks came out. "You certainly aren't doing a very good job of it now."

"Well, for instance…last week, when I was working on my car. I was just putting the engine back in for the third time, and I was explaining to the readers that this was a very delicate operation and had to be performed with the utmost care. Not funny at all."

"Charlie, you were pounding it in place with a sledge hammer. That's pretty funny. And calling it a delicate operation just makes it funnier."

Charlie stood stock-still for a moment, his lip quivering. Then he collapsed into his chair, his purple neck arching high as he dropped his head into his hands. "I know!" he sobbed, big blue teardrops running down between his fingers. "No matter what I do, no matter how hard I try to be serious, it comes out hilarious. And I'm tired of them laughing at me!"

Jerry offered his handkerchief, and Charlie blew his nose in it with an immense orange HONK.

"These 'readers'…can you hear them? Can you see them?"

"No." He didn't raise his head from his hands.

"Then how do you know they're laughing at you?"

"I just know. The same way I know they're there."

"Where are they, exactly?"

"Right now? Over there."

Jerry followed Charlie's pointing finger, but there was nothing there but the green and white flowered wallpaper. At least it was prettier than the pink and white polka-dots that had been there before. "I don't see anything."

"Neither do I. But they're there. They're always there."

"Always?"

"Well, most of the time." He lifted his head and tried to return the sodden handkerchief, but Jerry gestured to keep it. "I don't think they watch anyone else. I mean, they're watching you now, because you're with me. And they might watch you for a while after you leave here. But eventually they'll come back to me. I'm the main character in their little comic book."

Jerry's tail bristled. "Why you? Why not me?"

"I don't know. I wish I did. That's just the way it is, I guess."

Jerry paced back and forth on the table for a time, thinking. Finally he spoke. "I think you ought to talk with Dr Nocerous about this."

Charlie shook his head, a slow rueful motion. "Okay...but I don't think it will do any good."

Doctor Nocerous's office walls were completely covered in diplomas, from such institutions as THE SCHOOL OF AARD VARKS and WAZUP WITU. The doctor himself was a stout gray rhino, nearly as wide as he was tall, whose wire-rimmed glasses perched incongruously at the top of his horn. He wore a white lab coat, and a small round mirror was strapped to his forehead. He never used the mirror in any way.

"Hmm," he said as he held his stethoscope to the side of Charlie's neck, and "Hmm" again as he stood on a stepladder to peer down Charlie's throat, and "Hmm" one more time as he held Charlie's lapel between two fingers and looked at his watch.

"Well, doctor," said Jerry when the exam was finished, "what's wrong with him?"

"My examination has discovered no physical infirmities whatsoever. Superficially, he is salubrious as an equine."

"What?" said Charlie.

"Healthy as a horse," explained the doctor.

"I told you."

"But he's *seeing* things!" said Jerry.

"Indeed. These phantasmagorical manifestations are most worrisome," the doctor muttered, puffing on his pipe. A few small pink bubbles emerged as he pondered. "I recommend that we keep your friend under observation."

"How ironic," Charlie said to the wall, then returned his gaze to the doctor. "I am not seeing things, or hearing things! I just *know* things. Is that so bad?"

Jerry jumped up on the doctor's desk. "Charlie, listen to me. I'm your friend, right? I've never steered you wrong?"

"Of course not."

"Then get this through your thick purple skull: *there are no 'readers'.* You are not the 'main character' in anyone's 'comical book.' You're just a person like anyone else, and you're here to muddle through your life the same as the rest of us. Nothing more."

"The veracity of your diminutive companion's statement is incontrovertible," said the doctor, waving his pipe. "These megalomaniacal misapprehensions must be immediately terminated. They jeopardize your physical integrity and the overall stability of the community."

"What?"

"You're a danger to yourself and others."

Charlie jumped out of his seat. "I'm no danger to anyone! So what if I talk to myself? That doesn't mean I'm going to pick up a big mallet and start flattening people!"

"Solipsistic delusions are frequently merely the initial manifestation of a general insensitivity to the legitimacy, even the existence, of external personalities. If allowed to go unchecked, these tendencies could escalate into antisocial or even injurious behavior!"

"What?"

"He thinks you might pick up a big mallet and start flattening people," said Jerry.

Charlie stood with his feet planted wide and his fists clenched. The white fabric of his gloves was bunched and strained. He stared at the wall. "You think this is funny, don't you?"

"Nobody's making any jokes here, Charlie," said Jerry. "We're serious."

"I wasn't talking to you." He turned around, pointed at a different spot on the wall. "This has all been arranged for *your* amusement! Are you happy?"

Jerry and Dr Nocerous looked at each other.

Charlie pulled a big mallet from his pocket and began pounding on the wall. "Are you laughing now? Huh? Are you?" The WHAM of the mallet on the wall was huge and black. "Just let me get out there and I'll show you what comedy is all about!"

"This situation necessitates immediate incarceration!" said the doctor as he ran behind his desk.

"Ditto!" said Jerry as he dived under a chair.

The doctor pressed a button under the desk; no sound came out, but a few small lightning bolts appeared. Moments later two enormous gorillas, their white coats stretched taut over bulging muscles, burst through the door. There was a swirl of motion, and when it cleared Charlie was on the floor, trussed in a straitjacket.

"Don't let them put me away!" Charlie cried.

"It's for your own good," said Jerry, and waved encouragingly as the gorillas hustled Charlie away. But as soon as they were gone, Jerry's shoulders slumped. "What are you going to do, Doctor?"

"His prognosis is not encouraging. However, he will be the recipient of the most advanced experimental treatments modern medical technology has to offer." From his pocket, the doctor drew one end of a set of heavy jumper cables. Sparks flew from the sharp copper teeth as he touched them together, and a small strange grin appeared on his face.

Charlie's sad, desperate eyes peered through the slot in the metal door. "You've got to get me out of here, Jerry." His word balloons squeezed through the slot like bubbles from a sinking ship.

"Hang in there, buddy. Dr Nocerous tells me you're coming along nicely."

"He's been saying that for weeks." Charlie shook his head, bringing his blackened horns briefly into view. "But I know the score. I'm not going to get out of here until I show some improvement, but since there's nothing wrong with me I'm never going to get any better than I am now."

"Charlie, you must accept that you have a problem. It's the first step on the road to recovery."

Charlie chuckled ruefully. "I have a problem, all right. I've learned that there are worse things than being laughed at."

"Nobody's laughing at you, Charlie. You need to understand that these 'readers' are nothing more than a projection of your own feelings of self-doubt and inconsequentiality."

"That's just what the rhino told you to say. But you're right – nobody's laughing at me. The *readers* aren't laughing at me. And that's the problem."

"I thought you didn't want them to laugh at you."

"I didn't. But since I've been here in this padded cell, tied up in this straitjacket all day long with nothing to do…they're *bored*."

"Well, that's an improvement, isn't it? Maybe now they'll watch someone else instead."

"They've tried. But – no insult intended – none of you guys are as funny as I am." Jerry's tail bristled. "So they're leaving. They're going away completely. And that scares me."

"You should be glad to be rid of them!" Jerry fumed.

Charlie's eyes closed for a moment. When they opened again, Jerry saw a bit of the old manic fervor. "Listen…do you ever think about the nature of time?"

"What?"

"Time. How it passes, from moment to moment. Haven't you ever noticed how some things change when you aren't looking at them?"

"Like the wallpaper?"

"Exactly. I believe that time is...divided. Into moments, or segments. Within each segment we are alive and awake, but in between...there are gaps. That's when things change."

"What does this have to do with anything?"

"I think the readers live their lives in the gaps between our time segments. They live in our time too, somehow – I know because they can see us. But in the gaps...they have the universe to themselves."

"Charlie, you're not making any sense."

"I know it sounds crazy. But I'm dead serious. And here's the important part: when the readers aren't watching us...*we don't exist!*"

Jerry shook his head and turned away, but after a moment's thought he turned back. "OK. Suppose I accept this theory of yours. Suppose there *are* gaps between moments. But time still *feels* continuous to us. See?" He waved a paw rapidly back and forth. "So it doesn't really matter!"

"It doesn't matter as long as they keep coming back. But if too many of them get bored...if they all go away and don't come back...then the gap will just go on and on, and we'll never exist again. It'll be the end of the world, Jerry. Squashed flat in the dark, forever." Charlie's eyes were desperate, sincere, pleading. "You've got to get me out of here. I'll joke, I'll pratfall, I'll do anything to keep the readers coming back. To keep us all alive. Please."

Jerry closed his eyes, unable to bear his friend's gaze. "There are no readers, Charlie."

In the end, he was right.

MASTER LAO AND
THE FLYING HORROR
Lawrence Person

Lawrence Person (b. 1965) is, along with Paul Di Filippo, the only contributor in this volume who also appeared in the Mammoth Book of Extreme Science Fiction. *Person has been producing science fiction and fantasy since his first published story in 1990, though he may be better known for his genre criticism and commentary, partly through his many published essays and reviews but also as editor of the critical magazine* Nova Express, *which he took over in 1992. His stories have appeared in* Asimov's Science Fiction, Analog *and Peter Crowther's* Postscripts, *from which the following is taken. If you are fans of Chinese horror and fantasy films you are in for a treat.*

His website is at home.austin.rr.com/lperson/index.html

On the day Old Man Zhang was murdered, Orange Blossom was teaching me the ritual she called Butterfly Drinking Nectar.

Her mother had nicknamed her Orange Blossom because she was born the day of her village's Orange Blossom ritual. The other apprentices at the White Crane Temple called her Shaking Melons for current performances of far more interesting rituals.

Minutes earlier, I had made good use of her namesakes in a ritual called Bear Jumping Two Mountains, which I had found quite engrossing, though not half so much as Butterfly Drinking Nectar. Orange Blossom loved me for my strong and handsome body, my growing mastery of magic and kung fu, and my ability to pay her five coins every other week. I loved her not only for her namesakes, but also for her lovely peasant beauty, her delightful giggle, and her carefully honed talents, many of which had been learned in Shanghai.

Just then she was about to show me her most powerful and sacred ritual, Magic Sword Entering the Lotus, when our lovely interlude was most cruelly interrupted.

"Idiot! Dolt! Moron!" I heard a dreaded voice yell behind me, each word punctuated by a bamboo staff's painfully familiar blow to my naked back. I leapt off the bed, all the magic draining from my sword as I shielded my head from the wrathful blows of Master Lao.

"Harlot! Strumpet! Whore!" he yelled, wielding his bamboo against Orange Blossom's exposed bottom. (Thanks to ample padding there, his blows inflicted no lasting harm.) "I have told you before not to tempt my apprentices with your wickedness!"

"Their money is as good as anyone else's!" yelled Orange Blossom defiantly. It saddened me to hear her reduce our transcendent ecstasy to mere commerce, but I had more pressing concerns to worry about, as Master Lao turned his wrath, and staff, back to me.

"You were supposed to be back from the market half an hour ago!" he yelled, inflicting a most painful blow to my raised forearm. "And here I find you shirking your duties and cavorting with harlots!"

"Mercy, Master!" I yelled. "My spirit is willing but my flesh is weak!"

"Not nearly so weak as it will be after I get through with you!" he said, raising the staff again.

"What in the Nine Hells are you doing in here?" asked Dancing Petals from the doorway. Dancing Petals was the establishment's proprietress, though the other apprentices called her Lumbering Whale.

"He beat me with a bamboo cane!" yelled Orange Blossom.

"That's five coins extra, and only by appointment!" said Dancing Petals.

"Corrupt panderer! I am only here to retrieve my apprentice! We have no intention of staying in your vile den of iniquity!"

"That's not what you said the last time you were here!" Dancing Petals replied, causing my master's face to turn the most amazing shade of pale.

"Come, Chou Lin, we must leave this place immediately," said Master Lao, drawing himself up and speaking in the calm, dignified voice he used on rich businessmen. "Such houses of wickedness are often a magnet for evil spirits."

In my experience such houses are more often magnets for middle-aged husbands and government officials, but in this, as in so many things, I acceded to my master's greater wisdom. With a single, mournful glance at the lovely Orange Blossom, I struggled into my clothes, grabbed my bundle, and followed Master Lao out into the street.

"Chou Lin, what are the Three Great Sins for a temple apprentice?" he asked.

"Idleness, Drunkenness, and Lustfulness," I recited dutifully.

"And you have indulged in each during the last three days!" he said, striking my back another painful blow.

"Mercy, Master, mercy!" I cried. It seemed unfair for him to bring up Drunkenness, since the bottle had been Kua Qing's. Likewise, the Idleness had been a direct result of the Drunkenness, since next morning the sunlight had burned my eyes like hot pokers. I knew that when I became a White Crane priest, my chief duties would be battling evil and sin. While I understood evil, I still had an inadequate grasp of sin, and thus sought to study it at every opportunity.

"Stop cringing, you pathetic little insect! Your conduct is unbecoming a temple apprentice. Did you get the rice paper for the prayer offerings?"

"Yes, master."

"Did you get the joss sticks?"

"Yes, master."

"Did you get all three kinds of rice?"

"Yes, master."

"Did you get the steamed buns?"

"No master!"

Master Lao raised his staff again.

"I was unable to! Zu Bing's shop has closed!" And indeed, the latter was true. Rumor linked Zu Bing and his debts to several notorious gambling house owners with a mound of live ants in a most unpleasant fashion.

"Come then. There is a new place we can get sticky buns."

Spring Moon's noodle house had opened in what had once been the carpentry shop of Kao Ling. Kao Ling had been one of the first victims of the plague of snakes, an incident I have already related in great detail elsewhere.

From the many smiling customers assembled there, it seemed that no one missed Zu Bing. With an attractive atrium extending to the new second story, a bamboo-propped skylight letting in a flood of sunshine, bright tile floors and the beautiful screen paintings adorning the walls, Spring Moon's noodle house presented a most pleasing and cheerful atmosphere, and I resolved to take Orange Blossom there as soon as Master Lao's wrath (and watchfulness) had faded.

"Are you here for lunch?" asked a melodious voice. I turned and instantly all thoughts of Orange Blossom left my mind.

In our province, it is said that the Emperor of Heaven is attended by the nine most beautiful women in the world, each raised to Godhood that they might serve him on his dragon throne. However, on that day I knew he could have been attended by only eight. One must have slipped away back to earth while he was sleeping, for surely there could not be nine more beautiful women in all of Heaven and Earth than Autumn Wind.

"No, we are here to pick up some steamed buns," said Master Lao, smiling. This in and of itself was a sure sign of Autumn Wind's divinity, since I could count the number of times Master Lao had smiled in my presence on the fingers of a single hand. "Are you Spring Moon?"

"No, I am Autumn Wind, her daughter. Mother is helping out in the kitchen. Let me go get her."

I gazed longingly after her as her divine form glided as softly as her namesake back to the kitchen. Master Lao must have noticed my gaze. He held his staff across my chest and spoke in a grave tone.

"Chou Lin, I know what you're thinking, and I order you to stop at once!"

"Huh?" I replied cleverly.

"You have already fallen into lustfulness once today. Do not compound your sin with a second offense!"

"What?" was my witty retort.

"Autumn Wind is not one of Dancing Petals' girls! To pursue the wicked thoughts about her that I know are racing through your head can lead only to dishonor and ruin!"

"Hmm?" I said eloquently.

Master Lao lowered his staff and leaned forward on it. "Ah, youth," he sighed wistfully.

At that moment, Autumn Wind floated back to us. "Mother says she will be out here shortly."

Once more I mustered the masterful rhetorical skills I had so recently displayed. "Hello," I said, smiling.

"Hello," she said, smiling back so brightly I feared I would melt before her radiance. "Are you two from the village? I haven't seen you in here before."

"We are from the White Crane Temple. I am Master Lao, and this is my apprentice, Chou Lin."

"Hello," I said again, the sight of Autumn Wind evidently having driven all other words from my brain.

"Why don't you..." she began, to say, but just then our reverie was broken by a hideous, piercing scream.

Belying his white hair, Master Lao was instantly off and running in the direction of the terrible sound, and soon I, and half the village, followed in his wake.

The scream sounded once again, straight ahead, and Master Lao headed for Old Man Zhang's house.

In his youth, Zhang had made his fortune as a junk captain upon the Yangtzee, after which he had retired back to the village for a life of gambling and idle drunkenness, sins for which he was both condemned and envied in equal measure.

Spring Flower (who was now, if truth be told, more of an autumn weed) had been his cleaning woman, and it was she who stood just a few feet inside the door to Zhang's house, screaming again and again. Master Lao was through the door in an instant, then stopped, his face ashen. I was only a few steps behind.

"Chou Lin, escort her outside and bar the door," he said. I nodded dumbly and guided the still screaming Spring Flower out the door against the pressing throng, the terrible image of Old Man Zhang's body burned into my mind.

He sat facing the door, dark bloodstains down the front of his blue silk shirt and a bloody crater where his neck had been.

When we arrived back at the temple, Master Lao was in a foul mood. Not only had he administered purification rights to Zhang's body, but he had to wait nearly an hour for Policeman Ho to show up to examine it. Ho, who owed his job entirely to his uncle's position as assistant tax collector for the province, had done his usual cursory, bumbling job.

"This man has obviously been the victim of a crime of violence!" he said.

"Your powers of observation are unparalleled, Honorable Ho," said Master Lao.

All of these delays meant we, and the food, arrived back at the temple two hours later than Master Lao had planned on starting preparation for the feast.

"Master Lao," said Kua Qing, rushing up as we entered the temple, "we heard about the murder! What has happened?"

"Later!" bellowed Master Lao, thrusting the chicken cage into Kua Qing's hands. "We must start on the feast. Kill and pluck these chickens immediately!"

"But Master, why me?" asked Kua Qing in the honeyed voice he always used when attempting to evade honest work. "It is Chou Lin who should pluck the chickens in atonement for the sin of lustfulness." In a small village, news travels fast.

"No, *you* will pluck the chickens," said Master Lao sternly. "Chou Lin needs to perform a more important task."

At this, I puffed up my chest and smiled at Kua Qing. It is always heartening to have my position as Master Lao's Number One Apprentice confirmed.

"Chou Lin, start cleaning the chamber pots."

My smile faded.

Master Lao asserts that all work is honorable, and thus there is no shame in cleaning chamber pots. However, some honors smell better than others.

It was three days prior to the midsummer festival, time for The Feast of the Chicken, to be followed by The Feast of the Duck, The Feast of the Goose, and finally, on solstice eve, The Feast of the White Crane. (The last, being our namesake, was the only one not consumed.) It was a time to create charms to ward off pestilence, bad weather, and evil spirits.

After finishing the odious task and performing a purifying ritual with water and salt, Master Lao sent me back to the kitchen to help our cook Jade Willow with the preparations. Due to an unfortunate incident involving a simple fire spell and a pot of cooking oil, Jade Willow held an irrational and entirely unwarranted grudge against me. Upon entering, she gave me a deep frown, then set me tending no less than six pots.

After a good hour of vigorous stirring, Old Zhong, the temple servant, finally came to relieve me, and Master Lao had me change into my ceremonial robes of gold and cinnabar.

For the feast, the oldest apprentices sat closest to Master Lao, so I sat immediately to his right while Kua Qing sat to his left. Further down the table were Ba Le, Lai Wang, Dai Li, and Bang Zhou. At the end of the table were the four "tadpoles," the novitiates pledged to the temple just a month before. There had originally been six, but two had already hobbled home in splints, unable to stand up to Master Lao's rigorous training methods.

Once we were seated, Master Lao struck a small silver gong, then began the ritual invocation against evil.

When he reached the third stanza, someone chuckled.

Master Lao paused, then resumed the chant, looking from face to face, trying to determine the culprit. Because of certain unfortunate incidents in the past, I was frequently the subject of his scrutiny in such matters, but this time the voice was clearly too deep and far away to be my own.

The rest of the invocation passed without incident, until Master Lao finished up by burning a prayer offering. Then the same voice coughed.

Master Lao looked around again, craning his head to see if anyone was lurking around the rest of the temple, to no avail. Still perturbed, he rang the dinner gong, and Jade Willow and Old Zhong came out of kitchen bearing the feast.

Any lingering uneasiness over the odd voices dissipated as the steaming platters were laid before us. Though the temple diet usually consisted of meager portions of rice and fish, feast days always offered up a sumptuous and dizzying variety of food, as well as an opportunity to imbibe the rice and plum wine usually forbidden us. Moreover, on such days eating and drinking as much as possible was considered a sacred duty, a way of showing respect to the Celestial Masters, from whom all bounty flows. It was upon these occasions that my own devotion was unsurpassed.

Rice wine and jocularity flowed freely as we quickly slurped down gallons of noodles, devoured heaps of sticky buns, and consumed dozens of rice balls. Only Master Lao seemed lacking in festive spirit, still brooding over the mysterious voice.

Then Jade and Zhong brought out the chickens, laying them out along the table. Using my superior speed, I had just snagged a drumstick before Kua Qing could reach it, when a frightened cry at the other end of the table silenced our revelry.

Xau Qu, the roundest of the tadpoles, was backing away from the table. In front of him, the roast chicken he had been reaching for only moments before was moving.

Not just moving, *dancing*. It took two steps forward, then two back, then turned in a circle, all the while swinging its cooked wings as juice dripped down its still-moist carcass.

"Chou Lin, bring my pen and inkpot, quickly!" said Master Lao, and I scurried to obey. Thus armed, Master Lao quickly transcribed a prayer against evil on a sheet of rice paper, rolled it up in a ball of sticky rice, then cast it at the possessed bird.

The roast chicken gave a painful squawk, then flopped lifelessly back to the table. The younger apprentices who had been holding their breath let out a sigh of relief, but it was short-lived.

Another chicken, this one in front of Ba La, stood up and kicked over his wine cup. Master Lao dashed off and rolled up another prayer ball and dispatched this one as well, but he had no sooner vanquished that chicken when a third popped up.

After dispatching two more unnatural chickens, Master Lao changed tactics. "Chou Lin, fetch my silver rope.".

In the great prayer cabinet against the north wall were tucked many of the more esoteric tools of a White Crane priest. In one of the bottommost drawers was a thin rope of purest spun silver, knotted and braided for strength, its handle carved from the hardest of ram's horn, intricately carved with the most worthy verses of Lao Dan. It was this tool that I quickly retrieved and rushed to Master Lao's hands.

Master Lao whirled the silver rope around his head three times, chanting out an invocation to banish evil spirits, then launched it at the latest dancing chicken, ensnaring it.

There was a cry of pain high up in the rafters. Master Lao, slowly and with a surprisingly great effort for something so small, hauled the chicken towards him. As he pulled, an evil, leering face high in the temple shadows was pulled into the lantern-light.

It was Old Man Zhang's head. Or rather, slightly *more* than his head, as a long trail of writhing viscera snaked behind it.

"*Filthy priest! Your silver cord will not save you!*"

" Kua Qing! Begin the chant to drive out evil spirits!" said Master Lao, slowly pulling the roped chicken towards him, which also drew Zhang's head lower. "Quickly!"

Kua Qing began the chant, which was soon picked up, somewhat unsteadily, by the other apprentices.

"*Doom will come to your temple! I will eat your livers, and pluck out your eyes!*"

"Chou Lin, you know the first refrain of the third Crane Exorcism?"

"*Your corpses shall litter the earth, and I shall suck the marrow from your bones!*"

As Zhang was pulled closer, it became apparent that his eye teeth seemed unnaturally long and curved.

"Yes master!"

"Scribe it on the paper, then roll it up in a sticky rice ball as you saw me do!"

"*The Queen shall suck down all your souls, and you shall serve as her slaves in Hell!*"

I have always considered my calligraphy inferior to my martial arts, but never had I scribed ideograms so quickly in all my life. In ten seconds I had written out the refrain and rolled it into the center of a ball of sticky rice.

"Now, throw it at the head!"

With a stone I am regarded as a pretty fair shot, having once managed to destroy an expensive vase at no less than 50 paces. (My reasons for doing so were entirely salutary and justified, but too complex to relate here.) However, when I tossed the rice ball, Zhang's head jerked with an amazing fluidity, and my shot sailed just wide of the mark.

"Again!" said Master Lao, still slowly and carefully pulling the chicken, and Zhang, closer.

"*The worms shall eat your flesh, and your heads shall hunt the night at the Queen's command!*"

I completed and threw a second prayer ball, but Zhang again ducked out of the way.

"Again!" said Master Lao. The exertions of the chicken grew ever more frantic, and it was all he could do to keep it captive.

Once again I scribed and enclosed a prayer, took careful aim, and threw. This time the ball hit the upper left side of Zhang's face, disintegrating in a shower of smoke and rice as the impacted cheek caught fire.

Zhang screamed and jerked violently. At that jerk, the captive chicken went barreling over the edge of the table, slipping out of the silver loop. Still screaming, Zhang's burning head flew up and out one of the second floor windows. By the time Kua Qing and I had raced up the stair it had already escaped into the night.

"Close all the windows!" ordered Master Lao. During the summer, the screens were left open due to the heat, but none of us argued.

"Master Lao, what was it?" asked Ba Le. "And how could it have gotten into the temple?"

"And who is the queen it mentioned?" asked Bang Zhou.

"It must have flown in through a window," said Master Lao. "We have not blessed the charms there in over a year. As for what it is, I have an idea, but I shall have to consult the sacred texts. In the meantime, continue the feast. We'll deal with Zhang and his 'queen' tomorrow."

We resumed our seats, but the other apprentices only picked at their food, leaving their chickens untouched. Fortunately, my quick thinking in grabbing a drumstick as soon as it arrived meant our chicken was the only one not possessed, and thus still safe for consumption. However, my chain of logic seemed unconvincing to the others, leaving me the entire chicken.

Once again I proved unsurpassed in my devotion to the Celestial Masters.

Most of the next morning was taken up with making new charms and re-blessing the ones around the temple. Master Lao observed the rituals, then, content that Kua Qing was capable of supervising in his stead, pulled me aside to help him in his study.

Along with the standard works of Lao Dan, Zhuang Zhou and Confucius, Master Lao possessed a number of ancient books and scrolls, many of them on esoteric subjects. There was Hai Yan's important book detailing the many varieties of hopping vampires, Yu Wei's obscure treatise on magic involving turtles, and a mysterious volume written in an unreadable script by a mad Arab with an unpronounceable name.

After several minutes of study, Master Lao finally found what he was looking for in a particularly large leather-bound tome. "Here, take a look at this," he said, pointing to a woodcut depicting three flying heads trailing viscera behind them, with terrified villagers running about below.

"What are they?"

"Here they are called the Kongbu Feixing Tou. It says that they are demonic spirits which posses the heads of those who have died without being properly blessed. Those so possessed can infect others by biting their neck or wrist. Unless the wound is purified within an hour, the victim also turns into an evil flying creature enslaved by the one that bit it."

"How do we fight them?"

"They cannot stand sunlight, and strong light of any kind causes them pain, especially when reflected from a silver mirror. Prayers and charms can harm them, but because they are encased in human flesh, not actually kill them unless placed directly in the mouth. And the queen herself can only be killed by a blessed arrow carved from a branch of a weeping mulberry.

"It also says that once the Kongbu Feixing Tou queen has three servants to do her bidding, she can use them to consecrate an unholy temple, and from there open a gate to summon more of her kind."

"A temple? Like our own?"

"Perhaps. According to this, it must be equidistant from the sites of the three slain acolytes. Perhaps we can…"

I'll never know what Master Lao was going to say next, because at that very moment Kua Qing burst into the room, his face stricken.

"Master Lau, you and Chou Lin must come quickly! There's been another murder!"

"Another one?" Master Lao stood up. "Chou Lin, you stay here and supervise the other apprentices."

"No Master, Chou Lin should come as well," said Kua Qing, bowing sadly. "The murder was at Dancing Petals'. It was…it was…"

At that Kua Qing bowed and raced out of the room, unable to meet my eyes. It was then I knew.

It took all my training to stay composed as we ran to Dancing Petals'.

In the front room, her other girls issued wild lamentations and copious tears. Dancing Petals herself wore a mournful expression, and silently gestured for us to follow her up the stairs to Orange Blossom's room.

It pained me greatly to realize that the same room I had experienced such ecstasy in the day before had become the site of such a foul crime. The smell of her namesake perfume still lingered in the air, but was now mixed with an undertone of corruption and decay.

When Dancing Petals lifted the sheet away from the covered body I had to turn away, unable to look at the ruin where her head had been. I stood there staring at the wall while Master Lao administered the proper rituals. Then he finished and turned up the sheet.

"Tell undertaker Zu I will send him special charms and ointments to prepare the body with. In the meantime, there is a great evil loose. Tell all the girls to close their windows by sunset."

When Dancing Petals had left Master Lao turned back to me. "Chou Lin, do you see now why I said these places are magnets for evil spirits?"

"Master Lao, with all respect, I do not believe this is what you had in mind. Nor do you."

At that he looked nonplussed for a moment, his eyes showing a trace of the stormy look that usually preceded a beating. But this time he merely grunted and nodded, then turned away.

Soon the entire village had been instructed to close their windows by sunset, no matter how they might swelter in the summer heat.

Despite the tragic occurrences, it was the night for the Feast of the Duck, and preparations had to be undertaken. The seasons would not halt at our mortal problems, nor would the Celestial Masters step down from Heaven to dry our tears. In fact, with such evil abroad, it was all the more reason to seek their favour.

And so it was with heavy hearts that Master Lao and I once again found ourselves in Spring Moon's noodle house. Autumn Wind greeted us and I felt my spirits lift somewhat, though she was still struck by our long faces.

"Both of your faces are too sad for a festival day! You look like someone died!"

This caused a brief and uncomfortable silence as Master Lao and I looked at each other, then he started explaining Orange Blossom's death, though not the precise nature of her murderer, and Autumn Wind looked positively stricken. News travels fast, but evidently the doings at Dancing Petals' were not considered polite conversation in the company of one so ethereal as Autumn Wind.

"That's horrible! Oh, I'm so sorry! Did either of you know her?"

"Yes," I said, then immediately regretted it, fearful of what Autumn Wind might think of such a friendship, but she seemed far too good-natured to draw such scandalous (if admittedly correct) conclusions.

"Oh you poor man!" she said, giving me a hug. At that moment I must admit that thoughts of Orange Blossom moved very far away from my mind indeed. "Here, the two of you sit down. I'll go fetch mother and get you some tea."

Autumn Moon glided away from us in a way that confirmed, once again, her heavenly origin. I reflected that, if one of them had to survive, then better Autumn Wind than Orange Blossom. Then I immediately felt a sharp pang of guilt, for Autumn Wind, while beautiful, was someone I barely knew, while I had known Orange Blossom very well indeed. But then I thought that, on the strength of merit and virtue, Autumn Wind was clearly the more deserving. But *then* I thought...

There are times when I am proud of my learning. My father had been an illiterate ox-herd, while I was more than halfway to being a sage and respected White Crane Priest. However, at that moment I felt dumber than the dumbest ox, not knowing what I felt or thought.

Master Lao often said that the road to wisdom is a very long and painful one. I thought that was merely an easy way to justify our beatings, but the longer I live the more I fear he is right.

Spring Moon insisted on leaving the kitchen to serve us tea and sympathy. Like her daughter she was slim and graceful, and carried her mature beauty well. She asked us gently for details about the murder. Master Lao was circumspect about the cause, but emphasized that a killer was loose in the night, and that all window screens should be closed and doors locked.

After this genial chat, Spring Moon insisted on making this order of buns an offering to the temple. Master Lao refused twice, then graciously acceded the third time, offering to send charms and blessings over the next day.

Back at the temple, Master Lao pulled out the village map he used to advise businessmen on the most auspicious location for a new enterprise. He made a small mark for Zhang's house, then another for Dancing Petals' place, then laid a reed between them. Then he took out two more reeds of the same length to form a triangle, with the temple squarely in the middle.

"Just as I feared," said Master Lao.

"Who lives here?" I asked, pointing to an estate on the edge of town at the triangle's apex.

"Hmm, that would be Hu Feng's place," said Master Lao darkly. Feng ran a distillery which decanted plum wine of unusual potency. His position at the edge of town was necessitated by the unfortunate tendency of his production apparatus towards periodic explosions. Despite these occasional setbacks, Feng was a remarkably successful businessman, as his libations were a favourite throughout the province, and he had steadily improved his father's original recipe to the point where cases of permanent blindness resulting from its imbibing were now exceptionally rare.

"Obviously, someone will need to protect Honorable Feng's establishment," I said, rising, "So I'll just go over there and start..."

At that, Master Lao extended his bamboo staff and pushed me, quite forcefully, back into my seat.

"Neither you nor Kua Qing will defend Feng's, despite your obvious knowledge of his establishment. I will go myself and take Xau Qu with me. You and Kua Qing will guard the temple. But first, we must prepare the Feast of the Duck."

There followed more feast preparations, although this time I was not stirring pots but inspecting the temple to make sure charms had been appropriately situated and blessings properly scribed above all doors and windows. For once Kua Qing seems to have done a good job supervising the other apprentices, rather than his usual half-hearted and slip-shod efforts, perhaps because this time his own safety was at stake.

Some may believe that I have unfairly exaggerated Kua Qing's numerous deficiencies in these pages, but they don't know him as well as I, nor have they witnessed his underhanded dealings at close range as I have. It is true that I myself am not free of sin, and that I have not always followed the Celestial Masters in all things. However, there is an important difference: The errors I have committed have been but youthful indiscretions and small lapses in my otherwise laudable life, while Kua Qing's deplorable actions stem from deep and abiding flaws in his character.

Besides, as any number of bruises and scars on his body will attest, my kung fu is demonstrably superior.

The feast itself was more subdued than the night before. Because we would be taking turns guarding the temple, we were allowed only one cup of plum wine each. (There is one traveller of my acquaintance who claims that his kung fu is improved immeasurably by imbibing vast quantities of alcohol before every bout, but this person is known far and wide as a shameless braggart and liar, so I shall refrain from naming him here.) This time no supernatural forces interrupted either the blessing or the meal.

After a necessarily abbreviated feast, Master Lao went to his cabinet and withdrew several implements. For himself he pulled out the silver rope, a small whisk broom with bristles of tiger fur, and a slender bamboo rod covered with strange symbols. For myself and Kua Qing he pulled out a hooded prayer lantern and an octagonal silver mirror inscribed with the eight trigrams of the Bagua. The lantern he poured a measure of purified palm oil into, then lit. Next he wrote out a long prayer on a piece of vellum, chanting over it the entire time. When finished, he skillfully folded it into the shape of a crane, then inserted it into the flame. Suddenly, the lantern light seemed to increase ten fold, making it bright enough that I briefly shielded my eyes.

"If one of the Kongbu Feixing Tou attacks, shine the lantern off the mirror to reflect the beam onto them. It may not destroy them, but it should cause them great pain. Chou Lin, head the first watch, and Kua Qing the second." At that, Master Lao and Xau Qu headed off to Feng's.

That night was the first time I had ever viewed the wide courtyard of our temple as anything but an inviting refuge. One corner held the stumps we balanced upon for our White Crane training, we practiced our forms outside when the weather was good, and held the harvest festival for the whole village there in the fall. Yet tonight, despite torches burning in the corners, it seemed a strange and ominous place, filled with dancing shadows as the willow trees whispered in the breeze.

Bang Zhou was my companion for the first watch, and it was he who carried the silver mirror. Born the youngest of nine sons in a poor fisherman's family near Canton, Bang Zhou was thin as a rake and wore a perpetual hang-dog expression. Despite his slight build he was a sturdy fighter and a graceful acrobat.

"We'll patrol around the entire length of the temple together," I instructed Bang Zhou. "If we see anything, we'll use the lantern and mirror and call out for the other apprentices to help."

"What if it's not a demon? Or what if the lantern doesn't work? Shouldn't we have swords?" asked Bang Zhou.

"Master Lao said the lantern should be effective," I answered. But then a snake of doubt uncoiled its head as I remembered how unnaturally strong Old Man Zhang's head had been. "But it wouldn't hurt to have swords," I concluded. "Run in and fetch one for each of us."

"Chou Lin...." whispered a strangely familiar female voice as soon as Bang Zhou had disappeared.

"Who's there?" I asked shining my lantern into the gloom of the courtyard.

"Why, it's just me Chou Lin," answered the voice, and when I turned I saw Orange Blossom's face staring at me from the edge of the torchlight.

"Orange Blossom!" I said, stepping towards her, flooded with a feeling of relief. But then I stopped, uneasy. "But I thought you were dead!"

"Oh no, that wasn't me!" she said, laughing her delightful peasant giggle in a way that sounded slightly strange. "That was another girl that looked like me. When that horrible thing came in through the window I escaped out into the woods. I've been out there all day. Oh, Chou Lin I'm so cold! I wasn't able to grab any clothes before I escaped..."

This particular detail interested me greatly, but there was still something that didn't quite add up. "What was the other girl doing in your room?"

Orange Blossom laughed again. "We were doing something terribly naughty! So naughty I can only whisper it. Come closer and I'll tell you."

This too interested me greatly, but it was at this moment that I finally remembered to think with the large head rather than the small one. I held up the lantern and aimed it at Orange Blossom.

Orange Blossom's head recoiled and hissed at the sudden radiance, which revealed, just as I feared, the absence of her body and a long trail of viscera floating behind her. "You fool!" she screamed. "You had to go and ruin it! I'll do it the hard way!"

At that she flew straight for me, her unnaturally long teeth now visible. Her rush was so quick I had no time to think, whirling around and bringing the lantern in an arc head-on into her face, sending her recoiling away, a scream of pain on her lips.

"You wretched little worm!" she screamed, her pale face turning red where the lantern had connected. "You'll pay for that! Your pain will be unimaginable!"

"Orange Blossom, please, don't do this! Remember all we shared when you were alive!"

"Shared?" She let out a cruel, chilling laugh. "We never *shared* anything. You bought me like you bought chickens at the market! And I pretended to love you to keep the coins coming. 'Oh Chou Lin, you're the best! Of course I love you!'" She laughed again. "Look at the strutting, arrogant ox-herder, so proud of his kung fu, and his position at the temple, and his pitiful lovemaking. You weren't even the best among the temple apprentices! Kua Qing is a better lover than you'll ever be!" She lowered her voice to a whisper. "You know, he was so good, I often let him visit for free."

"Be gone, demon," I said, thrusting the lantern towards her again. "I will not listen to your lies!"

"What's the matter, Chou Lin, don't you have five coins on you to buy my body with? Oh wait, I don't have a body anymore." At that she let loose another cruel laugh, then snarled and dove for another attack.

I launched a palm-heel strike to send her spinning back, then grabbed the floating trail of viscera, swung her around a couple of times, sending her spinning out into the courtyard, a move I instantly regretted.

My hands, now covered with the vile, unnatural secretions of her demonic organs, immediately began to tingle unpleasantly, followed quickly by a painful burning sensation. I dropped the lantern and pulled off my robe, trying to dry my hands.

Orange Blossom took that opportunity to attack again. With my hands trapped, all I could do was wrap the rest of the robe around her.

There followed a most ignoble episode of my being dragged across the courtyard as Orange Blossom attempted to escape my robe's confines. I was shocked at the strength a single flying head could display, though in life certain parts of Orange Blossom's body had displayed a remarkably strong grip. She finally wriggled free, and I took this opportunity to race back to the lantern, Orange Blossom in hot pursuit.

"Chou Lin?" asked Bang Zhou incredulously, having finally located the swords.

"The mirror!" I screamed. "Quickly!"

For a moment, Bang Zhou looked stunned, then came to his senses and held up the mirror. I quickly directed the lantern's beam at it, which Bang Zhou moved to reflect squarely at Orange Blossom's head. She let out a scream as she burst into flames, then quickly fled over the wall, leaving a trail of sparks behind as she escaped into to the night.

"Are you hurt?" he asked.

"Just my pride."

Kua Qing and Dai Li relieved us at midnight, and the rest of the night passed without incident. The next morning, Jade Willow shot me a dirty look over the ruins of my robe, as if flying monsters were part of a complex plot to deplete the temple's meager clothing budget. (I will admit that a certain incident or two in the past requiring her to spend several hours removing plum wine stains from my robes may have contributed to her prejudice.)

Master Lao and Xau Qu returned from Feng's just as breakfast was being served. (Though Master Lao has the lean, muscled body appropriate to a kung fu master, I have noticed that he never misses a meal, and I have always sought to emulate him in this regard.) His night had passed without any sign from the Kongbu Feixing Tou, and Master Lao listened with great interest to my description of Orange Blossom's visit (though I did omit certain slanderous lies she told as not being relevant to the matter at hand).

"Maybe the worst is over," said Master Lao. "Without a third victim, they won't be able to consecrate their temple. But just in case, I want Kua

Qing and Bang Zhou to bring back branches from a weeping mulberry today."

That said, Master Lao wrote down the needs for that night's festival and sent me out to procure them, then went to his room to sleep while he could.

Kua Qing returned with the weeping mulberry branches, and Master Lao brought us into his study to observe how arrows were crafted and consecrated. First the ends were cut off with a blessed knife, then the bark was carefully stripped away with a special circular tool. Next the shafts were cleansed in purified water, then again in salt.

Master Lao wrote out several prayers against evil, burned each in a silver tray, sifted the ashes into the ink dish, then pricked his thumb and let a single drop of blood fall into the concoction. He wrote out a very specific prayer against evil in a tiny hand on a slip of parchment, then carefully rolled it around the arrow shaft, repeating the process until he had 20 blessed shafts laying in various states of drying.

Next he took out a bag of eagle feathers, sorting through it for suitable candidates. Finally, he feathered and pointed each shaft. Though I'm sure a true fletcher could have done better and quicker work, each seemed lethal and well-honed.

That accomplished, Master Lao placed the arrows in a quiver, then took down the ceremonial bow which hung on his west wall, both of which he handed over to Kua Qing. (As much as it pains me to admit it, bowmanship is the one area of martial arts where Kua Qing's prowess exceeds my own. However, I attribute this to an entirely inadvertent incident early in my apprenticeship that resulted in my being banned from using the bow for three months, thus allowing Kua Qing to gain an unfair advantage.)

However, any pleasure Kua Qing had in this assignment was short-lived. Since the events of the last few days had interrupted our usual kung fu training, Master Lao decided to put us through a particularly grueling two-hour workout.

As twilight descended, Widow Zi came waddling up to the temple. She was a pleasant, matronly woman whose husband had been executed for smuggling opium by a most unpleasant method involving blocks of granite, a brazier, and a long, thin metal rod. She arrived out of breath and Master Lao invited her in to sit down. While Jade Willow made tea, she asked if anyone had seen Gau Lou that day.

Gau Lou was a local handyman who lived in a shack at the far end of the village. He never did work at the temple because my fellow apprentices and I were always available to provide manual labour. He was supposed to visit that morning to help clear brush around her house, but had never shown up. The news seemed to disturb Master Lao, who sent me to fetch the village map.

"Can you show me where Gau Lou's shack is?" he asked.

Widow Zi took a few moments to find her own house on the map, then pointed to a clearing near the forest. "There."

Master Lao made a charcoal mark, then brought out and laid down his reeds again, forming another triangle. This time the center of the triangle was centered on a large building near the center of the village.

"What's that?" asked Kua Qing.

"Spring Moon's noodle house," said Master Lao. "Quick, gather everyone up! We must go over there immediately!"

Master Lao quickly sorted through his prayer cabinet, procuring items for the coming battle: his herbal medicine kit, the lantern and mirror, rice paper and ink, several swords, two spears made from an ash tree, a bowl of sticky rice, and Kua Qing's bow and arrows.

We raced over to Spring Moon's. When we arrived, the door was closed, the screens drawn and the lanterns off. Master Lao banged on the door several times. It was finally unlocked and Spring Moon, her hair down, looked out quizzically. "Oh, Master Lao, it's you. Is there something wrong?"

Master Lao bowed apologetically. "Very possibly, madam. Please allow us to inspect your premises to ensure you come to no harm."

We entered quickly and formed a circle around Master Lao and Spring Moon, scanning the area for signs of the Kongbu Feixing Tou in the flickering lantern light. Except for the lovely Autumn Wind walking out of the kitchen, the building seemed empty.

"Check the windows," said Master Lao, and we moved to comply.

"What's going on?" asked Autumn Wind.

"There's a great evil at loose in the night," said Master Lao. "Are all the windows barred and charmed?"

Each of us went forward to verify that each window was locked, and that charms against evil were situated in each corner, a silk string connecting each to each in the shape of an X. We all nodded in turn indicating that our window was secure.

"Let me check the windows upstairs," said Autumn Wind, already starting up.

"It might be dangerous…" Master Lao began, but by that time I was already racing up the stairs just behind her. I arrived at her side just as she reached the second floor.

"It is dangerous for you to be up here alone!"

At that she smiled and I felt my heart melt again. "I already feel safer with you here, though I think you're being silly. There's nothing up here, but we can check the windows together."

We did so, and each appeared to be closed and properly charmed. The building appeared to be protected.

"See? Nothing to worry about," she said, smiling.

I returned her smile, but something nagged the back of my mind. "Is there no other way in? How about a back door? Or the chimney?"

"No, the back door is locked. And the flue is always closed when we're not cooking."

I looked around, then up. "What about the skylight? Is it locked?"

She frowned. "No, I didn't think of that. But who could possibly get in from the roof?"

Faced with the difficulty of explaining the exact nature of the evil loose, I avoid it entirely. "It should be locked just like the windows and doors."

"There's no lock on it," she said, "but I suppose we can tie it down." At that she had me fetch a small ladder, which she braced against the nearest pillar and started up.

"Do you need any help?" I asked.

"No, I can do it," she said, reaching for a black rope caught under the edge of the skylight door.

Only it wasn't a rope.

Autumn Wind screamed as the thing coiled around her hand, then jerked her upward as the skylight door flew open. Instantly I leapt up onto the ladder and grabbed her foot before she could be pulled out by her inhuman assailant.

Whatever writhing thing that gripped her was strong, but not quite strong enough to lift both of us. Still gripping Autumn Wind's foot, I leapt up and wrapped my legs around the pillar, pulling against the creature with all my might. Inch by inch I gained against it, Autumn Wind screaming all the while. I began to think I might be able to best it, when another half-dozen ropy tentacles descended from the darkness to grip Autumn Wind's arms and head. Suddenly I was wrenched from the pillar by the unseen foe's inhuman strength, and feared that both of us were doomed to be pulled into the night when I felt two hands gripping each of my ankles.

I looked back and saw Xau Qu and Bang Zhou hanging on. For once Xau Qu's bulk served him well, as the fiend we fought was not strong enough to lift all four of us. However, it still lurched and heaved against us, causing us to jerk and ripple like a segmented festival dragon. Painful as this was, my discomfort was increased by the disparity in weight between Xau Qu and Bang Zhou. However, Xau Qu had his own cause of complaint, as every jerk sent his head crashing into the pillar, each eliciting most strong and unpriestly oaths from his lips. And I can only imagine how much more agonizing the entire struggle must have been for poor Autumn Wind.

My own discomfort increased momentarily when the limber Bang Zhou climbed up my body as though it were a rope, then gripped my hair most painfully with one hand while he pulled a sword from his belt. Then, timing the swings, he leapt up to slash through the tangle wrapped around Autumn Wind's head. For a moment we had the advantage, but Bang Zhou's blow caused the beast to jerk so violently that a momentarily stunned Xau Qu lost his grip.

Though her head was free, Autumn Wind's arms were still in the monster's clutches. Bang Zhou raised his sword for another chop, when the strands holding Autumn Wind's right hand suddenly let go, only to instantly wrap themselves around Bang Zhou's swordarm. With a wrenching jerk, the sword fell from his grasp. I caught it as it fell, and it was now my turn to leap up and grab Autumn Wind's arm with one hand, while severing the strands that bound Bang Zhou.

Suddenly, the beast released its last grip on Autumn Wind and all three of us fell heavily to floor, scattering tables and chairs in our wake.

"Are you all right?" I asked Autumn Wind.

"My ankles hurt, and I think I'm an inch taller," replied Autumn Wind, "but other than that I'm AGGGGGGHHHHHH!"

Autumn Wind held out her arm, and the source of her distress became apparent. The black, ropey strands entangling her were revealed to be braided hair. Moreover, the strands still wrapped around her wrists seemed alive, and slithered steadily up her arms like snakes up a tree branch.

Dai Li and Ba Le came running up the stairs, spears in hand, as Bang Zhou and I each pulled the animate hair off Autumn Wind. "Quick, get a prayer lantern!" I instructed as the braids writhed in our hands. When Lai Wang brought the lantern, Bang Zhou and I both consigned the unnatural locks to its flame. As they burned, there was a terrible scream above the noodle house.

Then the skylight door flew open, and *they* descended.

Orange Blossom was there, and Old Man Zhang, and Gau Lou, who I vaguely recognized. But all our eyes were inevitably drawn towards the inescapable presence of the Kongbu Feixing Tou Queen.

She possessed a cold, inhuman beauty, with pale skin, high cheekbones, long, thin fangs, and onyx eyes with cats-eye pupils of fire. All around her, several yards in every direction, floated myriad ropey tresses of lustrous black hair, each of which seemed to writhe of its own accord. However, it was what was *in* her hair which was most alarming of all.

Dozens of shriveled heads, pale skin stretched like parchment over their skulls, floated entangled in her hair. Their eyes were dead except for tiny flames in each orb, pale reflections of their Queen's fiery visage. Each of their mouths moved wordlessly, issuing the rattling, hissing sound of a dying old man's laboured breathing.

"Well, look what we have here!" she said in archaic Mandarin. "A clutch of fresh and juicy worms for the nest! If you think your old man's pathetic bush magic will thwart my will you are sadly mistaken!"

"Demon, I've faced far worse than you before," said Master Lao, raising his staff. "Be gone from this place, or face your own destruction!"

"Your soul will make a most splendid feast, little priest!" At that her unnatural hair convulsed, sending a screaming horde of her skull minions flying towards us, teeth bared.

Thrusting Autumn Wind towards the stairs behind me, I split the first attacker in half with Bang Zhou's sword, and then struck another a glancing blow. Ba Le managed to skewer still another, but both he and Dai Li were quickly forced to use their spears as staffs as more and more attacked. Behind us, the other apprentices lobbed sticky rice prayer balls at the horrors, and where their shots connected the skulls blackened and fell to the ground. But every time one was destroyed, two more seemed to take its place. Soon there were too many to stand against, and I and the other apprentices fought a desperate withdrawal down the stairway.

"The lantern!" cried Master Lao. "Quickly!"

Lai Wang unhooded the lantern and directed it towards Master Lao, who reflected the beam off the octagonal silver mirror and into the creatures. The beam caught one of the flying skulls squarely, and it uttered a horrifying shriek, then exploded in a shower of dust. So too, when the beam passed across Gau Lou's head, his hair burst into flame before he fled its radiance. Soon Gau Lou's panicked flight resulted in several small fires around the noodle house, Spring Moon and Autumn Wind following frantically in his wake with pitchers of water to douse the flames.

However, when Master Lao directed the beam against the Queen, she laughed as her hair readily blocked it.

"Your little mirror might work on the undead, little priest, but do you really think it would affect one forged in the Lower Hells?"

"Kua Qing, the bow!" cried Master Lao.

Kua Qing hopped up onto a table, pulled out an arrow, aimed, and fired all in one smooth motion. The arrow flew straight at the Queen, but she easily plucked it out of the air with her hair, then gasped in pain and dropped it as her strands caught fire.

"Weeping mulberry arrows!" hissed the Queen, shaking out the flames. "You're more clever than I thought! But it will avail you nothing. Get the bowman!"

The mob of skulls we had been fighting suddenly rose up and over our heads, making a beeline for Kua Qing. Chanting, Master Lao leapt up onto the table in front of him, assuming the crane stance as his palms took on the unmistakable glow of Lao Dan Hands.

And then the fight was *truly* on.

We raced back to form a protective perimeter around Kua Qing. Swords, hands and spears struck with all the skill we could muster, sending the skulls hurtling back from our blows. Gau Lou (his head finally extinguished), Orange Blossom and Old Man Zhang all swooped and dove, trying to sink their fangs into our necks, or, failing that, entangle us in their viscera. As Master Lao's glowing blows hurtled around him like a firework prayer wheel, Kua Qing hunkered low on the table, popping up every now and then to shoot another arrow, but none ever made it beyond the Queen's hair. Spring Moon and Autumn Wind cowered beneath the table, stabbing out with their kitchen knives anytime one of the horrors came near.

Alas, they had not counted on the speed of a White Crane apprentice, and an instant after I had kicked one of the skulls across the room, I received a painful but shallow wound in my right calf from Autumn Wind's knife.

"Sorry!" she cried, aghast. But there was no time for recriminations, as Gau Lou suddenly raced for my neck. I jerked back just in time for his lunge to miss, then slashed him with the sword. It connected cleanly, almost cleaving his face in two and getting stuck in his skull. Despite the blow he was far from finished, as his viscera snapped up and around my neck.

"You'll pay for that!" he said wetly.

There proceeded a most strange and desperate dance, as I simultaneously attempted to pull the sword free and remove Gau Lou's burning tendrils from around my throat, succeeding at neither task. Soon Bang Zhou and Ba Le came to my assistance.

"Is that my sword?" asked Bang Zhou, as Ba Le attempted to unwrap the tendrils.

I nodded and answered to the extent possible, but due to the circumstances my assent sounded rather like a choking sheep.

"May I have it back?"

I agreed as best I could, sinking to my knees as my sight started to dim.

Bang Zhou gripped his sword with both hands while levering his left foot firmly against Gau Lou's entrails. With a mighty tug he wrenched the sword free, then swiftly brought it to bear at the exposed length of viscera mere inches away from my throat.

I would have thought the blow sufficient to sever it, but it was unnaturally tough. However, it did cause the creature to let me loose and attempt to ensnare Bang Zhou instead. The three of us quickly wrestled it to the ground, ignoring the pain in our hands as we held it down, Bang Zhou bringing the sword down again and again without apparent effect.

"Quick, hand me a prayer ball!" I cried, and one of the younger apprentices complied. Avoiding Gau Lou's unnatural teeth, I spread apart his jaws.

"Happy festival day!" I said, then shoved the sticky-rice wrapped offering into his mouth. Gau Lou let out a horrific scream. Then exploded.

Whatever demonic magic had held Gao Lo's decay at bay ceased, and the three of us found ourselves covered in tiny bits of putrefying remains. As we attempted to wipe them off, the Kongbu Feixing Tou Queen screamed in rage. "You wretched little maggots! You think slaying a single acolyte will stop me? Your pain shall be legendary!"

The battle seemed to be turning, if ever so slightly, in our favour. The blackened remains of a dozen skull servants littered the floor, but more still swooped above our heads. Kua Qing was down to his last six arrows, having dispatched several of the skull minions, but unable to bring down the Queen. Encouraged by our example, he took aim at Orange Blossom's flying form, launching an arrow that missed by a hairsbreadth.

Master Lao leapt up yet again to dispatch two of the flying skulls trying to swoop in on Kua Qing, but as he landed the much abused table issued a loud *crack* and collapsed under him, and he and Kua Qing went crashing down upon Spring Moon and Autumn Wind.

Our enemies took that moment to redouble their assault, and it was all we could do to hold them back as Spring Moon and Autumn Wind sprinted for another table. However, Old Man Zhang managed to evade Dai Li's spear thrust and attached himself to Spring Moon, sinking his fangs into her neck as his tendrils wrapped around her body. In a flash, Kua Qing drew an arrow, aimed, and fired, striking Zhang 's head dead center. Zhang let out a bellow of pain as his head and viscera ignited, quickly burning down to ash in a matter of seconds.

Autumn Wind frantically batted out the tiny flames on her mother's dress caused by Zhang 's combustion. "Mother, are you all right? Mother? *Mother?*"

Spring Moon didn't answer, her breathing shallow and unnaturally raspy, a fine network of dark lines already starting to spread out from the wound in her neck. Seeing this, Master Lao sprung into action, laid out both his herbal kit and his brush and ink set, then instantly started to scribe runes around the wound. "Chou Lin, this will take several minutes. You must defend Kua Qing!"

I nodded and raced back to the fight. There seemed only a half dozen of the skull things left, in addition to Orange Blossom, but the Queen herself had waded into the fight. She had ensnared both of Xau Qu's arms, but was unable to bring her fangs to bear upon him due to the chair he held between them.

I quickly grabbed the prayer lantern from Lai Wang and raced to Xau Qu's side. As they struggled, I wrestled one of the ropey strands from his arms and stuck it into the lantern's opening. The Queen let out another below of rage as her hair ignited, letting loose of Xau Qu and knocking both of us across the room in her haste to shake out the flames.

"So you like fire, little man? Then have some fire!" At that the Queen opened her mouth and let loose a jet of flame, singeing my robes as I leapt away. I rolled across the floor to extinguish them, then scurried under a table to avoid the next fiery assault, which set it ablaze. Grabbing the table by its legs, I rushed back at her, using it as both a shield and weapon.

Unfortunately, I did not count on the Queen plucking the table from my grasp and tossing it back at me. I leapt just in time, receiving only a glancing blow to my left shoulder as it hurtled past.

Thinking the Queen distracted, Kua Qing let loose another arrow, but once again she snatched it from the air in mid-flight. Worse still, Orange Blossom chose that moment to swoop in on Kua Qing, wrapping her entrails around the bow. Kua Qing resisted with all his might, refusing to let the weapon be stolen from him without a fight. For a moment it was a tug-of-war.

Then the bow snapped in two.

Kua Qing went flying back, half of the broken bow still gripped in his hands, the remaining arrows in his quiver scattering across the floor. The Queen laughed, a sound inhumanly shrill and throaty at the same time. "Time's up, vermin! Your pathetic attempts have failed! You may have slain two of my acolytes, but it's easy enough to make more!"

At that the Queen rushed forward and snatched up Kua Qing, Autumn Wind and Master Lao, binding each so tightly with her hair that they were unable to free their arms no matter how hard they struggled.

"You've got spirit, little priest! That is why you shall make such a splendid slave when I eat your soul!"

As the Queen raised Master Lao to her lips, I grabbed one of the arrows off the floor, leapt up to grab his robe, and then clambered onto his shoulders just before the Queen bestowed her deadly kiss.

"Eat this!" I said, thrusting the arrow directly into her gaping maw.

The Queen let out a deafening bellow of pain and rage, dropping her captives (and myself) unceremoniously to the floor. Flames licked out of her mouth and the wound at the back of her neck where the arrow had pierced, and then expanded until an inferno raged where her head had been, her hair writhing madly in its death-throes. All around the noodle house, Orange Blossom and the remaining skull minions suffered a similar fiery fate. The Queen let out a last scream and exploded in a shower of vile dust and ash.

We lay on the floor for a long moment, victorious, befouled and exhausted. Bang Zhou took the initiative to grab a pitcher of water and extinguish those portions of the noodle house set alight by the final conflagration. Master Lao climbed unsteadily to his feet, dusting himself off and coughing, then turned to me and bowed, a gesture nearly as shocking and unusual as battle had been.

"Chou Lin, you are a credit to the temple, and it is an honour to have you as a White Crane apprentice."

For a moment I was struck entirely dumb, as Master Lao's compliments were nearly as rare as summer snow. Finally, I got unsteadily to my feet and returned the bow. "It is, and has always been, a great honour to serve as your apprentice."

Master Lao merely grunted, then returned to ministering to Spring Moon. "Will my mother be alright?" asked her daughter.

"Yes. Look, the unnatural infection is already starting to fade."

Autumn Wind sighed in relief, then wrapped her arms around and kissed me, an event as shocking as it was welcome. I could not tell you how long that kiss lasted, though it seemed as if several dynasties rose and fell during its duration. It was far too short.

"Thank you for saving us, Chou Lin," she said at last. I'm sure I made some reply to this, as I distinctly remember my mouth moving and sounds coming out of it, but I could not say with any certainty what was said for all the taels in Shanghai.

At that moment, exhausted and exultant, I truly knew what it was to be one with the Celestial Masters, to know the perfect contentment of balance and being, to move with the wind and be as still as the earth, to bask in the fullness of the world like a flower in the sun.

But even as I felt that moment of divine clarity passing, I thought I could see the path before me: a life together with Autumn Wind, a wedding presided over by Master Lao, a clutch of laughing, exasperating children, agile as cats and as mischievous as imps (how could they be otherwise, given their father?), growing old in joy and contentment.

Alas, it was not to be, as Autumn Wind and I would soon be ripped apart by the strange events surrounding an ancient scroll, a most unusual monkey, and three cursed coins.

But that's a story for another day.

USING IT AND LOSING IT
Jonathan Lethem

Stories by Jonathan Lethem (b. 1964) began to appear in the specialist science-fiction magazines in 1989 and they showed signs then of an especially radical talent, heavily influenced by Philip K Dick. His first novel, Gun, With Occasional Music *(1994), which blended hard-boiled detective fiction with bizarre images of science fiction, rapidly brought him to the attention of the literary scene and he has since gone on to establish a formidable reputation. His collection,* The Wall of the Sky, the Wall of the Eye *(1996), won the World Fantasy Award whilst his novel,* The Fortress of Solitude *(2003), where two children discover a means to become superheroes, became a* New York Times *bestseller. You can guarantee that every story by Lethem will be experimental or radical or surreal. Take the following, which considers the significance of language.*

They sent Pratt to Montreal for a three-day conference, but after the first day he stopped attending the meetings, and spent the remainder of the long weekend wandering around the streets of the city. He liked Montreal, though at first he didn't understand why. It reminded him of America, of the United States; not the least bit exotic – in fact it was startlingly familiar. The only difference was that he couldn't understand what other people were saying. And that was what he liked.

Pratt had taken Spanish in high school. He passed the classes, but only narrowly, and he didn't retain any memory of the language. He certainly didn't have any handle on the French he heard around him in

Montreal. He went to the store for cigarettes and pointed; first at the brand he wanted, then at the bowl of matches behind the cash register. He switched on the television in his hotel room and watched the news in French (weathermen gesturing at the odd Canadian-based map) and was unable to understand anything; all he could puzzle out were the categories: international news, local items, sports, weather, human interest. The news seemed very simple that way; reduced to a series of formats it became oddly small and comprehensible.

Pratt felt alone. He felt alone in New York, and it was a feeling he thrived on; his aloneness insulated him, made it possible for him to live in the city. Now, in Montreal, he felt the flowering within himself of a potential for a new kind of aloneness, something much deeper, and something more unique. Walking alone through a city of strangers, unable to share their language, suggested enticing possibilities to him.

Back in New York the following week Pratt walked the distance to work, stopped in at his accustomed cigar store to buy cigarettes, and rode the elevator upstairs to his office; in short, his standard routine, without deviation – yet it didn't feel right. Pratt felt hemmed in by the people around him for the first time, his invisible Gardol shield of isolation stripped mysteriously away. He heard snippets of conversation as he passed or was passed on the sidewalks, and the packets of language landed unbidden on the doorstep of his consciousness, and intruded on his cool solitary thoughts. The cigar man struck up a needless conversation about the humidity, despite Pratt's silently pointing at the desired items, the way he had in Montreal.

Pratt isolated himself in his office, put his folder of papers into the bottom drawer of his desk, then gathered the accumulated inter-office memos of the last week and balled them up and threw them away without reading them. Pratt had learned something about not being reached in Montreal, and he determined to apply it directly to his job. At some deeper level he knew that such an attitude would quickly mean the end of his job, but he could live with that. The path he was about to follow would lead him far beyond his job. He was on the verge, he felt, of developing a philosophy.

Pratt wondered what came next. He was carefully retying his shoelaces when the door to his office opened. It was Glock, Pratt's supervisor, and the man who'd chosen Pratt for the Montreal deal. Glock didn't come into the office; he leaned in the doorway, crossing his arms. His face was expressive and rubbery; now it expressed a scowl.

"You didn't find things interesting in Montreal? Geez. You should've called. Northern's guy really liked you, he really did, he called me to ask if anything was the matter. What's the matter? Didn't you like the guy? He said you two hit it off. That's a good connection, Pratt. You should've called, we could have talked about it. What's the matter?"

Pratt winced at the flood of language Glock undimmed in his direction. He couldn't even remember the guy from Northern. "I don't feel good," he told Glock.

"Geez. You don't look that good. You don't feel good? You didn't feel good?"

"I didn't feel good."

"You should have called. You don't feel good? Geez, go home. This isn't high school, Pratt. Go home if you don't feel good."

Pratt went home. He did his best to avoid overhearing conversations on the way back, taking side streets and veering wide when he passed couples or groups of people. A grey man with a tattered hat stepped up from against the side of a building and stuck his hand out at Pratt. "Spare change man? I gotta get something to eat." Pratt edged away from him without answering.

By the time he was safely back in his apartment Pratt had formulated his new ambition: he wanted a divorce from the English language. He felt amazed at the simplicity and grace of his plan. The relationship he strove to strike up with the world was uniquely shallow: the world consistently misunderstood, and pressed him for further commitment. Pratt wanted to turn the world down, definitively this time, and the abandonment of the language of his fellow men seemed to him the perfect embodiment of this ideal.

Pratt knew from lifelong experience that words sometimes slipped free of their meanings when he repeated them over and over, or wrote them down again and again; they became abstract, and refused to adhere. Words could hemorrhage, and bleed empty of their lifeblood meaning. He decided to perfect this technique, if it could be perfected, to systematize it, and through it, forget the entirety of the English language. The very thought of it made him hungry and impatient for this loss, for the empty completeness of it, like a man finally stepping free of his shadow, yet he knew it would take a long time – years perhaps. Pratt didn't mind. He knew he could rein in his impatience, he knew he had what it took. He knew he was good for it.

Nonetheless, Pratt shook with excitement. He went into the living room and sat down in the middle of the couch, fighting to breathe evenly and cleanly, struggling not to cross his legs. I'll start now, he told himself, and began searching for a word with which to begin. *I'll lose my first words first,* he thought; *that's the proper way to do it.*

Mommy, mommy, mommy, Pratt thought heavily and intentionally. He said it aloud: "Mommy, mommy, mommy, Mommy-mommymommy." He groped on the coffee table for a legal pad and scribbled the word again and again in looping script; mommy, mommy, mommy.

The syllables were perfect, near nonsense to begin with, and they lost their meaning for Pratt almost immediately. But he didn't stop there. He pressed on, his tongue swelling on big mommymommy syllables, spittle collecting in the corners of his mouth, four pages filled with illegible mommymommy and then on to the fifth, pencil point blunted fat like tongue, mommymommymommy.

He killed the word and flogged its corpse, only stopping when he couldn't go on, collapsing back on the couch, exhausted. The word was gone, eradicated, nowhere to be found. Pratt waited, but it didn't come back. He probed for it fearfully, turning over mossy stones in his consciousness, but no mommy crawled out. He looked at the pages of scribbled mommymommy but it seemed another language to him, unreadable, meaningless, baffling. The word was gone. *One down,* he thought.

The next word took less time, and the one after that even less. Pratt was suspicious; he checked each word for its absence, but each seemed obediently banished. He finished with dad, then cat, then man and bad and boy, then hat and hot together, repeating them alternately: hathothathothathothathot. He finished a dozen words before he felt his eyelids slipping down towards the floor, his grip loosening on his pencil. He put himself to bed.

The next morning he deliberately avoided the living room, where the coffee table sat littered with sheets of the yellow pad. The words – whichever words they had been – were gone, and he didn't want them back. As he sipped his coffee in the kitchen he grew increasingly pleased with the events of the previous night, and increasingly resolute. Waking with a smaller vocabulary was exhilarating; he felt lighter, freer, less hemmed in. The clear priority was to send the rest of the language packing, the sooner the better.

After cleaning up in the kitchen, Pratt went out for a walk in the park. The crisp air felt good in his lungs, and the sun felt good on his head. There was nobody in the park yet. Pratt warmed up by disposing of tree and sky, defying categorical reality by staring up at the oak leaves drifting in the wind against a backdrop of blue even as he eradicated the words. This done, he felt immediately ready for bigger things. He rid himself of a couple of unusual, once-in-a-while words: sundial and migraine, mixing them into midial and sungraine before allowing them to fade completely.

It got easier and easier. Even the most tenacious words proved banishable after fifteen or twenty repetitions, and some others slipped away after Pratt pronounced them twice. He'd developed a muscle for destroying language, and it grew strong through exercise. Pratt spent the day wandering through the park, forgetting words: he forgot words as he clambered over boulders and he forgot words while he lay with his eyes closed on the great lawn. When he got hungry he found a vendor and bought a hot dog, and in the process of eating it killed hot dog, killed frank, killed wiener and sausage and wurst, until all the words disappeared and he was left to finish a nameless tube of meat.

Things seemed to like being unnamed; they expanded, became at once more ambiguous and more real. The speech Pratt heard as people strolled past seemed littered with meaningless, musical phrases; their sentences were coming unhinged, and the less Pratt understood the more he liked. As meaningful words assailed his ears he spoke them and rendered them meaningless, then tossed away their empty husks to the invisible wind.

Pratt arrived home exhausted, yet buoyant. He no longer feared the yellow pad on the coffee table; he rushed in and happily made neither head nor tails of it. He opened a book from his shelf and read a sentence, delightedly baffled by most of it; when he found a word he knew he pronounced it and it disappeared. He had it down to a single utterance now. To use a word was to lose it.

Glock called. It jolted Pratt to be on the telephone. He hurriedly conducted a search for the words that were left, to try and patch together a response.

"You should see a doctor," said Glock. "It's paid for, it's taken out of your paycheck, so why not just go? Do you know a good doctor? Why don't you see mine?"

Pratt didn't understand. "Overabundant," he said. "Inconspicuous." He couldn't think of anything else to say.

"Dr Healthbronner, 548-7980," Glock went on. "He's good, I've known him for twenty years. I mean, Jeezus, take care of yourself. You sound like shit."

"Shit," repeated Pratt into the receiver. Without knowing it, Glock had opened up a whole new category of words. "Piss crap cunt prick snatch," said Pratt. The words disappeared as he mouthed them.

"Okay, okay, Jeezus," said Glock. "I was only trying to help. Stay home, for god's sake, stay home until you feel better. One hundred percent. Call me if you need anything." He hung up.

The call unnerved Pratt. His job, he saw, was lost to him forever. Quite a lot, in fact, was lost to him forever. He began to wish the process had not gotten so automatic. The few words left began to seem more and more like commodities, things to be treasured. Not that he didn't want to finish the job, eliminate the language entirely, but now it seemed important to savour its going, to draw the process out.

He slept fitfully that night, and although he had never been a somnolinguist he awoke several times, bathed in sweat and trembling slightly, to the sound of his own voice calling out some stray word into the darkness, always too late to know what he was losing. He felt he'd only slept an hour or two when the sun began to creep through the window.

Pratt showered, shaved, and flossed his teeth, trying to pull himself together. Words surfaced from the murk of his consciousness and he struggled not to say them aloud. He pushed them into a corner of his mind, a little file of what he had left, and like the tiles on a Scrabble tray he shuffled and reshuffled them, trying to form coherent sentences. It was a losing struggle. He could feel words receding, becoming abstract and meaningless just from his thinking about them over-strenuously; he reached the point where for a word to remain meaningful he needed to hear it spoken aloud, given the tangibility of speech, and he lost several words this way, because by now anything he spoke aloud destroyed itself, immediately and forever.

After a thin breakfast Pratt went downstairs, but after walking halfway to the park he was caught in a sudden rain shower, and forced back to his apartment. He was unlocking his apartment door when the phone began ringing, and fumbled impatiently at the lock while it rang, twice, three times, four times; he dropped his keys in the foyer and jogged through the dark apartment to the phone. It seemed suddenly terribly important to answer it.

It was a wrong number. "Dan Shard?" asked the voice on the other end.

Pratt had already surrendered *no* to the void. He made a guttural sound into the line.

"Dan Shard? Who's there? May I speak to Mr Shard?"

Pratt shook his head, made the sound again.

"Mr Shard?"

"Pratt," said Pratt, before he could stop himself. "Pratt," he said again, wonderingly, and then the word vanished.

"I'm sorry," said the voice on the line, and hung up.

Pratt saw now that he was painting himself into a corner, in a room where the paint would never dry, where he would have to climb onto the wall, and begin painting that, and then from there onto the ceiling. The horizon of consciousness grew nearer and nearer. The world at large might be round but Pratt's world was flat, and he was about to fall off the edge of it.

That night he watched the news on the television. The only words Pratt understood on the programme were the neologisms: Crisisgate, Lovemaker Missile, CLOTH Talks, Oopscam and Errscam. Advertisements seemed bewildering and surreal. Switching the channels Pratt eventually stumbled on a station consisting exclusively of these miniature epics, one ad after another. He watched this station, transfixed, for almost half an hour, when it came to him that they were rock videos.

He called Glock back, but got the answering machine. Pratt had saved up a last message, a cry for help, and felt deflated at not being able to deliver it. It was already losing its meaning in the storeroom of his consciousness, and he decided to leave it on Glock's tape.

"Well, I'm not home," went Glock's voice. "Relax. I'll be back. Just leave a message. Just leave a message, and I'll call, and we'll talk. Relax." The machine beeped.

"Ebbing," blurted Pratt. He felt proud at having saved such a simple word for so long. The rest of the message wasn't so easy. "John-Hancocked auto-mortality affidavit," he continued. "Disconsolate." He paused for effect, and then delivered the last word, the only word he had left, the payload. "Bereft," he said, giving it all he had, the full thespian treatment. The machine clicked off between the two syllables of the word.

Pratt put the phone down. He couldn't think of any more words. He went to the bathroom and brushed out his tired mouth with mint toothpaste, then went into the living room and gathered up the books on his shelves and carried them out to the incinerator.

Pratt slept surprisingly well that night, cool between the sheets, his mind empty. He didn't dream. When he awoke he felt cleansed; with the furniture of language finally cleared the movers' footprints could be wiped away, and the dust-bunnies swept out of the corners. There was nothing left to forget: English had become a foreign language to him, and the world was rendered innocent of connotation. His doubts about the process evaporated. He'd panicked momentarily, been a little weak in the knees, but now that he was language-free he knew how little cause he'd had for alarm. He awoke into a rightness, his wish granted. Like a snail with its shell Pratt now lugged his own private Montreal around on his back. He was a tourist everywhere, a tourist originating from a land so private and complete that it didn't require a language.

He went downstairs, and out. The sun was busy clearing the puddles away, and Manhattan warmed into activity. Pratt walked up Broadway, feeling confident. Everything seemed bigger now, more promising and mysterious, and, most importantly, further away. He considered going in to work; they couldn't harm him now that he'd become invulnerable. The air was filled with the musical chatter of conversation – the forest couldn't harm him now that he'd become invulnerable. The air was filled with the musical chatter of conversation as the forest air is filled with the singing of birds; New York transmuted itself into a wonderland of incomprehensibility.

Pratt passed a shopkeeper haggling with a fat black woman over the price of bananas; she waved her curled-up money and cradled the bananas like a long lost child. Pratt frowned disapprovingly at how much she communicated, beyond language, and at how much he picked it up despite himself. Pratt saw a teenage boy on a skateboard perform a flourish for a gaggle of girls who idled in a building entrance; transfixed by the subtleties of the interaction, Pratt had to tear himself away from it. Suddenly the walls of comprehension were closing in again.

A pair of businessmen with briefcases parted on the sidewalk to make room for Pratt to pass, and though their language seemed a babble of water-rushing-over-rocks, Pratt felt astonished at what he learned from their manner, their expressions and gesticulations. It was inescapable. Like a blind man whose other senses attune themselves in compensation, Pratt found himself involuntarily sensitized to non-verbal forms of communication.

He panicked, turned around and headed back towards his apartment, reverting to his former strategies of steering wide berths around groups of people who might be tainted with language. As he ran Pratt struggled to understand this new predicament, racking his brains like a snake-bit man who had once learned the formula for the antidote.

There was clearly more to communication than language; that had been an underestimation of his opponent, a mistake Pratt knew he couldn't afford to make twice. It seemed clear enough; he was going to have to forget body language.

Back safe in his apartment, Pratt sat on the couch and began shrugging mechanically.

THE ALL-AT-ONCE MAN
R A Lafferty

R A Lafferty (1914–2002) was unique amongst the annals of science fiction. It's almost impossible to categorise his work because although much of it uses the standard images and icons of science fiction, they are just pieces on a board game for which Lafferty seems to make up the rules as he goes along. His stories are anarchic and at times incomprehensible, and yet they can be compelling.

Their delight comes from Lafferty's acute observation of the illogicality of the lives we lead and his marvellous use of language. There are phrases dotted through his stories that make you stop in your tracks in amazement. Lafferty seldom starts from an obvious point and never takes an obvious route, and yet somehow you reach a natural conclusion in his stories.

The following, about a man's quest for immortality, is one of his more easily accessible stories, though it's no less extreme in its conclusion. There have been several collections of Lafferty's stories, many from specialist presses, and most are worth tracking down, including Nine Hundred Grandmothers (1970), Strange Doings (1972) and Through Elegant Eyes (1983), but there is so much more.

A fan website devoted to Lafferty and his work is www.mulle-kybernetik.com/RAL/

I

...let him know that the word translated "everlasting" by our writers is
what the Greeks term aionion, *which is derived from* aion, *the Greek for*
Saeculum, *an age. But the Latins have not ventured to translate this by*
secular, *lest they should change the meaning into something widely*
different. For many things are called secular which so happen in this
world as to pass away even in a short time; but what is termed aionion
either has no end, or lasts to the very end of this world.

The City of God – Saint Augustine

This is an attempt to assemble such facts (hard and soft) as may yet
be found about a remarkable man who seemed to be absolutely
balanced and integrated, yet who developed a schizo-gash deep as a
canyon right down the middle of his person. Dr George Drakos says he
developed three or four such schizo-gashes.

This is also an attempt to record some of the strange goings-on in the
house on Harrow Street – and it is a half-hearted (no, a faint-hearted or
downhearted) attempt to record the looser goings-on in the subsequently
forever house on Harrow Street. The subject is a man who had
everything, took hold of something beyond and was broken to pieces by
it. Or was not.

"I want to be the complete man," John Penandrew used to say to
himself. "I want to be the complete man," he would say to all of us who
would hear him. Well, he was already the most complete man that any
of us had ever seen. He had been a promising young man: as Don
Marquis has said of himself, and had been a promising young man for
twenty years. But Penandrew didn't show those twenty years at all, except
in his depth.

His eyes, his shape, his everything was just as all had been when he
left Monica Hall twenty years before: he had been a gilded youth then
– or at least he had been plated over with a very shiny substance. He

still was, he was still that youth, but in his depth he was a full man, sure and mature, and with the several appearances together and unconflicting. For he was also the boy he had been thirty years before, in no detail changed. He had been a loud-mouthed kid, but smart all the time and smooth when he wanted to be. Now there was a boy, a youth and a man, three non-contradictory stages of him looking out of his grey eyes. His complexity impressed me strongly. And it also impressed four men who were not as easily impressed as I was.

There were five men who knew everything; and there was myself. We met loosely two or three times a year. The five men who knew everything were this John Penandrew (he was in banks as his father had been); Dr George Drakos, who was Greek and who used to go to Greek school in the evenings; Harry O'Donovan, who was a politician as his fathers had been forever; Cris Benedetti, an ex-seminarian who taught literature and esoterica at the university; and Barnaby Sheen, who was owner of the Oklahoma Seismograph Enterprizes.

These five men were all rich, and they all knew everything. I wasn't and I didn't. I belonged to the loose group by accident: they had never noticed that I alone had not become rich or that there were evident gaps in my information.

We had all gone to school twenty years before to the Augustinians at Monica Hall and minds once formed by the Augustinians are Augustinian forever. We had learned to latch onto every sound idea and intuition and to hold on forever. At least we had more scope than those who went to school to the Jesuits or the Dominicans. This information is all pertinent. Without the Augustinian formation John Penandrew would never have shattered – he'd have bent.

"I've decided not to die in the natural course of things," John Penandrew said softly. The other four of those men who knew everything didn't seem at all surprised.

"You've given enough thought to it, have you?" Cris Benedetti asked him. "That's really the way you want it?"

"Yes, that's the way I want it," John Penandrew said. "And I've considered it pretty thoroughly."

"You've decided to live forever then, have you?" Barney Sheen asked with just a hint of boyish malice.

"Naturally not to live forever here," Penandrew attempted to explain. "I've decided to live only as long as the world lasts, unless I am called from my plan by peremptory order. I am resolved, however, to live for very many normal lifetimes. The idea appeals to me strongly."

"Have you decided just how you will bring this about?" Dr George Drakos asked.

"Not fully decided. I've begun to consider that part only recently. Of first importance is always the decision to do a thing. The means of carrying it out will have to follow that decision and flow from it. There is no real reason why I shouldn't be able to do it, though."

"No, I suppose not," Cris Benedetti said thoughtfully. "You're an intelligent man and you're used to tall problems. But there have been other intelligent men and, as far as I know, none of them has done this thing."

"Do you know of any really intelligent man who has decided to do this and then has failed in the doing?" Penandrew asked.

"No, not if you put it that way," Cris admitted. "Most problems remain unsolved simply because they have never been tried seriously and in the proper framework. And there are legends of men (I presume them to have been intelligent) who have done this thing and are doing it. Not very reputable legends, though."

"Well, what is it then, an elixir of youth that you'll be seeking?" Harry O'Donovan asked in his high voice.

"No, Harry, that idea is clearly unworkable. It couldn't be taken seriously by anyone except a youth," Penandrew talked it out carefully. "It will not be an elixir of youth: it will be an elixir of all ages – that, I believe, is the crux of the matter. I do not want to be only a youth forever or for a very long time – I am more than just a youth now. It would not be possible to remain a youth forever."

"Then what?" O'Donovan demanded. "I don't believe you've thought this out very thoroughly, John. Do you want to live for a very long time and you getting older and older and older all that time?"

"But I have thought it out pretty thoroughly, Harry. I will get old only at one end, only in depth. I will become a complete man – and then still more complete. I believe there is no record of any really complete man's ever dying – that's the thing."

"I believe there is no record of any complete man at all," George Drakos said. "That's really the thing."

"There's probably been a large handful of us," Penandrew said. "I know pretty well what I want to do and I know pretty well what it consists of. I will become every aeon of myself simultaneously; then I will have become a complete man – and then I will not die. There is a meaning within a meaning of the old word aeon. Aeon means ages. But the pleroma or plentitude is made up of substantial powers called aeons. I maintain that these two meanings are the same. In Gnosticism the aeon is one of the group of eternal beings that combine to form the supreme being – all are eternal and simultaneous but no one of them would be eternal out of combination. I believe that there is analogy on the human plain; and I intend to become that analogy, to be all my ages simultaneously and forever, to be every aeon of myself. I will be forever a boy, forever a youth, forever a man and forever an old man. I'm already something of this multiple appearance, I'm told. I guarantee that I'll be a boy forever. I'll nail down that end."

"And what happens when the old man in you gets older and older and dies?" Drakos said.

"I don't know what will happen but I'm certainly interested in knowing, George. Possibly I will assume a still older man and then a still older. I'm not sure there is a necessary connection between very old age and death. It may be, though, that the extreme aeons of me will pass over the edge and give me a foot in each world. I'd like that. The possibilities are almost endless. But I believe that the boy in me, the youth in me, the man in me will live for innumerable lifetimes."

"Oh brother!" Harry O'Donovan sounded in his high voice. "And how will you be doing it all? Not by talking about it, I'll bet."

"Yes, I will do it by considerable talking about it and by much more thinking about it," Penandrew ventured. "It is not a thing for gadgets or apparatuses, though I may employ them some. It is a thing, I believe, of mental and physical disposition and I tell you that I'm well disposed toward it."

This John Penandrew who lived in the big house on Harrow Street was married to Zoe Archikos. Barney Sheen would like to have been married to her. So would Cris Benedetti and Harry O'Donovan. So would George Drakos except that she was his cousin. Zoe was a creature that has become fairly rare these last twenty-five centuries: a blonde Grecian, a veritable Helen, a genuinely classic model with that brassiness that must go with it. The bronze age understood the necessity of this high brass, but we have forgotten.

Oh, she was form and life, she was perfection and brindled passion – and she was also the blast of a brass horn. John Penandrew was fortunate in having her; she should have been elixir enough for anyone. But he was fortunate in almost everything.

"The fathers tell us that Adam, in his preternatural state, enjoyed all ages at once," Barney Sheen said, "so it is not strictly true that he had no childhood, even though he was created adult. He was created all ages at once. It was a good trick till he broke it. And, by coincidence, I recently ran into the still surviving legend of the one man who, since Adam, is most persistently believed to have been all ages at once and to be still alive."

"Coincidence, which is simultaneity, is valid when it touches a simultaneous man as I am becoming," John Penandrew said with what would have been pomposity in another man. "Ah – where did you run into the latest legend of Prester John, Barney?"

"In Ethiopia. I have several crews doing petroleum exploration work there and I visited there recently. Some of the simple local workmen talk of the everlasting man as if he were a present-day presence."

"Near Magdala, was it?" John Penandrew asked with sudden eagerness.

"About seventy miles northwest of there, on the Guna slopes."

"I was sure it was near. Magdala, of course, is a modern name-form of old Mogadore, the legendary kingdom of Prester John."

"That's impossible," George Drakos cut in. "Anyone with even an elementary knowledge of the Amharic language would know that the one name could not change into the other."

"Anyone with even an elementary knowledge of anything would know that both names are from the Geez and not the Amharic language," Cris Benedetti sneered, "and there is a strong possibility that the two names are the same, George."

(It is sometimes confusing to have these acquaintances who know everything.)

"But *you* can't do it John, in Ethiopia or anywhere; you can't be the simultaneous man," Cris continued. "You haven't the integrity for it."

"Why not, Cris? I pay tithes of cummin and that other stuff. I love my wife and many other persons. I have a pleasant way with my money and I do not grind the faces of the poor. Why haven't I integrity?"

"You have common decency, John, but not integrity," Cris said. "I use the word to mean unified totality and scope – that is integrity in the theological sense. I use the word as Tanquerey uses it."

(They used to study Tanquerey's Dogmatic Theology in the seminaries. Now they study rubbish.)

"There are several ways I can go about this," Penandrew said. "I believe that we originally had this simultaneity and everlastingness as a preternatural gift. Then we were deprived of it. But it remains a part of our preternatural nature. This means that we must be deprived of it all over again every day or it will flow back into us. It could be as simple a thing as actinic rays depriving us of this handy gift of everlasting life. I've studied these possibilities a little. I could have a series of silver plates or baffles set into my head to combat the rays. That's one way."

"What's the other ways?" Barney Sheen asked.

"Oh, proper disposition of mind and body. Induced mystic states combined with my natural powers and proclivities. I believe that there may be gadgetry employed as a trigger – but only as a trigger for the alteration. I believer that it will be mostly realizing a state of being that already belongs to us, something that belongs to our preternatural nature."

"Or our unnatural nature," Barney said. "You didn't use to play so loose with words. What's the other way, John?"

"Oh, I may go and find Prester John and learn how he's been doing it these thousands of years," John Penandrew said. "And I will go and do likewise."

"Did you ever hear anything like that, Laff?" Barney asked me. "Has the subject ever been handled in your – ah, pardon my smile – field?"

"Several stories have handled the subject," I said, "but not in the variation that Penandrew wants to give it."

II

Saying: O grandfather,
the little ones have nothing of which to make a symbol.
He replied, saying:
…they shall make of me their symbol
…the four division of days (stages in life)
they shall enable themselves to reach and enter…
Legends. Appendix to a Dictionary of the Osage Language –
Francis La Flesche

John Penandrew was out of town for about a year. When he came back he had a different look to him. Oh, he had simultaneity now! He really had it. It was the boy he had been thirty years ago; he was the youth he had been twenty years ago; he was the man he should have been now and he was also an older man. He was all these several persons or ages at once, much more than he had been before – all of them, completely and unconflictingly. He had pulled it off. He was truly the simultaneous man. But that isn't exactly what we mean when we say that he had a different look to him.

In all his simultaneous persons he had something just a little bit lopsided about him. One eye was always just a little bit larger than the other. There was more than a hint of deformity and there shouldn't have been this in a complete man.

But he was the complete man now. He had done it. He had pulled the coup. He was wound up all the way and he would live forever unless he flew apart. This was no fakery. You could feel that he had done it.

He lived in the big house on Harrow Street with the brassy classy Zoe and they lived it to the hilt. There wasn't ever anyone in such a hurry to have so much fun so fast. They were perfervid about it. But why should he be in such a hurry when he had forever?

Well, he had money and he had talent and he had Zoe. The boy was strong in him now (he had been a loud-mouthed kid but smart all the time and smooth when he wanted to be); the youth was in him very strong (he had been a gilded youth or at least a very brassy one); and the man and the older man were vital and shouting in him. The Penandrews were cutting a wide swath and they were much in the papers. But what was John's big hurry now?

"Add one dimension, then you might as well add another." He grinned with a grin a little too lopsided for a complete and simultaneous man. "Speed, that's the thing. Speed forever and lean heavy on that hooting horn."

But it was another year before myself and those five men who knew everything were all together again.

John Penandrew lolled with his lopsided grin as though he were too full of mischief to talk. And Barnaby Sheen wound into one of his cosmic theses, of which he had hundreds:

"Just before the Beginning there was a perfect sphere and no other thing." Barney spoke in his rich voice. "At least it supposed itself to be a perfect sphere – it had no imperfect spheroid with which to compare itself. It suspected that it was revolving at a very high rate of speed, such a rate of speed that it would immediately fly apart if the rotation could be established as fact. But in relation to what point could it be rotating?

"It was not in space – there was no space beyond it; how could there be? It could not be in motion, of course, there being nothing relative to it. Neither could it be at rest – in relation to what could it be at rest? It was not in time nor in eternity, there being nothing to pose it against in either aspect. It had no size, for there was nothing to which it might be compared – it might be a pinhead in size, or a mega-megalo. It had no temperature, it had no mass, it had no gravity – all of these things are relative to other things.

"Then an exterior speck appeared. This was the Beginning, not the sphere's lone existence. The mere speck was less than one billionth to the billionth power the diameter of the sphere and was at much more than a billion billions of diameters from it. Now there was both contrast and relationship.

"Now there was size and mass and temperature, space, time and motion; for there was something to relate to. The sphere was indeed found to be in furious and powerful rotation, now that it could rotate in relation to something. It was in such rapid rotation that it deformed itself with its own centrifugal force, it ruptured itself, it flowed apart completely and everything thence is from its pieces.

"What happened to the speck? Was it consumed in the great explosion? Probably not. Likely it had never existed at all. It was a mere illusion to get things started. Say, I consider that an excellent 'In the Beginning' bit. Can you use that, Laff? Can you make a piece out of that piece?"

"I will use it some day," I said.

"The important thing about that speck was its duration." John Penandrew licked the words out with a tongue that now seemed a little lopsided. "It lasted for much less than a billionth of a billionth of a second. It was in contrast to the short-duration speck that the then-happening cosmos acquired its delusion of immortality."

"You are sure it is a delusion, Pen?" Cris Benedetti asked anxiously, as though much depended on the answer.

"Yes, all a delusion," Penandrew grinned. "We cosmic types call it the workable delusion, and we will work it for all it is worth."

"Tell us the truth, Penandrew," Barnaby Sheen said gruffly. "Did you really do it? And how did you do it?"

"I really did it, Barney. I'll not die. I'll dance on your graves and on the graves of your great-great-grandchildren. I'll make a point of it. I'll dance naked on the graves as David danced before the Ark."

"Why such frenzied pleasure in our going, Pen?" Cris asked with some hurt.

"It's the boy in me. He's a bit monstrous now and he's me. I can't change him or any of us or it will all collapse. It's mine. I'll hang onto it. I'll bow my back. I won't give an inch ever. I've got a mind-set in me now – that's a big part of it."

"Yes, I believe you did pull it off, Penandrew," Barney said slowly. "How did you do it, though? By elixir? By plates against the rays? By Prester John's secret? How?"

"Oh yes, I finally lifted the secret from Prester John himself and now I will not die in the natural course of things. But I'll not tell you about it. You don't need to know about it. Why should you want to know?"

"We also might want to avoid dying in the natural course of things," Doctor George Drakos said softly.

"No, no that's impossible," Penandrew shouted. "I won't be done out of it by anyone. I'll hold onto it for dear life – and that is exactly the case of it."

"Is it an exclusive thing?" Harry O'Donovan asked, "and it can't be shared?"

"It cannot be shared," Penandrew said harshly. "It isn't anything like you think it is. It isn't at all as I thought it might be. It became a freak in its general withdrawal. It's a jealous thing. It's a snake in the hand and it must be held tightly. It isn't the preternatural thing I thought it would be. It's an unnatural thing now – and only one person in the world can have it at a time, for all time. I won't let go of it. Hack my hands off – but I won't let go of it!"

"How *is* Prester John?" Barney Sheen asked in a strong low tone.

"Oh, leave off the legends," Harry O'Donovan sounded angrily. "If there was a Prester John ever – he's been dead these thousand year."

"No, About eighteen months," Penandrew said. "I found him alive. And now he is dead."

"You killed him," Barney said simply.

"How would I kill him?" Penandrew protested. "He died of old age and God knows that that is the truth. He crumbled to dust. Why should he not have died of old age? Do you know how long he had been around? He saw Rome fall. And Jerusalem."

"What did you take from him?" Barney Sheen asked.

" I took the jealous thing, the only thing. And now I will not die in the natural course of things. He wanted me to take it. He had been trying to give it to someone for a long time."

"That is the truth?" Sheen asked.

"That is the truth," Penandrew said. And it was the truth, we all knew that, but it was a lopsided truth. Penandrew left us suddenly then.

"May the sun come up on him crooked in the morning," Harry O'Donovan said bitterly.

But in the big house on Harrow Street, John and Zoe Penandrew lived it up to the haft. It was speed forever and lean heavy on the hooting horn. There was something a little disreputable about the couple now – if that word can be used of rich and positioned people.

John grew older only in the old man of him. The boy in him was still the boy, the youth still the youth, the man still the man. He was living at least four lives at once, all at high speed and all forever. Zoe became more buxom and more classic, more brassy, more lively. If she aged at all she did it entrancingly and disgracefully – but not ungracefully. There was nobody like her. She was full and overflowing always.

All the fun that could be crammed into every day and night! Speed, and the dangerous teetering that goes with very high speed. They went on forever.

Actually they went on for ten years. Then Zoe left him and he broke up.

No. He broke up first and then she left him.

"I lost it," he said, "and I couldn't have. Nobody could ever have got it out of my grip."

III

For his duration too there is a word – the word
Aevum or Aeviterntiy, the duration of that in which
its essence or substance knows no change:
though by its accidents it can know change...
Theology and Sanity – F J Sheed

It was then that the doings in the house on Harrow Street took a peculiar turn. Things had been hectic when Zoe was there; they had been noisy and publicized. But, whatever Zoe was, she was always High Brass. She'd had class. Now the house and happenings degenerated.

John Penandrew brought those three nephews of his into the big house to live with him. They were a crass bunch. There was something pretty low about them, and they brought John pretty low. A man should not be ashamed of his poor relations, of course: he should help them if they need help; and perhaps it was the essence of charity that John should take them into his own house. John had real charity in his heart; there is no taking that away from him. He also had baser things there and they began to pour out of it now. The three nephews were bums and John Penandrew became a bum along with them. Rich bums are the worst kind.

And there was no doubting the kinship. All three of the fellows had the family look strongly. They were loudmouths, as John had always been a little – but they were not smart and they were not smooth, as John could be when he wished. They all had what I can only call a facial deformity and they had it to a grotesque degree where John had it only to a minor extent. It was that lopsided look. It was that one eye bigger than the other. Coming out of that clan, John Penandrew came by his own slight deformity honestly.

There were low-life doings at the big house on Harrow Street. The four Penandrew males each seemed to bring in seven cronies worse than himself. There were riotous doings there and the black maria was a frequent visitor to those doors. There was the aroma of stale evil in all this and John hadn't used to be a bad sort of man.

John Penandrew talked rationally but sadly whenever we came across him.

"I should never have taken the thing," he said. "I knew before I finally seized it that it was wrong and unnatural. And, having taken it, I should have been willing to let it go easier when I found what deformity it really was. 'The corruption of the best is the worst –' do you remember when we were taught that? This excellent gift was taken away from us long ago, and for a reason. I had it as a tainted and forbidden remnant, and I held onto it like a snake in the hand. But I will not easily give up any strong idea that I have held. I have an intransigent mind. Do you remember when we were taught to have *that*? I held it too tight, and it shattered me."

And in fact John Penandrew was a shattered man now – or a splattered one. The sap had been all drained out of him, as though the nephews were sapsuckers or bloodsuckers who preyed on him. He weathered badly. Now he looked older than he was and he no longer looked all ages at once. He aged monstrously – he leered and lolled. He seemed to be returning to most unaromatic dust.

He had given up his chairmanships of the boards and his associations with the banks. It was their loss. He had always been very smart in matters of business and policy. He knew that that was finished with him now. He took his money and went home.

And that home was a shipwreck. The middle nephew was as queer as a glass-egg goose. He had a stack of morals charges against him and John Penandrew had thousands of dollars of bond out on him. He was an almost personable fellow, but he was slanted – how he was slanted!

The youngest nephew was no more than a boy – a cat-killing, window-breaking, arsonous vandal who led a wild pack and always left a trail right up to the Harrow Street house. What things he got away with because he was not yet adult! And him much more intricate than the adults who had to deal with him and much more deadly – it is pretty certain that he killed larger and higher things than cats and broke more fragile things than windows.

The oldest nephew, a twisted humorist, an almost good fellow, was the instigator of the endless series of sick parties held in the big house, the procurer of the dozen or so florid witches who always came with the dark. He was an experimenter in the vices, an innovator of reputation.

John Penandrew had become an old and dirty caricature of himself. There was something artificial about him now, as though he were no more than a mask and effigy propped up on a display float at some garish carnival. The shape he was in, John Penandrew surely could not go on forever and he didn't.

After about three years of cohabitation with the nephews, John Penandrew died. That should have wrecked the legend. Maybe not, though. Well, it really seemed that he did *not* die in the natural course of things. There was something most unnatural about the course of his dying, as though he had turned to dust before he died; as though what died was not himself at all; as though the dying were an incident, almost an afterthought.

He wasn't much more than fifty years old. He looked ninety. Zoe didn't come to the funeral.

"He isn't in very good shape right now," she said. "I'll wait a few months, and then go back to him when things are looking a little better with him." She wasn't at all distraught; she was just not making sense. She left the country the night before the funeral.

After the funeral mass, after the Zecharih Canticle when the body is taken out from the church, Barnaby Sheen whispered to the priest in the vestibule:

"I don't believe you've got him all there."

"I don't believe so either," the priest whispered back.

Zoe inherited.

The nephews? No, they didn't get anything.

There was something a little bit loose about those nephews. They weren't – ah – seen again. No trace was found of them, either backward or forward. They simply hadn't been. In the legal and recorded sense, at least, John Penandrew hadn't had any nephews. He had had attributes, we suppose, but not nephews. Well, peace to the pieces of the poor rich man!

———————————

It's a moral paradigm, really, of a man who reached for too much and was shattered by it. It's a neat instance of final moral compensation and seemliness. Yes, except that it wasn't near; that this wasn't the final part of it; and that the compensation was not particularly moral.

It was not neat because there were pieces left sticking out of it – a primordial brass horn that surely wasn't Gabriel's; and three, at least, noisy persons in the house on Harrow Street.

But it was not stated that the nephews were not heard from again. They *were* heard. Oh how they were heard! They were the noisiest unbodied bodies that ever assaulted honest ears. They and their florid witches (unseen also) made the nights – well – interesting for quite some months in that long block on Harrow Street.

This was the first phase of the Haunted House in Harrow Street. It was featured in Sunday supplements everywhere, likely in your own town paper. It was included in books like *Beyond the Strange*. It became a classic instance.

And that was only the first phase of the Haunted House episode. The next phase was not so loudly trumpeted (don't *use* that word in this case) to the world. There was a tendency to play it down. It was too hell-fire hot to handle.

Zoe came back to town, bright and big and brassy as ever. A classic personage. Zoe. How the classic has been underestimated and misunderstood! But she came in almost silently, muted brass with only a hint of the dazzle and blare.

"I believe that things will be looking a little better with my husband John now," she said. "He should be better composed by this time. I am his wife. I will just move in with him again and be the proper wife to him."

"Move in where?" Harry O'Donovan asked aghast, "into the grave?"

"Oh no, I'll move back into the house on Harrow Street and live there with my husband."

"Zoe, did you take the, well, thing from John?" Barney Sheen asked curiously.

"Yes, I took it, Barney, but only for this short while. I'll give it back to him now. He may be able to cope with it this time. I don't need such things for myself. This time I am certain that we will have a long and entertaining life together. All things coalesce for us now."

"Zoe, you're not making sense. John Penandrew is dead!" Cris Benedetti shouted.

"Who isn't?" she asked simply. "I'll be you though, Cris…" (raucous horn blowing in the far distance) "that he's more alive than you are at this minute. Or you or you or you or you. If any of you were as alive as he is, I'd have you."

"You're out of your wits, Zoe," George Drakos said and blinked. There was something the matter with Drakos' eyes, with all of our eyes. Somewhere a brassy shimmer of the second brightest light that human eyes will ever see. The four men who knew everything did not know Zoe Archikos: much less did I.

Zoe moved back into the house on Harrow Street. And how was it with her there? Noisy, noisy. Some things at least coalesced for her or into her: among these, the florid witches who used to come with the dark. Their voices had been so jangling because they were broken voices, part voices. Now they were together in that dozen-toned instrument, the red-brass, the flesh-brass. They had never been anything other than wraiths of her. Now she was all one again.

There was some evidence also (shouting, grisly evidence) that the aeons or nephews or attributes had all coalesced into John Penandrew again.

Well, that is the sort of thing that a town must live with, or die with; but it will not live on a normal course.

———————

Listen. No, not with your ears! Listen to your crawling flesh! Did you yourself ever meet a man after you had seen him dead? It does give you a dread, does it now? There was no need of elaboration. John Penandrew was a humorist but by the time he had become a little edgy of horror humor. There was none of that coming through the walls business. He came in normally by the door and sat down.

"Jesus Christ!" Barney Sheen moaned. "Are you a ghost, John?"

"The very opposite," Penandrew said softly. "In fact, I had to give up the ghost." Penandrew was *that* kind of humorist, but even bad jokes are shocking from a man who's supposed to be dead.

"It wasn't all of you in the coffin was it, John?" Barney asked in wonder.

"No. Only my older aspect went over the edge. I once thought that this would give me a foot in each world and I was curious about it. It didn't work that way. I have no consciousness of that aspect now; nor, I suppose, has he of me. I shuffled off the mortal coil there. I've won. That's something. Nobody else ever won at it, except those like Zoe who were already preternatural."

"You're a damned zombie, Penandrew!" Harry O'Donovan cried in shrill anger.

"Can a zombie be damned?" Penandrew asked. "I don't know. Tell me, Cris. You were the theology student. For damnation is there not required a nature of a certain moment? But I'm of another moment now. *Momentum,* I am saying, which means a movement and a power and a weight; and 'moment of time' is only part of its meaning and only part of mine."

"Damn your Latin! You're a deformity," O'Donovan cried.

"Yes, I'm a deformed curve, the one that never closes on itself," Penandrew said with his lopsided smile. "Barney Sheen's 'In the Beginning' bit left something out. There was what might have been a perfect sphere, yes. There was, possibly, an exterior speck for contrast. I say that there was something else, one curve that would not close when everything else closed into the rather neat package that called itself The Cosmos, the Beauty. There was one shape left over. I am part of that other shape. Try being a little lopsided sometimes, men. You'll live longer by it."

That was the last real talk that we ever had with John Penandrew. He never sought our company again and we sure never sought his.

———————————

Nobody else lives in that long block on Harrow Street now, but the noises are over-riding in that whole part of town. There is nothing the law can do. It is always that beautifully brassy woman there when they call and always with her artless answers:

"It is only myself and my husband together here," Zoe says, "and we taking our simple pleasures together. Is that so wrong?" Even coppers get that funny look in their eyes when they have been hexed by the prevading sound of the brass winds.

Old boys and young men often gather near that house at night and howl like wolves from the glandular ghosts that the strange flesh calls up in them. But even the most aroused of them will not attempt the house or the doors.

The Penandrews are a unique couple taking their pleasures together all at once forever, and so violently as to drive the whole town stone-deaf – like those old stone-deaf statues, their only real kindred? For these two will not die, in any natural course of things, not with that big loud bright brassy horn blowing in a distance, and at absolute close range, all at once, everywhere, unclosed, lopsided. It's the ending that hasn't any end. The Stone is found, and it's an older texture than the philosophers believed. The transmutation is accomplished, into brass. Classic and *koine*: this is the Zoe who dies hardly forever; this is the Penandrew, the man of the wrong shape.

The four men who know everything understand it now.

And I do not.

ELOI ELOI LAMA SABACHTHANI

William Hope Hodgson

This is the one classic story I chose to include because despite its age it remains a remarkable story. What's more, its author, William Hope Hodgson (1877–1918), who was killed in the First World War, was a writer of extraordinary gifts and produced what might well be classified as the most extreme fantasy ever written, The Night Land *(1912) set in an unimaginably distant future of perpetual darkness on an Earth inhabited by bizarre monsters.*

His other novels were The Boats of the "Glen Carrig" *(1907),* The House on the Borderland *(1908) and* The Ghost Pirates *(1909). He wrote many short stories, including a series featuring the investigations of an occult detective,* Carnacki the Ghost Finder *(1913). He had been a merchant seaman in the 1890s and produced many atmospheric strange stories of the sea, some collected as* Men of the Deep Waters *(1914).*

Almost all of his work has been reprinted in recent years, including a five-volume definitive series from Night Shade Books, and a volume of miscellaneous items, The Wandering Soul *(2005). Amongst the websites devoted to Hodgson and his work is www.thenightland.co.uk*

The following, apart from some slight comparison with the Carnacki stories, is unlike anything else Hodgson wrote. He completed the story in January 1912 but was unable to find a market. That's not too surprising, considering the subject matter, which some may have regarded as blasphemous. It was not until after his death that his widow, Betty, who meticulously kept track of Hodgson's writings and continued to try and sell them after the War, managed to place it with Nash's Illustrated Weekly. *It appeared there in the issue for 17 September 1919 under the title "The Baumoff Experiment".*

The story is reprinted here under Hodgson's original working title, which were amongst the last words Christ spoke on the cross, and translate as "My God, my God, why have You forsaken me?"

Dally, Whitlaw and I were discussing the recent stupendous explosion which had occurred in the vicinity of Berlin. We were marvelling concerning the extraordinary period of darkness that had followed, and which had aroused so much newspaper comment, with theories galore.

The papers had got hold of the fact that the War Authorities had been experimenting with a new explosive, invented by a certain chemist, named Baumoff, and they referred to it constantly as "The New Baumoff Explosive".

We were in the Club, and the fourth man at our table was John Stafford, who was professionally a medical man, but privately in the Intelligence Department. Once or twice, as we talked, I had glanced at Stafford, wishing to fire a question at him; for he had been acquainted with Baumoff. But I managed to hold my tongue; for I knew that if I asked out pointblank, Stafford (who's a good sort, but a bit of an ass as regards his almost ponderous code-of-silence) would be just as like as not to say that it was a subject upon which he felt he was not entitled to speak.

Oh, I know the old donkey's way; and when he had once said that, we might just make up our minds never to get another word out of him on the matter as long as we lived. Yet, I was satisfied to notice that he seemed a bit restless, as if he were on the itch to shove in his oar; by which I guessed that the papers we were quoting had got things very badly muddled indeed, in some way or other, at least as regarded his friend Baumoff. Suddenly, he spoke:

"What unmitigated, wicked piffle!" said Stafford, quite warm. "I tell you it is wicked, this associating of Baumoff's name with war inventions and such horrors. He was the most intensely poetical and earnest follower of the Christ that I have ever met; and it is just the brutal Irony of Circumstance that has attempted to use one of the products of his genius for a purpose of Destruction. But you'll find they won't be able to use it, in spite of their having got hold of Baumoff's formula. As an explosive it is not practicable. It is, shall I say, too impartial; there is no way of controlling it.

"I know more about it, perhaps, than any man alive; for I was Baumoff's greatest friend, and when he died, I lost the best comrade a man ever had. I need make no secret about it to you chaps. I was 'on duty' in Berlin, and I was deputed to get in touch with Baumoff. The government had long had an eye on him; he was an Experimental Chemist, you know, and altogether too jolly clever to ignore. But there was no need to worry about him. I got to know him, and we became enormous friends, for I soon found that *he* would never turn his abilities towards any new war-contrivance, and so, you see, I was able to enjoy my friendship with him, with a comfy conscience – a thing our chaps are not always able to do in their friendships. Oh, I tell you, it's a mean, sneaking, treacherous sort of business, ours, though it's necessary; just as some odd man, or other, has to be a hangsman. There's a number of unclean jobs to be done to keep the Social Machine running!

"I think Baumoff was the most enthusiastic *intelligent* believer in Christ that it will be ever possible to produce. I learned that he was compiling and evolving a treatise of most extraordinary and convincing proofs in support of the more inexplicable things concerning the life and death of Christ. He was, when I became acquainted with him, concentrating his attention particularly upon endeavouring to show that the Darkness of the Cross, between the sixth and the ninth hours, was a very real thing, possessing a tremendous significance. He intended at one sweep to smash utterly all talk of a timely thunderstorm or any of the other more or less inefficient theories which have been brought forward from time to time to explain the occurrence away as being a thing of no particular significance.

"Baumoff had a pet aversion, an atheistic Professor of Physics, named Hautch, who – using the "marvellous" element of the life and death of Christ, as a fulcrum from which to attack Baumoff's theories – smashed at him constantly, both in his lectures and in print. Particularly did he pour bitter unbelief upon Baumoff"s upholding that the Darkness of the Cross was anything more than a gloomy hour or two, magnified into blackness by the emotional inaccuracy of the Eastern mind and tongue.

"One evening, some time after our friendship had become very real, I called on Baumoff, and found him in a state of tremendous indignation over some article of the Professor's which attacked him brutally; using his theory of the *Significance* of the 'Darkness', as a target. Poor Baumoff! It was certainly a marvellously clever attack; the attack of a thoroughly trained, well-balanced Logician. But Baumoff was something more, he was Genius. It is a title few have any rights to, but it was his!

"He talked to me about his theory, telling me that he wanted to show me a small experiment, presently, bearing out his opinions. In his talk, he told me several things that interested me extremely. Having first reminded me of the fundamental fact that light is conveyed to the eye through the means of that indefinable medium, named the Æther. He went a step further, and pointed out to me that, from an aspect which more approached the primary, Light was a vibration of the Æther, of a certain definite number of waves per second, which possessed the power of producing upon our retina the sensation which we term Light.

"To this, I nodded; being, as of course is everyone, acquainted with so well-known a statement. From this, he took a quick, mental stride, and told me that an ineffably vague, but measurable, darkening of the atmosphere (greater or smaller according to the personality-force of the individual) was always evoked in the immediate vicinity of the human, during any period of great emotional stress.

"Step by step, Baumoff showed me how his research had led him to the conclusion that this queer darkening (a million times too subtle to be apparent to the eye) could be produced only through something which had power to disturb or temporally interrupt or break up the Vibration of Light. In other words, there was, at any time of unusual emotional activity, some disturbance of the Æther in the immediate vicinity of the person suffering, which had some effect upon the Vibration of Light, interrupting it, and producing the aforementioned infinitely vague darkening.

"'Yes?' I said, as he paused, and looked at me, as if expecting me to have arrived at a certain definite deduction through his remarks. 'Go on.'

"'Well,' he said, 'don't you see, the subtle darkening around the person suffering, is greater or less, according to the personality of the suffering human. Don't you?'

"'Oh!' I said, with a little gasp of astounded comprehension, 'I see what you mean. You – you mean that if the agony of a person of ordinary personality can produce a faint disturbance of the Æther, with a consequent faint darkening, then the Agony of Christ, possessed of the Enormous Personality of the Christ, would produce a terrific disturbance of the Æther, and therefore, it might chance, of the Vibration of Light, and that this is the true explanation of the Darkness of the Cross; and that the fact of such an extraordinary and apparently unnatural and improbable Darkness having been recorded is not a thing to weaken the Marvel of Christ. But one more unutterably wonderful, infallible proof of His God-like power? Is that it? Is it? Tell me?'

"Baumoff just rocked on his chair with delight, beating one fist into the palm of his other hand, and nodding all the time to my summary.

How he *loved* to be understood; as the Searcher always craves to be understood.

"'And now,' he said, 'I'm going to show you something.'

"He took a tiny, corked test-tube out of his waistcoat pocket, and emptied its contents (which consisted of a single, grey-white grain, about twice the size of an ordinary pin's head) on to his dessert plate. He crushed it gently to powder with the ivory handle of a knife, then damped it gently, with a single minim of what I supposed to be water, and worked it up into a tiny patch of grey-white paste. He then took out his gold tooth-pick, and thrust it into the flame of a small chemist's spirit lamp, which had been lit since dinner as a pipe-lighter. He held the gold tooth-pick in the flame, until the narrow, gold blade glowed whitehot.

"'Now look!' he said, and touched the end of the tooth-pick against the infinitesmal patch upon the dessert plate. There came a swift little violet flash, and suddenly I found that I was staring at Baumoff through a sort of transparent darkness, which faded swiftly into a black opaqueness. I thought at first this must be the complementary effect of the flash upon the retina. But a minute passed, and we were still in that extraordinary darkness.

"'My Gracious! Man! What is it?' I asked, at last.

"His voice explained then, that he had produced, through the medium of chemistry, an exaggerated effect which simulated, to some extent, the disturbance in the Æther produced by waves thrown off by any person during an emotional crisis or agony. The waves, or vibrations, sent out by his experiment produced only a partial simulation of the effect he wished to show me – merely the temporary interruption of the Vibration of Light, with the resulting darkness in which we both now sat.

"'That stuff,' said Baumoff, 'would be a tremendous explosive, under certain conditions.'

"I heard him puffing at his pipe, as he spoke, but instead of the glow of the pipe shining out visible and red, there was only a faint glare that wavered and disappeared in the most extraordinary fashion.

"'My Goodness!' I said, 'when's this going away?' And I stared across the room to where the big kerosene lamp showed only as a faintly glimmering patch in the gloom; a vague light that shivered and flashed oddly, as though I saw it through an immense gloomy depth of dark and disturbed water.

"'It's all right,' Baumoff's voice said from out of the darkness. 'It's going now; in five minutes the disturbance will have quieted, and the waves of light will flow off evenly from the lamp in their normal fashion. But, while we're waiting, isn't it immense, eh?'

"'Yes,' I said. 'It's wonderful; but it's rather unearthly, you know.'

"'Oh, but I've something much finer to show you,' he said. 'The real thing. Wait another minute. The darkness is going. See! You can see the light from the lamp now quite plainly. It looks as if it were submerged in a boil of waters, doesn't it? that are growing clearer and clearer and quieter and quieter all the time.'

"It was as he said; and we watched the lamp, silently, until all signs of the disturbance of the light-carrying medium had ceased. Then Baumoff faced me once more.

"'Now,' he said. 'You've seen the somewhat casual effects of just crude combustion of that stuff of mine. I'm going to show you the effects of combusting it in the human furnace, that is, in my own body; and then, you'll see one of the great wonders of Christ's death reproduced on a miniature scale.'

"He went across to the mantelpiece, and returned with a small, 120 minim glass and another of the tiny, corked test-tubes, containing a single grey-white grain of his chemical substance. He uncorked the test-tube, and shook the grain of substance into the minim glass, and then, with a glass stirring-rod, crushed it up in the bottom of the glass, adding water, drop by drop as he did so, until there were sixty minims in the glass.

"'Now!' he said, and lifting it, he drank the stuff. 'We will give it thirty-five minutes,' he continued; 'then, as carbonization proceeds, you will find my pulse will increase, as also the respiration, and presently there will come the darkness again, in the subtlest, strangest fashion; but accompanied now by certain physical and psychic phenomena, which will be owing to the fact that the vibrations it will throw off, will be blent into what I might call the emotional-vibrations, which I shall give off in my distress. These will be enormously intensified, and you will possibly experience an extraordinarily interesting demonstration of the soundness of my more theoretical reasonings. I tested it by myself last week' (He waved a bandaged finger at me), 'and I read a paper to the Club on the results. They are very enthusiastic, and have promised their co-operation in the big demonstration I intend to give on next Good Friday – that's seven weeks off, to-day.'

"He had ceased smoking; but continued to talk quietly in this fashion for the next thirty-five minutes. The Club to which he had referred was a peculiar association of men, banded together under the presidentship of Baumoff himself, and having for their appellation the title of – so well as I can translate it – 'The Believers And Provers Of Christ'. If I may say so, without any thought of irreverence, they were, many of them, men fanatically crazed to uphold the Christ. You will agree later, I think, that I have not used an incorrect term, in describing the bulk of the members of this extraordinary club, which was, in its way, well worthy of one of the religio-maniacal extrudences which have been forced into temporary being by certain of the more religiously-emotional minded of our cousins across the water.

"Baumoff looked at the clock; then held out his wrist to me. 'Take my pulse,' he said, 'it's rising fast. Interesting data, you know.'

"I nodded, and drew out my watch. I had noticed that his respirations were increasing; and I found his pulse running evenly and strongly at 105. Three minutes later, it had risen to 175, and his respirations to 41. In a further three minutes, I took his pulse again, and found it running at 203, but with the rhythm regular. His respirations were then 49. He had, as I knew, excellent lungs, and his heart was sound. His lungs, I may say, were of exceptional capacity, and there was at this stage no marked dyspnoea. Three minutes later I found the pulse to be 227, and the respiration 54.

"'You've plenty of red corpuscles, Baumoff!' I said. 'But I hope you're not going to overdo things.'

"He nodded at me, and smiled; but said nothing. Three minutes later, when I took the last pulse, it was 233, and the two sides of the heart were sending out unequal quantities of blood, with an irregular rhythm. The respiration had risen to 67 and was becoming shallow and ineffectual, and dyspnoea was becoming very marked. The small amount of arterial blood leaving the left side of the heart betrayed itself in the curious bluish and white tinge of the face.

"'Baumoff!' I said, and began to remonstrate; but he checked me, with a queerly invincible gesture.

"'It's all right!' he said, breathlessly, with a little note of impatience. 'I know what I'm doing all the time. You must remember I took the same degree as you in medicine.'

"It was quite true. I remembered then that he had taken his MD in London; and this in addition to half a dozen other degrees in different branches of the sciences in his own country. And then, even as the memory reassured me that he was not acting in ignorance of the possible danger, he called out in a curious, breathless voice:

"'The Darkness! It's beginning. Take note of every single thing. Don't bother about me. I'm all right!'

"I glanced swiftly round the room. It was as he had said. I perceived it now. There appeared to be an extraordinary quality of gloom growing in the atmosphere of the room. A kind of bluish gloom, vague, and scarcely, as yet, affecting the transparency of the atmosphere to light.

"Suddenly, Baumoff did something that rather sickened me. He drew his wrist away from me, and reached out to a small metal box, such as one sterilizes a hypodermic in. He opened the box, and took out four rather curious looking drawing-pins, I might call them, only they had spikes of steel fully an inch long, whilst all around the rim of the heads (which were also of steel) there projected downward, parallel with the central spike, a number of shorter spikes, maybe an eighth of an inch long.

"He kicked off his pumps; then stooped and slipped his socks off, and I saw that he was wearing a pair of linen inner-socks.

"'Antiseptic!' he said, glancing at me. 'Got my feet ready before you came. No use running unnecessary risks.' He gasped as he spoke. Then he took one of the curious little steel spikes.

"'I've sterilized them,' he said; and therewith, with deliberation, he pressed it in up to the head into his foot between the second and third branches of the dorsal artery.

"'For God's sake, what are you doing!' I said, half rising from my chair.

"'Sit down!' he said, in a grim sort of voice. 'I can't have any interference. I want you simply to observe; keep note of *everything*. You ought to thank me for the chance, instead of worrying me, when you know I shall go my own way all the time.'

"As he spoke, he had pressed in the second of the steel spikes up to the hilt in his left instep, taking the same precaution to avoid the arteries. Not a groan had come from him; only his face betrayed the effect of this additional distress.

"'My dear chap!' he said, observing my upsetness. 'Do be sensible. I know exactly what I'm doing. There simply *must be distress*, and the readiest way to reach that condition is through physical pain.'

"His speech had becomes a series of spasmodic words, between gasps, and sweat lay in great clear drops upon his lip and forehead. He slipped off his belt and proceeded to buckle it round both the back of his chair and his waist; as if he expected to need some support from falling.

"'It's wicked!' I said. Baumoff made an attempt to shrug his heaving shoulders, that was, in its way, one of the most piteous things that I have seen, in its sudden laying bare of the agony that the man was making so little of.

"He was now cleaning the palms of his hands with a little sponge, which he dipped from time to time in a cup of solution. I knew what he was going to do, and suddenly he jerked out, with a painful attempt to grin, an explanation of his bandaged finger. He had held his finger in the flame of the spirit lamp, during his previous experiment; but now, as he made clear in gaspingly uttered words, he wished to simulate as far as possible the actual conditions of the great scene that he had so much in mind. He made it so clear to me that we might expect to experience something very extraordinary, that I was conscious of a sense of almost superstitious nervousness.

"'I wish you wouldn't, Baumoff!' I said.

"'Don't – be – silly!' he managed to say. But the two latter words were more groans than words; for between each, he had thrust home right to the heads in the palms of his hands the two remaining steel spikes. He gripped his hands shut, with a sort of spasm of savage determination, and I saw the point of one of the spikes break through the back of his hand, between the extensor tendons of the second and third fingers. A drop of blood beaded the point of the spike. I looked at Baumoff's face; and he looked back steadily at me.

"'No interference,' he managed to ejaculate. 'I've not gone through all this for nothing. I know – what – I'm doing. Look – it's coming. Take note – everything!'

"He relapsed into silence, except for his painful gasping. I realised that I must give way, and I stared round the room, with a peculiar commingling of an almost nervous discomfort and a stirring of very real and sober curiosity.

"'Oh,' said Baumoff, after a moment's silence, 'something's going to happen. I can tell. Oh, wait – till I – I have my – big demonstration. I'll show that brute Hautch.'"

"I nodded; but I doubt that he saw me; for his eyes had a distinctly in-turned look, the iris was rather relaxed. I glanced away round the room again; there was a distinct occasional breaking up of the light-rays from the lamp, giving a coming-and-going effect.

"The atmosphere of the room was also quite plainly darker – heavy, with an extraordinary sense of gloom. The bluish tint was unmistakably more in evidence; but there was, as yet, none of that opacity which we had experienced before, upon simple combustion, except for the occasional, vague coming-and-going of the lamp-light.

"Baurnoff began to speak again, getting his words out between gasps. 'Th' – this dodge of mine gets the – pain into the – the – right place. Right association of – of ideas – emotions – for – best – results. You follow me? Parallelizing things – as – much as – possible. Fixing whole attention – on the – the death scene – '

"He gasped painfully for a few moments. 'We demonstrate truth of – of The Darkening; but – but there's psychic effect to be – looked for, through – results of parallelization of – conditions. May have extraordinary simulation of – the *actual thing*. Keep note. Keep note.' Then, suddenly, with a clear, spasmodic burst: 'My God, Stafford, keep note of everything. Something's going to happen. Something – wonderful – Promise not – to bother me. I know – what I'm doing.'

"Baurnoff ceased speaking, with a gasp, and there was only the labour of his breathing in the quietness of the room. As I stared at him, halting from a dozen things I needed to say, I realized suddenly that I could no longer see him quite plainly; a sort of wavering in the atmosphere, between us, made him seem momentarily unreal. The whole room had darkened perceptibly in the last thirty seconds; and as I stared around, I realized that there was a constant invisible swirl in the fast-deepening, extraordinary blue gloom that seemed now to permeate everything. When I looked at the lamp, alternate flashings of light and blue – darkness followed each other with an amazing swiftness.

"'My God!' I heard Baumoff whispering in the half-darkness, as if to himself, 'how did Christ bear the nails!'

"I stared across at him, with an infinite discomfort, and an irritated pity troubling me; but I knew it was no use to remonstrate now. I saw him vaguely distorted through the wavering tremble of the atmosphere. It was somewhat as if I looked at him through convolutions of heated air; only there were marvellous waves of blue-blackness making gaps in my sight. Once I saw his face clearly, full of an infinite pain, that was somehow, seemingly, more spiritual than physical, and dominating everything was an expression of enormous resolution and concentration, making the livid, sweat-damp, agonized face somehow heroic and splendid.

"And then, drenching the room with waves and splashes of opaqueness, the vibration of his abnormally stimulated agony finally broke up the vibration of Light. My last, swift glance round, showed me, as it seemed, the invisible Æther boiling and eddying in a tremendous fashion; and, abruptly, the flame of the lamp was lost in an extraordinary swirling patch of light, that marked its position for several moments, shimmering and deadening, shimmering and deadening; until, abruptly, I saw neither that glimmering patch of light, nor anything else. I was suddenly lost in a black opaqueness of night, through which came the fierce, painful breathing of Baumoff.

"A full minute passed; but so slowly that, if I had not been counting Baumoff's respirations, I should have said that it was five. Then Baumoff spoke suddenly, in a voice that was, somehow, curiously changed – a certain toneless note in it:

"'My God!' he said, from out of the darkness, 'what must Christ have suffered!'

"It was in the succeeding silence, that I had the first realization that I was vaguely afraid; but the feeling was too indefinite and unfounded, and I might say subconscious, for me to face it out. Three minutes passed, while I counted the almost desperate respirations that came to me through the darkness. Then Baumoff began to speak again, and still in that peculiarly altering voice:

"'By Thy Agony and Bloody Sweat,' he muttered. Twice he repeated this. It was plain indeed that he had fixed his whole attention with tremendous intensity, in his abnormal state, upon the death scene.

"The effect upon me of his intensity was interesting and in some ways extraordinary. As well as I could, I analyzed my sensations and emotions and general state of mind, and realized that Baumoff was producing an effect upon me that was almost hypnotic.

"Once, partly because I wished to get my level by the aid of a normal remark, and also because I was suddenly newly anxious by a change in the breathsounds, I asked Baumoff how he was. My voice going with a peculiar and really uncomfortable blankness through that impenetrable blackness of opacity.

"He said: 'Hush! I'm carrying the Cross.' And, do you know, the effect of those simple words, spoken in that new, toneless voice, in that atmosphere of almost unbearable tenseness, was so powerful that, suddenly, with eyes wide open, I saw Baumoff clear and vivid against that unnatural darkness, carrying a Cross. Not, as the picture is usually shown of the Christ, with it crooked over the shoulder; but with the Cross gripped just under the cross-piece in his arms, and the end trailing behind, along rocky ground. I saw even the pattern of the grain of the rough wood, where some of the bark had been ripped away; and under the trailing end there was a tussock of tough wire-grass, that had been uprooted by the lowing end, and dragged and ground along upon the rocks, between the end of the Cross and the rocky ground. I can see the thing now, as I speak. Its vividness was extraordinary; but it had come and gone like a flash, and I was sitting there in the darkness, mechanically counting the respirations; yet unaware that I counted.

"As I sat there, it came to me suddenly – the whole entire marvel of the thing that Baumoff had achieved. I was sitting there in a darkness which was an actual reproduction of the miracle of the Darkness of the

Cross. In short, Baumoff had, by producing in himself an abnormal condition, developed an Energy of Emotion that must have almost, in its effects, paralleled the Agony of the Cross. And in so doing, he had shown from an entirely new and wonderful point, the indisputable truth of the stupendous personality and the enormous spiritual force of the Christ. He had evolved and made practical to the average understanding a proof that would make to live again the *reality* of that wonder of the world – *CHRIST*. And for all this, I had nothing but admiration of an almost stupefied kind.

"But, at this point, I felt that the experiment should stop. I had a strangely nervous craving for Baumoff to end it right there and then, and not to try to parallel the psychic conditions. I had, even then, by some queer aid of sub-conscious suggestion, a vague reaching-out-towards the danger of 'monstrosity' being induced, instead of any actual knowledge gained.

"'Baumoff!' I said. 'Stop it.'

"But he made no reply, and for some minutes there followed a silence, that was unbroken, save by his gasping breathing. Abruptly, Baumoff said, between his gasps: 'Woman – behold – thy – son. ' He muttered this several times, in the same uncomfortably toneless voice in which he had spoken since the darkness became complete.

"'Baumoff.' I said again. 'Baumoff! *Stop it*.' " And as I listened for his answer, I was relieved to think that his breathing was less shallow. The abnormal demand for oxygen was evidently being met, and the extravagant call upon the heart's efficiency was being relaxed.

"'Baumoff!' I said, once more. 'Baumoff! Stop it!'

"And, as I spoke, abruptly, I thought the room was shaken a little.

"Now, I had already as you will have realized, been vaguely conscious of a peculiar and growing nervousness. I think that is the word that best describes it, up to this moment. At this curious little shake that seemed to stir through the utterly dark room, I was suddenly more than nervous. I felt a thrill of actual and literal fear; yet with no sufficient cause of reason to justify me; so that, after sitting very tense for some long minutes, and feeling nothing further, I decided that I needed to take myself in hand, and keep a firmer grip upon my nerves. And then, just as I had arrived at this more comfortable state of mind, the room was shaken again, with the most curious and sickening oscillatory movement, that was beyond all comfort of denial.

"'My God!' I whispered. And then, with a sudden effort of courage, I called: 'Baumoff! *For God's sake stop it.*'

"You've no idea of the effort it took to speak aloud into that darkness; and when I did speak, the sound of my voice set me afresh on edge. It went so empty and *raw* across the room; and somehow, the room seemed to be incredibly big. Oh, I wonder whether you realize how beastly I felt, without my having to make any further effort to tell you.

"And Baumoff never answered a word; but I could hear him breathing, a little fuller; though still heaving his thorax painfully, in his need for air. The incredible shaking of the room eased away; and there succeeded a spasm of quiet, in which I felt that it was my duty to get up and step across to Baumoffs chair. But I could not do it. Somehow, I would not have touched Baumoff then for any cause whatever. Yet, even in that moment, as now I know, I was not aware that I was *afraid to* touch Baumoff.

"And then the oscillations commenced again. I felt the seat of my trousers slide against the seat of my chair, and I thrust out my legs, spreading my feet against the carpet, to keep me from sliding off one way or the other on to the floor. To say I was afraid, was not to describe my state at all. I was terrified. And suddenly, I had comfort, in the most extraordinary fashion; for a single idea literally glazed into my brain, and gave me a reason to which to cling. It was a single line:

"'Æther, the soul of iron and sundry stuffs' which Baumoff had once taken as a text for an extraordinary lecture on vibrations, in the earlier days of our friendship. He had formulated the suggestion that, in embryo, Matter was, from a primary aspect, a localized vibration, traversing a closed orbit. These primary localized vibrations were inconceivably minute. But were capable, under certain conditions, of combining under the action of keynote-vibrations into secondary vibrations of a size and shape to be determined by a multitude of only guessable factors. These would sustain their new form, so long as nothing occurred to disorganize their combination or depreciate or divert their energy – their unity being partially determined by the inertia of the still Æther outside of the closed path which their area of activities covered. And such combination of the primary localised vibrations was neither more nor less than matter. Men and worlds, aye! and universes.

"And then he had said the thing that struck me most. He had said, that if it were possible to produce a vibration of the Æther of a sufficient energy, it would be possible to disorganize or confuse the vibration of matter. That, given a machine capable of creating a vibration of the Æther of a sufficient energy, he would engage to destroy not merely the world, but the whole universe itself, including heaven and hell themselves, if such places existed, and had such existence in a material form.

"I remember how I looked at him, bewildered by the pregnancy and scope of his imagination. And now his lecture had come back to me to help my courage with the sanity of reason. Was it not possible that the Æther disturbance which he had produced, had sufficient energy to cause some disorganization of the vibration of matter, in the immediate vicinity, and had thus created a miniature quaking of the ground all about the house, and so set the house gently a-shake?

"And then, as this thought came to me, another and a greater, flashed into my mind. 'My God!' I said out loud into the darkness of the room. It explains one more mystery of the Cross, the disturbance of the Æther caused by Christ's Agony, disorganized the vibration of matter in the vicinity of the Cross, and there was then a small local earthquake, which opened the graves, and rent the veil, possibly by disturbing its supports.

And, of course, the earthquake was an effect, and *not* a cause, as belittlers of the Christ have always insisted.

"'Baumoff!' I called. 'Baumoff, you've proved another thing. Baumoff! Baumoff! Answer me. Are you all right?'

"Baumoff answered, sharp and sudden out of the darkness; but not to me:

"'My God!' he said. 'My God!' His voice came out at me, a cry of veritable mental agony. He was suffering, in some hypnotic, induced fashion, something of the very agony of the Christ Himself.

"'Baumoff!' I shouted, and forced myself to my feet. I heard his chair clattering, as he sat there and shook. 'Baumoff!'

An extraordinary quake went across the floor of the room, and I heard a creaking of the woodwork, and something fell and smashed in the darkness. Baumoff's gasps hurt me; but I stood there. I dared not go to him. I knew *then* that I was afraid of him – of his condition, or something I don't know what. But, oh, I was horribly afraid of him.

"'Bau – ' I began, but suddenly I was afraid even to speak to him. And I could not move. Abruptly, he cried out in a tone of incredible anguish:

"'Eloi, Eloi, lama sabach*thani!* But the last word changed in his mouth, from his dreadful hypnotic grief and pain, to a scream of simply infernal terror.

"And, suddenly, a horrible mocking voice roared out in the room, from Baumoff's chair: 'Eloi, Eloi lama sabachthani!'

"Do you understand, the voice was not Baumoff's at all. It was not a voice of despair; but a voice sneering in an incredible, bestial, monstrous fashion. In the succeeding silence, as I stood in an ice of fear, I knew that Baumoff no longer gasped. The room was absolutely silent, the most dreadful and silent place in all this world. Then I bolted; caught my foot, probably in the invisible edge of the hearth-rug, and pitched headlong into a blaze of internal brain-stars. After which, for a very long time, certainly some hours, I knew nothing of any kind.

"I came back into this Present, with a dreadful headache oppressing me, to the exclusion of all else. But the Darkness had dissipated. I rolled over on to my side, and saw Baumoff and forgot even the pain in my head. He was leaning forward towards me: his eyes wide open, but dull. His face was enormously swollen, and there was, somehow, something *beastly* about him. He was dead, and the belt about him and the chairback, alone prevented him from falling forward on to me. His tongue was thrust out of one corner of his mouth. I shall always remember how he looked. He was leering, like a human-beast, more than a man.

"I edged away from him, across the floor; but I never stopped looking at him, until I had got to the other side of the door, and closed between us. Of course, I got my balance in a bit, and went back to him; but there was nothing I could do.

"Baumoff died of heart-failure, of course, obviously! I should never be so foolish as to suggest to any sane jury that, in his extraordinary, self-hypnotized, defenseless condition, he was 'entered' by some Christ-apeing Monster of the Void. I've too much respect for my own claim to be a common-sensible man, to put forward such an idea with seriousness! Oh, I know I may seem to speak with a jeer; but what can I do but jeer at myself and all the world, when I dare not acknowledge, even secretly to myself, what my own thoughts are. Baumoff did, undoubtedly die of heart-failure; and, for the rest, how much was I hypnotized into believing. Only, there was over by the far wall, where it had been shaken down to the floor from a solidly fastened-up bracket, a little pile of glass that had once formed a piece of beautiful Venetian glassware. You remember that I heard something fall, when the room shook. Surely the room *did* shake? Oh, I must stop thinking. My head goes round.

"The explosive the papers are talking about. Yes, that's Baumoff's; that makes it all seem true, doesn't it? They had the darkness at Berlin, after the explosion. There is no getting away from *that*. The Government know only that Baumoff's formulae is capable of producing the largest quantity of gas, in the shortest possible time. That, in short, it is ideally *explosive*. So it is; but I imagine it will prove an explosive, as I have already said, and as experience has proved, a little too impartial in its action for it to create enthusiasm on either side of a battlefield. Perhaps this is but a mercy, in disguise; certainly a mercy, if Baumoff's theories as to the possibility of disorganizing matter, be anywhere near to the truth.

"I have thought sometimes that there might be a more normal explanation of the dreadful thing that happened at the end. Baumoff *may* have ruptured a blood-vessel in the brain, owing to the enormous arterial pressure that his experiment induced; and the voice I heard and the mockery and the horrible expression and leer may have been nothing more than the immediate outburst and expression of the natural 'obliqueness' of a deranged mind, which so often turns up a side of a man's nature and produces an inversion of character, that is the very complement of his normal state. And certainly, poor Baumoff's normal religious attitude was one of marvellous reverence and loyalty towards the Christ.

"Also, in support of this line of explanation, I have frequently observed that the voice of a person suffering from mental derangement is frequently wonderfully changed, and has in it often a very repellant and inhuman quality. I try to think that this explanation fits the case. But I can never forget that room. Never."

BOATMAN'S HOLIDAY
Jeffrey Ford

Jeffrey Ford (b. 1955) is a professor of Writing and Literature at Brookdale Community College. Although he had been selling short fiction to various literary reviews and small-press magazines since 1981 his career as a writer did not really take off until 1996 with the publication of his first novel, The Physiognomy *(1997), which went on to win the World Fantasy Award. Ford has since won several more awards, including another World Fantasy for his collection* The Fantasy Writer's Assistant *(2002). His stories are seldom conventional and often exotic and elaborate. I could have chosen from any number to include in this anthology, but settled on this exploration of Hell and one of its most notable characters.*

Ford's website is at http://users.rcn.com/delicate/

Beneath a blazing orange sun, he maneuvered his boat between the two petrified oaks that grew so high their tops were lost in violet clouds. The vast trunks and complexity of branches were bone white, as if hidden just below the surface of the murky water was a stag's head the size of a mountain. Thousands of crows, like black leaves, perched amidst the pale tangle, staring silently down. Feathers fell, spiraling in their descent with the slow grace of certain dreams, and he wondered how many of these journeys he'd made or if they were all, always, the same journey.

Beyond the oaks, the current grew stronger, and he entered a constantly shifting maze of whirlpools, some spinning clock wise, some counter, as if to negate the passage of time. Another boatman might have given in to panic and lost everything, but he was a master navigator and knew the river better than himself. Any other craft would have quickly succumbed to the seething waters, been torn apart and its debris swallowed.

His boat was comprised of an inner structure of human bone lashed together with tendon and covered in flesh stitched by his own steady hand, employing a thorn needle and thread spun from sorrow. The lines of its contours lacked symmetry, meandered and went off on tangents.

Along each side, worked into the gunwales well above the waterline, was a row of eyeless, tongueless faces – the empty sockets, the gaping lips, portals through which the craft breathed. Below, in the hold, there reverberated a heart beat that fluttered randomly and died every minute only to be revived the next.

On deck, there were two long rows of benches fashioned from skulls for his passengers, and at the back, his seat at the tiller. In the shallows, he'd stand and use his long pole to guide the boat along. There was no need of a sail as the vessel moved slowly forward of its own volition with a simple command. On the trip out, the benches empty, he'd whisper, "There!" and on the journey back, carrying a full load, "Home!" and no river current could dissuade its progress. Still, it took a sure and fearless hand to hold the craft on course.

Charon's tall, wiry frame was slightly but irreparably bent from centuries hunched beside the tiller. His beard and tangled nest of snow white hair, his complexion the colour of ash, made him appear ancient. When in the throes of maneuvering around Felmian, the blue serpent, or in the heated rush along the shoals of the Island of Nothing; however, he'd toss one side of his scarlet cloak back over his shoulder, and the musculature of his chest, the coiled bulge of his bicep, the thick tendon in his forearm, gave evidence of the power hidden beneath his laconic façade. Woe to the passenger who mistook those outer signs of age for weakness and set some plan in motion, for then the boatman would wield his long shallows stick and shatter every bone in their body.

Each treacherous obstacle, the clutch of shifting boulders, the rapids, the waterfall that dropped into a bottomless star filled space, was expertly avoided with a skill born of intuition. Eventually a vague but steady tone like the uninterrupted buzz of a mosquito came to him over the water; a sign that he drew close to his destination. He shaded his eyes against the brightness of the flaming sun and spotted the dark, thin edge of shoreline in the distance. As he advanced, that whispered note grew steadily into a high keening, and then fractured to reveal itself a chorus of agony. A few more leagues and he could make out the legion of forms crowding the bank. When close enough to land, he left the tiller, stood, and used the pole to turn the boat so it came to rest sideways on the black sand. Laying down the pole, he stepped to his spot at the prow.

Two winged, toad faced, demons with talons for hands and hands for feet, Gesnil and Trinkthil, saw to the orderliness of the line of passengers that ran from the shore back a hundred yards into the writhing human continent of dead. Every day there were more travellers, and no matter how many trips Charon made, there was no hope of ever emptying the endless beach.

Brandishing cat-o-nine-tails with barbed tips fashioned from incisors, the demons lashed the "tourists," as they called them, subduing those unwilling to go.

"Another load of the falsely accused, Charon," said Gesnil, puffing on a lit human finger jutting from the corner of his mouth.

"Watch this woman, third back, in the blue dress," said Trinkthil, "her blithering lamentations will bore you to sleep. You know, she never really meant to add Belladonna to the recipe for her husband's gruel."

Charon shook his head.

"We've gotten word that there will be no voyages for a time," said Gesnil.

"Yes," said Charon, "I've been granted a respite by the Master. A holiday."

"A century's passed already?" said Gesnil. "My, my, it seemed no more than three. Time flies…"

"Travelling?" asked Trinkthil. "Or staying home?"

Charon ignored the question and said "Send them along."

The demons knew to obey, and they directed the first in line to move forward. A bald, overweight man in a cassock, some member of the clergy, stepped up. He was trembling so that his jowls shook. He'd waited on the shore in dire fear and anguish for centuries, milling about, fretting as to the ultimate nature of his fate.

"Payment," said Charon.

The man tipped his head back and opened his mouth. A round shiny object lay beneath his tongue. The boatman reached out and took the gold coin, putting it in the pocket of his cloak. "Next," called Charon as the man moved past him and took a seat on the bench of skulls.

Hell's orange sun screamed in its death throes every evening, a pandemonium sweeping down from above that made even the demons sweat and set the master's three headed dog to cowering. That horrendous din worked its way into the rocks, the river, the petrified trees, and everything brimmed with misery. Slowly, it diminished as the starless, moonless dark came on, devouring every last shred of light. With that infernal night came a cool breeze whose initial tantalizing relief never failed to deceive the damned, though they be residents for a thousand years, with a false promise of Hope. That growing wind carried in it a catalyst for memory, and set all who it caressed to recalling in vivid detail their lost lives – a torture individually tailored, more effective than fire.

Charon sat in his home, the skull of a fallen god, on the crest of a high flint hill, overlooking the river. Through the left eye socket glazed with transparent lies, he could be seen sitting at a table, a glutton's-fat tallow burning, its flame guttering in the night breeze let in through the

gap of a missing tooth. Laid out before him was a curling width of
tattooed flesh skinned from the back of an ancient explorer who'd no
doubt sold his soul for a sip from the Fountain of Youth. In the boat
man's right hand was a compass and in his left a writing quill. His gaze
traced along the strange parchment the course of his own river, Acheron,
the River of Pain, to where it crossed paths with Pyriphlegethon, the
River of Fire. That burning course was eventually quelled in cataracts of
steam where it emptied into and became the Lethe, River of Forgetting.

He traced his next day's journey with the quill tip, gliding it an inch
above the meandering line of vein blue. There, in the meager width of
that last river's depiction, almost directly half way between its origin and
end in the mournful Cocytus, was a freckle. Anyone else would have
thought it no more than a bodily blemish inked over by chance in the
production of the map, but Charon was certain after centuries of
overhearing whispered snatches of conversation from his unlucky
passengers that it represented the legendary island of Oondeshai.

He put down his quill and compass and sat back in the chair, closing
his eyes. Hanging from the center of the cathedral cranium above, the
wind chime made of dangling bat bones clacked as the mischievous
breeze that invaded his home lifted one corner of the map. He sighed at
the touch of cool wind as its insidious effect reeled his memory into the
past.

One night, he couldn't recall how many centuries before, he was
lying in bed on the verge of sleep, when there came a pounding at the
hinged door carved in the left side of the skull. "Who's there?" he called
in the fearsome voice he used to silence passengers. There was no verbal
answer, but another barrage of banging ensued. He rolled out of bed, put
on his cloak and lit a tallow. Taking the candle with him, he went to the
door and flung it open. A startled figure stepped back into the darkness.
Charon thrust the light forward and beheld a cowed, trembling man, his
naked flesh covered in oozing sores and wounds.

"Who are you?" asked the boat man.

The man stared up at him, holding out a hand.

"You've escaped from the pit, haven't you?"

The back side of the flint hill atop which his home sat overlooked the enormous pit, its circumference at the top, a hundred miles across. Spiraling along its inner wall was a path that led down and down in ever decreasing arcs through the various levels of Hell to end at a pin point in the very mind of the Master. Even at night, if Charon were to go behind the skull and peer out over the rim, he could see a faint reddish glow and hear the distant echo of plaintive wails.

The man finally nodded.

"Come in," said Charon, and held the door as the stranger shuffled past him.

Later, after he'd been offered a chair, a spare cloak, and a cup of nettle tea, the broken visitor began to come around.

"You know," said Charon, "there's no escape from Hell."

"This I know," mumbled the man, making a great effort to speak as if he'd forgotten the skill. "But there is an escape in Hell."

"What are you talking about? The dog will be here within the hour to fetch you back. He's less than gentle."

"I need to make the river," said the man.

"What's your name?" asked Charon.

"Wieroot," said the man with a grimace.

The boatman nodded. "This escape in Hell, where is it, what is it?"

"Oondeshai," said Wieroot, "an island in the River Lethe."

"Where did you hear of it?"

"I created it," he said, holding his head with both hands as if to remember. "Centuries ago, I wrote it into the fabric of the mythology of Hell."

"Mythology?" asked Charon. "I suppose those wounds on your body are merely a myth?"

"The suffering's real here, don't I know it, but the entire construction of Hell is, of course, man's own invention. The Pit, the three headed dog, the rivers, you, if I may say so, all sprung from the mind of humanity, confabulated to punish itself."

"Hell has been here from the beginning," said Charon.

"Yes," said Wieroot, "in one form or another. But when, in the living world, something is added to the legend, some detail to better convince believers or convert new ones, here it leaps into existence with a ready made history that instantly spreads back to the start and a guaranteed future that creeps inexorably forward." The escapee fell into a fit of coughing, smoke from the fires of the pit issuing in small clouds from his lungs.

"The heat's made you mad," said Charon. "You've had too much time to think."

"Both may be true," croaked Wieroot, wincing in pain, "but listen for a moment more. You appear to be a man, yet I'll wager you don't remember your youth. Where were you born? How did you become the boatman?"

Charon strained his memory, searching for an image of his past in the world of the living. All he saw was rows and rows of heads, tilting back, proffering the coin beneath the tongue. An image of him setting out across the river, passing between the giant oaks, repeated behind his eyes three dozen times in rapid succession.

"Nothing there, am I correct?"

Charon stared hard at his guest.

"I was a cleric," said Wieroot, "and in copying a sacred text describing the environs of Hell, I deviated from the disintegrating original and added the existence of Oondeshai. Over the course of years, decades, centuries, other scholars found my creation and added it to their own works and so, now, Oondeshai, though not as well known as yourself or your river, is an actuality in this desperate land."

From down along the river bank came the approaching sound of Cerberus baying. Wieroot stood, sloughing off the cloak to let it drop into his chair. "I've got to get to the river," he said. "But consider this.

You live in the skull of a fallen god. This space was once filled with a substance that directed the universe, no, was the universe. How does a god die?"

"You'll never get across," said Charon.

"I don't want to. I want to be caught in its flow."

"You'll drown."

"Yes, I'll drown, be bitten by the spiny eels, burned in the River of Fire, but I won't die, for I'm already dead. Some time ages hence, my body will wash up on the shore of Oondeshai, and I will have arrived home. The way I crafted the island, the moment you reach its shores and pull yourself from the River of Forgetting, you instantly remember everything."

"It sounds like a child's tale," Charon murmured.

"Thank you," said the stranger.

"What gave you cause to create this island?" asked the boatman.

Wieroot staggered towards the door. As he opened it and stepped out into the pitch black, he called back, "I knew I would eventually commit murder."

Charon followed out into the night and heard the man's feet pacing away down the flint hill towards the river. Seconds later, he heard the wheezing breath of the three headed dog. Growling, barking, sounded in triplicate. There was silence for a time, and then finally…a splash, and in that moment, for the merest instant, an image of a beautiful island flashed behind the boatman's eyes.

He'd nearly been able to forget the incident with Wieroot as the centuries flowed on, their own River of Pain, until one day he heard one of his passengers whisper the word "Oondeshai" to another. Three or four times this happened, and then, only a half century past, a young woman, still radiant though dead, with shiny black hair and a curious red dot of a birthmark just below her left eye, was ushered onto his boat. He requested payment. When she tilted her head back, opened her mouth and lifted her tongue, there was no coin but instead a small, tightly folded package of flesh. Charon nearly lost his temper as he retrieved it from her mouth, but she whispered quickly, "A map to Oondeshai."

These words were like a slap to his face. He froze for the merest instant, but then thought quickly, and, nodding, stepped aside for her to take a seat. "Next," he yelled and the demons were none the wiser. Later that night, he unfolded the crudely cut rectangle of skin, and after a close inspection of the tattoo cursed himself for having been duped. He swept the map onto the floor and the night breeze blew it into a corner. Weeks later, after finding it had been blown back out from under the table into the middle of the floor, he lifted it and searched it again. This time he noticed the freckle in the length of Lethe's blue line and wondered.

He kept his boat in a small lagoon hidden by a thicket of black poplars. It was just after sunrise, and he'd already stowed his provisions in the hold below deck. After lashing them fast with lengths of hangman's rope, he turned around to face the chaotically beating heart of the craft. The large blood organ, having once resided in the chest of the Queen of Sirens, was suspended in the center of the hold by thick branch-like veins and arteries that grew into the sides of the boat. Its vasculature expanded and contracted, and the heart itself beat erratically, undulating and shivering, sweating red droplets.

Charon waited until after it died, lay still, and then was startled back to life by whatever immortal force pervaded its chambers. Once it was moving again, he gave a high pitched whistle, a note that began at the bottom of the register and quickly rose to the top. At the sound of this signal, the wet red meat of the thing parted in a slit to reveal an eye.

The orb swiveled to and fro, and the boatman stepped up close with a burning tallow in one hand and the map, opened, in the other. He back lit the scrap of skin to let the eye read its tattoo. He'd circled the freckle that represented Oondeshai with his quill, so the destination was clearly marked. All he'd have to do is steer around the dangers, keep the keel in deep water and stay awake. Otherwise, the craft now knew the way to go.

Up on deck, he cast off the ropes, and instead of uttering the word "There," he spoke a command used less than once a century – "Away." The boat moved out of the lagoon and onto the river. Charon felt something close to joy at not having to steer between the giant white oaks. He glanced up to his left at the top of the flint hill and saw the huge skull, staring down at him. The day was hot and orange and all of Hell was busy at the work of suffering, but he, the boatman, was off on a holiday.

On the voyage out, he travelled with the flow of the river, so its current combined with the inherent, enchanted propulsion of the boat made for swift passage. There were the usual whirlpools, outcroppings of sulfur and brimstone to avoid, but these occasional obstacles were a welcome diversion. He'd never taken this route before when on holiday. Usually, he'd just stay home, resting, making minor repairs to the boat, playing knuckle bones with some of the bat winged demons from the pit on a brief break from the grueling work of torture.

Once, as a guest of the master during a holiday, he'd been invited into the bottommost reaches of the pit, transported in a winged chariot that glided down through the center of the great spiral. There, where the Czar of the Underworld kept a private palace made of frozen sighs, in a land of snow so cold one's breath fractured upon touching the air, he was led by an army of living marble statues, shaped like men but devoid of faces, down a tunnel that led to an enormous circle of clear ice. Through this transparent barrier he could look out on the realm of the living. Six days he spent transfixed between astonishment and fear at the sight of the world the way it was. That vacation left a splinter of ice in his heart that took three centuries to melt.

None of his previous getaways ever resulted in a tenth the sense of relief he already felt having gone but a few miles along the nautical route to Oondeshai. He repeated the name of the island again and again under his breath as he worked the tiller or manned the shallows pole, hoping to catch another glimpse of its image as he had the night Wieroot dove into the Acheron. As always, that mental picture refused to coalesce, but he'd learned to suffice with its absence, which had become a kind of solace in itself.

To avoid dangerous eddies and rocks in the middle flow of the river, Charon was occasionally forced to steer the boat in close to shore on the port side. There, he glimpsed the marvels of that remote, forgotten landscape – a distant string of smoldering volcanoes; a thundering herd of bloodless behemoths, sweeping like a white wave across the immensity of a fissured salt flat; a glittering forest of crystal trees alive with long tailed monkeys made of pitch. The distractions were many, but he struggled to put away his curiosity and concentrate for fear of running aground and ripping a hole in the hull.

He hoped to make the River of Fire before nightfall, so as to have light with which to navigate. To travel the Acheron blind would be sheer suicide, and unlike Wieroot, Charon was uncertain as to whether he was already dead or alive or merely a figment of Hell's imagination. There was the possibility of finding a natural harbour and dropping the anchor, but the land through which the river ran had shown him fierce and mysterious creatures stalking him along the banks and that made steering through the dark seem the fairer alternative.

As the day waned, and the sun began to whine with the pain of its gradual death, Charon peered ahead with a hand shading his sight in anticipation of a glimpse at the flames of Pyriphlegethon. During his visit to the palace of frozen sighs, the master had let slip that the liquid fire of those waters burned only sinners. Because the boat was a tool of Hell, made of Hell, he was fairly certain it could withstand the flames, but he wasn't sure if at some point in his distant past he had not sinned.

If he were to blunder into suffering, though, he thought that he at least would learn some truth about himself.

In the last moments of light, he lit three candles and positioned them at the prow of the boat. They proved ineffectual against the night, casting their glow only a shallows pole length ahead of the craft. Their glare wearied Charon's eyes. To distract himself from fatigue, he went below and brought back a dried, salted, Harpy leg to chew on.

In recent centuries the winged creatures had grown scrawny, almost thin enough to slip his snares. The meat was known to improve eyesight and exacerbate the mind. Its effect had nothing to do with clarity, merely a kind of agitation of thought that was, at this juncture, preferable to slumber. Sleep was the special benefit of the working class of Hell, and the boatman usually relished it. Dreams especially were an exotic escape from the routine of work. The sinners never slept, nor did the master.

Precisely at the center of the night Charon felt some urge, some pull of intuition to push the tiller hard to the left. As soon as he'd made the reckless maneuver, he heard from up ahead the loud gulping sound that meant a whirlpool laid in his path. The sound grew quickly to a deafening strength, and only when he was upon the swirling monster, riding its very lip around the right arc, was he able to see its immensity.

The boat struggled to free itself from the draw, and instead of being propelled by its magic it seemed to be clawing its way forward, dragging its weight free of the hopeless descent. There was nothing he could do but hold the tiller firm and stare with widened eyes down the long, treacherous tunnel. Not a moment passed after he was finally free of it than the boat entered the turbulent waters where Acheron crossed the River of Fire.

He released his grip on the tiller and let the craft lead him with its knowledge of the map he'd shown it. His fingers gripped tightly into the eye holes of two of the skulls that formed his seat, and he held on so as not to be thrown overboard. Pyriphlegethon now blazed ahead of him, and the sight of its roiling flames, some flaring high into the night, made him scream, not with fear but exhilaration. The boat forged forward, cleaved the burning surface, and then was engulfed in a yellow-orange brightness that gave no heat. The frantic illumination dazed Charon, and he sat as in a trance, dreaming wide awake. He no longer felt the passage of Time, the urgency to reach his destination, the weight of all those things he'd fled on his holiday.

Eventually, after a prolonged bright journey, the blazing waters became turbulent, lost their fire, and a thick mist rose off them. The mist quickly became a fog that seemed to have texture, brushing against his skin like a feather. He thought he might grab handfuls until it slipped through his fingers, leaked into his nostrils, and wrapped its tentacles around his memory.

When the boatman awoke to the daily birth cry of Hell's sun, he found himself lying naked upon his bed, staring up at the clutch of bat bones dangling from the cranial center of his skull home. He was startled at first, grasping awkwardly for a tiller that wasn't there, tightening his fist around the shaft of the absent shallows stick that instead rested at an angle against the doorway. As soon as the shock of discovery that he was home had abated, he sighed deeply and sat up on the edge of the bed. It struck him then that his entire journey, his holiday, had been for naught.

He frantically searched his thoughts for the slightest shred of a memory that he might have reached Oondeshai, but every trace had been forgotten. For the first time in centuries, tears came to his eyes, and the frustration of his predicament made him cry out. Eventually, he stood and found his cloak rolled into a ball on the floor at the foot of his bed. He dressed and without stopping to put on his boots or grab the shallows pole, he left his home.

With determination in his stride, he mounted the small rise that lay back behind the skull and stood at the rim of the enormous pit. Inching to the very edge, he peered down into the spiraled depths at the faint red glow. The screams of tortured sinners, the wailing laments of self-pity, sounded in his ears like distant voices in a dream. Beneath it all he could barely discern, like the buzzing of a fly, the sound of the master laughing uproariously, joyously, and that discordant strain seemed to lace itself subtly into everything.

Charon's anger and frustration slowly melted into a kind of numbness as cold as the hallways of Satan's palace, and he swayed to and fro, out over the edge and back, not so much wanting to jump as waiting to fall. Time passed, he was not aware how much, and then as suddenly as he had dressed and left his home, he turned away from the pit.

Once more inside the skull, he prepared to go to work. There was a great heaviness within him, as if his very organs were now made of lead, and each step was an effort, each exhalation a sigh. He found his eel skin ankle boots beneath the table at which he'd studied the flesh map at night. Upon lifting one, it turned in his hand, and a steady stream of blonde sand poured out onto the floor. The sight of it caught him off guard and for a moment he stopped breathing.

He fell to his knees to inspect the little pile that had formed. Carefully, he lifted the other boot, turned it over and emptied that one into its own neat little pile next to the other. He reached towards these twin wonders, initially wanting to feel the grains run through his fingers, but their stark proof that he had been to Oondeshai and could not recall a moment of it ultimately defeated his will and he never touched them. Instead, he stood, took up the shallows pole and left the skull for his boat.

As he guided the boat between the two giant oaks, he no longer wondered if all his journeys across the Acheron were always the same journey. With a dull aspect, he performed his duties as the boatman. His muscles, educated in the task over countless centuries, knew exactly how to avoid the blue serpent and skirt the whirlpools without need of a single thought. No doubt it was these same unconscious processes that had brought Charon and his craft back safely from Oondeshai.

Gesnil and Trinkthil inquired with great anticipation about his vacation when he met them on the far shore. For the demons, who knew no respite from the drudgery of herding sinners, even a few words about a holiday away would have been like some rare confection, but he told them nothing. From the look on Charon's face, they knew not to prod him and merely sent the travellers forward to offer coins and take their places on the benches.

During the return trip that morning, a large fellow sitting amongst the passengers had a last second attack of nerves in the face of an impending eternity of suffering. He screamed incoherently, and Charon ordered him to silence. When the man stood up and began pacing back and forth, the boat man ordered him to return to his seat. The man persisted moving about, his body jerking with spasms of fear, and it was obvious his antics were spooking the other sinners. Fearing the man would spread mutiny, Charon came forth with the shallows stick and bringing it around like a club, split the poor fellow's head. That was usually all the incentive a recalcitrant passenger needed to return to the bench, but this one was now insane with the horror of his plight.

The boatman waded in and beat him wildly, striking him again and again. With each blow, Charon felt some infinitesimal measure of relief from his own frustration. When he was finished, the agitator lay in a heap on deck, nothing more than a flesh bag full of broken bones, and the other passengers shuffled their feet sideways as not to touch it.

Only later, after he had docked his boat in the lagoon and the winged demons had flown out of the pit to lead the damned up the flint hill and down along the spiral path to their eternal destinies, did the boatman regret his rage. As he lifted the sac of flesh that had been his charge and dumped it like a bale of chum over the side, he realized that the man's hysteria had been one and the same thing as his own frustration.

The sun sounded its death cry as it sank into a pool of blood that was the horizon and then Hell's twilight came on. Charon dragged himself up the hill and went inside his home. Before pure night closed its fist on the river bank, he kicked off his boots, gnawed on a haunch of Harpy flesh, and lit the tallow that sat in its holder on the table. Taking his seat there he stared into the flame, thinking of it as the future that constantly drew him forward through years, decades, centuries, eons, as the past disappeared behind him. "I am nothing but a moment," he said aloud and his words echoed around the empty skull.

Some time later, still sitting at his chair at the table, he noticed the candle flame twitch. His eyes shifted for the first time in hours to follow its movement. Then the fire began to dance, the sheets of flesh parchment lifted slightly at their corners, the bat bones clacked quietly overhead. Hell's deceptive wind of memory had begun to blow. He heard it whistling in through the space in his home's grin, felt its coolness sweep around him. This most complex and exquisite torture that brought back to sinners the times of their lives, now worked on the boatman. He moved his bare feet beneath the table and realized the piles of sand lay beneath them.

The image began in his mind no more than a dot of blue and then rapidly unfolded in every direction to reveal a sky and crystal water. The sun there in Oondeshai had been yellow and it gave true warmth. This he remembered clearly. He'd sat high on a hill of blonde sand, staring out across the endless vista of sparkling water. Next to him on the left was Wieroot, legs crossed, dressed in a black robe and sporting a beard to hide the healing scars that riddled his face. On the right was the young woman with the shining black hair and the red dot of a birthmark beneath her left eye.

"…And you created this all by writing it in the other world?" asked Charon. There was a breeze blowing and the boatman felt a certain lightness inside as if he'd eaten of one of the white clouds floating across the sky.

"I'll tell you a secret," said Wieroot, "although it's a shame you'll never get a chance to put it to use."

"Tell me," said the boatman.

"God made the world with words," he said in a whisper.

Charon remembered that he didn't understand. He furrowed his brow and turned to look at the young woman to see if she was laughing. Instead she was also nodding along with Wieroot. She put her hand on the boatman's shoulder and said, "And man made God with words."

Charon's memory of the beach on Oondeshai suddenly gave violent birth to another memory from his holiday. He was sitting in a small structure with no door, facing out into a night scene of tall trees whose leaves were blowing in a strong wind. Although it was night, it was not the utter darkness he knew from his quadrant of Hell. High in the black sky there shone a bright disk, which cast its beams down onto the island. Their glow had seeped into the small home behind him and fell upon the forms of Wieroot and the woman, Shara was her name, where they slept upon a bed of reeds. Beneath the sound of the wind, the calls of night birds, the whirr of insects, he heard the steady breathing of the sleeping couple.

And one last memory followed. Charon recalled Wieroot drawing near to him as he was about to board his boat for the return journey.

"You told me you committed murder," said the boatman.

"I did," said Wieroot.

"Who?"

"That god whose skull you live in," came the words which grew faint and then disappeared as the night wind of Hell ceased blowing. The memories faded and Charon looked up to see the candle flame again at rest. He reached across the table and drew his writing quill and a sheaf of parchment towards him. Dipping the pen nib into the pot of blood that was his ink, he scratched out two words at the top of the page. My Story, he wrote, and then set about remembering the future. The words came, slowly at first, reluctantly, dragging their imagery behind them, but after a short while their numbers grew to equal the number of sinners awaiting a journey to the distant shore. He ferried them methodically, expertly, from his mind to the page, scratching away long into the dark night of Hell until down at the bottom of the spiral pit, in his palace of frozen sighs, Satan suddenly stopped laughing.

THE DETWEILER BOY
Tom Reamy

Tom Reamy's life was cut tragically short when he died in November 1977 aged only 42, only three years after his first professional story sale and a matter of months before his first novel, Blind Voices *was published. His few published stories were collected posthumously in* San Diego Lightfoot Sue and Other Stories *(1979). Reamy had been well known in science-fiction and fantasy fandom for some years, and published what many regarded as the most beautifully produced of all amateur magazines,* Trumpet. *This later metamorphosed into* Nickelodeon, *where Reamy helped encourage the careers of several local writers, including Howard Waldrop. Reamy worked in the aerospace industry, but when that wound down in the early seventies he turned his hand to printing and graphic design. He also helped publish another beautiful magazine of the seventies,* Shayol, *which published early material by Pat Cadigan and, again, Howard Waldrop. Reamy was a craftsman and seldom satisfied with his stories, and so completed only a few. Yet his work immediately attracted attention and in 1976 he won the Campbell Award as Best New Writer. I was keen to include one of Reamy's stories in this volume and settled on the following, which is the closest this anthology comes to extreme horror.*

The room had been cleaned with pine-oil disinfectant and smelled like a public toilet. Harry Spinner was on the floor behind the bed, scrunched down between it and the wall. The almost colourless chenille bedspread had been pulled askew exposing part of the clean but dingy sheet. All I could see of Harry was one leg poking over the edge of the bed. He wasn't wearing a shoe, only a faded brown and tan argyle sock with a hole in it. The sock, long bereft of any elasticity, was crumpled around his thin rusty ankle.

I closed the door quietly behind me and walked around the end of the bed so I could see all of him. He was huddled on his back with his elbows propped up by the wall and the bed. His throat had been cut. The blood hadn't spread very far. Most of it had been soaked up by the threadbare carpet under the bed. I looked around the grubby little room but didn't find anything. There were no signs of a struggle, no signs of forced entry – but then, my BankAmericard hadn't left any signs either. The window was open, letting in the muffled roar of traffic on the Boulevard. I stuck my head out and looked, but it was three stories straight down to the neon-lit marquee of the movie house.

It had been nearly two hours since Harry called me. "Bertram, my boy, I've run across something very peculiar. I don't really know what to make of it."

I had put away the report I was writing on Lucas McGowan's hyperactive wife. (She had a definite predilection for gas-pump jockeys, car-wash boys, and parking-lot attendants. I guess it had something to do with the Age of the Automobile.) I propped my feet on my desk and leaned back until the old swivel chair groaned a protest.

"What did you find this time, Harry? A nest of international spies or an invasion from Mars?" I guess Harry Spinner wasn't much use to anyone, not even himself, but I liked him. He'd helped me in a couple of cases, nosing around in places only the Harry Spinners of the world can nose around in unnoticed. I was beginning to get the idea he was trying to play Doctor Watson to my Sherlock Holmes.

"Don't tease me, Bertram. There's a boy here in the hotel. I saw something I don't think he wanted me to see. It's extremely odd."

Harry was also the only person in the world, except my mother, who called me Bertram. "What did you see?"

"I'd rather not talk about it over the phone. Can you come over?"

Harry saw too many old private-eye movies on the late show. "It'll be a while. I've got a client coming in in a few minutes to pick up the poop on his wandering wife."

"Bertram, you shouldn't waste your time and talent on divorce cases."

"It pays the bills, Harry. Besides, there aren't enough Maltese falcons to go around."

By the time I filled Lucas McGowan in on all the details (I got the impression he was less concerned with his wife's infidelity than with her taste; that it wouldn't have been so bad if she'd been shacking up with movie stars or international playboys), collected my fee, and grabbed a Thursday special at Colonel Sanders', almost two hours had passed. Harry hadn't answered my knock, and so I let myself in with a credit card.

Birdie Pawlowicz was a fat, slovenly old broad somewhere between forty and two hundred. She was blind in her right eye and wore a black felt patch over it. She claimed she had lost the eye in a fight with a Creole whore over a riverboat gambler. I believed her. She ran the Brewster Hotel the way Florence Nightingale must have run that stinking army hospital in the Crimea.

Her tenants were the losers habitating that rotting section of the Boulevard east of the Hollywood Freeway. She bossed them, cursed them, loved them, and took care of them. (Once, a couple of years ago, a young black buck thought an old fat lady with one eye would make easy pickings. The cops found him three days later, two blocks away, under some rubbish in an alley where he'd hidden. He had a broken arm, two cracked ribs, a busted nose, a few missing teeth, and was stone-dead from internal hemorrhaging.)

The Brewster ran heavily in the red, but Birdie didn't mind. She had quite a bit of property in Westwood which ran very, very heavily in the black. She gave me an obscene leer as I approached the desk, but her good eye twinkled.

"Hello, lover!" she brayed in a voice like a cracked boiler. "I've lowered my price to a quarter. Are you interested?" She saw my face and her expression shifted from lewd to wary. "What's wrong, Bert?"

"Harry Spinner. You'd better get the cops, Birdie. Somebody killed him."

She looked at me, not saying anything, her face slowly collapsing into an infinitely weary resignation. Then she turned and telephoned the police. Because it was just Harry Spinner at the Brewster Hotel on the wrong end of Hollywood Boulevard, the cops took over half an hour to get there. While we waited I told Birdie everything I knew, about the phone call and what I'd found.

"He must have been talking about the Detweiler boy," she said, frowning. "Harry's been kinda friendly with him, felt sorry for him, I guess."

"What's his room? I'd like to talk to him."

"He checked out."

"When?"

"Just before you came down."

"Damn!"

She bit her lip. "I don't think the Detweiler boy killed him."

"Why?"

"I just don't think he could. He's such a gentle boy."

"Oh, Birdie," I groaned, "you know there's no such thing as a killer type. Almost anyone will kill with a good enough reason."

"I know," she sighed, "but I still can't believe it." She tapped her scarlet fingernails on the dulled Formica desktop. "How long had Harry been dead?"

He had phoned me about ten after five. I had found the body at seven. "A while," I said. "The blood was mostly dry."

"Before six-thirty?"

"Probably."

She sighed again, but this time with relief. "The Detweiler boy was down here with me until six-thirty. He'd been here since about four-fifteen. We were playing gin. He was having one of his spells and wanted company."

"What kind of spell? Tell me about him, Birdie."

"But he couldn't have killed Harry," she protested.

"Okay," I said, but I wasn't entirely convinced. Why would anyone deliberately and brutally murder inoffensive, invisible Harry Spinner right after he told me he had discovered something "peculiar" about the Detweiler boy? Except the Detweiler boy?

"Tell me anything. If he and Harry were friendly, he might know something. Why do you keep calling him a boy; how old is he?"

She nodded and leaned her bulk on the registration desk. "Early twenties, twenty-two, twenty-three, maybe. Not very tall, about five-five or -six. Slim, dark curly hair, a real good-looking boy. Looks like a movie star except for his back."

"His back?"

"He has a hump. He's a hunchback."

That stopped me for a minute, but I'm not sure why. I must've had a mental picture of Charles Laughton riding those bells or Igor stealing that brain from the laboratory. "He's good-looking and he's a hunchback?"

"Sure." She raised her eyebrows. The one over the patch didn't go up as high as the other. "If you see him from the front, you can't even tell."

"What's his first name?"

"Andrew."

"How long has he been living here?"

She consulted a file card. "He checked in last Friday night. The twenty-second. Six days."

"What's this spell he was having?"

"I don't know for sure. It was the second one he'd had. He would get pale and nervous. I think he was in a lot of pain. It would get worse and worse all day; then he'd be fine, all rosy and healthy-looking."

"Sounds to me like he was hurtin' for a fix."

"I thought so at first, but I changed my mind. I've seen enough of that and it wasn't the same. Take my word. He was real bad this evening. He came down about four-fifteen, like I said. He didn't complain, but I could tell he was wantin' company to take his mind off it. We played gin until six-thirty. Then he went back upstairs. About twenty minutes later he came down with his old suitcase and checked out. He looked fine, all over his spell."

"Did he have a doctor?"

"I'm pretty sure he didn't. I asked him about it. He said there was nothing to worry about, it would pass. And it did."

"Did he say why he was leaving or where he was going?"

"No, just said he was restless and wanted to be movin' on. Sure hated to see him leave. A real nice kid."

When the cops finally got there, I told them all I knew – except I didn't mention the Detweiler boy. I hung around until I found out that Harry almost certainly wasn't killed after six-thirty. They set the time somewhere between five-ten, when he called me, and six. It looked like Andrew Detweiler was innocent, but what "peculiar" thing had Harry noticed about him, and why he had moved out right after Harry was killed? Birdie let me take a look at his room, but I didn't find a thing, not even an abandoned paper clip.

Friday morning I sat at my desk trying to put the pieces together. Trouble was, I only had two pieces and *they* didn't fit. The sun was coming in off the Boulevard, shining through the window, projecting the chipping letters painted on the glass against the wall in front of me. BERT MALLORY Confidential Investigations. I got up and looked out. This section of the Boulevard wasn't rotting yet, but it wouldn't be long.

There's one sure gauge for judging a part of town: the movie theatres.

It never fails. For instance, a new picture hadn't opened in downtown LA in a long, long time. The action ten years ago was on the Boulevard. Now it's in Westwood. The grand old Pantages, east of Vine and too near the freeway, used to be the site of the most glittering premieres. They even had the Oscar ceremonies there for a while. Now it shows exploitation and double-feature horror films. Only Graumann's Chinese and the once Paramount, once Loew's, now Downtown Cinema (or something) at the west end got good openings. The Nu-View, across the street and down, was showing an X-rated double feature. It was too depressing. So I closed the blind.

Miss Tremaine looked up from her typing at the rattle and frowned. Her desk was out in the small reception area, but I had arranged both desks so we could see each other and talk in normal voices when the door was open. It stayed open most of the time except when I had a client who felt secretaries shouldn't know his troubles. She had been transcribing the Lucas McGowan report for half an hour, *humph*ing and *tsk-tsk*ing at thirty-second intervals. She was having a marvelous time. Miss Tremaine was about forty-five, looked like a constipated librarian, and was the best secretary I'd ever had. She'd been with me seven years. I'd tried a few young and sexy ones, but it hadn't worked out. Either they wouldn't play at all, or they wanted to play all the time. Both kinds were a pain in the ass to face first thing in the morning, every morning.

"Miss Tremaine, will you get Gus Verdugo on the phone, please?"

"Yes, Mr Mallory." She dialed the phone nimbly, sitting as if she were wearing a back brace.

Gus Verdugo worked in R&I. I had done him a favour once, and he insisted on returning it tenfold. I gave him everything I had on Andrew Detweiler and asked him if he'd mind running it through the computer. He wouldn't mind. He called back in fifteen minutes. The computer had never heard of Andrew Detweiler and had only seven hunchbacks, none of them fitting Detweiler's description.

I was sitting there, wondering how in hell I would find him, when the phone rang again. Miss Tremaine stopped typing and lifted the receiver without breaking rhythm. "Mr Mallory's office," she said crisply, really letting the caller know he'd hooked onto an efficient organization. She put her hand over the mouthpiece and looked at me. "It's for you – an obscene phone call." She didn't bat an eyelash or twitch a muscle.

"Thanks," I said and winked at her. She dropped the receiver back on the cradle from a height of three inches and went back to typing. Grinning, I picked up my phone. "Hello, Janice," I said.

"Just a minute till my ear stops ringing," the husky voice tickled my ear.

"What are you doing up this early?" I asked. Janice Fenwick was an exotic dancer at a club on the Strip nights and was working on her master's in oceanography at UCLA in the afternoons. In the year I'd known her I'd seldom seen her stick her nose into the sunlight before eleven.

"I had to catch you before you started following that tiresome woman with the car."

"I've finished that. She's picked up her last parking-lot attendant – at least with this husband." I chuckled.

"I'm glad to hear it."

"What's up?"

"I haven't had an indecent proposition from you in days. So I thought I'd make one of my own."

"I'm all ears."

"We're doing some diving off Catalina tomorrow. Want to come along?"

"Not much we can do in a wetsuit."

"The wetsuit comes off about four; then we'll have Saturday night and all of Sunday."

"Best indecent proposition I've had all week."

Miss Tremaine *humph*ed. It might have been over something in the report, but I don't think it was.

I picked up Janice at her apartment in Westwood early Saturday morning. She was waiting for me and came striding out to the car all legs and healthy golden flesh. She was wearing white shorts, sneakers, and that damned Dallas Cowboys jersey. It was authentic. The name and number on it were quite well-known – even to non–football fans. She wouldn't tell me how she got it, just smirked and looked smug. She tossed her suitcase in the backseat and slid up against me. She smelled like sunshine.

We flew over and spent most of the day *glubb*ing around in the Pacific with a bunch of kids fifteen years younger than I and five years younger than Janice. I'd been on these jaunts with Janice before and enjoyed them so much I'd bought my own wetsuit. But I didn't enjoy it nearly as much as I did Saturday night and all of Sunday.

I got back to my apartment on Beachwood fairly late Sunday night and barely had time to get something to eat at the Mexican restaurant around the corner on Melrose. They have marvelous carne asada. I live right across the street from Paramount, right across from the door people go in to see them tape *The Odd Couple*. Every Friday night when I see them lining up out there, I think I might go someday, but I never seem to get around to it. (You might think I'd see a few movie stars living where I do, but I haven't. I did see Seymour occasionally when he worked at Channel 9, before he went to work for Gene Autry at Channel 5.)

I was so pleasantly pooped I completely forgot about Andrew Detweiler. Until Monday morning when I was sitting at my desk reading the *Times*.

It was a small story on page three, not very exciting or newsworthy. Last night a man named Maurice Milian, age 51, had fallen through the plate glass doors leading onto the terrace of the high rise where he lived. He had been discovered about midnight when the people living below him had noticed dried blood on *their* terrace.

The only thing to connect the deaths of Harry Spinner and Maurice

Milian was a lot of blood flowing around. If Milian had been murdered, there *might* be a link, however tenuous. But Milian's death was accidental – a dumb, stupid accident. It niggled around in my brain for an hour before I gave in. There was only one way to get it out of my head.

"Miss Tremaine, I'll be back in an hour or so. If any slinky blondes come in wanting me to find their kid sisters, tell 'em to wait."

She *humph*ed again and ignored me.

The Almsbury was half a dozen blocks away on Yucca. So I walked. It was a rectangular monolith about eight stories tall, not real new, not too old, but expensive-looking. The small terraces protruded in neat, orderly rows. The long, narrow grounds were immaculate with a lot of succulents that looked like they might have been imported from Mars. There were also the inevitable palm trees and clumps of birds of paradise. A small, discreet, polished placard dangled in a wrought-iron frame proclaiming, ever so softly, NO VACANCY.

Two willowy young men gave me appraising glances in the carpeted lobby as they exited into the sunlight like exotic jungle birds. It's one of those, I thought. My suspicions were confirmed when I looked over the tenant directory. All the names seemed to be male, but none of them was Andrew Detweiler.

Maurice Milian was still listed as 407. I took the elevator to four and rang the bell of 409. The bell played a few notes of Bach, or maybe Vivaldi or Telemann. All those old Baroques sound alike to me. The vision of loveliness who opened the door was about forty, almost as slim as Twiggy but as tall as I. He wore a flowered silk shirt open to the waist, exposing his bony hairless chest, and tight white pants that might as well have been made of Saran Wrap. He didn't say anything, just let his eyebrows rise inquiringly as his eyes flicked down, then up.

"Good morning," I said and showed him my ID. He blanched. His eyes became marbles brimming with terror. He was about to panic, tensing to slam the door. I smiled my friendly, disarming smile and went on as if I hadn't noticed. "I'm inquiring about a man named Andrew

Detweiler." The terror trickled from his eyes, and I could see his thin chest throbbing. He gave me a blank look that meant he'd never heard the name.

"He's about twenty-two," I continued, "dark, curly hair, very good-looking."

He grinned wryly, calming down, trying to cover his panic. "Aren't they all?" he said.

"Detweiler is a hunchback."

His smile contracted suddenly. His eyebrows shot up. "Oh," he said. "Him."

Bingo!

Mallory, you've led a clean, wholesome life and it's paying off.

"Does he live in the building?" I swallowed to get my heart back in place and blinked a couple of times to clear away the skyrockets.

"No. He was…visiting."

"May I come in and talk to you about him?"

He was holding the door three-quarters shut, and so I couldn't see anything in the room but an expensive-looking colour TV. He glanced over his shoulder nervously at something behind him. The inner ends of his eyebrows drooped in a frown. He looked back at me and started to say something, then, with a small defiance, shrugged his eyebrows. "Sure, but there's not much I can tell you."

He pushed the door all the way open and stepped back. It was a good-sized living room come to life from the pages of a decorator magazine. A kitchen behind a half wall was on my right. A hallway led somewhere on my left. Directly in front of me were double sliding glass doors leading to the terrace. On the terrace was a bronzed hunk of beef stretched out nude trying to get bronzer. The hunk opened his eyes and looked at me. He apparently decided I wasn't competition and closed them again. Tall and lanky indicated one of two identical orange-and-brown-striped couches facing each other across a football field–size marble and glass cocktail table. He sat on the other one, took a cigarette from an alabaster box and lit it with an alabaster lighter. As an afterthought, he offered me one.

"Who was Detweiler visiting?" I asked as I lit my cigarette. The lighter felt cool and expensive in my hand.

"Maurice – next door," he inclined his head slightly towards 407.

"Isn't he the one who was killed in an accident last night?"

He blew a stream of smoke from pursed lips and tapped his cigarette on an alabaster ashtray. "Yes," he said.

"How long had Maurice and Detweiler known each other?"

"Not long."

"How long?"

He snuffed his cigarette out on pure white alabaster and sat so prim and pristine I would have bet his feces came out wrapped in cellophane. He shrugged his eyebrows again. "Maurice picked him up somewhere the other night."

"Which night?"

He thought a moment. "Thursday, I think. Yes, Thursday."

"Was Detweiler a hustler?"

He crossed his legs like a forties pinup and dangled his Roman sandal. His lips twitched scornfully. "If he was, he would've starved. He was de-*formed!*"

"Maurice didn't seem to mind." He sniffed and lit another cigarette. "When did Detweiler leave?"

He shrugged. "I saw him yesterday afternoon. I was out last night…until quite late."

"How did they get along? Did they quarrel or fight?"

"I have no idea. I only saw them in the hall a couple of times. Maurice and I were…not close." He stood, fidgety. "There's really not anything I can tell you. Why don't you ask David and Murray. They and Maurice are…were thick as thieves."

"David and Murray?"

"Across the hall. 408."

I stood up. "I'll do that. Thank you very much." I looked at the plate glass doors. I guess it would be pretty easy to walk through one of them if you thought it was open. "Are all the apartments alike? Those terrace doors?"

He nodded. "Ticky-tacky."

"Thanks again."

"Don't mention it." He opened the door for me and then closed it behind me. I sighed and walked across to 408. I rang the bell. It didn't play anything, just went *bing-bong*.

David (or Murray) was about twenty-five, red-headed, and freckled. He had a slim, muscular body which was also freckled. I could tell because he was wearing only a pair of jeans, cut off very short, and split up the sides to the waistband. He was barefooted and had a smudge of green paint on his nose. He had an open, friendly face and gave me a neutral smile-for-a-stranger. "Yes?" he asked.

I showed him my ID. Instead of going pale he only looked interested. "I was told by the man in 409 you might be able to tell me something about Andrew Detweiler."

"Andy?" He frowned slightly. "Come on in. I'm David Fowler." He held out his hand.

I shook it. "Bert Mallory." The apartment couldn't have been more different from the one across the hall. It was comfortable and cluttered, and dominated by a drafting table surrounded by jars of brushes and boxes of paint tubes. Architecturally, however, it was almost identical.

The terrace was covered with potted plants rather than naked muscles. David Fowler sat on the stool at the drafting table and began cleaning brushes. When he sat, the split in his shorts opened and exposed half his butt, which was also freckled. But I got the impression he wasn't exhibiting himself; he was just completely indifferent.

"What do you want to know about Andy?"

"Everything."

He laughed. "That lets me out. Sit down. Move the stuff."

I cleared a space on the couch and sat. "How did Detweiler and Maurice get along?"

He gave me a knowing look. "Fine. As far as I know. Maurice liked to pick up stray puppies. Andy was a stray puppy."

"Was Detweiler a hustler?"

He laughed again. "No. I doubt if he knew what the word means."

"Was he gay?"

"No."

"How do you know?"

He grinned. "Haven't you heard? We can spot each other a mile away. Would you like some coffee?"

"Yes, I would. Thank you."

He went to the half wall separating the kitchen and poured two cups from a pot that looked like it was kept hot and full all the time. "It's hard to describe Andy. There was something very little-boyish about him. A real innocent. Delighted with everything new. It's sad about his back. Real sad." He handed me a cup and returned to the stool. "There was something very secretive about him. Not about his feelings; he was very open about things like that."

"Did he and Maurice have sex together?"

"No. I told you it was a stray puppy relationship. I wish Murray was here. He's much better with words than I am. I'm visually oriented."

"Where is he?"

"At work. He's a lawyer."

"Do you think Detweiler could have killed Maurice?"

"No."

"Why?"

"He was here with us all evening. We had dinner and played Scrabble. I think he was real sick, but he tried to pretend he wasn't. Even if he hadn't been here I would not think so."

"When was the last time you saw him?"

"He left about a half hour before they found Maurice. I imagine he went over there, saw Maurice dead, and decided to disappear. Can't say I blame him. The police might've gotten some funny ideas. We didn't mention him."

"Why not?"

"There was no point in getting him involved. It was just an accident."

"He couldn't have killed Maurice after he left here?"

"No. They said he's been dead over an hour. What did Desmond tell you?"

"Desmond?"

"Across the hall. The one who looks like he smells something bad."

"How did you know I talked to him and not the side of beef?"

He laughed and almost dropped his coffee cup. "I don't think Roy *can* talk."

"He didn't know nothin' about nothin'." I found myself laughing also. I got up and walked to the glass doors. I slid them open and then shut again. "Did you ever think one of these was open when it was really shut?"

"No. But I've heard of it happening."

I sighed. "So have I." I turned and looked at what he was working on at the drafting table. It was a small painting of a boy and girl, she in a soft white dress, and he in jeans and T-shirt. They looked about fifteen. They were embracing, about to kiss. It was quite obviously the first time for both of them. It was good. I told him so.

He grinned with pleasure. "Thanks. It's for a paperback cover."

"Whose idea was it that Detweiler have dinner and spend the evening with you?"

He thought for a moment. "Maurice." He looked up at me and grinned. "Do you know stamps?"

It took me a second to realize what he meant. "You mean stamp collecting? Not much."

"Maurice was a philatelist. He specialized in postwar Germany –

locals and zones, things like that. He'd gotten a kilo of buildings and wanted to sort them undisturbed."

I shook my head. "You've lost me. A kilo of buildings."

He laughed. "It's a set of twenty-eight stamps issued in the American Zone in 1948 showing famous German buildings. Conditions in Germany were still pretty chaotic at the time, and the stamps were printed under fairly makeshift circumstances. Consequently, there's an enormous variety of different perforations, watermarks, and engravings. Hundreds as a matter of fact. Maurice could spend hours and hours poring over them."

"Are they valuable?"

"No. Very common. Some of the varieties are hard to find, but they're not valuable." He gave me a knowing look. "Nothing was missing from Maurice's apartment."

I shrugged. "It had occurred to me to wonder where Detweiler got his money."

"I don't know. The subject never came up." He wasn't being defensive.

"You liked him, didn't you?"

There was a weary sadness in his eyes. "Yes," he said.

That afternoon I picked up Birdie Pawlowicz at the Brewster Hotel and took her to Harry Spinner's funeral. I told her about Maurice Milian and Andrew Detweiler. We talked it around and around. The Detweiler boy obviously couldn't have killed Harry *or* Milian, but it was stretching coincidence a little bit far.

After the funeral I went to the Los Angeles Public Library and started checking back issues of the *Times.* I'd only made it back three weeks when the library closed. The LA *Times* is *thick,* and unless the death is sensational or the dead prominent, the story might be tucked in anywhere except the classifieds.

Last Tuesday, the 26th, a girl had cut her wrists with a razor blade in North Hollywood.

The day before, Monday, the 25th, a girl had miscarried and hemorrhaged. She had bled to death because she and her boyfriend were stoned out of their heads. They lived a block off Western – very near the Brewster – and Detweiler was at the Brewster Monday.

Sunday, the 24th, a wino had been knifed in MacArthur Park.

Saturday, the 23rd, I had three. A knifing in a bar on Pico, a shooting in a rooming house on Irolo, and a rape and knifing in an alley off LaBrea. Only the gunshot victim had bled to death, but there had been a lot of blood in all three.

Friday, the 22nd, the same day Detweiler checked into the Brewster, a two-year-old boy had fallen on an upturned rake in his backyard on Larchemont – only eight or ten blocks from where I lived on Beachwood. And a couple of Chicano kids had had a knife fight behind Hollywood High. One was dead and the other was in jail. Ah, *machismo!*

The list went on and on, all the way back to Thursday, the 7th. On that day was another slashed-wrist suicide near Western and Wilshire.

The next morning, Tuesday, the 3rd, I called Miss Tremaine and told her I'd be late getting in but would check in every couple of hours to find out if the slinky blonde looking for her kid sister had shown up. She *humph*ed.

Larchemont is a middle-class neighbourhood huddled in between the old wealth around the country club and the blight spreading down Melrose from Western Avenue. It tries to give the impression of suburbia – and does a pretty good job of it – rather than just another nearly downtown shopping center. The area isn't big on apartments or rooming houses, but there are a few. I found the Detweiler boy at the third one I checked. It was a block and a half from where the little kid fell on the rake.

According to the landlord, at the time of the kid's death Detweiler was playing bridge with him and a couple of elderly old-maid sisters in number twelve. He hadn't been feeling well and had moved out later that evening – to catch a bus to San Diego, to visit his ailing mother. The landlord had felt sorry for him, so sorry he'd broken a steadfast rule and refunded most of the month's rent Detweiler had paid in advance. After all, he'd only been there three days. So sad about his back. Such a nice gentle boy – a writer, you know.

No, I didn't know, but it explained how he could move around so much without seeming to work.

I called David Fowler: "Yes, Andy had a portable typewriter, but he hadn't mentioned being a writer."

And Birdie Pawlowicz: "Yeah, he typed a lot in his room."

I found the Detweiler boy again on the 16th and the 19th. He'd moved into a rooming house near Silver Lake Park on the night of the 13th and moved out again on the 19th. The landlady hadn't refunded his money, but she gave him an alibi for the knifing of an old man in the park on the 16th and the suicide of a girl in the same rooming house on the 19th. He'd been in the pink of health when he moved in, sick on the 16th, healthy the 17th, and sick again on the 19th.

It was like a rerun. He lived a block away from where a man was mugged, killed, and robbed in an alley on the 13th – though the details of the murder didn't seem to fit the pattern. But he was sick, had an alibi, and moved to Silver Lake.

Rerun it on the 10th: a woman slipped in the bathtub and fell through the glass shower doors, cutting herself to ribbons. Sick, alibi, moved.

It may be because I was always rotten in math, but it wasn't until right then that I figured out Detweiler's timetable. Milian died the 1st, Harry Spinner the 28th, the miscarriage the 25th, the little kid on the 22nd, Silver Lake on the 16th and 19th, etc, etc, etc.

A bloody death occurred in Detweiler's general vicinity every third day.

But I couldn't figure out a pattern for the victims: male, female, little kids, old aunties, married, unmarried, rich, poor, young, old. No pattern of any kind, and there's *always* a pattern. I even checked to see if the names were in alphabetical order.

I got back to my office at six. Miss Tremaine sat primly at her desk, cleared of everything but her purse and a notepad. She reminded me quite a lot of Desmond. "What are you still doing here, Miss Tremaine? You should've left an hour ago." I sat at my desk, leaned back until the swivel chair groaned twice, and propped my feet up.

She picked up the pad. "I wanted to give you your calls."

"Can't they wait? I've been sleuthing all day and I'm bushed."

"No one is paying you to find this Detweiler person, are they?"

"No."

"Your bank statement came today."

"What's that supposed to mean?"

"Nothing. A good secretary keeps her employer informed. I was informing you."

"Okay. Who called?"

She consulted the pad, but I'd bet my last gumshoe she knew every word on it by heart. "A Mrs Carmichael called. Her French poodle has been kidnapped. She wants you to find her."

"Ye Gods! Why doesn't she go to the police?"

"Because she's positive her ex-husband is the kidnapper. She doesn't want to get him in any trouble; she just wants Gwendolyn back."

"Gwendolyn?"

"Gwendolyn. A Mrs Bushyager came by. She wants you to find her little sister."

I sat up so fast I almost fell out of the chair. I gave her a long, hard stare, but her neutral expression didn't flicker. "You're kidding." Her eyebrows rose a millimetre. "Was she a slinky blonde?"

"No. She was a dumpy brunette."

I settled back in the chair, trying not to laugh. "Why does Mrs Bushyager want me to find her little sister?" I sputtered.

"Because Mrs Bushyager thinks she's shacked up somewhere with *Mr* Bushyager. She'd like you to call her tonight."

"Tomorrow. I've got a date with Janice tonight." She reached in her desk drawer and pulled out my bank statement. She dropped it on the desk with a papery plop. "Don't worry," I assured her, "I won't spend much money. Just a little spaghetti and wine tonight and ham and eggs in the morning." She *humph*ed. My point. "Anything else?"

"A Mr Bloomfeld called. He wants you to get the goods on Mrs Bloomfeld so he can sue for divorce."

I sighed. Miss Tremaine closed the pad. "Okay. No to Mrs Carmichael and make appointments for Bushyager and Bloomfeld." She lowered her eyelids at me. I spread my hands. "Would Sam Spade go looking for a French poodle named Gwendolyn?"

"He might if he had your bank statement. Mr Bloomfeld will be in at two, Mrs Bushyager at three."

"Miss Tremaine, you'd make somebody a wonderful mother." She didn't even *humph;* she just picked up her purse and stalked out. I swiveled the chair around and looked at the calendar. Tomorrow was the 4th.

Somebody would die tomorrow and Andrew Detweiler would be close by.

I scooted up in bed and leaned against the headboard. Janice snorted into the pillow and opened one eye, pinning me with it. "I didn't mean to wake you," I said.

"What's the matter," she muttered, "too much spaghetti?"

"No. Too much Andrew Detweiler."

She scooted up beside me, keeping the sheet over her breasts, and turned on the light. She rummaged around on the nightstand for a cigarette. "Who wants to divorce him?"

"That's mean, Janice," I groaned.

"You want a cigarette?"

"Yeah."

She put two cigarettes in her mouth and lit them both. She handed me one. "You don't look a bit like Paul Henreid," I said.

She grinned. "That's funny. You look like Bette Davis. Who's Andrew Detweiler?"

So I told her.

"It's elementary, my dear Sherlock," she said. "Andrew Detweiler is a vampire." I frowned at her. "Of course, he's a *clever* vampire. Vampires are usually stupid. They always give themselves away by leaving those two little teeth marks on people's jugulars."

"Darling, even vampires have to be at the scene of the crime."

"He always has an alibi, huh?"

I got out of bed and headed for the bathroom. "That's suspicious in itself."

When I came out she said, "Why?"

"Innocent people usually don't have alibis, especially not one every three days."

"Which is probably why innocent people get put in jail so often."

I chuckled and sat on the edge of the bed. "You may be right."

"Bert, do that again."

I looked at her over my shoulder. "Do what?"

"Go to the bathroom."

"I don't think I can. My bladder holds only so much."

"I don't mean that. Walk over to the bathroom door."

I gave her a suspicious frown, got up, and walked over to the bathroom door. I turned around, crossed my arms, and leaned against the door frame. "Well?"

She grinned. "You've got a cute rear end. Almost as cute as Burt Reynolds'. Maybe he's twins."

"What?" I practically screamed.

"Maybe Andrew Detweiler is twins. One of them commits the murders and the other establishes the alibis."

"Twin vampires?"

She frowned. "That's a bit much, isn't it? Had they discovered blood groups in Bram Stoker's day?"

I got back in bed and pulled the sheet up to my waist, leaning beside her against the headboard. "I haven't the foggiest idea."

"That's another way vampires are stupid. They never check the victim's blood group. The wrong blood group can kill you."

"Vampires don't exactly get transfusions."

"It all amounts to the same thing, doesn't it?" I shrugged. "Oh, well," she sighed, "vampires are stupid." She reached over and plucked at the hair on my chest. "I haven't had an indecent proposition in hours," she said, grinning.

So I made one.

Wednesday morning I made a dozen phone calls. Of the nine victims I knew about, I was able to find the information on six.

All six had the same blood group.

I lit a cigarette and leaned back in the swivel chair. The whole thing was spinning around in my head. I'd found a pattern for the victims, but I didn't know if it was *the* pattern. It just didn't make sense. Maybe Detweiler *was* a vampire.

"Mallory," I said out loud, "you're cracking up."

Miss Tremaine glanced up. "If I were you, I'd listen to you," she said poker-faced.

The next morning I staggered out of bed at 6.00 am. I took a cold shower, shaved, dressed, and put Murine in my eyes. They still felt like I'd washed them in rubber cement. Mrs Bloomfeld had kept me up until two the night before, doing all the night spots in Santa Monica with some dude I hadn't identified yet. When they checked into a motel, I went home and went to bed.

I couldn't find a morning paper at that hour closer than Western and

Wilshire. The story was on page seven. Fortunately they found the body in time for the early edition. A woman named Sybil Herndon, age 38, had committed suicide in an apartment on Las Palmas. (Detweiler hadn't gone very far. The address was just around the corner from the Almsbury.) She had cut her wrists on a piece of broken mirror. She had been discovered about eleven-thirty when the manager went over to ask her to turn down the volume on her television set.

It was too early to drop around, and so I ate breakfast, hoping this was one of the times Detweiler stuck around for more than three days. Not for a minute did I doubt he would be living at the apartment court on Las Palmas, or not far away.

The owner-manager of the court was one of those creatures peculiar to Hollywood. She must have been a starlet in the twenties or thirties, but success had eluded her. So she had tried to freeze herself in time. She still expected, at any moment, a call from The Studio. But her flesh hadn't cooperated. Her hair was the colour of tarnished copper, and the fire-engine-red lipstick was painted far past her thin lips. Her watery eyes peered at me through a Lone Ranger mask of Maybelline on a plaster-white face. Her dress had obviously been copied from the wardrobe of Norma Shearer.

"Yes?" She had a breathy voice. Her eyes quickly traveled the length of my body. That happens often enough to keep me feeling good, but this time it gave me a queasy sensation, like I was being measured for a mummy case. I showed her my ID, and asked if I could speak to her about one of the tenants.

"Of course. Come on in. I'm Lorraine Nesbitt." Was there a flicker of disappointment that I hadn't recognized the name? She stepped back holding the door for me. I could tell that detectives, private or otherwise, asking about her tenants wasn't a new thing. I walked into the doilied room, and she looked at me from a hundred directions. The faded photographs covered every level surface and clung to the walls like leeches. She had been quite a dish – forty years ago. She saw me looking at the photos and smiled. The makeup around her mouth cracked.

"Which one do you want to ask about?" The smile vanished and the cracks closed.

"Andrew Detweiler." She looked blank. "Young, good-looking, with a hunchback."

The cracks opened. "Oh, yes. He's only been here a few days. The name had slipped my mind."

"He's still here?"

"Oh, yes." She sighed. "It's so unfair for such a beautiful young man to have a physical impairment."

"What can you tell me about him?"

"Not much. He's only been here since Sunday night. He's very handsome, like an angel, a dark angel. But it wasn't his handsomeness that attracted me." She smiled. "I've seen many handsome men in my day, you know. It's difficult to verbalize. He has such an incredible innocence. A lost, doomed look that Byron must have had. A vulnerability that makes you want to shield him and protect him. I don't know for sure what it is, but it struck a chord in my soul. Soul," she mused. "Maybe that's it. He wears his soul on his face." She nodded, as if to herself. "A dangerous thing to do." She looked back up at me. "If that quality, whatever it is, would photograph, he would become a star overnight, whether he could act or not. Except – of course – for his infirmity."

Lorraine Nesbitt, I decided, was as nutty as a fruitcake.

Someone entered the room. He stood leaning against the door frame, looking at me with sleepy eyes. He was about twenty-five, wearing tight chinos without underwear and a T-shirt. His hair was tousled and cut unfashionably short. He had a good-looking Kansas face. The haircut made me think he was new in town, but the eyes said he wasn't. I guess the old broad liked his hair that way.

She simpered. "Oh, Johnny! Come on in. This detective was asking about Andrew Detweiler in number seven." She turned back to me.

"This is my protégé, Johnny Peacock – a very talented young man. I'm arranging for a screen test as soon as Mr Goldwyn returns my calls." She lowered her eyelids demurely. "I was a Goldwyn girl, you know."

Funny, I thought Goldwyn was dead. Maybe he wasn't.

Johnny took the news of his impending stardom with total unconcern. He moved to the couch and sat down, yawning. "Detweiler? Don't think I ever laid eyes on the man. What'd he do?"

"Nothing. Just routine." Obviously he thought I was a police detective. No point in changing his mind. "Where was he last night when the Herndon woman died?"

"In his room, I think. I heard his typewriter. He wasn't feeling well," Lorraine Nesbitt said. Then she sucked air through her teeth and clamped her fingers to her scarlet lips. "Do you think he had something to do with *that?*"

Detweiler had broken his pattern. He didn't have an alibi. I couldn't believe it.

"Oh, Lorraine," Johnny grumbled.

I turned to him. "Do you know where Detweiler was?"

He shrugged. "No idea."

"They why are you so sure he had nothing to do with it?"

"She committed suicide."

"How do you know for sure?"

"The door was bolted from the inside. They had to break it down to get in."

"What about the window? Was it locked too?"

"No. The window was open. But it has bars on it. No way anybody could get in."

"When I couldn't get her to answer my knock last night, I went around to the window and looked in. She was lying there with blood all over." She began to sniffle. Johnny got up and put his arms around her. He looked at me, grinned, and shrugged.

"Do you have a vacancy?" I asked, getting a whiz-bang idea.

"Yes," she said, the sniffles disappearing instantly. "I have two. Actually three but I can't rent Miss Herndon's room for a few days – until someone claims her things."

"I'd like to rent the one closest to number seven," I said.

I wasn't lucky enough to get number six or eight, but I did get five. Lorraine Nesbitt's nameless, dingy apartment court was a fleabag. Number five was one room with a closet, a tiny kitchen, and a tiny bath – identical with the other nine units she assured me. With a good deal of tugging and grunting the couch turned into a lumpy bed. The refrigerator looked as if someone had spilled a bottle of Br'er Rabbit back in 1938 and hadn't cleaned it up yet. The stove looked like a lube rack. Well, I sighed, it was only for three days. I had to pay a month's rent in advance anyway, but I put it down as a bribe to keep Lorraine's and Johnny's mouths shut about my being a detective.

I moved in enough clothes for three days, some sheets and pillows, took another look at the kitchen and decided to eat out. I took a jug of Lysol to the bathroom and crossed my fingers. Miss Tremaine brought up the bank statement and *humph*ed a few times.

Number five had one door and four windows – identical to the other nine, Lorraine assured me. The door had a heavy-duty bolt that couldn't be fastened or unfastened from the outside. The window beside the door didn't open at all and wasn't intended to. The bathroom and kitchen windows cranked out and were tall and skinny, about twenty-four by six. The other living room window, opposite the door, slid upward. The iron bars bolted to the frame were so rusted I doubted if they could be removed without ripping out the whole window. It appeared Andrew Detweiler had another perfect alibi after all – along with the rest of the world.

I stood outside number seven suddenly feeling like a teenager about to pick up his first date. I could hear Detweiler's typewriter *tickety-tick*ing away inside. Okay, Mallory, this is what you've been breaking your neck on for a week.

I knocked on the door.

I heard the typewriter stop ticking and the scrape of a chair being scooted back. I didn't hear anything else for fifteen or twenty seconds, and I wondered what he was doing. Then the bolt was drawn and the door opened.

He was buttoning his shirt. That must have been the delay; he wouldn't want anyone to see him with his shirt off. Everything I'd been told about him was true. He wasn't very tall; the top of his head came to my nose. He was dark, though not as dark as I'd expected. I couldn't place his ancestry. It certainly wasn't Latin-American and I didn't think it was Slavic. His features were soft, without the angularity usually found in Mediterranean races. His hair wasn't quite black. It wasn't exactly long and it wasn't exactly short. His clothes were nondescript. Everything about him was neutral – except his face. It was just about as Lorraine Nesbitt had described it. If you called central casting and asked for a male angel, you'd get Andrew Detweiler in a blond wig. His body was slim and well-formed – from where I was standing I couldn't see the hump and you'd never know there was one. I had a glimpse of his bare chest as he buttoned his shirt. It wasn't muscular but it was very well made. He was very healthy-looking – pink and flushed with health, though slightly pale, as if he didn't get out in the sun much. His dark eyes were astounding. If you blocked out the rest of the face, leaving nothing but the eyes, you'd swear he was no more than four years old. You've seen little kids with those big, guileless, unguarded, inquiring eyes, haven't you?

"Yes?" he asked.

I smiled. "Hello. I'm Bert Mallory. I just moved in to number five. Miss Nesbitt tells me you like to play gin."

"Yes," he said, grinning. "Come on in."

He turned to move out of the way and I saw the hump. I don't know how to describe what I felt. I suddenly had a hurting in my gut. I felt the same unfairness and sadness the others had, the way you would feel about any beautiful thing with one overwhelming flaw.

"I'm not disturbing you, am I? I heard the typewriter." The room was indeed identical to mine, though it looked a hundred percent more livable. I couldn't put my finger on what he had done to it to make it that way. Maybe it was just the semidarkness. He had the curtains tightly closed and one lamp lit beside the typewriter.

"Yeah, I was working on a story, but I'd rather play gin." He grinned, open and artless. "If I could make money playing gin, I wouldn't write."

"Lots of people make money playing gin."

"Oh, I couldn't. I'm too unlucky."

He certainly had a right to say that, but there was no self-pity, just an observation. Then he looked at me with slightly distressed eyes. "You…ah…didn't want to play for money, did you?"

"Not at all," I said and his eyes cleared. "What kind of stories do you write?"

"Oh, all kinds." He shrugged. "Fantasy mostly."

"Do you sell them?"

"Most of 'em."

"I don't recall seeing your name anywhere. Miss Nesbitt said it was Andrew Detweiler?"

He nodded. "I use another name. You probably wouldn't know it either. It's not exactly a household word." His eyes said he'd really rather not tell me what it was. He had a slight accent, a sort of soft slowness, not exactly a drawl and not exactly Deep South. He shoved the typewriter over and pulled out a deck of cards.

"Where're you from?" I asked. "I don't place the accent."

He grinned and shuffled the cards. "North Carolina. Back in the Blue Ridge."

We cut and I dealt. "How long have you been in Hollywood?"

"About two months."

"How do you like it?"

He grinned his beguiling grin and picked up my discard. "It's very...unusual. Have you lived here very long, Mr Mallory?"

"Bert. All my life. I was born in Inglewood. My mother still lives there."

"It must be...unusual...to live in the same place all your life."

"You move around a lot?"

"Yeah. Gin."

I laughed. "I thought you were unlucky."

"If we were playing for money, I wouldn't be able to do anything right."

We played gin the rest of the afternoon and talked – talked a lot. Detweiler seemed eager to talk or, at least, eager to have someone to talk with. He never told me anything that would connect him to nine deaths, mostly about where he'd been, things he'd read. He read a lot, just about anything he could get his hands on. I got the impression he hadn't really *lived* life so much as he'd *read* it, that all the things he knew about had never physically affected him. He was like an insulated island. Life flowed around him but never touched him. I wondered if the hump on his back made that much difference, if it made him such a green monkey he'd had to retreat into his insular existence. Practically everyone I talked to liked him, mixed with varying portions of pity, to be sure, but liking nevertheless. Harry Spinner had liked him, but had discovered something "peculiar" about him; Birdie Pawlowicz, Maurice Milian, David Fowler, Lorraine Nesbitt, they all liked him.

And, God damn it, I liked him too.

At midnight I was still awake, sitting in number five in my jockey shorts with the light out and the door open. I listened to the ticking of the Detweiler boy's typewriter and the muffled roar of Los Angeles. And thought, and thought, and thought. And got nowhere.

Someone walked by the door, quietly and carefully. I leaned my head out. It was Johnny Peacock. He moved down the line of bungalows silent as a shadow. He turned south when he reached the sidewalk. Going to Selma or the Boulevard to turn a trick and make a few extra bucks. Lorraine must keep tight purse strings. Better watch it, kid. If she finds out, you'll be back on the streets again. And you haven't got too many years left where you can make good money by just gettin' it up.

I dropped in at the office for a while Friday morning and checked the first-of-the-month bills. Miss Tremaine had a list of new prospective clients. "Tell everyone I can't get to anything till Monday."

She nodded in disapproval. "Mr Bloomfeld called."

"Did you get my report?"

"Yes. He was very pleased, but he wants the man's name."

"Tell him I'll get back on it Monday."

"Mrs Bushyager called. Her sister and Mr Bushyager are still missing."

"Tell her I'll get on it Monday." She opened her mouth. "If you say anything about my bank account, I'll put Spanish fly in your Ovaltine." She didn't *humph,* she giggled. I wonder how many points *that* is?

That afternoon I played gin with the Detweiler boy. He was genuinely glad to see me, like a friendly puppy. I was beginning to feel like a son of a bitch.

He hadn't mentioned North Carolina except that once the day before, and I was extremely interested in all subjects he wanted to avoid. "What's it like in the Blue Ridge? Coon huntin' and moonshine?"

He grinned and blitzed me. "Yeah, I guess. Most of the things you read about it are pretty nearly true. It's really a different world back in there, with almost no contact with the outside."

"How far in did you live?"

"About as far as you can get without comin' out the other side. Did you know most of the people never heard of television or movies and some of 'em don't even know the name of the President? Most of 'em never been more than thirty miles from the place they were born, never saw an electric light? You wouldn't believe it. But it's more than just *things* that're different. People are different, think different – like a foreign country." He shrugged. "I guess it'll all be gone before too long though. Things keep creepin' closer and closer. Did you know I never went to school?" he said, grinning. "Not a day of my life. I didn't wear shoes till I was ten. You wouldn't believe it." He shook his head, remembering. "Always kinda wished I coulda gone to school," he murmured softly.

"Why did you leave?"

"No reason to stay. When I was eight, my parents were killed in a fire. Our house burned down. I was taken in by a balmy old woman who lived not far away. I had some kin, but they didn't want me." He looked at me, trusting me. "They're pretty superstitious back in there, you know. Thought I was…marked. Anyway, the old woman took me in. She was a midwife, but she fancied herself a witch or something. Always making me drink some mess she'd brewed up. She fed me, clothed me, educated me, after a fashion, tried to teach me all her conjures, but I never could take 'em seriously." He grinned sheepishly. "I did chores for her and eventually became a sort of assistant, I guess. I helped her birth babies…I mean, deliver babies a couple of times, but that didn't last long. The parents were afraid me bein' around might mark the baby. She taught me to read and I couldn't stop. She had a lot of books she'd dredged up somewhere, more of 'em published before the First World War. I read a complete set of encyclopedias – published in 1911."

I laughed.

His eyes clouded. "Then she…died. I was fifteen, so I left. I did odd jobs and kept reading. Then I wrote a story and sent it to a magazine. They bought it; paid me fifty dollars. Thought I was rich, so I wrote another one. Since then I've been travelling around and writing. I've got an agent who takes care of everything, and so all I do is just write."

Detweiler's flush of health was wearing off that afternoon. He wasn't ill, just beginning to feel like the rest of us mortals. And I was feeling my resolve begin to crumble. It was hard to believe this beguiling kid could possibly be involved in a string of bloody deaths. Maybe it was just a series of unbelievable coincidences. Yeah, "unbelievable" was the key word. He *had* to be involved unless the laws of probability had broken down completely. Yet I could swear Detweiler wasn't putting on an act. His guileless innocence was real, damn it, *real.*

Saturday morning, the third day since Miss Herndon died, I had a talk with Lorraine and Johnny. If Detweiler wanted to play cards or something that night, I wanted them to agree and suggest I be a fourth. If he didn't bring it up, I would, but I had a feeling he would want his usual alibi this time.

Detweiler left his room that afternoon for the first time since I'd been there. He went north on Las Palmas, dropped a large manila envelope in the mailbox (the story he'd been working on, I guess), and bought groceries at the supermarket on Highland. Did that mean he wasn't planning to move? I had a sudden pang in my belly. What if he was staying because of his friendship with *me?* I felt more like a son of a bitch every minute.

Johnny Peacock came by an hour later acting very conspiratorial. Detweiler had suggested a bridge game that night, but Johnny didn't play bridge, and so they settled on Scrabble.

I dropped by number seven. The typewriter had been put away, but the cards and score pad were still on the table. His suitcase was on the floor by the couch. It was riveted cowhide of a vintage I hadn't seen since I was a kid. Though it wore a mellow patina of age, it had been preserved with neat's-foot oil and loving care. I may have been mistaken about his not moving.

Detweiler wasn't feeling well at all. He was pale and drawn and fidgety. His eyelids were heavy and his speech was faintly blurred. I'm sure he was in pain, but he tried to act as if nothing were wrong.

"Are you sure you feel like playing Scrabble tonight?" I asked.

He gave me a cheerful, if slightly strained, smile. "Oh, sure. I'm all right. I'll be fine in the morning."

"Do you think you ought to play?"

"Yeah, it...takes my mind off my...ah...headache. Don't worry about it. I have these spells all the time. They always go away."

"How long have you had them?"

"Since...I was a kid." He grinned. "You think it was one of those brews the old witch-woman gave me caused it? Maybe I could sue for malpractice."

"Have you ever seen a doctor? A real doctor?"

"Once."

"What did he tell you?"

He shrugged. "Oh, nothing much. Take two aspirin, drink lots of liquids, get plenty of rest, that sort of thing." He didn't want to talk about it. "It always goes away."

"What if one time it doesn't?"

He looked at me with an expression I'd never seen before and I knew why Lorraine said he had a lost, doomed look. "Well, we can't live forever, can we? Are you ready to go?"

The game started out like a Marx Brothers routine. Lorraine and Johnny acted like two canaries playing Scrabble with the cat, but Detweiler was so normal and unconcerned they soon settled down. Conversation was tense and ragged at first until Lorraine got off on her "career" and kept us entertained and laughing. She had known a lot of famous people and was a fountain of anecdotes, most of them funny and libelous. Detweiler proved quickly to be the best player, but Johnny, to my surprise, was no slouch. Lorraine played dismally but she didn't seem to mind.

I would have enjoyed the evening thoroughly if I hadn't known someone nearby was dead or dying.

After about two hours, in which Detweiler grew progressively more ill, I excused myself to go to the bathroom. While I was away from the table, I palmed Lorraine's master key.

In another half hour I said I had to call it a night. I had to get up early the next morning. I always spent Sunday with my mother in Inglewood. My mother was touring Yucatán at the time, but that was neither here nor there.

I looked at Johnny. He nodded. He was to make sure Detweiler stayed at least another twenty minutes and then follow him when he did leave. If he went anywhere but his apartment, he was to come and let me know, quick.

I let myself into number seven with the master key. The drapes were closed, and so I took a chance and turned on the bathroom light. Detweiler's possessions were meager. Eight shirts, six pairs of pants, and a light jacket hung in the closet. The shirts and jacket had been altered to allow for the hump. Except for that, the closet was bare. The bathroom contained nothing out of the ordinary – just about the same as mine. The kitchen had one plastic plate, one plastic cup, one plastic glass, one plastic bowl, one small folding skillet, one small folding sauce pan, one metal spoon, one metal fork, and a medium-sized kitchen knife. All of it together would barely fill a shoebox.

The suitcase, still beside the couch, hadn't been unpacked – except for the clothes hanging in the closet and the kitchen utensils. There was underwear, socks, an extra pair of shoes, an unopened ream of paper, a bunch of other stuff necessary for writing, and a dozen or so paperbacks. The books were rubber-stamped with the name of a used-book store on Santa Monica Boulevard. They were a mixture: science fiction, mysteries, biographies, philosophy, several by Colin Wilson.

There was also a carbon copy of the story he'd just finished. The return address on the first page was a box number at the Hollywood post office. The title of the story was "Deathsong." I wish I'd had time to read it.

All in all, I didn't find anything. Except for the books and the deck of cards there was nothing of Andrew Detweiler personally in the whole apartment. I hadn't thought it possible for anyone to lead such a turnip existence.

I looked around to make sure I hadn't disturbed anything, turned off the bathroom light, and got in the closet, leaving the door open a crack. It was the only possible place to hide. I sincerely hoped Detweiler wouldn't need anything out of it before I found out what was going on. If he did, the only thing I could do was confront him with what I'd found out. And then what, Mallory, a big guilty confession? With what you've found out he could laugh in your face and have you arrested for illegal entry.

And what about this, Mallory. What if someone died nearby tonight while you were with Detweiler; what if he comes straight to his apartment and goes to bed; what if he wakes up in the morning feeling fine; what if nothing is going on, you son of a bitch?

It was so dark in there with the curtains drawn that I couldn't see a thing. I left the closet and opened them a little on the front window. It didn't let in a lot of light, but it was enough. Maybe Detweiler wouldn't notice. I went back to the closet and waited.

Half an hour later the curtains over the barred open window moved. I had squatted down in the closet and wasn't looking in that direction, but the movement caught my eye. Something hopped in the window and scooted across the floor and went behind the couch. I only got a glimpse of it, but it might have been a cat. It was probably a stray looking for food of hiding from a dog. Okay, cat, you don't bother me and I won't bother you. I kept my eye on the couch, but it didn't show itself again.

Detweiler didn't show for another hour. By that time I was sitting flat on the floor trying to keep my legs from cramping. My position wasn't too graceful if he happened to look in the closet, but it was too late to get up.

He came in quickly and bolted the door behind him. He didn't notice the open curtain. He glanced around, clicking his tongue softly. His eyes caught on something at the end of the couch. He smiled. At the *cat?* He began unfastening his shirt, fumbling at the buttons in his haste. He slipped off the shirt and tossed it on the back of the chair.

There were straps across his chest.

He turned towards the suitcase, his back to me. The hump was artificial, made of something like foam rubber. He unhooked the straps, opened the suitcase, and tossed the hump in. He said something, too soft for me to catch, and lay face down on the couch with his feet towards me. The light from the opened curtain fell on him. His back was scarred, little white lines like scratches grouped around a hole.

He had a hole in his back, between his shoulder blades, an unhealed wound big enough to stick your finger in.

Something came around the end of the couch. It wasn't a cat. I thought it was a monkey, and then a frog, but it was neither. It was human. It waddled on all fours like an enormous toad.

Then it stood erect. It was about the size of a cat. It was pink and moist and hairless and naked. Its very human hands and feet and male genitals were too large for its tiny body. Its belly was swollen, turgid and distended like an obscene tick. Its head was flat. Its jaw protruded like an ape's. It too had a scar, a big, white, puckered scar between its shoulder blades, at the top of its jutting backbone.

It reached its too-large hand up and caught hold of Detweiler's belt. It pulled its bloated body up with the nimbleness of a monkey and crawled onto the boy's back. Detweiler was breathing heavily, clasping and unclasping his fingers on the arm of the couch.

The thing crouched on Detweiler's back and placed its lips against the wound.

I felt my throat burning and my stomach turning over, but I watched in petrified fascination.

Detweiler's breathing grew slower and quieter, more relaxed. He lay with his eyes closed and an expression of almost sexual pleasure on his face. The thing's body got smaller and smaller, the skin on its belly growing wrinkled and flaccid. A trickle of blood crawled from the wound, making an erratic line across the Detweiler boy's back. The thing reached out a hand and wiped the drop back with a finger.

It took ten minutes. The thing raised its mouth and crawled over beside the boy's face. It sat on the arm of the couch like a little gnome and smiled. It ran its finger down the side of Detweiler's cheek and pushed his damp hair back out of his eyes. Detweiler's expression was euphoric. He sighed softly and opened his eyes sleepily. After a while he sat up.

He was flushed with health, rosy and clear and shining.

He stood up and went to the bathroom. The light came on and I heard water running. The thing was in the same place, watching him. Detweiler came out of the bathroom and sat back on the couch. The thing climbed onto his back, huddling between his shoulder blades, its hand on his shoulder. Detweiler stood up, the thing hanging onto him, retrieved the shirt, and put it on. He wrapped the straps neatly around the artificial hump and stowed it in the suitcase. He closed the lid and locked it.

I had seen enough, more than enough. I opened the door and stepped out of the closet.

Detweiler whirled, his eyes bulging. A groan rattled in his throat. He raised his hands as if fending me off. The groan rose in pitch, becoming an hysterical keening. The expression on his face was too horrible to watch. He stepped backward and tripped over the suitcase.

He lost his balance and toppled over. His arms flailed for equilibrium, but never found it. He struck the edge of the table. It caught him square across the hump on his back. He bounced and fell forward on his hands. He stood up agonizingly, like a slow motion movie, arching his spine backward, his face contorted in pain.

There were shrill, staccato shrieks of mindless torment, but they didn't come from Detweiler.

He fell again, forward onto the couch, blacking out from pain. The back of his shirt was churning. The scream continued, hurting my ears. Rips appeared in the shirt and a small misshapen arm poked out briefly. I could only stare, frozen. The shirt was ripped to shreds. Two arms, a head, a torso came through. The whole thing ripped its way out and fell onto the couch beside the boy. Its face was twisted, tortured, and its mouth kept opening and closing with screams. Its eyes looked uncomprehendingly about. It pulled itself along with its arms, dragging its useless legs, its spine obviously broken. It fell off the couch and flailed about on the floor.

Detweiler moaned and came to. He rose from the couch, still groggy. He saw the thing, and a look of absolute grief appeared on his face.

The thing's eyes focused for a moment on Detweiler. It looked at him, beseeching, held out one hand, pleading. Its screams became a breathless rasping. I couldn't stand it any longer. I picked up a chair and smashed it down on the thing. I dropped the chair and leaned against the wall and heaved.

I heard the door open. I turned and saw Detweiler run out.

I charged after him. My legs felt rubbery but I caught him at the street. He didn't struggle. He just stood there, his eyes vacant, trembling. I saw people sticking their heads out of doors and Johnny Peacock coming toward me. My car was right there. I pushed Detweiler into it and drove away. He sat hunched in the seat, his hands hanging limply, staring into space. He was trembling uncontrollably and his teeth chattered.

I drove, not paying attention to where I was going, almost as deeply in shock as he was. I finally started looking at the street signs. I was on Mulholland. I kept going west for a long time, crossed the San Diego Freeway, into the Santa Monica Mountains. The pavement ends a couple of miles past the freeway, and there's ten or fifteen miles of dirt road before the pavement picks up again nearly to Topanga.

The road isn't travelled much, there are no houses on it, and people don't like to get their cars dusty. I was about in the middle of the unpaved section when Detweiler seemed to calm down. I pulled over to the side of the road and cut the engine. The San Fernando Valley was spread like a carpet of lights below us. The ocean was on the other side of the mountains.

I sat and watched Detweiler. The trembling had stopped. He was asleep or unconscious. I reached over and touched his arm. He stirred and clutched at my hand. I looked at his sleeping face and didn't have the heart to pull my hand away.

The sun was poking over the mountains when he woke up. He roused and was momentarily unaware of where he was; then memory flooded back. He turned to me. The pain and hysteria were gone from his eyes. They were oddly peaceful.

"Did you hear him?" he said softly. "Did you hear him die?"

"Are you feeling better?"

"Yes. It's all over."

"Do you want to talk about it?"

His eyes dropped and he was silent for a moment. "I want to tell you. But I don't know how without you thinking I'm a monster."

I didn't say anything.

"He…was my brother. We were twins. Siamese twins. All those people who died so I could stay alive." There was no emotion in his voice. He was detached, talking about someone else. "He kept me alive. I'll die without him." His eyes met mine again. "He was insane, I think. I thought at first I'd go mad too, but I didn't. I think I didn't. I never knew what he was going to do, who he would kill. I didn't want to know. He was very clever. He always made it look like an accident or suicide when he could. I didn't interfere. I didn't want to die. We had to have blood. He always did it so there was lots of blood, so no one would miss what he took." His eyes were going empty again.

"Why did you need the blood?"

"We were never suspected before."

"Why did you need the blood?" I repeated.

"When we were born," he said, and his eyes focused again, "we were joined at the back. But I grew and he didn't. He stayed little bitty, like a baby riding around on my back. People didn't like me...us, they were afraid. My father and mother too. The old witch-woman I told you about, she birthed us. She seemed always to be hanging around. When I was eight, my parents died in a fire. I think the witch-woman did it. After that I lived with her. She was demented, but she knew medicine and healing. When we were fifteen she decided to separate us. I don't know why. I think she wanted him without me. I'm sure she thought he was an imp from hell. I almost died. I'm not sure what was wrong. Apart, we weren't whole. I wasn't whole. He had something I didn't have, something we'd been sharing. She would've let me die, but he knew and got blood for me. Hers." He sat staring at me blankly, his mind living the past.

"Why didn't you go to a hospital or something?" I asked, feeling enormous pity for the wretched boy.

He smiled faintly. "I didn't know much about anything then. Too many people were already dead. If I'd gone to a hospital they'd have wanted to know how I'd stayed alive so far. Sometimes I'm glad it's over, and, then, the next minute I'm terrified of dying."

"How long?"

"I'm not sure. I've never been more than three days. I can't stand it any longer than that. He knew. He always knew when I had to have it. And he got it for me. I never helped him."

"Can you stay alive if you get regular transfusions?"

He looked at me sharply, fear creeping back. "Please. No!"

"But you'll stay alive."

"In a cage! Like a freak! I don't want to be a freak anymore. It's over. I want it to be over. Please."

"What do you want me to do?"

"I don't know. I don't want you to get in trouble."

I looked at him, at his face, at his eyes, at his soul. "There's a gun in the glove compartment," I said.

He sat for a moment, then solemnly held out his hand. I took it. He shook my hand, then opened the glove compartment. He removed the gun and slipped out of the car. He went down the hill into the brush. I waited and waited and never did hear a shot.

THE FENCE AT THE END OF THE WORLD

Melissa Mia Hall

Melissa Mia Hall is not a prolific writer of fiction. Most of her work has been reviews and interviews in her career as a journalist, and she has sold a little less than thirty stories in almost as many years. But each story packs as much energy as a dozen ordinary tales. Melissa writes much of herself into her work and her stories are always memorable, even one as short as the following. It was the story's title that first caught my eye, but let it not delude you. It has a far harsher and more frightening meaning than you might expect, and is written straight from the heart. Melissa's website is at home.earthlink.net/~blackleatherrequired/hallofmia/

Every evening they go out to the fence, down where the world ends. Marla and Kay hold hands for luck. It takes courage to go down there. They take turns looking though a crack in one wooden plank, its tip sharp with splinters just begging to pierce their hands. They search the sometimes featureless darkness for clues.

"I see a spot of light."

"A lightning bug..."

"A lightning ball."

"No, you don't."

"I seen it. I seen it plain as day, that a UFO gonna come down and scoop us up, take us away to Alpha Centauri, or who knows, maybe Camelot. I got to get me a King Arthur."

"Liar, liar, pants on fire."

"You wish."

They can't open the gate that goes outside. Mama told them never to open the gate. They can never, ever go outside. They will live here forever until their bodies rot and their eyeballs fall out.

Marla turns away from the fence. She sits back on her haunches like their old Irish Setter Claude used to. The ritual is getting tiresome.

"Ain't you ever sick to death about all this?"

"If you want to fall off the edge of the world, you go right on ahead and do it. You want to go together?" Kay puts an arm around her older sister and Marla shivers. "We could fall through space together."

"We could go during the day. I can see more'n space out there then. The postman comes. So does all manner of folk. Everybody comes and goes. Why not us? I heard tell maybe somebody's gonna come and make Mama let us go to school this fall."

The postman says everyone's got to go to school. He's tall, brown and muscular. He looks good in his shorts. Name's Emmitt and he always talks to Marla like she's smart.

"We gonna look like fools. They'll think we retards," Kay says.

"I don't care. Mama can't make us stay here forever."

"But we will. We got to take care of Mama."

"Money ain't gonna last forever. We gots to pay bills," Marla sighs.

"No, we don't. Besides, nobody cares about white trash. We can just slide on by for awhile – just borrow from Peter to pay Paul – way we've always done."

"Don't be calling us white trash. Daddy was the trash. He shouldn't have gone off and left us." Marla says sharply.

The darkness seems to lift a little. Marla pushes Kay's arm away and stands up. She stretches her thin arms and Kay watches admiringly. Kay is smaller, chubbier.

"Did you hear her? Was that Mama?"

Behind them, the house appears to tilt as a sound whispers in the pecan trees drooping above it. "What if people never die, just seem like."

"You mean, play like they dead?" Marla doesn't like to talk about the dead. She heads for the porch bravely where Mama's old porch-swing moves in the breeze in lop-sided fashion. Kay follows her. They sit on the steps, waiting for the air to turn cooler, but it's August in East Texas and is not at all likely. "I don't know, but say we climbed the fence and went over tonight, Katykins, what do you think would really happen?"

"We'd fall into pitch darkness, into nothing. We'd fall and fall and never land."

Kay wraps her short arms around her knees and squeezes.

"Sure you would! I don't think Mama's right about this. It's crazy."

"She be bed bound. She can't make us do anything, that's for sure." Kay rubs her latest bruise and studies a scab on her knee. "Oh, who we kidding, yes, she can."

It's an eternal argument, what Mama can and can't do.

The old neon hand is no longer lit. Folks don't come anymore to visit Madame Clarice, Spiritual Advisor and Gifted Psychic. It's like a magical circle has been drawn around their house. It happened around the time Mama came back from the hospital after the fit. Doctors called it a stroke. The girls knew better. Mama got so mad at them one day she just sit down and screamed until she couldn't scream anymore.

Marla has considered turning the electricity on and becoming the next Spiritual Advisor. Every town needs one and they really like them to be exotic. Marla has taken to wearing some of Mama's old get-ups. She is aware of how pretty she is. Sometimes she just stares at herself naked in the hall mirror. She tries different earrings. Mama can't say anything. Mama was so greedy.

"Marla, we gots to do something. I want to go to school. If we can see the sun and it is out there, every morning…" Kay points towards the gate that for some peculiar reason, only the postman can open, "then hey, we can go out there. We've got to."

They used to go out. It's not like they've never been. But Marla believes Mama is right. After the fit, everything changed. The air shifted.

Spring became fall. Marla tried, one secret night to go outside and her foot fell on air. She slipped and fell, held on to the edge of the world by sheer determination and pulled herself back into yard. She looked down into nothing. The ground had given away. At first, she thought there'd been an earthquake or something. Magic. Mama never wanted them to leave her. They had to stay. Because the world had become an illusion. "No."

Marla leaves Kay. She goes inside to the bookshelves where all of Mama's magic books live. They are virtually unreadable. She decides it is time for a bonfire. It might please Kay, distract her from unholy thoughts.

"What you doing, Marla?"

She makes a neat stack and starts to strike a match.

"Firemen'll come," Kay says, smiling.

Marla freezes. "Mama might get mad."

"Oh, don't do that…" Kay pulls out her pocket knife and begins to cut her arm, just enough to make it bleed a little. Then Kay sucks the blood. A row of scars displays her predilection toward hurting herself is a constant in her young life.

"Don't do that."

"It feels good."

Silence descends as the darkness lightens. They've been up all night. Kay lies down on the old quilt in the porch swing and fluffs her old pillow. She never sleeps in the house anymore. "I'm going to sleep now."

Marla hasn't slept in a good while. She wonders if she is a vampire but really, only Kay likes the taste of blood. Marla might be a ghost. And she might just be crazy. Mama was. "Maybe it's time to leave Mama."

Kay has fallen asleep. Marla listens for Mama to make that almost breathless wheeze. She must listen very quietly. Mama only makes animal sounds now. Only silence answers. She creeps back to the fence. The light rises like fog off of the bayou.

The TV broke last winter and they don't get the newspaper. She can only guess what's been going on out there. People don't send them many letters, either. And Marla can only dream what it would be like to have a computer. Mama said computers were evil.

Mama's relatives gave up on them a long time ago. Just bills arrive and some circulars. The Reverend Cleveland used to come and try to save their souls till the winter Mama threw boiling water on him. The money is running out. She doesn't want to stay any longer. Certainly it is time to leave Mama. She undoes the latch on the gate and pushes. She puts one foot out. Air, still air.

You can't leave me, understand – I am all you have in the world. I am power. I am the source of your life. You are nothing without me. I am God's holy vessel, sent here to control things and you bastard chil'ren. I know everything. You must mind me.

Some say I be a Goddess. There are no names in the darkness, just truth, Marla Faith. And the truth binds. It does not set you free. Do you understand, spawn of man, the evil one?

Mama became like a devil at some point. She was always right. That's why the money held out for so long. She was good at guessing games. Folk came all the way from New Orleans, Houston and Dallas to listen to her prophecies. Marla believes it's not good to be right all the time. She thinks it does something to the heart, shrivels it somehow. Folks need to be surprised.

Marla looks at the palm of her hand. Mama read palms, did cards, looked in crystal balls and played with numbers but they did not tell her what she saw. Marla thinks the tongue told her. And the tongue twists things mean-like every once in awhile. She got too proud of it. Pride Goeth Before a Fall. Marla knows that must be true. That's why the fit came.

The Spirit took Mama's tongue. But she still speaks in Marla's head sometimes, especially when she's afraid she must do something Mama would not approve of.

"I guess it's time we told someone."

"No!" Behind her, Kay sticks her knife into Marla's back, just enough to prick and draw a bead of blood that trickles, like sweat into her panties.

"You've hurt me. Put that knife away." Marla puts her arms out like Jesus on the cross, keeping her back to her little sister.

"I've done decided the Spirit has entered me. Mama's Spirit has given me the Tongue."

"You're sleepwalking little sis."

"She's starting to stink."

"You're starting to stink." Like the voice…

MARLA FAITH and KAY ALBERTINE, I charge you with eternal damnation if you ever leave me. Kay Albertine, you are my youngest and the one who must watch the oldest. There is a darkness about her. I see her stepping into darkness and falling, falling because she has no faith despite all I have tried to teach her. She thinks she has power. I own the power. She is nothing without me. Remember this.

"Mama doesn't need us anymore – we've got to fend for ourselves now," Marla hurries, sidesteps the knife point and pushes the gate wider. One step. Two. She'll have to run. Her joy mixes with pure relief to be getting away from the old dead witch.

Kay screams like a banshee. If they only had neighbours to hear her, Marla could get help. "Mama is DEAD…" Marla says over her shoulder, "Come on, Kay, let's run…"

Dawn lifts the world into focus. Marla is thrilled with the light rising. The ground is strong. Her bare feet are free and then suddenly dropping into nothingness. Below her the cracked sidewalk becomes transparent with the promised void. "No…" Marla is sure the world is not an illusion. Mama can't be right all of the time. She looks back at the fence in shock.

Kay holds the bloodied knife aloft. "I told you – Mama told you – the fence is the only thing that be real, Marla. The world without Mama don't exist…"

Marla keeps falling.

ELRIC AT THE END OF TIME
Michael Moorcock

From the end of the World to the end of Time. It was impossible to compile this anthology without something by Michael Moorcock. Moorcock (b. 1939) has been a renegade in the field of science fiction ever since he took over editorship of New Worlds *in 1964 and revolutionized everything under the banner of the so-called "New Wave".*

He had already been producing heroic fantasy since the June 1961 issue of Science Fantasy *had introduced the character of Elric of Melniboné. Although Moorcock was inspired by the works of Robert E Howard and Edgar Rice Burroughs, Elric was no bulk-standard barbarian swordsman. Quite the contrary. He was a dispossessed prince and an albino who drew his strength from his sword, Stormbringer, which drank the souls of those it killed. Moorcock's original sequence of stories were collected together as* The Stealer of Souls *(1963) and* Stormbringer *(1965) at the end of which Elric met his inevitable fate. Everyone expected that was the end of Elric but, thankfully not.*

In his other book sequences, Moorcock was developing the idea of the Eternal Champion, a hero who exists in various incarnations throughout the many dimensions of the Multiverse, and who battles to ensure a balance between Law and Chaos. This character is known by different names and includes, amongst Moorcock's books, Dorian Hawkmoon, Corum Jhaelen, Jherek Carnelian and Elric himself. In a complex sequence Moorcock wrote several interweaving series which brought most of the characters together at one or more

*points in time. He continued this game in a further sequence called
the Dancers at the End of Time, and the following story features as
part of that series.*

*Sounds complex? It is, but it is immensely rewarding. Extreme?
Well, when I put this to Moorcock his response was, "I've never
thought anything I do is extreme. It's other people who seem to think
that." See what you think...*

I

IN WHICH MRS PERSSON DETECTS AN ABOVE AVERAGE
DEGREE OF CHAOS IN THE MEGAFLOW

Returning from China to London and the Spring of 1936, Una
Persson found an unfamiliar quality of pathos in most of the friends
she had last seen, as far as she recalled, during the Blitz on her way back
from 1970. Then they had been desperately hearty: it was a comfort to
understand that the condition was not permanent. Here, at present,
Pierrot ruled and she felt she possessed a better grip on her power. This
was, she admitted with shame, her favourite moral climate for it
encouraged in her an enormously gratifying sense of spiritual superiority:
the advantage of having been born, originally, into a later and probably
more sophisticated age. The 1960s. Some women, she reflected, were
forced to have children in order to enjoy this pleasure.

But she was uneasy, so she reported to the local Time Centre and
the bearded, sullen features of Sergeant Alvarez who welcomed her in
white, apologising for the fact that he had himself only just that morning
left the Lower Devonian and had not had time to change.

"It's the megaflow, as you guessed," he told her, operating toggles to
reveal his crazy display systems. "We've lost control."

"We never really had it." She lit a Sherman's and shook her long hair
back over the headrest of the swivel chair, opening her military overcoat
and loosening her webbing. "Is it worse than usual?"

"Much." He sipped cold coffee from his battered silver mug. "It cuts through every plane we can pick up – a rogue current swerving through the dimensions. Something of a twister."

"Jerry?"

"He's dormant. We checked. But it's like him, certainly. Most probably another aspect."

"Oh, sod." Una straightened her shoulders.

"That's what I thought," said Alvarez. "Someone's going to have to do a spot of rubato." He studied a screen. It was Greek to Una. For a moment a pattern formed. Alvarez made a note. "Yes. It can either be fixed at the nadir or the zenith. It's too late to try anywhere in between. I think it's up to you, Mrs P."

She got to her feet. "Where's the zenith?"

"The End of Time."

"Well," she said, "that's something."

She opened her bag and made sure of her jar of instant coffee. It was the one thing she couldn't get at the End of Time.

"Sorry," said Alvarez, glad that the expert had been there and that he could remain behind.

"It's just as well," she said. "This period's no good for my moral well-being. I'll be off, then."

"Someone's got to." Alvarez failed to seem sympathetic.

"It's Chaos out there."

"You don't have to tell me."

She entered the makeshift chamber and was on her way to the End of Time.

II

IN WHICH THE ETERNAL CHAMPION FINDS HIMSELF AT THE END OF TIME

Elric of Melniboné shook a bone-white fist at the greedy, glaring stars –

the eyes of all those men whose souls he had stolen to sustain his own enfeebled body. He looked down. Though it seemed he stood on something solid, there was only more blackness falling away below him. It was as if he hung at the centre of the universe. And here, too, were staring points of yellow light. Was he to be judged?

His half-sentient runesword, Stormbringer, in its scabbard on his left hip, murmured like a nervous dog.

He had been on his way to Imrryr, to his home, to reclaim his kingdom from his cousin Yyrkoon; sailing from the Isle of the Purple Towns where he had guested with Count Smiorgan Baldhead. Magic winds had caught the Filkharian trader as she crossed the unnamed water between the Vilmirian peninsula and the Isle of Melniboné. She had been borne into the Dragon Sea and thence to Sorcerers' Isle, so-called because that barren place had been the home of Cran Liret, the Thief of Spells, a wizard infamous for his borrowings, who had, at length, been dispatched by those he sought to rival. But much residual magic had been left behind. Certain spells had come into the keeping of the Krettii, a tribe of near-brutes who had migrated to the island from the region of The Silent Land less than fifty years before. Their shaman, one Grrodd Ybene Eenr, had made unthinking use of devices buried by the dying sorcerer as the spells of his peers sucked life and sanity from them. Elric had dealt with more than one clever wizard, but never with so mindless a power. His battle had been long and exhausting and had required the sacrifice of most of the Filkharians as well as the entire tribe of Krettii. His sorcery had become increasingly desperate. Sprite fought sprite, devil fell upon devil, in both physical and astral, all around the region of Sorcerers' Isle. Eventually Elric had mounted a massive Summoning against the allies of Grrodd Ybene Eenr with the result that the shaman had been at last overwhelmed and his remains scattered in limbo. But Elric, captured by his own monstrous magickings, had followed his enemy and now he stood in the Void, crying out into appalling silence, hearing his words only in his skull:

"*Arioch! Arioch! Aid me!*"

But his patron Duke of Hell was absent. He could not exist here. He could not, for once, even hear his favourite protégé.

"*Arioch! Repay my loyalty! I have given you blood and souls!*"

He did not breathe. His heart had stopped. All his movements were sluggish.

The eyes looked down at him. They looked up at him. Were they glad? Did they rejoice in his terror?

"*Arioch!*"

He yearned for a reply. He would have wept, but no tears would come. His body was cold; less than dead, yet not alive. A fear was in him greater than any fear he had known before.

"*Oh, Arioch! Aid me!*"

He forced his right hand towards the pulsing pommel of Stormbringer which, alone, still possessed energy. The hilt of the sword was warm to his touch and, as slowly he folded his fingers around it, it seemed to swell in his fist and propel his arm upwards so that he did not draw the sword. Rather the sword forced his limbs into motion.

And now it challenged the Void, glowing with black fire, singing its high, gleeful battle-song.

"Our destinies are intertwined, Stormbringer," said Elric. "Bring us from this place, or those destinies shall never be fulfilled."

Stormbringer swung like the needle of a compass and Elric's unfeeling arm was wrenched round to go with it. In eight directions the sword swung, as if to the eight points of Chaos. It was questing – like a hound sniffing a trail. Then a yell sounded from within the strange metal of the blade; a distant cry of delight, it seemed to Elric. The sound one would hear if one stood above a valley listening to children playing far below.

Elric knew that Stormbringer had sensed a plane they might reach. Not necessarily their own, but one which would accept them. And, as a drowning mariner must yearn for the most inhospitable rock rather than no rock at all, Elric yearned for that plane.

"*Stormbringer. Take us there!*"

The sword hesitated. It moaned. It was suspicious.

"*Take us there!*" whispered the albino to his runesword.

The sword struck back and forth, up and down, as if it battled invisible enemies. Elric scarcely kept his grip on it. It seemed that Stormbringer was frightened of the world it had detected and sought to drive it back but the act of seeking had in itself set them both in motion. Already Elric could feel himself being drawn through the darkness, towards something he could see very dimly beyond the myriad eyes, as dawn reveals clouds undetected in the night sky.

Elric thought he saw the shapes of crags, pointed and crazy. He thought he saw water, flat and ice-blue. The stars faded and there was snow beneath his feet, mountains all around him, a huge, blazing sun overhead – and above that another landscape, a desert, as a magic mirror might reflect the contrasting character of he who peered into it – a desert, quite as real as the snowy peaks in which he crouched, sword in hand, waiting for one of these landscapes to fade so that he might establish, to a degree, his bearings. Evidently the two planes had intersected.

But the landscape overhead did not fade. He could look up and see sand, mountains, vegetation, a sky which met his own sky at a point halfway along the curve of the huge sun – and blended with it. He looked about him. Snowy peaks in all directions. Above – desert everywhere. He felt dizzy, found that he was staring downwards, reaching to cup some of the snow in his hand. It was ordinary snow, though it seemed reluctant to melt in contact with his flesh.

"This is a world of Chaos," he muttered. "It obeys no natural laws." His voice seemed loud, amplified by the peaks, perhaps. "That is why you did not want to come here. This is the world of powerful rivals."

Stormbringer was silent, as if all its energy were spent. But Elric did not sheathe the blade. He began to trudge through the snow towards what seemed to be an abyss. Every so often he glanced upward, but the desert overhead had not faded; sun and sky remained the same. He wondered if he walked around the surface of a miniature world, that if he continued to go forward he might eventually reach the point where the two landscapes met. He wondered if this were not some punishment wished upon him by his untrustworthy allies of Chaos. Perhaps he must choose between death in the snow or death in the desert. He reached the edge of the abyss and looked down.

The walls of the abyss fell for all of five feet before reaching a floor of gold and silver squares which stretched for perhaps another seven feet before they reached the far wall, where the landscape continued – snow and crags – uninterrupted.

"This is undoubtedly where Chaos rules," said the prince of Melniboné. He studied the smooth, chequered floor. It reflected parts of the snowy terrain and the desert world above it. It reflected the crimson-eyed albino who peered down at it, his features drawn in bewilderment and tiredness.

"I am at their mercy," said Elric. "They play with me. But I shall resist them, even as they destroy me." And some of his wild, careless spirit came back to him as he prepared to lower himself onto the chequered floor and cross to the opposite bank.

He was halfway over when he heard a grunting sound in the distance and a beast appeared, its paws slithering uncertainly on the smooth surface, its seven savage eyes glaring in all directions as if it sought the instigator of its terrible indignity.

And, at last, all seven eyes focused on Elric and the beast opened a mouth in which row upon row of thin, vicious teeth were arranged, and uttered a growl of unmistakable resentment.

Elric raised his sword. "Back, creature of Chaos. You threaten the Prince of Melniboné!"

The beast was already propelling itself towards him. Elric flung his body to one side, aiming a blow with the sword as he did so, succeeding only in making a thin incision in the monster's heavily muscled hind leg. It shrieked and began to turn.

"Back!"

Elric's voice was the brave, thin squeak of a lemming attacked by a hawk. He drove at the thing's snout with Stormbringer. The sword was heavy. It had spent all its energy and there was no more to give. Elric wondered why he, himself, did not weaken. Possibly the Laws of Nature were entirely abolished in the Realm of Chaos. He struck and drew blood. The beast paused, more in astonishment than fear.

Then it opened its jaws, pushed its back legs against the snowy bank, and shot towards the albino who tried to dodge it, lost his footing, and fell, sprawling backwards, on the gold and silver surface.

III

IN WHICH UNA PERSSON DISCOVERS AN UNEXPECTED SNAG

The gigantic beetle, rainbow carapace glittering, turned as if into the wind, which blew from the distant mountains, its thick, flashing wings beating rapidly as it bore its single passenger over the queer landscape.

On its back Mrs Persson checked the instruments on her wrist. Ever since Man had begun to travel in time it had become necessary for the Guild to develop techniques to compensate for the fluctuations and disruptions in the space-time continua; perpetually monitoring the chronoflow and megaflow. She pursed her lips. She had picked up the signal. She made the semi-sentient beetle swing a degree or two SSE and head directly for the mountains. She was in some sort of enclosed (but vast) environment. These mountains, as well as everything surrounding them, lay in the territory most utilised by the gloomy, natural-born Werther de Goethe, poet and romantic, solitary seeker after truth in a world no longer differentiating between the degrees of reality.

He would not remember her, she knew, because, as far as Werther was concerned, they had not met yet. Had Werther even experienced his adventure with Mistress Christia, the Everlasting Concubine? A story on which she had dined out more than once, in duller eras.

The mountains drew closer. From here it was possible to see the entire arrangement (a creation of Werther's very much in character): a desert landscape, a central sun, and, inverted above it, winter mountains. Werther strove to make statements, like so many naïve artists before him, by presenting simple contrasts: The World is Bleak / The World is Cold / Barren am I As I Grow Old / Tomorrow I Die, Entombed in Cold / For Silver My Poor Soul Was Sold – she remembered he was perhaps the worst poet she had encountered in an eternity of meetings with bad poets. He had taught himself to read and write in old, old English so that he might carve those words on one of his many abandoned tombs (half his time was spent in composing obituaries for himself). Like so many others he seemed to equate self-pity with artistic inspiration. In an earlier age he might have discovered his public and become quite rich (self-pity passing for passion in the popular understanding). Sometimes she regretted the passing of Wheldrake, so long ago, so far away, in a universe bearing scarcely any resemblances to those in which she normally operated.

She brought her wavering mind back to the problem. The beetle dipped and circled over the desert, but there was no sight of her quarry.

She was about to abandon the search when she heard a faint roaring overhead and she looked up to see another characteristic motif of Werther's – a gold and silver chessboard on which, upside down, a monstrous doglike creature was bearing down on a tiny white-haired man dressed in the most abominable taste Una had seen for some time.

She directed the air car upwards and then, reversing the machine as she entered the opposing gravity, downwards to where the barbarically costumed swordsman was about to be eaten by the beast.

"Shoo!" cried Una commandingly.

The beast raised a befuddled head.

"Shoo."

It licked its lips and returned its seven-eyed gaze to the albino, who was now on his knees, using his large sword to steady himself as he climbed to his feet.

The jaws opened wider and wider. The pale man prepared, shakily, to defend himself.

Una directed the air car at the beast's unkempt head. The great beetle connected with a loud crack. The monster's eyes widened in dismay. It yelped. It sat on its haunches and began to slide away, its claws making an unpleasant noise on the gold and silver tiles.

Una landed the air car and gestured for the stranger to enter. She noticed with distaste that he was a somewhat unhealthy looking albino with gaunt features, exaggeratedly large and slanting eyes, ears that were virtually pointed, and glaring, half-mad red pupils.

And yet, undoubtedly, it was her quarry and there was nothing for it but to be polite.

"Do, please, get in," she said. "I am here to rescue you."

"*Shaarmraaam torjistoo quellahm vyeearrr,*" said the stranger in an accent that seemed to Una to be vaguely Scottish.

"Damn," she said, "that's all we need." She had been anxious to approach the albino in private, before one of the denizens of the End of Time could arrive and select him for a menagerie, but now she regretted that Werther or perhaps Lord Jagged were not here, for she realized that she needed one of their translation pills, those tiny tablets which could 'engineer' the brain to understand a new language. By a fluke – or perhaps because of her presence here so often – the people at the End of Time currently spoke formal early 20th-century English.

The albino – who wore a kind of tartan divided kilt, knee-length boots, a blue and white jerkin, a green cloak and a silver breastplate, with a variety of leather belts and metal buckles here and there upon his person – was vehemently refusing her offer of a lift. He raised the sword before him as he backed away, slipped once, reached the bank, scrambled through snow and disappeared behind a rock.

Mrs Persson sighed and put the car into motion again.

IV

IN WHICH THE PRINCE OF MELNIBONÉ ENCOUNTERS FURTHER TERRORS

Xiombarg herself, thought Elric as he slid beneath the snows into the cave. Well, he would have no dealings with the Queen of Chaos; not until he was forced to do so.

The cave was large. In the thin light from the gap above his head he could not see far. He wondered whether to return to the surface or risk going deeper into the cave. There was always the hope that he would find another way out. He was attempting to recall some rune that would aid him, but all he knew depended either upon the aid of elementals who did not exist on this plane, or upon the Lords of Chaos themselves – and they were unlikely to come to his assistance in their own realm. He was marooned here: the single mouse in a world of cats.

Almost unconsciously, he found himself moving downwards, realizing that the cave had become a tunnel. He was feeling hungry but, apart from the monster and the woman in the magical carriage, had seen no sign of life. Even the cavern did not seem entirely natural.

It widened; there was phosphorescent light. He realized that the walls were of transparent crystal, and behind the walls were all manner of artefacts. He saw crowns, sceptres and chains of precious jewels; cabinets of complicated carving; weapons of strangely turned metal; armour, clothing, things whose use he could not guess – and food. There were sweetmeats, fruits, flans and pies, all out of reach.

Elric groaned. This was torment. Perhaps deliberately planned torment. A thousand voices whispered to him in a beautiful, alien language.

"*Bie-meee... Bie-meee...*" the voices murmured. "*Baa-gen, baa-gen...*"

They seemed to be promising every delight, if only he could pass through the walls; but they were of transparent quartz, lit from within. He raised Stormbringer, half-tempted to try to break down the barrier, but he knew that even his sword was, at its most powerful, incapable of destroying the magic of Chaos.

He paused, gasping with astonishment at a group of small dogs which looked at him with large brown eyes, tongues lolling, and jumped up at him.

"*O, Nee Tubbens!*" intoned one of the voices.

"Gods!" screamed Elric. "This torture is too much!" He swung his body this way and that, threatening with his sword, but the voices continued to murmur and promise, displaying their riches but never allowing him to touch.

The albino panted. His crimson eyes glared about him. "You would drive me insane, eh? Well, Elric of Melniboné has witnessed more frightful threats than this. You will need to do more if you would destroy his mind!"

And he ran through the whispering passages, looking to neither his right nor his left, until, quite suddenly, he had run into blazing daylight and stood staring down into pale infinity – a blue and endless void. He looked up. And he screamed.

Overhead were the gentle hills and dales of a rural landscape, with rivers, grazing cattle, woods and cottages. He expected to fall, headlong, but he did not. He was on the brink of the abyss. The cliff-face of red sandstone fell immediately below and then was the tranquil void. He looked back:

"*Baa-gen... O, Nee Tubbens...*"

A bitter smile played about the albino's bloodless lips as, decisively, he sheathed his sword.

"Well, then," he said. "Let them do their worst!"

And, laughing, he launched himself over the brink of the cliff.

V

IN WHICH WERTHER DE GOETHE MAKES A WONDERFUL DISCOVERY

With a gesture of quiet pride, Werther de Goethe indicated his gigantic skull.

"It is very large, Werther," said Mistress Christia, the Everlasting Concubine, turning a power ring to adjust the shade of her eyes so that they perfectly matched the day.

"It is monstrous," said Werther modestly. "It reminds us all of the Inevitable Night."

"Who was that?" enquired golden-haired Gaf the Horse in Tears, at present studying ancient legendry. "Sir Lew Grady?"

"I mean Death," Werther told him, "which overwhelms us all."

"Well, not us," pointed out the Duke of Queens, as usual a trifle literal-minded. "Because we're immortal, as you know."

Werther offered him a sad, pitying look and sighed briefly. "Retain your delusions, if you will."

Mistress Christia stroked the gloomy Werther's long, dark locks. "There, there," she said. "We have compensations, Werther."

"Without Death," intoned the Last Romantic, "there is no point to Life."

As usual, they could not follow him, but they nodded gravely and politely.

"The skull," continued Werther, stroking the side of his air car (which was in the shape of a large flying reptile) to make it circle and head for the left eye-socket, "is a Symbol not only of our Mortality, but also of our Fruitless Ambitions."

"Fruit?" Bishop Castle, drowsing at the rear of the vehicle, became interested. His hobby was currently orchards. "Less? My pine trees, you know, are proving a problem. The apples are much smaller than I was led to believe."

"The skull is lovely," said Mistress Christia with valiant enthusiasm. "Well, now that we have seen it…"

"The outward shell," Werther told her. "It is what it hides which is more important. Man's Foolish Yearnings are all encompassed therein. His Greed, his Need for the Impossible, the Heat of his Passions, the Coldness which must Finally Overtake him. Through this eye-socket you will encounter a little invention of my own called The Bargain Basement of the Mind…"

He broke off in astonishment.

On the top edge of the eye-socket a tiny figure had emerged.

"What's that?" enquired the Duke of Queens, craning his head back. "A random thought?"

"It is not mine at all!"

The figure launched itself into the sky and seemed to fly, with flailing limbs, towards the sun. Werther frowned, watching the tiny man disappear. "The gravity field is reversed there," he said absently, "in order to make the most of the paradox, you understand. There is a snowscape, a desert…" But he was much more interested in the newcomer. "How do you think he got into my skull?"

"At least he's enjoying himself. He seems to be laughing." Mistress Christia bent an ear towards the thin sound, which grew fainter and fainter at first, but became louder again. "He's coming back."

Werther nodded. "Yes. The field's no longer reversed." He touched a power ring.

The laughter stopped and became a yell of rage. The figure hurtled down on them. It had a sword in one white hand and its red eyes blazed.

Hastily, Werther stroked another ring. The stranger tumbled into the bottom of the air car and lay there panting, cursing and groaning.

"How wonderful!" cried Werther. "Oh, this is a traveller from some rich, romantic past. Look at him! What else could he be? What a prize!"

The stranger rose to his feet and raised the sword high above his head, defying the amazed and delighted passengers as he screamed at the top of his voice:

"*Heeshgeegrowinaz!*"

"Good afternoon," said Mistress Christia. She reached in her purse for a translation pill and found one. "I wonder if you would care to swallow this – it's quite harmless…"

"*Yakoom, oom glallio,*" said the albino contemptuously.

"Aha," said Mistress Christia. "Well, just as you please."

The Duke of Queens pointed towards the other socket. A huge, whirring beetle came sailing from it. In its back was someone he recognized with pleasure. "Mrs Persson!"

Una brought her air car alongside.

"Is he in your charge?" asked Werther with undisguised disappointment. "If so, I could offer you…"

"I'm afraid he means a lot to me," she said.

"From your own age?" Mistress Christia also recognized Una. She still offered the translation pill in the palm of her hand. "He seems a mite suspicious of us."

"I'd noticed," said Una. "It would be useful if he would accept the pill. However, if he will not, one of us…"

"I would be happy," offered the generous Duke of Queens. He tugged at his green and gold beard. "Werther de Goethe, Mrs Persson."

"Perhaps I had better," said Una nodding to Werther. The only problem with translation pills was that they did their job so thoroughly. You could speak the language perfectly, but could speak no other.

Werther was, for once, positive. "Let's all take a pill," he suggested.

Everyone at the End of Time carried translation pills, in case of meeting a visitor from Space or the Past.

Mistress Christia handed hers to Una and found another. They swallowed.

"Creatures of Chaos," said the newcomer with cool dignity, "I demand that you release me. You cannot hold a mortal in this way, not unless he has struck a bargain with you. And no bargain was struck which would bring me to the Realm of Chaos."

"It's actually more orderly than you'd think," said Werther apologetically. "Your first experience, you see, was the world of my skull, which was deliberately muddled. I meant to show what Confusion was the Mind of Man…"

"May I introduce Mistress Christia, the Everlasting Concubine," said the Duke of Queens, on his best manners. "This is Mrs Persson, Bishop Castle, Gaf the Horse in Tears. Werther de Goethe – your unwitting host – and I am the Duke of Queens. We welcome you to our world. Your name, sir…?"

"You must know me, my lord Duke," said Elric. "For I am Elric of Melniboné, Emperor by Right of Birth, Inheritor of the Ruby Throne, Bearer of the Actorios, Wielder of the Black Sword…"

"Indeed!" said Werther de Goethe. In a whispered aside to Mrs Persson: "What a marvellous scowl! What a noble sneer!"

"You are an important personage in your world, then?" said Mistress Christia, fluttering the eyelashes she had just extended by half an inch. "Perhaps you would allow me…"

"I think he wishes to be returned to his home," said Mrs Persson hastily.

"Returned?" Werther was astonished. "But the Morphail Effect! It is impossible."

"Not in this case, I think," she said. "For if he is not returned there is no telling the fluctuations which will take place throughout the dimensions…"

They could not follow her, but they accepted her tone.

"Aye," said Elric darkly, "return me to my realm, so that I may fulfil my own doom-laden destiny…"

Werther looked upon the albino with affectionate delight. "Aha! A fellow spirit! I, too, have a doom-laden destiny."

"I doubt it is as doom-laden as mine." Elric peered moodily back at the skull as the two air cars fled away towards a gentle horizon where exotic trees bloomed.

"Well," said Werther with an effort, "perhaps it is not, though I assure you…"

"I have looked upon hellborn horror," said Elric, "and communicated with the very Gods of the Uttermost Darkness. I have seen things which would turn other men's minds to useless jelly…"

"Jelly?" interrupted Bishop Castle. "Do you, in your turn, have any expertise with, for instance, blackbird trees?"

"Your words are meaningless," Elric told him, glowering. "Why do you torment me so, my lords? I did not ask to visit your world. I belong in the world of men, in the Young Kingdoms, where I seek my weird. Why, I have but lately experienced adventures…"

"I do think we have one of those bores," murmured Bishop Castle to the Duke of Queens, "so common amongst time-travellers. They all believe themselves unique."

But the Duke of Queens refused to be drawn. He had developed a liking for the frowning albino. Gaf the Horse in Tears was also plainly impressed, for he had fashioned his own features into a rough likeness of Elric's. The Prince of Melniboné pretended insouciance, but it was evident to Una he was frightened. She tried to calm him.

"People here at the End of Time…" she began.

"No soft words, my lady." A cynical smile played about the albino's lips. "I know you for that great unholy temptress, Queen of the Swords, Xiombarg herself."

"I assure you, I am as human as you, sir…"

"Human? I, human? I am not human, madam – though I be a mortal, 'tis true. I am of older blood, the blood of the Bright Empire itself, the Blood of R'lin K'ren A'a which Cran Liret mocked, not understanding what it was he laughed at. Aye, though forced to summon aid from Chaos, I made no bargain to become a slave in your realm…"

"I assure you – um – your majesty," said Una, "that we had not meant to insult you and your presence here was no doing of ours. I am, as it happens, a stranger here myself. I came especially to see you, to help you escape…"

"Ha!" said the albino. "I have heard such words before. You would lure me into some worse trap than this. Tell me, where is Duke Arioch? He, at least, I owe some allegiance to."

"We have no-one of that name," apologised Mistress Christia. She enquired of Gaf, who knew everyone. "No time-traveller?"

"None," Gaf studied Elric's eyes and made a small adjustment to his own. He sat back, satisfied.

Elric shuddered and turned away mumbling.

"You are very welcome here," said Werther. "I cannot tell you how glad I am to meet one as essentially morbid and self-pitying as myself!"

Elric did not seem flattered.

"What can we do to make you feel at home?" asked Mistress Christia. She had changed her hair to a rather glossy blue in the hope, perhaps, that Elric would find it more attractive. "Is there anything you need?"

"Need? Aye. Peace of mind. Knowledge of my true destiny. A quiet place where I can be with Cymoril, whom I love."

"What does this Cymoril look like?" Mistress Christia became just a trifle overeager.

"She is the most beautiful creature in the universe," said Elric.

"It isn't very much to go on," said Mistress Christia. "If you could imagine a picture, perhaps? There are devices in the old cities which could visualize your thoughts. We could go there. I should be happy to fill in for her, as it were…"

"What? You offer me a simulacrum? Do you not think I should detect such witchery at once? Ah, this is loathsome! Slay me, if you will, or continue the torment. I'll listen no longer!"

They were floating now, between high cliffs. On a ledge far below a group of time-travellers pointed up at them. One waved desperately.

"You've offended him, Mistress Christia," said Werther pettishly. "You don't understand how sensitive he is."

"Yes I do." She was aggrieved. "I was only being sympathetic."

"Sympathy!" Elric rubbed at his long, somewhat pointed jaw. "Ha! What do I want with sympathy?"

"I never heard anyone who wanted it more." Mistress Christia was kind. "You're like a little boy, really, aren't you?"

"Compared to the ancient Lords of Chaos, I am a child, aye. But my blood is old and cold, the blood of decaying Melniboné, as well you know." And with a huge sigh the albino seated himself at the far end of the car and rested his head on his fist. "Well? What is your pleasure, my Lords and Ladies of Hell?"

"It is your pleasure we are anxious to achieve," Werther told him. "Is there anything at all we can do? Some environment we can manufacture? What are you used to?"

"Used to? I am used to the crack of leathery dragon wings in the sweet, sharp air of the early dawn. I am used to the sound of red battle, the drumming of hoofs on bloody earth, the screams of the dying, the yells of the victorious. I am used to warring against demons and monsters, sorcerers and ghouls. I have sailed on magic ships and fought hand to hand with reptilian savages. I have encountered the Jade Man himself. I have fought side by side with the elementals, who are my allies. I have battled black evil…"

"Well," said Werther, "that's something to go on, at any rate. I'm sure we can…"

"Lord Elric won't be staying," began Una Persson politely. "You see – these fluctuations in the megaflow – not to mention his own destiny… He should not be here, at all, Werther."

"Nonsense!" Werther flung a black velvet arm about the stiff shoulders of his new friend. "It is evident that our destinies are one. Lord Elric is as grief-haunted as myself!"

"How can you know what it is to be haunted by grief?" murmured the albino. His face was half-buried in Werther's generous sleeve.

Mrs Persson controlled herself. She rose from Werther's air car and made for her own. "Well," she said, "I must be off. I hope to see you later, everybody."

They sang out their farewells.

Una Persson turned her beetle westward, towards Castle Canaria, the home of her old friend Lord Jagged.

She needed help and advice.

VI

IN WHICH ELRIC OF MELNIBONÉ RESISTS THE TEMPTATIONS OF THE CHAOS LORDS

Elric reflected on the subtle way in which laughing Lords of Chaos had captured him. Apparently, he was merely a guest and quite free to wander where he would in their realm. Actually, he was in their power as much as if they had chained him, for he could not flee this flying dragon and they had already demonstrated their enormous magical gifts in subtle ways, primarily with their shape-changing. Only the one who called himself Werther de Goethe (plainly a leader in the hierarchy of Chaos) still had the face and clothing he had worn when first encountered.

It was evident that this realm obeyed no natural laws, that it was mutable according to the whims of its powerful inhabitants. They could destroy him with a breath and had, subtly enough, given him evidence of that fact. How could he possibly escape such danger? By calling upon the Lords of Law for aid? But he owed them no loyalty and they, doubtless, regarded him as their enemy. But if he were to transfer his allegiance to Law...

These thoughts and more continued to engage him, while his captors chatted easily in the ancient High Speech of Melniboné, itself a version of the very language of Chaos. It was one of the other ways in which they revealed themselves for what they were. He fingered his runesword, wondering if it would be possible to slay such a lord and steal his energy, giving himself enough power for a little while to hurl himself back to his own sphere...

The one called Lord Werther was leaning over the side of the beast-vessel. "Oh, come and see, Elric. Look!"

Reluctantly, the albino moved to where Werther peered and pointed.

The entire landscape was filled with a monstrous battle. Creatures of all kinds and all combinations tore at one another with huge teeth and claws. Shapeless things slithered and hopped; giants, naked but for helmets and greaves, slashed at these beasts with great broadswords and axes, but were borne down. Flame and black smoke drifted everywhere. There was a smell. The stink of blood?

"What do you miss most?" asked the female. She pressed a soft body against him. He pretended not to be aware of it. He knew what magic flesh could hide on a she-witch.

"I miss peace," said Elric almost to himself, "and I miss war. For in battle I find a kind of peace..."

"Very good!" Bishop Castle applauded. "You are beginning to learn our ways. You will soon become one of our best conversationalists."

Elric touched the hilt of Stormbringer, hoping to feel it grow warm and vibrant under his hand, but it was still, impotent in the Realm of Chaos. He uttered a heavy sigh.

"You are an adventurer, then, in your own world?" said the Duke of Queens. He was bluff. He had changed his beard to an ordinary sort of black and was wearing a scarlet costume; quilted doublet and tight-fitting hose, with a blue and white ruff, an elaborately feathered hat on his head. "I, too, am something of a vagabond. As far, of course, as it is possible to be here. A buccaneer, of sorts. That is, my actions are in the main bolder than those of my fellows. More spectacular. Vulgar. Like yourself, sir. I admire your costume."

Elric knew that this Duke of Hell was referring to the fact that he affected the costume of the southern barbarian, that he did not wear the more restrained colours and more cleverly wrought silks and metals of his own folk. He gave tit for tat at this time. He bowed.

"Thank you, sir. Your own clothes rival mine."

"Do you think so?" The hell-lord pretended pleasure. If Elric had not known better, the creature would seem to be swelling with pride.

"Look!" cried Werther again. "Look, Lord Elric – we are attacked." Elric whirled.

From below were rising oddly wrought vessels – something like ships, but with huge round wheels at their sides, like the wheels of water-clocks he had seen once in Pikarayd. Coloured smoke issued from chimneys mounted on their decks which swarmed with huge birds dressed in human clothing. The birds had multicoloured plumage, curved beaks, and they held swords in their claws, while on their heads were strangely shaped black hats on which were blazed skulls with crossed bones beneath.

"Heave to!" squawked the birds. "Or we'll put a shot across your bowels!"

"What can they be?" cried Bishop Castle.

"Parrots," said Werther de Goethe soberly. "Otherwise known as the hawks of the sea. And they mean us no good."

Mistress Christia blinked.

"Don't you mean pirates, dear?"

Elric took a firm grip on his sword. Some of the words the Chaos Lords used were absolutely meaningless to him. But whether the attacking creatures were of their own conception, or whether they were true enemies of his captors, Elric prepared to do bloody battle. His spirits improved. At least here was something substantial to fight.

VII

IN WHICH MRS PERSSON BECOMES ANXIOUS ABOUT
THE FUTURE OF THE UNIVERSE

Lord Jagged of Canaria was nowhere to be found. His huge castle, of gold and yellow spires, an embellished replica of Kings Cross station, was populated entirely by his quaint robots, whom Jagged found at once more mysterious and more trustworthy than android or human servants, for they could answer only according to a limited programme.

Una suspected that Jagged was, himself, upon some mission, for he, too, was a member of the Guild of Temporal Adventurers. But she needed aid. Somehow she had to return Elric to his own dimension without creating further disruptions in the fabric of time and space. The Conjunction was not due yet and, if things got any worse, might never come. So many plans depended on the Conjunction of the Million Spheres that she could not risk its failure. But she could not reveal too much either to Elric or his hosts. As a Guild member she was sworn to the utmost and indeed necessary secrecy. Even here at the End of Time there were certain laws which could be disobeyed only at enormous risk. Words alone were dangerous when they described ideas concerning the nature of time.

She racked her brains. She considered seeking out Jherek Carnelian, but then remembered that he had scarcely begun to understand his own destiny. Besides, there were certain similarities between Jherek and Elric which she could only sense at present. It would be best to go cautiously there.

She decided that she had no choice. She must return to the Time Centre and see if they could detect Lord Jagged for her.

She brought the necessary coordinates together in her mind and concentrated. For a moment all memories, all sense of identity left her.

Sergeant Alvarez was beside himself. His screens were no longer completely without form. Instead, peculiar shapes could be seen in the arrangements of lines. Una thought she saw faces, beasts, landscapes. That had never occurred before. The instruments, at least, had remained sane, even as they recorded insanity.

"It's getting worse," said Alvarez. "You've hardly any Time left. What there is, I've managed to borrow for you. Did you contact the rogue?"

She nodded. "Yes. But getting him to return… I want you to find Jagged."

"Jagged? Are you sure?"

"It's our only chance, I think."

Alvarez sighed and bent a tense back over his controls.

VIII

IN WHICH ELRIC AND WERTHER FIGHT SIDE BY SIDE AGAINST ALMOST OVERWHELMING ODDS

Somewhere, it seemed to Elric, as he parried and thrust at the attacking bird-monsters, rich and rousing music played. It must be a delusion, brought on by battle-madness. Blood and feathers covered the carriage. He saw the one called Christia carried off screaming. Bishop Castle had disappeared. Gaf had gone. Only the three of them, shoulder to shoulder, continued to fight.

What was disconcerting to Elric was that Werther and the Duke of Queens bore swords absolutely identical to Stormbringer. Perhaps they were the legendary Brothers of the Black Sword, said to reside in Chaos?

He was forced to admit to himself that he experienced a sense of comradeship with these two, who were braver than most in defending themselves against such dreadful, unlikely monsters – perhaps some creation of their own which had turned against them.

Having captured the Lady Christia, the birds began to return to their own craft.

"We must rescue her!" cried Werther as the flying ships began to retreat. "Quickly! In pursuit!"

"Should we not seek reinforcements?" asked Elric, further impressed by the courage of this Chaos Lord.

"No time!" cried the Duke of Queens. "After them!"

Werther shouted to his vessel. "Follow those ships!"

The vessel did not move.

"It has an enchantment on it," said Werther. "We are stranded! Ah, and I loved her so much!"

Elric became suspicious again. Werther had shown no signs, previously, of any affection for the female.

"You loved her?"

"From a distance," Werther explained. "Duke of Queens, what can we do? Those parrots will ransom her savagely and mishandle her objects of virtue!"

"Dastardly poltroons!" roared the huge duke.

Elric could make little sense of this exchange. It dawned on him, then, that he could still hear the rousing music. He looked below. On some sort of dais in the middle of the bizarre landscape a large group of musicians was assembled. They played on, apparently oblivious of what happened above. This was truly a world dominated by Chaos.

Their ship began slowly to fall towards the band. It lurched. Elric gasped and clung to the side as they struck yielding ground and bumped to a halt.

The Duke of Queens, apparently elated, was already scrambling overboard. "There! We can follow on those mounts."

Tethered near the dais was a herd of creatures bearing some slight resemblance to horses but in a variety of dazzling, metallic colours, with horns and bony ridges on their backs. Saddles and bridles of alien workmanship showed that they were domestic beasts, doubtless belonging to the musicians.

"They will want some payment from us, surely," said Elric, as they hurried towards the horses.

"Ah, true!" Werther reached into a purse at his belt and drew forth a handful of jewels. Casually he flung them towards the musicians and climbed into the saddle of the nearest beast. Elric and the Duke of Queens followed his example. Then Werther, with a whoop, was off in the direction in which the bird-monsters had gone.

The landscape of this world of Chaos changed rapidly as they rode. They galloped through forests of crystalline trees, over fields of glowing flowers, leapt rivers the colour of blood and the consistency of mercury, and their tireless mounts maintained a headlong pace which never faltered. Through clouds of boiling gas which wept, through rain, through snow, through intolerable heat, through shallow lakes in which oddly fashioned fish wriggled and gasped, until at last a range of mountains came in sight.

"There!" panted Werther, pointing with his own runesword. "Their lair. Oh, the fiends! How can we climb such smooth cliffs?"

It was true that the base of the cliffs rose some hundred feet before they became suddenly ragged, like the rotting teeth of the beggars of Nadsokor. They were of dusky, purple obsidian and so smooth as to reflect the faces of the three adventurers who stared at them in despair.

It was Elric who saw the steps put into the side of the cliff.

"These will take us up some of the way, at least."

"It could be a trap," said the Duke of Queens. He, too, seemed to be relishing the opportunity to take action. Although a Lord of Chaos there was something about him that made Elric respond to a fellow spirit.

"Let them trap us," said Elric laconically. "We have our swords."

With a wild laugh, Werther de Goethe was the first to swing himself from his saddle and run towards the steps, leaping up them almost as if he had the power of flight. Elric and the Duke of Queens followed more slowly.

Their feet slipping in the narrow spaces not meant for mortals to climb, ever aware of the dizzying drop on their left, the three came at last to the top of the cliff and stood clinging to sharp crags, staring across a plain at a crazy castle rising into the clouds before them.

"Their stronghold," said Werther.

"What are these creatures?" Elric asked. "Why do they attack you? Why do they capture the Lady Christia?"

"They nurse an abiding hatred for us," explained the Duke of Queens, and looked expectantly at Werther, who added:

"This was their world before it became ours."

"And before it became theirs," said the Duke of Queens, "it was the world of the Yargtroon."

"The Yargtroon?" Elric frowned.

"They dispossessed the bodiless vampire goat-folk of Kia," explained Werther. "Who, in turn, destroyed – or thought they destroyed – the Grash-Tu-Xem, a race of Old Ones older than any Old Ones except the Elder Old Ones of Ancient Thriss."

"Older even than Chaos?" asked Elric.

"Oh, far older," said Werther.

"It's almost completely collapsed, it's so old," added the Duke of Queens.

Elric was baffled. "Thriss?"

"Chaos," said the Duke.

Elric let a thin smile play about his lips. "You still mock me, my lord. The power of Chaos is the greatest there is, only equalled by the power of Law."

"Oh, certainly," agreed the Duke of Queens.

Elric became suspicious again. "Do you play with me, my lord?"

"Well, naturally, we try to please our guests…"

Werther interrupted. "Yonder doomy edifice holds the one I love. Somewhere within its walls she is incarcerated, while ghouls taunt at her and devils threaten."

"The bird-monsters…?" began Elric.

"Chimerae," said the Duke of Queens. "You saw only one of the shapes they assume."

Elric understood this. "Aha!"

"But how can we enter it?" Werther spoke almost to himself.

"We must wait until nightfall," said Elric, "and enter under the cover of darkness."

"Nightfall?" Werther brightened.

Suddenly they were in utter darkness.

Somewhere the Duke of Queens lost his footing and fell with a muffled curse.

IX

IN WHICH MRS PERSSON AT LAST MAKES CONTACT WITH HER OLD FRIEND

They stood together beneath the striped awning of the tent while a short distance away armoured men, mounted on armoured horses, jousted, were injured or died. The two members wore appropriate costumes for the period. Lord Jagged looked handsome in his surcoat and mail, but Una Persson merely looked uncomfortable in her wimple and kirtle.

"I can't leave just now," he was saying. "I am laying the foundations for a very important development."

"Which will come to nothing unless Elric is returned," she said.

A knight with a broken lance thundered past, covering them in dust.

"Well played Sir Holger!" called Lord Jagged. "An ancestor of mine, you know," he told her.

"You will not be able to recognize the world of the End of Time when you return, if this is allowed to continue," she said.

"It's always difficult, isn't it?" But he was listening to her now.

"These disruptions could as easily affect us and leave us stranded," she added. "We would lose any freedom we have gained."

He bit into a pomegranate and offered it to her. "You can only get these in this area. Did you know? Impossible to find in England. In the thirteenth century, at any rate. The idea of freedom is such a nebulous one, isn't it? Most of the time when angry people are speaking of 'freedom' what they are actually asking for is much simpler – respect. Do those in authority or those with power ever really respect those who do not have power?" He paused. "Or do they mean 'power' and not 'freedom'. Or are they the same…?"

"Really, Jagged, this is no time for self-indulgence."

He looked about him. "There's little else to do in the Middle East in the 13th century, I assure you, except eat pomegranates and philosophize…"

"You must come back to the End of Time."

He wiped his handsome chin. "Your urgency," he said, "worries me, Una. These matters should be handled with delicacy – slowly…"

"The entire fabric will collapse unless he is returned to his own dimension. He is an important factor in the whole plan."

"Well, yes, I understand that."

"He is, in one sense at least, your protégé."

"I know. But not my responsibility."

"You must help," she said.

There was a loud bang and a crash.

A splinter flew into Mrs Persson's eye.

"Oh, zounds!" she said.

X
IN WHICH THE CASTLE IS ASSAULTED AND THE PLOT THICKENED

A moon had appeared above the spires of the castle which seemed to Elric to have changed its shape since he had first seen it. He meant to ask his companions for an explanation, but at present they were all sworn to silence as they crept nearer. From within the castle burst light, emanating from guttering brands stuck into brackets on the walls. There was laughter, noise of feasting. Hidden behind a rock they peered through one large window and inspected the scene within.

The entire hall was full of men wearing identical costumes. They had black skull-caps, loose white blouses and trousers, black shoes. Their eyebrows were black in dead white faces, even paler than Elric's and they had bright red lips.

"Aha," whispered Werther, "the parrots are celebrating their victory. Soon they will be too drunk to know what is happening to them."

"Parrots?" said Elric. "What is that word?"

"Pierrots, he means," said the Duke of Queens. "Don't you, Werther?" There were evidently certain words which did not translate easily into the High Speech of Melniboné.

"Shh," said the Last Romantic, "they will capture us and torture us to death if they detect our presence."

They worked their way around the castle. It was guarded at intervals by gigantic warriors whom Elric at first mistook for statues, save that, when he looked closely, he could see them breathing very slowly. They were unarmed, but their fists and feet were disproportionately large and could crush any intruder they detected.

"They are sluggish, by the look of them," said Elric. "If we are quick, we can run beneath them and enter the castle before they realize it. Let me try first. If I succeed, you follow."

Werther clapped his new comrade on the back. "Very well."

Elric waited until the nearest guard halted and spread his huge feet apart, then he dashed forward, scuttling like an insect between the giant's legs and flinging himself through a dimly lit window. He found himself in some sort of store-room. He had not been seen, though the guard cocked his ear for half a moment before resuming his pace. Elric looked cautiously out and signalled to his companions. The Duke of Queens waited for the guard to stop again, then he, too, made for the window and joined Elric. He was panting and grinning. "This is wonderful," he said.

Elric admired his spirit. There was no doubt that the guard could crush any of them to a pulp, even if (as still nagged at his brain) this was all some sort of complicated illusion.

Another dash, and Werther was with them.

Cautiously, Elric opened the door of the store-room. They looked onto a deserted landing. They crossed the landing and looked over a balustrade. They had expected to see another hall, but instead there was a miniature lake on which floated the most beautiful miniature ship, all mother-of-pearl, brass and ebony, with golden sails and silver masts. Surrounding this ship were mermaids and mermen bearing trays of exotic food (reminding Elric how hungry he still was) which they fed to the ship's only passenger, Mistress Christia.

"She is under an enchantment," said Elric. "They beguile her with illusions so that she will not wish to come with us even if we do rescue her. Do you know no counter-spells?"

Werther thought for a moment. Then he shook his head.

"You must be very minor Lords of Chaos," said Elric, biting his lower lip.

From the lake, Mistress Christia giggled and drew one of the mermaids towards her. "Come here, my pretty piscine!"

"Mistress Christia!" hissed Werther de Goethe.

"Oh!" The captive widened her eyes (which were now both large and blue). "At last!"

"You wish to be rescued?" said Elric.

"Rescued? Only by you, most alluring of albinos!"

Elric hardened his features. "I am not the one who loves you, madam."

"What? I am loved? By whom? By you, Duke of Queens?"

"Sshh," said Elric. "The demons will hear us."

"Oh, of course," said Mistress Christia gravely, and fell silent for a second. "I'll get rid of all this, shall I?"

And she touched one of her rings.

Ship, lake and merfolk were gone. She lay on silken cushions, attended by monkeys.

"Sorcery!" said Elric, "if she has such power, then why…?"

"It is limited," explained Werther. "Merely to such tricks."

"Quite," said Mistress Christia.

Elric glared at them. "You surround me with illusions. You make me think I am aiding you, when really…"

"No, no!" cried Werther. "I assure you, Lord Elric, you have our greatest respect — well, mine at least — we are only attempting to…"

There was a roar from the gallery above. Rank upon rank of grinning demons looked down upon them. They were armed to the teeth.

"Hurry!" The Duke of Queens leapt to the cushions and seized Mistress Christia, flinging her over his shoulder. "We can never defeat so many!"

The demons were already rushing down the circular staircase. Elric, still not certain whether his new friends deceived him or not, made a decision. He called to the Duke of Queens. "Get her from the castle. We'll keep them from you for a few moments, at least." He could not help himself. He behaved impulsively.

The Duke of Queens, sword in hand, Mistress Christia over the other shoulder, ran into a narrow passage. Elric and Werther stood together as the demons rushed down on them. Blade met blade. There was an unbearable shrilling of steel mingled with the cacklings and shrieks of the demons as they gnashed their teeth and rolled their eyes and slashed at the pair with swords, knives and axes. But worst of all was the smell. The dreadful smell of burning flesh which filled the air and threatened to choke Elric. It came from the demons. The smell of hell.

He did his best to cover his nostrils as he fought, certain that the smell must overwhelm him before the swords. Above him was a set of metal rungs fixed into the stones, leading high into a kind of chimney. As a pause came he pointed upwards to Werther, who understood him.

For a moment they managed to drive the demons back. Werther jumped onto Elric's shoulders (again displaying a strange lightness) and reached down to haul the albino after him.

While the demons wailed and cackled below, they began to climb the chimney.

They climbed for nearly fifty feet before they found themselves in a small, round room whose windows looked out over the purple crags and, beyond them, to a scene of bleak rocky pavements pitted with holes, like some vast, unlikely cheese.

And there, rolling over this relatively flat landscape, in full daylight (for the sun had risen) was the Duke of Queens in a carriage of brass and wood, studded with jewels, and drawn by two bovine creatures which looked to Elric as if they might be the fabulous oxen of mythology who had drawn the war-chariot of his ancestors to do battle with the emerging nations of mankind.

Mistress Christia was beside the Duke of Queens. They seemed to be waiting for Elric and Werther.

"It's impossible," said the albino. "We could not get out of this tower, let alone across those crags. I wonder how they managed to move so quickly and so far. And where did the chariot come from?"

"Stolen, no doubt, from the demons," said Werther. "See, there are wings here." He indicated a heap of feathers in the corner of the room. "We can use those."

"What wizardry is this?" said Elric. "Man cannot fly on bird wings."

"With the appropriate spell he can," said Werther. "I am not that well versed in the magic arts, of course, but let me see…" He picked up one set of wings. They were soft and glinted with subtle, rainbow colours. He placed them on Elric's back, murmuring his spell:

"*Oh, for the wings, for the wings of a dove,*
To carry me to the one I love…

"There!" He was very pleased with himself. Elric moved his shoulders and his wings began to flap. "Excellent! Off you go, Elric. I'll join you in a moment."

Elric hesitated, then saw the head of the first demon emerging from the hole in the floor. He jumped to the window ledge and leapt into space. The wings sustained him. Against all logic he flew smoothly towards the waiting chariot and behind him came Werther de Goethe. At the windows of the tower the demons crowded, shaking fists and weapons as their prey escaped them.

Elric landed rather awkwardly beside the chariot and was helped aboard by the Duke of Queens. Werther joined them, dropping expertly amongst them. He removed the wings from the albino's back and nodded to the Duke of Queens who yelled at the oxen, cracking his whip as they began to move.

Mistress Christia flung her arms about Elric's neck. "What courage! What resourcefulness!" she breathed. "Without you, I should now be ruined!"

Elric sheathed Stormbringer. "We all three worked together for your rescue, madam." Gently he removed her arms. Courteously he bowed and leaned against the far side of the chariot as it bumped and hurtled over the peculiar rocky surface.

"Swifter! Swifter!" called the Duke of Queens, casting urgent looks backwards. "We are followed!"

From the disappearing tower there now poured a host of flying, gibbering things. Once again the creatures had changed shape and had assumed the form of striped, winged cats, all glaring eyes, fangs and extended claws.

The rock became viscous, clogging the wheels of the chariot, as they reached what appeared to be a silvery road, flowing between the high trees of an alien forest already touched by a weird twilight.

The first of the flying cats caught up with them, slashing.

Elric drew Stormbringer and cut back. The beast roared in pain, blood streaming from its severed leg, its wings flapping in Elric's face as it hovered and attempted to snap at the sword.

The chariot rolled faster, through the forest to green fields touched by the moon. The days were short, it seemed, in this part of Chaos. A path stretched skyward. The Duke of Queens drove the chariot straight up it, heading for the moon itself.

The moon grew larger and larger and still the demons pursued them, but they could not fly as fast as the chariot which went so swiftly that sorcery must surely speed it. Now they could only be heard in the darkness behind and the silver moon was huge.

"There!" called Werther. "There is safety!"

On they raced until the moon was reached, the oxen leaping in their traces, galloping over the gleaming surface to where a white palace awaited them.

"Sanctuary," said the Duke of Queens. And he laughed a wild, full laugh of sheer joy.

The palace was like ivory, carved and wrought by a million hands, every inch covered with delicate designs.

Elric wondered. "Where is this place?" he asked. "Does it lie outside the Realm of Chaos?"

Werther seemed nonplussed. "You mean our world?"

"Aye."

"It is still part of our world," said the Duke of Queens.

"Is the palace to your liking?" asked Werther.

"It is lovely."

"A trifle pale for my own taste," said the Last Romantic. "It was Mistress Christia's idea."

"You built this?" The albino turned to the woman. "When?"

"Just now." She seemed surprised.

Elric nodded. "Aha. It is within the power of Chaos to create whatever whims it pleases."

The chariot crossed a white drawbridge and entered a white

courtyard. In it grew white flowers. They dismounted and entered a huge hall, white as bone, in which red lights glowed. Again Elric began to suspect mockery, but the faces of the Chaos Lords showed only pleasure. He realized that he was dizzy with hunger and weariness, as he had been ever since he had been flung into this terrible world where no shape was constant, no idea permanent.

"Are you hungry?" asked Mistress Christia.

He nodded. And suddenly the room was filled by a long table on which all kinds of food were heaped – and everything, meats and fruits and vegetables, was white.

Elric moved to take the seat she indicated and he put some of the food on a silver plate and he touched it to his lips and he tasted it. It was delicious. Forgetting suspicion, he began to eat heartily, trying not to consider the colourless quality of the meal. Werther and the Duke of Queens also took some food, but it seemed they ate only from politeness. Werther glanced up at the faraway roof. "What a wonderful tomb this would make," he said. "Your imagination improves, Mistress Christia."

"Is this your domain?" asked Elric. "The moon?"

"Oh no," she said. "It was all made for the occasion."

"Occasion?"

"For your adventure," she said. Then she fell silent.

Elric became grave. "Those demons? They were not your enemies. They belong to you!"

"Belong?" said Mistress Christia. She shook her head.

Elric frowned and pushed back his plate. "I am, however, most certainly your captive." He stood up and paced the white floor. "Will you not return me to my own plane?"

"You would come back almost immediately," said Werther de Goethe. "It is called the Morphail Effect. And if you did not come here, you would yet remain in your own future. It is in the nature of time."

"This is nonsense," said Elric. "I have left my own realm before and returned – though admittedly memory becomes weak, as with dreams poorly recalled."

"No man can go back in time," said the Duke of Queens. "Ask Brannart Morphail."

"He, too, is a Lord of Chaos?"

"If you like. He is a colleague."

"Could he not return me to my realm? He sounds a clever being."

"He could not and he would not," said Mistress Christia. "Haven't you enjoyed your experiences here so far?"

"Enjoyed?" Elric was astonished. "Madam, I think… Well, what has happened this day is not what we mortals would call 'enjoyment'!"

"But you *seemed* to be enjoying yourself," said the Duke of Queens in some disappointment. "Didn't he, Werther?"

"You were much more cheerful through the whole episode," agreed the Last Romantic. "Particularly when you were fighting the demons."

"As with many time-travellers who suffer from anxieties," said Mistress Christia, "you appeared to relax when you had something immediate to capture your attention…"

Elric refused to listen. This was clever Chaos talk, meant to deceive him and take his mind from his chief concern.

"If I was any help to you," he began, "I am, of course…"

"He isn't very grateful," Mistress Christia pouted.

Elric felt madness creeping nearer again. He calmed himself.

"I thank you for the food, madam. Now, I would sleep."

"Sleep?" she was disconcerted. "Oh! Of course. Yes. A bedroom?"

"If you have such a thing."

"As many as you like." She moved a stone on one of her rings. The walls seemed to draw back to show bedchamber after bedchamber, in all manner of styles, with beds of every shape and fashion. Elric controlled his temper. He bowed, thanked her, said goodnight to the two lords and made for the nearest bed.

As he closed the door behind him, he thought he heard Werther de Goethe say: "We must try to think of a better entertainment for him when he wakes up."

XI

IN WHICH MRS PERSSON WITNESSES THE FIRST SIGN OF THE MEGAFLOW'S DISINTEGRATION

In Castle Canaria Lord Jagged unrolled his antique charts. He had had them drawn for him by a baffled astrologer in 1950. They were one of his many affectations. At the moment, however, they were of considerably greater use than Alvarez's electronics.

While he used a wrist computer to check his figures, Una Persson looked out of the window of Castle Canaria and wondered who had invented this particular landscape. A green and orange sun cast sickening light over the herds of grazing beasts who resembled, from this distance at any rate, nothing so much as gigantic human hands. In the middle of the scene was raised some kind of building in the shape of a vast helmet, vaguely Greek in conception. Beyond that was a low, grey moon. She turned away.

"I must admit," said Lord Jagged, "that I had not understood the extent…"

"Exactly," she said.

"You must forgive me. A certain amount of amnesia – euphoria, perhaps? – always comes over one in these very remote periods."

"Quite."

He looked up from the charts. "We've a few hours at most."

Her smile was thin, her nod barely perceptible.

While she made the most of having told him so, Lord Jagged frowned, turned a power ring and produced an already lit pipe which he placed thoughtfully in his mouth, taking it out again almost immediately. "That wasn't Dunhill Standard Medium." He laid the pipe aside.

There came a loud buzzing noise from the window. The scene outside was disintegrating as if melting on glass. An eerie golden light spread everywhere, flooding from an apex of deeper gold, as if forming a funnel.

"That's a rupture," said Lord Jagged. His voice was tense. He put his arm about her shoulders. "I've never seen anything of the size before."

Rushing towards them along the funnel of light there came an entire city of turrets and towers and minarets in a wide variety of pastel colours. It was set into a saucer-shaped base which was almost certainly several miles in circumference.

For a moment the city seemed to retreat. The golden light faded. The city remained, some distance away, swaying a little as if on a gentle tide, a couple of thousand feet above the ground, the grey moon below it.

"That's what I call megaflow distortion," said Una Persson in that inappropriately facetious tone adopted by those who are deeply frightened.

"I recognize the period." Jagged drew a telescope from his robes. "Second Candlemaker's Empire, mainly based in Arcturus. This is a village by their standards. After all, Earth was merely a rural park during that time." He retreated into academe, his own response to fear.

Una craned her head. "Isn't that some sort of vehicle heading towards the city? From the moon – good heavens, they've spotted it already. Are they going to try to put the whole thing into a menagerie?"

Jagged had the advantage of the telescope. "I think not." He handed her the instrument.

Through it she saw a scarlet and black chariot borne by what seemed to be some form of flying fairground horses. In the chariot, armed to the teeth with lances, bows, spears, swords, axes, morningstars, maces and almost every other barbaric hand-weapon, clad in quasi-mythological armour, were Werther de Goethe, the Duke of Queens and Elric of Melniboné.

"They're attacking it!" she said faintly. "What will happen when the two groups intersect?"

"Three groups," he pointed out. "Untangling that in a few hours is going to be even harder."

"And if we fail?"

He shrugged. "We might just as well give ourselves up to the biggest chronoquake the universe has ever experienced."

"You're exaggerating," she said.

"Why not? Everyone else is."

XII

THE ATTACK ON THE CITADEL OF THE SKIES

"Melniboné! Melniboné!" cried the albino as the chariot circled over the spires and turrets of the city. They saw startled faces below. Strange engines were being dragged through the narrow streets.

"Surrender!" Elric demanded.

"I do not think they can understand us," said the Duke of Queens. "What a find, eh? A whole city from the past!"

Werther had been reluctant to embark on an adventure not of his own creation, but Elric, realizing that here at last was a chance of escape, had been anxious to begin. The Duke of Queens had, in an instant, aided the albino by producing costumes, weapons, transport. Within minutes of the city's appearance, they had been on their way.

Exactly why Elric wished to attack the city, Werther could not make out, unless it was some test of the Melnibonéan's to see if his companions were true allies or merely pretending to have befriended him. Werther was learning a great deal from Elric, much more than he had ever learned from Mongrove, whose ideas of angst were only marginally less notional than Werther's own.

A broad, flat blue ray beamed from the city. It singed one wheel of the chariot.

"Ha! They make sorcerous weapons," said Elric. "Well, my friends. Let us see you counter with your own power."

Werther obediently imitated the blue ray and sent it back from his fingers, slicing the tops off several towers. The Duke of Queens typically let loose a different coloured ray from each of his extended ten fingers and bored a hole all the way through the bottom of the city so that fields could be seen below. He was pleased with the effect.

"This is the power of the Gods of Chaos!" cried Elric, a familiar elation filling him as the blood of old Melniboné was fired. "Surrender!"

"Why do you want them to surrender?" asked the Duke of Queens in some disappointment.

"Their city evidently has the power to fly through the dimensions. If I became its lord I could force it to return to my own plane," said Elric reasonably.

"The Morphail Effect..." began Werther, but realized he was spoiling the spirit of the game. "Sorry."

The blue ray came again, but puttered out and faded before it reached them.

"Their power is gone!" cried Elric. "Your sorcery defeats them, my lords. Let us land and demand they honour us as their new rulers."

With a sigh, Werther ordered the chariot to set down in the largest square. Here they waited until a few of the citizens began to arrive, cautious and angry, but evidently in no mood to give any further resistance.

Elric addressed them. "It was necessary to attack and conquer you, for I must return to my own realm, there to fulfil my great destiny. If you will take me to Melniboné, I will demand nothing further from you."

"One of us really ought to take a translation pill," said Werther. "These people probably have no idea where they are."

A meaningless babble came from the citizens. Elric frowned. "They understand not the High Speech," he said. "I will try the common tongue." He spoke in a language neither Werther, the Duke of Queens nor the citizens of this settlement could understand.

He began to show signs of frustration. He drew his sword Stormbringer. "By the Black Sword, know that I am Elric, last of the royal line of Melniboné! You must obey me. Is there none here who understands the High Speech?"

Then, from the crowd, stepped a being far taller than the others. He was dressed in robes of dark blue and deepest scarlet and his face was haughty, beautiful and full of evil.

"I speak the High Tongue," he said.

Werther and the Duke of Queens were nonplussed. This was no-one they recognized.

Elric gestured. "You are the ruler of the city?"

"Call me that, if you will."

"Your name?"

"I am known by many names. And you know me, Elric of Melniboné, for I am your lord and your friend."

"Ah," said Elric lowering his sword, "this is the greatest deception of them all. I am a fool."

"Merely a mortal," said the newcomer, his voice soft, amused and full of a subtle arrogance. "Are these the renegades who helped you?"

"Renegades?" said Werther. "Who are you, sir?"

"You should know me, rogue lords. You aid a mortal and defy your brothers of Chaos."

"Eh?" said the Duke of Queens. "I haven't got a brother."

The stranger ignored him. "Demigods who thought that by helping this mortal they could threaten the power of the Greater Ones."

"So you did aid me against your own," said Elric. "Oh, my friends!"

"And they shall be punished!"

Werther began: "We regret any damage to your city. After all, you were not invited…"

The Duke of Queens was laughing. "Who are you? What disguise is this?"

"Know me for your master." The eyes of the stranger glowed with myriad fires. "Know me for Arioch, Duke of Hell!"

"Arioch!" Elric became filled with a strange joy. "Arioch! I called upon thee and was not answered!"

"I was not in this realm," said the Duke of Hell. "I was forced to be absent. And while I was gone, fools thought to displace me."

"I really cannot follow all this," said the Duke of Queens. He set aside his mace. "I must confess I become a trifle bored, sir. If you will excuse me."

"You will not escape me." Arioch lifted a languid hand and the Duke of Queens was frozen to the ground, unable to move anything save his eyes.

"You are interfering, sir, with a perfectly…" Werther too was struck dumb and paralyzed.

But Elric refused to quail. "Lord Arioch, I have given you blood and souls. You owe me…"

"I owe you nothing, Elric of Melniboné. Nothing I do not choose to owe. You are my slave…"

"No," said Elric. "I serve you. There are old bonds. But you cannot control me, Lord Arioch, for I have a power within me which you fear. It is the power of my very mortality."

The Duke of Hell shrugged. "You will remain in the Realm of Chaos for ever. Your mortality will avail you little here."

"You need me in my own realm, to be your agent. That, too, I know, Lord Arioch."

The handsome head lowered a fraction as if Arioch considered this. The beautiful lips smiled. "Aye, Elric. It is true that I need you to do my work. For the moment it is impossible for the Lords of Chaos to interfere directly in the world of mortals, for we should threaten our own existence. The rate of entropy would increase beyond even our control.

The day has not yet come when Law and Chaos must decide the issue once and for all. But it will come soon enough for you, Elric."

"And my sword will be at your service, Lord Arioch."

"Will it, Elric?"

Elric was surprised by this doubting tone. He had always served Chaos, as his ancestors had. "Why should I turn against you? Law has no attractions for one such as Elric of Melniboné."

The Duke of Hell was silent.

"And there is the bargain," added Elric. "Return me to my own realm, Lord Arioch, so that I might keep it."

Arioch sighed. "I am reluctant."

"I demand it," bravely said the albino.

"Oho!" Arioch was amused. "Well, mortal, I'll reward your courage and I'll punish your insolence. The reward will be that you are returned whence you came, before you called on Chaos in your battle with that pathetic wizard. The punishment is that you will recall every incident that occurred since then – but only in your dreams. You will be haunted by the puzzle for the rest of your life – and you will never for a moment be able to express what mystifies you."

Elric smiled. "I am already haunted by a curse of that kind, my lord."

"Be that as it may, I have made my decision."

"I accept it," said the albino, and he sheathed his sword, Stormbringer.

"Then come with me," said Arioch, Duke of Hell. And he drifted forward, took Elric by the arm, and lifted them both high into the sky, floating over distorted scenes, half-formed dream-worlds, the whims of the Lords of Chaos, until they came to a gigantic rock shaped like a skull. And through one of the eye-sockets Lord Arioch bore Elric of Melniboné. And down strange corridors that whispered and displayed all manner of treasures. And up into a landscape, a desert in which grew many strange plants, while overhead could be seen a land of snow and mountains, equally alien. And from his robes Arioch, Duke of Hell, produced a wand and he bade Elric to take hold of the wand, which was hot to the touch and glittered, and he placed his own slender hand at the other end, and he murmured words which Elric could not understand and together they began to fade from the landscape, into the darkness of limbo where many eyes accused them, to an island in a grey and storm-tossed sea; an island littered with destruction and with the dead.

Then Arioch, Duke of Hell, laughed a little and vanished, leaving the Prince of Melniboné sprawled amongst corpses and ruins while heavy rain beat down upon him.

And in the scabbard at Elric's side, Stormbringer stirred and murmured once more.

XIII

IN WHICH THERE IS A SMALL CELEBRATION AT THE END OF TIME

Werther de Goethe and the Duke of Queens blinked their eyes and found that they could move their heads. They stood in a large, pleasant room full of charts and ancient instruments. Mistress Christia was there, too.

Una Persson was smiling as she watched golden light fade from the sky. The city had disappeared, hardly any the worse for its existence. She had managed to save the two friends without a great deal of fuss, for the citizens had still been bewildered by what had happened to them. Because of the megaflow distortion, the Morphail Effect would not manifest itself. They would never understand where they had been or what had actually happened.

"Who on earth was that fellow who turned up?" asked the Duke of Queens. "Some friend of yours, Mrs Persson? He's certainly no sportsman."

"Oh, I wouldn't agree. You could call him the ultimate sportsman," she said. "I am acquainted with him, as a matter of fact."

"It's not Jagged in disguise is it?" said Mistress Christia who did not really know what had gone on. "This is Jagged's castle – but where is Jagged?"

"You are aware how mysterious he is," Una answered. "I happened to be here when I saw that Werther and the Duke were in trouble in the city and was able to be of help."

Werther scowled (a very good copy of Elric's own scowl). "Well, it isn't good enough."

"It was a jolly adventure while it lasted, you must admit," said the Duke of Queens.

"It wasn't meant to be jolly," said Werther. "It was meant to be significant."

Lord Jagged entered the room. He wore his familiar yellow robes. "How pleasant," he said. "When did all of you arrive?"

"I have been here for some time," Mrs Persson explained, "but Werther and the Duke of Queens…"

"Just got here," explained the Duke. "I hope we're not intruding. Only we had a slight mishap and Mrs Persson was good enough…"

"Always delighted," said the insincere lord. "Would you care to see my new…"

"I'm on my way home," said the Duke of Queens. "I just stopped by. Mrs Persson will explain."

"I, too," said Werther suspiciously, "am on my way back."

"Very well. Goodbye."

Werther summoned an air car, a restrained figure of death, in rags with a sickle, who picked the three up in his hand and bore them towards a bleak horizon.

It was only days later, when he want to visit Mongrove to tell him of his adventures and solicit his friend's advice, that Werther realised he was still speaking High Melnibonéan. Some nagging thought remained with him for a long while after that. It concerned Lord Jagged, but he could not quite work out what was involved.

After this incident there were no further disruptions at the End of Time until the conclusion of the story concerning Jherek Carnelian and Mrs Amelia Underwood.

XIV

IN WHICH ELRIC OF MELNIBONÉ RECOVERS FROM A VARIETY OF ENCHANTMENTS AND BECOMES DETERMINED TO RETURN TO THE DREAMING CITY

Elric was awakened by the rain on his face. Wearily he peered around him. To left and right there were only the dismembered corpses of the dead, the Krettii and the Filkharian sailors destroyed during his battle with the half-brute who had somehow gained so much sorcerous power. He shook his milk-white hair and he raised crimson eyes to the grey, boiling sky.

It seemed that Arioch had aided him, after all. The sorcerer was destroyed and he, Elric, remained alive. He recalled the sweet, bantering tones of his patron demon. Familiar tones, yet he could not remember what the words had been.

He dragged himself over the dead and waded through the shallows towards the Filkharian ship which still had some of its crew. They were, by now, anxious to head out into open sea again rather than face any more terrors on Sorcerers' Isle.

He determined to see Cymoril, whom he loved, to regain his throne from Yyrkoon, his cousin...

XV

IN WHICH A BRIEF REUNION TAKES PLACE AT THE TIME CENTRE

With the manuscript of Colonel Pyat's rather dangerous volume of memoirs safely back in her briefcase, Una Persson decided it was the right moment to check into the Time Centre. Alvarez should be on duty again and his instruments should be registering any minor imbalances resulting from the episode concerning the gloomy albino.

Alvarez was not alone. Lord Jagged was there, in a disreputable Norfolk jacket and smoking a battered briar. He had evidently been holidaying in Victorian England. He was pleased to see her.

Alvarez ran his gear through all functions. "Sweet and neat," he said. "It hasn't been as good since I don't know when. We've you to thank for that, Mrs P."

She was modest.

"Certainly not. Jagged was the one. Your disguise was wonderful, Jagged. How did you manage to imitate that character so thoroughly? It convinced Elric. He really thought you were whatever it was – a Chaos Duke?"

Jagged waved a modest hand.

"I mean," said Una, "it's almost as if you *were* this fellow 'Arioch'…"

But Lord Jagged only puffed on his pipe and smiled a secret and superior smile.

CUP AND TABLE
Tim Pratt

Our curve of extremeness has been rising steadily, but has started to rise sharply over the last few stories, and takes a further leap here. I reprinted Tim Pratt's "The Witch's Bicycle", which is almost as extreme as this story, in The Mammoth Book of Sorcerer's Tales. *At that time I said of Pratt (b. 1976) that he is "a poet, author and reviewer from Oakland, California. He currently works as an associate editor at* Locus, *the news magazine of the science-fiction field, and co-edits the little magazine* Flytrap. *Although still quite new to the game his work is being noticed." Well, indeed it has.*

He was shortlisted for the Campbell Award for best new writer in 2004, his poem "Destination" won the Rhysling Award for Best Long Poem in 2005 and his short story, "Impossible Dreams", a beautiful romance between alternate worlds, won the Hugo Award in 2007.

Tim's website is at www.sff.net/people/timpratt/

Sigmund stepped over the New Doctor, dropping a subway token onto her devastated body. He stepped around the spreading shadow of his best friend, Carlsbad, who had died as he'd lived: inconclusively, and without fanfare. He stepped over the brutalized remains of Ray, up the steps, and kept his eyes focused on the shrine inside.

This room in the temple at the top of the mountain at the top of the world was large and cold, and peer as he might back through the layers of time – visible to Sigmund as layers of gauze, translucent as sautéed onions, decade after decade peeling away under his gaze – he could not see a time when this room had not existed on this spot, bare but potent, as if only recently vacated by the God who'd created and abandoned the world.

Sigmund approached the shrine, and there it was. The cup. The prize and goal and purpose of a hundred generations of the Table. The other members of the Table were dead, the whole *world* was dead, except for Sigmund.

He did not reach for the cup. Instead, he walked to the arched window and looked out. Peering back in time he saw mountains and clouds and the passing of goats. But in the present he saw only fire, twisting and writhing, consuming rock as easily as trees, with a few mountain peaks rising as-yet-untouched from the flames. Sigmund had not loved the world much – he'd enjoyed the music of Bach, violent movies, and vast quantities of cocaine – and by and large he could have taken or left civilization. Still, knowing the world was consumed in fire made him profoundly sad.

Sigmund returned to the shrine and seized the cup – heavy, stone, more blunt object than drinking vessel – and prepared to sip.

But then, at the last moment, Sigmund didn't drink. He did something else instead.

But first:

Or, arguably, later:

Sigmund slumped in the back seat, Carlsbad lurking on the floorboards in his semi-liquid noctilescent form, Carlotta tapping her razored silver fingernails on the steering wheel, and Ray – the newest member of the Table – fiddling with the radio. He popped live scorpions from a plastic bag into his mouth. Tiny spines were rising out of Ray's skin, mostly on the nape of his neck and the back of his hands, their tips pearled with droplets of venom.

"It was a beautiful service," Sigmund said. "They sent the Old Doctor off with dignity."

Carlsbad's tarry body rippled. Ray turned around, frowning, face hard and plain as a sledgehammer, and said "What the shit are you talking about, junkie? We haven't even gotten to the funeral home yet."

Sigmund sank down in his seat. This was, in a way, even more embarrassing than blacking out.

"Blood and honey," Carlotta said, voice all wither and bile. "How much of that shit did you snort this morning that you can't even remember what day it is?"

Sigmund didn't speak. They all knew he could see into the past, but none of them knew the full extent of his recent gyrations through time. Lately he'd been jerking from future to past and back again without compass or guide. Only the Old Doctor had known about that, and now that he was dead, it was better kept a secret.

They reached the funeral home, and Sigmund had to go through the ceremony all over again. Grief – unlike sex, music, and cheating at cards – was not a skill that could be honed by practice.

The Old Doctor welcomed Sigmund, twenty years old and tormented by visions, into the library at the Table's headquarters. Shelves rose everywhere like battlements, the floors were old slate, and the lights were ancient crystal-dripping chandeliers, but the Old Doctor sat in a folding chair at a card table heaped with books.

"I expected, well, something *more*," Sigmund said, thumping the rickety table with his hairy knuckles. "A big slab of mahogany or something, a table with authority."

"We had a fine table once," the Old Doctor said, eternally middle-aged and absently professorial. "But it was chopped up for firewood during a siege in the 1600s." He tapped the side of his nose. "There's a lesson in that. No asset, human or material, is important compared to the continued existence of the organization itself."

"But surely *you're* irreplaceable," Sigmund said, awkward attempt at job security through flattery. The room shivered and blurred at the edges of his vision, but it had not changed much in recent decades, a few books moving here and there, piles of dust shifting across the floor.

The Old Doctor shook his head. "I am the living history of the Table, but if I died, a new doctor would be sent from the archives to take over operations, and though his approach might differ from mine, his role would be the same – to protect the cup."

"The cup," Sigmund said, sensing the cusp of mysteries. "You mean the Holy Grail."

The Old Doctor ran his fingers along the spine of a dusty leatherbound book. "No. The Table predates the time of Christ. We guard a much older cup."

"The cup, is it here, in the vaults?"

"Well." The Old Doctor frowned at the book in his hands. "We don't actually know where the cup is anymore. The archives have... deteriorated over the centuries, and there are gaps in my knowledge. It would be accurate to say the agents of the Table now *seek* the cup, so that we may protect it properly again. That's why you're here, Sigmund. For your ability to see into the past. Though we'll have to train you to narrow your focus to the here-and-now, to peel back the gauze of time at will." He looked up from the book and met Sigmund's eyes. "As it stands, you're almost useless to me, but I've made useful tools out of things far more broken than you are."

Some vestigial part of Sigmund's ego bristled at being called broken, but not enough to stir him to his own defense. "But I can only look back thirty or forty years. How can that help you?"

"I have...a theory," the Old Doctor said. "When you were found on the streets, you were raving about gruesome murders, yes?"

Sigmund nodded. "I don't know about *raving*, but yes."

"The murders you saw took place over a hundred years ago. On that occasion, you saw back many more years than usual. Do you know why?"

Sigmund shook his head. He thought he *did* know, but shame kept him from saying.

"I suspect your unusual acuity was the result of all that speed you snorted," the Old Doctor said. "The stimulants enabled you to see deeper into the past. I have, of course, vast quantities of very fine methamphetamines at my disposal, which you can use to aid me in my researches."

Sigmund said "Vast quantities?" His hands trembled, and he clasped them to make them stop.

"Enough to let you see *centuries* into the past," the Old Doctor said. "Though we'll work up to that, of course."

"When I agreed to join the Table, I was hoping to do field work."

The Old Doctor sniffed. "That business isn't what's important, Sigmund. Assassination, regime change, paltry corporate wars – that's just the hackwork our agents do to pay the bills. It's not worthy of your gifts."

"Still, it's what I want. I'll help with your research if you let me work in the field." Sigmund had spent a childhood in cramped apartments and hospital wards, beset by visions of the still-thrashing past. In those dark rooms he'd read comic books and dreamed of escaping the prison of circumstance – of being a superhero. But heroes like that weren't real. Anyone who put on a costume and went out on the streets to fight crime would be murdered long before morning. At some point in his teens Sigmund had graduated to spy thrillers and Cold War history, passing easily from fiction to non-fiction and back again, reading about double- and triple-agents with an interest that bordered on the fanatical. Becoming a spy – that idea had the ring of the plausible, in a way that becoming a superhero never could. Now, this close to that secret agent dream, he wouldn't let himself be shunted into a pure research position. This was his chance.

The Old Doctor sighed. "Very well."

"What's it like?" Carlotta said, the night after their first mission as a duo. She'd enthralled a Senator while Sigmund peered into the past to find out where the microfilm was hidden. Now, after, they were sitting at the counter in an all-night diner where even *they* didn't stand out from the crowd of weirdoes and freaks.

Sigmund sipped decaf coffee and looked around at the translucent figures of past customers, the crowd of nights gone by, every booth and stool occupied by ghosts. "It's like layers of gauze," he said. "Usually I just see the past distantly, shimmering, but if I concentrate I can sort of…shift my focus." He thumped his coffee cup and made the liquid inside ripple. "The Old Doctor taught me to keep my eyes on the here-and-now, unless I *need* to look back, and then I just sort of…" He gestured vaguely with his hands, trying to create a physical analogue for a psychic act, to mime the metaphysical. "I guess I sort of twitch the gauze aside, and pass through a curtain, and the present gets blurrier while the past comes into focus."

"That's a shitty description," Carlotta said, sawing away at the rare steak and eggs on her plate.

The steak, briefly, shifted in Sigmund's vision and became a living, moving part of a cow. Sigmund's eyes watered, and he looked away. He mostly ate vegetables for that very reason. "I've never seen the world any other way, so I don't know how to explain it better. I can't imagine what it's like for you, seeing just the present. It must seem very *fragile*."

"We had a guy once who could see into the future, just a little bit, a couple of minutes at most. Didn't stop him from getting killed, but he wet himself right before the axe hit him. He was a lot less boring than you are." Carlotta belched.

"Why haven't I met you before?" Sigmund shrank back against the cushions in the booth.

"I'm heavy ordnance," Carlsbad said, his voice low, a rumble felt in Sigmund's belly and bones as much as heard by his ears. "I've been with the Table since the beginning. They don't reveal secrets like me to research assistants." Carlsbad was tar-black, skin strangely reflective, face eyeless and mouthless, blank as a minimalist snowman's, human only in general outline. "But the Old Doctor says you've exceeded all expectations, so we'll be working together from time to time."

Sigmund looked into Carlsbad's past, as far as he could – which was quite far, given the cocktail of uppers singing in his blood – and Carlsbad never changed; black, placid, eternal. "What…" *What are you*, he'd nearly asked. "What do you do for the Table?"

"Whatever the Old Doctor tells me to," Carlsbad said.

Sigmund nodded. "Carlotta told me you're a fallen god of the underworld."

"That bitch lies," Carlsbad said, without disapproval. "I'm no god. I'm just, what's that line – 'the evil that lurks in the hearts of men.' The Old Doctor says that as long as one evil person remains on Earth, I'll be alive."

"Well," Sigmund said. "I guess you'll be around for a while, then."

The first time Carlsbad saved his life, Sigmund lay panting in a snowbank, blood running from a ragged gash in his arm. "You could have let me die just then," Sigmund said. Then, after a moment's hesitation: "You could have benefited from my death."

Carlsbad shrugged, shockingly dark against the snow. "Yeah, I guess."

"I thought you were *evil*," Sigmund said, lightheaded from blood loss and exertion, more in the *now* than he'd ever felt before, the scent of pines and the bite of cold air immediate reminders of his miraculously ongoing life. "I mean, you're *made* of evil."

"You're made mostly of carbon atoms," Carlsbad said. "But you don't spend all your time thinking about forming long-chain molecules, do you? There's more to both of us than our raw materials."

"Thank you for saving me, Carlsbad."

"Anytime, Sigmund." His tone was laid-back but pleased, the voice of someone who'd seen it all but could still sometimes be pleasantly surprised. "You're the first Table agent in four hundred years who's treated me like something other than a weapon or a monster. I know I scare you shitless, but you *talk* to me."

Exhaustion and exhilaration waxed and waned in Sigmund. "I like you because you don't change. When I look at most people I can see them as babies, teenagers, every step of their lives superimposed, and if I look back far enough they disappear – but not you. You're the same as far back as I can see." Sigmund's eyelids were heavy. He felt light. He thought he might float away.

"Hold on," Carlsbad said. "Help is on the way. Your death might not diminish me, but I'd still like to keep you around."

Sigmund blacked out, but not before hearing the whirr of approaching helicopters coming to take him away.

"I'm the New Doctor," the New Doctor said. Willowy, brunette, young, she stood behind a podium in the briefing room, looking at the assembled Table agents – Sigmund, Carlotta, Carlsbad, and the recently-promoted Ray. They were the alpha squad, the apex of the organization, and the New Doctor had not impressed them yet. "We're going to have some changes around here. We need to get back to basics. We need to find the *cup*. These other jobs might fill our bank accounts, but they don't further our cause."

Ray popped a wasp into his mouth, chewed, swallowed, and said "Fuck that mystic bullshit." His voice was accompanied by a deep, angry buzz, a sort of wasp-whisper in harmony with the normal workings of his voicebox. Ray got nasty and impatient when he ate wasps. "I joined up to make money and get a regular workout, not chase after some imaginary Grail." Sigmund knew Ray was lying – that he had a very specific interest in the cup – but Sigmund also understood why Ray was keeping that interest a secret. "You just stay in the library and read your books like the Old Doctor did, okay?"

The New Doctor shoved the podium over, and it fell towards Ray, who dove out of the way. While he was moving, the New Doctor came around and kicked him viciously in the ribs, her small boots wickedly pointed and probably steel-toed. Ray rolled away, panting and clutching his side.

Sigmund peered into the New Doctor's past. She looked young, but she'd looked young for *decades*.

"I'm not like the Old Doctor," she said. "He missed his old life in the archives, and was content with his books, piecing together the past. But I'm glad to be out of the archives, and under my leadership, we're going to make history, not study it."

"I'll *kill* you," Ray said. Stingers were growing out of his fingertips, and his voice was all buzz now.

"Spare me," the New Doctor said, and kicked him in the face.

By spying on their pasts and listening in on their private moments, Sigmund learned why the other agents wanted to find the cup, and see God:

Carlotta whispered to one of her lovers, the shade of a great courtesan conjured from an anteroom of Hell: "I want to castrate God, so he'll never create another world."

Ray told Carlotta, while they disposed of the body of a young archivist who'd discovered their secret past and present plans: "I want to eat God's heart and belch out words of creation."

Carlsbad, alone, staring at the night sky (a lighted void, while his own darkness was utter), had imaginary conversations with God that always came down, fundamentally, to one question: "Why did you make me?"

The New Doctor, just before she poisoned the Old Doctor (making it look like a natural death), answered his bewildered plea for mercy by saying "No. As long as you're alive, we'll *never* find the cup, and I'll *never* see God, and I'll *never* know the answers to the ten great questions I've composed during my time in the archives."

Sigmund saw it all, every petty plan and purpose that drove his fellows, but he had no better purpose himself. The agents of the Table might succeed in finding the cup, not because they were worthy, but simply because they'd been trying for years upon years, and sometimes persistence led to success.

Sigmund knew their deepest reasons, and kept all their secrets, because past and present and cause and effect were scrambled for him. The Old Doctor's regime of meth, cocaine, and more exotic uppers had ravaged Sigmund's nasal cavities and set him adrift in time. At first, he'd only been able to *see* back in time, but sometimes taking the Old Doctor's experimental stimulants *truly* sent him back in time. Sometimes it was just his mind that travelled, sent back a few days to relive past events again in his own body, but other times, rarely, he physically travelled back, just a day or two at most, just for a little while, before being wrenched back to a present filled with headaches and nosebleeds.

On one of those rare occasions when he travelled physically back in time, Sigmund saw the Old Doctor's murder, and was snapped back to the future moments before the New Doctor could kill him, too.

Ray ate a Sherpa's brain two days out of base camp, and after that, he was able to guide them up the crags and paths toward the temple perfectly, though he was harder to converse with, his speech peppered with mountain idioms. He developed a taste for barley tea flavored with rancid yak butter, and sometimes sang lonely songs that merged with the sound of the wind.

"We're going to Hell," the New Doctor said.

"Probably," Sigmund said, edging away.

She sighed. "No, really – we're going into the underworld. Or, well, sort of a visiting room for the underworld."

"I've heard rumors about that." Hell's anteroom was where Carlotta found her ghostly lovers. "One of the Table's last remaining mystic secrets. I'm surprised they didn't lose that, too, when they lost the key to the moon and the scryer's glass and all those other wonders in the first war with the Templars."

"Much has been lost." The New Doctor pushed a shelf, which swung easily away from the wall on secret hinges, revealing an iron grate. "But that means much can be regained." She pressed a red button. "Stop fidgeting, Sigmund. I'm not going to kill you. But I do want to know, how did you get into the Old Doctor's office and see me kill him, when I *know* you were on assignment with Carlsbad in Belize at the time? And how did you disappear afterwards? Bodily bilocation? Ectoplasmic projection? What?"

"Time travel," Sigmund said. "I don't just see into the past. Sometimes I travel into the past physically."

"Huh. I didn't see anything about that in the Old Doctor's notes."

"Oh, no. He kept the most important notes in his head. So why aren't you going to kill me?"

Something hummed and clattered beneath the floor.

"Because I can use you. Why haven't you turned me in?"

Sigmund hesitated. He'd liked the Old Doctor, who was the closest thing he'd ever had to a father. He hated to disrespect the old man's memory, though he knew the Old Doctor had seen him as a research tool, a sort of ambulatory microfiche machine, and nothing more. "Because I'm ready for things to change. I thought I wanted to be an operative, but I'm tired of the endless pointless round-and-round, not to mention being shot and stabbed and thrown from moving trains. Under your leadership, I think the Table might actually *achieve* something."

"We will." The grinding and humming underground intensified, and she raised her voice. "We'll find the cup, and see God, and get answers. We'll find out why he created the world, only to immediately abandon his creation, letting chaos fill his wake. But first, to Hell. Here." She tossed something glittering toward him, a few old subway tokens. "To pay the attendant."

The grinding stopped, the grate sliding open to reveal a tarnished brass elevator car operated by a man in a cloak the color of dust and spiderwebs. He held out his palm, and Sigmund and the New Doctor each dropped a token into his hand.

"Why are we going…down there?" Sigmund asked.

"To see the Old Doctor, and get some of that information he kept only in his head. I know where to find the cup – or where to find the map that leads to it, anyway – but I need to know what will happen once I have the cup in hand."

"Why take me?"

"Because only insane people, like Carlotta, risk going to Hell's anteroom alone. And if I took anyone else, they'd find out I was the one who killed the Old Doctor, and they might be less understanding about it than you are."

She stepped into the elevator car, and Sigmund followed. He glanced into the attendant's past, almost reflexively, and the things he saw were so horrible that he threw himself back into the far corner of the tiny car; if the elevator hadn't already started moving, he would have pried open the doors and fled. The attendant turned his head to look at him, and

Sigmund squeezed his eyes shut so that he didn't have to risk seeing the attendant frown, or worse, smile.

"Interesting," the New Doctor said.

After they returned from Hell, Sigmund and the New Doctor fucked furiously beneath the card table in the Old Doctor's library, because sex is an antidote to death, or at least, an adequate placebo.

"That's it, then," the New Doctor said. "We're going to the Himalayas."

"Great," Ray said. "I always wanted to eat a Yeti."

"I think you're hairy enough already," Carlotta said.

Sigmund and the New Doctor sat beneath a ledge of rock, frigid wind howling across the face of the mountain. Carlsbad was out looking for Ray and Carlotta, who had stolen all the food and oxygen and gone looking for the temple of the cup alone. They wanted to kill God, not ask him questions, so their betrayal was troublesome but not surprising. Sigmund probably should have told someone about their planned betrayal, but he felt more and more like an actor outside time – a position which, he now realized, was likely to get him killed. He needed to take a more active role.

"Ray and Carlotta don't know the prophecy," Sigmund said. "Only the Old Doctor knew, and he only told *us*. They have no idea what they're going to cause, if they reach the Temple first."

"If they reach the Temple first, we'll die along with the rest of the world." The New Doctor was weak from oxygen deficiency. "If Carlsbad doesn't find them, we're doomed." She looked older, having left the safety of the library and the archives, and the past two years had been hard. They'd travelled to the edges and underside of the Earth, gathering fragments of the map to the temple of the cup, chasing down the obscure references the New Doctor had uncovered in the archives.

First they'd gone deep into the African desert, into crumbling palaces carved from sentient rock; then they'd trekked through the Antarctic, looking for the secret entrance to the Earth's war-torn core, and finding it; they'd projected themselves, astrally and otherwise, into the mind of a sleeping demigod from the jungles of another world; and two months ago they'd descended to crush-depth in the Pacific Ocean to find the last fragment of the map in a coral temple guarded by spined, bioluminescent beings of infinite sadness. Ray had eaten one of those guardians, and ever since he'd been sweating purple ink and taking long, contemplative baths in salt water.

The New Doctor had ransacked the Table's coffers to pay for this last trip to the Himalayas, selling off long-hoarded art objects and dismissing even the poorly-paid hereditary janitorial staff to cover the expenses. And now they were on the edge of total failure, unless Sigmund did something.

Sigmund opened his pack and removed his last vial of the Old Doctor's most potent exotic upper. "Wish me bon voyage," he said, and snorted it all.

Time unspooled, and Sigmund found himself beneath the same ledge, but earlier, the ice unmarked by human passage, the weather more mild. Moving manically, driven by drugs and the need to stay warm, he piled up rocks above the trail and waited, pacing in an endless circle, until he heard Carlotta and Ray approaching, grunting under the weight of stolen supplies.

He pushed rocks down on them, and the witch and the phage were knocked down. Sigmund made his way to them, hoping they would be crushed – that the rocks would have done his work for him. Carlotta was mostly buried, but her long fingernails scraped furrows in the ice, and Sigmund gritted his teeth, cleared away enough rocks to expose her head, and finished her off with the ice axe.

She did not speak, but Sigmund almost thought he saw respect in her expression before he obliterated it. Ray was only half-buried, but unmoving, his neck twisted unnaturally. Sigmund sank the point of the axe into Ray's thigh to make sure he was truly dead, and the phage did not react. Sigmund left the axe in Ray's leg. He turned his back on the dead and crouched, waiting for time to sweep him up again in its flow.

Carlsbad found Ray and Carlotta dead, and brought back the supplies. By then Sigmund was back from the past, and while the New Doctor ate and rested, he took Carlsbad aside to tell him the truth: "There's a good chance we might destroy the world."

"Hmm," Carlsbad said.

"There's a prophecy, in the deep archives of the Table, that God will only return when the world is destroyed by fire. But it's an article of faith – the *basis* of our faith – that when the contents of the cup are swallowed by an acolyte of the Table, God will return. So by approaching the cup – by *intending* to drink from it – we might collapse the probability wave in such a way that the end of the world begins, fire and all, in the moments before we even touch the cup."

"And you and the New Doctor are okay with that?"

"The New Doctor thinks she can convince God to spare the world from destruction, retroactively, if necessary."

"Huh," Carlsbad said.

"She can be very persuasive," Sigmund said.

"I'm sure," Carlsbad replied.

The fire began to fall just as they reached the temple, a structure so old it seemed part of the mountain itself. The sky went red, and great gobbets of flame cascaded down, the meteor shower to end all others.

Snow flashed instantly to steam on all the surrounding mountains, though the temple peak was untouched, for now.

"That's it, then," Carlsbad said. "Only the evil in you two is keeping me alive."

"No turning back now," the New Doctor said, and started up the ancient steps to the temple.

Ray, bloodied and battered, left arm hanging broken, stepped from the shadows beside the temple. He held Sigmund's ice axe in his good hand, and he swung it at the New Doctor's head with phenomenal force, caving in her skull. She fell, and he fell upon her, bringing the axe down again and again, laying her body open. He looked up, face bruised and swollen, fur sprouting from his jaw, veins pulsing in his forehead, poison and ink and pus and hallucinogens oozing from his pores. "You can't kill me, junkie. I've eaten wolverines. I've eaten giants. I've eaten *angels*." As he said this last, he began to glow with a strange, blue-shifted light.

"Saving your life again," Carlsbad said, almost tenderly, and then he did what the Table always counted on him to do. He swelled, he stormed, he smashed, he tore Ray to pieces, and then tore up the pieces.

After that he began to melt. "Ah, shit, Sigmund," he said. "You just aren't *evil* enough." Before Sigmund could say thank you, or goodbye, all that remained of Carlsbad was a dark pool, like a slick of old axle grease on the snow.

There was nothing for Sigmund to do but go on.

"The cup holds the blood of God," the Old Doctor said. "Drink it, and God will return, and as you are made briefly divine by swallowing the substance of his body, he will treat you as an equal, and answer questions, and grant requests. For that moment, God will do whatever you ask." The Old Doctor placed his hand on Sigmund's own. "The Table exists to make sure the cup's power is not used for evil or trivial purposes. The question asked, the wish desired, has to be worth the cost, which is the world."

"What would you ask?" Sigmund said.

"I would ask why God created the world and walked away, leaving only a cupful of blood and a world of wonders behind. But that is only curiosity, and not a worthy question."

"So anyway," Sigmund said, sniffing and wiping at his nose. "When can I start doing field work?" He wished he could see the future instead of the past. He thought this was going to be a lot of fun.

The cup in Sigmund's hands held blood, liquid at the center, but dried and crusted on the cup's rim. Sigmund scraped the residue of dried blood up with his long pinky fingernail. He took a breath. Let it out. And snorted God's blood.

Time *snapped*.

Sigmund looked around the temple. It was white, bright, clean, and no longer on a mountaintop. The windows looked out on a placid sea. He was not alone.

God looked nothing like Sigmund had imagined, but at the same time, it was impossible to mistake him for anyone else. It was clear that God was on his way out, but he paused, and looked at Sigmund expectantly.

Sigmund had gone from the end of the world to the beginning. He was so high from snorting God's blood that he could see individual atoms in the air, vibrating. He knew he could be jerked back to the top of the ruined world at any moment.

Sigmund tried to think. He'd expected the New Doctor to ask the questions, to make the requests, so he didn't know what to say. God was clearly growing impatient, ready to leave his creation forever behind. If Sigmund spoke quickly, he could have anything he wanted. Anything at all.

"Hey," Sigmund said. "Don't go."

I, HARUSPEX
Christopher Priest

Yes, I had to look the word "haruspex" up in a dictionary as, in my ignorance and before reading the story, I thought it might be someone's name. In fact it was a diviner amongst the ancient Romans who sought to interpret omens from a study of the entrails of sacrificed animals. Its relevance in the following powerful story will soon become apparent. Christopher Priest (b. 1943) is one of Britain's most accomplished writers of science fiction and fantasy. He is perhaps best known for his novel The Prestige *(1995), which was filmed to much critical success in 2006, but he had been writing short fiction for over thirty years.*

Priest has never followed fashion and has defiantly produced material of striking originality and high quality. Other books include A Dream of Wessex *(1977),* The Glamour *(1984) and* The Separation *(2002), though perhaps his strangest book remains* Inverted Island *(1974), which won the British Science Fiction Award as that year's best novel. Priest's website is at www.christopher-priest.co.uk*

The morning of that January day was icy cold with bright but slanting sunlight, the blue sky lending an electric radiance to the hoar frost that lay sharply on the grass and shrubs of the Abbey grounds. Earlier I had taken a brief walk across the Long Lawn, but the pre-dawn chill had driven me indoors again after a few minutes. Now I waited in the draughty main entrance hall of the Abbey, behind the closed double doors, listening for the sound of tyres on the gravel drive outside.

The car sent by the solicitor arrived punctually, only a few seconds after the clock in the stairwell had finished chiming nine o'clock. I snatched the doors open as soon as I heard the car come to a halt. The frozen air swirled in and around me.

The simple formality began.

The chauffeur climbed out of the driver's seat, lowering his head to one side to avoid dislodging his cap, then straightened his full-buttoned jacket with a jerking motion at the hem. He stood erect. Without looking in my direction he walked smartly to the rear compartment of the car, and held the door open. He stared into the distance. Miss Wilkins stepped down: a brief vision of silken stockings, a tight black skirt, glossy shoes, mousquetaire gloves, a discreet hat with a wide brim and a veil. She was clutching the small, box-shaped parcel I was expecting.

As she climbed the double flight of steps towards the main door the chauffeur followed. He stood protectively behind her as she confronted me. As usual she did not look directly at me but held out the package for me to take. She was looking down at the steps, a parody of demureness. Intoxicating waves of her civet-based perfume drifted across to me, and I could not suppress a relishing sniff.

I took the package from her, and also the release form that required my signature, but now I had the parcel in my hands I was no longer in any hurry. I shook the package beside my ear, listening to the satisfying, provocative sound of the hard little pellets rattling around inside. All that potential locked within! I stared directly at Miss Wilkins, challenging her to look back at me, but her expression remained frightened and evasive. She could not leave without my signature on the release, so naturally I made her wait.

I like to see fear in another person's face, and in spite of her seeming composure, and her deliberate avoidance of my gaze, Miss Wilkins could hide her apprehension no better than she could conceal her youthful allure. She was trembling, a hint of convulsive movement that induced a terrible bodily craving in me. As usual, she had gone to manifest efforts to make herself unattractive to me. The jacket and skirt of her suit, made of heavy, businesslike serge, and of forbidding stiffness, for me only served to emphasize the hint of feminine ripeness that lay beneath. The delay I was causing interested me, the fear in the young woman stimulated me, and her scents were all but irresistible.

I said softly, "Will you enter my house, Miss Wilkins?"

Beneath the veil, her steadfast gaze at the ground was briefly interrupted; I saw her long lashes flicker.

"I dare not," she said, in a whisper.

"Then…"

The moment was interrupted by the chauffeur, who shifted his weight in an impatient, threatening manner.

"Please just sign the receipt, Mr Owsley," he said.

I did not mind him intervening, although I resented the sense of intimidation. He had his job to do; I expected only that he should do it civilly. I gave the young woman an appreciative smile for bringing me my pellets, hoping to excite another response, perhaps even a glimpse of her eyes, but during the many brief visits she had made in the last few months she had never once looked straight at me. I fussed with my pen, making it seem that it was unexpectedly dry of ink, but I must have tried this once before in the past. Miss Wilkins had another pen at the ready, concealed in her gloved hand, and she moved deftly to provide me with it.

I took it from her, contriving to brush my fingers against the soft fabric covering the palm of her hand, but once I had the thing in my hand there were no more excuses for delay. I signed the receipt for the package, and Miss Wilkins seized it from me with a fearful sweep of her hand.

There was a momentary unavoidable collision of her fingers with mine, but she turned back to the steps and at once hurried down them to the car. The chauffeur strode beside her. Her last scents briefly swirled around me, and I darted my face through them, sniffing them up: not everything of the flesh she exuded was concealed by the bottled perfume.

I went to the parapet to watch her, again admiring her silk-clad legs as she climbed elegantly into the rear compartment of the limousine. Although blinds obscured most of the windows, I could make out her head and shoulders as she settled back into the seat. I could not fail to notice the shudder that convulsed her when the chauffeur closed the door on her. He hurried to his cab, climbed stiffly inside, and started the engine at once. Neither of them glanced back at me or the Abbey. Miss Wilkins lowered her face, brought a folded white handkerchief to her eyes, held it there.

The silver-grey Bentley Providence swung around the ornamental sundial, then accelerated down the drive towards the gates. Gravel flew behind it. I could hear the sound of the tyres long after the car had passed behind St Matrey's Stump and out of my sight.

Aware of the importance to me of the day, Mrs Scragg had arrived at work early that morning and was already in the kitchen, waiting for me to bring the pellets to her. What she did not know was that I had mystical evaluations of the pellets to perform first.

I hurried as quietly as I could to the conservatory at the far end of the East Wing and locked the connecting door behind me. I glanced in all directions from the windows to make sure I was unobserved.

Across the Long Lawn, in the hollow beyond the trees, morning mist hung in evil shroud above the Beckon Slough. I stared across at it for a moment, trying to detect any sign of movement from within the cover of thick trees. It was a windless day and the mist was persisting well into the morning, the sunlight as yet too weak to disperse it. I shivered, knowing that I would soon have to venture that way.

I was in the cooler part of the conservatory, the one that faced down towards the Slough. In the normal course tropical plants could be expected to thrive in a glass enclosure on the south face of any house in this part of England, but here on the Beckon Slough side the air was inexplicably chilly and condensation usually clung to the panes. No specimens from the equatorial rain forests would grow in the mysterious dankness, so here were kept the pots of common ivy, the thick-leaved ficus, the fatsia japonica in its huge cauldron. Even hardy plants like these had to struggle to maintain life.

I squatted on the floor beneath the fatsia, first checking the most basic of facts, that no error had been made and that the package was appropriately addressed to me: *Mr James Owsley, Beckon Abbey, Beckonfield, Suffolk.* Of course it was correct; who else would receive such a package? But like everyone else I had my fantasies.

Inside, as I rocked the parcel to and fro, I could feel the loose movement of the pellets, their deadly weights knocking about in their separate protective compartments. The medical staff at the Trust had for some reason sealed up today's consignment more securely than usual, itself an intriguing augury. I was forced to tear at the stiff brown sealing tape, accidentally bending back the nail of my middle finger as I did so. Sucking at it to try to assuage the pain I got the lid open and shot a glance inside to be certain as quickly as possible that everything was in order and as I required.

A faint chemical smell, with its hint of preservatives masking the truer stench, drifted promisingly around my nostrils. Beneath it, the darker, headier fragrance of putrid organics. The muscles of my throat tightened in a gagging reflex, and I felt the familiar conflict of terror against rapture, both hinting at different kinds of oblivion.

The sixteen compartments on the top layer, four by four, each contained a pellet, brown-red or grey-pink, the exact shade indicating to me from which part of the source it had been removed. Every pellet had undergone primary compression by the Trust staff, bringing it down to the approximate size of a large horse-chestnut, but their methods had not yet become systematized or a matter of routine and the results were uneven in shape and size. I knew that the compression was one of the means by which the staff tried to distance themselves from their work, but I cared only about the vital essence. Each pellet was the result of individual sacrifice and surgical endeavour.

Satisfied already with the contents of the package, I pushed my fingers down the sides of the box and with immense care lifted away the top layer. I placed it gingerly aside on the stone-flagged conservatory floor. Underneath was the carton's second level, also arranged four by four, and here the pellets were less well formed than the ones on the top, closer in shape to their clinical origins. Rapture and terror again took hold of me.

I touched one of the pellets at random and found it bewitchingly hard and resilient to my touch, as if it had been allowed to dehydrate. I picked it up and pressed it gently beneath my nostril, inhaling its subtle fragrance. The hardening process had made the release of its essence more reluctant, but even so I could sense the death of the person who had grown the pellet for me. I knew that this pellet had struggled for months in the silent but unceasing contest of decay, and as a consequence it was empowered with the ineluctable life-rage of the dying.

I returned the pellet to its tiny compartment, then lifted aside the second layer. Two more layers were below, also arranged in sixteen square compartments. All of them were filled. For once the Trust had sent me not only quality and diversity, but quantity too. Sixty-four pellets were more than enough to get me through the week that lay ahead. A new and surprising sense of optimism surged through me.

I wondered: could this be the time I had been waiting for, perhaps? If I regulated my appetites, partook steadily of the pellets, varied my intake, started with the most powerful to make up for the unsatisfactory week I had recently endured, then gradually moderated my intake so that I used only the grey slices of tissue until I had the pit under control, then took the rest in a rush, dosing myself until insensate on the most potent of the reddish ones…?

Could the nightmare reach its hitherto unimaginable end?

This sudden rush of optimism came because I knew my strength was starting to decline. I could not continue to struggle alone much longer.

Many aspects of my life were a source of consternation to me. My father, who as a young man had been employed as a sin eater in the six parishes in the vicinity of the Abbey, often spoke of his wish for me to follow his way, while warning me of the attendant dangers. As he saw me growing up with a greater haruspical power than his own I knew he realized that I was overtaking him. The conflict of parental hope against fear helped destroy him, and in his last years he slumped into hopelessness and melancholy. In the final twelve months of his life his madness took hold completely and he taunted me with grotesque descriptions of what befell those who perceived the powers of entrails in their efforts to control past and future. That I was already one such was a fact he could never entirely accept. He had had his own arcane methods; I had mine. It was the duty and curse of the male line of our family to stand on the brink of the abyss and repel the incursion from hell. When he perforce abandoned the struggle, I took his place. I remain in that role, following my ancestors, until someone else replaces me. There is no alternative, no end to the struggle.

I was brought out of my reverie by a staccato rapping sound on the glazed door that led back into the house. Mrs Scragg was standing beyond it, her hand raised, the bulging signet ring she had used to rap on the glass glinting in the daylight. I moved my chest and arms around to shield what I had been doing and quickly returned the trays of pellets to their carton.

I stood up and unlocked the door.

"Mr Owsley, I must speak to…"

"I have obtained some more supplies, as expected," I said, walking through and closing the conservatory door behind me. I proffered the parcel of pellets to her. "You know what to do with them. The rest may be kept in the cold store until later."

"Mr Owsley. James…"

"Yes?"

"Whatever you instruct, of course,' she said. She glanced at the parcel in her hands, and I heard a deep intake of breath. 'I am ready for that. Also, should you…"

Our eyes met and her unspoken meaning was clear. The arrival of the packages from the Trust often had a disturbing effect on us both, and sometimes, unpredictably to outsiders had they been there to see it, but memorably for us both, alone together in the house, violent sexual coupling would follow in the minutes after I received the pellets. Our physical encounters were so spontaneous that they often occurred wherever we happened to be: once against a bookcase in my library, another time on the snooker table in the Great Hall, actually beneath the eye of the hagioscope hidden there.

We rarely alluded explicitly to the darker side of our relationship, so this morning's invitation from her was a novelty. Normally, we played the roles of master and servant, she with an undercurrent of resentment I was never quite sure was genuine or assumed, I with a lofty disdain that sometimes I truly felt, sometimes I put on for her benefit or mine. It was my place to make the first move, but today I was full of haruspical hope, not bodily lust.

"No, Patricia," I said as gently and quietly as I could. "Not today."

Anger briefly flared in her eyes; I knew she hated sexual rejection. But I was feeling calm and positive, excited by the realization of what the new pellets would mean for my destiny.

"Then allow me to cook for you…sir."

"If you would."

"Do you have a preference today?"

"A ragout," I said, having already considered the various choices. "Do you have a suitable recipe?"

"Mr Owsley," she said. "Don't you recall the stew I cooked for you last week?"

"I do," I said, for it had been a memorable experience. "I do not wish you to try that recipe again."

"It was not the method but the ingredients."

"But it is the ingredients I must consume," I said. "No matter what your damned method might be, I require the pellets to be appetizingly prepared."

She walked away from me with bad grace.

At times like this I cared little for her feelings, because I knew she was being well remunerated under the terms of the Trust. The mortgage on her house had been repaid in full to the loan corporation and invalid John Scragg, her husband whose health had been ruined during his service in the Great War, was more comfortable than he could ever once have dreamed of.

I was the greatest good fortune to the family Scragg. In this light the additional pleasures I took with her were a small price for her to pay. None the less, she continued to resent me. My father once told me that he and my mother had also had problems with servants, until they found the remedy.

With the domestic arrangements taken care of for the remainder of the day – indeed, for the rest of the week – I was determined that my optimistic mood should not be broken. I felt that if I could not confront the mystery of the Beckon Slough on a morning like today, then I might never in any conscience be able to again. I found my warmest coat, and left directly.

The day was bright, icy and shimmering with the promise of deeper winter weather to come. The frosted grass crunched enticingly under my shoes as I strode down the slope of the Long Lawn. I knew I was counting on the buoyancy of a passing mood to bear me through the dread of what lay ahead. As I passed from the blue-white, winter-sunlit slopes of frosted grass close to the house, and went along the cinder track that led into the dark wood, the cooler fears of my mystical calling returned. My pace slowed.

Soon the first tendrils of mist were reaching out above my head. Around my ankles eddies of whiteness dashed like slinking fish. The temperature had dropped ten or fifteen degrees since I had left the house. Above, in the gaunt branches of the trees, rooks cawed their melancholy warnings.

The slope was steeper now and where the path lay in permanent shadow the frozen soil was slippery and treacherous. Brambles grew thickly on each side, the dormant shoots lying across the path, their buds and thorns already worn away in several places by my frequent passing.

The Beckon Slough was ahead.

I smelt it before I could see it, a dull stench drifting out with the mist, a dim reminder of the pellets' own putrid reek. Then I could see it, the dark stretch of mud and water, overgrown with reeds and rushes, and the mosses and fungi that surrounded it.

Life clung torpidly and uselessly to the shifting impermanence of the bog. Saplings grew further back around the edge of the marsh, although even here the ground was too sodden to hold the weight of full-grown trees. The young shoots never grew to more than twelve or fifteen feet before they tipped horribly into the muck below. Roots and branches protruded muddily all around the periphery of the consuming quagmire, along with the sheets of broken ice, slanting up at crazy angles, broken by the sheer weight of the intrusion from above, the machine that had descended so catastrophically into the vegetating depths. It remained in place, an enigma that fate had selected me to unravel.

About a third of the way across the Slough were the remains of the crashing German aircraft. Now it rested, frozen in time. It was painted in mottled shades of dark brown and green, and it had made its first shattering impact. It had been immobilized as it rebounded, rising in plumes of icy spray from the frozen muck. The plane's back had broken, but because the process of disintegration was still taking place it remained recognizable. A few seconds into the future the plane would inevitably become a heap of twisted, burning wreckage amongst the trees, but because it had been immobilized in some fantastic way it was for the moment apparently whole.

The wing closer to me had broken where it entered the fuselage. It and its engine would soon cartwheel dangerously into the trees as the terrible stresses of the crash continued. The propeller of this engine was already broken: it had two blades instead of three, the missing one apparently trapped somewhere in the mud, but the spindle was still rotating with sufficient speed that the remaining two blades were throwing a spray of mud in a soaring vane through the mist above.

The other wing was out of sight, below the surface, its presence evinced by a swollen bulge of water, about to break out in an explosion of filthy spray.

The perspex panes of the cockpit cover were starred where machine-gun bullets had left their trail across the upper fuselage. Mud had already sprayed across what was left of the canopy. Inside, horribly and inexplicably, crouched the figure of the man who waved to me.

He waved again now.

I stared, I raised one hand. I raised another. Uncertainty froze me. What would a wave from me mean? What would it imply?

I briefly averted my gaze and lowered my arms, embarrassed by my weakness of will. When I looked back the man inside the aircraft waved again, pointing up at the perspex canopy with his other hand.

I had been visiting the scene of this frozen crash for several weeks and by careful measurement and reckoning had worked out roughly where the plane's final resting place was likely to be. Every day the tableau I saw had moved forward a few more instants of time, heading for its final surcease. Throughout the gradual process the man remained in the cockpit, signalling to me. His face was distorted, but whether it was with pain, or anger, or fear, or all three, I could not tell. All I knew was that he was imploring me to help him in some way.

But how? And who was he? For some reason he was standing in the cramped cockpit, not in one of the two seats where the pilot and another crewman would normally be positioned. I knew he was not one of them, because I could also see their bodies, strapped into the seats, their heads slumped forward.

The tail of the aircraft was intact, painted dark green with paler speckles, and bearing a geometrical device that already had such profound terror and significance that I could only stare at it in awe. It was the sign of the swastika, the broken four-legged cross, once a symbol of prosperity and creativity, Celtic, Buddhist, Hindu, revered by ancient peoples of all kinds, but recently suborned by the vile National Socialists in Germany and made a token of suppression, brutality and tyranny.

It was an aircraft of the German Air Force, the *Luftwaffe*, the Air Weapon, that was crashing here. It was rising out of Beckon Slough, immobilized by my attention to it. Somehow, my interest in it held it here. Soon, if I were to release it, presumably by inattention, the plane would conclude its dying fall: the broken wing would cartwheel into the woods, the fuselage would complete its rebounding lurch into the air before sinking finally beneath the filthy mud, and the spilling aviation spirit would explode in a deadly ball of white flame, detonating the hidden load of bombs that were carried aboard.

But not yet. I had its mysteries to fathom first.

They were focused on the presence of the man who watched me from the damaged cockpit, signalling desperately to me. But how could I reach him? Did he expect me to walk across the wreckage, in hazard to myself, to free him? There was a violent dynamic in the plane: to try to enter it might embroil me in its destructive end. The only logical way for me to scramble across to the cockpit would be along the unbroken wing, but this, as I have said, was half-submerged in the frozen slime.

I felt no urgency to respond to the man's pleas. Anyway, there was a larger mystery.

Five weeks earlier I had spotted what I thought must be a serial number stencilled on the side of the plane's fin, beneath the swastika. I had since spent many hours in my library, and in correspondence with other scholars and investigators, some of them abroad, and had established beyond doubt that such a plane with such a registration number did not exist! Indeed, the Heinkel company, whose serial number sequence it turned out to be, was at present several hundred units short of such a number.

Moreover, it was self-evidently a warplane, apparently shot down while flying over Britain, and therefore in itself a riddle. No state of war existed. Peace remained in this year 1937, fragile and tentative, but peace none the less.

The inexplicable German warplane was moving through time in diverse directions. Forward, at fractional speed, into its own oblivion, throwing up the sludge of the marsh in a fountain of vile spray, killing the occupants, detonating the store of bombs it carried in its bay and felling a giant swathe of Beckon Wood as it did so.

But it had also moved *back* through time, perplexingly, impossibly. Europe was at peace, Chancellor Hitler's armies of workers, thugs and soldiers were not as yet on the march, the boot of the tyrant was still at rest within the borders of the old Reich. The Nazi cry was for *lebensraum*, living space for the German race, and a deadly spreading of the nationalist poison through Europe must inevitably follow. Total war against Germany might indeed lie somewhere ahead, as the politicians warned, inevitably, devastatingly. As yet, though, in the quiet time in which I lived, Britain and Germany and much of Europe, clung to peace, brittle but miraculously persisting.

Out of that future, floating back to its own destructive destiny in the wood that grew in the grounds of my family's house, came this German bomber, victim of a machine-gun attack. By British defenders? How could I possibly tell? But it had fallen into my terrible domain, and consequently I had inadvertently sealed it in my present, slowing the plunge into its own final future.

I was a man of certainties: good and bad, order and chaos, liberty and death. These were my concerns. I cared not for enigmas, even though this one could exert a deadly fascination over me.

I could feel the haruspical strength in me waning and knew I must hurry back to the house for Patricia Scragg's meal. In recent days a demon in me had sometimes urged me to delay while I regarded the German bomber. As the essential power of the pellets faded – my last meal had been eaten more than twelve hours before – so my ability to halt or reverse time failed in me. I knew that if I were simply to stand here at the fringe of Beckon Slough for the rest of the afternoon I would likely see the final destructive moments of the aircraft enacted before my eyes. The prospect of such a spectacle was an undeniable temptation.

I had other masters, though.

I turned and walked back through the trees towards the house. At the point where the track curved to the right, taking me out of sight of the plane, I turned to look back. The man in the cockpit was waving frantically at me, apparently urging me not to leave. I pondered his plight again for a few moments – nothing ever occurred in my life without mystical significance – but continued on towards the house.

Mrs Scragg's cooking was sufficient, but only just. Today she had soaked the pellets in a dark brown gravy, rather lumpy for my taste but otherwise acceptable. She was employed to provide me with food that gave nourishment, not pleasure. When I had prepared myself in the Great Hall she brought me the dish under its silver chafing lid, placed it before my seat at the long table and then hovered expectantly.

"Will there be anything else, Mr Owsley?"

"Not, I think, at present."

"A little later, perhaps?"

Her gaze was steady, determined. I said, "I don't know, Patricia. I have to work. If you could stay late this evening, maybe when I have finished…?"

Again, I knew I was hurtfully rejecting an overt offer, but now she had laid the pellets before me I was single-minded, as she must have known.

"Whatever pleases you, sir."

She left. I followed her to the double doors, trying to seem courteous, and closed them behind her.

I listened for the sound of her steps receding along the uncarpeted corridor, then I locked the doors and bolted them top and bottom. I gave them a forceful testing shake to be certain they were securely closed against her or anyone else who tried to interrupt what I was about to do. I put in place my secret anti-tamper seals, then returned to the dish waiting for me at the table.

I quickly removed the chafing cover and seasoned the food with several vigorous shakes of the pepper pot, and three long scoops with the knife into the mustard jar. With one last glance behind me to make certain I was not being observed I picked up the plate, dropped a knife and fork into my breast pocket, and went to the raised dais at the gallery end of the Hall. I worked the mechanism of the concealed door in the panelling of the wall and passed through into the hagioscope that lay behind. I took up my position.

From here I was afforded a double view: the cell was a squint, to use the term that the original masons themselves would have employed. On one side of me, through a slit cunningly contrived in the stone wall and the wooden panelling was a narrow, restricted view back into the Great Hall I had left moments before. It was only through this narrow aperture that the dim ambient light inside the hagioscope arose. On the other side, through a much larger gap, a mere turn of the head away, was a glimpse into hell.

There was no light down there, in the great abyss lying beneath the Abbey. I could see nothing in the impenetrable black, nor was I intended to see. Whatever inhabited that sunken void required no light to give itself life. It, they, existed in a dark of such profundity that all human feeling or emotion was extinguished too. However, my presence in the hagioscope enabled me, Janus-like, to sit at the gateway between past and present, guarding the way. Behind me, the present world; before me, the denizens of an ancient past and a deplorable future. I was suspended in time, like the dying aircraft that even now was arrested in the mire of Beckon Slough.

I was still cradling the plate of cooked meat. I knew that it was cooling quickly. Difficult to eat even when hot and freshly served, the pellets were nauseating if they were allowed to cool down. I retrieved the knife and fork from my pocket and began to eat the ragout as quickly as possible.

With Mrs Scragg's artful culinary techniques, and the more brutal coverings of spices I had latterly applied, the food was just about edible. Even so, it required an inhuman will to be able to put the pellets in my mouth. Instinctively, for there were still vestiges of the human in me, I looked first for the smaller pieces, the ones most likely to have had their fibres cooked down into masticable form, or the ones which would yield easiest to the knife, or the ones which I could see had received the greatest share of the pepper. While I chewed steadily through the stuff, feeling the sense of evil power growing in me, I tried to distract myself with childish mnemonics – old nursery rhymes, playground chants – in a vain attempt to postpone the imminent confrontation, distract myself not only from the knowledge of what I was putting into my mouth, but also from the growing malignity that took shape whenever I ate.

I could unerringly sense the fiends of the nether world, rousing themselves for our fray, in the same way as I had to relish the rubbery gristle of the pellets and the vile flavours of death that were released with their juices.

Even so, I could take comfort from the consequence of the grotesque meal. I had the transcendent knowledge that time was being reversed by my actions, that evil was being repulsed and that the lurkers of the pit were being held back. On the colossal scale of the vasty death-universe, the delay was breathtakingly short, but enough, enough, all I could do. I alone, haruspex against evil.

Continuing life was my reward; life denied would be my punishment.

As I worked the meat between my jaws I began to sense action and reaction below. I heard discarnate screams, the fury of the frustrated malignity of evil embodied, of the dashing of whatever hopes such monstrous skulkers could entertain, as their slow attempts to claw their way up and out of the pit towards the surface of the world were suddenly thwarted. Most of the meal would be used up pushing them back down to the level at which I had left them the day before, but with this new potency I believed there would be enough energy to force larger reversals on them. I chewed steadily, drawing every iota of flavour from the pellets, returning the beings whence they had come. Every time I swallowed I felt the peristaltic thrust of my oesophagus, forcing down the meat. My mind's eye glimpsed in fitful bursts the outlines of their noisome forms as they surrendered to the release of the death-force I was sucking from the pellets.

Their calling threats, echoing hoarsely around the slime-caked walls of the pit, gave aural shape to their forms!

They were low, flat, many-legged beings, each forelimb and hindlimb jointed at horrible double knees, like immense arthropods. Their limbs extruded to small claws, with which they flailed at the rubbery walls, trying to gain purchase. Each one of the beings was more than two yards in length, far too large for reason! I shuddered to perceive them!

Their heads, sunk low towards the part that could only be the abdomen, were wreathed in cilia, flailing as the angry brows swung from side to side. They had deep mandibles, their maws perpetually slack-jawed and drooling, emitting their beastly howls of anger, vengeance and threat. And the rattling! How they clattered! Some large part of their arthropodic bodies was chitinous, perhaps a loosely connected cuticle or carapace, so that each thrusting step produced a loud, ghastly clicking as they moved their ill-formed frames. It was the cacophony of sticks, of staves flailed against each other, of bones breaking in a yard.

And their relentless, ineluctable climbing would bring them, if not halted or at least given pause, into the world of men, women and children. I and only I stood before these denizens of the pit, barring their way, reversing their quest for escape.

Into this, my long-suffered private world of struggle with stasis, had come by some freakish chance a modern-day intrusion. It was itself as baffling as the creeping horrors I was doomed to obstruct. Somehow, from a militarized future that was conceivable only to a few, had appeared a German warplane. This, shot down and crashing into the Beckon Slough, had become frozen by the same distortions of time that I, haruspical mystic, used to repel the underworld invaders. What was the link?

Because I could never see the dwellers of the world beneath me, inevitably I often wondered whether my loathsome toil might be the product of delusion. Only I, aberrant haruspex from an ancient family of mystics, scholars, clairvoyants, contemplatives, could deal with the threat they presented, but equally it was only my family who had divined their presence.

The crashing German warplane was the first evidence of third-party recognition, incomprehensible though it might be. The plane must have come to Beckon Abbey either because I was in it, or because the pit was to be found beneath it. Now, whether or not this was the intention, it was held frozen in time not unlike the way the repugnant dwellers of the pit were halted.

Furthermore, I knew, as I chewed stoically on the pellets, that not only were the malignant beasts being forced back into their abyss, so the warplane too would at this moment be inching back in time, plotting a reversal of its catastrophic arrival.

First it would sink briefly but necessarily into the mud, where its broken components would start to reassemble, then there would come an abrupt and cataclysmic reverse lifting out of the mud, and it would begin the long backwards tracing of its crash from the sky.

Seven days before, while cheerlessly consuming the pellets of last week's inferior consignment, I had found entirely by chance a uniquely potent example. In devouring it I recognized that the disturbing potency within was having a powerful effect on the arthropodous horrors inside the pit. The moment the eating ritual had been completed I rushed down to the Slough to see for myself. I found I had managed to reverse the bomber's path so far that the doomed machine was actually hovering briefly in the air above the mire, returning for an inert instant to its role as a dweller of the skies. Both of its propellers were intact at this moment before final impact (and to my perception slowly turning), but from the nacelle of the engine on my side was streaming some kind of transparent liquid, presumably the fuel, and behind that a searing whiteness of flame, and flowing behind that was a long trail of black smoke. This traced the aircraft's final path: an almost straight line backwards and up at an angle of some forty-five degrees to the horizontal, past the treetops, into the blue sky, into the unseen flying formation of its fellow bombers, and, for all I knew, back thence into the heart of the German nation.

It was this action of mine that had alerted the man in the cockpit. He had been invisible to me until that day, presumably crouching or lying on the floor, but in some amazing way he had become aware of my actions. Ever since then, his signalling for help had been distraught and constant.

As the days passed, and I eked out my supply of pellets, the Heinkel had gradually returned to its inexorable collision with the bog, while the man within gestured towards me with increasing consternation. Soon the plane had reached the position in which I had seen it this morning, not more than a second or two from its final destruction.

For the first time I had a kind of yardstick to judge my progress. It had seemed to me until today that if I allowed the aircraft to continue on into oblivion the other struggle too would end, but in that case with the catastrophic escape of the horrors into the world. This was the true significance to me of the new consignment of pellets.

I was saving the largest, juiciest, most deadly pellet to last. Earlier in the meal, as I began eating, I had sensuously stroked the cutting edge of my knife across it and nothing of its sinewy texture had succumbed. It was tough, perfectly shaped! A streak of gristle, unreduced by Mrs Scragg's cooking, ran through it from side to side. When I finally took the pellet into my mouth, whole, as it had been found, it was the gristle that produced the tensile strength. It stayed stubbornly in my mouth, distending and bulging while I chewed, but retaining its overall shape. Juices in it were nevertheless released, and as I worked horribly at my task I could taste their exotic menace as they flowed over my tongue.

The final pellet at last produced a reaction from one of my enemies lurking in the dark. In my mind, a dread familiar voice:

"Owsley, Owsley, abandon this work and surrender to the pit!"

"Leave me!" I cried aloud.

"You can never prevail," came the mentally perceived tones of my accuser. "Flesh is weak, life is short, we are forever! Tighten your gut muscles, Owsley!"

"I shall not!"

"Do you not feel the nausea creeping within you? Do you not taste the fleshly residues of what you have consumed? Are they not churning within you, indigestible, disgusting, sickening, wrenching your gut into coils of vomitory? Puke up the cancers, Owsley! Vomit them up!"

I lurched back from the gap that led to hell. I could hardly breathe and nausea had me in its grip. If I stayed where I was I would doubtless spew up everything I had eaten, as often before I had found myself doing. But if I did eject the half-digested tumours all my work would be undone. This my hellish interlocuter knew full well. He came for me on most days, but always when my haruspical work was being most effective. If I were to vomit up the epitheliomata of the meal I would lose almost everything I had just achieved.

So I retreated. The only way I could ignore the terrible voice was to leave the hagioscope, and this I did.

Once I had regained the comparative normality of the Great Hall, it was not difficult to regain control over the feelings of nausea. After I had taken several deep breaths I made sure that the concealed door had closed firmly behind me, and also that no one had entered the Great Hall while I had been in the hagioscope. I lit a candle and hurried to the main door to check the locks, then examined my secretly placed seals, a disturbance to which would reveal if someone had tried to force their way in. Of course, only Mrs Scragg was generally with me at the house, and she could probably be trusted, but the way time was dilated by my struggles inside the hagioscope meant I had to be sure. Hours of subjective time could pass imperceptibly, because my own sense of it was as distorted by the ingestion of the cancers as was that of the devilish creatures I was repulsing.

Now it had become night and the Hall was in darkness. I remembered my half-promise of an assignation with Patricia Scragg when I had completed my work, but there was no sign of her. She normally left the Abbey halfway through the afternoon, and today would probably not be prepared to face what might be a third rejection.

Thoughts of her were distracting me. The important matter was that the pit was secure again, or reasonably so, and would remain in that condition until the next day at least. If the new intestinal epithelial pellets were as powerful as I suspected, it was even possible that another visit to the squint might not be necessary until the day after.

I moved swiftly around the Great Hall, lighting more candles, pulling the blinds across the tall windows, blocking out the night, the glimpse of the moon and the stars, but most of all the white ground-mist that moved in across the valley at this time of the year, to lie like a winding-sheet across the grounds of the Abbey.

After I had checked once more that the door to the hagioscope was sealed, I went through the gloomy corridors to the domestic wing of the house, returning my platter, glass and cutlery to the scullery. Of Mrs Scragg there was still no sign. I left everything by the sink, then ascended to my apartment on the second floor. I stripped off all my clothes (as usual at this time of day they were sodden with old sweat and the seams scuffed uncomfortably against my flesh), and immersed myself in a bath of hot water.

When I went into my chamber afterwards, Patricia Scragg was there. She had lit my paraffin lamps and was waiting by the side of my bed, naked but for the sheet she held against her body. I glared at her, resenting her persistence, but even so unable to deny the animal lusts she aroused in me. She lowered the sheet so that I might gaze at her body. I relished the sight of her tired face, her pale heavy thighs, her dimpled elbows and knees, the girdle of fat about her waist, her large drooping breasts, the pasture of black curling bristle at the junction of her legs where soon I would gladly graze.

I placed my hands on her shoulders, then ran my tongue down her face and body, pausing to nuzzle on her heavy breasts with their tiny but tempting lumps of hard fibre buried deep within. I pushed her down on the bed and quickly serviced her, thrusting with greedy passion at her ample body.

I was exhausted afterwards, but my need to study was constant, so leaving Patricia Scragg to make her own way out of the house I pulled on my reading gown. With tremendous weariness of tread I went up to the next floor to the library. Here I took down several volumes of psychology: on the meaning of revenge, of fear, of repulsion. I glanced through them drowsily in the inadequate lamplight for half an hour. My books were the sole comfort of my life, but so drained was I by the encounter in the hagioscope, and by satisfying Patricia Scragg's agitated sexual needs, that I found it impossible to concentrate.

Later I returned to my chamber and slept.

In the morning I discovered a singular fact: part of one of the pellets from the day before had been packed between two of my lower back teeth and was still firmly in place. Neither pushing at it with my tongue nor scraping with a fingernail could dislodge it. When I had dressed I took a match, broke off the head to make a tiny jagged spear, and tried to pick out the compacted meat with that. Again, no success, but I did finally manage to shift it far enough to release some of the juices that by some marvel it still contained. They trickled across my taste buds.

Twelve minutes flashed by in a subjective moment! I checked the lapse of time, then returned the watch to my waistcoat pocket, still only half-believing that the act of consuming necrotic flesh should have such a potent effect on my mind. No matter how frequently the time distortion occurred it invariably astonished me.

I realized I was entering a familiar state of mind, in which starkest gloom jostled with boundless optimism. I therefore decided to measure the effect of the pellets I had eaten the previous day. Since it had obtruded itself into my life, the German bomber had come to signify a kind of yardstick of temporal motion. Its advances and reverses were a guide to the progress of the main conflict. Now that I had realized this connection it made no sense to subject myself needlessly to the torments of the pit. I could gain the reassurance I sought with much less risk to my sanity.

It was raining when I left the house and the crisp frosts of the previous few days were no more. The sloping sward of the Long Lawn was already sodden in its lower reaches. I was glad to reach the cinder path that led into the trees.

The Slough, when I came to it, lay undisturbed, the surface calm and untrammelled, apart from the constant patterns of overlapping circles made by the rain on the few stretches of clear water. Above the muddy water, a precious few inches above it, lay the plummeting body of the doomed warplane. At once my spirits lifted! The latent power of the pellets now in my possession was beyond doubt.

In the latest manifestation, the aircraft was more or less physically intact, not counting the visible damage the machine-gun rounds had caused to the cockpit cover and engine cowling. Both wings were attached, and although the spilling fuel, the blazing fire and the black smoke streamed back from the engine, it was possible to see it as still a fighting plane, not a broken wreck.

The tip of the wing closer to me – the one that I knew within a second or two of real time would break off catastrophically as the plane ploughed into the mud – was only two or three inches from the solid ground on which I stood.

A single session in the hagioscope, and this! One meal of the new pellets! Fifty or sixty more such pieces still to come!

Was it at last the final stage of the bitter struggle against the chaos of the pit?

Then, immediately banishing the heady optimism, a voice said in my mind, "Get me out of here!"

It was the same voice as that familiar, loathsome cry from the heart of the pit. My first thought: *It cannot be!* Had the monster found a way to track me beyond the hagioscope, away from the house, to here?

It came again, more urgently, "I am about to perish! I implore you! The canopy is jammed! Can't you do something?"

I realized that it was the helmeted figure who stood in the cockpit. His face was pressed desperately against the perspex panes of the cockpit cover and both of his arms were reaching up, struggling to release the catches that held it in place. His movements were frenzied, panicky.

"I can't help you!" I shouted at him.

"Yes you can! Find something with which to release me. I beg you! Save me from this!"

"What are you?" I cried. "Who are you? What do you want?"

"I am an emissary from the future."

I am strong with mysticism, not with physical or muscular development. The predicament of the man on the aircraft wrenched at me, but it was not in my power to assist him. He wanted me to wrestle with the jammed cockpit cover? Or to try to cut my way through the metal side of the fuselage? I regarded him across the short distance that separated us. He was locked in a time and destiny of his own, an alien intruder, subject to the will of a universe fundamentally different from mine.

His voice came at me repeatedly, a sane but desperate plea for help. Wondering what if anything I could do, I stood there regarding him, playing at the soreness of my gum with the tip of my tongue, fretting at the piece of pellet that had become lodged in my teeth the day before. It seemed to have worked a little more loose since waking this morning, and when I sucked at it I distinctly felt it shift. Still watching the man in the aircraft I picked at the fragment of meat with the nail of my ring finger, and in a moment it was out. The familiar essence lifted like gas against my taste sensors.

The plane moved back.

"You are who I am seeking!" the voice cried in my mind. "You are Owsley!"

"I am."

I recoiled with shock from the discovery that he knew my name!

"And you are haruspical!" he called.

"I am."

Now he stood erect, abandoning his panicky efforts to release the cockpit cover. His demeanour was strangely calm. "You must release me if you can. You doubtless know why."

"I believe I do," I said, responding to the composure that had come over him and which was also now surrounding me. 'But there are questions…"

"None matters!"

"How did you…?"

"Owsley, be silent!" His mood had abruptly changed again. "Release me from this aircraft! Then perhaps we might have reasons to converse."

Disliking the authoritative tone, yet even so respecting it, I turned away from him and followed the long path back in the direction of the Abbey. I looked around me as I walked, hoping to spot something hard and heavy and made of metal. Nothing offered itself as suitable. When I entered the house I noticed at once from the clock in the stairwell that more time had fled while the pellet juices flowed in my mouth. It was already past noon and as I went along the ground floor corridors I glimpsed Mrs Scragg pacing impatiently in the short passage outside the kitchen. Fortunately, she happened to have her back towards me at that moment, so I was able to pass unseen beyond her.

In the utility room, after a search, I found a long steel spanner or wrench, I knew not which, apparently left behind by a workman at some time in the past. I assumed it would be sufficient for the task of breaking through the thick perspex, but my skills, as I say, are not those of the physical body. As I carried the heavy implement back down the lawns towards Beckon Wood I felt self-conscious with it and knew that it hung at an unnatural angle in my grasp. The weather was still cold and unpleasant: it was raining persistently and the damp twigs on the drooping branches of the trees brushed against my face and hair. As I followed the bend in the path and again saw Beckon Slough, I raised the spanner in my hand. Holding it before me I strode across the muddy ground to the site of the wreck.

The man remained standing within the cockpit, calm and poised, awaiting my return. I went to where the tip of the wing hovered a few inches above the muddy ground.

"While you were gone," the man said, in my mind, "I was trying to establish how best to force the canopy."

"Don't you know already?" I said, facing him.

"Why should I?"

"You are a member of the Air Force, are you not? The German *Luftwaffe*?"

My mind seemed to laugh mockingly. "I, an aviator? I have never before been inside such a thing. I am a man of learning and of the spirit, as you."

"Who are you?"

"My name is Tomas Bauer. You, I know, are James Owsley." Amazement stirred again in me, but at once the man added, "Of course, you are the one I have travelled to find."

Since the death of my father I had known that I was upholding a tradition, one that I had to honour, and one which eventually I should have to pass on to another. I had expected, though, that such release would not come for many years or decades. Tomas Bauer's words, and the mystical circumstances of his arrival, informed me that the moment had come. Waves of relief, excitement and a distinct tremor of fear passed through me.

However, the immediate problem remained of what to do to release Tomas Bauer from the aircraft. I was still holding the spanner aloft, but the feeling of foolish physical ineptitude was still paralysing me.

I heard in my mind, "James Owsley, you must do as I direct. No more words!"

I tried to assent, but it was as if a sponge flooded with chloroform had been pressed irresistibly over my mind, making it insensible. I felt myself propelled forward, raising my right foot like an automaton to step on the very tip of the wing itself. It took my weight, without dipping. I stepped forward and walked across the curved upper surface of the wing towards the bullet-riven cockpit. When I reached the curved housing of the engine I had to scramble over the hot metal case, carefully not placing any part of my body in the dangerous stream of escaping fuel.

The propeller, still turning slowly a few inches away from me as I passed, set up a torrent of forced air behind it, neither to my perception moving nor turbulent but somehow compressed by the rotation of the airscrew.

Then I was against the side of the cockpit cover itself, looking in at the man who had taken control of my mind. Tomas had removed his leather helmet and I could see his features clearly. He was a young man, tall and ruggedly built, with a shock of blond hair and a sturdily jutting jaw. He stared at me with an intent frown, exercising his mental will against mine.

There was a part of the transparent canopy where two panels of it overlaid each other, apparently the place where the two halves joined after the front part had been slid forward and locked in position. Tomas directed me towards it. I slipped the edge of the spanner against what crack I could see, then heaved at it with all my might, trying to use it as a lever.

When the thick perspex did not shift I felt my arms swing backwards, raising the spanner above my head. I brought it down with a tremendous blow, one far more heavy than anything I would have believed myself capable before now. The cockpit cover shattered at once, a large star-shaped hole appearing in the flattened top. Three more blows forced an irregular aperture large enough for a man to escape through.

I reached down and held Tomas's arms as he found footholds in the cramped cockpit and pushed himself up and through to freedom. As he clambered around I could not help looking down and past him, to where I could see the bodies of the two German aviators. The one in the left-hand seat had clearly suffered a direct hit from a bullet, because a large part of his helmet and skull had been broken away. He was slumped against his dashboard of instruments. I could see a bulge of blood rising through the gap in his head and knew it soon to be a fountaining gout to join the soak of blood that already covered his flying suit. From this evidence of a pumping heart I realized that the pilot must be, in a way, still alive. The other aviator, who outwardly appeared uninjured, although my view of him was restricted, also was leaning forward with his face against the instruments. His body was broken in some horrible way I shrank from trying to imagine. I had to assume he was dead or unconscious, even though there were no apparent wounds on him.

While I was regarding this disagreeable sight with a sense of increasing horror, Tomas had climbed swiftly out of the cockpit and was standing on the wing beside me. He tugged at my arm, swinging me round.

"We leave," he said peremptorily. These were the first words he had so far uttered while I had a clear sight of his face. As I hastened to follow him, down the wing and through the turbulent stream of compressed air behind the propeller, I realized that the words I was hearing in my mind were not the same as those forming in his mouth. The words did not move with his lips.

As I thought about this, he instantly replied, "I speak in German. You will hear, I believe, English. It is the same for me, in reverse. It is best, I think."

He jumped down from the wing. After a few uncertain steps on the muddy bank of the Slough he strode off along the cinder pathway. His long black coat swung in the air behind him. Now he was freed from the aircraft he was walking with easy, powerful grace, like an athlete. From his gait I would not have credited that he was haruspical: others of my calling that I had met were, like me, small in stature, bookish, introspective, timid in all matters that required strenuous activity.

Tomas had implied that he was no better equipped to contend with problems of the physical world – otherwise, surely, he could have escaped from that plane without my help? – but even so nature had apparently blessed him with a strong and agile body.

When we reached the part of the path where I normally struck up the Long Lawn towards the house, Tomas Bauer came to a halt. He turned towards me as I caught up with him. The dark shape of the Abbey, squatting on the brow of Beckon Hill, loomed up behind him. He extended a hand of friendship towards me.

"I thank you James Owsley," he said, and now that I was only a few inches away from him I found distracting the dissonance there was between the words I heard and the movements of his lips. "To you I owe my life."

"Why were you on the aircraft?" I said. "It makes no sense to me. Where was the aircraft going and who sent it? How was it shot down? How did you contrive it to crash on my property? What…?"

He held up the palms of his hands to silence me.

"Nor does it make sense to me," he said. "I was in Germany, you are in England. The war was running its course and I could find no other way to reach England…"

"To which war do you refer?"

"The war between our two countries, of course."

"There is no war,' I said. 'True, there are portents, but the German Chancellor would not be so insane…"

"He is mad enough," said Tomas. "You can be sure of that. In my time his madness has led to a war that is engulfing most of Europe. It is irrelevant to the greater struggle, the one in which you and I engage, but there is no avoiding it for practical matters. I was effectively trapped in my homeland, while my true work was here. The German army is poised to invade England…"

"But this is fantasy!" I cried.

"To you it might seem so. But I speak of what is a grim reality of the time in which I live. Four, maybe five years from this moment. Madness? Yes it is! Engines of war are turning, but they are not such deadly machineries as the ones you and I face. We confront a larger madness, a virulent incursion whose terrors would dwarf in significance a mere military conquest by one nation of another. You reside above the pit of hell and its denizens seek release. The portents have been written in texts since the dawn of time. I have studied many such texts and so, I know, have you. Our task is beyond history! War, pestilence, genocide, famine…these are trivial concerns, compared with what we confront! I had no alternative: I had to escape to England to be with you. After much doubt I came to the conclusion that the only way was to travel with one of the planes that was flying to bomb your English towns. I knew there would be risks, but in my desperation I saw no alternative."

"You raise more questions than you answer," I said.

"And I have told you they are of no account. I am here; that is sufficient. Are we at last to unite and engage together in our struggle against the creatures of the pit?"

"In my life there is no other concern," I said.

"Nor in mine. So we must address ourselves to it."

He turned from me and strode purposefully up the lawn towards the Abbey. Once again I found myself following in his wake. His manner was decisive, arrogant, imperious. He behaved as if I had been merely caretaking the house until the moment of his arrival. As I trotted behind him, already furious with myself for allowing him to dominate me, flashing memories of the years I had endured alone were shining in my mind, almost dazzling me. Was Tomas Bauer somehow projecting them at me?

No matter the source: I could not ignore them. I remembered the first time my father took me into the squint, so that I might experience the raw evil of the pit's emanations and truly learn what it would mean to follow him there. He thrust my face against the opening so that I had to stare down into the merciless darkness, and while he held me with his knee against the small of my back he began an endless braying sermon. His leg moved up and down against me, his yelling voice becoming a terrifying stridulation. It was a new and stunning insight into my father.

When I managed to free myself and struggle round to face him in the confined space of the hagioscope, he was looming over me, lit from all sides by the candles that guttered from every crevice in the rock walls. He bellowed his ranting, maniacal entreaties into the pit, swaying horribly from side to side, a Bible held aloft in one hand, a glistering golden crucifix in the other.

I also could not forget the physical after-effect that the first experience had on me: the long hours that followed while I retched disconsolately into the pewter bowl beside my bed, a purging that was a making-ready of my body for the fray that on some dark level it must have known would be coming. Then there were those few precious weeks when my father allowed me to work alongside him, and when I, in my naïveté, had believed he was encouraging me and that we would work together for years to come.

I did not realize straight away that his sudden interest in me was only a preliminary to a greater event: his resolution suddenly collapsed and he subsided into insanity. The disintegration of his will happened, so it seemed, overnight. Another glimpse of memory: a terrible confrontation with him in the Great Hall, when in the boiling rage of his madness he beset me with what he interpreted as my sacrilegious mystical leanings and physically threw at me the entrails on which I had been preparing the day's labours in the pit, challenging me to consume them while he watched. Impossible, of course. He desperately wanted me to follow him, but my calling stood like a barrier between us, blocking his sight of me.

After this confrontation, a hiatus. There was my father gibbering quietly and in solitude while nurses worked in relays to minister to his needs, while I stood alone at the gate of the pit, attempting for the first time to thwart the malignant ones below in the only way I knew, and not doing too well.

My father's death came as a release for me. Mostly at first it was a release from the guilt that I felt about our relationship, but in more practical terms his death freed the financial fruits of the estate. These were now mine to enjoy. Before his decline, while he yet retained ambitions for me, my father had had the foresight to endow a family Trust to finance an independent pathology research laboratory in a London clinic.

This act not only revealed to me that in his last months he had come to terms with what I might be capable of, but also ensured that our family's material wealth, otherwise so ineffectual against the denizens of the sunken world, could be applied to the production of a steady supply of scientifically reliable epitheliomata.

The first consignment of cancerous bowel growths and malignant intestinal tumours had arrived at Beckon Abbey within three weeks of my father's burial. Thereafter they were delivered at a rate of approximately one package every ten days. The supply was erratic, both in haruspical suitability and in time of delivery, but in recent weeks both matters had greatly improved.

All this was mine. My life, my sacrifice, my commitment and dedication. My father, his father, the generations of the family before us; we had all stood at the dreadful portal and resisted the earthly incursion of the Old Ones.

Now Tomas Bauer had entered our private hell. He arrived in a bizarre warping of time and space, stepping out of some unimaginable future, then arrogantly removed my sense of primacy. I watched him as he walked ahead of me. His able body took him in swift strides up the Long Lawn to the house, while I, the overweight and physically frail product of a lifetime of poring over books and of consuming protein-rich foods, was soon a considerable distance behind him and in a great deal of discomfort. I never ran or exercised, rarely took my body to its limits. My energies had to be conserved for my work. My only physical activity was the hasty, frenzied, irregular satisfaction of Patricia Scragg's sexual needs.

Tomas reached the door on this garden side of the house and passed within as if he had been accustomed to going in and out of my house for all his life. I was so far behind him that by the time I stumbled up to the door, winded and dishevelled, he had been inside for two or three minutes. I allowed the door to slam closed behind me. I leaned against the jamb, coughing helplessly while I tried unsuccessfully to steady my breathing.

I looked feebly into the vestibule that opened out in this part of the building. Sweat was streaming down my temples and into my collar and every inhalation was a painful labour. I could feel my heart pounding like a fist within my chest cavity, beating to be released.

Tomas Bauer had already ascended the flight of steps that led to the upper hallway, from which, after passing along a wide corridor where most of my family's art treasures were displayed, he would eventually gain access to the Great Hall and the terrors within. He was standing on the top step of the flight and Patricia Scragg was with him. I could not hear his voice, but she was nodding compliantly. She heard my arrival and glanced down the stairs towards me. As our eyes briefly met I heard Tomas's mentally projected voice:

"...from now, if you please, Herr Owsley is no longer..."

The weirdly disembodied voice faded again as she turned away, like a lighthouse beam sweeping by. I heard her say, in English, "Very well, sir. I understand."

I called up to her, "What is it you understand, Mrs Scragg?"

She made no answer, but the newcomer inclined his head more closely to hers, speaking softly and urgently. As he did so she turned again to look down the steps in my direction, a look of conspiratorial attention on her face. Although the lids of her eyes were suggestively half closed, the fact that she again turned towards me accidentally opened up his words through her consciousness.

He was saying, "—tonight it will change, for I have ransacked his mind and I know what he is to you, but now you are mine, if you come to me when I will, I shall take you as mine, for you are the ravishing prize I have sought in return for the sacrifice I make in this quest, but you will be rewarded with such pleasures as you cannot easily imagine, for I have the power..."

And on, glibly and pressingly, suggestions and innuendos and flattering promises. I heard them all until the moment when at last she looked away from me and the torrent of intimations was silenced.

I was recovering my wind at last and I began to mount the stairs.

"Patricia," I called. "What is he saying to you?"

She glanced at me again (his oleaginous insinuations had temporarily ceased), and she said, "Mr Owsley, I must ask you not to approach!"

"I am still the master of the house, Patricia," I said. "I want you to accord our visitor every courtesy, but you will continue to take instructions only from me."

She spoke, but I knew at once that the words were not hers. She was mouthing them on behalf of Tomas Bauer. Her voice had taken on a deeper timbre than usual.

She said, (Tomas said), "You have failed to stem the tide of evil that flows beneath this mound. Your efforts have been insufficient to the task. I shall assume responsibility. You may assist me if you wish, but I should prefer you to stay away. This is no longer a matter for your family, but concerns the world. It is my mission to seal the pit forever."

"You don't know how!" I shouted. "You have no experience!"

He stared directly at me.

"No experience? What then is this?" With both of his strong hands he ripped at the front of his tunic, pulling it open. The buttons on his shirt followed, and his broad, hairless chest was revealed. A misshapen, reddened mound disfigured the area around his left aureole and a grotesquely enlarged nipple drooped horribly. Brown traces of a stain from some bodily discharge lay on the pale skin beneath. "You, haruspex, have consumed many such tumours. But this one, I say, is upon me and within me and it is consuming me. What better way is there to know evil than to have it upon you? And you say I know nothing!"

I was, in truth, stunned by his revelation. Tears were welling in his eyes and his head was shaking uncontrollably, as if with a nervous tic. His chest rose and fell with his suddenly stertorous breathing. I knew beyond question that he was not deceiving me. His bared chest made him vulnerable, piteous, the red carcinomatous flare marking his flesh like the petals of a burgeoning flower. He was a man who already stood on the brink of his own hellish pit.

"Tomas," I said after a long silence. "Would we not be better co-operating?"

"I think not. I am here to take your place, Owsley."

I detected, though, a softening of tone, a decrease in his arrogance.

"But surely…" I indicated his infected chest. "How long can you survive?"

"Long enough. Or do you propose to eat my entrails too?"

I was shocked again, this time by the candour of his reply. It did mean, as he had claimed, that in addition to placing words in my mind he could listen to what I was thinking. I had been unable to suppress my inner excitement when I saw the rich potential of the tumour he had revealed on his breast. Doubtless he had sensed that too.

"Eventually, I should have to," I admitted. "You must know that, Tomas. You are haruspical too."

"Not as you."

"You eat human flesh!"

Mrs Scragg gasped and turned away from us both. Tomas grabbed her arm, and spun her around.

"To your work, woman! Never mind what methods we use. I am hungry! I have not eaten in days."

She looked imploringly at me. "Mr Owsley, is this right?"

"Do as he instructs, Patricia."

"You concede my mastery, then?" cried Tomas, looking directly at me. Triumph charged his eyes.

"Mrs Scragg, prepare the next meal," I said. "You may use the usual ingredients. Places should be laid for two. We shall dine in the Great Hall."

I noticed she hesitated for a second or two longer. I recalled our usual conversations at this point when we discussed the way in which she was to prepare the pellets, but I nodded noncommittally at her and she left. Tonight of all nights I was prepared to let her cook in whatever way she felt best.

Feeling that a new understanding had been reached with Tomas Bauer, and even that some sympathy might be possible between us, I climbed the remainder of the steps to join him. He had lost interest in me, though, and was already striding away. Maddened again by his disdainful behaviour, first seemingly vulnerable, then almost without warning as overbearing as ever, I at first made to follow him but immediately decided against it.

Instead, I went downstairs, walked through to the kitchen to speak quietly to Patricia Scragg, then went to my library. I closed and locked the door, and with a dread feeling that Tomas Bauer would inevitably know what I was doing took out the final volume of my father's irreplaceable set of haruspical grimoires, written in Latin.

The task of translation, started by his own grandfather and as yet only partly accomplished, was familiar and necessary, but also unfinishable. I sought only distraction. The abstruseness of the text never did help me concentrate at the best of times and on this evening my mind was racing with feelings of anxiety and conflict. I knew Tomas Bauer was somewhere in the Abbey, prowling around, investigating every corner of the old building.

At odd moments I could detect his thoughts, and they came at me in distracting bursts of non-sequitur. Fear was coursing through me: it was almost as if one of the monsters below had at last broken out of the pit and invaded this continuum of reality. Tomas's intrusion was of that magnitude. Nothing was going to be the same again.

Unless he died. I could not rid myself of the memory of his horribly inflamed chest, the cancer bursting through the flesh and skin. It was surely a terminal ailment? If so, how long would it be before he became too ill to function?

Was his inexplicable arrival from "the future" connected somehow with his illness? From what was he really trying to escape when he travelled to England? Did he have one final destiny to fulfil? Was it involved with my haruspical mysticism, so that, in effect, it was not he himself who was taking control but the cancer he bore?

Mrs Scragg came hesitantly to the door of the library, calling my name. I laid aside the precious tome with a sense of finality and eased open the door. The candle flames bent to the side of their wicks in the sudden draught from the corridor, and wax ran in floods down the guttered stems.

"The meal is ready, Mr Owsley," she said. "Do you still want me to serve it in the Great Hall?"

"Yes, I do. I shall have to unlock the door for you."

"Sir, that's what concerns me. Our visitor has already found a way inside."

"He is in the hall *alone*?"

"I could do nothing about it. I knew you would be angry."

"Very well, Patricia. I am not angry with you. Is the food ready to be eaten?"

"As I said."

"And you have prepared two portions?" She nodded, and I regarded her thoughtfully. "If the meal is still in the kitchen, let me come with you so that I might inspect it…"

A voice came: "If you are thinking of tampering, Owsley…"

Mrs Scragg and I both started with surprise. I know not what was in her thoughts, but to me it was further proof that the end of my era as custodian must almost be upon me. Tomas Bauer had invaded everything and I could not function like that. The feelings that welled up in me were a confusion of relief, dismay and anger.

When we reached the kitchen Mrs Scragg took up the large japanned tray bearing the dishes and we both set off towards the Great Hall. I scurried before her to push open and hold each of the doors along the corridors. When we reached the entrance to the Hall I saw that the reinforced locks had been burst asunder by main force. I immediately saw Tomas within, standing in an aggressive manner with his arms folded and his legs braced, staring at the place from where the hagioscope viewed the room.

I said quietly to Mrs Scragg, "As soon as you have left the Hall, I want you to collect your personal belongings and depart the house. Do you understand?"

"Yes, Mr Owsley."

"I suggest you do it as soon as possible. Do not delay for anything."

"When should I return?"

I was about to reply that Tomas Bauer would surely let her know, when his supplanting voice burst into my mind.

"I'll call her when and if I'm ready! Bring the food!"

"Let me take the tray," I said to Mrs Scragg. "You should leave at once."

Her gaze briefly met mine. I had never before seen such a frank, unguarded look from her.

"I shouldn't say it, sir, but the best of good fortune to you."

"Fortune is not what I want, Patricia, but I thank you for that. I need strength, and the resolve to stand up to this man."

Tomas Bauer was moving towards us, so I turned decisively away from her and walked into the main part of the Hall. Tomas indicated with his hand that I should carry the tray to the long oaken table, then he stepped close beside me as I walked nervously across the polished boards of the floor. I set down the tray and lifted away the chafing covers. I saw at once that Patricia had done us proud, and prepared all the most powerful of the pellets. She had cooked them by the simplest of means, boiling them up with a selection of garden vegetables into a stew which would be appetizing were it not for the main ingredient.

Tomas Bauer said in my mind, "In spite of what you think, I am here to salute you, James Owsley. In your country, honour is for many people a matter of pride, and to others self-sacrifice is a privilege. Although I have come to replace you, it is not out of contempt. How may I best show my esteem?"

"Why can we not work together?" I said. "This talk of replacing me is inappropriate. You have come at a moment when I am certain the course of the battle is about to turn. Look at what lies before us." I gently waved the palm of my hand above the protein-rich stew that Patricia Scragg had cooked for us. "To work beside me would be the greatest honour you could pay me."

"That would not be possible," Tomas said, and I sensed a trace of sadness in his tone. "Your way is not the right way. You have to depart."

"Can I not even show you of what I am capable?" I said. "Let us take our meal into the hagioscope and partake of it together. Then you will realize how the fiends' movements inside the pit will not only be reversed, but placed so far back that a final sealing of the pit might conceivably be possible, and soon."

Tomas replaced the chafing lids on the plates.

"Let us indeed visit the hagioscope," he said. "But not for what you propose. I must inspect the pit for myself, try to comprehend it. I have to set about planning my defence against whatever it contains."

Once again I found my own ideas and wishes swept aside by his imperious manner. He thrust one of the covered plates into my hands, then took the other and walked steadfastly towards the entrance to the squint. I followed, my heart already beating faster in anticipation of confronting again what I knew was beyond its narrow confines.

It turned out that although Tomas clearly knew of the existence of the hagioscope, and indeed its approximate position in the wall, he had not worked out how to gain entrance to it. He made me show him how to operate the concealed mechanism, then tried it for himself once or twice. With the main panel set to one side he glanced briefly into the space beyond, before stepping aside to allow me to enter first. I already knew that there was only enough comfortable space for one person at a time, so as Tomas squeezed in behind me I was already pressing myself against the cold stone wall at the back. The aperture that opened to the pit was at my shoulder and I could hear once again the familiar and disgusting movements of the beasts below. Inexplicably, they seemed much closer than ever before. I had spent too much time, too much energy, releasing this man from the crashing plane. How I regretted that!

"Sir, I request you to eat," Tomas said in my mind.

I raised my arms awkwardly, trying to manoeuvre the plate around to a position in which I could take away the chafing cover again, but to do so meant I had to pass it directly in front of Tomas Bauer's face. To my amazement he jerked his forehead sharply forward, banging the plate in my hand, making it spin away in the confined space. The pellets, my precious and powerful tumours, burst out wetly in their gravy and spilled messily down my clothes and on the dark floor.

I smelt Tomas's breath, so close was his face to mine. In the wan light that seeped in from the Hall I could see his face, maniacally grinning.

"You will never have to taste your beloved pellets again, Owsley. Your purpose is more personal." He was still holding his own plate and as he forced his body round in the cramped space he was able to place the dish on the narrow stone shelf I had myself been trying to reach. "I shall come to those later, if they remain necessary. First, you must eat, sir, and do so until you are replete!"

"You have spilled my plate!" I cried.

"And deliberately!"

To my horror, Tomas once again ripped open the fastenings of his shirt and exposed his diseased chest to me. It was only six inches away from my face. The efflorescence of his cancerous breast gleamed in the dim light from the Hall. I madly glimpsed chasing patterns of conflict: life against death, blood pumping through diseased cells, grisly malignant tendrils reaching out like pollen-laden anthers to impregnate the as-yet normal flesh that surrounded the deathly bloom.

Neither of us moved, while I regarded this object of allure and repulsion. A thrill of anticipation was pouring through me like liquid fire.

Tomas raised both his hands and put them behind my head, a

gesture that was partly a restraint, partly a caress. When he spoke next his words had a tender quality that until this moment I had never heard from him.

"I shall if you wish hold you, James. You may take what you will from what you see."

"I have never divined with flesh that is still alive," I said softly, and in awe of what he was offering me.

"Then do so now."

Whether he drew my head forward with his hands or I moved of my own volition is something I shall never know, but next my teeth had sunk into the soft flesh of his swollen breast. His strong hands supported my head, while his fingers sensually stroked my hair. I used my tongue to explore the texture of the tumour, sensing its preternatural heat, its tenacious grip on its host, the way it spread like an unfolding corolla. Soon I had found its heart, the pistil, where lay the passive organs of love and reproduction, and final decay and death.

As Tomas Bauer's hands tightened on the back of my head I lunged forward, my jaw opened wide, my tongue guiding, my teeth easily piercing the thin wasted skin that still managed somehow to contain the tumour. I bit into the heart of the cancer. Tomas gasped with pain or passion, and I, sublimely, felt myself release wetly and sweetly. With the access of intoxicating pleasure, came the clarity of perception of the little death: Tomas had brought me to this!

His talk of working alone, without me, had never been true! My role was to release him from death. The thrill of the realization urged me on to abandonment: I buried my face ever deeper into his chest as the ecstasy coursed through me. The blackness of the malignancy surged forward to take me, seeming to open up around my eyes like a long dark cylinder, rotating, drawing me through the all-enveloping abyss of night.

I, haruspex, had entered the darkest entrail of all.

Time went past. Minutes, hours, days, years; none held meaning any longer. I had moved to a plane where the mere counting of time was irrelevant. I knew only the gushing flood of death, pumping out around my face, a warm nectar, blinding me, drawing me down, drowning me.

I could no longer see. I was in terminal darkness and I was leaning on, resting on, a slope that was nearly vertical. It was warm and fleshly, coated in slime, lacking anywhere I could obtain a good hold. I felt the terror of what might lie below me and yearned to climb away from it.

A vertical undulation rippled down the slope, shifting me out and back over the abyss below. Panic flooded through me. I was starting to slide, so I held on, paralysed by the abject terror of what would happen to me if my grip weakened. My hands had become claws, their long tines sinking ineffectually into the slimy membrane to which I clung. Oblivion was below. I reached forward and up, trying to gain purchase on the greasy slope. One of my claws felt as if it had found a firmer place, and, thus encouraged, I shifted my weight below, my doubly articulated legs stretching and pushing.

I clicked. I moved.

Another peristaltic undulation came heaving down. This time I was dislodged! I fell, my limbs waving in terror, my unwieldy body curling instinctively into a defensive hump. Only by great good fortune did one of my claws make fleeting contact with the membranous wall. I slashed in the claws and held on with all my strength, and as my body thrashed and collapsed against the scummy gradient I heard others of my kind clicking and clattering with their fright as they too struggled to hold on.

Their panicky sounds swelled around me, muted by the slime around us, but echoing brightly off our chitinous carapaces. The being closest to me, clinging on not far above in the darkness, turned a grotesquely swollen head towards me. Its two rear legs were raised, their horrid inverted knees braced against each other. With a violent spasm the legs rubbed together, setting off a shrieking stridulation.

Around us, the other arthropods took up the rasping chorus, the endless braying sermon; I too felt my rear legs twitching unstoppably against each other. My father, my ancestors, my damned destiny!

By the time the next peristaltic convulsion rolled down towards us I was ready for it, and rode the attack without losing any more ground. The stridulations changed pitch as the slimy wall rippled against us. I shuffled my legs, croaking and belching with the effort, determined never again to fall.

Soon, I started to climb. Beside me, above me, below, the other damned beings climbed too. Ahead was a glimmer of light, a suggestion of final release from the pit, an invitation to life. I knew only the urge to escape and climbed grimly on.

With the next surge of peristalsis a torrent of vile fluids washed down from above, a raging flood of slime and acidic liquid. I held on, while others fell. A violent contraction shook the wall and a great eructation of gases roared past me, carrying with it a fine spray of much of the slime. Again, others around me were dislodged. In my mind I heard their dying fall as at last they entered the abyss.

I resumed my climb, following my father.

RADIO WAVES
Michael Swanwick

Michael Swanwick (b. 1950) became a writer to watch from his first story sales in 1980. Though he works with the traditional motifs of science fiction and fantasy they are often only superficial to allow Swanwick to explore the depths beneath.

His books can at once be technofantasies and humanist as the following shows only too well. Swanwick's primary fantasy novel – though it's as much an anti-fantasy – is The Iron Dragon's Daughter *(1993), though he is probably best known for* Vacuum Flowers *(1987) and* Stations of the Tide *(1991), which won him the Nebula as that year's best sf novel. He has continued to win awards including the World Fantasy Award for the following, which the author still ranks as amongst his favourites.*

His website is www.michaelswanwick.com

I was walking the telephone wires upside down, the sky underfoot cold and flat with a few hard bright stars sparsely scattered about it, when I thought how it would take only an instant's weakness to step off to the side and fall up forever into the night. A kind of wildness entered me then and I began to run.

I made the wires sing. They leapt and bulged above me as I raced past Ricky's Luncheonette and up the hill. Past the old chocolate factory and the IDI Advertising Display plant. Past the body shops, past A J LaCourse Electric Motors-Controls-Parts. Then, where the slope steepened, along the curving snake of rowhouses that went the full quarter-mile up to the Ridge. Twice I overtook pedestrians, hunched and bundled, heads doggedly down, out on incomprehensible errands. They didn't notice me, of course. They never do.

The antenna farm was visible from here. I could see the Seven Sisters spangled with red lights, dependent on the Earth like stalactites. "Where are you running to, little one?" one tower whispered in a crackling, staticky voice. I think it was Hegemone.

"Fuck off," I said without slackening my pace, and they all chuckled.

Cars mumbled by. This was ravine country, however built-up, and the far side of the road, too steep and rocky for development, was given over to trees and garbage. Hamburger wrappings and white plastic trash bags rustled in their wake. I was running full-out now.

About a block or so from the Ridge, I stumbled and almost fell. I slapped an arm across a telephone pole and just managed to catch myself in time. Aghast at my own carelessness, I hung there, dizzy and alarmed.

The ground overhead was black as black, an iron roof that somehow was yet as anxious as a hound to leap upon me, crush me flat, smear me to nothingness. I stared up at it, horrified.

Somebody screamed my name.

I turned. A faint blue figure clung to a television antenna atop a small, stuccoed brick duplex. Charlie's Widow. She pointed an arm that flickered with silver fire down Ripka Street. I slewed about to see what was coming after me.

It was the Corpsegrinder.

When it saw that I'd spotted it, it put out several more legs, extended a quilled head, and raised a howl that bounced off the Heaviside layer. My nonexistent blood chilled.

In a panic, I scrambled up and ran toward the Ridge and safety. I had a squat in the old Roxy, and once I was through the wall, the Corpsegrinder would not follow. Why this should be so, I did not know. But you learn the rules if you want to survive.

I ran. In the back of my head I could hear the Seven Sisters clucking and gossiping to each other, radiating television and radio over a few dozen frequencies. Indifferent to my plight.

The Corpsegrinder churned up the wires on a hundred needle-sharp legs. I could feel the ion surge it kicked up pushing against me as I reached the intersection of Ridge and Leverington. Cars were pulling up to the pumps at the Atlantic station. Teenagers stood in front of the A-Plus Mini Market, flicking half-smoked cigarettes into the street, stamping their feet like colts, and waiting for something to happen. I couldn't help feeling a great longing disdain for them. Every last one worried about grades and drugs and zits, and all the while snugly barricaded within hulking fortresses of flesh.

I was scant yards from home. The Roxy was a big old movie palace, fallen into disrepair and semi-converted to a skateboarding rink which had gone out of business almost immediately. But it had been a wonderful place once, and the terra cotta trim was still there: ribbons and river gods, great puffing faces with panpipes, guitars, flowers, wyverns. I crossed the Ridge on a dead telephone wire, spider-web delicate but still usable.

Almost there.

Then the creature was upon me, with a howl of electromagnetic rage that silenced even the Sisters for an instant. It slammed into my side, a storm of razors and diamond-edged fury, hooks and claws extended.

I grabbed at a rusty flange on the side of the Roxy.

Too late! Pain exploded within me, a sheet of white nausea. All in an instant I lost the name of my second daughter, an April morning when the world was new and I was five, a smoky string of all-nighters in Rensselaer Polytech, the jowly grin of Old Whatsisface the German who lived on LaFountain Street, the fresh pain of a sprained ankle out back of a Banana Republic warehouse, fishing off a yellow rubber raft with my old man on Lake Champlain. All gone, these and a thousand things more, sucked away, crushed to nothing, beyond retrieval.

Furious as any wounded animal, I fought back. Foul bits of

substance splattered under my fist. The Corpsegrinder reared up to smash me down, and I scrabbled desperately away. Something tore and gave.

Then I was through the wall and safe among the bats and the gloom. "*Cobb!*" the Corpsegrinder shouted. It lashed wildly back and forth, scouring the brick walls with limbs and teeth, as restless as a March wind, as unpredictable as ball lightning.

For the moment I was safe. But it had seized a part of me, tortured it, and made it a part of itself. I could no longer delude myself into thinking it was simply going to go away. "Cahawahawbb!" It broke my name down to a chord of overlapping tones. It had an ugly, muddy voice. I felt dirtied just listening to it. "Caw…" A pause. "…awbb!"

In a horrified daze, I stumbled up the Roxy's curving patterned-tin roof until I found a section free of bats. Exhausted and dispirited, I slumped down.

"Caw aw aw awb buh buh!"

How had the thing found me? I'd thought I'd left it behind in Manhattan. Had my flight across the high-tension lines left a trail of some kind? Maybe. Then again, it might have some special connection with me. To follow me here it must have passed by easier prey. Which implied it had a grudge against me. Maybe I'd known the Corpsegrinder back when it was human. We could once have been important to each other. We might have been lovers. It was possible. The world is a stranger place than I used to believe.

The horror of my existence overtook me then, an acute awareness of the squalor in which I dwelt, the danger which surrounded me, and the dark mystery informing my universe.

I wept for all that I had lost.

Eventually, the sun rose up like God's own Peterbilt and with a triumphant blare of chromed trumpets, gently sent all of us creatures of the night to sleep.

When you die, the first thing that happens is that the world turns upside down. You feel an overwhelming disorientation and a strange sensation that's not quite pain as the last strands connecting you to your body part, and then you slip out of physical being and fall from the planet.

As you fall, you attenuate. Your substance expands and thins, glowing more and more faintly as you pick up speed. So far as can be told, it's a process that doesn't ever stop. Fainter, thinner, colder…until you've merged into the substance of everyone else who's ever died, spread perfectly uniformly through the universal vacuum, forever moving toward but never arriving at absolute zero.

Look hard, and the sky is full of the Dead.

Not everyone falls away. Some few are fast-thinking or lucky enough to maintain a tenuous hold on earthly existence. I was one of the lucky ones. I was working late one night on a proposal when I had my heart attack. The office was empty. The ceiling had a wire mesh within the plaster, and that's what saved me.

The first response to death is denial. *This can't be happening*, I thought. I gaped up at the floor where my body had fallen, and would lie undiscovered until morning. My own corpse, pale and bloodless, wearing a corporate tie and sleeveless grey Angora sweater. Gold Rolex, Sharper Image desk accessories, and of course I also thought: *I died for THIS?*

By which of course I meant my entire life.

So it was in a state of both personal and ontological crisis that I wandered across the ceiling to the location of an old pneumatic message tube, removed and casually plastered over some fifty years before. I fell from the seventeenth to the twenty-fifth floor, and I learned a lot in the process.

Shaken, startled, and already beginning to assume the wariness that the afterlife requires, I went to a window to get a glimpse of the outer world. When I tried to touch the glass, my hand went right through. I jerked back. Cautiously, I leaned forward, so that my head stuck out into the night.

What a wonderful experience Times Square is when you're dead! There is ten times the light a living being sees. All metal things vibrate with inner life. Electric wires are thin blue scratches in the air. Neon *sings*. The world is filled with strange sights and cries. Everything shifts from beauty to beauty.

Something that looked like a cross between a dragon and a wisp of smoke was feeding in the Square. But it was lost among so many wonders that I gave it no particular thought.

Night again. I awoke with Led Zeppelin playing in the back of my head. "Stairway to Heaven." Again. It can be a long wait between Dead Milkmen cuts.

"Wakey-risey, little man," crooned one of the Sisters. It was funny how sometimes they took a close personal interest in our doings, and other times ignored us completely. "This is Euphrosyne with the red-eye weather report. The outlook is moody with a chance of existential despair. You won't be going outside tonight if you know what's good for you. There'll be lightning within the hour."

"It's too late in the year for lightning," I said.

"Oh dear. Should I inform the weather?"

By now I was beginning to realize that what I had taken on awakening to be the pressure of the Corpsegrinder's dark aura was actually the high-pressure front of an advancing storm. The first drops of rain pattered on the roof. Wind skirled and the rain grew stronger. Thunder growled in the distance. "Why don't you just go fuck your…"

A light laugh that trilled up into the supersonic, and she was gone.

I was listening to the rain underfoot when a lightning bolt screamed into existence, turning me inside out for the briefest instant then cartwheeling gleefully into oblivion. In the femtosecond of restoration following the bolt, the walls were transparent and all the world made of glass, its secrets available to be snooped out. But before comprehension was possible, the walls opaqued again and the lightning's malevolent aftermath faded like a madman's smile in the night.

Through it all the Seven Sisters were laughing and singing, screaming with joy whenever a lightning bolt flashed, and making up nonsense poems from howls, whistles, and static. During a momentary lull, the flat hum of a carrier wave filled my head. Phaenna, by the feel of her. But instead of her voice, I heard only the sound of fearful sobs.

"Widow?" I said. "Is that you?"

"She can't hear you," Phaenna purred. "You're lucky I'm here to bring you up to speed. A lightning bolt hit the transformer outside her house. It was bound to happen sooner or later. Your Nemesis – the one you call the Corpsegrinder, such a cute nickname, by the way – has her trapped."

This was making no sense at all. "Why would the Corpsegrinder be after her?"

"Why why why why?" Phaenna sang, a snatch of some pop ballad or other. "You didn't get answers when you were alive, what made you think you'd get any *now*?"

The sobbing went on and on. "She can sit it out," I said. "The Corpsegrinder can't – hey, wait. Didn't they just wire her house for cable? I'm trying to picture it. Phone lines on one side, electricity on the other, cable. She can slip out on his blind side."

The sobs lessened and then rose in a most unWidowlike wail of despair.

"Typical," Phaenna said. "You haven't the slightest notion of what you're talking about. The lightning stroke has altered your little pet. Go out and see for yourself."

My hackles rose. "You know damned good and well that I can't..."

Phaenna's attention shifted and the carrier beam died. The Seven

Sisters are fickle that way. This time, though, it was just as well. No way was I going out there to face that monstrosity. I couldn't. And I was grateful not to have to admit it.

For a long while I sat thinking about the Corpsegrinder. Even here, protected by the strong walls of the Roxy, the mere thought of it was paralyzing. I tried to imagine what Charlie's Widow was going through, separated from this monster by only a thin curtain of brick and stucco. Feeling the hard radiation of its malice and need… It was beyond my powers of visualization. Eventually I gave up and thought instead about my first meeting with the Widow.

She was coming down the hill from Roxborough with her arms out, the inverted image of a child playing at tightrope walker. Placing one foot ahead of the other with deliberate concentration, scanning the wire before her so cautiously that she was less than a block away when she saw me.

She screamed.

Then she was running straight at me. My back was to the transformer station – there was no place to flee. I shrank away as she stumbled to a halt.

"It's you!" she cried. "Oh God, Charlie, I knew you'd come back for me, I waited so long, but I never doubted you, never, we can…" She lunged forward as if to hug me. Our eyes met.

All the joy in her died.

"Oh," she said. "It's not you."

I was fresh off the high-tension lines, still vibrating with energy and fear. My mind was a blaze of contradictions. I could remember almost nothing of my post-death existence. Fragments, bits of advice from the old dead, a horrifying confrontation with…something, some creature or phenomenon that had driven me to flee Manhattan. Whether it was this event or the fearsome voltage of that radiant highway that had scoured me of experience, I did not know. "It's me," I protested.

"No, it's not." Her gaze was unflatteringly frank. "You're not Charlie and you never were. You're – just the sad remnant of what once was a man, and not a very good one at that." She turned away. She was leaving me! In my confusion, I felt such a despair as I had never known before.

"Please…" I said.

She stopped.

A long silence. Then what in a living woman would have been a sigh. "You'd think that I – well, never mind." She offered her hand, and when I would not take it, simply said, "This way."

I followed her down Main Street, through the shallow canyon of the business district to a diner at the edge of town. It was across from Hubcap Heaven and an automotive junkyard bordered it on two sides. The diner was closed. We settled down on the ceiling.

"That's where the car ended up after I died," she said, gesturing toward the junkyard. "It was right after I got the call about Charlie. I stayed up drinking and after a while it occurred to me that maybe they were wrong, they'd made some sort of horrible mistake and he wasn't really dead, you know? Like maybe he was in a coma or something, some horrible kind of misdiagnosis, they'd gotten him confused with somebody else, who knows? Terrible things happen in hospitals. They make mistakes.

"I decided I had to go and straighten things out. There wasn't time to make coffee so I went to the medicine cabinet and gulped down a bunch of pills at random, figuring *some*thing among them would keep me awake. Then I jumped into the car and started off for Colorado."

"My God."

"I have no idea how fast I was going – everything was a blur when I crashed. At least I didn't take anybody with me, thank the Lord. There was this one horrible moment of confusion and pain and rage and then I found myself lying on the floor of the car with my corpse just inches beneath me on the underside of the roof." She was silent for a moment. "My first impulse was to crawl out the window. Lucky for me I didn't." Another pause. "It took me most of a night to work my way out of the yard. I had to go from wreck to wreck. There were these gaps to jump. It was a nightmare."

"I'm amazed you had the presence of mind to stay in the car."

"Dying sobers you up fast."

I laughed. I couldn't help it. And without the slightest hesitation, she joined right in with me. It was a fine warm moment, the first I'd had since I didn't know when. The two of us set each other off, laughing louder and louder, our merriment heterodyning until it filled every television screen for a mile around with snow.

My defenses were down. She reached out and took my hand.

Memory flooded me. It was her first date with Charlie. He was an electrician. The people next door were having the place rehabbed. She'd been working in the back yard and he struck up a conversation. Then he asked her out. They went to a disco in the Adam's Mark over on City Line Avenue.

She wasn't eager to get involved with somebody just then. She was still recovering from a hellish affair with a married man who'd thought that since he wasn't available for anything permanent, that made her his property. But when Charlie suggested they go out to the car for some coke – it was the Seventies – she'd said sure. He was going to put the moves on her sooner or later. Might as well get this settled early so they'd have more time for dancing.

But after they'd done up the lines, Charlie had shocked her by taking her hands in his and kissing them. She worked for a Bucks County pottery in those days and her hands were rough and red. She was very sensitive about them.

"Beautiful hands," he murmured. "Such beautiful, beautiful hands."

"You're making fun of me," she protested, hurt.

"No! These are hands that *do* things, and they've been shaped by the things they've done. The way stones in a stream are shaped by the water that passes over them. The way tools are shaped by their work. A hammer is beautiful, if it's a good hammer, and your hands are too."

He could have been scamming her. But something in his voice, his manner, said no, he really meant it. She squeezed his hands and saw that they were beautiful too. Suddenly she was glad she hadn't gone off the pill when she broke up with Daniel. She started to cry. Her date looked alarmed and baffled. But she couldn't stop. All the tears she hadn't cried in the past two years came pouring out of her, unstoppable.

Charlie-boy, she thought, you just got lucky.

All this in an instant. I snatched my hands away, breaking contact. "*Don't do that*!" I cried. "Don't you *ever* touch me again!"

With flat disdain, the Widow said, "It wasn't pleasant for me either. But I had to see how much of your life you remember."

It was naive of me, but I was shocked to realize that the passage of memories had gone both ways. But before I could voice my outrage, she said, "There's not much left of you. You're only a fragment of a man, shreds and tatters, hardly anything. No wonder you're so frightened. You've got what Charlie calls a low signal-to-noise ratio. What happened in New York City almost destroyed you."

"That doesn't give you the right to…"

"Oh be still. You need to know this. Living is simple, you just keep going. But death is complex. It's so hard to hang on and so easy to let go. The temptation is always there. Believe me, I know. There used to be five of us in Roxborough, and where are the others now? Two came through Manayunk last spring and camped out under the El for a season and they're gone too. Holding it together is hard work. One day the stars start singing to you, and the next you begin to listen to them. A week later they start to make sense. You're just reacting to events – that's not good enough. If you mean to hold on, you've got to know why you're doing it."

"So why are *you*?"

"I'm waiting for Charlie," she said simply.

It occurred to me to wonder exactly how many years she had been waiting. Three? Fifteen? Just how long was it possible to hold on? Even in my confused and emotional state, though, I knew better than to ask. Deep inside, she must've known as well as I did that Charlie wasn't coming. "My name's Cobb," I said. "What's yours?"

She hesitated and then, with an odd sidelong look, said, "I'm Charlie's Widow. That's all that matters." It was all the name she ever gave, and Charlie's Widow she was to me from then onward.

I rolled onto my back on the tin ceiling and spread out my arms and legs, a phantom starfish among the bats. A fragment, she had called me, shreds and tatters. No wonder you're so frightened! In all the months since I'd been washed into this backwater of the power grid, she'd never treated me with anything but a condescension bordering on contempt.

So I went out into the storm after all.

The rain was nothing. It passed right through me. But there were ion-heavy gusts of wind that threatened to knock me right off the lines, and the transformer outside the Widow's house was burning a fierce actinic blue. It was a gusher of energy, a flare star brought to earth, dazzling. A bolt of lightning unzipped me, turned me inside out, and restored me before I had a chance to react.

The Corpsegrinder was visible from the Roxy, but between the burning transformer and the creature's metamorphosis, I was within a block of the monster before I understood exactly what it was I was seeing.

It was feeding off the dying transformer, sucking in energy so greedily that it pulsed like a mosquito engorged with blood. Enormous plasma wings warped to either side, hot blue and transparent. They curved entirely around the Widow's house in an unbroken and circular wall. At the resonance points they extruded less detailed versions of the Corpsegrinder itself, like sentinels, all facing the Widow.

Surrounding her with a prickly ring of electricity and malice.

I retreated a block, though the transformer fire apparently hid me from the Corpsegrinder, for it stayed where it was, eyelessly staring inward. Three times I circled the house from a distance, looking for a way in. An unguarded cable, a wrought-iron fence, any unbroken stretch of metal too high or too low for the Corpsegrinder to reach.

Nothing.

Finally, because there was no alternative, I entered the house across the street from the Widow's, the one that was best shielded by the spouting and stuttering transformer. A power line took me into the attic crawl space. From there I scaled the electrical system down through the second and first floors and so to the basement. I had a brief glimpse of a man asleep on a couch before the television. The set was off but it still held a residual charge. It sat quiescent, smug, bloated with stolen energies. If the poor bastard on the couch could have seen what I saw, he'd've never turned on the TV again.

In the basement I hand-over-handed myself from the washing machine to the main water inlet. Straddling the pipe, I summoned all my courage and plunged my head underground.

It was black as pitch. I inched forward on the pipe in a kind of panic. I could see nothing, hear nothing, smell nothing, taste nothing. All I could feel was the iron pipe beneath my hands. Just beyond the wall the pipe ended in a T-joint where it hooked into a branch line under the drive. I followed it to the street.

It was awful: Like suffocation infinitely prolonged. Like being wrapped in black cloth. Like being drowned in ink. Like strangling noiselessly in the void between the stars.

To distract myself, I thought about my old man.

When my father was young, he navigated between cities by radio. Driving dark and usually empty highways, he'd twist the dial back and forth, back and forth, until he hit a station. Then he'd withdraw his hand and wait for the station ID. That would give him his rough location – that he was somewhere outside of Albany, say. A sudden signal coming in strong and then abruptly dissolving in groans and eerie whistles was a fluke of the ionosphere, impossibly distant and easily disregarded.

One that faded in and immediately out meant he had grazed the edge of a station's range. But then a signal would grow and strengthen as he penetrated its field, crescendo, fade, and collapse into static and silence. That left him north of Troy, let's say, and making good time. He would begin the search for the next station.

You could drive across the continent in this way, passed from hand to hand by local radio, and tuned in to the geography of the night.

I went over that memory three times, polishing and refining it, before the branch line abruptly ended. One hand groped forward and closed upon nothing.

I had reached the main conduit. For a panicked moment I had feared that it would be concrete or brick or even one of the cedar pipes the city laid down in the nineteenth century, remnants of which still linger here and there beneath the pavement. But by sheer blind luck, the system had been installed during that narrow window of time when the pipes were cast iron. I crawled along its underside first one way and then the other, searching for the branch line to the Widow's. There was a lot of crap under the street. Several times I was blocked by gas lines or by the high-pressure pipes for the fire hydrants and had to awkwardly clamber around them.

At last I found the line and began the painful journey out from the street again.

When I emerged in the Widow's basement, I was a nervous wreck. It came to me then that I could no longer remember my father's name. A thing of rags and shreds indeed!

I worked my way up the electrical system, searching every room and unintentionally spying on the family who had bought the house after the

Widow's death. In the kitchen a puffy man stood with his sleeves rolled up, elbow-deep in the sink, angrily washing dishes by candlelight. A woman who was surely his wife expressively smoked a cigarette at his stiff back, drawing in the smoke with bitter intensity and exhaling it in puffs of hatred. On the second floor a preadolescent girl clutched a tortoise-shell cat so tightly it struggled to escape, and cried into its fur. In the next room a younger boy sat on his bed in earphones, Walkman on his lap, staring sightlessly out the window at the burning transformer. No Widow on either floor.

How, I wondered, could she have endured staying in this entropic oven of a blue-collar rowhouse, forever the voyeur at the banquet, watching the living squander what she had already spent? Her trace was everywhere, her presence elusive. I was beginning to think she'd despaired and given herself up to the sky when I found her in the attic, clutching the wire that led to the antenna. She looked up, silenced and amazed by my unexpected appearance.

"Come on," I said. "I know a way out."

Returning, however, I couldn't retrace the route I'd taken in. It wasn't so much the difficulty of navigating the twisting maze of pipes under the street, though that was bad enough, as the fact that the Widow wouldn't hazard the passage unless I led her by the hand.

"You don't know how difficult this is for me," I said.

"It's the only way I'd dare." A nervous, humorless laugh. "I have such a lousy sense of direction."

So, steeling myself, I seized her hand and plunged through the wall.

It took all my concentration to keep from sliding off the water pipes, I was so distracted by the violence of her thoughts. We crawled through a hundred memories, all of her married lover, all alike.

Here's one:

Daniel snapped on the car radio. Sad music – something classical –

flooded the car. "That's bullshit, babe. You know how much I have invested in you?" He jabbed a blunt finger at her dress. "I could buy two good whores for what that thing cost."

Then why don't you, she thought. Get back on your Metroliner and go home to New York City and your wife and your money and your two good whores. Aloud, reasonably, she said, "It's over, Danny, can't you see that?"

"Look, babe. Let's not argue here, okay? Not in the parking lot, with people walking by and everybody listening. Drive us to your place, we can sit down and talk it over like civilized human beings."

She clutched the wheel, staring straight ahead. "No. We're going to settle this here and now."

"Christ." One-handed he wrangled a pack of Kents from a jacket pocket and knocked out a cigarette. Put the end in his lips and drew it out. Punched the lighter. "So talk."

A wash of hopelessness swept over her. Married men were supposed to be easy to get rid of. That was the whole point. "Let me go, Danny," she pleaded. Then, lying, "We can still be friends."

He made a disgusted noise.

"I've tried, Danny, I really have. You don't know how hard I've tried. But it's just not working."

"All right, I've listened. Now let's go." Reaching over her, Daniel threw the gearshift into reverse. He stepped on her foot, mashing it down on the accelerator.

The car leapt backwards. She shrieked and in a flurry of panic swung the wheel about and slammed on the brake with her free foot.

With a jolt and a crunch, the car stopped. There was the tinkle of broken plastic. They'd hit a lime-green Hyundai.

"Oh, that's just perfect!" Daniel said. The lighter popped out. He lit his cigarette and then swung open the door. "I'll check the damage."

Over her shoulder, she saw Daniel tug at his trousers' knees as he crouched to examine the Hyundai. She had a sudden impulse to slew the car around and escape. Step on the gas and never look back. Watch his face, dismayed and dwindling, in the rear-view mirror. Eyes flooded with tears, she began quietly to laugh.

Then Daniel was back. "It's all right, let's go."

"I heard something break."

"It was just a taillight, okay?" He gave her a funny look. "What the hell are you laughing about?"

She shook her head hopelessly, unable to sort out the tears from the laughter. Then somehow they were on the Expressway, the car humming down the indistinct and warping road. She was driving but Daniel was still in control.

We were completely lost now and had been for some time. I had taken what I was certain had to be a branch line and it had led nowhere. We'd been tracing its twisty passage for blocks. I stopped and pulled my hand away. I couldn't concentrate. Not with the caustics and poisons of the Widow's past churning through me. "Listen," I said. "We've got to get something straight between us."

Her voice came out of nowhere, small and wary. "What?"

How to say it? The horror of those memories lay not in their brutality but in their particularity. They nestled into empty spaces where memories of my own should have been. They were as familiar as old shoes. They *fit*.

"If I could remember any of this crap," I said, "I'd apologize. Hell, I can't blame you for how you feel. Of course you're angry. But it's gone, can't you see that, it's over. You've got to let go. You can't hold me accountable for things I can't even remember, okay? All that shit happened decades ago. I was young. I've changed." The absurdity of the thing swept over me. I'd have laughed if I'd been able. "I'm dead, for pity's sake!"

A long silence. Then, "So you've figured it out."

"You've known all along," I said bitterly. "Ever since I came off of the high-tension lines in Manayunk."

She didn't deny it. "I suppose I should be flattered that when you were in trouble you came to me," she said in a way that indicated she was not.

"Why didn't you tell me then? Why drag it out?"

"Danny…"

"Don't call me that!"

"It's your name. Daniel. Daniel Cobb."

All the emotions I'd been holding back by sheer force of denial closed about me. I flung myself down and clutched the pipe tight, crushing myself against its unforgiving surface. Trapped in the friendless wastes of night, I weighed my fear of letting go against my fear of holding on.

"Cobb?"

I said nothing.

The Widow's voice took on an edgy quality. "Cobb, we can't stay here. You've got to lead me out. I don't have the slightest idea which way to go. I'm lost without your help."

I still could not speak.

"*Cobb*!' She was close to panic. "I put my own feelings aside. Back in Manayunk. You needed help and I did what I could. Now it's your turn."

Silently, invisibly, I shook my head.

"God damn you, Danny," she said furiously. "I won't let you do this to me again! So you're unhappy with what a jerk you were – that's not my problem. You can't redeem your manliness on me any more. I am not your fucking salvation. I am not some kind of cosmic last chance and it's not my job to talk you down from the ledge."

That stung. "I wasn't asking you to," I mumbled.

"So you're still there! Take my hand and lead us out."

I pulled myself together. "You'll have to follow my voice, babe. Your memories are too intense for me."

We resumed our slow progress. I was sick of crawling, sick of the dark, sick of this lightless horrid existence, disgusted to the pit of my soul with who and what I was. Was there no end to this labyrinth of pipes?

"Wait." I'd brushed by something. Something metal buried in the earth.

"What is it?"

"I think it's..." I groped about, trying to get a sense of the thing's shape. "I think it's a cast-iron gatepost. Here. Wait. Let me climb up and take a look."

Relinquishing my grip on the pipe, I seized hold of the object and stuck my head out of the ground. I emerged at the gate of an iron fence framing the minuscule front yard of a house on Ripka Street. I could see again! It was so good to feel the clear breath of the world once more that I closed my eyes briefly to savor the sensation.

"How ironic," Euphrosyne said.

"After being so heroic," Thalia said.

"Overcoming his fears," Aglaia said.

"Rescuing the fair maid from terror and durance vile," Cleta said.

"Realizing at last who he is," Phaenna said.

"Beginning that long and difficult road to recovery by finally getting in touch with his innermost feelings," Auxo said.

Hegemone giggled.

"What?" I opened my eyes.

That was when the Corpsegrinder struck. It leapt upon me with stunning force, driving spear-long talons through my head and body. The talons were barbed so that they couldn't be pulled free and they burned like molten metal. "Ahhhh, Cobb," the Corpsegrinder crooned. "Now this is *sweet*."

I screamed and it drank in those screams, so that only silence escaped into the outside world. I struggled and it made those struggles its own, leaving me to kick myself deeper and deeper into the drowning pools of its identity. With all my will I resisted. It was not enough. I experienced the languorous pleasure of surrender as that very will and resistance were sucked down into my attacker's substance. The distinction between *me* and *it* weakened, strained, dissolved. I was transformed.

I was the Corpsegrinder now.

Manhattan is a virtual school for the dead. Enough people die there every day to keep any number of monsters fed. From the store of memories the Corpsegrinder had stolen from me, I recalled a quiet moment sitting cross-legged on the tin ceiling of a sleaze joint while table dancers entertained Japanese tourists on the floor above and a kobold instructed me on some of the finer points of survival. "The worst thing you can be hunted by," he said, "is yourself."

"Very aphoristic."

"Fuck you. I used to be human too."

"Sorry."

"Apology accepted. Look, I told you about Salamanders. That's a shitty way to go, but at least it's final. When they're done with you, nothing remains. But a Corpsegrinder is a parasite. It has no true identity of its own, so it constructs one from bits and pieces of everything that's unpleasant within you. Your basic greeds and lusts. It gives you a particularly nasty sort of immortality. Remember that old cartoon? This hideous toad saying 'Kiss me and live forever – you'll be a toad, but you'll live forever.'" He grimaced. "If you get the choice, go with the Salamander."

"So what's this business about hunting myself?"

"Sometimes a Corpsegrinder will rip you in two and let half escape. For a while."

"Why?"

"I dunno. Maybe it likes to play with its food. Ever watch a cat torture a mouse? Maybe it thinks it's fun."

From a million miles away, I thought: So now I know what's happened to me. I'd made quite a run of it, but now it was over. It didn't matter. All that mattered was the hoard of memories, glorious memories, into which I'd been dumped. I wallowed in them, picking out here a winter sunset and there the pain of a jellyfish sting when I was nine. So what if I was already beginning to dissolve? I was intoxicated, drunk, stoned with the raw stuff of experience. I was high on life.

Then the Widow climbed up the gatepost looking for me.

"Cobb?"

The Corpsegrinder had moved up the fence to a more comfortable spot in which to digest me. When it saw the Widow, it reflexively parked me in a memory of a grey drizzly day in a Ford Fiesta outside of 30th Street Station. The engine was going and the heater and the windshield wiper too, so I snapped on the radio to mask their noise. Beethoven filled the car, the Moonlight Sonata.

"That's bullshit, babe," I said. "You know how much I have invested in you? I could buy two good whores for what that dress cost."

She refused to meet my eyes. In a whine that set my teeth on edge, she said, "Danny, can't you see that it's over between us?"

"Look, babe, let's not argue in the parking lot, okay?" I was trying hard to be reasonable. "Not with people walking by and listening. We'll go someplace private where we can talk this over calmly, like two civilized human beings."

She shifted slightly in the seat and adjusted her skirt with a little tug. Drawing attention to her long legs and fine ass. Making it hard for me to think straight. The bitch really knew how to twist the knife. Even now, crying and begging, she was aware of how it turned me on. And even though I hated being aroused by her little act, I was. The sex was always best after an argument; it made her sluttish.

I clenched my anger in one hand and fisted my pocket with it. Thinking how much I'd like to up and give her a shot. She was begging for it. Secretly, maybe, it was what she wanted; I'd often suspected she'd enjoy being hit. It was too late to act on the impulse, though. The memory was playing out like a tape, immutable, unstoppable.

All the while, like a hallucination or the screen of a television set receiving conflicting signals, I could see the Widow, frozen with fear half in and half out of the ground. She quivered like an acetylene flame. In the memory she was saying something, but with the shift in my emotions came a corresponding warping-away of perception. The train station, car, the windshield wipers and music, all faded to a murmur in my consciousness.

Tentacles whipped around the Widow. She was caught. She struggled helplessly, deliciously. The Corpsegrinder's emotions pulsed through me and to my remote horror I found that they were identical to my own. I *wanted* the Widow, wanted her so bad there were no words for it. I wanted to clutch her to me so tightly her ribs would splinter and for just this once she'd know it was real. I wanted to own her. To possess her. To put an end to all her little games. To know her every thought and secret, down to the very bottom of her being.

No more lies, babe, I thought, no more evasions. You're mine now.

So perfectly in synch was I with the Corpsegrinder's desires that it shifted its primary consciousness back into the liquid sphere of memory, where it hung smug and lazy, watching, a voyeur with a willing agent. I was in control of the autonomous functions now. I reshaped the tentacles, merging and recombining them into two strong arms. The claws and talons that clutched the fence I made legs again. The exterior of the Corpsegrinder I morphed into human semblance, save for that great mass of memories sprouting from our back like a bloated spider-sack. Last of all I made the head.

I gave it my own face.

"Surprised to see me again, babe?" I leered.

Her expression was not so much fearful as disappointed. "No," she said wearily. "Deep down, I guess I always knew you'd be back."

As I drew the Widow closer, I distantly knew that all that held me to the Corpsegrinder in that instant was our common store of memories and my determination not to lose them again. That was enough, though.

I pushed my face into hers, forcing open her mouth. Energies flowed between us like a feast of tongues.

I prepared to drink her in.

There were no barriers between us. This was an experience as intense as when, making love, you lose all track of which body is your own and thought dissolves into the animal moment. For a giddy instant I was no less her than I was myself. I was the Widow staring fascinated into the filthy depths of my psyche. She was myself witnessing her astonishment as she realized exactly how little I had ever known her. We both saw her freeze still to the core with horror. Horror not of what I was doing.

But of what I was.

I can't take any credit for what happened then. It was only an impulse, a spasm of the emotions, a sudden and unexpected clarity of vision. Can a single flash of decency redeem a life like mine? I don't believe it. I refuse to believe it.

Had there been time for second thoughts, things might well have gone differently. But there was no time to think. There was only time enough to feel an upwelling of revulsion, a visceral desire to be anybody or anything but my own loathsome self, a profound and total yearning to be quit of the burden of such memories as were mine. An aching need to *just once* do the moral thing.

I let go.

Bobbing gently, the swollen corpus of my past floated up and away, carrying with it the parasitic Corpsegrinder. Everything I had spent all my life accumulating fled from me. It went up like a balloon, spinning, dwindling…gone. Leaving me only what few flat memories I have narrated here.

I screamed.

And then I cried.

I don't know how long I clung to the fence, mourning my loss. But when I gathered myself together, the Widow was still there.

"Danny," the Widow said. She didn't touch me. "Danny, I'm sorry."

I'd almost rather that she had abandoned me. How do you apologize for sins you can no longer remember? For having been someone who, however reprehensible, is gone forever? How can you expect forgiveness from somebody you have forgotten so completely you don't even know her name? I felt twisted with shame and misery. "Look," I said. "I know I've behaved badly. More than badly. But there ought to be some way to make it up to you. For, you know, everything. Somehow. I mean…"

What do you say to somebody who's seen to the bottom of your wretched and inadequate soul?

"I want to apologize," I said.

With something very close to compassion, the Widow said, "It's too late for that, Danny. It's over. Everything's over. You and I only ever had the one trait in common. We neither of us could ever let go of anything. Small wonder we're back together again. But don't you see, it doesn't matter what you want or don't want – you're not going to get it. Not now. You had your chance. It's too late to make things right." Then she stopped, aghast at what she had just said.

But we both knew she had spoken the truth.

"Widow," I said as gently as I could, "I'm sure Charlie…"

"Shut up."

I shut up.

The Widow closed her eyes and swayed, as if in a wind. A ripple ran through her and when it was gone her features were simpler, more schematic, less recognizably human. She was already beginning to surrender the anthropomorphic.

I tried again. "Widow…" Reaching out my guilty hand to her.

She stiffened but did not draw away. Our fingers touched, twined, mated. "Elizabeth," she said at last. "My name is Elizabeth Connelly."

We huddled together on the ceiling of the Roxy through the dawn and the blank horror that is day. When sunset brought us conscious again, we talked through half the night before making the one decision we knew all along that we'd have to make.

It took us almost an hour to reach the Seven Sisters and climb down to the highest point of Thalia.

We stood holding hands at the top of the mast. Radio waves were gushing out from under us like a great wind. It was all we could do to keep from being blown away.

Underfoot, Thalia was happily chatting with her sisters. Typically, at our moment of greatest resolve, they gave us not the slightest indication of interest. But they were all listening to us. Don't ask me how I knew.

"Cobb?" Elizabeth said. "I'm afraid."

"Yeah, me too."

A long silence, and then she said, "Let me go first. If you go first, I won't have the nerve."

"Okay."

She took a deep breath – funny, if you think about it – and then she let go, and fell into the sky.

First she was like a kite, and then a scrap of paper, and finally she was a rapidly tumbling speck. I stood for a long time watching her falling, dwindling, until she was lost in the background flicker of the universe, just one more spark in infinity.

She was gone and I couldn't help wondering if she had ever really been there at all. Had the Widow truly been Elizabeth Connelly? Or was she just another fragment of my shattered self, a bundle of related memories that I had to come to terms with before I could bring myself to finally let go?

A vast emptiness seemed to spread itself through all of existence. I clutched the mast spasmodically then, and thought: *I can't!*

But the moment passed. I've got a lot of questions, and there aren't any answers here. In just another instant, I'll let go and follow Elizabeth (if Elizabeth she was) into the night. I will fall forever and I will be converted to background radiation, smeared ever thinner and cooler across the universe, a smooth, uniform, and universal message that has only one decode. Let Thalia carry my story to whoever cares to listen. I won't be here for it.

It's time to go now. Time and then some to leave. I'm frightened, and I'm going.

Now.

TOWER OF BABYLON
Ted Chiang

Ted Chiang (b. 1967) is a technical writer, producing documentation for programmers, and only occasionally turns his hand to fiction, but when he does it always results in something special. The following story was Chiang's first appearance in print, after several unsuccessful attempts. It was bought by Ellen Datlow for Omni *and promptly went on to win the Nebula Award presented by the Science Fiction Writers of America.*

The next year Chiang won the Campbell Award as Best New Writer. Since then it became almost an annual event that each new story would win one or other award, most recently the Locus Award for his collection Stories of Your Life and Others *(2002). The following story, at its simplest level, is about faith but, of course, it isn't that simple.*

W‌ere the tower to be laid down across the plain of Shinar, it would be two days' journey to walk from one end to the other. While the tower stands, it takes a full month and a half to climb from its base to its summit, if a man walks unburdened. But few men climb the tower with empty hands; the pace of most men is slowed by the cart of bricks that they pull behind them. Four months pass between the day a brick is loaded onto a cart, and the day it is taken off to form a part of the tower.

Hillalum had spent all his life in Elam, and knew Babylon only as a buyer of Elam's copper. The copper ingots were carried on boats that travelled down the Karun to the Lower Sea, headed for the Euphrates. Hillalum and the other miners travelled overland, alongside a merchant's caravan of loaded onagers. They walked along a dusty path leading down from the plateau, across the plains, to the green fields sectioned by canals and dikes.

None of them had seen the tower before. It became visible when they were still leagues away: a line as thin as a strand of flax, wavering in the shimmering air, rising up from the crust of mud that was Babylon itself. As they drew closer, the crust grew into the mighty city walls, but all they saw was the tower.

When they did lower their gazes to the level of the river-plain, they saw the marks the tower had made outside the city: the Euphrates itself now flowed at the bottom of a wide, sunken bed, dug to provide clay for bricks. To the south of the city could be seen rows upon rows of kilns, no longer burning.

As they approached the city gates, the tower appeared more massive than anything Hillalum had ever imagined: a single column that must have been as large around as an entire temple, yet rising so high that it shrank into invisibility. All of them walked with their heads tilted back, squinting in the sun.

Hillalum's friend Nanni prodded him with an elbow, awestruck. "We're to climb that? To the top?"

"Going *up* to dig. It seems…unnatural."

The miners reached the central gate in the western wall, where another caravan was leaving. While they crowded forward into the narrow strip of shade provided by the wall, their foreman Beli shouted to the gatekeepers who stood atop the gate towers. "We are the miners summoned from the land of Elam."

The gatekeepers were delighted. One called back, "You are the ones who are to dig through the vault of heaven?"

"We are."

The entire city was celebrating. The festival had begun eight days ago, when the last of the bricks were sent on their way, and would last two more. Every day and night, the city rejoiced, danced, feasted.

Along with the brickmakers were the cart-pullers, men whose legs were roped with muscle from climbing the tower. Each morning a crew began its ascent; they climbed for four days, transferred their loads to the next crew of pullers, and returned to the city with empty carts on the fifth. A chain of such crews led all the way to the top of the tower, but only the bottommost celebrated with the city. For those who lived upon the tower, enough wine and meat had been sent up earlier to allow a feast to extend up the entire pillar.

In the evening, Hillalum and the other Elamite miners sat upon clay stools before a long table laden with food, one table among many laid out in the city square. The miners spoke with the pullers, asking about the tower.

Nanni said, "Someone told me that the bricklayers who work at the top of the tower wail and tear their hair when a brick is dropped, because it will take four months to replace, but no one takes notice when a man falls to his death. Is that true?"

One of the more talkative pullers, Lugatum, shook his head. "Oh no, that is only a story. There is a continuous caravan of bricks going up the tower; thousands of bricks reach the top each day. The loss of a single brick means nothing to the bricklayers." He leaned over to them. "However, there is something they value more than a man's life: a trowel."

"Why a trowel?"

"If a bricklayer drops his trowel, he can do no work until a new one is brought up. For months he cannot earn the food that he eats, so he must go into debt. The loss of a trowel is cause for much wailing. But if a man falls, and his trowel remains, men are secretly relieved. The next one to drop his trowel can pick up the extra one and continue working, without incurring debt."

Hillalum was appalled, and for a frantic moment he tried to count how many picks the miners had brought. Then he realized. "That cannot be true. Why not have spare trowels brought up? Their weight would be nothing against all the bricks that go up there. And surely the loss of a man means a serious delay, unless they have an extra man at the top who is skilled at bricklaying. Without such a man, they must wait for another one to climb from the bottom."

All of the pullers roared with laughter. "We cannot fool this one," Lugatum said with much amusement. He turned to Hillalum. "So you'll begin your climb once the festival is over?"

Hillalum drank from a bowl of beer. "Yes. I've heard that we'll be joined by miners from a western land, but I haven't seen them. Do you know of them?"

"Yes, they come from a land called Egypt, but they do not mine ore as you do. They quarry stone."

"We dig stone in Elam, too," said Nanni, his mouth full of pork.

"Not as they do. They cut granite."

"Granite?" Limestone and alabaster were quarried in Elam, but not granite. "Are you certain?"

"Merchants who have travelled to Egypt say that they have stone ziggurats and temples, built with limestone and granite, huge blocks of it. And they carve giant statues from granite."

"But granite is so difficult to work."

Lugatum shrugged. "Not for them. The royal architects believe such stoneworkers may be useful when you reach the vault of heaven."

Hillalum nodded. That could be true. Who knew for certain what they would need? "Have you seen them?"

"No, they are not here yet, but they are expected in a few days' time. They may not arrive before the festival ends, though; then you Elamites will ascend alone."

"You will accompany us, won't you?"

"Yes, but only for the first four days. Then we must turn back, while you lucky ones go on."

"Why do you think us lucky?"

"I long to make the climb to the top. I once pulled with the higher crews, and reached a height of twelve days' climb, but that is as high as I have ever gone. You will go far higher." Lugatum smiled ruefully. "I envy you, that you will touch the vault of heaven."

To touch the vault of heaven. To break it open with picks. Hillalum felt uneasy at the idea. "There is no cause for envy..." he began.

"Right," said Nanni. "When we are done, all men will touch the vault of heaven."

The next morning, Hillalum went to see the tower. He stood in the giant courtyard surrounding it. There was a temple off to one side that would have been impressive if seen by itself, but it stood unnoticed beside the tower.

He could sense the utter solidity of it. According to all the tales, the tower was constructed to have a mighty strength that no ziggurat possessed; it was made of baked brick all the way through, when ordinary ziggurats were mere sun-dried mud brick, having baked brick only for the facing. The bricks were set in a bitumen mortar, which soaked into the fired clay, forming a bond as strong as the bricks themselves.

The tower's base resembled the first two platforms of an ordinary ziggurat. There stood a giant square platform some two hundred cubits on a side and forty cubits high, with a triple staircase against its south face. Stacked upon that first platform was another level, a smaller platform reached only by the central stair. It was atop the second platform that the tower itself began.

It was sixty cubits on a side, and rose like a square pillar that bore the weight of heaven. Around it wound a gently inclined ramp, cut into the side, that banded the tower like the leather strip wrapped around the handle of a whip. No; upon looking again, Hillalum saw that there were two ramps, and they were intertwined. The outer edge of each ramp was studded with pillars, not thick but broad, to provide some shade behind them. In running his gaze up the tower, he saw alternating bands, ramp, brick, ramp, brick, until they could no longer be distinguished. And still the tower rose up and up, farther than the eye could see; Hillalum blinked, and squinted, and grew dizzy. He stumbled backwards a couple steps, and turned away with a shudder.

Hillalum thought of the story told to him in childhood, the tale following that of the Deluge. It told of how men had once again populated all the corners of the earth, inhabiting more lands than they ever had before. How men had sailed to the edges of the world, and seen the ocean falling away into the mist to join the black waters of the Abyss far below. How men had thus realized the extent of the earth, and felt it to be small, and desired to see what lay beyond its borders, all the rest of Yahweh's Creation. How they looked skyward, and wondered about Yahweh's dwelling place, above the reservoirs that contained the waters of heaven. And how, many centuries ago, there began the construction of the tower, a pillar to heaven, a stair that men might ascend to see the works of Yahweh, and that Yahweh might descend to see the works of men.

It had always seemed inspiring to Hillalum, a tale of thousands of men toiling ceaselessly, but with joy, for they worked to know Yahweh better. He had been excited when the Babylonians came to Elam looking for miners. Yet now that he stood at the base of the tower, his senses rebelled, insisting that nothing should stand so high. He didn't feel as if he were on the earth when he looked up along the tower.

Should he climb such a thing?

On the morning of the climb, the second platform was covered, edge to edge, with stout two-wheeled carts arranged in rows. Many were loaded with nothing but food of all sorts: sacks filled with barley, wheat, lentils, onions, dates, cucumbers, loaves of bread, dried fish. There were countless giant clay jars of water, date wine, beer, goat's milk, palm oil. Other carts were loaded with such goods as might be sold at a bazaar: bronze vessels, reed baskets, bolts of linen, wooden stools and tables. There was also a fattened ox and a goat that some priests were fitting with hoods so that they could not see to either side, and would not be afraid on the climb. They would be sacrificed when they reached the top.

Then there were the carts loaded with the miners' picks and hammers, and the makings for a small forge. Their foreman had also ordered a number of carts be loaded with wood and sheaves of reeds.

Lugatum stood next to a cart, securing the ropes that held the wood. Hillalum walked up to him. "From where did this wood come? I saw no forests after we left Elam."

"There is a forest of trees to the north, which was planted when the tower was begun. The cut timber is floated down the Euphrates."

"You planted a entire *forest*?"

"When they began the tower, the architects knew that far more wood would be needed to fuel the kilns than could be found on the plain, so they had a forest of trees planted. There are crews whose job is to provide water, and plant one new tree for each that is cut."

Hillalum was astonished. "And that provides all the wood needed?"

"Most of it. Many other forests in the north have been cut as well, and their wood brought down the river." He inspected the wheels of the cart, uncorked a leather bottle he carried, and poured a little oil between the wheel and axle.

Nanni walked over to them, staring at the streets of Babylon laid out before them. "I've never before been even this high, that I can look down upon a city."

"Nor have I," said Hillalum, but Lugatum simply laughed.

"Come along. All of the carts are ready."

Soon all the men were paired up and matched with a cart. The men stood between the cart's two pull rods, which had rope loops for pulling. The carts pulled by the miners were mixed in with those of the regular pullers, to ensure that they would keep the proper pace. Lugatum and another puller had the cart right behind that of Hillalum and Nanni.

"Remember," said Lugatum, "stay about ten cubits behind the cart in front of you. The man on the right does all the pulling when you turn corners, and you'll switch every hour."

Pullers were beginning to lead their carts up the ramp. Hillalum and Nanni bent down and slung the ropes of their cart over their opposite shoulders. They stood up together, raising the front end of the cart off the pavement.

"Now PULL," called Lugatum.

They leaned forward against the ropes, and the cart began rolling. Once it was moving, pulling seemed to be easy enough, and they wound their way around the platform. Then they reached the ramp, and they again had to lean deeply.

"This is a light wagon?" muttered Hillalum.

The ramp was wide enough for a single man to walk beside a cart if he had to pass. The surface was paved with brick, with two grooves worn deep by centuries of wheels. Above their heads, the ceiling rose in a corbelled vault, with the wide, square bricks arranged in overlapping layers until they met in the middle. The pillars on the right were broad enough to make the ramp seem a bit like a tunnel. If one didn't look off to the side, there was little sense of being on a tower.

"Do you sing when you mine?" asked Lugatum.

"When the stone is soft," said Nanni.

"Sing one of your mining songs, then."

The call went down to the other miners, and before long the entire crew was singing.

As the shadows shortened, they ascended higher and higher. Shaded from the sun, with only clear air surrounding them, it was much cooler than in the narrow alleys of a city at ground level, where the heat at midday could kill lizards as they scurried across the street. Looking out to the side, the miners could see the dark Euphrates, and the green fields stretching out for leagues, crossed by canals that glinted in the sunlight. The city of Babylon was an intricate pattern of closely set streets and buildings, dazzling with gypsum whitewash; less and less of it was visible, as it seemingly drew nearer the base of the tower.

Hillalum was again pulling on the right-hand rope, nearer the edge, when he heard some shouting from the upward ramp one level below. He thought of stopping and looking down the side, but he didn't wish to interrupt their pace, and he wouldn't be able to see the lower ramp clearly anyway. "What's happening down there?" he called to Lugatum behind him.

"One of your fellow miners fears the height. There is occasionally such a man among those who climb for the first time. Such a man embraces the floor, and cannot ascend further. Few feel it so soon, though."

Hillalum understood. "We know of a similar fear, among those who would be miners. Some men cannot bear to enter the mines, for fear that they will be buried."

"Really?" called Lugatum. "I had not heard of that. How do you feel yourself about the height?"

"I feel nothing." But he glanced at Nanni, and they both knew the truth.

"You feel nervousness in your palms, don't you?" whispered Nanni.

Hillalum rubbed his hands on the coarse fibers of the rope, and nodded.

"I felt it too, earlier, when I was closer to the edge."

"Perhaps we should go hooded, like the ox and the goat," muttered Hillalum jokingly.

"Do you think we too will fear the height, when we climb further?"

Hillalum considered. That one of their comrades should feel the fear so soon did not bode well. He shook it off; thousands climbed with no fear, and it would be foolish to let one miner's fear infect them all. "We are merely unaccustomed. We will have months to grow used to the height. By the time we reach the top of the tower, we will wish it were taller."

"No," said Nanni. "I don't think I'll wish to pull this any further." They both laughed.

In the evening they ate a meal of barley and onions and lentils, and slept inside narrow corridors that penetrated into the body of the tower. When they woke the next morning, the miners were scarcely able to walk, so sore were their legs. The pullers laughed, and gave them salve to rub into their muscles, and redistributed the load on the carts to reduce the miners' burden.

By now, looking down the side turned Hillalum's knees to water. A wind blew steadily at this height, and he anticipated that it would grow stronger as they climbed. He wondered if anyone had ever been blown off the tower in a moment of carelessness. And the fall; a man would have time to say a prayer before he hit the ground. Hillalum shuddered at the thought.

Aside from the soreness in the miners' legs, the second day was similar to the first. They were able to see much farther now, and the breadth of land visible was stunning; the deserts beyond the fields were visible, and caravans appeared to be little more than lines of insects. No other miner feared the height so greatly that he couldn't continue, and their ascent proceeded all day without incident.

On the third day, the miners' legs had not improved, and Hillalum felt like a crippled old man. Only on the fourth day did their legs feel better, and they were pulling their original loads again. Their climb continued until the evening, when they met the second crew of pullers leading empty carts rapidly along the downward ramp. The upward and downward ramps wound around each other without touching, but they were joined by the corridors through the tower's body. When the crews had intertwined thoroughly on the two ramps, they crossed over to exchange carts.

The miners were introduced to the pullers of the second crew, and they all talked and ate together that night. The next morning, the first crew readied the empty carts for their return to Babylon, and Lugatum bid farewell to Hillalum and Nanni.

"Take care of your cart. It has climbed the entire height of the tower, more times than any man."

"Do you envy the cart, too?" asked Nanni.

"No, because every time it reaches the top, it must come all the way back down. I could not bear to do that."

When the second crew stopped at the end of the day, the puller of the cart behind Hillalum and Nanni came over to show them something. His name was Kudda.

"You have never seen the sun set at this height. Come, look." The puller went to the edge and sat down, his legs hanging over the side. He saw that they hesitated. "Come. You can lie down and peer over the edge, if you like." Hillalum did not wish to seem like a fearful child, but he could not bring himself to sit at a cliff face that stretched for thousands of cubits below his feet. He lay down on his belly, with only his head at the edge. Nanni joined him.

"When the sun is about to set, look down the side of the tower." Hillalum glanced downward, and then quickly looked to the horizon.

"What is different about the way the sun sets here?"

"Consider, when the sun sinks behinds the peaks of the mountains to the west, it grows dark down on the plain of Shinar. Yet here, we are higher than the mountaintops, so we can still see the sun. The sun must descend further for us to see night."

Hillalum's jaw dropped as he understood. "The shadows of the mountains mark the beginning of night. Night falls on the earth before it does here."

Kudda nodded. "You can see night travel up the tower, from the ground up to the sky. It moves quickly, but you should be able to see it."

He watched the red globe of the sun for a minute, and then looked down and pointed. "Now!"

Hillalum and Nanni looked down. At the base of the immense pillar, tiny Babylon was in shadow. Then the darkness climbed the tower, like a canopy unfurling upward. It moved slowly enough that Hillalum felt he could count the moments passing, but then it grew faster as it approached, until it raced past them faster than he could blink, and they were in twilight.

Hillalum rolled over and looked up, in time to see darkness rapidly ascend the rest of the tower. Gradually, the sky grew dimmer as the sun sank beneath the edge of the world, far away.

"Quite a sight, is it not?" said Kudda.

Hillalum said nothing. For the first time, he knew night for what it was: the shadow of the earth itself, cast against the sky.

After climbing for two more days, Hillalum had grown more accustomed to the height. Though they were the better part of a league straight up, he could bear to stand at the edge of the ramp and look down the tower. He held on to one of the pillars at the edge, and cautiously leaned out to look upwards. He noticed that the tower no longer looked like a smooth pillar.

He asked Kudda, "The tower seems to widen further up. How can that be?"

"Look more closely. There are wooden balconies reaching out from the sides. They are made of cypress, and suspended by ropes of flax."

Hillalum squinted. "Balconies? What are they for?"

"They have soil spread on them, so people may grow vegetables. At this height water is scarce, so onions are most commonly grown. Higher up, where there is more rain, you'll see beans."

Nanni asked, "How can there be rain above that does not just fall here?"

Kudda was surprised at him. "It dries in the air as it falls, of course."

"Oh, of course." Nanni shrugged.

By the end of the next day they reached the level of the balconies. They were flat platforms, dense with onions, supported by heavy ropes from the tower wall above, just below the next tier of balconies. On each level the interior of the tower had several narrow rooms inside, in which the families of the pullers lived. Women could be seen sitting in the doorways sewing tunics, or out in the gardens digging up bulbs.

Children chased each other up and down the ramps, weaving amidst the pullers' carts, and running along the edge of the balconies without fear. The tower dwellers could easily pick out the miners, and they all smiled and waved.

When it came time for the evening meal, all the carts were set down and food and other goods were taken off to be used by the people here. The pullers greeted their families, and invited the miners to join them for the evening meal. Hillalum and Nanni ate with the family of Kudda, and they enjoyed a fine meal of dried fish, bread, date wine, and fruit.

Hillalum saw that this section of the tower formed a tiny kind of town, laid out in a line between two streets, the upward and downward ramps. There was a temple, in which the rituals for the festivals were performed; there were magistrates, who settled disputes; there were shops, which were stocked by the caravan. Of course, the town was inseparable from the caravan: neither could exist without the other. And yet any caravan was essentially a journey, a thing that began at one place and ended at another. This town was never intended as a permanent place, it was merely part of a centuries-long journey.

After dinner, he asked Kudda and his family, "Have any of you ever visited Babylon?"

Kudda's wife, Alitum, answered, "No, why would we? It's a long climb, and we have all we need here."

"You have no desire to actually walk on the earth?"

Kudda shrugged. "We live on the road to heaven; all the work that we do is to extend it further. When we leave the tower, we will take the upward ramp, not the downward."

As the miners ascended, in the course of time there came the day when the tower appeared to be the same when one looked upward or downward from the ramp's edge. Below, the tower's shaft shrank to nothing long before it seemed to reach the plain below. Likewise, the miners were still far from being able to see the top. All that was visible was a length of the tower. To look up or down was frightening, for the reassurance of continuity was gone; they were no longer part of the ground. The tower might have been a thread suspended in the air, unattached to either earth or to heaven.

There were moments during this section of the climb when Hillalum despaired, feeling displaced and estranged from the world; it was as if the earth had rejected him for his faithlessness, while heaven disdained to accept him. He wished Yahweh would give a sign, to let men know that their venture was approved; otherwise how could they stay in a place that offered so little welcome to the spirit?

The tower dwellers at this altitude felt no unease with their station; they always greeted the miners warmly and wished them luck with their task at the vault. They lived inside the damp mists of clouds, they saw storms from below and from above, they harvested crops from the air, and they never feared that this was an improper place for men to be. There were no divine assurances or encouragements to be had, but the people never knew a moment's doubt.

With the passage of the weeks, the sun and moon peaked lower and lower in their daily journeys. The moon flooded the south side of the tower with its silver radiance, glowing like the eye of Yahweh peering at them. Before long, they were at precisely the same level as the moon when it passed; they had reached the height of the first of the celestial bodies. They squinted at the moon's pitted face, marveled at its stately motion that scorned any support.

Then they approached the sun. It was the summer season, when the sun appears nearly overhead from Babylon, making it pass close by the tower at this height. No families lived in this section of the tower, nor were there any balconies, since the heat was enough to roast barley. The mortar between the tower's bricks was no longer bitumen, which would have softened and flowed, but clay, which had been virtually baked by the heat. As protection against the day temperatures, the pillars had been widened until they formed a nearly continuous wall, enclosing the ramp into a tunnel with only narrow slots admitting the whistling wind and blades of golden light.

The crews of pullers had been spaced regularly up to this point, but here an adjustment was necessary. They started out earlier and earlier each morning, to gain more darkness for when they pulled. When they were at the level of the sun, they traveled entirely at night. During the day, they tried to sleep, naked and sweating in the hot breeze. The miners worried that if they did manage to sleep, they would be baked to death before they awoke. But the pullers had made the journey many times, and never lost a man, and eventually they passed above the sun's level, where things were as they had been below.

Now the light of day shone *upward*, which seemed unnatural to the utmost. The balconies had planks removed from them so that the sunlight could shine through, with soil on the walkways that remained; the plants grew sideways and downward, bending over to catch the sun's rays.

Then they drew near the level of the stars, small fiery spheres spread on all sides. Hillalum had expected them to be spread more thickly, but even with the tiny stars invisible from the ground, they seemed to be thinly scattered. They were not all set at the same height, but instead occupied the next few leagues above. It was difficult to tell how far they were, since there was no indication of their size, but occasionally one would make a close approach, evidencing its astonishing speed. Hillalum realized that all the objects in the sky hurtled by with similar speed, in order to travel the world from edge to edge in a day's time.

During the day, the sky was a much paler blue than it appeared from the earth, a sign they were nearing the vault. When studying the sky, Hillalum was startled to see that there were stars visible during the day. They couldn't be seen from the earth amidst the glare of the sun, but from this altitude they were quite distinct.

One day Nanni came to him hurriedly and said, "A star has hit the tower!"

"What!" Hillalum looked around, panicked, feeling like he had been struck by a blow.

"No, not now. It was long ago, more than a century. One of the tower dwellers is telling the story; his grandfather was there."

They went inside the corridors, and saw several miners seated around a wizened old man. "...lodged itself in the bricks about half a league above here. You can still see the scar it left; it's like a giant pockmark."

"What happened to the star?"

"It burned and sizzled, and was too bright to look upon. Men considered prying it out, so that it might resume its course, but it was too hot to approach closely, and they dared not quench it. After weeks it cooled into a knotted mass of black heaven-metal, as large as a man could wrap his arms around."

"So large?" said Nanni, his voice full of awe. When stars fell to the earth of their own accord, small lumps of heaven-metal were sometimes found, tougher than the finest bronze. The metal could not be melted for casting, so it was worked by hammering when heated red; amulets were made from it.

"Indeed, no one had ever heard of a mass of this size found on the earth. Can you imagine the tools that could be made from it!"

"You did not try to hammer it into tools, did you?" asked Hillalum, horrified.

"Oh no. Men were frightened to touch it. Everyone descended from the tower, waiting for retribution from Yahweh for disturbing the workings of Creation. They waited for months, but no sign came. Eventually they returned, and pried out the star. It sits in a temple in the city below."

There was silence. Then one of the miners said, "I have never heard of this in the stories of the tower."

"It was a transgression, something not spoken of."

As they climbed higher up the tower, the sky grew lighter in color, until one morning Hillalum awoke and stood at the edge and yelled from shock: what had before seemed a pale sky now appeared to be a white ceiling stretched far above their heads. They were close enough now to perceive the vault of heaven, to see it as a solid carapace enclosing all the sky. All of the miners spoke in hushed tones, staring up like idiots, while the tower dwellers laughed at them.

As they continued to climb, they were startled at how *near* they actually were. The blankness of the vault's face had deceived them, making it undetectable until it appeared, abruptly, seeming just above their heads. Now instead of climbing into the sky, they climbed up to a featureless plain that stretched endlessly in all directions.

All of Hillalum's senses were disoriented by the sight of it. Sometimes when he looked at the vault, he felt as if the world had flipped around somehow, and if he lost his footing he would fall upwards to meet it. When the vault did appear to rest above his head, it had an oppressive *weight*. The vault was a stratum as heavy as all the world, yet utterly without support, and he feared what he never had in the mines: that the ceiling would collapse upon him.

Too, there were moments when it appeared as if the vault were a vertical cliff face of unimaginable height rising before him, and the dim earth behind him was another like it, and the tower was a cable stretched taut between the two. Or worst of all, for an instant it seemed that there was no up and no down, and his body did not know which way it was drawn. It was like fearing the height, but much worse. Often he would wake from an unrestful sleep, to find himself sweating and his fingers cramped, trying to clutch the brick floor.

Nanni and many of the other miners were bleary-eyed too, though no one spoke of what disturbed their sleep. Their ascent grew slower, instead of faster as their foreman Beli had expected; the sight of the vault inspired unease rather than eagerness. The regular pullers became impatient with them. Hillalum wondered what sort of people were forged by living under such conditions; how did they escape madness? Did they grow accustomed to this? Would the children born under a solid sky scream if they saw the ground beneath their feet?

Perhaps men were not meant to live in such a place. If their own natures restrained them from approaching heaven too closely, then men should remain on the earth.

When they reached the summit of the tower, the disorientation faded, or perhaps they had grown immune. Here, standing upon the square platform of the top, the miners gazed upon the most awesome scene ever glimpsed by men: far below them lay a tapestry of soil and sea, veiled by mist, rolling out in all directions to the limit of the eye. Just above them hung the roof of the world itself, the absolute upper demarcation of the sky, guaranteeing their vantage point as the highest possible. Here was as much of Creation as could be apprehended at once.

The priests led a prayer to Yahweh; they gave thanks that they were permitted to see so much, and begged forgiveness for their desire to see more.

And at the top, the bricks were laid. One could catch the rich, raw smell of tar, rising out of the heated cauldrons in which the lumps of bitumen were melted. It was the most earthy odour the miners had smelled in four months, and their nostrils were desperate to catch a whiff before it was whipped away by the wind. Here at the summit, where the ooze that had once seeped from the earth's cracks now grew solid to hold bricks in place, the earth was growing a limb into the sky.

Here worked the bricklayers, the men smeared with bitumen who mixed the mortar and deftly set the heavy bricks with absolute precision. More than anyone else, these men could not permit themselves to experience dizziness when they saw the vault, for the tower could not vary a finger's width from the vertical. They were nearing the end of their task, finally, and after four months of climbing, the miners were ready to begin theirs.

The Egyptians arrived shortly afterwards. They were dark of skin and slight of build, and had sparsely bearded chins. They had pulled carts filled with dolerite hammers, and bronze tools, and wooden wedges.

Their foreman was named Senmut, and he conferred with Beli, the Elamites' foreman, on how they would penetrate the vault. The Egyptians built a forge with what they had brought, as did the Elamites, for recasting the bronze tools that would be blunted during the mining.

The vault itself remained just above a man's outstretched fingertips; it felt smooth and cool when one leapt up to touch it. It seemed to be made of fine-grained white granite, unmarred and utterly featureless. And therein lay the problem.

Long ago, Yahweh had released the Deluge, unleashing waters from both below and above; the waters of the Abyss had burst forth from the springs of the earth, and the waters of heaven had poured through the sluice gates in the vault. Now men saw the vault closely, but there were no sluice gates discernible. They squinted at the surface in all directions, but no openings, no windows, no seams interrupted the granite plain.

It seemed that their tower met the vault at a point between any reservoirs, which was fortunate indeed. If a sluice gate had been visible, they would have had to risk breaking it open and emptying the reservoir. That would mean rain for Shinar, out of season and heavier than the winter rains; it would cause flooding along the Euphrates. The rain would most likely end when the reservoir was emptied, but there was always the possibility that Yahweh would punish them and continue the rain until the tower fell and Babylon was dissolved into mud.

Even though there were no visible gates, a risk still existed. Perhaps the gates had no seams perceptible to mortal eyes, and a reservoir lay directly above them. Or perhaps the reservoirs were huge, so that even if the nearest sluice gates were many leagues away, a reservoir still lay above them.

There was much debate over how best to proceed.

"Surely Yahweh will not wash away the tower," argued Qurdusa, one of the bricklayers. "If the tower were sacrilege, Yahweh would have destroyed it earlier. Yet in all the centuries we've been working, we have never seen the slightest sign of Yahweh's displeasure. Yahweh will drain any reservoir before we penetrate it."

"If Yahweh looked upon this venture with such favor, there would already be a stairway ready-made for us in the vault," countered Eluti, an Elamite. "Yahweh will neither help or hinder us; if we penetrate a reservoir, we will face the onrush of its waters."

Hillalum could not keep his doubts silent at such a time. "And if the waters are endless?" he asked. "Yahweh may not punish us, but Yahweh may allow us to bring our judgment upon ourselves."

"Elamite," said Qurdusa, "even as a newcomer to the tower, you should know better than that. We labor for our love of Yahweh, we have done so for all our lives, and so have our fathers for generations back. Men as righteous as we could not be judged harshly."

"It is true that we work with the purest of aims, but that doesn't mean we have worked wisely. Did men truly choose the correct path when they opted to live their lives away from the soil from which they were shaped? Never has Yahweh said that the choice was proper. Now we stand ready to break open heaven, even when we know that water lies above us. If we are misguided, how can we be sure Yahweh will protect us from our own errors?"

"Hillalum advises caution, and I agree," said Beli. "We must ensure that we do not bring a second Deluge upon the world, nor even dangerous rains upon Shinar. I have conferred with Senmut of the Egyptians, and he has shown me designs which they have employed to seal the tombs of their kings. I believe their methods can provide us with safety when we begin digging."

The priests sacrificed the ox and the goat in a ceremony in which many sacred words were spoken and much incense was burned, and the miners began work.

Long before the miners reached the vault it had been obvious that simple digging with hammers and picks would be impractical: even if they were tunneling horizontally, they would make no more than two fingers' width of progress a day through granite, and tunneling upward would be far, far slower. Instead, they employed fire-setting.

With the wood they had brought, a bonfire was built below the chosen point of the vault, and fed steadily for a day. Before the heat of the flames, the stone cracked and spalled. After letting the fire burn out, the miners splashed water onto the stone to further the cracking. They could then break the stone into large pieces, which fell heavily onto the tower. In this manner they could progress the better part of a cubit for each day the fire burned.

The tunnel did not rise straight up, but at the angle a staircase takes, so that they could build a ramp of steps up from the tower to meet it. The fire-setting left the walls and floor smooth; the men built a frame of wooden steps underfoot, so that they would not slide back down. They used a platform of baked bricks to support the bonfire at the tunnel's end.

After the tunnel rose ten cubits into the vault, they leveled it out and widened it to form a room. After the miners had removed all the stone that had been weakened by the fire, the Egyptians began work. They used no fire in their quarrying. With only their dolerite balls and hammers, they began to build a sliding door of granite.

They first chipped away stone to cut an immense block of granite out of one wall. Hillalum and the other miners tried to help, but found it very difficult: one did not wear away the stone by grinding, but instead pounded chips off, using hammer blows of one strength alone, and lighter or heavier ones would not do.

After some weeks, the block was ready. It stood taller than a man, and was even wider than that. To free it from the floor, they cut slots around the base of the stone and pounded in dry wooden wedges. Then they pounded thinner wedges into the first wedges to split them, and poured water into the cracks so that the wood would swell. In a few hours, a crack travelled into the stone, and the block was freed.

At the rear of the room, on the right-hand side, the miners burned out a narrow upward-sloping corridor, and in the floor in front of the chamber entrance they dug a downward-sloping channel into the floor for a cubit. Thus there was a smooth continuous ramp that cut across the floor immediately in front of the entrance, and ended just to its left. On this ramp the Egyptians loaded the block of granite. They dragged and pushed the block up into the side corridor, where it just barely fit, and propped it in place with a stack of flat mud bricks braced against the bottom of the left wall, like a pillar lying on the ramp.

With the sliding stone to hold back the waters, it was safe for the miners to continue tunneling. If they broke into a reservoir and the waters of heaven began pouring down into the tunnel, they would break the bricks one by one, and the stone would slide down until it rested in the recess in the floor, utterly blocking the doorway. If the waters flooded in with such force that they washed men out of the tunnels, the mud bricks would gradually dissolve, and again the stone would slide down. The waters would be retained, and the miners could then begin a new tunnel in another direction, to avoid the reservoir.

The miners again used fire-setting to continue the tunnel, beginning at the far end of the room. To aid the circulation of air within the vault, ox hides were stretched on tall frames of wood, and placed obliquely on either side of the tunnel entrance at the top of the tower. Thus the steady wind that blew underneath the vault of heaven was guided upward into the tunnel; it kept the fire blazing, and it cleared the air after the fire was extinguished, so that the miners could dig without breathing smoke.

The Egyptians did not stop working once the sliding stone was in place. While the miners swung their picks at the tunnel's end, the Egyptians labored at the task of cutting a stair into the solid stone, to replace the wooden steps. This they did with the wooden wedges, and the blocks they removed from the sloping floor left steps in their place.

Thus the miners worked, extending the tunnel on and on. The tunnel always ascended, though it reversed direction regularly like a thread in a giant stitch, so that its general path was straight up. They built other sliding door rooms, so that only the uppermost segment of the tunnel would be flooded if they penetrated a reservoir. They cut channels in the vault's surface from which they hung walkways and platforms; starting from these platforms, well away from the tower, they dug side tunnels, which joined the main tunnel deep inside. The wind was guided through these to provide ventilation, clearing the smoke from deep inside the tunnel.

For years the labour continued. The pulling crews no longer hauled bricks, but wood and water for the fire-setting. People came to inhabit those tunnels just inside the vault's surface, and on hanging platforms they grew downward-bending vegetables. The miners lived there at the border of heaven; some married, and raised children. Few ever set foot on the earth again.

With a wet cloth wrapped around his face, Hillalum climbed down from wooden steps onto stone, having just fed some more wood to the bonfire at the tunnel's end. The fire would continue for many hours, and he would wait in the lower tunnels, where the wind was not thick with smoke.

Then there was a distant sound of shattering, the sound of a mountain of stone being split through, and then a steadily growing roar. And then a torrent of water came rushing down the tunnel.

For a moment, Hillalum was frozen in horror. The water, shockingly cold, slammed into his legs, knocking him down. He rose to his feet, gasping for breath, leaning against the current, clutching at the steps.

They had hit a reservoir.

He had to descend below the highest sliding door, before it was closed. His legs wished to leap down the steps, but he knew he couldn't remain on his feet if he did, and being swept down by the raging current would likely batter him to death. Going as fast as he dared, he took the steps one by one.

He slipped several times, sliding down as many as a dozen steps each time; the stone steps scraped against his back, but he felt no pain. All the while he was certain the tunnel would collapse and crush him, or else the entire vault would split open, and the sky would gape beneath his feet, and he would fall down to earth amidst the heavenly rain. Yahweh's punishment had come, a second Deluge.

How much further until he reached the sliding stone? The tunnel seemed to stretch on and on, and the waters were pouring down even faster now. He was virtually running down the steps.

Suddenly he stumbled and splashed into shallow water. He had run down past the end of the stairs, and fallen into the room of the sliding stone, and there was water higher than his knees.

He stood up, and saw Damqiya and Ahuni, two fellow miners, just noticing him. They stood in front of the stone that already blocked the exit.

"No!" he cried.

"They closed it!" screamed Damqiya. "They did not wait!"

"Are there others coming?" shouted Ahuni, without hope. "We may be able to move the block."

"There are no others," answered Hillalum. "Can they push it from the other side?"

"They cannot hear us." Ahuni pounded the granite with a hammer, making not a sound against the din of the water.

Hillalum looked around the tiny room, only now noticing that an Egyptian floated facedown in the water.

"He died falling down the stairs," yelled Damqiya.

"Is there nothing we can do?"

Ahuni looked upward. "Yahweh, spare us."

The three of them stood in the rising water, praying desperately, but Hillalum knew it was in vain: his fate had come at last. Yahweh had not asked men to build the tower or to pierce the vault; the decision to build it belonged to men alone, and they would die in this endeavor just as they did in any of their earthbound tasks. Their righteousness could not save them from the consequences of their deeds.

The water reached their chests. "Let us ascend," shouted Hillalum.

They climbed the tunnel laboriously, against the onrush, as the water rose behind their heels. The few torches illuminating the tunnel had been extinguished, so they ascended in the dark, murmuring prayers that they couldn't hear. The wooden steps at the top of the tunnel had dislodged from their place, and were jammed farther down in the tunnel. They climbed past them, until they reached the smooth stone slope, and there they waited for the water to carry them higher.

They waited without words, their prayers exhausted. Hillalum imagined that he stood in the black gullet of Yahweh, as the mighty one drank deep of the waters of heaven, ready to swallow the sinners.

The water rose, and bore them up, until Hillalum could reach up with his hands and touch the ceiling. The giant fissure from which the waters gushed forth was right next to him. Only a tiny pocket of air remained. Hillalum shouted, "When this chamber is filled, we can swim heavenward."

He could not tell if they heard him. He gulped his last breath as the water reached the ceiling, and swam up into the fissure. He would die closer to heaven than any man had ever before.

The fissure extended for many cubits. As soon as Hillalum passed through, the stone stratum slipped from his fingers, and his flailing limbs touched nothing. For a moment he felt a current carrying him, but then he was no longer sure. With only blackness around him, he once again felt that horrible vertigo that he had experienced when first approaching the vault: he could not distinguish any directions, not even up or down. He pushed and kicked against the water, but did not know if he moved.

Helpless, he was perhaps floating in still water, perhaps swept furiously by a current; all he felt was numbing cold. Never did he see any light. Was there no surface to this reservoir that he might rise to?

Then he was slammed into stone again. His hands felt a fissure in the surface. Was he back where he had begun? He was being forced into it, and he had no strength to resist. He was drawn into the tunnel, and was rattled against its sides. It was incredibly deep, like the longest mine shaft: he felt as if his lungs would burst, but there was still no end to the passage. Finally his breath would not be held any longer, and it escaped from his lips. He was drowning, and the blackness around him entered his lungs.

But suddenly the walls opened out away from him. He was being carried along by a rushing stream of water; he felt air above the water! And then he felt no more.

Hillalum awoke with his face pressed against wet stone. He could see nothing, but he could feel water near his hands. He rolled over and groaned; his every limb ached, he was naked and much of his skin was scraped raw or wrinkled from wetness, but he breathed air.

Time passed, and finally he could stand. Water flowed rapidly about his ankles. Stepping in one direction, the water deepened. In the other, there was dry stone; shale, by the feel of it.

It was utterly dark, like a mine without torches. With torn fingertips he felt his way along the floor, until it rose up and became a wall. Slowly, like some blind creature, he crawled back and forth. He found the water's source, a large opening in the floor. He remembered! He had been spewed up from the reservoir through this hole. He continued crawling for what seemed to be hours; if he was in a cavern, it was immense.

He found a place where the floor rose in a slope. Was there a passage leading upwards? Perhaps it could still take him to heaven.

Hillalum crawled, having no idea of how much time passed, not caring that he would never be able to retrace his steps, for he could not return whence he had come. He followed upward tunnels when he found them, downward ones when he had to. Though earlier he had swallowed more water than he would have thought possible, he began to feel thirst, and hunger.

And eventually he saw light, and raced to the outside.

The light made his eyes squeeze closed, and he fell to his knees, his fists clenched before his face. Was it the radiance of Yahweh? Could his eyes bear to see it? Minutes later he could open them, and he saw desert. He had emerged from a cave in the foothills of some mountains, and rocks and sand stretched to the horizon.

Was heaven just like the earth? Did Yahweh dwell in a place such as this? Or was this merely another realm within Yahweh's Creation, another earth above his own, while Yahweh dwelled still higher?

A sun lay near the mountaintops behind his back. Was it rising or falling? Were there days and nights here?

Hillalum squinted at the sandy landscape. A line moved along the horizon. Was it a caravan?

He ran to it, shouting with his parched throat until his need for breath stopped him. A figure at the end of the caravan saw him, and brought the entire line to a stop. Hillalum kept running.

The one who had seen him seemed to be man, not spirit, and was dressed like a desert-crosser. He had a waterskin ready. Hillalum drank as best he could, panting for breath.

Finally he returned it to the man, and gasped, "Where is this place?"

"Were you attacked by bandits? We are headed to Erech."

Hillalum stared. "You would deceive me!" he shouted. The man drew back, and watched him as if he were mad from the sun. Hillalum saw another man in the caravan walking over to investigate. "Erech is in Shinar!"

"Yes it is. Were you not travelling to Shinar?" The other man stood ready with his staff.

"I came from – I was in– " Hillalum stopped. "Do you know Babylon?"

"Oh, is that your destination? That is north of Erech. It is an easy journey between them."

"The tower. Have you heard of it?"

"Certainly, the pillar to heaven. It is said men at the top are tunneling through the vault of heaven."

Hillalum fell to the sand.

"Are you unwell?" The two caravan drivers mumbled to each other, and went off to confer with the others. Hillalum was not watching them.

He was in Shinar. He had returned to the earth. He had climbed above the reservoirs of heaven, and arrived back at the earth. Had Yahweh brought him to this place, to keep him from reaching further above? Yet Hillalum still hadn't seen any signs, any indication that Yahweh noticed him. He had not experienced any miracle that Yahweh had performed to place him here. As far as he could see, he had merely swum up from the vault and entered the cavern below.

Somehow, the vault of heaven lay beneath the earth. It was as if they lay against each other, though they were separated by many leagues. How could that be? How could such distant places touch? Hillalum's head hurt trying to think about it.

And then it came to him: *a seal cylinder*. When rolled upon a tablet of soft clay, the carved cylinder left an imprint that formed a picture. Two figures might appear at opposite ends of the tablet, though they stood side by side on the surface of the cylinder. All the world was as such a cylinder. Men imagined heaven and earth as being at the ends of a tablet, with sky and stars stretched between; yet the world was wrapped around in some fantastic way so that heaven and earth touched.

It was clear now why Yahweh had not struck down the tower, had not punished men for wishing to reach beyond the bounds set for them: for the longest journey would merely return them to the place whence they'd come. Centuries of their labour would not reveal to them any more of Creation than they already knew. Yet through their endeavor, men would glimpse the unimaginable artistry of Yahweh's work, in seeing how ingeniously the world had been constructed. By this construction, Yahweh's work was indicated, and Yahweh's work was concealed.

Thus would men know their place.

Hillalum rose to his feet, his legs unsteady from awe, and sought out the caravan drivers. He would go back to Babylon. Perhaps he would see Lugatum again. He would send word to those on the tower. He would tell them about the shape of the world.

JACK NECK AND
THE WORRY BIRD
Paul Di Filippo

Paul Di Filippo (b. 1954) is a remarkable writer who despite being enviably prolific always manages to produce fiction that is fresh, original and unusual. When I reprinted one of his stories in The Mammoth Book of Extreme Science Fiction *I said that he writes as if someone had scrunched up Harlan Ellison, Philip K Dick, Philip José Farmer and Roger Zelazny into a ball of dough, rolled it out and cut out pastry cakes that are then filled with a mix of sweetmeats of S J Perelman, Jerry Seinfeld, Tim Powers and Bruce Sterling all baked in an oven heated by that unique essence of Di Filippo's own imagination. The result is a party tray of delicacies that taste different at every bite. Perhaps I left out Lewis Carroll and Edward Lear because the following story reads as if Paul had commandeered those two writers to produce something in the vein of Roald Dahl.*

There's just no end to Paul's abilities. You can sample him at his most varied in his collections Fractal Paisleys *(1997),* Strange Trades *(2001) and* Little Doors *(2002) as well as his first book* The Steampunk Trilogy *(1994).*

O n the western edge of putty-coloured Drudge City, in the neighborhood of the Stoltz Hypobiological Refinery ("The lowest form of intelligent life – the highest form of dumb matter!"), not far from Newspaper Park and Boris Crocodile's Beanery and Caustics Bar

– both within a knucklebone's throw of the crapulent, crepitant Isinglass River – lived mawkly old Jack Neck, along with his bat-winged and shark-toothed bonedog, Motherway.

Jack Neck was retired now, and mighty glad of it. He'd put in many a lugubrious lustrum at Krespo's Mangum Exordium, stirring the slorq vats, cleaning the lard filters, sweeping up the escaped tiddles. Plenty of work for any man's lifetime. Jack had busted his hump like a shemp to earn his current pension (the hump was just now recovering; it didn't wander so bad like it used to), and Jack knew that unlike the lazy young and fecund time-eaters and space-sprawlers whom he shared his cheapjack building with, he truly deserved his union stipend, all 500 crones per moon (except once a year, during the Short Thirteenth, when he only got 495). Why, it had taken him a whole year of retirement just to forget the sound of the tiddles crying out for mercy. Deadly core-piercing, that noise was, by Saint Fistula's Nose!

But now, having survived the rigours of the Exordium (not all his buddies had lived to claim their Get-gone Get-by; why, his pal Slam Slap could still be seen as a screaming bas-relief in the floor tiles of Chamber 409), Jack could take life slow and easy. During daylight hours, he could loll around his bachelor-unclean flat (chittering dustbunnies prowling from couch to cupboard; obscurantist buildup on the windows, sulfur-yellow sweatcrust on the inside, pinky-grey smogma on the outside), quaffing his Anonymous Brand Bitterberry Slumps (2 crones per sixpack, down at Batu Truant's Package Parlor) and watching the televised Motorball games. Lookit that gracefully knurltopped Dean Tesh play, how easily he scored, like a regular Kuykendall Canton pawpaw!

Ignoring his master's excited rumbles and despairing whoops, Motherway the steel-coloured bonedog would lie peacefully by the side of Jack's slateslab chair, mostly droop-eyed and snore-birthing, occasionally emitting a low growl directed at a more-than-usually daring dustbunny, the bonedog's acutely articulated leathery wings reflexively snickersnacking in stifled pursuit.

Three times daily Motherway got his walkies. Down the four flights of badly lit, incongruently angled stairs Jack and his pet would clomber, Motherway's cloven chitin hooves scrabbling for purchase on the scarred boards. Last time down each day, Jack would pause in the lobby and check for mail. He never got anything, barring his moonly check, but it was good to clear the crumblies out of his wall-adherent mailsack. Dragoman Mr Spiffle wouldn't leave the mail if contumacious crumblies nested within Jack's fumarole-pocked personal mailsack. And Jack didn't blame him! One or two migrant crumblies a day could be dealt with – but not a whole moonly nest!

Outside on Marmoreal Boulevard, Jack and Motherway always turned left, towards Newspaper Park. Marmoreal Boulevard paralleled the Isinglass River, which gurgled and chortled in its high-banked channel directly across the Boulevard from Jack's flat. The mean and treacherous slippery river was further set off from foot and vehicle traffic by a wide promenade composed of earth-mortared butterblox and a rail of withyweave. Mostly, the promenade remained vacant of strollers. It didn't pay to get too close to the Isinglass, as more than one uncautious twitterer had discovered, when – peering curiously over the rail to goggle at the rainbowed plumduff sluicejuice pouring from the Stoltz Refinery pipes – he or she would be looped by a long suckered manipulator and pulled down to eternal aquatic slavery on the spillichaug plantations. GAWPERS AND LOOKYLOOS, BEWARE! read the numerous signage erected by the solicitous Drudge City Constabulary.

(Boating on the Isinglass held marginally fewer risks. Why, people were still talking about the event that quickly came to be known throughout Drudge City and beyond as "Pale Captain Dough's Angling Dismay," an event that Jack had had the misfortune to witness entire from his own flat. And he had thought the squeaky pleas of the tiddles were hard to dislodge from his mind–!)

Moving down the body- and booth-crowded sidewalk with a frowsty and jangly galumph that was partially a result of his fossilized left leg and partially attributable to the chunk-heeled, needle-toed boots which compressed his tiny feet unmercifully, Jack would enjoy the passing sights and sounds and smells of his neighbourhood. A pack of low-slung Cranials surged by, eliciting a snap and lunge from the umbilical-restrained Motherway.

From the peddle-powered, umbrella-shielded, salted-chickpea cart operated by Mother Gimlett wafted a delectable fragrance that always convinced Jack to part with a thread or two, securing in return a greasy paper cone of crispy steaming legumes. From the door of Boris Crocodile's poured forth angular music, the familiar bent notes and goo-modulated subsonics indicating that Stinky Frankie Konk was soloing on the hookah-piped banjo. Jack would lick his bristly nodule-dotted lips, anticipating his regular visit that evening to the boisterous Beanery and Caustics Bar, where he would be served a shot of his favourite dumble-rum by affable bartender Dinky Pachinko.

On the verges of Newspaper Park, beneath the towering headline tree, Jack would let slip Motherway's umbilical, which would retract inside the bonedog's belly with a whir and a click like a rollershade pull. Then Motherway would be off to romp with the other cavorting animals, the gilacats and sweaterbats, the tinkleslinks and slithersloths. Jack would amble over to his favourite bench, where reliably could be found Dirty Bill Brownback. Dirty Bill was more or less permanently conjoined with his bench, the man's indiscriminate flesh mated with the porously acquisitive material of the seat. Surviving all weathers and seasons, subsisting on a diet scrounged from the trashcan placed conveniently at his elbow, Dirty Bill boasted cobwebbed armpits and crumbly-infested trousers, but was nonetheless an affable companion. Functioning as a center of fresh gossip and rumors, news and notions, Dirty Bill nevertheless always greeted Jack Neck with the same stale jibe.

"Hey, Neck, still wearing those cellbug togs? Can't you afford better on your GGGB?"

True, Jack Neck's outfit went unchanged from one moon to the next. His ivory-and-ash-striped shirt and identically patterned leggings were the official workwear of his union, the MMMM, or Mangum Maulers Monitoring Moiety, and Jack's body had grown accustomed to the clothes through his long employment. Of course, the clothes had also grown accustomed to Jack's body, fusing in irregular lumpy seams and knobbly patches to his jocund, rubicund, moribund flesh.

That was just the way it went these days, in the midst of the Indeterminate. The stability of the Boredom was no more. Boundaries were flux-prone, cause-and-effect ineffectual, and forms not distinct from ideations. You soon got used to the semi-regular chaos, though, even if, like Jack, you had been born "way back" in the Boredom.

With the same predictability exhibited by Dirty Bill (human social vapidity remained perhaps the most stable force in the Indeterminate), Jack would consistently reply, "Happens I fancy these orts, Dirty Bill. And they fancy me!"

With a chuckle and a snaggletooth snigger, Dirty Bill would pat the bench beside him and offer, "Sit a spell then, neckless Jack Neck – not too long though, mind you! – and I'll fill you in on my latest gleanings. That is, if you'll share a salty chickpea or two!"

"Gladly, you old plank-ass!" Diverting as the perpetual Motorball Tourneys on television were, Jack relished simple human intercourse. So while Motherway chased six-legged squirrels (all four of the mature bonedog's feet an inch or two off the ground; only bonedog pups could get much higher), Jack and Dirty Bill would confab the droogly minutes away.

After his supper each night – commonly a pot of slush, slumgullion or a frozen precooked bluefish fillet heated in the hellbox, whichever being washed down with a tankard of Smith's Durian Essence – Jack would leave Motherway behind to lick doggy balls and umbilical while the bonedog's master made his visit to Boris Crocodile's. There on his reserved barstool, while empty-eyed Nori Nougat danced the latest fandango or barcarole with beetle-browed Zack Zither, Jack Neck would nod his own disproportionate head in time to the querulous squeegeeing of Stinky Frankie Konk and affirm to all who would pay any heed to the elderly GGGB-er, "Yessir, assuming you can get through the rough spots, life can turn out mighty sweet!"

But all that, of course, was before the advent of the Worrybird.

That fateful morning dawned nasty, low-hanging hieratic skies and burnt-toast clouds, an ugly odour like all the rain-drenched lost stuffed-toys of childhood seeping in from the streets. Upon opening first his good left eye, then his bad right ('twasn't the eye itself that was dodgy, but only the nacreous cheek-carbuncle below it that was smooshing the orb closed), Jack Neck experienced a ripe intestinal feeling telling him he should stay in bed. Just huddle up 'neath his checkerboard marshmallow quilt, leaving his beleathered feet safe in the grooves they had worn in the milkweed-stuffed mattress. Yes, that seemed just the safest course on a day like today, so pawky and slyboots.

But the allure of the common comforts awaiting him proved stronger than his intuition. Why, today was a Motorball matchup made in heaven! The Chlorine Castigators versus Dame Middlecamp's Prancers! And then there was Motherway to be walked, Dirty Bill's dishy yatterings, that Dinky-Pachinko-poured tot of dumble-rum to welcome midnight in. Surely nothing mingy nor mulcting would befall him, if he kept to his established paths and habits...

So out of his splavined cot old bunion-rumped Jack Neck poured himself, heavy hump leading Lady Gravity in an awkward pavane. Once standing, with minor exertions Jack managed to hitch his hump around, behind and upward to a less unaccomodatingly exigent position. Then he essayed the palpable trail midst the debris of his domicile that led to the bathroom.

As soon as Jack entered the WC, he knew his vague forebodings had been spot on. But it was now too late to return to the safety of his blankets. For Jack saw with dismay that out of his chipped granite commode, like a baleful excremental spirit, there arose a Smoking Toilet Puppet.

The rugose figure was composed of an elongated mud-colored torso, sprouting two boneless and sinuous claw-fingered arms, and topped by a rutted warpy face. The Puppet's head was crowned by a small fumey crater, giving its kind their name.

"Ja-a-ack," wailed the Puppet. "Jack Neck! Step closer! I have a message for you."

Jack knew that although the creature might indeed have a valid and valuable delphic message for him, to heed the Puppet's summons was to risk being abducted down to the gluck-mucky Septic Kingdom ruled by Baron Sugarslinger. So with an uncommon burst of energy, Jack grabbed up a wood-hafted sump-plunger and whanged the Puppet a good one on its audacious incense-dispensing bean.

While the Puppet was clutching its abused noggin and sobbing most piteously, Jack stepped around it and flushed. Widdershins and downward swirled the invader, disappearing with a liquidly dopplering "Nooooooo…!"

Jack did his old man's business quickly while the runnels still gurgled, then lowered the heavy toilet lid against further home invasions. He stepped to the sink and the sweatcrusted mirror above it, where he flaked scales off his reflection. He shaved his forehead, restoring the pointy dimensions of his once-stylish hairline, plucked some eelgrass out of his ears, lacquered his carbuncle, and congratulated himself on meeting so forcefully the first challenge of the day. If nothing else adventured, he would be polly-with-a-lolly!

Back through the bedroom and out into his sitting sanctuary, where

Motherway lay snoozily on his fulsome scrap of Geelvink carpet. Approaching the dirty window that looked out upon Marmoreal Boulevard and the Isinglass, the incautious and over-optimistic Jack Neck threw open the wormy sash and shouldered forward, questing additional meaning and haruspices from the day.

And that was precisely the moment the waiting Worrybird chose to land talon-tight upon the convenient perch of Jack's hapless hump!

Jack yelped and with an instinctive yet hopeless shake of his hump withdrew into the refuge of his apartment, thinking to disconcert and dislodge the Worrybird by swift maneuvers. But matters had already progressed beyond any such simple solution. The Worrybird was truly and determinedly ensconced, and Jack realized he was doomed.

Big as a turkey, with crepe-like vulture wings, the baldy Worrybird possessed a dour human face exhibiting the texture of ancient overwaxed linoleum, and exuded a stench like burning crones. Jack had seen the ominous parasites often, of course, riding on their wan, slumpy victims. But never had he thought to be one such!

Awakened by the foofraraw, Motherway was barking and leaping and snapping, frantically trying to drive the intruder off. But all the bonedog succeeded in doing was gouging his master's single sensible leg with his hooves. Jack managed to calm the bonedog down, although Motherway continued to whimper while anxiously fidgeting.

Now the Worrybird craned its paste-pallid pug-ugly face around on its long sebaceous neck to confront Jack. It opened its hideous rubbery mouth and intoned a portentous phrase.

"Never again, but not yet!"

Jack threw himself into his slateslab chair, thinking to crush the grim bird, but it leaped nimbly atop Jack's skull. By Saint Foraminifer's Liver, those scalp-digging claws hurt! Quickly Jack stood, prefering to let the bird roost on his hump. Obligingly, the Worrybird shifted back.

"Oh, Motherway," Jack implored, "what a fardelicious grievance has been construed upon us! What oh what are we to do?"

Motherway made inutile answer only by a plangent sympathetic whuffle.

The first thought to form in the anxious mind of bird-bestridden Jack Neck was that he should apply to the local Health Clinic run by the Little Sisters of Saint Farquahar. Surely the talented technicians and charity caregivers there would have a solution to his grisly geas! (Although at the back of his mind loomed the pessimistic question, perhaps Worrybird implanted, *Why did anyone suffer from Worrybird-itis if removal of same were so simple?*)

So, leaving Motherway behind to guard the apartment from any further misfortunes which this inopportune day might bring, Jack and his randomly remonstrative rider ("Never again, but not yet!") clabbered down the four flights of slant stairs to the street.

Once on Marmoreal (where formerly friendly or neutral neighbours now winced and retreated from sight of his affliction), Jack turned not happy-wise left but appointment-bound right. At the intersection of the Boulevard and El Chino Street, he wambled south on the cross-street. Several blocks down El Chino his progress was arrested by the sloppy aftermath of an accident: a dray full of Smith's Durian Essence had collided with one loaded with Walrus Brand Brochettes. The combination of the two antagonistic spilled foodstuffs had precipitated something noxious: galorping mounds of quivering dayglo cartiplasm that sought to ingest any flesh within reach. (The draft-animals, a brace of Banana Slugs per dray, had already succumbed, as had the blindly argumentative drivers, one Pheon Ploog and a certain Elmer Sourbray.)

Responding with the nimble reflexes and sassy footwork expected from any survivor of Drudge City's ordinary cataclysms, Jack dodged into a nearby building, rode a Recirculating Transport Fountain upward and took a wayward rooftop path around the crisis before descending, all the while writing a hundred times on the blackboard of his mind an exclamation-punctuated admonition never to mix internally his favourite suppertime drink with any iota of Walrus Brand Brochettes.

Encountering no subsequent pandygandy, Jack Neck and his foul avian passenger arrived at the Health Clinic on Laguna Diamante Way. Once inside, he was confronted with the stern and ruleacious face of Nurse Gwendolyn Hindlip, Triage Enforcement Officer. From behind her rune-carven desk that seemed assembled of poorly chosen driftwood fragments, Nurse Gwendolyn sized up Jack and his hump-burden, then uttered a presumptuous pronouncement.

"You might as well kill yourself now, you old mummer, and free up your GGGB for a younkling!"

Jack resented being called a mummer – a mildly derisive slang term derived from his union's initials – almost more than he umbrigated at the suicidal injunction.

"Shut up, you lava-faced hincty harridan! Just take my particulars, slot my citizen-biscuit into the chewer, and mind your own business!"

Nurse Gwendolyn sniffed with bruised emotionality. Jack had scored a mighty blow on a tender spot with his categorical comment "lava-faced." For Nurse Gwendolyn's scare-making and scarified visage did indeed reflect her own childhood brush with a flesh-melting disease that still occasionally plagued Drudge City. Known as Trough'n'Slough, the nonfatal disease left its victims with a stratified trapunto epidermis. Nurse Gwendolyn forever attributed her sour old-maidhood to the stigma of this pillowpuff complexion, although truth be told, her vile tongue had even more to do with her empty bed.

Snuffling aggrievedly, Nurse Gwendolyn now did as she was bade, at last dispatching a newly ID-braceleted Jack to a waiting area with the final tart remark, "You'll surely have a long uncomfortable wait, Mr Neck, for many and more seriously afflicted – yet naytheless with a better prognosis – are the helpseekers afore you!"

Coercing his fossil leg into the waiting room, Jack saw that Nurse Gwendolyn had not been merely flibbering. Ranked and stacked in moaning drifts and piles were a staggering assortment of Drudge City's malfunctioners. Jack spotted many a one showing various grades of Maskelyne's Curse, in which the face assumed the characteristics of a thickly blurred latex mold of the actual submerged features beneath. The false countenance remained connected by sensory tendrils, yet was migratory, so that one's visage slopped about like warm jello, eyes peeking from nostrils or ears, nose poking from mouth. Other patients showed plain signs of Exoskeletal Exfoliation, their limbs encased in osteoclastic armor. One woman – dressed in a tattered shift laterally patterned blue and gold – could only be host to Dolly Dwindles Syndrome: as she approached over months her ultimate doll-like dimensions, her face simultaneously grew more lascivious in a ghoulish manner.

Heaving a profound sigh at the mortal sufferings of himself and his fellows, Jack sat himself saggingly down in a low-backed chair that permitted the Worrybird to maintain its grip upon Jack's hump and resigned himself to a long wait.

On the seven-hundredth-and-forty-ninth "Never again, but not yet!", Jack's name was called. He arose and was conducted to a cubicle screened from an infinity of others by ripped curtains the colour of old tartar sauce. Undressing was not an option, so he simply plopped down on a squelchy examining table and awaited the advent of a healer. Before too long the curtains parted and a lab-coated figure entered.

This runcible-snouted doctor himself, thought Jack, should have been a patient, for he was clearly in an advanced state of Tessellated Scale Mange, as evidenced by alligatored wrists and neck poking from cuff and collar. Most horridly, the medico dragged behind him a long ridged tail, ever-extending like an accumulating stalactite from an infiltrated organ at the base of the spine.

"Doctor Weighbend," said the professional in a confident voice, extending a crocodile paw. Jack shook hands happily, liking the fellow's vim. But Doctor Weighbend's next question shattered Jack's sanguinity.

"Now, what seems to be the matter with you, Mr Neck?"

"Why – why, Doc, there's an irksome and grotty Worrybird implacably a-sway upon my tired old hump!"

Doctor Weighbend made a suave dismissive motion. "Oh, that. Since there's no known cure for the Worrybird, Mr Neck, I assumed there was another issue to deal with, some unseen plaque or innervation perhaps."

"No known cure, Doc? How can that be?"

Doctor Weighbend cupped his dragonly chin. "The Worrybird has by now slyly and inextricably mingled his Akashic Aura with yours. Were we to kill or even remove the little vampire-sparrow, you too would perish. Of course, you'll perish eventually anyway, as the lachrymose-lark siphons off your vitality. But that process could take years and years. 'Never again will you smile, but not yet shall you die.' That's the gist of it, I fear, Mr Neck."

"What – what do you recommend then?"

"Many people find some small palliation in building a festive concealing shelter for their Worrybird. Securely strapped to your torso bandolier-style and gaily decorated with soothing icons, it eases social functioning to a small degree. Now, I have other patients to attend to, if you'll permit me to take my leave by wishing you a minimally satisfactory rest of your life."

Doctor Weighbend spun around – his massive tail catching a cart of instruments and beakers and sending glassware smashing to the floor – and was gone. Jack sat wearily and down-in-the-dumpily for a few long minutes, then levered himself up and trudged off down the aisle formed by the curtained wards.

Almost to the exit, Jack's attention was drawn between two parted drapes.

On a table lay the Motorball Champion Dean Tesh! Bloodied and grimacing, his signature cornucopia-shaped head drooping, sparks and fizzles spurting from his numerous lumpy adjuncts, Jack Neck's hero awaited his own treatment. Assuredly, that day's game had been a rumbunctious and asgardian fray! And Jack had missed it!

Impulsively, Jack entered the Champion's cubicle. "Superlative Dean Tesh, if I may intrude briefly upon your eminence. I'm one of your biggest fans, and I wish to offer my condolences on your lapsarian desuetude."

Dean Tesh boldly smiled like the rigorous roughrider he was. "'Tis nothing, really, old mummenschanz. Once they jimmy open my cranial circuit flap and insert a few new wigwags, I'll be right as skysyrup!"

Jack blushed to be addressed by his union's highest title, in actuality undeserved. "Your magnificent spirit inspires me, lordly Dean Tesh! Somehow I too will win through my own malediction!"

Dean Tesh's ocular lenses whirred for a better look. "Worrybird, is it? I've heard Uncle Bradley has a way with them."

"Uncle Bradley! Of course! Did he not design your own world-renowned servos and shunts? If medicine holds no answers to my problem, then surely Uncle Bradley's Syntactical Fibroid Engineering must!"

And so bidding Dean Tesh a heartfelt farewell replete with benisonical affirmations of the Champion's swift recovery, Jack Neck set out for Cementville.

Soon Jack's trail of tiny archless footprints – outlined in fast-growing sporulating molds and luminescent quiverslimes – could be traced through many an urban mile. Behind him already lay the evil precincts of Barrio Garmi, where the Stilt-legged Spreckles were prone to drop rotten melons from their lofty vantages upon innocent passersby. Jack had with wiles and guiles eluded that sloppy fate. The district of Clovis Points he had also cunningly circumnavigated, wrenching free at the last possible moment from the tenebrous grasp of a pack of Shanghai Liliths, whose lickerish intention it was to drag innocent Jack to their spraddleskirted leader, Lil' Omen, for the irreligious ceremony known as the Ecstatic Excruciation.

For several blocks thereafter he had dared to ride the Henniker Avenue Slantwise Subway, disembarking hastily through his car's emergency exit and thence by escape-ready ladder-chute when he spotted a blockade across the tracks surely erected by the muskageous minions of Baron Sugarslinger. Luckily, Jack had had the foresight to obtain a transfer-wafer and so was able to board the Baba Wanderly Aerial Viaticum for free, riding high and safe above the verdigrised-copper-colored towers and chimney-pots, gables and garrets of Doo-Boo-Kay Flats.

At last, as a pavonine dusk was o'erspreading the haze-raddled, swag-bellied firmament, Jack Neck and his endlessly asseverating Worrybird – its face like a hairless druid's, its folded wings gloomy as a layoff notice from Krespo's – arrived at the premises of Uncle Bradley.

The largest employer in gritty Cementville, the firm of Bradley and His Boyo-Boys, experts in SFE, ran round the erratic clock all thirteen moons a year, turning out many and many a marvelous product, both luxuries and essentials, the former including Seductive Bergamot Filters and the latter notable for Nevermiss Nailguns. Renowned for accepting any and all engineering challenges, the more intractable the more alluring, Uncle Bradley represented Jack's best hope in the Worrybird-Removal Department.

At the towering portal to the lumbering and rachitic nine-storey algae-brick-fronted manufactory that occupied ten square blocks of Dimmig Gardens, Jack made free with the bellpull: the nose of a leering brass jackanapes. A minidoor opened within the gigundo pressboard entrance, and a functionary appeared. As the employee began to speak, Jack noted with dismay that the fellow suffered from Papyrus Mouth: his words emerged not as ordinary vocables but as separate words printed in blearsome bodily inks upon shoddy scraps of organic-tissue paper.

Jack sought to catch the emergent syllables as they spelunked bucally forth, but some eluded him and whitted away on the diddling breezes. Nervously assembling the remaining message, Jack read: *business state Bradley please with.*

"I need to solicit dear Uncle Bradley's genius in the area of invasive parasite disengagement." Jack jerked a thick split-nailed thumb backward at his broodsome rider.

A gush of flighty papyri: *Follow Bradley Uncle free see if me.*

Most gladfully, Jack Neck entered the dynamic establishment and strode after the Papyrus Mouther. Through humming, thrumming offices and sparky workshops – where crucibles glowed with neon-tinted polymeric compounds and, under the nimble fingers of Machine Elves, transistors danced the Happy Chicken Trot with capacitors and optical-fluid valves – Jack and his guide threaded, until at last they stood before a ridged and fumarole-pocked door with a riveted steel rubric announcing it as UNCLE BRADLEY'S CARBON CAVE.

Wait here.

Alone, Jack hipper-hopped nervously from toe to toe. He prayed to all the Saints whose names he could remember – Fimbule and Flubber, Flacken and Floss, Fluffie and Farina – that Uncle Bradley possessed the secret of his salvation – and at a price he could afford.

After an almost unsquingeable wait, the Papyrus Mouther returned.

with Bradley will now you Uncle meet.

"Oh, thank you, kind underling! A myriad blessings of the Yongy-bongy-bo descend upon you!"

Into the fabled Hades-embered Carbon Cave now, whose inward-seeming rattled Jack's sensory modes. The walls and ceiling of the vasty deep were layered with snivelling encrustations of Syntactical Fibroid Engineering at its most complex. Flickering readouts and mumbling speaker-grilles obtruded their cicatrice-bordered surfaces from amongst switches and pulls, toggles and knife-throws, fingering-holes and mentation-bands. Innumerable crystal monitors studded all surfaces, displaying upon their garnet and amethyst faces scenes from across

Drudge City. For a briefer-than-brief second, a shot of Marmoreal
Boulevard – right in front of Boris Crocodile's! – flashed across one, and
Jack nearly wept for the nostalgic past of mere yesterday!

In the middle of the Carbon Cave, on his numinous, numbly throne,
sat Uncle Bradley. Almost totally overwhelmed with layers of SFE
extrudements, a helpful carapace of gadgetry, the master of the Boyo-
Boys showed bare only his snaggle-toothed and wildly inventive face,
and his two striped arms, one of which terminated in chromium piratical
hook. Dangling all around inspiration-eyed Uncle Bradley were speakers
and microphones, mini-monitors, telefactored manipulators and sniff-
sources, allowing him to run his many-branched enterprise without
leaving his cozy sanctum.

As Jack approached tentatively across the wide checkerboard floor, he
could hear from Uncle Bradley a constant stream of queries, advice and
commands.

"Lay on ten thousand more karma-watts to the Soul Furnace! Process
Violet-Hundred is failing? Six hundred kilograms of Charm Catalyst
into the mix! Eureka! Start a new assembly line: personal Eyeblink
Moderators! Has the Bloodwort stabilized yet? No? Lash it with the
Zestful Invigorators! Cancel the Corndog Project, and feed the
experimental subjects to the Hullygees! How are the Pull Hats selling
this season? That poorly? Try them with claw-tassels in plaid!"

Jack and his momentarily silent Worrybird had reached the base of
Uncle Bradley's seat of power, and now the edisonical eminence took
notice of the supplicant. Before Jack could even state his need, Uncle
Bradley, laying a machicolated salesman's smile upon him, was offering
a concise prix-fixe of options.

"Worrybird, correct? Of course! Obviousness obtrudes! Here are
your recoursical tactics, in order of cost and desirability. For five
thousand crones, we inject the bird with a Circuitry Virus. In three days
the bird is totally roboticized. Still unremovable, of course, but its
lethality is slowed by fifty percent. For three thousand crones, we attach

a Secondary Imagineer to your cerebrumal interstices. You promptly forget the bird is there for the rest of your allotted span. For eight hundred crones, a simple cable allows you to share the bird's own mentation. Thus you enjoy your own death, and feel it to be darwinically mandated. Lastly, for a piddling three hundred crones, we remand one of our novice Boyo-Boys to stay by your side till you succumb to the inevitable wastage. He plys you with personalized jest and frolic, and remonstrates with anyone who dares to offer you contumely!"

Jack could barely conceal his dismay. "Those – those are my only choices?"

"What more could a sensible man want? The Worrybird is an incorrigable opponent, and no one besides the recondite and rascally Uncle Bradley dares even to tamper with one! Be quick now, old gansel! Which will it be?"

Jack wimbled and wambled pitifully. "I have not even the three hundred crones for the humblest palliation. I was hoping for more triumphalist affronts and easier terms…"

"What! You dare to waste Uncle's invaluable chronospasms without funds in reserve! And then to derogate my nostrums as if you were a fellow engineer at a throwdown session of the Tinkerer's Sodality! Away with you, laggardly old momerath!"

Suddenly, the Papyrus Mouther was by Jack's elbow. Without pleasant hostly ado, Jack was spun about and frog-marched from the Cave of the SFErical Monarch. Just before the heavy door slammed behind him, Jack could hear Uncle Bradley resume his litany of savantical willfullness: "Engage the services of ten thousand more Glissandos, and another dozen Kriegsteins!"

Summarily and insultively ejected onto the cheesily porous cobbled terrace before the SFErical Emporium, true night pressing down from above like a corpulent lover, Jack knew himself at the end of both his abilities and the universe's possibilities. The weight of the Worrybird seemed suddenly Atlasian. At the first "Never again, but not yet!", every nerve in Jack's poor frame thrilled with galvanic imbroglication. He hung his head, able to focus only on the snailslick cobbles.

Three tags of payrus skittered by just then, and without much hope Jack used the last of his scanty vigor to retrieve them.

Seek Saint Fiacre.

Now was veracious and lordly midnight come without fear of fleering misrecognition to occupy Drudge City like a famously conquering cubic khan. Much too low in the sky hung a sherberty scoop-hollowed partial moon like a slice of vanilla-icecream-sheened cantaloupe half-eaten by a finicky godling. Stars shown in the space between the tips of the errant satellite's horns. Insect-seeking sweaterbats, their calls of "stitch-stitch!" leavening the mist, thronged the curvaceous canyons formed by the tottering towers of home and office, both kinds of hobbledehoy establishment darkened as their inhabitants blissfully or troubledly slept. Only meeps and monks, strumpets and troubadors, witlings and mudlarks were abroad at this hour – at least in this dismal section of Drudge City. Perhaps among the delightful theaters in the district known as Prisbey's Heaves, or in the saucer-slurping cafes of Mechanics' Ramble, good citizens yet disported themselves without fear of encountering lurking angina-anklers or burrow-bums. And surely – most sadly of a certainty – at Boris Crocodile's Beanery and Caustics Bar, ghosty-eyed Nori Nougat was even at this moment frugging with ledge-browed Zack Zither, while Stinky Frankie Konk tortured banshee wails from his hybrid instrument.

But out here, where putrid Ashmolean Alley and rancid Rotifer Gangway ranked as the only streets of distinction, no such gaiety could be found. There lolloped only a besmirched and bedaubed and bedemoned Jack Neck, bustedly dragging himself down block after block, in search of Saint Fiacre.

The last Jack had heard – from Dirty Bill Brownback, in fact – rumors of a Saint sighting had recently wafted from out Ubidio way. No guarantee that said sighted Saint was named Fiacre, or that he was even still present. Saints had a disconcerting propensity to phase-shift at random. Yet poor Jack Neck had no other phantom to pursue, so thence he now leathered.

Two hours past the night's navel, Jack Neck emerged from encircling buildings onto bare-tiled Pringle Plaza. In the middle of the civic space ruminated an eyelid-shuttered naked Saint.

The Saint had once been human. After much spiritual kenning and abstemious indulgences, making the choice to give him or herself up entirely to the avariciously bountiful forces of the Indeterminate, the human had morpholyzed into a Saint. The Saint's trunk had widened and spread into a bulbous heap, from which sprouted withered legs and off-kilter arms, but no visible generative parts. Instead, out of the trunk at queer angles protruded numerous quasi-organic spouts and intakes similar to rusty gutter-pipes. The Saint's neck was a corded barrel supporting a pointy-peaked head on which the features had wandered north, south, east and west. Overall, the creature was a pebbled mushroom-white, and three times the size of Jack. Around this living interface with the Indeterminate, the air wavered whorlfully.

Humble as a wet cat, Jack approached the Saint. When the Worrybird-carrier was within a few yards of the strange being, the Saint opened his eyes.

"Are thee Fiacre?" nervously intoned Jack, who had never cozened with a Saint before, nor ever thought to.

"Aye."

"I was sent to thee. This bumptious bird I would begone."

The Saint pondered for a chronospasm. "You must perambulate round the Inverted Stupa for three hours, reciting without cease, 'Always once again, and perhaps now.'"

"This will cause the Worrybird to relinquish its hold?"

"Not at all. The procedure will simply give me further time to peer into the Indeterminate. But nonetheless, you must attend with precision to my instructions, upon pain of rasterbation."

"As you say, oh Saint."

Luckily, the Inverted Stupa was only half a league onward. Hurrying with renewed hope, Jack soon reached the famous monument. In the middle of another peopleless plaza, lit fitfully by torches of witch's-hair, was a railed pit of no small dimensions. Looking down over the rail, Jack saw the vertiginous walls of the Inverted Stupa, lighted windows stretching down to the earth's borborygmous bowels, deeper by far than even Baron Sugarslinger's realm.

Without delay, Jack began his circular hegira, chanting his Saintly mantra.

"Always once again, and perhaps now. Always once again, and perhaps now…"

The Worrybird seemed in no wise discommoded by Jack's croaking exertions. Jack tried not to lose his resurgent tentative cheer. At long last, just when Jack's legs – both good and bad – felt ready to snap, a nearby clock tolled five, releasing him to return to the Saint.

Saint Fiacre sat unchanged, a yeasty enigmatic effigy with a face like an anthropomorphic cartoon breadloaf.

"You have done well, old mockmurphy. Come close now, and cover my sacred Intake Number Nine with your palm."

Jack sidle-stepped up to the Saint, entering the zone where his vision burbled. He raised his hand toward the properly labelled bodypipe, then capped the opening with the flat of his permanently work-roughened hand.

Instantly, the insidious and undeniable vacuum-suck of ten dozen black holes!

Jack's hand was quickly pulled in. Before he could even gasp, his shoulder was pressed to the treacherous Intake Number Nine. Then Jack felt himself drawn even further in! Oddly he experienced no pain. Only, he was sure, because he was already dead.

Soon Jack was ingulped headwise up to both shoulders. His hump delayed his swallowment slightly, but then, thanks to a swelling surge of pull-power, even his abused hump was past the rim.

And the Worrybird too? Apparently not! Peeled off like a potato skin was that manfaced mordaunt! But what of their commingled Akashic Aura? Only Gossip Time would tell...

Within seconds, Jack was fully through Intake Number Nine. Then began a journey of sense-thwarting intricacy. Through a maze of bloodlit veiny pipes Jack flowed like the slorq at Krespo's, until he finally shot out of a funnel-mouth into ultracoloured drifts of sheer abundant nothingness that smelled like a bosomy woman and tasted like Shugwort's Lemon Coddle. Here existence was a matter of wayward wafts and dreamy enticements, so connubially unlike the pestiferous hurlyburly of mundane existence. Time evaporated, and soon Jack did too...

Early morning in Pringle Plaza, sunlight like the drip of candyapple glaze. Sanitation chimps were about their cleaning, sweeping litter and leaf into the open mouths of attendant roadhogs. A travelling preacher had unfolded his pocket altar and was preaching the doctrine of Klacktoveedsedsteen to a yawning group of bow-tied office dandies. Saint Fiacre, having just given a lonely little girl the second head she had requested, suddenly quivered all over as if stricken by Earthquake Ague, then decoted a real-as-mud, sprightly-as-fleas Jack Neck from Outflow Number Three.

Jack got woozily to his tiny feet. "Saint Fiacre, I thank thee!"

"Say twenty-seven Nuclear Novenas nightly, invoking the names of Gretchen Growl, Mercy Luna and the Rowrbazzle. And do not stick your foolish mummer's head out any more windows without forethought."

And then Saint Fiacre was gone.

Having polished off his supper and seen the merry Motherway lickily attending to his bonedog privates, mawkly old Jack Neck now commonly got to Boris Crocodile's a little later each night. Those Nuclear Novenas took time, and he did not trust either his tongue or his pledged determination after a shot of Dinky Pachinko's dumble-rum. Neither could his saviorology be allowed to interfere during the day with Jack's ardent eyeballing of the exploits of the mighty Dean Tesh, Motorball Mauler! So postprandial were his doxologies.

But despite the slight change in his schedule, Jack still entered the Beanery and Caustics Bar in mid-stridulation of hookah-banjo, still found his favourite reserved barstool awaiting him, still feasted his rheumy eyes on the flirtsome gavotteners atrot, and still affirmed to any and all who would lend an ear, "Yessir, assuming you can get through the rough spots, life can turn out mighty sweet!"

This story was inspired by the paintings of Chris Mars.

THE DARK ONE
A A Attanasio

Our extreme curve has now reached its apex. The following story may not seem challenging at first but you will later find yourself drawn personally into the story. On his website, at www.aaattanasio.com, Attanasio states: "I'm a novelist obsessed with the power of fiction to impart strangeness, hermetic wisdom and, above all, wonder."

All of his books have reflected his fascination with what drives the wheels of history to bring us where we are today and take us beyond. Initially drawn by an interest in Lovecraftian fiction and horror, Alfred Attanasio (b. 1951), sold his first stories in 1972. His first published novel was Radix *(1981), the start of what became the Radix Tetrad. Its exploration of a young man's voyage of self-discovery bears some comparison with the following story. His other books include the Arthor series, starting with* The Dragon and the Unicorn *(1994), which recasts the Arthurian legend on a cosmic scale, and the historical fantasy swashbuckler* Wyvern *(1988). Attanasio never does things by halves, as you will see.*

"Time is thingless," the old sorcerer told his last disciple. "Yet, you are about to see the source of it."

Tall, gaunt and completely bald, the sorcerer stood against the night dressed in straw sandals and a simple white robe. Narrow as a wraith, his raiment glowing gently in the starlight on the steep cliff above the temple city, he seemed about to blow away.

The disciple, a blue-eyed barbarian boy named Darshan, knelt before him on his bare knees, the hem of his kilt touching the ground. He lowered his face and closed his eyes. Whatever curiosity he had for why his masters, the priests, had awakened and brought him here stilled momentarily in the chill desert air, and he awaited his fate with expectant submission.

"Look at me!" the old man demanded, his voice resonant among the vacancies of the cliffs.

Darshan lifted his gaze hesitantly toward the withered figure and saw in the slim light that the sorcerer was smiling. He had a face as hewn as a temple stone, and it was a strange experience for the boy to find a friendly smile in that granite countenance. During the four years that Darshan had served as floor-scrubber and acolyte at the Temple of the Sun, he had seen the sorcerer often in the royal processions and ceremonies – but the haughty old man had always appeared in public garbed in cobra-hood mantle and plumed headdress. Now he was bare-shouldered, his skeletal chest exposed, reptilian flesh hanging like throat frills from his jaw.

"Why are you here?" the old man asked.

"The priests of Amon-Re sent me, lord."

"Yes – they sent you. Because I ordered them to. Do you know who I am?" He peered at the boy, the whole immense dark sky glistening in his eyes.

"Lord, you are the supreme vizier. The man of the high places."

"Yes. That is who I am." He stood taller, stretched out his bony arms, and spoke in a flat voice: "Supreme vizier of the People, counsel to kings, master sorcerer." Without warning, he sat down in the dust, and Darshan's shock at the sight of the holy man squat-legged on the ground almost toppled him. He had to touch the earth with one hand to stay on his knees. The sorcerer's sagacious grin thickened. "And you are Darshan. I know, for I am the one who sent the ships to seek you."

Darshan leaned back under the weight of his puzzlement.

"Well, not you specifically," the sorcerer added, hunching his frail body under the night. He looked tiny. "Just a child, boy or girl, *any* child, as long as the tyke was wild and not of the People. The child had to belong to no one. You are the one they found."

Darshan thought back, remembering the few fleeting memories and scraps of idle speculation an old priest had once offered him of the boy's young, insignificant life. He had been born on a heath in a northern land, in a bracken hovel with many mouths for the wind to sing through. His birth mother had been an outcast from her clan, exiled for madness but sane enough in the way of animals to survive on the wind-trampled moorlands.

His first memory was of her scent – a bog musk, creaturely, hot. Even now, he was fond of the fragrance of rain-wet fur. His second memory was of her telling him that she had never known a man. She had told him this many times, her simple speech gusty with fervor, saying it over and over again until she had become as redundant as the lamentations of the wind. To the day she died trying to cross an iced river, she had moved and talked in a frenzied rush. Ranting about never knowing a man, about beast eyes in the sky, about the smell of darkness in the sun-glare, and the thunder of hooves when the wind stilled, clearly she had been mad. He had realized this only years later, living among the People, though at the time, when he had first begun to reflect on his life, he knew nothing of madness, only that his mother had been true in her devotion to him, and he to her.

In his seventh winter, she fell into the river and vanished under the ice, all in an instant, right before his eyes. Standing three feet behind her, he had been attentive only to the twine net where she carried their next meal, a dead badger, the blood not yet frozen on its head where she had stoned it. That was the last he saw of her, the dead creature caught for an instant at the broken edge of the ice. He remembered clutching for it and it jumping from him, sliding into the black water as though it were yet alive.

After she was gone, he had survived only because he had pretended she was still with him, instructing him what to do. With the thaw, he had followed the river, looking for her body. He never found her. The corpses of animals still frozen or caught in the floods kept him alive. Moving with the river, he never went back.

He had stayed in the wilderness, avoiding contact with all people, and he had moved south to escape the winter that had killed his mother. For two years, he had stayed hidden, and then on a rocky coast by a sun-brassed sea, he spied his first boats. He didn't know what they were. He had thought them to be great floating beasts. He could not see that they were carrying men until they had spotted him also. He had fled, but the men had horses and cunning, and eventually they found him hiding in a tide cave.

Taken as a slave and brought to this great kingdom of the south, at first he had behaved like a caught animal – but his ferocity had been matched by the awe he felt for his captors. Their kingdom was a fabulous river valley of boats, armies, slave-hordes, and immense stone temples.

Many of the slaves were driven to labor like beasts, yet the boy himself was never beaten. He was employed by the priests as a floor-scrubber, and in return he was fed well, clothed, and bunked with the young students of the temple. They had given him a name, and eventually he had learned their language and their ways.

And now, four years later and a lifetime wiser, here he was under the smoldering stars with the kingdom's supreme vizier – a man too holy to stare at directly, too divine to touch earth – an old man sitting in the dust beside him and telling him not only that he was aware of the boy's lowly presence but that in fact he had ordered his capture! The thought filled Darshan with dread, for he had delighted in his anonymity. Being chosen implied a mission, and he had neither the desire nor the belief in himself to think he was capable of doing anything heroic for these great people.

"Do you know why I sent for you?" the sorcerer asked with a glimmering intensity.

"No, lord," the boy replied, peering at him from the sides of his eyes.

"You are to take my place." Another smile tautened the waxy flesh across the old man's skull-face, and he hissed with small, tight laughter when he saw the boy's look of utter incredulity. "Believe me, I am not toying with you. Nor am I mad. You will have plenty of time to get used to being a sorcerer. Time, that thingless word – there is plenty of that."

The boy's hands opened futilely before him. "I am but a slave…"

"So it seems to the present generation. But you shall outlive them and their grandchildren and their grandchildren's great-grandchildren."

At the boy's gasp, another of the old man's smiles flickered in the darkness. "I am not speaking symbolically, Darshan. I do not mean your works shall outlive them – for you shall do no works." His voice assumed a ritual cadence. "Symbols are a substitute for works. Works are a substitute for power. Power resides in stillness. That is the secret of the universe."

Truly, Darshan thought, *the vizier is mad!* He dared not voice that doubt. Rather, he mustered his courage to say, "I do not understand, lord."

The sorcerer moved closer and put a dry hand on the boy's shoulder. A coldness flowed from it. "Speak to me about what you do not understand."

Darshan shivered. Words came quickly into his head but moved slowly to his mouth. "Lord, I am but a barbarian. I am a child, and from the Outside. I am nothing."

"And so power resides in you." The sorcerer's hand squeezed the boy's shoulder with a firm gentleness, and the cold sharpened. "Speak."

"Lord, I do not understand what power would reside in a worthless outsider."

"The power you are made empty to receive." The hand on Darshan's shoulder became ice, and when it lifted away blue fire sheathed it.

A scream balked in the boy's throat, hindered by the benignity of the sorcerer's expression.

"You see?" the old man chuckled. "The power is already leaving me and going to you."

Rainbow light flowed like smoke from the upheld hand and coiled toward Darshan's face. He pulled away, horrified, and the spectral vapor shot at him like a viper, striking him between the eyes.

Cold fire paralyzed the boy, and his vision burst into a tunnel of infalling flames and shadows. The rush stalled abruptly, and, in an instant, the desert skyline vanished and the span of night deepened. Sun feathers lashed the darkness, ribbons of starsmoke furling into the reaches of the night.

"This is the raith," the sorcerer's voice lit up within him. "This is the Land of the Gods!"

Together, wordlessly, they advanced among rivers of light that poured like bright fumes into a golden sphere of billowy energy. A dissolving sun, the sphere radiated pollen sparks in a slow flux against the blackness. Each spark was the surface of a mirror, the other side of which opened into a biological form.

"Touch one," the sorcerer commanded, and when the boy did as he was told, he found himself inside the grooved sight of an antelope bounding through white grass. Touching another, he was among swerving schools of fish.

"Life. All of it." The sorcerer's voice pulled Darshan away from touching another spark. "I am not taking you there. But once you establish yourself where we are going, all of this is yours." The weltering surface of the gold sphere spun serenely before them in the haze of its rendings.

They drifted away from it, across spans of darkness vapory with fire. Alternating ice-winds and desert-blasts looped over their raith-senses. For a long time, they soared, pummeled by brutal gusts, until they burst into a darkness set at the back of the stars.

Darshan's flight stopped abruptly, and stillness seized him. He floated, alertly poised at the crystalcut center of clarity, so still that empty space itself seemed to writhe like a jammed swarming of eels. Flamboyant bliss saturated him. The was the top of the eagle's arc, the salmon's leap, the peak of midnight extending forever.

Immovable as the darkness of space, Darshan exulted. His life had suddenly become too minuscule to remember. The life of the People, too, had become the fleetest thought. Even the stones of their temples and tombs were breathing, their packed atoms shivering and blowing against the gelatinous vibrations of dark space.

Awe pierced the boy with the abrupt realization that the tumult of life, of existence itself, was far apart from him. He had become absolutely motionless.

Yet, with that very thought, the spell ended, and he found himself immediately back in his body on his knees before the aged sorcerer. With painful reluctance, Darshan peered about. The clamor of stars and the stink of dust nauseated him. He closed his eyes and groped inside himself for the eagle's poise.

"That stillness is your power," the sorcerer said in an urgent voice that made Darshan open his eyes. The old man's face glittered with tears. "It lies at the heart of everything." He gestured at the temples' torchlights and the lanterns and lamps of the city that shone in the dark valley like spilled jewels. Then, he looked up at the dangling stars. "Even the gods."

The barbarian boy gazed at the old man with unabashed amazement. "Then why is this stillness no longer yours?"

The sorcerer swelled closer, expansive in his joy, and he took Darshan's chilled hands in his icy ones and shook them with the emphasis of his words: "It *chose* me – as it now chooses you!" His voice hushed confidentially. "Ten thousand years ago, in a region that we presently call Cush, I too was an orphan, as you are, a savage, alone with the wilderness. Wholly by chance, as happened with you, I was led to the master of stillness who had come before me. He was thousands of years old then, as I am now. He had found his fulfillment after millennia of grounding the stillness in time. That thingless word. Thingless for those such as we who have know the stillness. It is only the combat of the gods that makes time a thing for everyone else. Time is the dimension of the gods' battlefield. Their clashes for dominance stir people's hearts with dreams. Those dreams, in turn, frenzy into ideas: tools are discovered, animals domesticated, royalty invented, religion, sacrifices, war. Now, even cities are called into being."

Tears gleamed silverly in the creases of his broad grinning. "Who cares? I certainly don't. My time is up. I have lived the stillness – right here in the middle of the battlefield! I have seen the gods aspire. I have seen generations sacrificed to their grand schemes. A great empire has risen from the red dust. The People think their empire will endure forever. But I tell you, you will see all this as dust again and all the People forgotten. Only the gods will go on. The dreaming will continue.

"Other empires will appear and disappear among the battling gods. You alone, alone as you have always been, will live the stillness – an enemy to the gods. For you alone, time will be thingless, for you will know the source of it. You will have been inside the mother of the gods. You will have the power to live the stillness."

Darshan was thirteen-years-old that night when the sorcerer, sitting in the dust, spoke to him. Nothing in his four years of scouring temple floors had prepared him for it. The priests who had sent him to the sorcerer had wondered about that meeting. Some had leered, suspecting lewdness. The sorcerer himself soon disappeared mysteriously. Yet, the boy went on scrubbing floors. And the raith went on dreaming him.

After that night, however, the work became immeasurably easier. Body dazzling with a vigor he mistook for approaching manhood,

Darshan excelled at athletics. And he astonished even the arrogant lector-scribes with his mental stamina as he absorbed everything they dared teach him.

Several years later, the raith's dream shifted, and Darshan became a certifiable wonder, the countenance of the gods, the boy who never aged. The priests worshipped him. Warlords offered tribute. Every difficulty in the region required his assuaging presence.

For a long time, Darshan prayed to the gods to restore his former life. But his prayers had no wings. The king learned of him, and he was removed from the temple and taken upriver to the royal city. There, he became a child-divinity sent by the gods to affirm the ancestral sorcery of the kings.

Life became a ceremony of walled gardens, incense-tattered rooms and banquets. Twice a year, he was portaged into the green of the fields to release a falcon that carried the prayers of the People to the sun god. Well-being clouded about him like an electric charge, and he was revered by the aristocracy even as the court aged and their tombs rose on the desert floor.

The years flowed by, and he grew wise on the dying of others. He took wives who bore his children, and he loved them all with sentimental delirium. His family shared riverboat mansions and superficialities, all of life's caprices, as they aged beyond him and shriveled away. He took younger wives and had more children. And all the while, he blessed the People and the riverland, and the kingdom prospered. He himself did not know how. He had forgotten the words of the sorcerer. He thought he was a child-god.

Three kings and a century later, with his first grandchildren's grandchildren older than he, he had aged a year. His body was fourteen-years-old.

Not until he was seventeen and two dynasties had risen and collapsed did he begin to remember. Dreams were ephemera. Families, kings, dynasties were ghosts, incidental to the emptiness in which they teemed.

Another six hundred years of orchard gardens and ripening families and he saw through to this truth.

He gave up family life. Rubbed smooth like a river stone after spawning forty generations of sons and daughters, children who grew up to be wives, warriors, queens, merchants, priestesses, all fossils now, and even their children fossils, he felt carnal desire slide away from him. He wanted no more lovers or children, and the machinations of power bored him.

For the next thousand years, he retreated into anonymity, seeking unity with the People. In various guises, he wandered the earth questing experience and knowledge. Eventually, the dreams themselves began to wear thin for Darshan. Experience turned out to be suffering. Knowledge was boundaries.

After long centuries of striving, Darshan finally accepted that he was no godling. He was a ghost. He returned to the river kingdom where the cursed gift had come to him. He searched for the sorcerer and after many years found him – not in the world but in his dreaming.

The sorcerer came to him one evening at sea. Darshan, serving on a freight boat hauling giant cedar timbers from the eastern forests back to the kingdom, dozed in a cord hammock slung between the prow and a shaggy log. Through half-lidded eyes, he stared ahead at the rinds of daylight in the west until sleep swelled in him and the raith uncurled.

All at once, his body unfurled and he found himself rushing headlong through windy darkness and fuming leakages of light. A gold sphere swirled before him veiled in a misty flotage of sparks. His flight slowed, and he hung among the tiny pieces of light until he remembered this vision from hundreds of lifetimes back, from his one short interview with the sorcerer.

The sun-round glare inside the starmist was Re, the god of his first learning. This was the creator immersed in his creation, each gempoint of the endless glittering a mind. The fulgurant light blazed with all being. And the drift of the sparks, stately as clouds, revealed the invisible spiral of time.

A religious hush thrummed to a droneful music in Darshan's bones. Here was deity! Here was the source of his own unreckonable fate. He knew that he had to keep his wits about him and remember everything of this great darkness fizzling with scattered light. This was the place that the sorcerer had called the raith.

Smoldering hulks of color and brightness fumed against the utter black. These, he recognized as the gods with their gloaming abstract bodies. All he had to do was stare at them to feel who they were: the crimson smoke and slithering banners of War, the green simmering vibrations of Plants, the surging floral hues of Sex, the ruffling blue flow of River, endless gods arrayed in smoky radiance as far as he could see.

All being burns! he marveled, drifting through the blaze, awed by the apparently random yet balanced pattern of the raith. Alongside the red feathered energy of War drizzled the violet realm of the dead. And above it all shone the blue depths of Peace.

He descended into the gray flutter of the dead with the image of the sorcerer firmly in his mind. Many familiar faces rose toward him through the trickling light, the shivering shapes of all his many families, all the lovers and children who had lived ahead of him into death. They tangled like entrails, shifted like weather, speaking to him in hurt voices not their own. He recognized then the filthy face of the dead. They were melting into each other! They were dissolving and being reabsorbed into the swirl of tenuous light.

Some of the dirty light drifted in a haze of limbs and faces toward the blue embers of Peace. Some smoked toward the red ranges of War. The rest dithered in human shapes.

Darshan lifted away, soaring over the gray pastures of snaggled bodies. The sorcerer wasn't among the dead. The sorcerer had belonged to the dark spaces and not the light. Just as he had said.

Darshan expanded into the dark, and the gold sphere of Re in its aura of sparkling lives loomed into view. But now only the darkness enwombing the light seemed real. He flung himself into the emptiness.

His eyes shattered, his atoms flew apart. He disappeared.

But the wind of the emptiness whirled all his parts together and blew him back into alertness. Stunned, he hung in the raith-dark before the fiery mist of Re – and the words of the sorcerer returned to him: "You alone, alone as you have always been, will live the stillness – an enemy to the gods."

Darshan woke. He was still a young sailor on a cargo boat ladened with cedars sailing into the night. He was still a man with a thousand years of memories. But the memories were weightless in the expansive silence. The night sea would become a dawn landfall. The cedars, faithful to their doom, already lived as rafters and pillars on their way to the termite's ravenous freedom or an enemy's torch. And the cargo boat would find its way to the bottom of the sea and give its shape to a vale of kelp and polyps. And the young sailor would weary of the sea and be forgotten. And Darshan, too, would be forgotten, swept away in the great migrations of Asian tribes that swarmed across Europe and North Africa a millennium before Christ.

He roamed among the different peoples, unseen, or seen in a peaceable light. The stillness threading through his eyes and pores and atom-gaps protected him: Its lack drew energy to him wherever he was, and the energy was health, ample food, treasures, and the fealty and love of others. Despite this abundance, he felt nothing for others. He felt nothing but serene emptiness. And when he did somehow fall in love with someone or a cause, the stillness vanished, and he was left hungering and at the mercy of others.

Sometimes even that was good. Though he had exhausted every kind of living during his first thousand years in the river kingdom, he was occasionally nostalgic for passion. And he was still aging a year for every century. Hence, even he was aware of his mortality. Pain and peril, too, had their appetites for him. More of the gods' dreaming.

Darshan had never been seriously ill or injured. The stillness protected him. The mangling forces ignored him even when he was stupid with his passions.

As a wanderer, he never thought much about his fate. Often, he surged into trances, swooping through the abysses of the raith, trembling with the malice and insane love of the gods until he could stand no more, and then plunging into utter black nothing.

He cohabited with a dim awareness that he served some function for the stillness. The old sorcerer had spoken of grounding the stillness in time. But at the time that he had heard this, rational thought had not been one of the gods feeding off of him.

Darshan lived his fate as a watcher, letting the ubiquitous nothing appear before him as anything at all. His personality changed with his name and place. For more than a century, he lived as a wealthy Phoenician purple manufacturer, hiring a complex of villages to harvest the banded dye-murex and create the most demanded colour in the world.

After that, he dwelt alone on the barren, wind-cumbered coasts of the Orkneys for two centuries, living off nettles and fish, sleepy and holy in the amplitude of winter.

Then, yearning company, he went south and wandered through Europe as a seer with the Celtic droves.

At the time of the Buddha, he was a twenty-eight year-old warrior prince in Persia. Five centuries later, he wandered with the gypsies through the Balkans when Christ was in Jerusalem. Another four hundred years and he was among the gangs that toppled Rome.

Once, he sailed with a Palestinian crew across the Atlantic and lived for several more centuries as a nomad in the jungles, deserts and grasslands of the western continents. He was at the crestpoint of the falcon's dive, suspended in time almost wholly timeless.

The nothing became well grounded in him. His very poise within the seething temporality grew steady enough that it created a pattern in the raith. Over his twenty-five centuries on earth, his power in the hidden reality had grown sufficient resonant to match the harmonies of the masters of stillness who had come before him.

Wrapped in the skin of a jaguar, shivering on a mountain scarp in the Andes, his sacrifice fulfilled itself. The mind of the dark spaces entered him, and his surrender became total. Now, he was the Dark One. Made of light slowed down to matter like everyone else, he had given all of himself to nothing like no one else. Given? More like, taken. He had been chosen from among the rays of creation by the space that the rays cut. He had become the wound, the living nothing.

Curious about the old world, he returned to Europe with the Norsemen who had been sent by their Christian king to Greenland to spread the gospel and whom a storm had carried west to Vinland. Europe in the High Middle Ages reminded him of the river valley kingdom where his power had begun. There, the temple of Amon-Re had competed with feudal lords for control of the domain. Here, the papacy served as the temple and the warlords remained the same, only the trappings had changed. Cathedrals instead of pyramids.

He wandered nameless for a long time as the power within him continued making its connections between earth and raith. He was a tinker, a minstrel, a carnival clown. His raith dreams fell into darkness. He entered the space between the enmeshing archons, the interstice of being and non, between the stars and the buried – where the Dark One watched.

When the dreams of the gold sphere in its mist of sparks began again, he was a Danish village's latrine ditch keeper, mulching the sewage with forest debris for use in the fields. The Dark One's thoughts began thinking him. Always before, there had been living and silence – the living given, thick with health and stamina, the silence bright with raith light and comfort. Now, there was something new.

Thoughts began crystallizing out of the inner dark. He needed a wide space of time in which to simply sit and face the immensity of them; so, he went into the mountains and let his dreams lead him to gold. Afterward, he settled in Italy, where he established himself as a wealthy nobleman from the north.

Sitting in his enclosed garden in Firenze, guarded from the outside world by courtyards and loggia, he opened himself to the clear music of thoughts emerging from the raith. The archons of precision and rational thought, simultaneously hampered and encouraged by the archon of war, had begun fusing into the complex of science.

Initially, he did not see the point of it all. Advances in boat design increased his revenues as a merchant, but that wealth was offset by advances in weaponry, which intensified the civil wars and cost him several of his estates. Nonetheless, he remained open to the thought-shaping patterns that the Dark One was thinking.

He was very good at being the stillness by this time. Everything floated through him: his body, his very awareness. The archons of protein synthesis and digestion, of ever-shifting emotions and thoughts, created him. The archons of wealth and poverty, power and impuissance, governed him. He was the battlefield of the gods.

The most powerful of all the gods was the Dark One – the uncreated and uncreating. More than a destroyer or death and its dissolvings. Void.

He began thinking about the Dark One. He wondered about its source and end, and who he was in that synapse, hemi-divine, living centuries as years, free of disease, protected from accidents and violence...

Over time, before the profound and absolutely unalterable flow of generations, his memories and rationalities froze into constellations as coldly distant and immutable as the stars.

Empires crossed Europe like shadows of the shifting stars. Science invented itself. By 1700, the Dark One had established a trading company in London, and he called himself Arthur Stilmanne. Privately, he funded research in every branch of science. A way was becoming clear. After aeons, a way was opening for the Dark One.

The sorcerer returned among the black gulfs of the raith. Almost four thousand years after he had initiated Darshan as an embodiment of the nothing, the old man reappeared in a raith dream. His body loomed out of the astral dark bound in shroudings. That, Arthur knew from his years of symbol-gazing in the raith, meant his master's limbs, his extension into the four dimensions, were restrained – he belonged to the void. But the sorcerer's head was clear – his knowledge and intent were accessible. His bald head gleamed in the gray light like a backlit bacterium: His knowing shone radiantly, suffused with the living energy of the void.

Arthur willed himself to touch the specter. Immediately, a voice came to him whose familiarity twitched in him like his own nerves: "Darshan, you have served the stillness well. The centuries have emptied you, and now you are full of your own power." The sorcerer's face pressed closer in the dream, gloomy with sleep, his stare an aching wakefulness. "Who are you?" the old visage asked.

Arthur responded instantly, "The Dark One."

A breath slipped from the sorcerer's gray lips, "It is so." And his countenance slackened with stupor.

After that encounter, Arthur's mind turned in on itself. The constellations of his long-thinking connected, looping into the veins and arteries of a body of knowledge. He saw himself finally as a response to the dialectic of life. Others just like he was now had existed before, randomly selected organisms, each metaordered not by life but by an intelligence equal and opposite to life.

Newton's work on vector forces inspired him. He had been given a shape by emptiness so that he might bring all shapes back to emptiness. Guided by Leibniz's exploration of the binary system of Asian philosophy, he began thinking of himself as a dot of ordered chaos in a world of chaotic order. His mission became clear. He and all the others who had preceded him had come to end existence. But how could that be?

During the nineteenth century, Stillman Trading Company flourished, and he kept himself moving around the continent to obscure the fact that he was continually succeeding himself as his own son. Arthur Stillman VI, of Victoria's Britain, poured vast sums into biological research, believing the insane rush of evolution could be ended by a virulent plague hostile to all forms of life. Not until Arthur Stillman VIII and the quantum research of the early twentieth century did he realize – with an authoritative irony – that the weapon he sought was not in the world but in the atoms of the world.

Arthur learned more about himself and the nature of reality in the last forty years than he had in the previous four thousand. The means to exterminate life and end the four billion year-old torment had emerged on its own. Arthur had done nothing to anticipate or promote it.

Reflecting on that, he came to see that he had never had any real influence in history. He was inert, like a stone time had swallowed. Eventually, time would void him. Inside the stone was a secret silence. Some Zen monks had alluded to it. But all others kept it hidden, even from themselves. He stayed close to that silence, and everything came to him.

In the mid-twentieth century, death itself came to Arthur Stillman, approaching closer than ever before. Accidents stalked him. A milk bottle teetered off a window ledge nine stories above his head and smashed at his feet. Lightning punched through the roof of his house and blasted the reading lamp at his bedside. On the highway, a tire exploded and sent him hurtling helplessly off the road and into a forest, where his car erupted into a fireball the instant after he was hurled through the windshield. During his six week hospital stay, mix-ups in medication nearly killed him twice.

Arthur understood that he had an enemy powerful enough to break the stillness that had protected him for several thousand years. Somewhere, lightworkers had begun working very hard indeed to destroy the Dark One. He knew why. Science had become his latest, most deadly weapon, and if the lightworkers did not stop him now, he would soon have the technology to destroy all of creation.

"Science," he became fond of saying as the doomful promise of the millennium approached yet again, "is heavy enough to bend every path toward it into circles. We'll never understand it all, never reach the center of omniscience. But we've circled close enough to science, to objective knowledge, to realize that whatever we thought we knew about reality we can throw away. With science, the human spirit stands with the creator spirit in the grave of everything that came before, in the midden heap of religion and superstition, on the dunghill of all past cultures. Science reveals the truth of things as they always were, to the beginning and the end. Science creates with a beauty as ancient as we are new."

Arthur burned with a passion for science, because it explained to him his singularity and his origin. From biologists, who studied the DNA differences in mitochondria of people from across the world and who traced human lineage back to one female ancestress hundreds of thousands of years ago, he came to accept the importance of his uniqueness. As Eve had mothered the mutants who would evolve into war-frenzied humans, he would father the energies that would return them all to nothing.

From physicists, who discovered that the four dimensions people experienced were actually projections of other compacted dimensions in a space smaller than 10^{-33} centimeter, he found the raith. The radii of curvature of all the dimensions except the familiar four of spacetime were smaller than atoms – in fact, smaller than the grain of spacetime itself. In that compact region, spacetime quantized, that is, space and time separated into realms of their own. That he knew had to be the raith, where omnipresent archons floated timelessly and evolving beings extended into endless distances.

Science even explained his existence. He had emerged as an epiphenomenon of a symmetry event: particles appeared spontaneously in the void all the time, leaking out of the vacuum, out of nothing, but always in pairs – electrons and positrons, negative and positive, existing separately for an interval, then annihilating each other. He was one of those particles, compelled into existence by the appearance of his opposite. The other was light itself, never still, energizing endless forms and activities.

He was the Dark One, yearning for quiescent timelessness. Light was the many. He was the one. Light was life. He was death.

To amplify his power in the raith, Stillman began creating power cells of human minds entrained to his will. He built a group-mind that he could control. There was no dearth of material. Authorized as a psychiatrist by the finest medical institutions in the United States, where he had effortlessly earned numerous degrees in medicine, psychopathology, and neural chemistry, he used his multibillion dollar trust to found Stillman Psychiatric Hostels. The hostels were free of charge and open to anyone with a mental health problem, with or without insurance.

By the mid-nineties, Arthur had a hostel in each state and dozens overseas, all of them packed. He hired the best qualified staff at competitive salaries, and many hundreds of people benefited. Hundreds of others were personally attended to by Arthur Stillman himself, who used drugs and hypnosis to open their psychic centers to his preternatural will. Once a subject had been treated by Arthur, that personality bonded to him in the raith. They appeared outwardly healed – but within, they belonged to the Dark One.

When the accidents began, Arthur knew that he was closing in on the means to destroy creation. He knew that by using his powerful group mind to feed power to the archons of war and chaos in the raith, he had alerted lightworkers across time and space to the real threat of his presence.

His true archenemies, he knew, were the progenitors of the world's lightworkers – the cave masters. They were the first humans who, a hundred thousand years ago and more, had learned to enter the raith and identify with the radiant diamondshape of the original light, the creation fire in its first instant out of the singularity that had birthed the cosmos. Their initial link with this preterit force, when all things were pure light, spanned time. The cave masters' early spells had revealed the secrets of fire, songdances, healing, and – as their raith-work widened through the ages – stoneworking, planting and the wondrous mystery of metals with its powers of purity and combination. Their identification with the light expanded and cooled into the shapes of all things and made them the natural nemesis of the Dark One.

Time, that thingless word, was an illusion. Arthur learned that in the twentieth century and began to use that potent knowledge to reach across time and strike directly at his enemies with his raith power. And they, successively, strove to reach forward into their future and destroy him before he annihilated them and all the dreamwork humanity had made of the cold light in the void of space.

But subversive attacks against the Dark One in the raith were useless, for the Dark One was dark – he belonged to the black spaces, and no one could see him if he did not want to be seen. To be effective, the lightworkers had to focus their attack in the physical world. And so they employed channelers – or, as the cave masters called them, the adepts – gentle people usually unaware that they served as antennae for the power of the cave masters. Through the adepts, the lightworkers found their way to Arthur in the world and then attacked him in the raith. By distracting his raith-self, they had several times come close to destroying his physical body. But with each assault, the Dark One grew cleverer.

He learned about the cave masters, and he discovered how to use their adepts as conduits into the far past, where he could strike directly at the extinct race whose intelligence continued fostering civilization through the raith. If the cave masters had their way, war, disease, even involuntary death would be abolished. The human genome project existed because of their hope to shape healthier, more intelligent people. With the help of the lightworkers, humans could eventually carry their archons to the stars, and then the dreaming would never end. The torment for him and those like him who embodied the dark would be forever.

The latest adept arrived as a word-processor from Indiana, Eleanor Chevsky, divorced and with no children, whom his mental health foundation had hired. The symmetry law that had created the Dark One also allowed only one adept to exist at a time, and there was never any doubt for Arthur when the cave masters selected that time. Usually a blur of dizziness cued him to the process. A mess of vertigo flung him into a chair the day that Eleanor began channeling the lightworkers' murderous intent.

She was five ten, a natural blonde whose gray eyes had a slight slant, as though she were part Asian or up to some mischief. Voluminously bosomed and globe-bottomed as any goddess, she caught the fancy of most of the men and the envy of many of the women in the main office, who assumed her rapid promotion to Stillman's personal data manager had little to do with her computer skills.

In fact, Arthur's relationship with Eleanor was solely business, a job that situated her where he could watch her and wait for the cave masters to open her as a channel. She was a dangerous adversary, because she had no notion of her role as a raith-warrior. Yet, this sword cut both ways. Here was another chance for Arthur to push deep into the Ice Age when cortical complexity reached its peak with the large-brained Neanderthals, the first hominids to enter the raith. He kept her close and waited. Not that he wasn't sexually attracted to her himself. Over the ages, his sex drive waned and flourished in long, arrhythmic cycles. Lately, since the revelation of atomic weapons, his sexual appetite had been insatiable. But he denied himself Eleanor – for the time being. He needed her working in the world and accessible, a lure for the cave masters.

When she began to channel the lightworkers' homicidal purpose, he invited her to dinner at an opulent restaurant. He selected this restaurant, with its indoor waterfall and arbors of hanging blossoms, especially for its allusion to temporality. He ordered a meal of traditional depth-food: a timbale of bay scallops in green pepper sauce and paupiette of trout served in a hollowed blood orange – a minceur meal as sparse in calories as the last supper.

Eleanor dazzled in the presence of Arthur. Over the years, she had seen him numerous times at foundation functions and she had even chatted with him at his mansion during a diplomatic reception several years ago, and, though she had been working in the office adjacent to his for several months, this was her first meal with the notable man.

He spoke a soulful poetry to her that moved her deeply, "All of us under the sprawl of the sun are such provisional bodies, Eleanor – and by that truth alone we can honestly say that we are true friends to the beginning and the end. I'm glad to include you in my circle and to share with you what Shelley somewhere calls these dreams and visions that flower from the beds our bodies are."

Charmingly, he had invited her to bring a guest to share their meal

– a request he made her believe was a commonplace courtesy between him and those who had worked as hard for his foundation as she had. Her intention was to bring her latest beau, but, at the last minute, he took ill. Not wanting to show up alone and give the wrong impression, she asked her friends. All had other plans. Finally, a friend of a friend recommended you. And though you knew her not at all, the idea of an elegant meal and a pleasant evening with new people and one of them something of a luminary appealed to you.

You arrived early and were seated at the table when Eleanor arrived in the company of a skinny man with a starved monk's face, wispy gray hair, and startling blue eyes. At your first sight of him, a wash of pity soaked you, for he seemed so frail a man. Gently, you touched the delicate fellow's pallid hand.

Over the dainty fish dinner, while Doctor Stillman prattled on about mental hygiene and the usefulness of recording one's dreams, you kept noticing how his pink features seemed tremulous as a husked shellfish. Several times in his eagerness to make a point, the doctor went faint, his eyelids fluttered and his wide British vowels softened.

"It's too easy to get dispirited in this cruel and hazardous world," he said, looking at you trustfully. "Yet, we must carry on with our lives, and, more than that, we must find the strength to create. As I remind my patients, bitterness, depression, even shattering despair are transfiguring powers that potentially accompany and corrupt every creative endeavour, because creativity is, as the mythologists insist, an intrusion into the inviolable realm of deity – of abstraction – where we with our spastic actuality can never fully go. How dare we grotesque notochords create anything in this frigid and entropic universe? It takes a lot of arrogance, don't you think? One has to give everything to create anything."

He gestured to the elegant dinner on the table. "Out of many grains, one bread. Out of many grapes, one wine. Out of many words, one story. The only important story, needless to say, is the one we tell ourselves. In our time, the story that science tells makes clear that our literal kingdoms are only shadows of an invisible reality. We ourselves are then part of a much vaster totality. *Pars pro toto*, the part sacrificed for the whole – the grain, the grape, the word for the bread, the wine and the story that sustain us during our time in this wilderness of vacuum and gamma rays."

"You make it all sound so grim, Dr Stillman," you said as you buttered your bread. "What then is the purpose of life? Merely to endure?"

"Purpose?" Stillman shook his head sullenly and a remote gaze opened in those arctic eyes. "Alone in the wind with our dance, humanity seems like an old medicine dancer on the sliding scree of a mountainside under the vacant swirl of the failing heavens, all of our soul hovering in our incantation. To what shall we dedicate the palsy of our dance? Hm? To God? Is there a God? Science reveals nothing of that. No, my friends. We dance under the eternal night of space. We dance on a rock spinning around a nondescript star. We dance for ourselves alone. And by this solitude and pain, we learn the extremity of love."

By the time the second course was served – a Thai vegetable roll in peanut sauce – you were far more interested in the food than in listening to Arthur Stillman discourse on the purpose of life. But he was just warming up.

"Epistrophe," he acclaimed while pouring Fuilly-Roux into a crystal glass. "That's what psychiatry is all about. Art, too, for that matter. And madness."

"Excuse me," Eleanor interrupted, accepting the glass. It was her third. You were still lipping your first, and Stillman wasn't drinking. "Epistrophe?"

"Multiplicity, correspondence, reversion…" He felt for the meaning in the air with his long fingers, the nails precise. "No thing is just a thing. It's also a symbol, a sign for a complex of other things. So that everything that we know, everything we are, reverts to the unknown. Epistrophe is what keeps us running in circles."

"What makes the world go round," you quipped, not quite following him or caring. It was just an inconsequential evening in a formal setting, something to say you did.

While the waiter poured coffee, Arthur excused himself and went to the restroom. Sitting in a stall with the door closed, he removed the small compact he had surreptitiously extracted from Eleanor's purse and held it up before his face. His vicaresque features hardened, took on the taut fixity of a predator's attention. In the raith, the crystals of glare tensed into view, and the dark strata between the floating archons received him. Blustery colours whipped past, and he flared through cold time and an outer space darkness that split open into the huge clarity of a noon sky.

A dozen men and women in animal hides circled with dancing a pole stuck through its shadow into the earth. Their graven faces frowned, intent on this one instant – noon at the midpoint between equinox and solstice – while their arms frenzied and their quick footwork kicked up the long-suffering earth in dust and pebbles. Their song shimmered with their exertion and then broke off entirely as the Dark One's blur of stormlight gushed from the pole. Noon went black, and screams slipped in the air.

Killing was easy. With a raith-blade of electric shock, the Dark One hit the people at the back of their heads as they fled, and the jigsaw parts of their skulls flew apart. In the thundery, rolling darkness, barbed wires of lightning lashed, and the bodies scattered like petals. Moments later, the inksmoke darkness coiled in on itself and drained back into the wooden pole piercing its shadow. A dozen corpses lay in the thick sunlight.

A hungry shrike noticed and began to turn on the pivot of the wind.

Arthur bobbed out of his trance and observed that the mirror of the compact had turned liver red. The focus of raith energy on the silver nitrate of the mirror had been strong enough to dent the orthorhombic crystal molecules of the mirror into flakes of hexagonal red corundum. The geometry of the change displayed itself stereoscopically in his mind's eye, and a serene psychic clarity permeated him. He had killed many of his enemies. To maintain the symmetry, it was time now to make a new friend, to create an ally out of some mind in its squirrel cage.

The after effects of the power he had released accompanied Arthur back to the table, and both Eleanor and you remarked on the brightened vigor in him. When the dessert trolley came by, he selected a velvety chocolate mud pie, black as earth. You lifted your water glass to your lips. The ice clicked against your teeth and went still as a snapshot. Fear grabbed your heart as you realized you were paralyzed, as frozen as the air rays in the ice under your nose.

And in the next leaden moment, the room turned gold. By an alchemy you suddenly knew too well, you understood everything. Arthur's whole story entered your consciousness. In that one slow second, quick centuries of telepathy invaded you, and you took in all that Arthur knew. The swerve of terror that followed would have knocked you unconscious had you not been held firmly in the Dark One's superconscious grip, its power black, the nothing colour, absorbing your horrified feelings and their children, the frenzied motes of thoughts seeking a way for you to escape.

But there was no escape. It was not Eleanor the Dark One wanted. She had already fulfilled her usefulness for him. It was you he was after all along, though it could have been any stranger. Numb-edged, you understood how deep in your luck you had lived your whole life – until now.

The gold light snapped off, and colours abruptly found their way back to their places. The silence you hadn't noticed vanished in a clamor of conversation and dinner noise. You spilled your water, and Eleanor made a small embarrassed cry. A waiter rushed to lift the tablecloth and staunch the cold flow draining into your lap. You hardly noticed. Your eyes were fixed on him, Darshan, the Dark One.

He smiled back, a knowing, wicked smile, confirming the terrible truth. That had been no electrical misfiring in your brain, no hallucinatory adumbration of madness. He nodded with interest, once, to acknowledge his transmission of destiny, of the fate-bond that now and forever would unite you, and then returned his attention to his mud pie.

What did he want of you? You got up at once and hurried to the restroom. Your pulse knocked painfully under your collarbone as you stared at yourself in the mirror and saw the scream in your eyes. Why had this happened to you? Shock glazed your mind. What had you to do with the cave masters and the apocalyptic yearnings of the Dark One? How could any of this mean anything to you? Its absurdity ravaged your mind, and you wept and laughed at the same time, not wanting to believe. You pressed your hands against the mirror and stared hard at the greedy fear you saw there. The lizards in your face coupled, and you knew you would go mad.

But you didn't. That, in part, was why he had selected you, or so you assumed when reason asserted itself. Later, back at the table, as he signed a credit slip for the meal, you expected more: a telepathic voice, an apparition from the raith, another knowing look – anything to reinforce the adrenalin-charged event that had carried you to a higher form of life.

Nothing.

At the door, Eleanor took his arm, drunk and amorous, and he offered you his hand. Everything in that firm handshake made you realize you were wrong to take pity on him.

A RING OF GREEN FIRE

Sean McMullen

---

*Time to wind down, and there's no better way than with this story
by Australian writer Sean McMullen. McMullen (b. 1948) was, for
many years, a professional musician before turning to writing, and
that helped inspire one of his early stories, "The Colours of the
Masters" (1988) where modern technology revives performances by
classical musicians. McMullen was one of the co-authors of a history
of Australian science fiction,* Strange Constellations *(1999). More
recently he has concentrated on fiction, both fantasy and science
fiction, which includes the Greatwinter trilogy, starting with* Souls
in the Great Machine *(1999) and the Moonworlds Saga, starting
with* Voyage of the Shadowmoon *(2002). McMullen's website is at
www.seanmcmullen.net.au*

*Some of McMullen's shorter fiction betrays a fascination with
history and the development of science from alchemy, cleverly
blending scientific and magical concepts, as the following story shows.*

*I was tempted, given the subject of the story, to remark that it is
time to go down under, but since McMullen has a black belt in
karate, I won't.*

"As I was travelling through Westbury forest, I met with a man
with a ring of green fire around his penis," Avenzoar's visitor
said casually.

The poet-physician looked up at his friend and stroked his beard,
then gazed wistfully across to the partially built minaret of Caliph al-
Mansur's huge mosque.

"Such a wonder," sighed Avenzoar, then turned to his visitor and raised an eyebrow. "I suppose you did not bring him here for this poor physician and poet turned bureaucrat to examine?"

His friend glanced away, and seemed troubled. "Alas, it was not possible."

"Such a pity. It may be an honour to be entrusted with the completion of this great mosque of Ishbiliyah, but I miss the wider world. Is England really such a cold, rainswept place?"

"When I was there, yes."

"What of your patient? Was he a traveller from even more exotic regions?"

"Not at all, yet the story of his curse is fascinating."

Avenzoar clapped his hands. Honey pastries and ripe fruit were brought in by a servant and placed before them.

"My friend, show kindness to a captive of the Caliph's goodwill and tell me this magical story."

"There was no magic, Avenzoar, nor was the curse any more than an exotic disease. Still, the story will afford you an hour's wonder."

How to begin? Affliction with the green fire was growing common in the midlands of England in the Christian year of 1188. The man in Westbury forest was a tinker, I saw that from his pack. He approached a tollbridge where I was resting in the dim light of late evening, and he drew his cloak tightly about himself as he came near.

His name was Watkin, and he was a small, thin but very energetic man, a little over thirty years of age. I introduced myself as a physician, and offered him the protection of my five men-at-arms while we camped for the night. He was glad to accept, as the forest was full of outlaws and we had also rigged a shelter against the rain. As we ate the night's meal I raised the subject of illness with him.

"You have an affliction, I can tell that," I said. He made no reply, yet his face was sad. He shaved slivers of cheese from a rind with his knife but did not eat them.

"Your affliction is distressing, but without pain," I continued. "I have learned to read the signs of distress in sick people."

He tossed the rind into the fire and wiped his knife on a crust. "You have never seen the like of my complaint," he said miserably. "Nobody can help me. I went to the physicians of the Church and they said that I was possessed by a devil. They wanted to torture me until it was driven out, but I'd have none of that. I broke free and ran. I run very fast."

"Wise of you, but there are other ways."

"I'm afeared of witchcraft too."

"I am no sorcerer, I am a physician who has studied under some of the greatest Moorish and Jewish masters of the day, including Maimonides himself."

"Who is Maimonides?"

"Ah, a great Jewish teacher and man of medicine. He is court physician to the great Saladin."

"Saladin! So…you have Moorish training."

"Why yes. I went to the Holy Land with the Crusade of 1147. I was badly wounded, then captured. The enemy physicians tended me so well that I resolved to learn their ways."

"You place no faith in torture to rid a man of demons?"

"Oh no, I have been trained in far more civilized means."

"Then I'll show you…"

"No! Wait, and let me examine you first. I wager that I can tell your affliction in moments."

I felt the glands beneath his jaw, looked into his eyes in the firelight and sniffed his breath. He was in good health, I could see that at once, yet I had to make a show of skill to gain his trust. He did not realise that I have acute vision at a distance, and had noticed a faint green glow through the cloth of his trews before he had wrapped himself in his cloak.

"You have a circlet of green fire about your penis," I announced calmly. "It has been slowly moving higher, and in its wake your skin has lost all feeling."

He gasped, then looked down to see if his glow was showing, which it was not. "Truly a man of great medical arts," he said in awe. "What – what are your fees? I'm but a poor tinker, yet I'd give anything to be rid of the fire and numbness."

I laughed disarmingly. "I have yet to meet a rich tinker, but do not worry. Your earnings for the week past will suffice. Open your robes, lower your trews, let me see your affliction."

He stood, opened his cloak, raised his tunic, then pulled on the drawstring of his trews. They dropped, but only as far as his knees: cleverly placed straps held them just high enough for him to run. What manner of man might need to run while his trews were down, I mused.

His ring was brighter than any others that I had seen, and had moved so far up the shaft that it was almost at the base and glowed through his pubic hair. My companions looked up from their meal in surprise.

"Can you break this spell?" Watkin babbled eagerly. "Have you seen the like before?"

"Ah yes, and I have had great success where all others have failed."

He sighed with relief as he raised his trews and retied them. "So, you have secret incantations and philtres, perhaps?"

"I have those, but they are for later. The real mode of breaking a spell is to learn the circumstances of its casting in the fullest detail possible. An honest, truthful account of the casting weakens the grip of the devil, who is behind all curses and spells. One lie, one slight deviation from the truth, however, and his grip is strengthened. How did you acquire your ring, Watkin?"

"It...appeared a month ago, after I bedded my wife, and each time that I enjoy her it moves a little higher..."

"Stop, stop," I laughed. "Three lies within one breath! Watkin, you will have to do better than that. The ring of green fire begins at the tip of one's member and moves higher only when you bed a woman for the first time. It also becomes brighter as time passes. In women the glow is all internal, yet there is also numbness and other such effects that increase with time and new lovers. I would say that you acquired it around May last year, and since then you have mounted eight dozen women. As to being married, no, not you. Am I wrong?"

He slowly shook his head and stared at his boots. "To my shame, no."

"Then tell the truth, however reproachful your conduct has been."

"It would burn the ears of a good Christian."

"But Watkin, I am not a Christian." He gaped at me. "When I was in the Holy Land I adopted more than the medical scholarship of Islam. Now tell me of how you were first snared by the ring, and tell the truth."

"It was in a village called Delmy, to the south, near the coast. I arrived there early one afternoon, during the May festival. The villagers were celebrating the victory of summer over winter with feasting, May carols and dancing. Strangers were welcome, especially an honest tinker like myself.

"For a time I sampled the tartlets, manchets, fried figs and ales, then I turned my thoughts to a companion for a little frolic. I'd been travelling for a long time, I was lonely, it was spring..."

"I am not too old to know the needs and urgings of the flesh, Watkin. Go on."

"It seemed easy pickings. Many young folk of the village were dancing and fondling most intimately, raising my hopes of a quick and easy conquest. Alas, no girl would spare me the deeper smile, indeed there seemed no girls unpaired at all. After so long tramping the road I was lonely, and with so many pairs of lovers cavorting before me I was quite beside myself to be part of it.

"At last I saw one girl who was unpaired, a big-boned, hairy-armed wench with a face that only a beard could have improved. She was alone, tending the tables, and she smiled broadly whenever I came near. At first it seemed worse to mount her than no wench at all, yet the fire of spring burned within me.

"I made up my mind, approached her, whispered words of compliment, then with unseemly haste did I shepherd her away from the fair – more in shame of being seen with her than in shame of the act to come. I chose a place among bushes behind a broad oak. I – I could not bear to look upon her, I just bent her over a rack of poles and flung her skirts up."

He paused for a long drink from the crock. "And you did the deed with her?" I prompted.

"Ah yes, master physician, and she was a virgin, wouldn't you know it? Hah, it was wearisome work, yet I am a diligent tradesman. To the beat of the distant village band, I placed my rivet and began tapping. At last I was spent. I eased back as she stood panting, then I slipped away as if I had been a wood sprite vanishing into air – lest she have thoughts about wedding me. I skirted the village, took up my pack and trotted away briskly.

"By evening I was five leagues gone and some way contented. My hammer had been well worked, in fact he even felt a little numb, so hard had I clinked the pan – or so I thought. Imagine my alarm when I unlaced to piss and saw a ring of cold, faint green fire encircling his head."

"The girl was a virgin, you say?"

"Indeed, no doubt of it, I have initiated many. Alas, she passed this cold glow to me, and soon I noticed that as I worked the pots of goodwives and maids on my travels, the ring would move a little further up each time. Where it had been the feeling that is lust's reward was no more."

"But surely the women you have bedded since then noticed your green glow?"

"Ah no master, you are obviously not a tradesman. We visit houses and cottages during the day, when the menfolk are in the fields and their women are at home, alone. Most times will there be a sly look, or even a saucy suggestion, then we will be coupled on the hearthrug in the light of day. Since the ring was slipped upon me, I have shared the glow to, oh, ninety five women, mostly lowborn, though some were of no mean rank." He nudged me, winking suavely. "Master, if foolish knights would do no better than fight and drink, well someone must plant the seeds of future knights."

"One last question, Watkin. Could you write down the names and villages of all the women that you have bedded since the stout maid gave you the green fire?"

"Alas, Master, I cannot write, yet I could recite the names of all! When I lie alone at night I like to recall each wench that I have ever mounted and set a name against a star, but of late the number of stars has grown insufficient. Since the stout virgin of Delmy there have been...now let me think...one hundred and five, yes. Ah, but it is becoming difficult now, as so much of my hammer has no feeling."

Without any warning I seized his wrist and twisted his arm hard behind his back. He cried out in surprise and pain as I shouted "A firebrand! A firebrand! Quickly!"

My men at arms jumped to their feet at once but Watkin tumbled in mid-air, twisted his arm free of my grip and darted for the woods with speed of a startled hind. Worse luck for him, the sentry had been alert for just such a flight. His hand-axe went spinning flat after him, tangled his legs and sent him sprawling in the mud with a cry of pain. We soon had him in hand and dragged him back to the fire.

"A good throw, Sir Phillip," I said as they held him down and I tended the gashes and cuts in Watkin's legs. "The great tendon is severed in his right leg, he will never again run from cuckolded husbands with such speed."

Watkin's moaning suddenly died away as he realized that something else was not as it seemed. Beneath their shabby robes my men-at-arms were well dressed warriors with fine weapons. They stood before us, glaring, their eyes sparkling with fury in the firelight.

"What – who are you?" the tinker stammered.

One of the men began to unlace, and the others followed his example. A moment later the light of five rings of green fire glowed steadily from their loins.

"Lied…you lied to me!" gasped Watkin.

"Lied, Watkin? I am indeed a physician and breaker of curses, and my faith is the Way of Islam."

"Then who are these men?"

"You may call this man Sir Robert," I said as he brought a coil of rope to tie the tinker's hands. "This fine, burly warrior is Sir Peter, and Sir Phillip was the sentry who brought you down. Sir Charles is the blonde man, and Sir Douglas has the black beard and is scowling as if he would cheerfully cut your heart out. You may call me William."

"Those are not your real names," he said fearfully.

"Those names will suffice for you, false or not. Speaking for myself, I really am an Englishman, and although I do have an Islamic name now, I was christened William when I was born. I have returned to England at the request of Sir Peter here."

"A Christian physician could well have had us denounced or burned for demonic possession," Sir Peter explained. "Some folk afflicted by the green fire have already suffered such a fate. This infidel, who is also my friend, can be trusted not to do that. On your feet now!"

The nobles tied him spreadeagled in the rain between two trees. "False physician, you betrayed me!" wailed Watkin.

"And how many women did you betray by passing the green fire on to them?" I asked.

"No, no, I have ceased to spread the green fire," he cried. "Look in my pack."

"You certainly have," I agreed as I rummaged through his goods. "Just look at these knick-knacks. All manner of little presents as might please a wench and entice her into bed. Aromatic oils and scents, and, and…less savoury items."

There it was, in his pack, the sheepgut device. I sat back, and examined the sheath while my companions cheerily tormented Watkin with what was to come. With such a plague as the green fire to be caught from casual dalliance it was only a matter of time before these sheaths of sheepgut became very popular. Still, that was not my concern. Watkin was the man I had been seeking, the Alpha firebrand, the butterfly king. The plague of green fire was about to end and he would play a role.

I stood up. Sir Douglas had just proposed a crude surgical operation to rid Watkin of his green fire and the others were roaring their approval. "Stop! Stop!" I shouted, rushing forward to seize Sir Peter's arm. "My good lords, this one is not to be killed."

"But he's the one who began it all," exclaimed Sir Peter, so hot with anger that the rain steamed from his face.

"Precisely. Other firebrands may be killed for spreading the green glow, but this one might well be used for a cure."

Their hard and vengeful glares were at once softened by amazement and hope. Even revenge took second place to removing the glowing green shackle from their manhood.

Watkin was bound, gagged and bagged, then taken to Sir Peter's castle some seventy miles away. The journey was done in a single stretch, with no sleep, and even meals were had in the saddle. It rained for most of the way.

The castle was no great wonder, it was a mean, low fortification of rammed earth, logs and stone blocks from ancient Roman ruins. The thatch and log roofs leaked, and it rained most of the time that I was there.

Although surly at first Watkin became wonderfully cooperative after a single touch of the torturer's red-hot iron. We wrote down the details of his 105 seductions, and in the weeks that followed established that only sixty two of the infected women had survived beatings by their husbands and attempts at exorcism by religious healers. Ten had escaped ensnarement by the green ring since he had begun to use his sheepgut armour.

In the months past we had travelled far and wide killing firebrands who had spread the green fire, and thanks to the fire their trails were easy to follow. With Watkin safely in chains we now visited Delmy, the village from where he had borne the green fire to torment the world. The stout virgin that Watkin had seduced was named Gerelde, but while she was indeed not comely, she was skilled with herbal cures and was a surpassing good cook.

Her mother was buried nearby. The woman had once lived alone in a forest some way up the coast, and was reputed to have been a witch. Cornish brigands had raided the area and seized her, and their leader had ravished her until she was some months swelling with his child.

He had then taken her out to sea and cast overboard to drown, yet she lived to struggle ashore and be found by the villagers of Delmy. The village midwife said that she had treated herself with a glowing green paste to ease the pain of the birth. It was a difficult delivery, as Gerelde was a very big baby for such a small mother as she was. The witch had died of the stresses of birth and cursing her ravisher.

Sir Peter assembled a squad of men while I went with Sir Phillip to locate the witch's house, a ransacked shell by now. We exhumed the witch's bones and reburied them in the overgrown garden of her old home. In the meantime Sir Peter had attacked and annihilated the brigand stronghold, avenging the witch after eighteen years. Every one of his fighting men had the ring of green fire and was frantic for revenge against anyone connected with it.

On the evening that we returned to Sir Peter's castle, I spoke with him in his dining hall. Rain dripped from the roof beams as we sat before the fire.

"That was clever work, finding the first firebrand of the green ring," he said to me. "Why didn't you tell us that we were on such a quest?"

"If I had told that I wanted a man of such-and-such a description you would have tortured dozens into confessing to be him. Better to take you on a vendetta against all firebrands and do the questioning myself."

"Well then, what good came of it? We avenged the witch, yet her magical ring still glows on my gronnick, and the ring on Watkin the Tinker is still bright enough to light his way on a moonless night. What sort of a sorcerer are you…"

"I am a physician, not a sorcerer. Magic does not exist, only illness in all its guises. The full cure for the ring of green fire is close. I have made progress."

"What kind of progress?"

"I returned the witch's bones to her garden and reburied them there. A month has passed since then, so the aura from her bones will have permeated the roots of her herbs and be taken up into the leaves. I shall soon return to her grave and harvest some leaves to grind into a paste."

"Will that be enough? Leaves?"

"There is more, Sir Peter, much more. Even though she is dead she is trying to teach us something of the new notion of chivalry – it's new to you English at least, us Saracenic scholars have taught it for years."

"That's why we employed you, dammit!"

"And your faith in me is not misplaced. I can see some kind of symbolism of pain being avenged while its resulting sorrow still lives on. The witch wanted you to do more than just avenge her."

"Well what did she damn well want?" shouted Sir Peter, pounding the table so hard with his goblet that a gemstone fell out of the silver filigree.

"Patience, patience, I dare not tell you everything yet."

Sir Peter had a mistress as well as his wife, and it was this woman that Watkin had bedded one afternoon in the summer past. The noble had argued with her a little earlier, and she felt lonely and neglected. Watkin had arrived, and cleverly spoke in a cultivated voice, as if by accident. Then he hinted that he was himself a noble on some secret mission, and so he won her trust and bedded her. Understandably, Sir Peter was all for impaling Watkin on a stake at the castle gate until the crows pecked his bones clean, but I restrained him.

"Why do you have such sympathy for the little wretch?" asked Sir Phillip the next morning as we squelched our way through the muddy grounds of the castle, holding sodden cloaks up against the rain. We were on our way to visit the tinker.

"Sympathy? I have no sympathy for Watkin, but I do have a use for him."

"The talk is that you are sorry for him."

"Sorry? Me? Not likely. I once suffered because of his kind. I was a young merchant's scribe in love with my master's daughter. Although she cared for me, our courtship was slow. I did not have skill with the words and gestures of seduction. My master took her on a journey to Normandy, he had trade business there. She met one such as Watkin, but this youth was a noble.

"He charmed her with talk as sweet as a nightingale's song, and settled upon her as softly as a butterfly. When she returned to England she grew round with child, and was desolate with remorse. I petitioned to marry her and the merchant consented, yet even then I was aflame with rage.

"I travelled to Normandy and sought out her seducer. Although a mere scribe I was skilled in the use of shortswords. I killed a guard and wounded several more, but the butterfly nobleman escaped and I was wounded. I became a fugitive and outlaw, I could never return to my young wife. She gave birth some months later, then flung herself from a cliff and was drowned in the sea."

"When did all this take place?"

"Your Christian year of 1150."

"But that was three years after the Crusade of 1147."

"Certainly. With a history like mine, would you let the truth be known? I began working aboard merchant ships, they were always in need of people who could write. After five years I had earned enough silver and learned sufficient Arabic to settle in the Zangid Sultanate and study medicine. I had an impressive wound, so I made up that tale of being on the crusade. Now you know my background, Sir Phillip. Please preserve my secret, yet reassure your folk about my intentions. A butterfly killed my sweetheart, and Watkin is another such butterfly. "

"But why do you stay Sir Peter's hand?"

"As I said, Watkin has his uses. Although a mere tinker he is magnificent, the ultimate seducer. He can affect the voices and manners of all types of people, from nobles to ploughmen. His trews have a double strap, so that he can lower them to his knees for a dalliance, yet they stay high enough for him to run unencumbered from an outraged husband. He is a master of escape and could run like the wind until your axe severed his hamstring. He cleans his teeth with soft bark, he washes, and he scents himself with aromatic oils. His trade is tinking, yet even that takes him roving to meet an endless bevy of women."

We had reached the dungeon, a squat blockhouse of stone with a log roof and narrow slits for windows. I made to enter, but Sir Phillip barred my way. "I'm with Sir Peter, I'm for killing the little rat," he declared. "He…"

"He seduced a maid on intimate terms with your seneschal, and your seneschal then passed the fire on to his wife – who was already your secret lover. If the green fire has done anything, it has traced out a fine trail of humpery bumpery at all stations of society."

"So what are you saying? Are we no better than Watkin?"

"I am saying that you can learn from Watkin. In spite of being a short, scrawny, low-born tinker, he charms greatly."

"He preys upon the most vulnerable of women."

"True, but were you English noblemen to clean your teeth, change your clothing at least weekly and take the care to give ladies little compliments instead of kicks, curses and belches, why the likes of Watkin would have no market for their charms. He is poor, but it costs him nothing to speak charmingly and wash. If you did the same, you would still be rich and powerful as well. Who would then choose Watkin over you?

"A hot iron can wound Watkin's type, but with good manners and clean fingernails you can hurt them a lot more. You English are adopting our Saracenic cooking, mathematics and music. Why not our chivalry as well?"

Sir Phillip glared at me from under his cloak, but he was obviously thinking.

"There is a lot of merit in what you say...but it's hard to think chivalrous thoughts with a ring of green fire about my gronnick! What can I do about that?"

"The tinker took a curse upon himself when he bundled into the witch's daughter. He then dispersed that curse to nearly every woman he seduced in his travels, and hence to all their lovers. That has formed quite an avenging army."

"And we did avenge her!"

"Yes, but there is more to it than that, so the glow remains. The green fire is a tool to force us to do certain tasks, and even teach us about the ways of men and women."

We entered the dungeon, where the tinker was practicing walking with a crutch and in good spirits.

"Have you caught the Delmy witch?" he asked.

"We found her grave and exhumed it. She is nought but bones after these eighteen years."

"Eighteen years? Bones? She was as well fleshed as a prize sow when I mounted her the May before last."

"That was her daughter. The witch herself died in childbirth, but her daughter unknowingly carried a curse. You turned that curse loose upon the world. Gerelde was raised by a peasant family, and has come to be a fine cook. I tasted her food, it was fine fare for a peasant table. She wants for nought but a husband. She's plain of face and is built as solidly as Sir Peter, yet for all that she is a kindly girl."

Watkin sneered. "Why are you telling me about her? I'd never touch her again, she's as ugly as a goat's backside."

"She was quite taken by you, Watkin, and she is very concerned that you are imprisoned here. Still, you are more fortunate than the brigand who raped her mother. Sir Peter caught him, did you know? He was a great slab of a man, massive rather than fat, full of life and defiance, even eighteen years after the deed that caused all this. He was confident that we would not kill him because he knew where sundry hoards of gold and silver loot lay buried. Sir Peter had him taken to the graveside of his victim, and there his gronnick was sliced from between his legs and rammed down his windpipe so that he choked on it and died most horribly. Those of his men as were watching quickly babbled the location of hoards of coin, plate and jewelry, yet none heeded them. Sir Peter had to kill him with the same weapon that killed Gerelde's mother."

Watkin was deathly pale by now, and had slumped against the wall. "Mother of God, but why?"

"He was a link in the chain that ignited the green fire. You are another link."

"Me? But, but…"

"You bedded Sir Peter's mistress. That alone should have you in fear for your life, but you also passed the fire to her."

The tinker cowered, but said no more. Sir Phillip lurked in the shadows, smirking at his discomfort.

"I need tears of pity that have been wept for you and no other. In all the world, Watkin, would anyone weep for you?"

"Many regard me as comely."

"Someone must *weep* for you, Watkin. Your flesh is about to hiss with the touch of the red iron."

"No! As God is merciful, no! Take my pack, sell me into slavery! I'll do anything…"

"For the final ingredient to quench the ring of green fire you *will* be able to choose between death and a less daunting fate, but for now you will be tortured. I require that it be done, Watkin, and believe me that there are thousands of men and women who would fight to the death for the pleasure of holding the glowing iron to you. You have often been bold, now you must learn to be brave."

Once we were well away from the dungeon and Watkin's hysterical pleading Sir Phillip took me by the arm.

"That brigand was killed in battle by one of Sir Peter's archers. It was a shaft through his skull, he died at once."

"True."

"Then what was that story about choking him on his own gronnick?"

"Watkin has the attention span of a butterfly. I meant to…focus his mind."

"To what end?"

"That is between myself and Allah. Rest assured, however, that Watkin will be tortured."

"And you will savour his screams with the rest of us?"

"Oh no, I shall be hard at work, preparing certain ingredients to quench the ring of green fire."

"Lord physician, I don't follow."

"You will never follow, Sir Phillip, but your ring of green fire shall be quenched, rely on my word for that."

By the time I had left Sir Peter's castle for Delmy, Watkin had faced the first of the silent, hooded men that were to torment him. Thousands gathered outside the castle to hear his screams, but these did not last. After he was blinded, the tendons at the source of his voice were cut. This produced such a riot outside that all Watkin's subsequent tortures had to be on public display. As I rode off for Delmy hot irons were being applied to the soles of his feet by the second torturer, Sir Douglas, while Sir Phillip held up a cloak up to keep the rain from cooling the red-hot metal.

I returned after three days, bringing Gerelde with me. Watkin was, of course, the only lover she had ever known, so he was a lot more special to her than the other way about. She was blind to his disfigurements, and she made heartfelt pleas for her feckless tinker. It was an impressive sight, for even on her knees she was taller than Sir Peter. I stood by and collected her tears on a small cloth. At a nod from me Sir Peter relented – on the condition that Watkin marry her, and that he never leave the village of Delmy under pain of death by torture. Watkin could only nod his head by way of agreement. Now Gerelde wept tears of joy, and I wiped these from her face as well.

A great marriage feast was held, and a good many folk with the ring of green fire were brought in to participate. Before Sir Peter's eyes I ground the cloth with its tears into a paste, then added cuttings of herbs taken from the witch's garden. The food at the feast was wonderful village fare, and to this I added my mixture. All ate heartily, and by evening the green fire was gone from every afflicted man and woman at the feast. There were, well, unseemly celebrations in spite of the rain, but that was only to be expected. The following day I called upon Sir Peter.

"Now that the curse is broken, a simple remedy can be used to quench the green fire in all others who still have it," I told him. "I have trained several clerks and midwives in its preparation already, and they will train more. Soon the green fire will be no more, so my work here is done."

Sir Peter embraced me so strongly that I heard the joints of my spine pop. I was the physician who had returned the feeling to his penis, and he was brimming with gratitude.

"You must have a reward, honours, you have done more good for this land than words can say."

"There is my agreed fee, of course."

"That? A mere trifle! Here's twice your fee." He tossed me a bag of gold. "Now, my Lord physician, if you could but renounce the faith of Islam you could also be given great rank."

"My faith is Islam, please respect that, and rank does not interest me. I am a physician, so although I find it an honour to treat caliphs and kings, I do not aspire to their thrones."

"Then treat a king you will! Our King Henry lies sick at Chinon, a town in his French provinces. I'm his trusted adviser, I'll recommend you to him, I'll recommend you in the very highest words of praise."

"I would be honoured to treat your king, Sir Peter."

Avenzoar gazed at the fountain at the centre of the courtyard for some moments before turning back to his guest. The constant rain, the glowing green fire, all the strange horrors of his visitor's tale slowly retreated before the warm Spanish sunshine.

"So the girl's tears broke the curse," he said.

"No. My 'other remedy' would have worked by itself."

"Then you could have stopped the green fire months earlier. Why the charade?"

The visitor paused to select a ripe fig, frowning as if troubled. "I was Watkin's first torturer." Avenzoar gasped with surprise. "Yes, I blinded him to Gerelde's face and I silenced his voice that he might never abuse her."

"I see. You made him a match for her and no other."

"I did more than that. The ring of green fire was a type of purgative, it flushed out those men with great skill in coldly manoeuvring women into bed. Watkin was not the only firebrand, we discovered nearly two dozen men, and a few women too, who had hundreds of seductions behind them. They are all dead now, save for Watkin. Many other diseases are spread by the loveless lust of Watkin's kind. We culled in the interests of good health."

Avenzoar considered this. "True, too much of any skill can be dangerous. Perhaps the witch did some good after all."

"The witch was no witch, and there was no curse. She was my dead wife's daughter, sired by a butterfly and born just before her mother cast herself into the ocean. Gerelde was my step-grandaughter, but even though she and her mother were no flesh and blood of mine, I loved them as my own. I provided for them and visited them every few years."

"Ah yes, now it all makes sense. The green fire was a medicine to deaden the pain of childbirth. Your step-daughter died before she could give the antidote to herself and her baby. The fire escaped when Watkin mounted Gerelde."

The visitor nodded. Avenzoar stood up slowly and looked across to the delicate tracery and interlaced arches of the partly built minaret. He glanced at a nearby sundial.

"It is time for my daily inspection of the minaret," he said with his back to his guest, then he turned. "But first I must reproach you for mutilating in the name of medicine."

The guest remained calm, as if he had expected Avenzoar's reaction, yet he did not meet his friend's eyes. "No, not in the name of medicine. I disfigured Watkin to have my step-grandaughter married and happy. She has a lame, blind, mute tinker who is nevertheless a prince of seducers, and she has him all to herself. He will be grateful for all that she does for him until the day he dies. Yes, it was evil of me, but perhaps good has come of it. Watkin's wings have been clipped, but at least he has his life."

Avenzoar sat down and fanned himself. "But what of my original question? You have not yet explained why you took so long to release your cure for the green fire? Surely it was not just to mark and slay the promiscuous?"

"You are right, Avenzoar, as usual. I withheld the cure to increase its worth. That increased my reward, in turn."

"Reward? To treat King Henry? It must have been of little comfort to you. I learned recently that he died barely a fortnight after midsummer."

"Precisely," the visitor agreed solemnly, and Avenzoar felt a sudden chill in spite of the bright sunshine. "As a teenage prince of Normandy he seduced my sweetheart. I spent a lifetime hating that royal butterfly, yet it was the accidental spread of the green fire that gave me a chance to get past his guards. Gerelde is his granddaughter, yes, and Watkin is unknowingly married to a princess."

He reached into his robes and took out a folded parchment, which he placed on the tray beside the pastries. "This details a cure for the mould that causes the ring of green fire." Avenzoar unfolded the parchment and read it slowly. Suddenly he looked up in astonishment.

"This also makes your fortune over to me!" he exclaimed.

"That is because I am going now, and I shall never return," said the visitor. "Our people will see no more of me. Use my fortune to train needy students and to foster the arts of healing in whatever way you will. Should any woman come to you complaining of numbness within, or any man disrobe to reveal a ring of green fire about his penis, well, you now have the cure."

"You cannot be serious!" exclaimed Avenzoar. "The loss of your skills would be a crime in itself."

"I killed under the guise of healing," the visitor replied firmly. "To strike at King Henry I destroyed my integrity as a physician. Now I must pay...but I knew that all along."

He stood slowly and shuffled across to the fountain, with Avenzoar following. The poet put a hand on his shoulder as he washed the crumbs from his hands.

"Accepting that you have done evil is a step towards atoning for it, my friend. Stay here for a while, rest and talk with Avenzoar, your friend and fellow physician."

"No, no. Have you not noticed that I cannot meet your eyes for more than a moment? Whenever I see a fellow physician I am shamed to remember that I have murdered, and I must hang my head."

"But where will you go?"

"To places where I shall meet no other physicians. Along the salt road to the barren granite mountains of Aghadez and the marshy shores of Lake Tchad, then deep into the great deserts of Africa. My skills may find a welcome there."

"But this is terrible. Your very words show you to be of good heart. Please stay."

Now Avenzoar's visitor held him by both arms and looked fleetingly into his eyes. "If I agreed to stay, you would despise me in the depths of your heart, where your goodwill cannot reach."

"This is not the best way..."

"My friend, it is the *only* way."

Later that afternoon, when his guest had departed, Avenzoar toured the partly completed Minaret with Ali al-Ghumari, his architect. As the sun's disk shimmered near the horizon they gazed out across the capital of al-Andalus.

"It is safe for now," said Avenzoar, "but one day a green fire may come to blight this fair city."

"Is it a weapon?" asked the architect with mild interest. "Is it like Greek fire?"

"It is English fire," replied Avenzoar.

"Hah! It must be fierce indeed to burn in spite of their rain," the architect laughed. "What is its fuel?"

Avenzoar fingered the scrap of folded parchment for reassurance. "Neglect and hatred," he said softly.

The architect pondered this for a moment, running his hand along the newly laid brickwork. "A cheap and plentiful fuel," he replied at last, and Avenzoar nodded.